PENGUIN BOOKS

STORIES OF THE MODERN SOUTH

Ben Forkner is professor of English and American literature at the University of Angers in France. A graduate of Stetson University in Florida, he received his M.A. and Ph.D. from the University of North Carolina at Chapel Hill. He has published articles on writers from Ireland and from the American South and has edited two anthologies of Irish short stories: *Modern Irish Short Stories* (Penguin) and *A New Book of Dubliners*. Professor Forkner has also edited *Louisiana Stories* and with Patrick Samway, S.J., has co-edited three other anthologies of Southern literature, *Stories of the Old South* (Penguin), *A Modern Southern Reader*, and *A New Reader of the Old South*. In addition, he edits the *Journal of the Short Story in English* published biannually by the University of Angers Press.

Patrick Samway, S.J., received his B.A. and M.A. from Fordham University, his M. Div. from Woodstock College, and his Ph.D. in English from the University of North Carolina at Chapel Hill. Father Samway taught for eight years at Le Moyne College in Syracuse, New York, and also has received two Fulbright lectureships to France (universities of Nantes and Paris VII), in addition to having been a Bannan Fellow at the University of Santa Clara in California and Visiting Associate Professor at both Boston College and Loyola University in New Orleans. He is the Literary Editor of *America* and author of *Faulkner's "Intruder in the Dust": A Critical Study of the Typescripts* and co-editor with Michel Gresset of *Faulkner and Idealism: Perspectives From Paris*.

STORIES OF THE MODERN SOUTH

Expanded Edition

Edited by

Ben Forkner

and

Patrick Samway, S. J.

PENGUIN BOOKS

PENGUIN BOOKS
Published by the Penguin Group
Viking Penguin, a division of Penguin Books USA Inc.,
375 Hudson Street, New York, New York 10014, U.S.A.
Penguin Books Ltd, 27 Wrights Lane,
London W8 5TZ, England
Penguin Books Australia Ltd, Ringwood,
Victoria, Australia
Penguin Books Canada Ltd, 2801 John Street,
Markham, Ontario, Canada L3R 1B4
Penguin Books (N.Z.) Ltd, 182–190 Wairau Road,
Auckland 10, New Zealand

Penguin Books Ltd, Registered Offices:
Harmondsworth, Middlesex, England

First published in the United States of America by Bantam Books, Inc., 1977
An edition with three new stories published in Penguin Books 1981
This expanded edition with six additional stories published in
Penguin Books 1986
Published simultaneously in Canada

5 7 9 10 8 6 4

LIBRARY OF CONGRESS CATALOGING IN PUBLICATION DATA
Stories of the modern South.
1. Short stories, American—Southern States.
2. Southern States—Fiction. 3. American fiction—
20th century. I. Forkner, Ben. II. Samway, Patrick H.
PS551.S75 1986 813'.01'08975 86-9515
ISBN 0 14 00.9695 7

Printed in the United States of America
Set in Times Roman

Copyright Notices and Acknowledgments

Contents

Introduction

The natural response to an anthology of modern Southern short stories is likely to focus on two questions. Are there enough good short stories by Southern writers in the 20th century to merit a full volume of their work? And what distinguishes these stories as Southern? The best reply to the first question is a quick glance at the table of contents. The reputations of at least a third of the names are already firmly rooted in the history of modern letters. They are recognized and acclaimed wherever there are readers of English literature. The books of William Faulkner, Flannery O'Connor, Robert Penn Warren, Carson McCullers, Katherine Anne Porter, James Agee, Eudora Welty, and John Barth are found in bookshops in Paris, London, Munich, Dublin, and Rome, as well as in New York and San Francisco. As editors, our main problem was not with finding enough representative stories, but with setting up a principle of selection.

One helpful consideration was chronological. The sudden flowering of Southern writing in the 1920s and '30s had been felt mainly in the poem and the novel. John Crowe Ransom, Allen Tate, Robert Penn Warren, William Faulkner, and Thomas Wolfe published important poems and novels almost yearly. Good stories were certainly being written, but the great period of the Southern short story began later, in the 1940s and '50s. It was as if a conscious effort had been made in the South to choose one genre and to excel in it. New original talent appeared constantly and the already established writers confirmed their reputations with one important collection after another. This anthology concentrates on that period. Most of the stories gathered here were written after World War II, and their rich and diverse presence testifies to a Southern literary tradition that not only continues today, but thrives.

This brings us back to the second question. In what ways are these stories Southern? It is a complex question because the South is a deceptively complex area, varied in its people and its climate, and marked by strong differences of racial origins, social values, temperaments, and landscapes. There are as many moods and contrasts in the South as there are in the blues guitar, the mountain banjo, the Negro spiritual, and the Cajun fiddle. And in a domain like the short story where the individual voice dominates all other matters, it is best to be wary of collective accents. In general, the South, from Baltimore to New Orleans, has always been one of the most creative sections of American society, to such an extent that critics normally refer to "Southern literature" without hesitation. Though all who admit its existence would not explain it in exactly the same way, most would agree that the Southern cultural and literary heritage stems from an environment where states' rights are important; where the Bible is read, memorized, and cherished; where decentralized government is seen as something valuable; where families tend to live by traditional agricultural means; where a code of honor and polite manners have been traditionally expected of everyone; where Elizabethan literature and the works of Sir Walter Scott were esteemed for decades; and where slavery and the effects of the Civil War have left a definite mark on *mores* and attitudes. Today's Southern writers, whether they were actually born in the South or whether they spent part of their lives there, continue to draw their inspiration from this unique section of the United States.

Though the stories in this volume owe much to a strong oral tradition of storytelling in the South, they do emerge out of a distinctly Southern literary history. Settled in the early part of the 17th century by men and women from England and Scotland, the South has always had a potential for a rich cultural development. For example, William Byrd (1674–1744), one of the most prominent men of early Virginia and author of the *History of the Dividing Line,* an account of the survey done to determine the boundary between Virginia and North Carolina, had a personal library of over 3600 volumes. A century later, once slavery had developed and the South had expanded because of the Louisiana Purchase in 1803, small regional pockets were created, determined partly by such physical surroundings as the Smoky Mountains and the Mississippi River. As some landowners grew richer, a leisure class developed which had the time, money, and energy to pursue higher forms of education. Though the early settlers had brought with them songs, poetry, religious tracts, political pamphlets, and drama from their native regions, the literature of the South, and particularly the Southern short story, did not really start until the early part of the 19th century.

The ante-bellum writers of the South, many whose names are barely remembered any more—writers such as Thomas Holley Chivers, Philip Pendleton Cooke, John Pendleton Kennedy, William Gilmore Simms, Johnson Jones Hooper, George Washington Harris—definitely provided a literary climate for the short story as they emphasized in their poetry and fiction their own geographical regions and various social classes within those regions. Two writers, in particular, captured the spirit of the pre-Civil War days. Augustus Baldwin Longstreet (1790–1870), a native of Georgia, served as a judge on the Georgia superior court before becoming president of four institutes of higher education. His *Georgia Scenes,* a series of sketches of popular life and tales that appeared in book form in 1835, provides a contrast to the historical romances that Kennedy and Simms were writing in the 1830s. Later, Joseph Glover Baldwin (1815–1864), Southern humorist and author of *The Flush Times of Alabama and Mississippi* (1853), describes the South from a slightly different perspective. Partly because of his legal background and interest in politics, Baldwin tended to focus his sketches on courtroom situations in which the characters often converse in tireless digressions and constantly swap jokes. Unlike some of the other writers of this period, Baldwin does not hesitate to make critical judgments about the South against which we can read his contemporaries.

The stories of the flush times of the ante-bellum South, as do many modern stories, revolve around small towns and villages where the interaction of the townsfolk with each other, with animals, with politicians, with outsiders, and with preachers provides an unusual variety of anecdotes. The comedy in these stories reflects the manners of the times where possum hunting, military escapes, courting, funerals, and family gatherings were ordinary events. The picaresque hero who stole, swindled, or cheated his neighbor or enemy was a common literary subject. In a sense, these authors were realists as they attempted to look at their own milieu, use dialect, and shy away from the techniques used by the romantic novelists. These humorists prepared the way not only for Mark Twain's books where the attitudes and comic situations in works like *The Adventures of Huckleberry Finn* and "Old Times on the Mississippi" embody much of the type of humor that characterized the ante-bellum South, but also for the stories of New York's demimonde written at the turn of the century by William Sidney Porter (O. Henry), a native of North Carolina.

The South in the mid-1800s was a predominantly agrarian society dependent on a large mass of slaves for its economic strength. With its large, feudal plantations—first in the rich coastal lands of the Tidewater, and later, as the cultivation of King Cotton spread, in the lush lowlands in and around the Mississippi Delta—with its scattered, isolated small towns, and with its rough-hewn backcountry, upland farms, the South gradually assumed an independence that finally asserted itself against the rest of the Union. At first, the rebel states had every intention of remaining a separate nation. But after the first exuberant months of the Confederacy when the Southern army in its surprising victories seemed blessed by a reckless grace that could do no wrong, there followed the series of devastating losses, the final defeat, and the bitter aftermath of guilt, poverty, and a kind of permanent religious fatalism. It is hard to realize the profound impact of slavery, war, and defeat on the Southern mind, not only during Reconstruction and the early days of the "New South," but even today. The names of Southern leaders still seem names that are remembered rather than learned from history books.

After the War, the writers of the New South, Walter Hines Page, Henry W. Grady, and Sidney Lanier, had to build on the literary heritage of their predecessors, but with a difference: they had to look to the future of the South and of the entire United States knowing and having experienced the defeat of the Civil War. Among the new breed of writers, George Washington Cable (1844–1925), who served in the Confederate Army but later considered slavery a great wrong, continued the short story tradition by writing about Creole society in Louisiana in *Old Creole Days* (1879); "Posson Jone'," "Jean-ah Poquelin," and "'Sieur George" describe those who frequent the Rue de Canal and the Faubourg Ste-Marie in New Orleans in much the same way that earlier in the century Washington Irving looked carefully at New York society. Joel Chandler Harris (1848–1908) was the author of the famous Uncle Remus stories which first appeared as a collection in 1880. In particular "The Wonderful Tar-Baby Story" and "Mr. Terrapin Shows His Strength" reveal the fantasy world of the imagination in the animal kingdom and show a remarkable desire to handle dialect. Harris, however, was quite versatile and wrote what might be considered more traditional stories about slavery, Reconstruction, and the poor white farmer in such works as *Free Joe, and Other Georgian Sketches* (1887). Thus, roughly between 1870 and 1900 these two local-color writers, in addition to three women writers, Kate Chopin, Grace King, and Mary Noailles Murfree (under the pseudonym of Charles Egbert Craddock), imaginatively recorded the dramatic scenes and speech patterns of their various locales.

None of these writers, however, can be said to have addressed the full complexity of the post-bellum South. The mood that prevailed for years after the War was a curious mixture of pride and guilt. There were those who locked themselves in the elegant myth of an idealized ante-bellum aristocracy and who refused to live in the present, and there were those who zealously, often blindly, sought to remake the South after the model of the industrial North. And there were those who, embittered with hate, and heedless of their own responsibility, blamed everything on the Negro.

One good explanation of what is sometimes called the Southern literary Renascence in the 1920s and '30s is that it was a critical reaction to these extremes. For much of the 19th century, the writing that came out of the South was generally content to reflect a pleasing image of civilizing society, high ideals, and an amusingly eccentric population of contented folk. The Southern writer of the early 20th century grew up in a time when the South he read about was largely denied by what he experienced.

What is perhaps most characteristic of the modern Southern writer is an urgent need to describe the world he knows and lives in, as immediately, as uncompromisingly, and as fully as he can. And since his world was a world of change and contradiction—the slowly embroidered, front-porch legends of the War suddenly juxtaposed with the hurried forward march of the new Chambers of Commerce, and all this under the deep shadow of racial discrimination—his art was complex, ironical, and unsentimental. He was as openly critical of the false images associated with the Old South as he was of the shamefaced imitations of the North.

But there were important attachments to match his repudiations, a personal vision of the South to counter the public myths. If he attacked the illusions and failures of the South, and often left his birthplace to live elsewhere, he usually affirmed the traditional values of a rural, small-town community, where individual acts and individual words still counted, and where large passions and large gestures were still recognized as such. The Southern scholar, Louis D. Rubin, Jr., points out the small-town context as a characteristic feature of Southern writing after World War I: "What has distinguished the body of literature produced by the writers of the Southern Renascence has been the extent to which, for all its modernity of technique and attitude, it continued to be grounded in the regional experience. . . ."

Indeed, most of the first generation of modern Southern writers, Ransom, Tate, Warren, Faulkner, Wolfe, and Ellen Glasgow in her later novels, saw the danger for the South less in a debilitating dream of the past than in the empty, crude materialism of the future. Faulkner, for example, as his career advanced, became much more preoccupied with the irresistible rise of the acquisitive Snopes family than with the decayed aristocracy of the Compsons. Nowhere else in the United States was the intrusion of the 20th century as latecoming, and as brutal. And it is perhaps this conflict between the fatal flaws of the old order and the corrupt values of the new that accounts for the stress Southern art places on the tragic on one hand, and on the satiric and the grotesque on the other.

Certainly the post-World War II South offers little to allay the fears of the 1920s and '30s. The New South of commerce, speculation, and industrial growth has become a permanent reality. Of course no one would argue that the rapid development of the South in the 20th century has been without its advantages. Southern universities have prospered. And many of the negative legacies of the past, the oppressive poverty, the vicious sharecropping system, the rural isolation and illiteracy, the crimes of segregation, are gradually disappearing. But the necessary changes have brought their modern plagues, and no Southerner, no matter how enthusiastic he may be about progress and the new wealth, would deny that the face of his land has lost something of its old character.

The last few decades have brought more jobs and more

money, but they have also brought the interstate, mass advertising, commercial television, the shopping center, rampant tourism, and the general desolate urban-suburban sprawl. A modern Southern city begins to resemble anywhere and nowhere, a bleak uniformity of chain stores, parking lots, motels, pizza parlors, high-rise apartments, and the mobile home. This is, at least, the South most visitors would see, and the South that most Southerners confront daily when leaving their suburban neighborhoods on the way to work.

Certainly, outside the commercial centers, vestiges of the old South still persist. And if the farms are larger and less populous, the farmlands continue to flourish. Almost any back road in North Carolina or Mississippi will eventually lead past a rotting cabin, an abandoned mansion, and perhaps an old flop-eared mule; but it will also lead past country stores, well-kept white wooden churches, and small towns full of large porches. Southern evenings continue to come alive with the nervous ritual dance of fireflies and with the voluminous drone of crickets. And along the country roads, the Southern landscape, in all its variety and lushness and mystery, still overwhelms, still remains a supreme presence.

But the South has changed, perhaps more in the last thirty years than in its entire history, and it has changed toward the rest of the United States, toward a uniform existence of the same desires and the same tastes. Because of this, not a few Southern writers, even those who continue to write about the South, are left to rely on their memories. In a recent interview, Robert Penn Warren explained why he still lives in Connecticut, even though he did try to make the move home: "I began to look for a place down there, but suddenly I saw it was a different world. The people aren't the same people. Oh, more prosperous and all that, but not the kind I had known—with a certain personal worth. So we are stuck with a new world. With certain virtues, I'd be the first to grant, but perhaps some fatal defects."

If this is the case, how does one explain the continuing vitality of Southern literature, even in the present decade when the changes in the South toward a standardized America now seem beyond control? No literary tradition can survive merely because the times are ripe for satire. One good reason is that the South is still nourished by strong folk traditions, traditions that are preserved mainly through music and language. For if the visual community has changed, even disappeared, a certain communal identity remains alive, and it remains alive especially in the act of speech.

The first difference that strikes a visitor to the South is the language, the accents, the tones, the vocabulary, and the rhythms. It is an English as distinct as the English of Ireland. Unlike the stage Southern accent made popular by commercial television, the best of Southern speech is rooted in a rural, oral tradition where the expressive power of language is highly prized. Characterized by concrete, sensual detail, sly humor, and vivid, dramatic images, the folk speech of both black and white can attain a rich evocative beauty, as anyone who has listened to Mississippi John Hurt or Doc Watson can attest.

The South has always sustained a strong verbal awareness, with a conscious self-delight in creating new expressive forms. It is no accident that three of the most original forms of popular music in the 20th century, jazz, the blues, and bluegrass, had their beginnings in the South. The two dominant folk cultures of the South, the Negro and the Scotch-Irish, brought with them already richly developed oral traditions in which those with special gifts for expression were praised and publicly encouraged. Negro slaves, forced into a position where English had to be learned, breathed into it their own nature and their own experiences, and created an English as vital and as expressive as the Anglo-Irish speech of the white settler. The presence and creative force of these two cultures, their intermingling and mutual influence especially in the 20th century, may help explain the special skills the South demonstrates in the short story.

In the South, as in certain other regions of the United States where people have inhabited the land for long periods, the art of storytelling, whether it be the accounts of fathers and grandfathers who have gone off to war, or the passing on of local folk tales, has helped to shape the expectation of the short story. The short story originates in the told tale; the written story's concentration of plot, the literary skills needed to stimulate interest and to hold it without waste, all these are conversational skills as well. Always, the short story in the oral tradition demands fewer words to relate the fullness of the story than does, for example, the epic or the novel form. But just as the length of the novel does not guarantee a richer literary experience, so too, brevity and conciseness do not automatically make a story successful. What is of prime importance is that the teller or author know almost instinctively how short or long a particular story should be.

Two authors, William Faulkner and Flannery O'Connor, deserve special mention as masters of the short story of the modern South. Although Faulkner considered himself at times a poet who never lived up to his promise, he is without doubt one of the South's most brilliant short story writers as the forty-two stories in his volume of collected stories bear witness. Often thought of as a strictly regional writer whose focus was entirely on the South, as the highly popular "Barn Burning" and "A Rose for Emily" might suggest, Faulkner's stories show considerable scope, particularly those written about the Choctaw and Chickasaw Indians and those about the soldiers and pilots of World War I. As he did in his novels, Faulkner wrote many of his stories about his apocryphal Yoknapatawpha County. Characters in one story sometimes appear in one or more stories or novels so that many of these works of fiction mutually illuminate one another; for example, the young Quentin Compson who originally appears in "That Evening Sun" is later developed in *The Sound and the Fury* and *Absalom, Absalom!*. In addition to an intricate narrative style fused with a strong moral sense, Faulkner's stories dramatize the vitality of what he called his "little postage stamp of native soil"; yet his stories transcend the particular to reveal a universal significance in what his characters say and do. One story or one novel could not exhaust the depth and richness of Yoknapatawpha County.

Unlike Faulkner, Flannery O'Connor did not attempt to create an imaginative geographical area for her fiction. Rather her principal works, *The Violent Bear It Away, A Good Man Is Hard to Find and Other Stories,* and *Everything That Rises Must Converge,* reflect a different literary sensibility in which an orthodox view of Catholicism is tempered by the biblical preaching of Southern Protestantism. In her stories, Miss O'Connor sees her characters as sinners who have the possibility of being saved, as human beings who have the freedom of opting for the plausibility of the lower choice, and as individuals in need of divine grace. For example, in her "The Displaced Person," masterfully transformed into a television show with the support of The National Endowment for the Humanities, when Mrs. McIntyre discusses with Father Flynn about Mr. Guizac, a newly arrived Pole who is working for her, Father Flynn gazes at a peacock unfolding his tail. "Christ will come like that," he says. Suddenly, like an epiphany, a moment of glorious insight, the reader identifies Mr. Guizac with Christ—both are displaced persons. And with this, the story is charged with a new precision and destiny. In this way, Flannery O'Connor's fiction has a calculated sense of ambiguity about it which makes her stories appear as modern allegories of Southern spirituality.

Despite differences in theme or style, all the stories in this volume reflect or depend on some distinctly Southern experience. All but one of the authors, Anne Tyler, were born in the South, and Tyler has spent most of her life there. Three stories do take place outside the geographical boundaries of the Southern states, but in all three the South plays an important role. In James Agee's "1928 Story," a relatively unknown story that combines some of the best narrative writing of *A Death in the Family* with the aesthetic sensibility of *Let Us Now Praise Famous Men,* an adolescent's love of jazz and his vision of a Southern city are ways of describing his imaginative life. And in Carson McCullers' "The Sojourner" and Andre Dubus' "Over the Hill," the memory of the South is a central element in the plot: in the first, the nostalgia for the fallow fields of Georgia is felt from New York and Paris; and in the second, the thoughts of a young Louisiana sailor in Japan are jolted back home with the news of his wife's infidelity.

Since the days of the ante-bellum South, one characteristic of Southern literature has always been the various relationships between blacks and whites. Though contact between the races often takes the form of conflict and confrontation, it can provide the possibility of deeper understanding. It is probably not too much of a coincidence then, that in terms of publication dates, the first and last stories collected here dramatize racial differences. William Faulkner's "Pantaloon in Black," first published in 1940 in *Harper's* and later revised slightly and incorporated in the novel-like collection of stories, *Go Down, Moses,* describes the progressive isolation of a black sawmill worker unable to accept the sudden death of his wife. In Faulkner's portrayal of grief, one of the most powerful in modern literature, Rider's love and bereavement are made even more intense when measured by the unfeeling, though comic version the white sheriff gives to his own indifferent wife. Anne Tyler's "The Geologist's Maid," published in 1975 in *The New Yorker,* raises the problem of racial misunderstanding in a contemporary urban context. The story takes place appropriately in Baltimore, a borderline city between the North and South, and describes a household where Dr. Johnson, a sick, white geology professor and Maroon, his black maid, live in completely different worlds, though each is entirely dependent on the other. Similarly, Peter Taylor's "What You Hear from 'Em?" and Reynolds Price's "The Warrior Princess Ozimba" are magnificent portraits of black servants; Taylor's ironic, unaffected prose charts out the effects of a long-standing illusion and Price's story pays homage to a blind warrior-servant with blue tennis shoes.

Perhaps even more characteristic of the South, however, are the stories that deal with a locale, with Southern town life and backcountry, especially when a stranger of some sort enters into the rural community. Truman Capote's "Children on Their Birthdays" describes Miss Lily Jane Bobbit from Memphis, a ten-year-old who, with the help of two friends, Billy Bob and Preacher Star, outwits a con man, Manny Fox, and his wife, "the Fan Dancer Without the Fan." Capote portrays the reactions of Southern townfolk to the dynamic presence of little Miss Bobbit as she tries to convince the regular beer drinkers at the Hangman's Club to finance her trip to Hollywood where she hopes to audition and become a movie star. In Robert Penn Warren's "Blackberry Winter," already a classic of modern fiction, a young boy is confronted with change and death everywhere he looks. Unlike Capote's story which likewise focuses on a young person, Warren's story is filtered through thirty-five years of experience as the narrator remembers his childhood experiences back in 1910 when an evil-speaking day-laborer, a cold spell in June, and a devastating flood seem to emerge out of the North. There is a haunting sense of nostalgia in this story; each character is presented as being unique and unpredictable whether he or she was known to the narrator for many years or only for a few short, fleeting hours.

In "Good Country People," Flannery O'Connor also presents a situation whereby a stranger makes a difference in the lives and attitudes of a certain type of country folk in the red hills of Georgia. This story, an excellent exposure of frustration and religious dupery, has certainly been influenced by the oral tradition of the folk tale where the stress is on deliberate exaggeration and grotesque situations. It also demonstrates

Miss O'Connor's belief that the artist penetrates the concrete world in order to find at its depths the image of ultimate reality. "This in no way hinders his perception of evil but rather sharpens it, for only when the natural world is seen as good does evil become intelligible as a destructive force and a necessary result of our freedom." Katherine Anne Porter's "Holiday" is the story of a young woman's stay with a warm and compassionate German family who live on a large farm in East Texas not far from the Louisiana line. Like Flannery O'Connor, Miss Porter has a tremendous feeling for human mystery and individuality, especially as she portrays the primal experiences of birth and death. In a different vein, David Madden's highly original and instructive satire on the art of storytelling, "The Singer," takes place in the impoverished mountain communities of eastern Kentucky. In this story, the stranger is The Singer, a character who really does not pertain to the "film-lecture" which is the basis of the story, yet who gives dramatic unity to the audience's experience as she appears and disappears in the film.

Another story that recalls the folk tale tradition is Alice Walker's "Strong Horse Tea" in which a desperate mother takes a chance on an old folk remedy to save her sick son. In Eudora Welty's "The Wide Net," a fine literary folk tale set in the lush countryside of southern Mississippi, the story begins with the disappearance of a pregnant wife and goes on to ring bright changes on the mythic modes of quest, initiation, and discovery. Here the sensual landscape of the Pearl River becomes a magical place of mystery and transformation, where the individual, the community, and the forces of nature seem equally involved in a single effort. One other story, Tennessee Williams' life of Alma Tutwiler in "The Yellow Bird," brings to mind folk tale tones, especially in its natural fusion of fantasy and realism. What is unusual here is that Williams unites the New England transcendentalist mode of storytelling as found in the short fiction of Nathaniel Hawthorne, for example, with the story of a prostitute who resides in New Orleans' French Quarter.

The present-day South of contradiction and excessive changes seems especially vivid in the stories by Kay, Jones, Betts, Hannah, and Shelnutt. In Kay's "The Fifth Generation," a young college graduate discovers himself caught between the established, uninteresting world of his father, a wealthy banker, and the rough, emotional, rootless world of the modern cowboy in a hardhat. In Jones' "The Fugitive," a mountain boy on the run and a dead grandfather awaken doubts in a city boy from Memphis. Doris Betts' "The Ugliest Pilgrim" portrays the drama of a note-taking girl from the Carolina mountains on her way to Tulsa for a religious "cure." Violet Karl's encounter with Grady Fliggins and Monty Harrill, her card-playing bus companions, makes her a more loving and lovable person. Finally, the stories of Hannah and Shelnutt, "Testimony of Pilot" and "Angel," are powerful subjective visions of some of the strange confusions that reign in the contemporary South. Hannah's story combines the form of the comic, freewheeling literary yarn with the destructive forces of Southern mythomania. In a more abstract way, the thoughts of the women in "Angel" as they prepare for Claire's recital seem to flow from the past into a liquid future to create a powerfully dense story in the present tense.

If the short stories presented here are characteristically Southern because of a shared history, and because of a shared experience of contemporary social change and contradiction, perhaps what unites them most strongly is a need for language to delight, to give shape to experience, and to reveal meaning. What is most Southern about this and most universal as well lies in its communal foundations, as a recognition by the artist that the reader shares the same need, and that the end of all art is a new communion. The Southern writers in this volume have known, each in his or her own way, what Eudora Welty says about the short story: "Stories are *new* things, stories make words new; that is one of their illusions and part of their beauty. And of course the great stories of the world are the ones that seem new to their readers on and on, always new because they keep their power of revealing something."

Note to the Revised Edition

In the few years since this collection was first published there has been no slacking off of the remarkable number of good stories written by writers from the American South. There is perhaps no final explanation of this continuing vitality and achievement, but it seems to us that at least two factors are worth considering. To begin with, there continues to exist in the contemporary South a special confederate union between a stubbornly oral society—even at this late date and against powerful odds—and the active speculative life available on university campuses and in university journals all over the Southern states. Nowhere else in the world does the university play such a large role in promoting a single literary genre. Naturally, a main thrust of the role is academic and scholarly, and during the past several years there have been many new studies of the major Southern writers. But more importantly for the young contemporary writer in the South, new writing is energetically encouraged and above all published. Southern university journals, *The Southern Review, The Sewanee Review, The Virginia Quarterly Review,* and *The Georgia Review,* among others, continue to publish new short stories by young writers, and Southern university presses regularly bring out new collections by both new and established writers.

A second factor is perhaps more compelling and deep-seated than the encouraging presence of universities and their presses. It may be that the modern Southern story, however much it shares with the related impulses of the modern Southern novel or poem, has sustained itself at such a high level of achievement simply because it is the most congenial form to the Southern literary mind. Certainly it is the genre most capable of fusing modern literary concerns and techniques with a native Southern idiom and oral storytelling tradition. But whatever explanation can be given, the palpable fact is there: modern Southern writers excel most consistently in a single genre.

In going through the mass of new stories available our principle of selection remained the same as that of the original edition: find the best Southern stories we could, one story for each author. Though we found many good stories, the six we have added very quickly ranked themselves at the top of the list. They could not be more different in their variety of styles and subjects; but they are all indelibly and immediately Southern, and in each an individual voice—the touchstone of all great stories—is distinctly heard. They are all, we feel, worthy of the best stories in the original edition.

Fred Chappell's "Blue Dive" is taken from his collection *Moments of Light,* a volume that contains at least one other Southern masterpiece, the short, searing "Children of Strikers," a description of two poor children walking along a "black chemical river" in a Southern mill town. "Blue Dive" is a longer, slower story, one of the few successful stories about Southern music; Eudora Welty's miraculous "Powerhouse" is another that comes immediately to mind. "Blue Dive" is the story of Stovebolt Johnson, an old-time bluesman who has been in prison, and who is now walking the roads trying to find a job. Nothing rings false in his story, neither the speech nor the music, and Stovebolt's performance at the Blue Dive, which pleases the people but fails to land him a job, convincingly dramatizes one of the central themes of Southern writing—the lasting seductive force of man's value expressed in his art even in a world where the most powerful means are used to deprive him of it. When we last see Stovebolt he is all by himself again, but he is nonetheless right at home and still thinking.

George Garrett is best known for his historical novels, *Death of the Fox,* and *The Succession,* but he has been writing short stories and writing about short stories for the past thirty years. "Time of Bitter Children" is a bleak story of nighttime highways, hitchhiking, and the disinherited, but the irresistible impulse to make a test of each new encounter curiously makes these drivers and hitchhikers more human, somehow subverting the story's dominant note of negation and hopelessness.

Ellen Gilchrist's story "Revenge" describes the coming of age of a ten-year-old-girl, Rhoda, in Mississippi during World War II. Left to herself in a household full of male cousins, she finally casts off the unwanted roles her family and community offer, and asserts herself by running away from a wedding reception and vaulting over the pole-vault bar in the field where her cousins had kept her out all summer. Along with Rhoda's solitary triumph of selfhood what strikes the reader most is Gilchrist's gift at brief characterizations. For a short story there are a surprising number of brilliant period portraits: Baby Doll, the housekeeper and dancer; Lauralee, Rhoda's whiskey-drinking older cousin who had joined the WAVES after her young husband had been killed in the war; and Lauralee's new husband-to-be from Florida who has flat feet and a reassuring laugh.

Breece D'J Pancake's story "Trilobites" is probably one of the most autobiographical stories he wrote, and the tensions between desire and fate that haunt the entire story show a psychological maturity in narration that Pancake, even in his early twenties, was capable of achieving. "Trilobites" is the story of Colly, a young man whose father has died and whose mother wants to sell the farm he has lived on all his life. His former girlfriend, Ginny, has left to go to Florida, though on the day of the story she is back in town. With everything fleeing his grasp, the fossil stones, the trilobites of the title, remote and inhuman as they are, seem signs of a lost permanence his own life now lacks. Sadly, because his posthumous collection of stories shows Pancake to be an accomplished writer with a promising career, he killed himself in 1979 at the age of 27.

Jayne Anne Phillips could be paired with Breece Pancake since she, too, is a West Virginian born in 1952. But whereas Pancake limits himself to a fairly restricted territory of West Virginia mines and adolescent frustration, Phillips reaches out all over the United States, and shows a remarkable gift for imagining a variety of types and situations. Her best Southern story is "1934," a finely drawn period piece of insanity and the Depression in Virginia. In it the subjective narrative of a daughter's love for her insane father is traced out in the public history of his suicide, making the inner and outer versions of the father halves of a single reality.

John McCluskey, Jr., in "The Best Teacher in Georgia," has written perhaps the most meditative story of the new group. Two black women, an old blind mother and her ill daughter, a retired teacher, both fall off the back porch onto the yard below. Temporarily immobilized, they talk to each other about sickness, the past, old age, and loneliness; and finally, the mother's moral strength and the daughter's renewed will seem to join together in a new affirmation of kinship and understanding as they raise themselves up without any help from the outside.

With writers such as Chappell, Garrett, Gilchrist, Pancake, Phillips, and McCluskey, not to mention all the other first-rate writers of short stories already represented in *Stories of the Modern South* and now working on their second, third, or fourth collections, there is nothing to complain about in the literary South. Whatever the state of the contemporary story in the rest of the world, or in the rest of the United States, in today's South it continues to be the most living literary form, still capable of bringing together, in fresh new narratives, the communal mind and the individual voice.

Ben Forkner
Patrick Samway, S.J.

STORIES OF THE MODERN SOUTH

1928 STORY
by *James Agee*

He had not been home long when he found that one of the things he cared most for was playing the old records. His wife liked some of them too, very much, and when he put on the oldest of them she remembered, he could see, how pleased he had been that she recognized how much better they were than most of the later ones. But now that he was playing them again, and she showed how warmly she enjoyed them, he had to realize that her associations were very different from his own, referring entirely to their times together just before the war; and that she was using these already different and inadequate associations a little too eagerly, to get close to him. He knew, sadly enough, that it was still not easy for either of them to get close to each other, and he felt gentle towards her for taking whatever means she could. But he knew too that it was worthless to try to exploit this music, and its so very different associations, for any such purpose. She was badly mistaken to try. And he had to realize that he was badly mistaken himself, to use the records in his own way: that whatever was done about this music, estranged them still further, rather than bringing them together. It seemed quite possible, for that matter, that he was using them as a way of retreating from her, and from everything else. He felt that he had no business doing it, to her, or for that matter to himself. He had to get used to living in the world again, after all. And when he thought of it at all he realized that the world he had once lived in, and could never live in again, and that could never again exist, was no great loss, to him or anyone else. He had better recognize this fact; he knew that very well. Even the nineteen thirties had been increasingly distasteful, one year worse than the next before it; then the war, which in one curious sense hardly counted as a part of living—or how much did it count? He still did not know. He wondered whether he was ever likely to. And now, the middle, the last half, of the nineteen forties. Only the meanness, and fatness, and insanity seemed to survive, as it had also survived the Depression; and in whatever ways these had changed, they seemed to have changed for the worse. There had been a kind of innocence in everything about the old years, that gave some sort of charm even to the worst of it. In a way, of course, the innocence had survived everything too. But it seemed a kind of innocence, now, that has no business being so innocent. And the sophistication, such as it was, was the most blinding thing of all. (What do I mean, he thought; but lacked the energy to specify.) Very likely, he realized, all this was purely subjective—a matter simply of his having been young during certain years, older during certain other years, and, God knew, older still right now. That, and beginning to learn about himself that he was infantile, to use a word out of a vocabulary which sickened him; that he had never really grown up, whatever that might mean, or even wanted. Good Lord, he thought, if I'm not careful I'm going to find out I'm a Conservative, after all.

Or was he. Was it ever true that he had not grown up, or hadn't wanted to? He had certainly been filled with a lot of easy hope, back during the Depression, when he and practically everyone else he knew had gone Left. And even when he found he was far less sanguine than most of his friends he had for a long time remained hopeful, and active. For several years his reflexes and ideas had been as thoroughly Marxian as they were Freudian, in the purely smattering way, that is, that he knew anything about either. Then his Freudian ideas had frayed out among the renegades and the schools, and his Marxian ideas had frayed out to something, he supposed, that was most easily defensible as political agnosticism, and for some years now, though he still used the same vocabulary and reacted to a great extent, he was afraid, according to the same reflexes—with a few additions which he supposed and hoped were his own—he had found it almost never possible to trust either his own judgments or those of anybody else. Certainly, by now, he felt no trust or hope in anything, that anyone might do or even say. It was a stupefied country, and evidently a stupefied world, and as stupefied as anything else was his sense of universal mistrust and of hopeless regret, his dependence on mere taste, his pleasure in the sensuous, his miserable reluctance to live in the world as it was, and to discard the pleasures of recall.

If I could write about this, he thought, maybe it would amount to something, or maybe at least it would help clear my mind. But he knew that he was quite unqualified to write it, and that he had no heart even to try, or even to think about it in terms of writing. It was so long since he had really felt any heart for that. During the war it had seemed, for a while, as if something had returned—yes, actually, for a while, he knew it had returned. First industriously, then more and more irregularly, finally petering out, all but entirely. He had kept a journal—which as it petered out turned more and more into guide notes—and he realized that there had been some pretty good things in the journal, here and there anyhow. Yet he was not sorry that he had destroyed it. And he was rather more sorry than glad that of the five poems he had written he had sent one, the Christmas one, to his wife, and that she had sent it along, without asking him, to *Partisan Review*, which had printed it. He remembered rather bitterly the letter a quite good poet (but not after all so *God* damned good himself) had sent him: the poem was not thoroughly finished—understandably enough under the circumstances, and was indeed in many respects a remarkably fine job—in some respects, in the poet's opinion, "far and away ahead of anything else you've done." He was delighted to see new work after so long a silence, and hoped that Irvine would remember that he, the poet, too, was an editor, and that poems as good as that don't grow on trees. He might, he said, take issue on one matter, if he felt that discussion of anything besides pure questions of technique were not hopelessly presumptuous and beside the point. He referred, of course, to the disturbing hint in lines 4–7 that Irvine was beginning perhaps to take a polite interest in God. That way, the poet begged leave to advise, madness lay, in his humble opinion—though one could if one liked (and indeed must, whether one liked or not) remember Dante and, if you insist, Eliot. But for a truly contemporary man, such as Irvine? But he would say no more. And it was in every important respect a welcome and truly superb poem.

He looked forward to a resumption of their old bouts, "when this indecent mess is over."

He was just as glad he had destroyed the other four—though one, anyhow, was probably a better poem anyway than The Nativity. And he was not at all sorry that he hadn't bothered to answer the letter—though it did embarrass him to remember his embarrassment over that, the evening they met.

He had no interest in talking about poetry, and very little interest in reading it—or anything else, for that matter, of contemporary work anyhow. Some of it was good, he supposed, a damn sight better, anyhow, than *he* had ever done. But he had no trust in it—or to put it more simply, no interest whatever. He detected in this lack of interest some element of jealousy, of self-pity; though he had long ago pretty thoroughly given up the idea that he was a writer. Or had he? If I haven't, he thought, it's high time I did. Like so many of the others, he realized, he had just been one of the overliterate "sensitive" middle-class boys with a great deal of adolescent excitement and a certain facility of the senses and with words and forms. Of most of them he couldn't see that they were anything more than this. The difference was, simply, that they had kept on producing. Maybe the difference was, that essentially it was they who had remained adolescent, that it was he, comparatively (oh *very* comparatively) speaking, who had grown up. In any case he saw nothing in their work (what little of it, he took care to remind himself, I've read), that could convince him that any one of them, except unquestionably Auden, was in the least what he meant by being a good artist. Smooth craftsmen, adroit—well *fairly* adroit—intellectuals, experienced manipulators of images that came too easily; producers of no doubt perfectly creditable work that didn't have an ounce wit to the ton, of even the most modest, minor art. Certainly it was impossible to regret not being one of them. The thing to regret was: was he not something more than that? He could not entirely, or permanently anyhow, get over the feeling that he was. And this feeling persisted even though he realized, thinking back over the writing he had done, that nothing existed in that writing—or at best very little and very debatable—to indicate it. It settled nothing either, to remind himself that no matter how glib the nonartists were, a good artist too is a man who constantly produces.

Why did that make no difference?

Melville? Coleridge?

He caught himself in shame: the old adolescent has it.

He realized that each of these producers whom he held, yes, more or less in contempt, must certainly have in themselves that confidence that they at least, no matter about the others, were true artists, which for all his own years-long stultification, he could not get rid of.

So what, he thought. And suddenly, with incredible sadness, he remembered a morning out at the shore, when, though the paper was soft with dampness, he had sat on through lunch (eating the sandwiches his mother brought), until he had finished the story of the girls and boys and of the rat—so tired that several times he put his forehead down on to the paper and stayed there several minutes, and nauseated with chain smoking (it was his first summer of being open with tobacco), but during the six and a half hours the job had taken, not once getting out of the chair except to go to the bathroom. Towards the end he had felt almost irresistible haste to finish so that he could read it to his mother; and had successfully resisted the haste and finished it as it ought to be finished; in spite of the speed, it had been a really carefully written story. And how proudly and unexpectedly he realized, once it was done, that for the first time in his life he felt very well in control of his eagerness to read it to his mother or to anyone else—in fact, it became clear to him that he really had no desire to read it, to anyone except himself, and that very likely he would not bother to read to her, either, the things he had brought along from school, that hadn't been printed yet. He read the story over, coldly, correcting and recasting with a feeling of perfect professionalism, and at the same time with the coldness and the resourceful proficiency, felt complete enjoyment and satisfaction. He clipped it, transferred the spring's work to a lower drawer, and laid the manuscript carefully into the empty, upper left-hand drawer. He stood up, stiff, slightly dazed, swollen with self-delight, and walked quietly back into the kitchen to the gin bottle. He was already allowed to drink, moderately, and might with impunity have made himself a highball, but he felt for some reason, doubtless connected with the lack of need to read the story to his mother, more triumphant in deceit. He poured an inch into a tumbler, added a little water, and drank it down rather quickly. Then he put ice and ginger ale into a glass and, his head swimming quietly, went out onto the screened porch. He cranked up the portable, put on *West Side Blues,* sat down and looked around him through the three screens, feeling like a king.

It was going to be a wonderful summer.

He heard the delicate, passionate music through, now, in a strange state of mind: perfectly, fiber by fiber, in cold and helpless regret; perfectly, at the same time, recalling, re-experiencing, the best that he had ever heard in it. The record had been new to him that spring, and he had first heard it at a perfect time to hear it, when his delight in jazz music was experienced but still fresh, in opening bloom. The record had seemed to him the best that need ever be asked for, of jazz, or of any other music. He had tried to use it to prove to his mother and father that jazz is as pure a lyric art as can exist, and that it can reach, among several men at once, improvising at that, great subtlety of mood, and beautiful development and integrity within that mood—as thorough and as good, he insisted, as anything in Mozart, and as distinct in every way, not a chance missed or soft pedaled, not a superfluous note. His father grinned and said he agreed there was nothing soft-pedaled about it anyhow, and sipped his highball. He replied, with astonishment and almost with rage, as to someone who sneers comfortably at one's close friend, that at least half of that record was played mezzo-piano or still more quietly, as anyone who had any ears could hear. His father, sorry for having sneered, answered this affront gently, saying that he guessed he just didn't have the right kind of ear for jazz, though he thought it was pleasant enough to listen to. Disheartened, and ashamed of his vehemence, Irvine then avoided asking his mother for her comment; but at the first rebalancing of feelings that seemed to her appropriate (and she had a fairly careful though far from adequate intuition for this) she said, also gently, that while perhaps she liked it better than Irvine's father, and thought it very pretty and pleasing indeed, and in places really *talented,* she could perfectly well see what Irvine meant about the lyricism, she certainly couldn't feel that it was possible to compare it with *Mozart,* or really that you could call it an art, perhaps. Irvine said quietly, all but interrupting her that he hadn't at all meant an out-and-out, all-round comparison with Mozart, and also he didn't mean "art," at all the way she said, that the worst thing that could happen to jazz would be, if people got to thinking of it as an "art," and he hated to think what any jazz musician would feel about anyone who said so—not that he knew any—but all the same in its own entirely distinct way it obviously *was* an art, with very strong and distinct disciplines of its own, and one that could be very eloquent and accurate about emotions and states of mind, too, like the one he had just played, and—. She interrupted, again gently, to say that though very likely, in the special sense he meant, it was an art, she supposed the real trouble, the real reason she wasn't as appreciative of it as she'd like to be, was a difference in generations. He asked, again too quietly, what kind of really good music she thought that could be said of: Mozart? And she replied, trying not to be rough or complacent in her triumph, that that was exactly the difference she meant, between Louis Armstrong and Mozart. "For East is East and West is West," Irvine's father said, smiling in a friendly way. And he hastened to add that he had said this not to make a comparison, to the disadvantage of either musician (here he could not wholly restrain his slight but not malevolent amusement), it simply came into his head anent the differences between the generations. ("Anent," a word which amused him, did not amuse his son.) The conversation then became general, as both parents remembered popular songs they had liked, which had not been enjoyed by their parents, and songs their parents had liked, which had seemed, at best, prettily old-fashioned to them. They began to hum and sing these songs, some of which interested and pleased Irvine, and before long, regretting that he had laid himself open, and had been so talkative (for his new motto was "silence, exile and cunning"), he decided not to try to bring it up again, listened with real pleasure to their singing, and even joined in, where he could.

The music had developed in him a distinct image of a place he had never known. When he tried to take the image apart, he realized that nothing much like it was, for that matter, likely to exist. But in the course of taking it apart, and imagining what was likely in it and what was not so likely, he only made it the less likely, and was satisfied that his changes were improvements. It was not a large room, and was not decorated. It had a quality of semilegality.

It was very late. Nearly everyone had gone home. Those who stayed were those who were there for the night. They were nearly all around thirty—on Irvine's scale of age, neither young nor old. Most of them were Negroes. Most of them were also poor people, working people, but not of a kind to work any harder than was absolutely necessary; not of a kind, in fact, to work for security. Though they were of an age when most people, of whatever degree of wealth or poverty, have become responsible, and careful, it had never occurred to them to live for anything other than enjoyment, and it probably never would. In a sense they were as unquestionably dedicated as the musicians themselves—who would now, like them, soon be quitting for the night. Those who had to, musicians and listeners alike, would go straight on from here to their day's work. Those who could afford to would soon be asleep.

Now they were all at the most beautiful time of the night, and in the most beautiful of states of being: full of gin, but no longer at all drunk; deeply tired, and quiet; completely gentle. Some kept on drinking gin; others drank black coffee; the place was never at its worst very professional, except when the unliked type of white came in; now it was as filled with easy fondness, and a lack of commercialism as the best kind of love. Faces which more normally might be sharp, clownish, brutal, demanding, suspicious were all perfected, now: responsive as drumbeats; yet as peaceful as sleep. The waiter, bringing more drinks and more coffee, walked in perfect silence; the drinking too was silent: not one noise of china. Some watched the musicians, or lifted their eyes and watched, smiling slightly, during the best moments. Most were looking at nothing; they were simply listening. A girl moved softly against the man she sat with; he put his hand along the side of her head and brought her head against his chest. The singer and the clarinetist, both low, sank lower, through chromatic minor thirds; the pianist picked it up. Two simple chords, a strong bass note; a bass tenth and the swung chord, against descending lacework, sharply, softly played. Now the tenths descending, the right hand rising—and in both hands, a sudden few chords of chisel-like energy, dissolving into tremolos. The bass again, squaring it out for the steep run down, to the low meeting of the hands; then a climb of arpeggio chords, major, and the trumpeter takes it off the last, flatted note, lifting, a half tone, another, a third high, the note held, the trombone gathered beneath that, and the clarinet, and the guitar, and the brushes, and the piano at its most elementary, while the held note holds, intensifies, enlarges, shines, in the pulsing of the other instruments, a full eight beats: to burst open at length into a rapturously gentle, spasmic figure, built on that high note and down from it, five times repeated, then climbing a full tone and down again, down, well into the low register and flaring up again, and down, an octave—to the piano's bell-like left hand, deep, and ringing right, five octaves up, flaring its chords out of its shaking heart, descending with each, shading over into minor, imitating the trumpet's opening salute as it comes into middle voice, flatting: a held breath, and the trumpet's imitation of the imitation, at the most simple possible, as simple as falling at last to sleep.

The window shades were drawn; daylight came through the cracks in them. There was dew on the rails of the track and on the weeds, and now that the music was over, you could hear roosters crowing.

The cornetist had drained his horn. Now he wrapped it in an old silk scarf and snapped it into its case.

It was time to go to work, but nobody was moving yet.

He cranked the machine, and started again with the piano solo, and sat back again. He had never been to a place like the one he imagined, yet it was more familiar to him than any place he had ever known. He tried taking it apart again, and realized, as he had often before, that it was not likely that there was any place like it. [But that did not impress him.] Musicians as good as those earned their living by it; even when they played for pleasure, even if they were Negroes, they probably never played in a place so poor. Or even if they did, it was not situated as this was, in a great field at the edge of the city, near the tracks; a field of dump-heaps, rusty iron, wild grasses and rough flowers, great lonely signboards, a few mysteriously flashing stalks of corn. You did not look out through the shade into the shining morning and watch hundreds of men, along the tracks, and the paths invisible along the great field, on their way to work. You did not see, so clearly, like the most beautiful closeup, the dew on the shine and oily rust of a section of rail and frogplate, the gravelly cinders and the oak tie, the dew on the spikey, flowering weed. Nor was it likely, in the Southern city he was thinking of—New Orleans? Algiers?—that whites and Negroes, however fond of the same music, would be so thoroughly at ease together as this. And if such an outlandish outsider as he should find his way there, would he ever be allowed to come in? Or if allowed, wouldn't he manage to destroy the spirit, quality and ease of everything?

But none of these doubts made any difference. With each critical repetition, in fact, he only added further detail to the reality of the place—a calendar against the wall, the picture of a girl in a great red hat; a cockroach on the electric light wire; the subdued sound of eggs frying back in the little kitchen; the cook leaning his face at his window during the final solo; the way it sounded to a man on his way to work, a quarter of a mile up the track, and the fleck of steam above the starting locomotive, far down at the roundhouse. You could see a little of the river from there, like moving putty, but guess its grandeur mainly by the smallness of everything on the far side. If it didn't exist, it ought to, and that suited him. But of course it did exist, and so did ten thousand other things as good, in just this kind of music.

He turned back the pickup and put the record back in its folder.

There was no chance, for him at least, he knew, of ever being a hundredth as good as that, in the art he worked at, and hoped to practice; but today, and still at his age in general, his own confidence was untroubled, even by such knowledge. He was glad there were such musicians in the world, and hoped he might learn something from them, and felt no fear for himself; only great sureness and pleasure.

He leaned back once more in the noisy wicker chair and looked through the three screened sides of the porch at the screened, shingled cottages along the irregular shore. Salt had made patterns on the screen on the sea side; there was already a little sand along the porch. It was a dull, cool day, and the cottages too looked dull—even boring, he supposed; but he liked the way they looked, and the silly caps and suits hung out in the back.

It was going to be a wonderful summer.

He thought of the new story he had finished earlier in the afternoon, secure in its otherwise empty drawer, the first work of the vacation—very possibly his best so far, the first day. He felt too pleased and too mature even to reread it. He thought of the gin in the kitchen cupboard, and the whiskey hidden (not too secretively) in the sideboard; he felt too well even to take another drink.

He went upstairs and changed into his bathing suit.

Like most of the beaches along this rough section of the shore, the one just below Irvine's cottage, to which he came now, was a makeshift, hundred-foot crescent along which sand had been dumped. The sand was renewed every spring, and stayed fairly well, but even by this time of year, late June, you could feel the rocks under foot and see them working through. A small sign freshly painted each spring, appealed to the bathers as gentlemen and ladies with the single word: PLEASE! and on the whole the beach was kept quite tidy. A life-preserver, also freshly painted, hung from a T-shaped oak stand; by the preceding summer, it had begun to appeal to Irvine as an esoteric emblem. Except at high tide it was necessary to wade on rocks and to get off your feet as soon as the water would hold you. This, in turn, was uncomfortable, except for the proudly brash, for even in sunny weather the water was cold. Those who intended to spend much time swimming and sun bathing went to the Yacht Club float, a quarter of a mile downshore, or drove three miles upshore, in their bathing suits, to the broad public beach; or those few who knew the wealthier families of the neighborhood well enough used their small, expensively developed private beaches, taking care not to invite themselves too often. But for casual swimming, everybody was used to and even rather fond of the deficiencies of these small semi-public ledges of discouraged sand which, like the small neat yacht clubs, were maintained by and for the cottage owners of the middle class.

There was practically nobody out on this cloudy afternoon, and Irvine was glad; the first few days of vacation always involved many exchanges of senseless courtesies, and the longer they were put off the better. His family had been spending summers here since he was five, among other equally stable cottage-owners. Everyone knew everyone else, amiably enough but in general, quite avoidance, without interest or fondness. For as Irvine had only lately begun to realize, most people of his parents' generation cared for privacy almost as thoroughly as he did, and made these crowded vacation compromises chiefly because they could afford nothing better—though he was still unable to understand how they could endure the uses they made of such privacy and leisure as they had. Mrs. Dart and her son Eddie and her daughter Anna were on the beach, and Irvine said hello to them, and talked with them, emptily but pleasantly enough, while he smoked half a cigarette; then excused himself, put it out, and made for the water a little sooner than he wanted to.

It was even colder than he had expected. He swam out as fast as he could until he was winded, turned over and floated, and looked back at the shore. The Darts, to his satisfaction, were picking their way up to the duckboard between the high rocks. He watched Eddie help his heavy mother over a difficult place. It was a natural enough courtesy, and he would have done it himself without a second or even a first thought; but it had a look of unquestioned servility and of tedium, which he disliked. He watched Anna's too-short, dabbing steps in her white rubber bathing slippers.* He could not feel the least interest in her, either, though he reflected now that she had developed a good deal, over the winter, and had watched him surreptitiously, while he talked with her brother and mother, in a way which would have made the coming summer look exciting, if she had been any girl less dull. For the first time he felt restive and uneasy, almost imprisoned, in the prospect of a whole summer in this place.

He warmed himself by swimming some more, and lay over and looked back again. Now he could see the whole range of middle-sized, somewhat too closely crowded cottages, stepped up-and-down, back-and-forth, along the rock

---

*Since this story was first published posthumously, there are a number of textual difficulties. Here, the word was originally "suits."

bluffs; and, down to the left, the compact, rather intricate yacht club, with its staring coat of new paint. Under this clouded light the brown and gray shingled cottages, and the brown and gray rocks, and the vegetation were particularly drab, whereas the white on the water and on the clubhouse and the intense perfect ring of the life-preserver on his beach glowed like white cloths at dusk. He saw a sedan turn in from the highway. George Helms was gassing his launch. Jordan Reid was already mooring; the main sail, weltering, sank without a sound. Four people whom he could not quite recognize, but knew were no strangers, lolled rather disconsolately on the float. Far behind his floating head, like a lost cowbell, a buoy drizzled its warnings. Down between the rocks, along the section of duckboard, came two more people to his empty beach.

Both were female; and even at this distance, he knew they were strangers. He wanted to swim to shore as quickly as possible. Though he was suddenly very cold, he waited, while they laid aside their robes and walked cautiously into the water. One, in dark blue, was a mature body; the other, he was sure now, was young. Her bathing suit was the color of cedar. As soon as they were sufficiently absorbed in swimming not to notice him, he hurried in, dried himself, lighted a cigarette, and carefully examined a barnacle cut in his heel. By the time he was able to taste the tobacco, they were coming in. They looked studiously into the water as if they were trying not to admit that they were dismayed to have committed themselves to such a place for the summer. Irvine suddenly realized that the life-preserver was badly corroded; a bottle, emptied of sun tan oil, leaned against a rock. The older woman had a hard well-kept body and a hard well-kept face which were unpleasantly masculine. Irvine did his best not to look at either the girl, or too pointedly away from her: but their eyes met, on her part cooly, he could see, on his, in a frightening spasm of hopeless joy. Instantly, proudly, yet gently, and he suspected, contemptuously, she looked away. He looked as quickly away; he felt as if she had slapped him.

He knew he must be calm, and courteous; he took care to catch the older woman's eye. "How do you do," he said, smiling gravely, and bowing his head, he realized too late, with a much too presumptuous graciousness. Her eyes were knowing and impersonal. "How do you do," she said, and turned from him to pick up her towel. She and the girl dried themselves in vigorous silence, put on their robes and sat down, their backs to him, a little ahead of him and to the right. The line of the girl's cheek and her [ ]* rubber cap were very cold and remote as she looked away at the water. Then as she drew up one knee and, putting both hands beneath her left ear unfastened the chin-strap, he saw the subtly vigilent turning of the older woman's head. But the woman said nothing, and the girl removed her cap and, her fingers spread from the nape, shook the damp hair lose. It was fine, flowerlike, full of golden light, the color of brown sugar. Irvine felt again, but more gently, the incredulous fear and kindliness of the moment when their eyes met. He knew by their voices that, so long as he remained, they were able only to make conversation. He put on his sneakers and laced them, carefully took apart and scattered his cigarette, caped his towel over his shoulders, and started towards the duckboard, stooping as he walked, to pick up the empty oil bottle. As he passed behind them he murmured, "good afternoon," in the inflection appropriate to withdrawal. The woman replied in the same tone, but when, a second later, the girl said it, the words had become a salutation, to which he felt, as he climbed the duckboard, the back of his neck burning, he should have replied.

Normally, showering after a swim, he merely rinsed off the brine. Now he used soap as well, and was more than usually interested in his body; and as he combed his hair, he watched himself carefully in the mirror. But his mind was so absorbed in her image, as she came out of the water, that he hardly saw himself. It was awkward and unpleasant, wading on rocks which were not only sharp but unfamiliar; but her awkwardness continually suggested her grace. For all her restraint, her breath was shakey and her teeth rattled. Her chilled lips were almost the color of her eyes. She had the kind of delicate skin which shows cold readily, and beautifully; her thighs were a mulled, marbled net of rose and azure. Tight with cold, and caught small in the gray-gold bathing-cap, her features, and her head were at once nun-like and saurian. Her breasts were also tight-

* Adjectives illegible.

ened with the cold, and he tried hard not to either remember them, or imagine them.

But even better was the moment in which she had shown her hair.

Had she known? Or done it unconsciously, because unconsciously she was attracted to him? Or was she unconscious of his existence? Or had she done this in deliberate contempt?

She had spoken to him; he remembered her voice; it was as startling as her eyes, and as impossible to deduce.

Don't be a fool, he kept warning himself. Take your time. Don't ask questions, or give yourself away. Don't try to force yourself on her. It's a long summer. You'll know her, soon enough.

But it was even harder to keep to himself a matter of such importance, than it would have been to betray himself. All during supper he was as silent, and as secret, as if he had just committed murder, and as elegant as if he were dining among princes. He gathered that his father honestly did not notice it, and saw that his mother was doing her best not to show that she did, was trying, even, to restrain her private curiosity; but it was as obvious and painful to him as if he were shouting about it, and he found that his efforts to appear casual were even more stupid. He even began to realize, with something of the helpless shame which one feels in dreams of nakedness, that he had dressed for this purely domestic meal, almost as scrupulously as if he were going to a party. He began to resent the girl, to try at least to reduce her to what she really was. There was nothing, actually, at all remarkable about her. It was a perfectly ordinary voice, when he remembered it with any detachment. This idea that she was unusually graceful was just so much adolescent illusion (but then he remembered the moment in which, in one motion, she had drawn up her left knee and loosened her chin strap; even the elbows alone were very graceful, there was no use doubting that). That kind of skin, in a way, which got so mottled with cold, was actually rather ugly, under those conditions, anyhow (but under other conditions, he had to admit, it might not be so ugly; in fact it was very attractive, perhaps even beautiful, under any condition, at all, so far as he was concerned). He did not at all like the way she had looked away from him; after all, they were in a sense neighbors already as she must have realized, and there had certainly been no possible grounds for showing contempt; it suggested that she was a cold, prim, narrow sort of girl—very much the kind, in fact, you might expect of that kind of mother. One thing was clear enough, anyway; he did not like the mother, anymore than the mother liked him. He did not like the strong line of muscle down the outside of her thigh, or her dark face, which looked almost shaven, or that cold, hard, dark eye. There was no reason for that kind of coldness. It was perfectly true that he had overdone the kind of *grand-seigneur* act, the old whatsitact business! when he spoke to her, but was he not expected to speak to her at all? There was such a thing as courtesy, after all, and it seemed very much of his place to speak and to speak first, since they were new here; also, he had taken natural care to address the older woman, and even more care not to seem to demand any further conversation by doing so. So why would it have hurt her, to say a little more than that cold how do you do in return—the absolute minimum required of her? Why couldn't she have at least given an opening for something more he might say himself? Or at least have smiled? And come to think of it, why had the girl said nothing? If either of them knew even the elements of common courtesy, they would realize that when he was addressing the older of the two he was addressing both of them; that in fact he had no right to address the younger one directly, in the presence of the older one, but certainly meant it to be for both of them. Then what was one to make of that silence, on the part of the one he was really interested in, and that coldness, on the part of the other? One had to make just this of it: that they were either people of no kind of breeding at all, or snobs. Well, it wasn't exactly a period of history where snobbery was appreciated. It—

Don't be a fool, he insisted again. You're making a mountain out of a molehill. She's just another girl; she may be a very nice one, she may stink. You'll find out.

Within half an hour after the meal he heard himself say, in a voice at which he wanted to shout his ridicule: "Some new people down at the beach, this afternoon." His mother looked at him. He detested himself. "Woman and her daughter." He felt himself blushing and quickly got up, to be above the line of the light. "At least I suppose it was her daughter," he said.

"New people?" his mother said, taking care not to watch him. "Who would they be, Burt?"

His father paused. "Must be the Parkers," he said. "Linton T. Parker. Rented the Fowler's cottage. Only new people *I've* heard of."

"Then the Fowlers *did* go abroad?"

"I don't know whether they went aboard. I know they rented their cottage."

"They were talking about it so much, last summer."

His father looked at her sharply, and grinned. "Don't worry," he said. "We'll go one of these days. Might as well wait until Irvine is old enough to get the most out of it."

"I think I'll go over to Ed's," Irvine said.

"Don't stay out too late," his mother called, as the screen door shut.

His father shook his head at her. "Don't nag at him," he said. "He's not a baby anymore."

Irvine's cottage was set high, quartered towards the sea and overlooking the Yacht Club. The Fowler's cottage was further from the shore, near the bottom of an opposite slope. Irvine could see its lights as he shut the porch door, and they were as startling among all the other lights he could see, and as quietly handsome as his name had been when he had first seen it in print in his school's literary magazine.

Don't be completely childish, he told himself, and started walking towards the lights. Even when the time came to choose the path to the Dart's cottage, he made no effort to choose, but, repeating, for God's sake don't be *utterly* childish, kept on towards the lights, the pit of his stomach cold.

Before he got near enough possibly to be seen, he cut off to the right, behind several cottages, and approached the Fowler cottage from the rear, which was dark. It was the front room which was lighted. The girl sat on a wicker couch with her feet drawn up and her skirt tucked carefully around her knees. The woman sat in another wicker chair next to one of the Fowler's bridge-lamps. A man sat with his back to Irvine, in a morris-chair. He was reading *The Boston Herald* and smoking a cigar, and Irvine could see only his cheek, which looked square, beefy, and truculent. The mother was playing Canfield and letting cigarette smoke through her nostrils like a quiet oath. The girl was reading; he could not see what. Taking care to stay out of the light, he came closer. She read in a way that fascinated and satisfied him, detachedly, yet in complete absorption. Each time she turned a page, it was like watching someone take another mouthful of food, with perfect elegance. Then, with the same elegance, she put her fingertip into one nostril, and worked, patiently, without interrupting her reading, until she had extracted the annoyance. Still reading, she rolled it between the tips of her forefinger and thumb, until it was dry, smelled of it, and flicked it to the jute carpet. God, Irvine thought: she's wonderful! He felt ashamed of himself; for now he waited, hoping that she would do this or something like it again; and when he became sufficiently aware of his shame, he withdrew, to past the rear of the cottage. There on the line, he could see bathing suits. He struck a match so that he might enjoy the cedar color. Suddenly he* wanted to smell the suit. What sort of a Peeping Tom am I, he said to himself, touched it—it was a fine silk-wool—and walked away.

He remembered the school word: Furter. Runs around smelling girls' bicycle-saddles.

"Nice going," he said scornfully, aloud.

So he sat and played bridge with the Darts, as a form of penance and because he could think of no better way to pass the time; but he left early, afraid he might already be too late, and ran all the way to the rear of the Fowlers'—Parkers'—cottage. He was too late. Mr. and Mrs. Parker were still up, but the girl was nowhere in sight, and there were no lights on upstairs.

It serves me right, he thought.

The bathing suit smelled of its own fabric and of the sea, and again he remembered the delicate discoloration of her thighs.

She is like the sea herself, he thought.

Where I waited, listlessly,
On Summer's unportentuous brink,
You stepped up out of the sea.
Now I can no longer think

---

* Original word is "we."

Of any [idleness] on earth*
Which once beguiled my wasted days.
When the quiet sea gave you birth,
I too was born, to sing your praise.

Born for that, and that alone.
Here for all time I dedicate
Heart and mind, and blood and bone,
Wholly to our mutual fate.

Like a wild creature of the sea,
Colored like the sea at dawn,
So you first appeared to me:
Just so, would I see you drawn,

Had I the knowledge and the art
A hundredth, toward that [peerless] task.**
Dear, I have neither, but my heart
Is wholly yours; you've but to ask.

Nuts, he said to himself.

He changed *idleness* to *idle dreams,* and back to *idleness; peerless* to *matchless.*

"You've but to ask," he thought, "Who's doing the asking around here anyway!"

He had seldom written a worse poem. But he did not destroy it. Instead, he gave it the title, *On First Watching A Young Woman Come Out of the Sea,* and went to bed. Five minutes later he turned on the light, deleted this title, wrote *Sea Piece,* changed *a hundredth* to *one thousandth,* and again shut off the light.

It was nearly four o'clock.

---

*The original words are "idle dream." Note the explanation of the change made in this poem by the narrator.

**The original word is "matchless." Note the explanation of the change made in this poem by the narrator.

WATER-MESSAGE
by *John Barth*

❀

Which was better would be hard to say. In the days when Uncle Konrad let out all five grades at once, Ambrose worried that he mightn't see Peter in time or that Peter mightn't stick up for him the way a brother ought. Sheldon Turley, who'd been in reform school once, liked to come up to him and say, "Well if it ain't my old pal Amby!" and give him a great whack in the back. "How was school today, Amby old boy?" he'd ask and give him another whack in the back, and Ambrose was obliged to return, "How was school for you?" Whereupon Sheldon Turley would cry, "Just swell, old pal!" and whack the wind near out of him. Or Sandy Cooper would very possibly sic his Chesapeake Bay dog on him—but if he joked with Sandy Cooper correctly, especially if he could get a certain particular word into it, Sandy Cooper often laughed and forgot to sic Doc on him.

More humiliating were the torments of Wimpy James and Ramona Peters: Wimpy was only in second grade, but he came from the Barracks down by the creek where the oyster-boats moored; his nose was wet, his teeth were black, one knew what his mother was; and he would make a fourth-grader cry. As for Ramona, Peter and the fellows teased her for a secret reason. All Ambrose knew was that she was a most awful tomboy whose pleasure was to run up behind and shove you so hard your head would snap back, and down you'd go breathless in the schoolyard clover. Her hair was as white as the Arnie twins'; when the health nurse had inspected all the kids' hair, Ramona was one of the ones that were sent home.

Between Sheldon Turley and Sandy Cooper and Wimpy James and Ramona Peters there had been so much picking on the younger ones that Uncle Konrad said one night at supper, "I swear to God, Marie, I'm the principal of a zoo!" So now the grades were let out by two's, ten minutes apart, and Ambrose had only to fear that Wimpy, who could seldom be mollified by wit or otherwise got next to, might be laying for him in the hollyhocks off the playground. If he weren't there would be no tears, but the blocks between East Dorset School and home were still by no means terrorless. Just past the alley in the second block was a place he had named Scylla and Charybdis after reading *The Book of Knowledge:* on one side of the street was a Spitz dog that snarled from his house and flung himself at any passing kid, and even Peter said the little chain was going to break one day, and then look out. While across the street was the yard of Crazy Alice, who had not hurt anybody *yet.* Large of pore and lip, tangly of hair and mind, she wore men's shoes and flowered chick-linen; she played with dolls in her backyard; she laughed when the kids would stop to razz her. But Marie declared that Alice had her spells and was sent to the Asylum out by Shoal Creek, and Ambrose himself had seen her once down at the rivershore loping along in her way and talking to herself a blue streak.

What was more, the Arnie twins were in fourth grade with him, though half again his age and twice his size; like Crazy Alice they inspired him with no great fear if Peter was along, but when he was alone it was another story. The Arnie twins lived God knows where: pale as two ghosts they shuffled through the alleys of East Dorset day and night, poking in people's trash cans. Their eyes were the faintest blue, red about the rims; their hair was a pile of white curls, unwashed, unbarbered; they wore what people gave them—men's vests over B.V.D. shirts, double-breasted suit coats out at the elbows, shiny trousers of mismatching stripe, the legs rolled up and the crotch hung half to their knees—and ghostlike too they rarely spoke, in class or out. Many a warm night when Ambrose had finished supper and homework, had his bath, gone to bed, he'd hear a clank in the alley and rise up on one elbow to look: like as not, if it wasn't the black dogs that run loose at night and howl to one another from ward to ward, it would be the Arnie twins exploring garbage. Their white curls shone in the moonlight; on the breeze that moved off the creek he could hear them murmur to each other over hambones, coffee grounds, nested halves of eggshells. Next morning they'd be beside him in class, and he who may have voyaged in dreams to Sumatra or the hot Arabian Sea would wonder where those two had prowled in fact, and what-all murmured.

"The truth of the matter is," he said to his mother on an April day, "you've raised your son for a sissy. I hope you're proud."

That initial phrase, like the word *facts,* was a favorite; they used it quite a lot on the afternoon radio serials, and it struck him as openhanded and mature. The case with *facts* was a little different: his mother and Uncle Konrad would smile when they mentioned "the facts of life," and he could elicit that same smile from them by employing the term himself. It had been amusing when Mr. Erdmann borrowed their *Cyclopedia of Facts* and Aunt Rosa had said, "It's time Willy Erdmann was learning a fact or two"; but when a few days later Ambrose had spied a magazine called *Facts About Your Diet* in a drugstore rack, and hardly able to contain his mirth had pointed it out to his mother, she had said "Mm hm" and bade him have done with his Dixie-cup before it was too late to stop at the pie-woman's.

This afternoon he had meant to tell her the truth of the matter in an offhand way with a certain sigh that he could hear clearly in his fancy, but in the telling his sigh choked in his throat, and such a hurt came there that he remarked to himself, "This is what they mean when they say they have *a lump in their throat*."

Two wretched mischances had disgraced him on the way from school. Midway through Scylla and Charybdis, on the Scylla side, he had heard a buzzing just behind his hip, which taking for a bumblebee he had spun round in mortal alarm and flailed at. No bee was there, but at once the buzzing recurred behind him. Again he wheeled about—was the creature in his pocket!—and took quick leaps forward; when the bee only buzzed more menacingly, he sprinted to the corner, heedless of what certain classmates might think. He had to wait for passing traffic, and observed that as he slowed and halted, so did the buzzing. It was the loose chain of his own jackknife had undone him.

"What's eating you?" Wimpy James hollered, who till then had been too busy with Crazy Alice to molest him.

Ambrose had frowned at the pointing fingers of his watch. "Timing myself to the corner!"

But at that instant a loose lash had dropped into his eye, and his tears could be neither hidden nor explained away.

"Scared of Kocher's dog!" one had yelled.

Another then sing-sang: "Sissy on Am-brose! Sissy on Am-brose!"

And Wimpy James, in the nastiest of accents:

"Run home and git
A sugar tit,
And don't let go of it!"

There was no saving face after that except by taking on Wimpy, for which he knew he had not the courage. Indeed, so puissant was that fellow, who loved to stamp on toes with all his might or twist the skin of arms with a warty Hothand, Ambrose was obliged to clown most ignominiously to escape. His uncle, thanks to the Kaiser, walked with a limp famous among the schoolboys of East Dorset, scores of whom had been chastised for mocking it; but none could imitate that walk as could his nephew. Ambrose stiffened his leg so, hunched his shoulders and pumped his arms, frowned and bobbed with every step—the image of Old Man Mensch! Just so, when the highway cleared, he had borne down upon his house as might a gimpy robin on a worm, or Uncle Konrad on some youthful miscreant, and Wimpy had laughed instead of giving chase. But the sound went into Ambrose like a blade.

"You are not any such thing!" his mother cried, and hugged him to her breast. "What you call brave, a little criminal like Wimpy James?"

He was ready to defend that notion, but colored Hattie walked in then, snapping gum, to ask what wanted ironing, and so he had to leave the subject.

"You go on upstairs and put your playclothes on if you're going down to the Jungle with Peter."

"Yes'm." He was not deaf to the solicitude in his mother's voice, but lest she fail to appreciate the measure of his despair he climbed the stairs with leaden foot. However, she had to go straighten Hattie out.

When Hattie was in the kitchen Mother's afternoon programs went by the board. Uncle Konrad called her a yellow gal, though to Ambrose's mind her skin was the shade of vanilla fudge. She had worked for them since a girl, and currently supported three children and a husband who lost her money on the horses. No one knew how much if anything Hattie grasped about his betting, but throughout the afternoons she insisted on the Baltimore station that broadcast results from Bowie and Pimlico, and Mrs. Mensch had not the heart to protest. Hattie's reaction was invariable: when a race began she would upend the electric iron and squint at the refrigerator, snapping ferociously her gum; then she acknowledged each separate return with a *hum* and a shake of the head.

"Warlord paid four-eighty, three-forty, and two-eighty . . ."

"Mm hm."

"Navaho, four-sixty and three-forty . . ."

"Mm *hm.*"

"Sal's Pride, two-eighty . . ."

"Mmmm *hm!*"

After which she resumed her labors and the radio its musical selections until the next race. This music affected Ambrose strongly: it was not at all the kind they played on the Fitch Bandwagon or the National Barn Dance, nor yet of a stripe with the "headache shows" of Sunday afternoons, whereon shrill-warbling ladies and three-named men sang songs that gave him headaches; this between races was classical music, as who should say, the sort upper-graders had to listen to in class. There was no singing to it whatever. Up through the floor of his bedroom came the rumble of great drums and a brooding figure in low strings. Ambrose paused in his dressing to listen, and thinking on his late disgrace frowned: the figure stirred a dark companion in his soul. No man at all, no man at all!

His family, shaken past tears, was in attendance at his graveside.

"I'll kill that Wimpy," Peter muttered, and for shame at not having lent his Silver King bike more freely to his late brother, could never bring himself to ride it again.

"Too late," his father mourned. Was he not reflecting how the dear dead boy had pled for a Senior Erector Set last Christmas, only to receive a Junior Erector Set with neither electric motor nor gearbox?

And outside the press of mourners, grieving privately,

was a brown-haired young woman in the uniform of a student nurse: Peggy Robbins from beside Crazy Alice's house. Gone now the smile wherewith she'd used to greet him on her way to the Nurses' Home; the gentle voice that answered, "How's my lover today?" when he said hello to her—it was shaken by rough, secret sobs. Too late she saw: that what she had favored him with in jest he had received with adoration. Then and there she pledged never to marry, fate having taken from her him who loved her most.

But now stern and solemn horns empowered the theme; abject no more, it grew rich, austere. Cymbals struck and sizzled. He was Jason steering the *Argo* under anvil-clouds like those in *Nature's Secrets.* A reedy woodwind warned of hidden peril; on guard, he crept to the closet with the plucking strings.

"Quick!" hissed he to his corduroy knickers inside, who were the undeserving Wimpy. If they could tiptoe from that cave before the lean hounds waked.

"But why are you saving my life?"

"No time for talk, Wimp! Follow me!"

Yet there! The trumpets flashed, the low horns roared, and it was slash your way under portcullis and over moat, it was lay about with mace and halberd, bearing up a fainting Peggy on your left arm while your right cut a swath through the chainmailed host. And at last, to the thrill of flutes, to the high strings' tremble, he reached the auditorium. His own tunic was rent, red; breath came hard; he was—*more weary than exultant.*

"The truth of the matter is," he declared to the crowd, "I'm just glad I happened to be handy."

But the two who owed him their lives would not be gainsaid! Before the assembled students and the P.T.A. Wimpy James begged his pardon, while Peggy Robbins—well, she hugged and kissed him there in front of all and whispered something in his ear that made him blush! The multitude rose to applaud, Father and Mother in the forefront, Uncle Konrad and Aunt Rosa beside them; Peter winked at him from the wings, proud as punch. Now brass and strings together played a recessional very nearly too sublime for mortal ears: like the word *beyond,* it sounded of flight, of vaulting aspiration. It rose, it soared, it sang; in the van of his admirers it bore him transfigured from the hall—beyond, beyond East Dorset, and aloft to the stars.

For all it was he and not his brother Peter who had suggested the gang's name, the Occult Order of the Leopard judged Ambrose too young for membership and forbade his presence at their secret meetings. He was permitted to accompany Peter and the others down to the rivershore and into the Jungle as far as to the Den; he might swing with them on the creepers like Tarzan of the Apes, slide down and scale the rooty banks; but when the Leopards had done with playing and convened the Occult Order, Peter would say, "You and Perse skeedaddle now," and he'd have to go along up the beach with Herman Goltz's little brother from the crabfat-yellow shacks beside the boatyard.

"Come on, pestiferous," he would sigh then to Perse. But indignifying as it was to be put thus with a brat of six, who moreover had a stye in his eye and smelled the year round like pee and old crackers, at bottom Ambrose approved of their exclusion. Let little kids into your Occult Order, and there would go your secrets all over school.

And the secrets were the point of the thing. When Peter had mentioned one evening that he and the fellows were starting a club, Ambrose had tossed the night through in a perfect fever of imagining. It would be a secret club, that went without saying, and there must be secret handshakes, secret passwords, secret initiations. But these he felt meant nothing except to remind you of the really important thing, which was—ah well, hard to find words for, but there had to be the *real* secrets, dark facts known to no one but the members. You had to have been initiated to find them out, and when you were a member you'd know the truth of the matter and smile in a private way when you met another member of the Order, because you both knew what you knew. All night and for awhile after, Ambrose had wondered whether Peter and the fellows could understand that that was the important thing. He ceased to wonder when he began to see just that kind of look on their faces sometimes; certain words and little gestures set them laughing; they absolutely barred outsiders from the Jungle and said nothing to their parents about the Occult Order of the Leopard, and Ambrose was satisfied. To make his own position bearable he gave Perse to understand that he himself was in on the secrets; was in fact a special kind of initiate whose job was to patrol the beach and make sure that no spies or brats got near the Den.

By the time he came downstairs from changing his clothes Peter and the gang had gone on ahead, and even at a run he couldn't catch up to them before they had got to the seawall and almost into the Jungle. The day was warm and windy; the river blue-black, afroth with whitecaps. Out in the channel the bell buoy clanged, and the other buoys leaned seaward with the tide. They had special names like Red Nun and Black Can, and sailors knew what each one stood for.

"Hey, Peter, wait up!"

Peter turned a bit and lifted his chin to greet him, but didn't wait up because Herman Goltz hit him one then where the fellows did, just for fun, and Peter had to go chase after him into the Jungle. Sandy Cooper was the first to speak to him: they called him Sandy on account of his freckles and his red hair, which was exactly as stiff and curly as the fur of his Chesapeake Bay dog, but Ambrose had always thought there was something gritty too in the feel of Sandy Cooper's hands, and his voice had a grainy sound as if there were sand on his tonsils.

"I hear you run home bawling today."

Sandy Cooper's dog was not about, and Peter was. Ambrose said, "That's a lie."

"Perse says you did."

"You did, too," Perse affirmed from some yards distant. "If Wimpy James was here he'd tell you."

Ambrose reflected on their narrow escape from the Cave of Hounds and smiled indulgently. "That's what *you* think."

"That's what I know, big sis!"

One wasn't expected to take on a little pest like Perse. Ambrose shied a lump of dirt at him, and when Perse shied back an oystershell that cut past like a knife, the whole gang called it a dirty trick and ran him across Erdmann's Cornlot. Then they all went in among the trees.

The Jungle, which like the Occult Order of the Leopard had been named by Ambrose, stood atop the riverbank between the Nurses' Home and the new bridge. It was in fact a grove of honey-locusts, in area no larger than a big backyard, bounded on two of its inland sides by Erdmann's Cornlot and on the third by the East Dorset dump. But it was made mysterious by rank honeysuckle that covered the ground and shrouded every tree, and by a labyrinth of intersecting footpaths. Jungle-like too, there was about it a voluptuous fetidity: gray rats and starlings decomposed where they fell B-B'd; curly-furred retrievers left their spoor about the footpaths; there were to be seen on occasion, stuck on twig-ends or flung amid the creepers, ugly little somethings in whose presence Ambrose snickered with the rest; and if you parted the vines at the base of any tree, you might find a strew of brown pellets and field-mouse bones, disgorged by feasting owls. Ambrose thought it the most exciting place he knew, in a special way. Its queer smell could retch him if he breathed too deeply, but in measured inhalations it had a rich, peculiarly stirring savor. And had he dared ask he would have very much liked to know whether the others, when they hid in the viny bowers from whoever was It, felt as he did the urging of that place upon his bladder!

With whoops and Tarzan-cries they descended upon the Den, built of drift-timber and carpeting from the dump and camouflaged with living vines. Peter and Herman Goltz raced to get there first, and Peter would have won, because anybody beat fat Herman, but his high-top came untied, and so they got there at the same time and dived to crawl through the entrance.

"Hey!"

They stopped in mid-scramble, backed off, and stood up quickly.

"There's somebody in there!" Herman hollered. Peter blushed and batted at him to be silent. All stared at the entryway of the hut.

A young man whom Ambrose did not recognize came out first. He had dark eyes and hair and a black mustache, and though he was clean-shaved his jaw was blue with coming whiskers. He wore a white shirt and a tie and a yellow sweater under his leather jacket, and had dirtied his clean trousers on the Den floor. He stood up and scowled at the ring of boys as if he were going to be angry—but then grinned and brushed his pants-knees.

"Sorry, mates. Didn't know it was your hut."

The girl climbed out after. Her brown hair was mussed,

her face drained of color, there were pieces of dead leaf upon her coat. The fellow helped her up and she walked straight off without looking at any of them, keeping her right hand stuffed into her coat pocket the whole time. The fellow winked at Peter and hurried to follow.

"Hey, gee!" Herman Goltz whispered. "That was Peggy Robbins!"

"Who was the guy?" Sandy Cooper wanted to know.

Someone declared it was Tommy James, just out of the U.S. Navy.

Peter said that Peggy Robbins would get kicked out of nurse's training if they found out, and Herman told how his big sister had been kicked out of nurse's training with only four months to go.

"A bunch went buckbathing one night down to Shoal Creek, and Sis was the only one was kicked out for it."

The Leopards all got to laughing and horsing around about Herman Goltz's sister and about Peggy Robbins and her boyfriend. Some of the fellows wanted to take after them and razz them, but it was agreed that Tommy James was a tough customer. Somebody believed there had been a scar across his temple.

Herman wailed, "Oh lover, will you marry me?" and collapsed against Peter, who wrestled him down into the creepers.

Cheeks burning, Ambrose joined in the merriment. "We ought to put a sign up!" he cried. *"Private Property: No Smooching Allowed."*

The fellows laughed. But not in just the right way.

"Smooching!" Sandy Cooper said. "Hey, guys! Amby Mensch says they was smooching!"

Ambrose quickly grinned and cried, "Like a duck! Like a duck!"; whenever a person said a thing just to fool you, he'd say, "Like a duck!" afterward to let you know you'd been fooled.

"Like a duck nothing," Sandy Cooper rasped. "I bet I know what we'll find inside."

"Hey, yeah!" said Peter.

Sandy Cooper had an old flashlight that he carried on his belt, and so they let him go in first, and Peter and Herman and the others followed after. In just an instant Ambrose heard Sandy shout "Woo-hoo!" and there was excitement inside the Den. He heard Peter cry, "Let me see!"

and Herman Goltz commence to giggle like a girl. Peter said, "Let *me* see, damn it!"

"Go to Hell," said the gritty voice of Sandy Cooper.

"Go to Hell your own self."

Perse Goltz had scrambled into the Den unnoticed with the rest, but now a Leopard spied him.

"Get out of here, Perse. I thought I smelt something."

"You smelt your own self," the little boy retorted.

"Go on, get out, Perse," Herman ordered. "You stink."

"You stink worst."

Somebody said, "Bust him once," but Perse was out before they could get him. He stuck out his tongue and made a great blasting raspberry at Peter, who had dived for his leg through the entrance.

Then Peter looked up at Ambrose from where he lay and said, "Our meeting's started."

"Yeah," someone said from inside. "No babies allowed."

"No smooching allowed," another Leopard ventured, mocking Ambrose in an official tone. Sandy Cooper added that no something-else was allowed, and what it was was the same queer word that would make him laugh sometimes instead of sicking his Chesapeake Bay dog on you.

"You and Perse skeedaddle now," Peter said. His voice was not unkind, but there was an odd look on his face and he hurried back into the Den, from which now came gleeful whispers. The name *Peggy Robbins* was mentioned, and someone dared, and double-dared, and dee-double-dared someone else, in vain, to go invite Ramona Peters to the meeting.

Perse Goltz had already gone a ways up the beach. Ambrose went down the high bank, checking his slide with the orange roots of undermined trees, and trudged after him. Peter had said, "Go to Hell your own self," in a voice that told you he was used to saying such things. And the cursing wasn't the worst of it.

Ambrose's stomach felt tied and lumpy; by looking at his arm a certain way he could see droplets standing in the cracks and pores. It was what they meant when they spoke of *breaking out in a cold sweat:* very like what one felt in school assemblies, when one was waiting in the wings for the signal to step out onto the stage. He could not bear to think of the mustachioed boyfriend: that fellow's wink, his curly hair, his leather jacket over white shirt and green tie filled Ambrose's heart with comprehension; they whispered to him that whatever mysteries had been in progress in the Leopard's Den, they did not mean to Wimpy James's brother what they meant to Peggy Robbins.

Toward her his feelings were less simple. He pictured them kicking her out of the Nurses' Home: partly on the basis of Herman Goltz's story about his sister, Ambrose rather imagined that disgraced student nurses were kicked out late at night, without any clothes on; he wondered who did the actual kicking, and where in the world the student nurses went from there.

Every one of the hurricanes that ushered in the fall took its toll upon the riverbank, with the result that the upper beach was strewn with trees long since fallen from the cliff. Salt air and water quickly stripped their bark and scoured the trunks. They seemed never to decay; Ambrose could rub his hands along the polished gray wood with little fear of splinters. One saw that in years to come the Jungle would be gone entirely. He would be a man then, and it wouldn't matter one way or the other. Only his children, he supposed, might miss the winding paths and secret places—but of course you didn't miss what you'd never had or known about.

On the foreshore, in the wrack along the high-water line where sandfleas jumped, were empty beer cans, grapefruit rinds, and hosts of spot and white perch poisoned by the runoff from the canneries. All rotted together. But on the sand beach, in the sun and wind, Ambrose could breathe their odor deeply. Indeed, with the salt itself and the pungent oils of the eelgrass they made the very flavor of the shore exhilarating to his spirit.

It was a bright summer night. Peggy Robbins had just been kicked out of the Nurses' Home, and the only way she could keep everybody from seeing her was to run into the Jungle and hide in the Leopards' Den. As it happened, Ambrose had been waked by a clanking in the alleyway and had gone outside to drive off the black dogs or the Arnie twins, whichever were rooting in the garbage. And finding the night so balmy he strolled down to the rivershore and entered the Jungle, where he heard weeping. It was pitch black in the Den; she cringed against the far wall.

"Who is it?"

"It is the only man who ever really loved you, Peggy."

She hugged and kissed him; then, overcome by double shame, drew away. But if he had accepted her caresses coolly, still he would not scorn her now. He took her hand.

"Ah Peggy. Ah Peggy."

She wept afresh, and then one of two things happened. Perhaps she flung herself before him, begging forgiveness and imploring him to love her. He raised her up and staunched her tears.

"Forgive you?" he repeated in a very kind voice. "Love forgives everything, Peggy. But the truth of the matter is, I can't forget."

He held her head in both his hands; her bitter tears splashed upon his wrists. He left the Den and walked to the edge of the bank, where leaning against a tree he stared seaward. Presently Peggy grew quiet and went her way. But he stayed a long time in the Jungle.

On the other hand, perhaps it was that he drew her to him in the dark, held her close, and gave her to know that while he could never feel just the same respect for her, he loved her nonetheless. They kissed. Tenderly together they rehearsed the secrets; long, long they lingered in the Leopards' Den, and then he bore her from the Jungle, lovingly to the beach, into the water. They swam until her tears were commingled with the sea, made a part of Earth's black waters; then hand in hand they waded shoreward on the track of the moon. In the shallows they paused to face each other. Warm waves flashed about their feet; waterdrops sparkled on their bodies. Washed of shame, washed of fear. Nothing was but sweetest knowledge.

In the lumberyard down past the hospital they used square pine sticks between the layers of drying boards to let air through. The beach was littered with such sticks, three and four and five feet long, and if you held one by the back end and threw it like a spear into the water, nothing made a better submarine. Perse Goltz had started launching submarines and following them down toward the Jungle as they floated on the tide.

"Don't go any farther," Ambrose said when he drew near.

"Why don't you shut up?" Perse asked indifferently.

"All I've got to do is give the sign," Ambrose declared, "and they'll know you're sneaking up to spy."

As they talked they launched more submarines. The object was to see how far you could make them go under water before they surfaced: if you launched them too flat they'd skim along the top, and if too deeply they'd nose under and slide up backward. But if you did it just right they'd straighten out and glide several yards under water before they came up. Ambrose's arms were longer and he knew the trick, so his went farther than Perse's.

"There ain't no sign," Perse said.

"There is so. Plenty of them."

"Well, you don't know none of them, anyhow."

"That's what you think. Watch this." He raised his hand toward the Jungle and made successive gestures with his fingers in the manner of Mister Neal the deaf and dumb eggman. "I told them we were just launching submarines and not to worry."

"You did not." But Perse left off his launching for a moment to watch, and moved no farther down the beach.

"Wait a minute." Ambrose squinted urgently toward the trees. "*Go . . . up . . . the . . . beach.* They want us to go on up the beach some more." He spoke in a matter-of-fact tone, and even though Perse said, "What a big fake you are," he followed Ambrose in the direction of the new bridge.

If Ambrose was the better launcher, Perse was by far the better bombardier: he could throw higher, farther, and straighter. The deep shells they skipped out for Ducks and Drakes; the flat ones they sailed top-up to make them climb, or straight aloft so that they'd cut water without a splash. Beer cans if you threw them with the holes down whistled satisfactorily as they flew. They went along launching and bombarding, and then Ambrose saw a perfectly amazing thing. Lying in the seaweed where the tide had left it was a bottle with a note inside.

"Look here!"

He rushed to pick it up. It was a clear glass bottle, a rum or gin bottle, tightly capped. Dried eelgrass full of sand and tiny musselshells clung round it. The label had been scraped off, all but some white strips where the glue was thickest, and the paper inside was folded.

"Gee *whiz!*" Perse cried. At once he tried to snatch the bottle away from Ambrose, but Ambrose held it well above his reach.

"No, sir! Finders keepers!"

Perse forgot to be cynical. "Where in the *world* do you think it come from?"

"Anywhere!" Ambrose's voice was thick. "It could've been floating around for years!" He removed the cap and tipped the bottle downward, but the note couldn't pass through the neck. "Get a little stick!"

They cast about for a straight twig, and Ambrose fished into the bottle with it.

"Aw!" they breathed at each near catch.

Ambrose's heart shook. For the moment Scylla and Charybdis, the Occult Order of the Leopard, his brother Peter—all were forgotten. Peggy Robbins, too, though she did not vanish altogether from his mind's eye, was caught up into the greater vision, vague and splendrous, whereof the sea-wreathed bottle was the emblem. Westward it lay, to westward, where the tide ran from East Dorset. Past the river and the Bay, from continents beyond the seas this messenger had made its way. Borne by currents as yet uncharted, nuzzled by great fishes as yet unnamed, it had bobbed and tossed for ages beneath strange constellations. Then out of the oceans it had strayed; past cape and cove, Black Can, Red Nun, the miracle had wandered willy-nilly to lay its word on his threshold.

"For pity's sake bust it!" Perse shouted. Holding the bottle by the neck Ambrose banged it on a mossed and barnacled brickbat. Not hard enough. His face perspired. On the third swing the bottle smashed and the note fell out.

"I got it!" Perse cried, but before he could snatch it up Ambrose sent him flying onto the sand.

The little boy's face screwed up with tears. "I'll get you!"

But Ambrose paid him no heed. As he picked up the paper Perse flew into him, and received such a swat from Ambrose's free hand that he ran bawling down the beach.

The paper was half a sheet of coarse ruled stuff, torn carelessly from a tablet and folded three times. Ambrose uncreased it. The message itself was penned in light blue ink athwart the lines.

It was Bill Bell

The four words could be held at once before the eye. In a number of places, owing to the coarseness of the paper, the ink had spread from the lines in fibrous blots.

It was Bill Bell

An oystershell zipped past and plicked into the sand behind him: a hundred feet away Perse Goltz thumbed his nose and stepped a few steps back. Ambrose ignored him, but moved slowly down the shore. Up in the Jungle the Leopards had adjourned their meeting and were playing King of the Hill on the riverbank. Perse threw another oystershell and half-turned to run, but he was not pursued.

The heart of Ambrose Mensch bore a new and subtle burden: neither despair nor yet disappointment, but a sweet melancholy. He would not tattle on Peter for cursing and the rest of it. The thought of his brother's deeds no longer troubled him or even greatly moved his curiosity. Tonight, tomorrow night, unhurriedly, he would find out from Peter just what it was they had discovered in the Den, and what-all done: the things he'd learn would not surprise now nor much disturb him, for though as yet he was still innocent of that knowledge, he had the feel of it in his heart, and of other, yet farther-reaching truth.

He changed the note to his left hand, the better to wing an oystershell at Perse. As he did so, some far corner of his mind remarked that those shiny bits in the paper's texture were splinters of wood-pulp. Often as he'd seen them before in the leaves of cheap tablets, he had not hitherto embraced that fact.

THE UGLIEST PILGRIM

by *Doris Betts*

❀

I sit in the bus station, nipping chocolate peel off a Mounds candy bar with my teeth, then pasting the coconut filling to the roof of my mouth. The lump will dissolve there slowly and seep into me the way dew seeps into flowers.

I like to separate flavors that way. Always I lick the salt off cracker tops before taking my first bite.

Somebody sees me with my suitcase, paper sack, and a ticket in my lap. "You going someplace, Violet?"

Stupid. People in Spruce Pine are dumb and, since I look dumb, say dumb things to me. I turn up my face as if to count those dead flies piled under the light bulb. He walks away—a fat man, could be anybody. I stick out my tongue at his back; the candy oozes down. If I could stop swallowing, it would drip into my lung and I could breathe vanilla.

Whoever it was, he won't glance back. People in Spruce Pine don't like to look at me, full face.

A Greyhound bus pulls in, blows air; the driver stands by the door. He's black-headed, maybe part Cherokee, with heavy shoulders but a weak chest. He thinks well of himself—I can tell that. I open my notebook and copy his name off the metal plate so I can call him by it when he drives me home again. And next week, won't Mr. Wallace Weatherman be surprised to see how well I'm looking!

I choose the front seat behind Mr. Weatherman, settle my bag with the hat in it, then open the lined composition book again. Maybe it's half full of writing. Even the empty pages toward the back have one repeated entry, high, printed off Mama's torn catechism: GLORIFY GOD AND ENJOY HIM FOREVER.

I finish Mr. Weatherman off in my book while he's running his motor and getting us onto the highway. His nose is too broad, his dark eyes too skimpy—nothing in his face I want—but the hair is nice. I write that down: "Black hair?" I'd want it to curl, though, and be soft as a baby's.

Two others are on the bus, a nigger soldier and an old woman whose jaw sticks out like a shelf. There grow, on the backs of her hands, more veins than skin. One fat blue vessel, curling from wrist to knuckle, would be good; so on one page I draw a sample hand and let blood wind across it like a river. I write at the bottom: "Praise God, it is started. May 29, 1969," and turn to a new sheet. The paper's lumpy and I flip back to the thick envelope stuck there with adhesive tape. I can't lose that.

We're driving now at the best speed Mr. Weatherman can make on these winding roads. On my side there is nothing out the bus window but granite rock, jagged and wet in patches. The old lady and the nigger can see red rhododendron on the slope of Roan Mountain. I'd like to own a tight dress that flower color, and breasts to go under it. I write in my notebook, very small, the word "breasts," and turn quickly to another page. AND ENJOY HIM FOREVER.

The soldier bends as if to tie his shoes, but instead zips open a canvas bag and sticks both hands inside. When finally he sits back, one hand is clenched around something hard. He catches me watching. He yawns and scratches his ribs, but the right fist sets very lightly on his knee, and when I turn he drinks something out of its cup and throws his head quickly back like a bird or a chicken. You'd think I could smell it, big as my nose is.

Across the aisle the old lady says, "You going far?" She shows me a set of tan, artificial teeth.

"Oklahoma."

"I never been there. I hear the trees give out." She pauses so I can ask politely where's she's headed. "I'm going to Nashville," she finally says. "The country-music capital of the world. My son lives there and works in the cellophane plant."

I draw in my notebook a box and two arrows. I crisscross the box.

"He's got three children not old enough to be in school yet."

I sit very still, adding new boxes, drawing baseballs in some, looking busy for fear she might bring out their pictures from her big straw pocketbook. The funny thing is she's looking past my head, though there's nothing out that window but rock wall sliding by. I mumble, "It's hot in here."

Angrily she says, "I had eight children myself."

My pencil flies to get the boxes stacked, eight-deep, in a pyramid. "Hope you have a nice visit."

"It's not a visit. I maybe will move." She is hypnotized by the stone and the furry moss in its cracks. Her eyes used to be green. Maybe, when young, she was red-haired and Irish. If she'll stop talking, I want to think about trying green eyes with that Cherokee hair. Her lids droop; she looks drowsy. "I am right tired of children," she says and lays her head back on the white rag they button on these seats.

Now that her eyes are covered, I can study that face—china white, and worn thin as tissue so light comes between her bones and shines through her whole head. I picture the light going around and around her skull, like water spinning in a jar. If I could wait to be eighty, even my face might grind down and look softer. But I'm ready, in case the Preacher mentions that. Did Elisha make Naaman bear into old age his leprosy? Didn't Jesus heal the withered hand, even on Sunday, without waiting for the work week to start? And put back the ear of Malchus with a touch? As soon as Job had learned enough, did his boils fall away?

Lord, I have learned enough.

The old lady sleeps while we roll downhill and up again; then we turn so my side of the bus looks over the valley and its thickety woods where, as a girl, I pulled armloads of galax, fern, laurel, and hemlock to have some spending money. I spent it for magazines full of women with permanent waves. Behind us, the nigger shuffles a deck of cards and deals to himself by fives. Draw poker—I could beat him. My papa showed me, long winter days and nights snowed in on the mountain. He said poker would teach me arithmetic. It taught me there are four ways to make a royal flush and, with two players, it's an even chance one of them holds a pair on the deal. And when you try to draw from a pair to four of a kind, discard the kicker; it helps your odds.

The soldier deals smoothly, using his left hand only with his thumb on top. Papa was good at that. He looks up and sees my whole face with its scar, but he keeps his eyes level as if he has seen worse things; and his left hand drops cards evenly and in rhythm. Like a turtle, laying eggs.

I close my eyes and the riffle of his deck rests me to the next main stop where I write in my notebook: "Praise God for Johnson City, Tennessee, and all the state to come. I am on my way."

At Kingsport, Mr. Weatherman calls rest stop and I go straight through the terminal to the ladies' toilet and look hard at my face in the mirror. I must remember to start the Preacher on the scar first of all—the only thing about me that's even on both sides.

Lord! I am so ugly!

Maybe the Preacher will claim he can't heal ugliness. And I'm going to spread my palms by my ears and show him—this is a crippled face! An infirmity! Would he do for a kidney or liver what he withholds from a face? The Preacher once stuttered, I read someplace, and God bothered with that. Why not me? When the Preacher labors to heal the sick in his Tulsa auditorium, he asks us at home to lay our fingers on the television screen and pray for God's healing. He puts forth his own ten fingers and we match them, pad to pad, on that glass. I have tried that, Lord, and the Power was too filtered and thinned down for me.

I touch my hand now to this cold mirror glass, and cover all but my pimpled chin, or wide nose, or a single red-brown eye. And nothing's too bad by itself. But when they're put together?

I've seen the Preacher wrap his hot, blessed hands on a club foot and cry out "HEAL!" in his funny way that sounds like the word "Hell" broken into two pieces. Will he not cry out, too, when he sees this poor, clubbed face? I will be to him as Goliath was to David, a need so giant it will drive God to action.

I comb out my pine-needle hair. I think I would like blond curls and Irish eyes, and I want my mouth so large it will never be done with kissing.

The old lady comes in the toilet and catches me pinching my bent face. She jerks back once, looks sad, then pets me with her twiggy hand. "Listen, honey," she says, "I had looks once. It don't amount to much."

I push right past. Good people have nearly turned me against you, Lord. They open their mouths for the milk of human kindness and boiling oil spews out.

So I'm half running through the terminal and into the café, and I take the first stool and call down the counter, "Tuna-fish sandwich," quick. Living in the mountains, I eat fish every chance I get and wonder what the sea is like. Then I see I've sat down by the nigger soldier. I do not want to meet his gaze, since he's a wonder to me, too. We don't have many black men in the mountains. Mostly they live east in Carolina, on the flatland, and pick cotton and tobacco instead of apples. They seem to me like foreigners. He's absently shuffling cards the way some men twiddle thumbs. On the stool beyond him is a paratrooper, white, and they're talking about what a bitch the army is. Being sent to the same camp has made them friends already.

I roll a dill-pickle slice through my mouth—a wheel, a bitter wheel. Then I start on the sandwich and it's chicken by mistake when I've got chickens all over my back yard.

"Don't bother with the beer," says the black one. "I've got better on the bus." They come to some agreement and deal out cards on the counter.

It's just too much for me. I lean over behind the nigger's back and say to the paratrooper, "I wouldn't play with him." Neither one moves. "He's a mechanic." They look at each other, not at me. "It's a way to cheat on the deal."

The paratrooper sways backward on his stool and stares around out of eyes so blue that I want them, right away, and maybe his pale blond hair. I swallow a crusty half-chewed bite. "One-handed grip; the mechanic's grip. It's the middle finger. He can second-deal and bottom-deal. He can buckle the top card with his thumb and peep."

"I be damn," says the paratrooper.

The nigger spins around and bares his teeth at me, but it's half a grin. "Lady, you want to play?"

I slide my dishes back. "I get mad if I'm cheated."

"And mean when you're mad." He laughs a laugh so deep it makes me retaste that bittersweet chocolate off the candy bar. He offers the deck to cut, so I pull out the center and restack it three ways. A little air blows through his upper teeth. "I'm Grady Fliggins and they call me Flick."

The paratrooper reaches a hand down the counter to shake mine. "Monty Harrill. From near to Raleigh."

"And I'm Violet Karl. Spruce Pine. I'd rather play five-card stud."

By the time the bus rolls on, we've moved to its wider back seat, playing serious cards with a fifty-cent ante. My money's sparse, but I'm good and the deck is clean. The old lady settles into my front seat, stiffer than plaster. Sometimes she throws back a hurt look.

Monty, the paratrooper, plays soft. But Flick's so good he doesn't even need to cheat, though I watch him close. He drops out quick when his cards are bad; he makes me bid high to see what he's got; and the few times he bluffs, I'm fooled. He's no talker. Monty, on the other hand, says often, "Whose play is it?" till I know that's his clue phrase for a pair. He lifts his cards close to his nose and gets quiet when planning to bluff. And he'd rather use wild cards but we won't. Ah, but he's pretty, though!

After we've swapped a little money, mostly the paratrooper's, Flick pours us a drink in some cups he stole in Kingsport and asks, "Where'd you learn to play?"

I tell him about growing up on a mountain, high, with Mama dead, and shuffling cards by a kerosene lamp with my papa. When I passed fifteen, we'd drink together, too. Applejack or a beer he made from potato peel.

"And where you headed now?" Monty's windburned in a funny pattern, with pale goggle circles that start high on his cheeks. Maybe it's something paratroopers wear.

"It's a pilgrimage." They lean back with their drinks. "I'm going to see this preacher in Tulsa, the one that heals, and I'm coming home pretty. Isn't that healing?" Their still faces make me nervous. "I'll even trade if he says. . . . I'll take somebody else's weak eyes or deaf ears. I could stand limping a little."

The nigger shakes his black head, snickering.

"I tried to get to Charlotte when he was down there with his eight-pole canvas cathedral tent that seats nearly fifteen thousand people, but I didn't have money then. Now what's so funny?" I think for a minute I am going to have to take out my notebook, and unglue the envelope and read them all the Scripture I have looked up on why I should be healed. Monty looks sad for me, though, and that's worse. "Let the Lord twist loose my foot or give me a cough, so long as I'm healed of my looks while I'm still young enough—" I stop and tip up my plastic cup. Young enough for you, blue-eyed boy, and your brothers.

"Listen," says Flick in a high voice. "Let me go with you and be there for that swapping." He winks one speckled eye.

"I'll not take black skin, no offense." He's offended, though, and lurches across the moving bus and falls into a far seat. "Well, you as much as said you'd swap it off!" I call. "What's wrong if I don't want it any more than you?"

Monty slides closer. "You're not much to look at," he grants, sweeping me up and down till I nearly glow blue from his eyes. Shaking his head, "And what now? Thirty?"

"Twenty-eight. His drink and his cards, and I hurt Flick's feelings. I didn't mean that." I'm scared, too. Maybe, unlike Job, I haven't learned enough. Who ought to be expert in hurt feelings? Me, that's who.

"And you live by yourself?"

I start to say "No, there's men falling all over each other going in and out my door." He sees my face, don't he? It makes me call, "Flick? I'm sorry." Not one movement. "Yes. By myself." Five years now, since Papa had heart failure and fell off the high back porch and rolled downhill in the gravel till the hobblebushes stopped him. I found him past sunset, cut from the rocks but not much blood showing. And what there was, dark, and already jellied.

Monty looks at me carefully before making up his mind to say, "That preacher's a fake. You ever see a doctor agree to what he's done?"

"Might be." I'm smiling. I tongue out the last liquor in my cup. I've thought of all that, but it may be what I believe is stronger than him faking. That he'll be electrified by my trust, the way a magnet can get charged against its will. He might be a lunatic or a dope fiend, and it still not matter.

Monty says, "Flick, you plan to give us another drink?"

"No." He acts like he's going to sleep.

"I just wouldn't count on that preacher too much." Monty cleans his nails with a matchbook corner and sometimes gives me an uneasy look. "Things are mean and ugly in this world—I mean *act* ugly, do ugly, be ugly."

He's wrong. When I leave my house, I can walk for

miles and everything's beautiful. Even the rattlesnakes have grace. I don't mind his worried looks, since I'm writing in my notebook how we met and my winnings—a good sign, to earn money on a trip. I like the way army barbers trim his hair. I wish I could touch it.

"Took one furlough in your mountains. Pretty country. Maybe hard to live in? Makes you feel little." He looks toward Flick and says softer, "Makes you feel like the night sky does. So many stars."

"Some of them big as daisies." It's easy to live in, though. Some mornings a deer and I scare up each other in the brush, and his heart stops, and mine stops. Everything stops till he plunges away. The next pulsebeat nearly knocks you down. "Monty, doesn't your hair get lighter in the summers? That might be a good color hair to ask for in Tulsa. Then I could turn colors like the leaves. Spell your last name for me."

He does, and says I sure am funny. Then he spells Grady Fliggins and I write that, too. He's curious about my book, so I flip through and offer to read him parts. Even with his eyes shut, Flick is listening. I read them about my papa's face, a chunky block face, not much different from the Preacher's square one. After Papa died, I wrote that to slow down how fast I was forgetting him. I tell Monty parts of my lists: that you can get yellow dye out of gopherwood and Noah built his ark from that, and maybe it stained the water. That a cow eating snakeroot might give poison milk. I pass him a pressed maypop flower I'm carrying to Tulsa, because the crown of thorns and the crucifixion nails grow in its center, and each piece of the bloom stands for one of the apostles.

"It's a mollypop vine," says Flick out of one corner of his mouth. "And it makes a green ball that pops when you step on it." He stretches. "Deal you some blackjack?"

For no reason, Monty says, "We oughtn't to let her go."

We play blackjack till supper stop and I write in my book, "Praise God for Knoxville and two new friends." I've not had many friends. At school in the valley, I sat in the back rows, reading, a hand spread on my face. I was smart, too; but if you let that show, you had to stand for the class and present different things.

When the driver cuts out the lights, the soldiers give me a whole seat, and a duffelbag for a pillow. I hear them whispering, first about women, then about me; but after awhile I don't hear that anymore.

By the time we hit Nashville, the old lady makes the bus wait while she begs me to stop with her. "Harvey won't mind. He's a good boy." She will not even look at Monty and Flick. "You can wash and change clothes and catch a new bus tomorrow."

"I'm in a hurry. Thank you." I have picked a lot of galax to pay for this trip.

"A girl alone. A girl that maybe feels she's got to prove something?" The skin on her neck shivers. "Some people might take advantage."

Maybe when I ride home under my new face, that will be some risk. I shake my head, and as she gets off she whispers something to Mr. Weatherman about looking after me. It's wasted, though, because a new driver takes his place and he looks nearly as bad as I do—oily-faced and toad-shaped, with eyeballs a dingy color and streaked with blood. He's the flatlands driver, I guess, because he leans back and drops one warty hand on the wheel and we go so fast and steady you can hardly tell it.

Since Flick is the tops in cards and we're tired of that, it's Monty's turn to brag on his motorcycle. He talks all across Tennessee till I think I could ride one by hearsay alone, that my wrist knows by itself how far to roll the throttle in. It's a Norton and he rides it in Scrambles and Enduro events, in his leathers, with spare parts and tools glued all over him with black electrician's tape.

"So this bastard tells me, 'Zip up your jacket because when I run over you I want some traction.' "

Flick is playing solitaire. "You couldn't get me on one of them killing things."

"One day I'm coming through Spruce Pine, flat out, throw Violet up behind me! We're going to lean all the way through them mountains. Sliding the right foot and then sliding the left." Monty lays his head back on the seat beside me, rolls it, watches. "How you like that? Take you through creeks and ditches like you was on a skateboard. You can just holler and hang on."

Lots of women have, I bet.

"The Norton's got the best front forks of anybody. It'll nearly roll up a tree trunk and ride down the other side." He demonstrates on the seat back. I keep writing. These are new things, two-stroke and four-stroke, picking your line on a curve, Milwaukee iron. It will all come back to me in the winters, when I reread these pages.

Flick says he rode on a Harley once. "Turned over and got drug. No more."

They argue about what he should have done instead of turning over. Finally Monty drifts off to sleep, his head leaning at me slowly, so I look down on his crisp, light hair. I pat it as easy as a cat would, and it tickles my palm. I'd almost ask them in Tulsa to make me a man if I could have hair like his, and a beard, and feel so different in so many places.

He slides closer in his sleep. One eyebrow wrinkles against my shoulder. Looking our way, Flick smokes a cigarette, then reads some magazine he keeps rolled in his belt. Monty makes a deep noise against my arm as if, while he slept, his throat had cleared itself. I shift and his whole head is on my shoulder now. Its weight makes me breathe shallow.

I rest my eyes. If I should turn, his hair would barely touch my cheek, the scarred one, like a shoebrush. I do turn and it does. For miles he sleeps that way and I almost sleep. Once, when we take a long curve, he rolls against me, and one of his hands drifts up and then drops in my lap. Just there, where the creases are.

I would not want God's Power to turn me, after all, into a man. His breath is so warm. Everywhere, my skin is singing. Praise God for that.

When I get my first look at the Mississippi River, the pencil goes straight into my pocketbook. How much praise would that take?

"Is the sea like this?"

"Not except they're both water," Flick says. He's not mad anymore. "Tell you what, Vi-oh-LETTE. When Monty picks you up on his cycle" ("sickle," he calls it), "you ride down to the beaches—Cherry Grove, O.D., around there. Where they work the big nets in the fall and drag them up on the sand with trucks at each end, and men to their necks in the surf."

"You do that?"

"I know people that do. And afterward they strip and dress by this big fire on the beach."

And they make chowder while this cold wind is blowing! I know that much, without asking. In a big black pot that sits on that whipping fire. I think they might let me sit with them and stir the pot. It's funny how much, right now, I feel like praising all the good things I've never seen, in places I haven't been.

Everybody has to get off the bus and change in Memphis, and most of them wait a long time. I've taken the long way, coming here; but some of Mama's cousins live in Memphis and might rest me overnight. Monty says they plan to stay the night, too, and break the long trip.

"They know you're coming, Violet?" It's Flick says my name that way, in pieces, carefully: Vi-oh-LETTE. Monty is lazier: Viii-lut. They make me feel like more than one.

"I've never even met these cousins. But soon as I call up and tell them who I am and that I'm here . . ."

"We'll stay some hotel tonight and then ride on. Why don't you come with us?" Monty is carrying my scuffed bag. Flick swings the paper sack. "You know us better than them."

"Kin people," grunts Flick, "can be a bad surprise."

Monty is nodding his head. "Only cousin I had got drunk and drove this tractor over his baby brother. Did it on purpose, too." I see by his face that Monty has made this up, for my sake.

"Your cousins might not even live here anymore. I bet it's been years since you heard from a one."

"We're picking a cheap hotel, in case that's a worry."

I never thought they might have moved. "How cheap?"

When Flick says, "Under five," I nod; and my things go right up on their shoulders as I follow them into a Memphis cab. The driver takes for granted I'm Monty's afflicted sister and names a hotel right off. He treats me with pity and good manners.

And the hotel he chooses is cheap, all right, where ratty salesmen with bad territories spend half the night drinking in their rooms. Plastic palm bushes and a worn rug the color of wet cigars. I get Room 210 and they're down the hall in the teens. They stand in my doorway and watch me drop both shoes and walk the bed in bare feet. When Monty opens my window, we can hear some kitchen underneath—a fan, clattering noise, a man's crackly voice singing about the California earthquake.

It scares me, suddenly, to know I can't remember how home sounds. Not one bird call, nor the water over rocks. There's so much you can't save by writing down.

"Smell that grease," says Flick, and shakes his head till his lips flutter. "I'm finding an ice machine. You, Vi-oh-LETTE, come on down in a while."

Monty's got a grin I'll remember if I never write a word. He waves. "Flick and me going to get drunker than my old cousin and put wild things in your book. Going to draw dirty pictures. You come on down and get drunk enough to laugh."

But after a shower, damp in my clean slip, even this bed like a roll of fence wire feels good, and I fall asleep wondering if that rushing noise is a river wind, and how long I can keep it in my mind.

Monty and Flick edge into my dream. Just their voices first, from way downhill. Somewhere in a Shonny Haw thicket. "Just different," Monty is saying. "That's all. Different. Don't make some big thing out of it." He doesn't sound happy. "Nobody else," he says.

Is that Flick singing? No, because the song goes on while his voice says, "Just so . . ." and then some words I don't catch. "It don't hurt?" Or maybe, "You don't hurt?" I hear them climbing my tangled hill, breaking sticks and knocking the little stones loose. I'm trying to call to them which way the path is, but I can't make noise because the Preacher took my voice and put it in a black bag and carried it to a sick little boy in Iowa.

They find the path, anyway. And now they can see my house and me standing little by the steps. I know how it looks from where they are: the wood rained on till the siding's almost silver; and behind the house a wet-weather waterfall that's cut a stream bed downhill and grown pin cherry and bee balm on both sides. The high rock walls by the waterfall are mossy and slick, but I've scraped one place and hammered a mean-looking gray head that leans out of the hillside and stares down the path at whoever comes. I've been here so long by myself that I talk to it sometimes. Right now I'd say, "Look yonder. We've got company at last!" if my voice wasn't gone.

"You can't go by looks," Flick is saying as they climb. He ought to know. Ahead of them, warblers separate and fly out on two sides. Everything moves out of their path if I could just see it—tree frogs and mosquitoes. Maybe the worms drop deeper just before a footstep falls.

"Without the clothes, it's not a hell of a lot improved," says Monty, and I know suddenly they are inside the house with me, inside my very room, and my room today's in Memphis. "There's one thing, though," Monty says, standing over my bed. "Good looks in a woman is almost like a wall. She can use it to shut you outside. You never know what she's like, that's all." He's wearing a T-shirt and his dog tags jingle. "Most of the time I don't even miss knowing that."

And Flick says, disgusted, "I knew that much in grammar school. You sure are slow. It's not the face you screw." If I opened my eyes, I could see him now, behind Monty. He says, "After a while, you don't even notice faces. I always thought, in a crowd, my mother might not pick Daddy out."

"*My* mother could," says Monty. "He was always the one *started* the fight."

I stretch and open my eyes. It's a plain slip, cotton, that I sewed myself and makes me look too white and skinny as a sapling.

"She's waking up."

When I point, Monty hands me the blouse off the doorknob. Flick says they've carried me a soda pop, plus something to spruce it up. They sit stiffly on two hard chairs till I've buttoned on my skirt. I sip the drink, cold but peppery, and prop on the bed with the pillows. "I dreamed you both came where my house is, on the mountain, and it had rained so the waterfall was working. I felt real proud of that."

After two drinks we go down to the noisy restaurant with that smelly grease. And after that, to a picture show. Monty grins widely when the star comes on the screen. The spit on his teeth shines, even in the dark. Seeing what kind of woman he really likes, black-haired as a gypsy and with a juicy mouth, I change all my plans. My eyes, too, must turn up on the ends and when I bend down my breasts must fall forward and push at each other. When the star does that in the picture, the cowboy rubs his mustache low in the front of her neck.

In the darkness, Monty takes my hand and holds it in his swelling lap. To me it seems funny that my hand, brown and crusty from hoeing and chopping, is harder than his. I guess you don't get calluses rolling a motorcycle throttle. He rubs his thumb up and down my middle finger. Oh, I would like to ride fast behind him, spraddle-legged, with my arms wrapped on his belt, and I would lay my face between his sharp shoulder blades.

That night, when I've slept awhile, I hear something brushing the rug in the hall. I slip to my door. It's very dark. I press myself, face first, to the wood. There's breathing on the other side. I feel I get fatter, standing there, that even my own small breasts might now be made to touch. I round both shoulders to see. The movement jars the door and it trembles slightly in its frame.

From the far side, by the hinges, somebody whispers, "Vi-oh-LETTE?"

Now I stand very still. The wood feels cooler on my skin, or else I have grown very warm. Oh, I could love anybody! There is so much of me now, they could line up strangers in the hall and let me hold each one better than he had ever been held before!

Slowly I turn the knob, but Flick's breathing is gone. The corridor's empty. I leave the latch off.

Late in the night, when the noise from the kitchen is over, he comes into my room. I wake when he bumps on a chair, swears, then scrabbles at the footboard.

"Viii-lut?"

I slide up in bed. I'm not ready, not now, but he's here. I spread both arms wide. In the dark he can't tell.

He feels his way onto the bed and he touches my knee and it changes. Stops being just my old knee, under his fingers. I feel the joint heat up and bubble. I push the sheet down.

He comes onto me, whispering something. I reach up to claim him.

One time he stops. He's surprised, I guess, finding he isn't the first. How can I tell him how bad that was? How long ago? The night when the twelfth grade was over and one of them climbed with me all the way home? And he asked. And I thought, *I'm entitled*. Won him a five-dollar bet. Didn't do nothing for me.

But this time I sing out and Monty says, "Shh" in my ear. And he starts over, slow, and makes me whimper one other time. Then he turns sideways to sleep and I try my face there, laid in the nest on his damp back. I reach out my tongue. He is salty and good.

Now there are two things too big for my notebook but praise God! And for the Mississippi, too!

There is no good reason for me to ride with them all the way to Fort Smith, but since Tulsa is not expecting me, we change my ticket. Monty pays the extra. We ride through the fertile plains. The last of May becomes June and the Arkansas sun is blazing. I am stunned by this heat. At home, night means blankets and even on hot afternoons it may rain and start the waterfall. I lie against my seat for miles without a word.

"What's wrong?" Monty keeps asking; but, under the heat, I am happy. Sleepy with happiness, a lizard on a rock. At every stop Monty's off the bus, bringing me more than I can eat or drink, buying me magazines and gum. I tell him and Flick to play two-handed cards, but mostly Flick lectures him in a low voice about something.

I try to stop thinking of Memphis and think back to Tulsa. I went to the Spruce Pine library to look up Tulsa in their encyclopedia. I thought sure it would tell about the Preacher, and on what street he'd built his Hope and Glory Building for his soul crusades. Tulsa was listed in the *Americana,* Volume 27, Trance to Venial Sin. I got so tickled with that I forgot to write down the rest.

Now, in the hot sun, clogged up with trances and venial sins, I dream under the drone of their voices. For some reason I remember that old lady back in Nashville, moved in with Harvey and his wife and their three children. I hope she's happy. I picture her on Harvey's back porch, baked in the sun like me, in a rocker. Snapping beans.

I've left my pencil in the hotel and must borrow one from Flick to write in my book. I put in, slowly: "This is the day which the Lord hath made." But, before Monty, what kind of days was He sending me? I cross out the line. I have this wish to praise, instead of Him, the littlest things. Honeybees, and the wet slugs under their rocks. A gnat in some farmer's eye.

I give up and hand Flick his pencil. He slides toward the aisle and whispers, "You wish you'd stayed in your mountains?"

I shake my head and a piece of my no-color hair falls into the sunlight. Maybe it even shines.

He spits on the pencil point and prints something inside a gum wrapper. "Here's my address. You keep it. Never can tell."

So I tear the paper in half and give him back mine. He reads it a long time before tucking it away, but he won't send a letter till I do—I can tell that. Through all this, Monty stares out the window. Arkansas rolls out ahead of us like a rug.

Monty has not asked for my address, nor how far uphill I live from Spruce Pine, though he could ride his motorcycle up to me, strong as its engine is. For a long time he has been sitting quietly, lighting one cigarette off another. This winter, I've got to learn smoking. How to lift my hand up so every eye will follow it to my smooth cheek.

I put Flick's paper in my pocketbook and there, inside, on a round mirror, my face is waiting in ambush for me. I see the curved scar, neat as ever, swoop from the edge of one nostril in rainbow shape across my cheek, then down toward the ear. For the first time in years, pain boils across my face as it did that day. I close my eyes under that red drowning, and see again Papa's ax head rise off its locust handle and come floating through the air, sideways, like a gliding crow. And it drops down into my face almost daintily, the edge turned just enough to slash loose a flap of skin the way you might slice straight down on the curve of a melon. My papa is yelling, but I am under a red rain and it bears me down. I am lifted and run with through the woodyard and into the barn. Now I am slumped on his chest and the whipped horse is throwing us down the mountainside, and my head is wrapped in something big as a wet quilt. The doctor groans when he winds it off and I faint while he lifts up my flesh like the flap of a pulpy envelope, and sews the white bone out of sight.

Dizzy from the movement of the bus, I snap shut my pocketbook.

Whenever I cry, the first drop quivers there, in the curving scar, and then runs crooked on that track to the ear. I cry straight-down on the other side.

I am glad this bus has a toilet. I go there to cool my eyes with wet paper, and spit up Monty's chocolate and cola.

When I come out, he's standing at the door with his fist up. "You all right, Viii-lut? You worried or something?"

I see he pities me. In my seat again, I plan the speech I will make at Fort Smith and the laugh I will give. "Honey, you're good," I'll say, laughing, "but the others were better." That ought to do it. I am quieter now than Monty is, practicing it in my mind.

It's dark when we hit Fort Smith. Everybody's face looks shadowed and different. Mine better. Monty's strange. We're saying goodbyes very fast. I start my speech twice and he misses it twice.

Then he bends over me and offers his own practiced line that I see he's worked up all across Arkansas, "I plan to be right here, Violet, in this bus station. On Monday. All day. You get off your bus when it comes through. Hear me, Viii-lut? I'll watch for you?"

No. He won't watch. Nor I come. "My schedule won't take me this road going back. Bye, Flick. Lots of good luck to you both."

"Promise me. Like I'm promising."

"Good luck to you, Vi-oh-LETTE." Flick lets his hand fall on my head and it feels as good as anybody's hand.

Monty shoves money at me and I shove it back. "Promise," he says, his voice furious. He tries to kiss me in the hair and I jerk so hard my nose cracks his chin. We stare, blurry-eyed and hurting. He follows Flick down the aisle, calls back, "I'm coming here Monday. See you then, hear? And you get off the bus!"

"No! I won't!"

He yells it twice more. People are staring. He's out of the bus pounding on the steel wall by my seat. I'm not going to look. The seats fill up with strangers and we ride away, nobody talking to anyone else. My nose where I hit it is going to swell—the Preacher will have to throw that in for free. I look back, but he's gone.

The lights in the bus go out again. Outside they bloom thick by the streets, then thinner, then mostly gone as we pass into the countryside. Even in the dark, I can see Oklahoma's mountains are uglier than mine. Knobs and hills, mostly. The bus drives into rain which covers up everything. At home I like that washing sound. We go deeper into the downpour. Perhaps we are under the Arkansas

River, after all. It seems I can feel its great weight move over me.

Before daylight, the rain tapers off and here the ground looks dry, even barren. Cattle graze across long fields. In the wind, wheat fields shiver. I can't eat anything all the way to Tulsa. It makes me homesick to see the land grow brighter and flatter and balder. That old lady was right—the trees do give out—and oil towers grow in their place. The glare's in my eyes. I write in my notebook: "Praise God for Tulsa; I am nearly there," but it takes a long time to get the words down.

One day my papa told me how time got slow for him when Mama died. How one week he waded through the creek and it was water, and the next week cold molasses. How he'd lay awake a year between sundown and sunup, and in the morning I'd be a day older and he'd be three hundred and sixty-five.

It works the other way, too. In no time at all, we're into Tulsa without me knowing what we've passed. So many tall buildings. Everybody's running. They rush into taxis before I can get one to wait for me long enough to ask the driver questions. But still I'm speeded to a hotel, and the elevator yanks me to a room quicker than Elijah rode to Heaven. The room's not bad. A Gideon Bible. Inside are lots of dirty words somebody wrote. He must have been feeling bad.

I bathe and dress, trembling from my own speed, and pin on the hat which has traveled all the way from Spruce Pine for this. I feel tired. I go out into the loud streets full of fast cars. Hot metal everywhere. A taxi roars me across town to the Preacher's church.

It looks like a big insurance office, though I can tell where the chapel is by colored glass in the pointed windows. Carved in an arch over the door are the words: "HOPE OF GLORY BUILDING." Right away, something in me sinks. All this time I've been hearing it on TV as the Hope *and* Glory Building. You wouldn't think one word could make that much difference.

Inside the door, there's a list of offices and room numbers. I don't see the Preacher's name. Clerks send me down long, tiled halls, past empty air-conditioned offices. One tells me to go up two flights and ask the fat woman, and the fat woman sends me down again. I'm carrying my notebook in a dry hand, feeling as brittle as the maypop flower.

At last I wait an hour to see some assistant—very close to the Preacher, I'm told. His waiting room is chilly, the leatherette chairs worn down to the mesh. I try to remember how much TB and cancer have passed through this very room and been jerked out of people the way Jesus tore out a demon and flung him into a herd of swine. I wonder what he felt like to the swine.

After a long time, the young man calls me into his plain office—wood desk, wood chairs. Shelves of booklets and colored folders. On one wall, a colored picture of Jesus with that fairy ring of light around His head. Across from that, one of His praying hands—rougher than Monty's, smoother than mine.

The young man wears glasses with no rims. In this glare, I am reflected on each lens, Vi-oh-LETTE and Viii-lut. On his desk is a box of postcards of the Hope and Glory Building. *Of* Glory. *Of* Glory.

I am afraid.

I feel behind me for the chair.

The man explains that he is presently in charge. The Preacher's speaking in Tallahassee, his show taped weeks ahead. I never thought of it as a show before. He waits.

I reach inside my notebook where, taped shut, is the thick envelope with everything written down. I knew I could never explain things right. When have I ever been able to tell what I really felt? But it's all in there—my name, my need. The words from the Bible which must argue for me. I did not sit there nights since Papa died, counting my money and studying God's Book, for nothing. Playing solitaire, then going back to search the next page and the next. Stepping outside to rest my eyes on His limitless sky, then back to the Book and the paper, building my case.

He starts to read, turns up his glitter-glass to me once to check how I look, then reads again. His chair must be hard, for he squirms in it, crosses his legs. When he has read every page, he lays the stack down, slowly takes off his glasses, folds them shining into a case. He leaves it open on his desk. Mica shines like that, in the rocks.

Then he looks at me, fully. Oh. He is plain. Almost

homely. I nearly expected it. Maybe Samuel was born ugly, so who else would take him but God?

"My child," the man begins, though I'm older than he is, "I understand how you feel. And we will most certainly pray for your spirit. . . ."

I shut my eyes against those two flashing faces on his spectacles. "Never mind my spirit." I see he doesn't really understand. I see he will live a long life, and not marry.

"Our Heavenly Father has purpose in all things."

Stubbornly, "Ask Him to set it aside."

"We must all trust His will."

After all these years, isn't it God's turn to trust mine? Could He not risk a little beauty on me? Just when I'm ready to ask, the sober assistant recites, " 'Favor is deceitful and beauty is vain.' That's in Proverbs."

And I cry, " 'The crooked shall be made straight!' Isaiah said that!" He draws back, as if I had brought the Gideon Bible and struck him with its most disfigured pages. "Jesus healed an impediment in speech. See my impediment! Mud on a blind man's eyes was all He needed! Don't you remember?" But he's read all that. Everything I know on my side lies, written out, under his sweaty hand. Lord, don't let me whine. But I whine, "He healed the ten lepers and only one thanked. Well, I'll thank. I promise. All my life."

He clears his long knotty throat and drones like a bee, " 'By the sadness of the countenance the heart is made better.' Ecclesiastes. Seven. Three."

Oh, that's not fair! I skipped those parts, looking for verses that suited me! And it's wrong, besides.

I get up to leave and he asks will I kneel with him? "Let us pray together for that inner beauty."

No, I will not. I go down that hollow hall and past the echoing rooms. Without his help I find the great auditorium, lit through colored glass, with its cross of white plastic and a pinker Jesus molded onto it. I go straight to the pulpit where the Preacher stands. There is nobody else to plead. I ask Jesus not to listen to everything He hears, but to me only.

Then I tell Him how it feels to be ugly, with nothing to look back at you but a deer or an owl. I read Him my paper, out loud, full of His own words.

"I have been praising you, Lord, but it gets harder every

year." Maybe that sounds too strong. I try to ease up my tone before the Amens. Then the chapel is very quiet. For one minute I hear the whir of many wings, but it's only a fan inside an air vent.

I go into the streets of Tulsa, where even the shade from a building is hot. And as I walk to the hotel I'm repeating, over and over, "Praise God for Tulsa in spite of everything."

Maybe I say this aloud, since people are staring. But maybe that's only because they've never seen a girl cry crooked in their streets before.

Monday morning. I have not looked at my face since the pulpit prayer. Who can predict how He might act—with a lightning bolt? Or a melting so slow and tender it could not even be felt?

Now, on the bus, I can touch in my pocketbook the cold mirror glass. Though I cover its surface with prints, I never look down. We ride through the dust and I'm nervous. My pencil is flying: "Be ye therefore perfect as your Heavenly Father is perfect. Praise God for Oklahoma. For Wagoner and Sapulpa and Broken Arrow and every other name on these signs by the road."

Was that the wrong thing to tell Him? My threat that even praise can be withheld? Maybe He's angry. "Praise God for oil towers whether I like them or not." When we pass churches, I copy their names. Praise them all. I want to write, "Bless," but that's *His* job.

We cross the cool Arkansas River. As its damp rises into the bus and touches my face, something wavers there, in the very bottom of each pore; and I clap my rough hands to each cheek. Maybe He's started? How much can He do between here and Fort Smith? If He will?

For I know what will happen. Monty won't come. And I won't stop. That's an end to it.

No, Monty is there. Waiting right now. And I'll go into the bus station on tiptoe and stand behind him. He'll turn, with his blue eyes like lamps. *And he won't know me!* If I'm changed. So I will explain myself to him: how this gypsy hair and this juicy mouth is still Violet Karl. He'll say, "Won't old Flick be surprised?" He'll say, "Where is that place you live? Can I come there?"

But if, while I wait and he turns, he should know me by

my old face . . . If he should say my name or show by recognition that my name's rising up now in his eyes like something through water . . . I'll be running by then. To the bus. Straight out that door to the Tennessee bus, saying, "Driver, don't let that man on!" It's a very short stop. We'll be pulling out quick. I don't think he'll follow, anyhow.

I don't even think he will come.

One hundred and thirty-one miles to Fort Smith. I wish I could eat.

I try to think up things to look forward to at home. Maybe the sourwoods are blooming early, and the bees have been laying-by my honey. If it's rained enough, my corn might be in tassel. Wouldn't it be something if God took His own sweet time, and I lived on that slope for years and years, getting prettier all the time? And nobody to know?

It takes nearly years and years to get to Fort Smith. My papa knew things about time. I comb out my hair, not looking once to see what color sheddings are caught in the teeth. There's no need feeling my cheek, since my finger expects that scar. I can feel it on me almost anywhere, by memory. I straighten my skirt and lick my lips till the spit runs out.

And they're waiting. Monty at one door of the terminal and Flick at another.

"Ten minutes," the driver says when the bus is parked, but I wait in my seat till Flick gets restless and walks to the cigarette machine. Then I slip through his entrance door and inside the station. Mirrors shine everywhere. On the vending machines and the weight machines and a full-length one by the phone booth. It's all I can do not to look. I pass the ticket window and there's Monty's back at the other door. My face remembers the shape of it. Seeing him there, how he's made, and the parts of him fitted, makes me forget how I look. And before I can stop, I call out his name.

Right away, turning, he yells to me, "*Viii*-lut!"

So I know. I can look, then, in the wide mirror over a jukebox. Tired as I am and unfed, I look worse than I did when I started from home.

He's laughing and talking. "I been waiting here since daylight scared you wouldn't . . ." but by then I've run past the ugly girl in the glass and I race for the bus, for the road, for the mountain.

Behind me, he calls loudly, "Flick!"

I see that one step in my path like a floating dark blade, but I'm faster this time. I twist by him, into the flaming sun and the parking lot. How my breath hurts!

Monty's between me and my bus, but there's time. I circle the cabstand, running hard over the asphalt field, with a pain ticking in my side. He calls me. I plunge through the crowd like a deer through fetterbush. But he's running as hard as he can and he's faster than me. And, oh!

Praise God!

He's catching me!

CHILDREN ON THEIR BIRTHDAYS
by *Truman Capote*

❀

(This story is for Andrew Lyndon)

Yesterday afternoon the six-o'clock bus ran over Miss Bobbit. I'm not sure what there is to be said about it; after all, she was only ten years old, still I know no one of us in this town will forget her. For one thing, nothing she ever did was ordinary, not from the first time that we saw her, and that was a year ago. Miss Bobbit and her mother, they arrived on that same six-o'clock bus, the one that comes through from Mobile. It happened to be my cousin Billy Bob's birthday, and so most of the children in town were here at our house. We were sprawled on the front porch having tutti-frutti and devil cake when the bus stormed around Deadman's Curve. It was the summer that never rained; rusted dryness coated everything; sometimes when a car passed on the road, raised dust would hang in the still air an hour or more. Aunt El said if they didn't pave the highway soon she was going to move down to the seacoast; but she'd said that for such a long time. Anyway, we were sitting on the porch, tutti-frutti melting on our plates, when suddenly, just as we were wishing that something would happen, something did; for out of the red road dust appeared Miss Bobbit. A wiry little girl in a starched, lemon-colored party dress, she sassed along with a grown-up mince, one hand on her hip, the other supporting a spinsterish umbrella. Her mother, lugging two cardboard valises and a wind-up victrola, trailed in the background. She was a gaunt shaggy woman with silent eyes and a hungry smile.

All the children on the porch had grown so still that when a cone of wasps started humming the girls did not set up their usual holler. Their attention was too fixed upon the approach of Miss Bobbit and her mother, who had by now reached the gate. "Begging your pardon," called Miss Bobbit in a voice that was at once silky and childlike, like a pretty piece of ribbon, and immaculately exact, like a movie star or a schoolmarm, "but might we speak with the grown-up persons of the house?" This, of course, meant Aunt El; and, at least to some degree, myself. But Billy Bob and all the other boys, no one of whom was over thirteen, followed down to the gate after us. From their faces you would have thought they'd never seen a girl before. Certainly not like Miss Bobbit. As Aunt El said, whoever heard tell of a child wearing makeup? Tangee gave her lips an orange glow, her hair, rather like a costume wig, was a mass of rosy curls, and her eyes had a knowing, penciled tilt; even so, she had a skinny dignity, she was a lady, and, what is more, she looked you in the eye with manlike directness. "I'm Miss Lily Jane Bobbit, Miss Bobbit from Memphis, Tennessee," she said solemnly. The boys looked down at their toes, and, on the porch, Cora McCall, who Billy Bob was courting at the time, led the girls into a fanfare of giggles. "*Country* children," said Miss Bobbit with an understanding smile, and gave her parasol a saucy whirl. "My mother," and this homely woman allowed an abrupt nod to acknowledge herself, "my mother and I have taken rooms here. Would you be so kind as to point out the house? It belongs to a Mrs. Sawyer." Why, sure, said Aunt El, that's Mrs. Sawyer's, right there across the street. The only boarding house around here, it is an old tall dark place with about two dozen lightning rods scattered on the roof: Mrs. Sawyer is scared to death in a thunderstorm.

Coloring like an apple, Billy Bob said, please ma'am, it being such a hot day and all, wouldn't they rest a spell and have some tutti-frutti? and Aunt El said yes, by all means, but Miss Bobbit shook her head. "Very fattening, tutti-frutti; but *merci* you kindly," and they started across the road, the mother half-dragging her parcels in the dust. Then, and with an earnest expression, Miss Bobbit turned back; the sunflower yellow of her eyes darkened, and she rolled them slightly sideways, as if trying to remember a poem. "My mother has a disorder of the tongue, so it is necessary that I speak for her," she announced rapidly and heaved a sigh. "My mother is a very fine seamstress; she has made dresses for the society of many cities and towns, including Memphis and Tallahassee. No doubt you have noticed and admired the dress I am wearing. Every stitch of it was handsewn by my mother. My mother can copy any pattern, and just recently she won a twenty-five-dollar prize from the *Ladies' Home Journal.* My mother can also crochet, knit, and embroider. If you want any kind of sewing done, please come to my mother. Please advise your friends and family. Thank you." And then, with a rustle and a swish, she was gone.

Cora McCall and the girls pulled their hair-ribbons nervously, suspiciously, and looked very put out and prune-faced. I'm *Miss* Bobbit, said Cora, twisting her face into an evil imitation, and I'm Princess Elizabeth, that's who I am, ha, ha, ha. Furthermore, said Cora, that dress was just as tacky as could be; personally, Cora said, all my clothes come from Atlanta; plus a pair of shoes from New York, which is not even to mention my silver turquoise ring all the way from Mexico City, Mexico. Aunt El said they ought not to behave that way about a fellow child, a stranger in the town, but the girls went on like a huddle of witches, and certain boys, the sillier ones that liked to be with the girls, joined in and said things that made Aunt El go red and declare she was going to send them all home and tell their daddies, to boot. But before she could carry forward this threat Miss Bobbit herself intervened by traipsing across the Sawyer porch, costumed in a new and startling manner.

The older boys, like Billy Bob and Preacher Star, who had sat quiet while the girls razzed Miss Bobbit, and who had watched the house into which she'd disappeared with misty, ambitious faces, they now straightened up and ambled down to the gate. Cora McCall sniffed and poked out her lower lip, but the rest of us went and sat on the steps. Miss Bobbit paid us no mind whatever. The Sawyer yard is dark with mulberry trees and it is planted with grass and sweet shrub. Sometimes after a rain you can smell the sweet shrub all the way into our house; and in the center of this yard there is a sundial which Mrs. Sawyer installed in 1912 as a memorial to her Boston bull, Sunny, who died after having lapped up a bucket of paint. Miss Bobbit pranced into the yard toting the victrola, which she put on the sundial; she wound it up, and started a record playing, and it played the Court of Luxemborg. By now it was almost nightfall, a firefly hour, blue as milkglass; and birds like arrows swooped together and swept into the folds of trees. Before storms, leaves and flowers appear to burn with a private light, color, and Miss Bobbit, got up in a little white skirt like a powderpuff and with strips of gold-glittering tinsel ribboning her hair, seemed, set against the darkening all around, to contain this illuminated quality. She held her arms arched over her head, her hands lily-limp, and stood straight up on the tips of her toes. She stood that way for a good long while, and Aunt El said it was right smart of her. Then she began to waltz around and around, and around and around she went until Aunt El said, why, she was plain dizzy from the sight. She stopped only when it was time to rewind the victrola; and when the moon came rolling down the ridge, and the last supper bell had sounded, and all the children had gone home, and the night iris was beginning to bloom, Miss Bobbit was still there in the dark turning like a top.

We did not see her again for some time. Preacher Star came every morning to our house and stayed straight through to supper. Preacher is a rail-thin boy with a butchy shock of red hair; he has eleven brothers and sisters, and even they are afraid of him, for he has a terrible temper, and is famous in these parts for his green-eyed meanness: last fourth of July he whipped Ollie Overton so bad that Ollie's family had to send him to the hospital in Pensacola; and there was another time he bit off half a mule's ear, chewed it, and spit it on the ground. Before Billy Bob got his growth, Preacher played the devil with him, too. He used to drop cockleburrs down his collar, and rub pepper in his eyes, and tear up his homework. But now they are the biggest friends in town; talk alike, walk alike, and occasionally they disappear together for whole days, Lord knows where to. But during these days when Miss Bobbit did not appear they stayed close to the house. They would stand around in the yard trying to slingshot sparrows off telephone poles; or sometimes Billy Bob would play his ukulele, and they would sing so loud Uncle Billy Bob, who is Judge for this county, claimed he could hear them all the way to the courthouse: *send me a letter, send it by mail, send it in care of the Birming-ham jail.* Miss Bobbit did not hear them; at least she never poked her head out the door.

Then one day Mrs. Sawyer, coming over to borrow a cup of sugar, rattled on a good deal about her new boarders. You know, she said, squinting her chicken-bright eyes, the husband was a crook, uh huh, the child told me herself. Hasn't an ounce of shame, not a mite. Said her daddy was the dearest daddy and the sweetest singing man in the whole of Tennessee. . . . And I said, honey, where is he? and just as off-hand as you please she says, Oh, he's in the penitentiary and we don't hear from him no more. Say, now, does that make your blood run cold? Uh huh, and I been thinking, her mama, I been thinking she's some kinda foreigner: never says a word, and sometimes it looks like she don't understand what nobody says to her. And you know, they eat everything *raw*. *Raw* eggs, *raw* turnips, carrots—no meat whatsoever. For reasons of health, the child says, but ho! she's been straight out on the bed running a fever since last Tuesday.

That same afternoon Aunt El went out to water her roses, only to discover them gone. These were special roses, ones she'd planned to send to the flower show in Mobile, and so naturally she got a little hysterical. She rang up the Sheriff, and said, listen here, Sheriff, you come over here right fast. I mean somebody's got off with all my Lady Anne's that I've devoted myself to heart and soul since early spring. When the Sheriff's car pulled up outside our house, all the neighbors along the street came out on their porches, and Mrs. Sawyer, layers of cold cream whitening her face, trotted across the road. Oh shoot, she said, very disappointed to find no one had been murdered, oh shoot, she said, nobody's stole them roses. Your Billy Bob brought them roses over and left them for little Bobbit. Aunt El did not say one word. She just marched over to the peach tree, and cut herself a switch. Ohhh, Billy Bob, she stalked along the street calling his name, and then she found him down at Speedy's garage where he and Preacher were watching Speedy take a motor apart. She simply lifted him by the hair and, switching blueblazes, towed him home. But she couldn't make him say he was sorry and she couldn't make him cry. And when she was finished with him he ran into the backyard and climbed high into the tower of a pecan tree and swore he wasn't ever going to come down. Then his daddy stood at the window and called to him: Son, we aren't mad with you, so come down and eat your supper. But Billy Bob wouldn't budge. Aunt El went and leaned against the tree. She spoke in a voice soft as the gathering light. I'm sorry, son, she said, I didn't mean whipping you so hard like that. I've fixed a nice supper, son, potato salad and boiled ham and deviled eggs. Go away, said Billy Bob, I don't want no supper, and I hate you like all-fire. His daddy said he ought not to talk like that to his mother, and she began to cry. She stood there under the tree and cried, raising the hem of her skirt to dab at her eyes. I don't hate you, son. . . . If I didn't love you I wouldn't whip you. The pecan leaves began to rattle; Billy Bob slid slowly to the ground, and Aunt El, rushing her fingers through his hair, pulled him against her. Aw, Ma, he said, Aw, Ma.

After supper Billy Bob came and flung himself on the foot of my bed. He smelled all sour and sweet, the way boys do, and I felt very sorry for him, especially because he looked so worried. His eyes were almost shut with worry. You're s'posed to send sick folks flowers, he said righteously. About this time we heard the victrola, a lilting faraway sound, and a night moth flew through the window, drifting in the air delicate as the music. But it was dark now, and we couldn't tell if Miss Bobbit was dancing. Billy Bob, as though he were in pain, doubled up on the bed like a jackknife; but his face was suddenly clear, his grubby boy-eyes twitching like candles. She's so cute, he whispered, she's the cutest dickens I ever saw, gee, to hell with it, I don't care, I'd pick all the roses in China.

Preacher would have picked all the roses in China, too. He was as crazy about her as Billy Bob. But Miss Bobbit did not notice them. The sole communication we had with her was a note to Aunt El thanking her for the flowers. Day after day she sat on her porch, always dressed to beat the band, and doing a piece of embroidery, or combing curls in her hair, or reading a Webster's dictionary—formal, but friendly enough; if you said good-day to her she said good-day to you. Even so, the boys never could seem to get up the nerve to go over and talk with her, and most of the time she simply looked through them, even when they tomcatted up and down the street trying to get her eye. They wrestled, played Tarzan, did foolheaded bicycle tricks. It was a sorry business. A great many girls in town strolled by the Sawyer house two and three times within an hour just on the chance of getting a look. Some of the girls who did this were: Cora McCall, Mary Murphy Jones, Janice Ackerman. Miss Bobbit did not show any interest in them either. Cora would not speak to Billy Bob any more. The same was true with Janice and Preacher. As a matter of fact, Janice wrote Preacher a letter in red ink on lace-trimmed paper in which she told him he was vile beyond all human beings and words, that she considered their engagement broken, that he could have back the stuffed squirrel he'd given her. Preacher, saying he wanted to act nice, stopped her the next time she passed our house, and said, well, hell, she could keep that old squirrel if she wanted to. Afterwards, he couldn't understand why Janice ran away bawling the way she did.

Then one day the boys were being crazier than usual; Billy Bob was sagging around in his daddy's World War khakis, and Preacher, stripped to the waist, had a naked woman drawn on his chest with one of Aunt El's old lipsticks. They looked like perfect fools, but Miss Bobbit, reclining in a swing, merely yawned. It was noon, and there was no one passing in the street, except a colored girl, baby-fat and sugar-plum shaped, who hummed along carrying a pail of blackberries. But the boys, teasing at her like gnats, joined hands and wouldn't let her go by, not until she paid a tariff. I ain't studyin' no tariff, she said, what kinda tariff you talkin' about, mister? A party in the barn, said Preacher, between clenched teeth, mighty nice party in the barn. And she, with a sulky shrug, said, huh, she intended studyin' no barn parties. Whereupon Billy Bob capsized her berry pail, and when she, with despairing, piglike shrieks, bent down in futile gestures of rescue, Preacher, who can be mean as the devil, gave her behind a kick which sent her sprawling jellylike among the blackberries and the dust. Miss Bobbit came tearing across the road, her finger wagging like a metronome; like a schoolteacher she clapped her hands, stamped her foot, said: "It is a well-known fact that gentlemen are put on the face of this earth for the protection of ladies. Do you suppose boys behave this way in towns like Memphis, New York, London, Hollywood, or Paris?" The boys hung back, and shoved their hands in their pockets. Miss Bobbit helped the colored girl to her feet; she dusted her off, dried her eyes, held out a handkerchief and told her to blow. "A pretty pass," she said, "a fine situation when a lady can't walk safely in the public daylight."

Then the two of them went back and sat on Mrs. Sawyer's porch; and for the next year they were never far apart, Miss Bobbit and this baby elephant, whose name was Rosalba Cat. At first, Mrs. Sawyer raised a fuss about Rosalba being so much at her house. She told Aunt El that it went against the grain to have a nigger lolling smack there in plain sight on her front porch. But Miss Bobbit had a certain magic, whatever she did she did it with completeness, and so directly, so solemnly, that there was nothing to do but accept it. For instance, the tradespeople in town used to snicker when they called her *Miss* Bobbit; but by and by she was Miss Bobbit, and they gave her stiff little bows as she whirled by spinning her parasol. Miss Bobbit told everyone that Rosalba was her sister, which caused a good many jokes; but like most of her ideas, it gradually seemed natural, and when we would overhear them calling each other Sister Rosalba and Sister Bobbit none of us cracked a smile. But Sister Rosalba and Sister Bobbit did some queer things. There was the business about the dogs. Now there are a great many dogs in this town, rat terriers, bird dogs, bloodhounds; they trail along the forlorn noon-hot streets in sleepy herds of six to a dozen, all waiting only for dark and the moon, when straight through the lonesome hours you can hear them howling: someone is dying, someone is dead. Miss Bobbit complained to the Sheriff; she said that certain of the dogs always planted themselves under her window, and that she was a light sleeper to begin with; what is more, and as Sister Rosalba said, she did not believe they were dogs at all, but some kind of devil. Naturally the Sheriff did nothing; and so she took the matter into her own hands. One morning, after an especially loud night, she was seen stalking through the town with Rosalba at her side, Rosalba carrying a flower basket filled with rocks; whenever they saw a dog they paused while Miss Bobbit scrutinized him. Sometimes she would shake her head, but more often she said, "Yes, that's one of them, Sister Rosalba," and Sister Rosalba, with ferocious aim, would take a rock from her basket and crack the dog between the eyes.

Another thing that happened concerns Mr. Henderson. Mr. Henderson has a back room in the Sawyer house; a tough runt of a man who formerly was a wildcat oil prospector in Oklahoma, he is about seventy years old and, like a lot of old men, obsessed by functions of the body. Also, he is a terrible drunk. One time he had been drunk for two weeks; whenever he heard Miss Bobbit and Sister Rosalba moving around the house, he would charge to the top of the stairs and bellow down to Mrs. Sawyer that there were midgets in the walls trying to get at his supply of toilet paper. They've already stolen fifteen cents' worth, he said. One evening, when the two girls were sitting under a tree in the yard, Mr. Henderson, sporting nothing more than a nightshirt, stamped out after them. Steal all my toilet paper, will you? he hollered, I'll show you midgets. . . . Somebody come help me, else these midget bitches are liable to make off with every sheet in town. It was Billy Bob and Preacher who caught Mr. Henderson and held him until some grown men arrived and began to tie him up. Miss Bobbit, who had behaved with admirable calm, told the men they did not know how to tie a proper knot, and undertook to do so herself. She did such a good job that all the circulation stopped in Mr. Henderson's hands and feet and it was a month before he could walk again.

It was shortly afterwards that Miss Bobbit paid us a call. She came on Sunday and I was there alone, the family having gone to church. "The odors of a church are so offensive," she said, leaning forward and with her hands folded primly before her. "I don't want you to think I'm a heathen, Mr. C.; I've had enough experience to know that there is a God and that there is a Devil. But the way to tame the Devil is not to go down there to church and listen to what a sinful mean fool he is. No, love the Devil like you love Jesus: because he is a powerful man, and will do you a good turn if he knows you trust him. He has frequently done me good turns, like at dancing school in Memphis. . . . I always called in the Devil to help me get the biggest part in our annual show. That is common sense; you see, I knew Jesus wouldn't have any truck with dancing. Now, as a matter of fact, I have called in the Devil just recently. He is the only one who can help me get out of this town. Not that I live here, not exactly. I think always about somewhere else, somewhere else where everything is dancing, like people dancing in the streets, and everything is pretty, like children on their birthdays. My precious papa said I live in the sky, but if he'd lived more in the sky he'd be rich like he wanted to be. The trouble with my papa was he did not love the Devil, he let the Devil love him. But I am very smart in that respect; I know the next best thing is very often the best. It was the next best thing for us to move to this town; and since I can't pursue my career here, the next best thing for me is to start a little business on the side. Which is what I have done. I am sole subscription agent in this county for an impressive list of magazines, including *Reader's Digest, Popular Mechanics, Dime Detective,* and *Child's Life*. To be sure, Mr. C., I'm not here to sell you anything. But I have a thought in mind. I was thinking those two boys that are always hanging around here, it occurred to me that they are men, after all. Do you suppose they would make a pair of likely assistants?"

Billy Bob and Preacher worked hard for Miss Bobbit, and for Sister Rosalba, too. Sister Rosalba carried a line of cosmetics called Dewdrop, and it was part of the boys' job to deliver purchases to her customers. Billy Bob used to be so tired in the evening he could hardly chew his supper. Aunt El said it was a shame and a pity, and finally one day when Billy Bob came down with a touch of sunstroke she said, all right, that settled it, Billy Bob would just have to quit Miss Bobbit. But Billy Bob cussed her out until his daddy had to lock him in his room; whereupon he said he was going to kill himself. Some cook we'd had told him once that if you ate a mess of collards all slopped over with molasses it would kill you sure as shooting; and so that is what he did. I'm dying, he said, rolling back and forth on his bed, I'm dying and nobody cares.

Miss Bobbit came over and told him to hush up. "There's nothing wrong with you, boy," she said. "All you've got is a stomach ache." Then she did something that shocked Aunt El very much: she stripped the covers off Billy Bob and rubbed him down with alcohol from head to toe. When Aunt El told her she did not think that was a nice thing for a little girl to do, Miss Bobbit replied: "I don't know whether it's nice or not, but it's certainly very refreshing." After which Aunt El did all she could to keep Billy Bob from going back to work for her, but his daddy said to leave him alone, they would have to let the boy lead his own life.

Miss Bobbit was very honest about money. She paid Billy Bob and Preacher their exact commission, and she would never let them treat her, as they often tried to do, at the drugstore or to the picture show. "You'd better save your money," she told them. "That is, if you want to go to college. Because neither one of you has got the brains to win a scholarship, not even a football scholarship." But it was over money that Billy Bob and Preacher had a big falling out; that was not the real reason, of course: the real reason was that they had grown cross-eyed jealous over Miss Bobbit. So one day, and he had the gall to do this right in front of Billy Bob, Preacher said to Miss Bobbit that she'd better check her accounts carefully because he had more than a suspicion that Billy Bob wasn't turning over to her *all* the money he collected. That's a damned lie, said Billy Bob, and with a clean left hook he knocked Preacher off the Sawyer porch and jumped after him into a bed of nasturtiums. But once Preacher got a hold on him, Billy Bob didn't stand a chance. Preacher even rubbed dirt in his eyes. During all this, Mrs. Sawyer, leaning out an upper-story window, screamed like an eagle, and Sister Rosalba, fatly cheerful, ambiguously shouted, Kill him! Kill him! Kill him! Only Miss Bobbit seemed to know what she was doing. She plugged in the lawn hose, and gave the boys a close-up, blinding bath. Gasping, Preacher staggered to his feet. Oh, honey, he said, shaking himself like a wet dog, honey, you've got to decide. "Decide *what?*" said Miss Bobbit, right away in a huff. Oh, honey, wheezed Preacher, you don't want us boys killing each other. You got to decide who is your real true sweetheart. "Sweetheart, my eye," said Miss Bobbit. "I should've known better than to get myself involved with a lot of country children. What sort of businessman are you going to make? Now, you listen here, Preacher Star: I don't want a sweetheart, and if I did, it wouldn't be you. As a matter of fact, you don't even get up when a lady enters the room."

Preacher spit on the ground and swaggered over to Billy Bob. Come on, he said, just as though nothing had happened; she's a hard one, she is, she don't want nothing but to make trouble between two good friends. For a moment it looked as if Billy Bob was going to join him in a peaceful togetherness; but suddenly, coming to his senses, he drew back and made a gesture. The boys regarded each other a full minute, all the closeness between them turning an ugly color: you can't hate so much unless you love, too. And Preacher's face showed all of this. But there was nothing for him to do except go away. Oh, yes, Preacher, you looked so lost that day that for the first time I really liked you, so skinny and mean and lost going down the road all by yourself.

They did not make it up, Preacher and Billy Bob; and it was not because they didn't want to, it was only that there did not seem to be any straight way for their friendship to happen again. But they couldn't get rid of this friendship: each was always aware of what the other was up to; and when Preacher found himself a new buddy, Billy Bob moped around for days, picking things up, dropping them again, or doing sudden wild things, like purposely poking his finger in the electric fan. Sometimes in the evenings Preacher would pause by the gate and talk with Aunt El. It was only to torment Billy Bob, I suppose, but he stayed friendly with all of us, and at Christmas time he gave us a huge box of shelled peanuts. He left a present for Billy Bob, too. It turned out to be a book of Sherlock Holmes; and on the flyleaf there was scribbled: "Friends Like Ivy on the Wall Must Fall." That's the corniest thing I ever saw, Billy Bob said. Jesus, what a dope he is! But then, and though it was a cold winter day, he went in the backyard and climbed up into the pecan tree, crouching there all afternoon in the blue December branches.

But most of the time he was happy, because Miss Bobbit was there, and she was always sweet to him now. She and Sister Rosalba treated him like a man; that is to say, they allowed him to do everything for them. On the other hand, they let him win at three-handed bridge, they never questioned his lies, nor discouraged his ambitions. It was a happy while. However, trouble started again when school began. Miss Bobbit refused to go. "It's ridiculous," she said, when one day the principal, Mr. Copland, came around to investigate, "really ridiculous; I can read and write and there are *some* people in this town who have every reason to know that I can count money. No, Mr. Copland, consider for a moment and you will see neither of us has the time nor energy. After all, it would only be a matter of whose spirit broke first, yours or mine. And besides, what is there for you to teach me? Now, if you knew anything about dancing, that would be another matter; but under the circumstances, yes, Mr. Copland, under the circumstances, I suggest we forget the whole thing." Mr. Copland was perfectly willing to. But the rest of the town thought she ought to be whipped. Horace Deasley wrote a piece in the paper which was titled "A Tragic Situation." It was, in his opinion, a tragic situation when a small girl could defy what he, for some reason, termed the Constitution of the United States. The article ended with a question: *Can she get away with it?* She did; and so did Sister Rosalba. Only she was colored, so no one cared. Billy Bob was not as lucky. It was school for him, all right; but he might as well have stayed home for the good it did him. On his first report card he got three F's, a record of some sort. But he is a smart boy. I guess he just couldn't live through those hours without Miss Bobbit; away from her he always seemed half-asleep. He was always in a fight, too; either his eye was black, or his lip was split, or his walk had a limp. He never talked about these fights, but Miss Bobbit was shrewd enough to guess the reason why. "You are a dear, I know, I know. And I appreciate you, Billy Bob. Only don't fight with people because of me. Of course they say mean things about me. But do you know why that is, Billy Bob? It's a compliment, kind of. Because deep down they think I'm absolutely wonderful."

And she was right: if you are not admired no one will take the trouble to disapprove. But actually we had no idea of how wonderful she was until there appeared the man known as Manny Fox. This happened late in February. The first news we had of Manny Fox was a series of jovial placards posted up in the stores around town: Manny Fox Presents the Fan Dancer Without the Fan; then, in smaller print: Also, Sensational Amateur Program Featuring Your Own Neighbors—First Prize, A Genuine Hollywood Screen Test. All this was to take place the following Thursday. The tickets were priced at one dollar each, which around here is a lot of money; but it is not often that we get any kind of flesh entertainment, so everybody shelled out their money and made a great todo over the whole thing. The drugstore cowboys talked dirty all week, mostly about the fan dancer without the fan, who turned out to be Mrs. Manny Fox. They stayed down the highway at the Chucklewood Tourist Camp; but they were in town all day, driving around in an old Packard which had Manny Fox's full name stenciled on all four doors. His wife was a deadpan pimento-tongued redhead with wet lips and moist eyelids; she was quite large actually, but compared to Manny Fox she seemed rather frail, for he was a fat cigar of a man.

They made the pool hall their headquarters, and every afternoon you could find them there, drinking beer and joking with the town loafs. As it developed, Manny Fox's business affairs were not restricted to theatrics. He also ran a kind of employment bureau: slowly he let it be known that for a fee of $150 he could get for any adventurous boys in the county high-class jobs working on fruit ships sailing from New Orleans to South America. The chance of a lifetime, he called it. There are not two boys around here who readily lay their hands on so much as five dollars; nevertheless, a good dozen managed to raise the money. Ada Willingham took all she'd saved to buy an angel tombstone for her husband and gave it to her son, and Acey Trump's papa sold an option on his cotton crop.

But the night of the show! That was a night when all was forgotten: mortgages, and the dishes in the kitchen sink. Aunt El said you'd think we were going to the opera, everybody so dressed up, so pink and sweet-smelling. The Odeon had not been so full since the night they gave away the matched set of sterling silver. Practically everybody had a relative in the show, so there was a lot of nervousness to contend with. Miss Bobbit was the only contestant we knew real well. Billy Bob couldn't sit still; he kept telling us over and over that we mustn't applaud for anybody but Miss Bobbit; Aunt El said that would be very rude, which sent Billy Bob off into a state again; and when his father bought us all bags of popcorn he wouldn't touch his because it would make his hands greasy, and please, another thing, we mustn't be noisy and eat ours while Miss Bobbit was performing. That she was to be a contestant had come as a last-minute surprise. It was logical enough, and there were signs that should've told us; the fact, for instance, that she had not set foot outside the Sawyer house in how many days? And the victrola going half the night, her shadow whirling on the window shade, and the secret, stuffed look on Sister Rosalba's face whenever asked after Sister Bobbit's health. So there was her name on the program, listed second, in fact, though she did not appear for a long while. First came Manny Fox, greased and leering, who told a lot of peculiar jokes, clapping his hands, ha, ha. Aunt El said if he told another joke like that she was going to walk straight out: he did, and she didn't. Before Miss Bobbit came on there were eleven contestants, including Eustacia Bernstein, who imitated movie stars so that they all sounded like Eustacia, and there was an extraordinary Mr. Buster Riley, a jug-eared old wool-hat from way in the back country who played "Waltzing Matilda" on a saw. Up to that point, he was the hit of the show; not that there was any marked difference in the various receptions, for everybody applauded generously, everybody, that is, except Preacher Star. He was sitting two rows ahead of us, greeting each act with a donkey-loud boo. Aunt El said she was never going to speak to him again. The only person he ever applauded was Miss Bobbit. No doubt the Devil was on her side, but she deserved it. Out she came, tossing her hips, her curls, rolling her eyes. You could tell right away it wasn't going to be one of her classical numbers. She tapped across the stage, daintily holding up the sides of a cloud-blue skirt. That's the cutest thing I ever saw, said Billy Bob, smacking his thigh, and Aunt El had to agree that Miss Bobbit looked real sweet. When she started to twirl the whole audience broke into spontaneous applause; so she did it all over again, hissing, "Faster, faster," at poor Miss Adelaide, who was at the piano doing her Sunday-school best. "I was born in China, and raised in Jay-pan . . ." We had never heard her sing before, and she had a rowdy sandpaper voice. ". . . if you don't like my peaches, stay away from my can, o-ho o-ho!" Aunt El gasped; she gasped again when Miss Bobbit, with a bump, up-ended her skirt to display blue-lace underwear, thereby collecting most of the whistles the boys had been saving for the fan dancer without the fan, which was just as well, as it later turned out, for that lady, to the tune of "An Apple for the Teacher" and cries of gyp gyp, did her routine attired in a bathing suit. But showing off her bottom was not Miss Bobbit's final triumph. Miss Adelaide commenced an ominous thundering in the darker keys, at which point Sister Rosalba, carrying a lighted Roman candle, rushed onstage and handed it to Miss Bobbit, who was in the midst of a full split; she made it, too, and just as she did the Roman candle burst into fiery balls of red, white, and blue, and we all had to stand up because she was singing "The Star Spangled Banner" at the top of her lungs. Aunt El said afterwards that it was one of the most gorgeous things she'd ever seen on the American stage.

Well, she surely did deserve a Hollywood screen test and, inasmuch as she won the contest, it looked as though she were going to get it. Manny Fox said she was: honey, he said, you're real star stuff. Only he skipped town the next day, leaving nothing but hearty promises. Watch the mails, my friends, you'll all be hearing from me. That is what he said to the boys whose money he'd taken, and that is what he said to Miss Bobbit. There are three deliveries daily, and this sizable group gathered at the post office for all of them, a jolly crowd growing gradually joyless. How their hands trembled when a letter slid into their mailbox. A terrible hush came over them as the days passed. They all knew what the other was thinking, but no one could bring himself to say it, not even Miss Bobbit. Postmistress Patterson said it plainly, however: the man's a crook, she said, I knew he was a crook to begin with, and if I have to look at your faces one more day I'll shoot myself.

Finally, at the end of two weeks, it was Miss Bobbit who broke the spell. Her eyes had grown more vacant than anyone had ever supposed they might, but one day, after the last mail was up, all her old sizzle came back. "O.K., boys, it's lynch law now," she said, and proceeded to herd the whole troupe home with her. This was the first meeting of the Manny Fox Hangman's Club, an organization which, in a more social form, endures to this day, though Manny Fox has long since been caught and, so to say, hung. Credit for this went quite properly to Miss Bobbit. Within a week she'd written over three hundred descriptions of Manny Fox and dispatched them to Sheriffs throughout the South; she also wrote letters to papers in the larger cities, and these attracted wide attention. As a result, four of the robbed boys were offered good-paying jobs by the United Fruit Company, and late this spring, when Manny Fox was arrested in Uphigh, Arkansas, where he was pulling the same old dodge, Miss Bobbit was presented with a Good Deed Merit award from the Sunbeam Girls of America. For some reason, she made a point of letting the world know that this did not exactly thrill her. "I do not approve of the organization," she said. "All that rowdy bugle blowing. It's neither good-hearted nor truly feminine. And anyway, what is a good deed? Don't let anybody fool you, a good deed is something you do because you want something in return." It would be reassuring to report she was wrong, and that her just reward, when at last it came, was given out of kindness and love. However, this is not the case. About a week ago the boys involved in the swindle all received from Manny Fox checks covering their losses, and Miss Bobbit, with clodhopping determination, stalked into a meeting of the Hangman's Club, which is now an excuse for drinking beer and playing poker every Thursday night. "Look, boys," she said, laying it on the line, "none of you ever thought to see that money again, but now that you have, you ought to invest it in something practical—like me." The proposition was that they should pool their money and finance her trip to Hollywood; in return, they would get ten percent of her life's earnings which, after she was a star, and that would not be very long, would make them all rich men. "At least," as she said, "in this part of the country." Not one of the boys wanted to do it: but when Miss Bobbit looked at you, what was there to say?

Since Monday, it has been raining buoyant summer rain shot through with sun, but dark at night and full of sound, full of dripping leaves, watery chimings, sleepless scuttlings. Billy Bob is wide-awake, dry-eyed, though everything he does is a little frozen and his tongue is as stiff as a bell tongue. It has not been easy for him, Miss Bobbit's going. Because she'd meant more than that. Than what? Than being thirteen years old and crazy in love. She was the queer things in him, like the pecan tree and liking books and caring enough about people to let them hurt him. She was the things he was afraid to show anyone else. And in the dark the music trickled through the rain: won't there be nights when we will hear it just as though it were really there? And afternoons when the shadows will be all at once confused, and she will pass before us, unfurling across the lawn like a pretty piece of ribbon? She laughed to Billy Bob; she held his hand, she even kissed him. "I'm not going to die," she said. "You'll come out there, and we'll climb a mountain, and we'll all live there together, you and me and Sister Rosalba." But Billy Bob knew it would never happen that way, and so when the music came through the dark he would stuff the pillow over his head.

Only there was a strange smile about yesterday, and that was the day she was leaving. Around noon the sun came out, bringing with it into the air all the sweetness of wisteria. Aunt El's yellow Lady Anne's were blooming again, and she did something wonderful, she told Billy Bob he could pick them and give them to Miss Bobbit for goodbye. All afternoon Miss Bobbit sat on the porch surrounded by people who stopped by to wish her well. She looked as though she were going to Communion, dressed in white and with a white parasol. Sister Rosalba had given her a handkerchief, but she had to borrow it back because she couldn't stop blubbering. Another little girl brought a baked chicken, presumably to be eaten on the bus; the only trouble was she'd forgotten to take out the insides before cooking it. Miss Bobbit's mother said that was all right by her, chicken was chicken; which is memorable because it is the single opinion she ever voiced. There was only one sour note. For hours Preacher Star had been hanging around down at the corner, sometimes standing at the curb tossing a coin, and sometimes hiding behind a tree, as if he didn't want anyone to see him. It made everybody nervous. About twenty minutes before bus time he sauntered up and leaned against our gate. Billy Bob was still in the garden picking roses; by now he had enough for a bonfire, and their smell was as heavy as wind. Preacher stared at him until he lifted his head. As they looked at each other the rain began again, falling fine as sea spray and colored by a rainbow. Without a word, Preacher went over and started helping Billy Bob separate the roses into two giant bouquets: together they carried them to the curb. Across the street there were bumblebees of talk, but when Miss Bobbit saw them, two boys whose flower-masked faces were like yellow moons, she rushed down the steps, her arms outstretched. You could see what was going to happen; and we called out, our voices like lightning in the rain, but Miss Bobbit, running toward those moons of roses, did not seem to hear. That is when the six-o'clock bus ran over her.

BLUE DIVE

by *Fred Chappell*

❀

His name that was ever used was Stovebolt Johnson and he was a short black man, heavily muscled, a chunk of a man. In the middle of nowhere he clambered gingerly down the steps of the Greyhound. As he stepped onto the ground the round bottom of his guitar clipped the bus door, twanged softly. The guitar was tied over his shoulder with seagrass twine and was enveloped in a washed and faded flour sack. He grunted involuntarily when he heard the knock of it against the metal. When at last he was all the way down he kept his back to the bus as it hissed and shivered and roared, then plowed away into the gray east wind. Stovebolt wasn't studying any bus; he was looking at the horizon, staring away as far as his eyesight would reach.

There was nothing anybody else would have remarked. The two-lane asphalt highway stretched from one end of his vision to the other, narrowing to a pencil mark as it went on in this flat country. On both sides of the road newly turned dark brown fields rolled on endlessly. In the gray late morning sky to the north six blackbirds pursued a hawk, skimming and swooping. When the bus had gone, there was no other sound and no other sight but the fields and the sky and the birds and telephone poles and a few lines of bushes and this man, Stovebolt Johnson. Still he stood for a minute or two, gazing toward the edge of the world, and then he unslung the guitar from his heavy torso and pulled away the flour sack and examined the guitar until he was satisfied there was no damage. "Mm hmm," he murmured, "that's all right." Testing, he struck three chords on the strings and out here in the wind and the flatness they sounded as lonesome as starlight. Then he tied the guitar back in its sack and thumbed it over his shoulder.

He reached into the breast pocket of his khaki wool jacket and took out a mint bar of Red Coon. From his pants he produced a pocket knife and cut away a rounded corner with the hawkbill blade and slipped the tobacco into the right side of his mouth and commenced chewing very slowly. Even now he was still looking at the horizon and he turned softly on his heel to take the whole of it in. He breathed deeply; his ripply shoulders rose and fell. Something there in the dirt by the edge of the highway caught his attention and he squatted and eyed the ground for a moment, but it was nothing more than a scrap of tin foil from a cigarette package. He grunted again. He had thought he'd found him a dime.

Now he began walking. A little puddly car lane divided two fields and he crossed the highway and began to follow it. He took short but leisurely strides, making good steady time going along, and the rhythm of his walking brought words into his mind and an old tune.

> Going down this road feeling bad,
> O Lord,
> I'm going down this road feeling bad.
> Down this road feeling bad,
> Lord Lord,
> I ain't going to be treated this way.

But when he thought about it he decided he wasn't feeling bad at all; he felt open and free and truly pleasured by the quiet country about him and he brushed his thighs with his fingertips as he walked. Still that song persisted in his head.

He went about a quarter of a mile before he came to another car lane branching left. He turned and went down this way. The ground was softer here and the ruts were sharper and the puddles wider and deeper. Now and again he hitched at the weight of the guitar and now and again he snapped his fingers to the tune in his mind. There was no doubt in him how good he felt; maybe he had never felt better than right now.

After another thousand yards or so this road straggled into the front yard of a house. It was a shackly little house, smudged white asbestos shingles and a tin roof and a short front porch with narrow splintery pine planks eaten away at the outer edges by weather. There were two trees, a spindly little pecan and a grandly spreading water oak with a rubber tire swing hanging down by a frayed cotton rope. There was an outbuilding, a little shed open on this side to the sky, but there was no car under it. He hadn't expected the car to be gone and he halted at the indefinable border of the yard. He spat a dollop of juice and considered.

But there was no place else to go. So he walked on up and stepped to the door and knocked smartly. For a moment there was no sound, and then children's voices chirruped inside. "Mama, Mama, there's a man here now." "Mama, Mama." And then silence again, but he could feel in his shoesoles the slight quiver of someone walking from the back of the house, from the kitchen, he guessed.

She opened the glass-paned door and stood inside the shadow of the room, and it was hard to make her out through the bulging rusty screen door.

"What is it you want?" Her voice was soft and carefully matter-of-fact.

"Excuse me," Stovebolt said. He tried to peer. "Donna? Is that you, Donna?"

"I suppose you've got the wrong house," she said, as if there were dozens of them scattered up and down these broad empty fields.

"Excuse me," he said again. "I'm Stovebolt Johnson here, and I'm looking for the man name of Franklin Childress. Pointy, some folks call him."

"I don't know that man."

"Well now, wait a minute. This here is his house, or leastways it used to be his house. And it's urgent to me to find Pointy Childress because he can give me a job. He promised he could give me a job."

"I don't know any of that," she said. "We took this house from Charlie James after he went to work for the furniture factory up in High Point."

"That's him, that's one," Stovebolt said. "He was an old buddy of Pointy's. I recall I've met him before. He must have took this house from Pointy, whatever happened to Pointy. And I've got an awful need to see Pointy because I have to have that job."

"I don't know."

"Look now," he said. "Maybe you've heard of Pointy Childress and forgot about it. He was a big tall bald man with two gold teeth right in front. He was running a little roadhouse up the highway here. It was a little concrete block place, sky-blue painted, and it was called the Blue Dive and folks used to come in there and drink beer and all."

"I know the Blue Dive," she said. "Everybody knows that place a long time. But I never heard of that man you name."

"This is a puzzler, ain't it?" He tried to smile as friendly as he could, though he couldn't tell what she could see through the screen. "I've come a long way on the hopes of that job."

"Well, come in the house," she said. "Maybe we can find out something." She held the screen door open a few inches and he opened it all the way and entered.

As his eyes were adjusting to the dimness of the room it seemed for a moment that this comely young woman was dividing into three. But it was two children who separated themselves from her skirt to stand apart regarding him, their eyes big and bright in their dark faces.

"Hello there, younguns," Stovebolt said.

The little boy stepped back a few steps and stood watching him gravely, his finger hooked in the corner of his mouth. His sister, who looked to be about a year older, clapped her hand to her forehead and turned twice about on her toes; she was trying hard not to giggle.

The handsome young woman was talking again. "My husband ought to be home for dinner in a few minutes," she said. "He might can help you with what you want to find out."

"I'm thanking you," he said. "Looks like I've kind of got in a bind here."

The living room was small and no lights were on. There was a sagging reddish sofa and an upholstered rocking chair and two straight chairs, and here and there over the patchy linoleum lay soiled and broken toys. On the screen of a little television set in the corner a gray animated cartoon fluttered frenziedly, cat and mouse.

"Can I give you a cup of coffee?" she asked. "Always I keep some heating on the stove."

"I could use a cupful if it ain't no trouble. I been walking in the cool wind."

"What do you take?"

"Whole lot of sugar, is all."

The little boy popped his finger out of his mouth and pointed it, gleaming wet, at Stovebolt's shoulder. "Can you play that thing?" he asked. His manner of inquiring was sharp and belligerent, a dare.

"Yes I can."

"What can you play?"

"I can play anything," Stovebolt said. "I can play the best music there is in the world. I can play happy and sad and in-between."

"Like what?"

"I can play," he said, "to beat anything you'll ever hear off of *that.*" He nodded his head at a giant box of cornflakes glimmering on the television screen.

"I want to see you play it."

The mother came in with a steaming white coffee mug which she held cradled at the bottom as well as by the handle. "I hope I've got it sweet enough for you."

"Oh it's fine," Stovebolt said. "And I sure do appreciate it." He turned back to the little boy. "If you want to hear me play you'll have to come out here on the porch. I've got to have me some working room when I play my guitar."

He pushed through the door to go and sit on the edge of the porch. He had been reflecting that if he was a woman's husband driving up from work at noontime he might not be overcome with joy to find a strange man and a guitar in his house. He spat out his chew of tobacco and worked up all the juice he could and spat that out too. The first sip of coffee he wallowed about in his mouth, rinsing, and then got rid of. He'd known any number of men who could chew and drink at the same time, but he'd never got the hang of it. He took a swallow. It was strong and sweet as molasses. "You mama makes a fine cup of coffee," he said to the boy. "What kind of music do you like to listen?" He took the guitar out and fingered a few aimless notes.

"Knock Three Times," the boy said.

Stovebolt grinned, thinking he might have guessed that would be it or something pretty near. "I never heard of that one," he said. "I'm going to play you a song called *One Dime Blues.* You ever hear that one?"

The boy shook his head.

"Well, you listen now and see if you don't think it's a mighty fine song." He got down another swallow of coffee and launched out with a startling bright chromatic run, playing quite loudly.

The little boy's mouth slackened to a red astonished O and he clasped his hands behind his neck. His sister standing behind him waited until she could bear it no longer and then she began to dance. She pirouetted, the five white-cotton-ribboned braids of hair spinning like the horses on a toy carousel; her bony knees jerked upward and her heels in her worn red tennis shoes slapped sounding on the porch boards. Stovebolt could feel without turning the presence of the young mother behind him in the doorway. He kept playing for maybe five minutes and as he played he felt happier and happier. He finished and damped the strings quickly with the heel of his palm.

"There you go now," Stovebolt said. "How you like that one?"

The little girl stood stockstill and looked at him and giggled, bubbled over with giggles like a flowing fountain. The little boy was grave and his voice still belligerent. "Now play *Knock Three Times,"* he said. "Or play any damn thing, I don't care."

Stovebolt threw his head back and laughed. "That's the way to talk," he said. "When the music is good, there ain't no reason to be too choicy about what songs." He drank half the coffee left in the mug.

The girl had stopped giggling and was looking out down the road. "Daddy's coming," she said in a placid dreamy voice.

It was a rust-pitted yellow Dodge pickup bobbing and floundering through the ruts and puddles. It veered from side to side in the lane as the driver tried to escape the larger holes.

"Is that your daddy's truck?" Stovebolt asked.

"I don't know," the little boy said.

The truck stopped in front of the shed and a man got out. He was a shorter man than Stovebolt had expected—he couldn't be much taller than his wife—but there was no mistaking the loosely flowing strength in him. He came toward the porch, glancing questioningly at each of the group gathered there.

The mother stepped out onto the porch. "Hello, honey," she said.

"Darlene," the man said. But his eyes rested steadily on Stovebolt and he didn't appear to be thinking about anything else.

She came to the porch edge. "Honey, this here is Stovebolt Johnson and he's looking for a man and we was hoping maybe you could help him."

He halted directly in front of him and Stovebolt stood up and put out his hand. "Howdy. I'm Stovebolt, like she says."

The other man hesitated, then shook hands. "I'm B.J., like I guess she's told *you.*"

"No," he said. "I hadn't been here long enough to get acquainted. Except maybe a little bit with him." With his head he indicated the man's son.

B.J. glanced at the boy, then back at Stovebolt. "Are you some kind of music man?"

"Yes," he said, "it's the truth I am."

The little boy shouted. "Daddy, he can play the *blue pee* out of that thing!"

B.J. smiled, and seemed at last to relax. "That right?" he murmured. He took a Camel out of his shirt pocket and turned out of the wind to light it.

"What was the name of that song? Play that song one time for him." Stovebolt reached over and squeezed the boy at the back of his neck. "Ooh," he squeaked.

The mother said, "Mr. Stovebolt has come looking for a man that promised him a job. And I didn't know who it was."

"Who was that, then?" B.J. asked.

"Pointy Childress he was called," Stovebolt said. "He offered me a job playing music at a little roadhouse beer joint he had around here. I mean to say, he downright promised me."

"I've heard of him," B.J. said. "When would this be that he promised you?"

"This is going back three years now."

"You a little late showing up. That man has been gone from here a good year and a half, anyhow. He was gone after the first week we moved into the house here. I didn't know him myself but just to nod at."

"Uh oh, that don't sound so fine. Kind of hard to find a job sometimes in my line of business."

"Is that right?" said B.J. "Seems to me most people kind of like Rafer here, they just crazy about hearing music." He grinned at his son.

"Well, but these days now, mostly it's the TV they got turned on in the places. Or they've got them a record box where the customers have to pay for the music. But what I play, the way I play it, you can't get out of no machine."

Rafer shouted again. "Daddy, make him play that guitar for you. You ought to hear the way he does."

"What happened to the man you want I don't have no impression. It's another man entirely running the Blue Dive. It might be he'd want to hire him some music and he might not. Hard to say about him."

"Where would he be that I could talk to him?"

"Right now he wouldn't be nowhere. But he'll show up at his place about two o'clock and you can talk to him then, I expect."

"I reckon I'll do it," Stovebolt said. "What's he called by?"

"His name is Locklear Hawkins," B.J. said. "I can't tell you much about him to help you out, because I ain't been able to figure him all that close. He's a new kind of man, Hawk is."

"Folks name him Hawk, do they?"

B.J. smiled. "Yeah, he kind of likes that. He's younger than you and me."

"B.J.," the mother said, "ain't you going to ask Mr. Stovebolt to come in and have dinner with us?"

"Sure I am. I was just fixing to."

"I'll go in and set it then. It's already on the stove and waiting." She went into the house.

Stovebolt was wrapping his guitar again. "I thank you awful kindly," he said, "but I can't stay. If I want to be meeting this here Hawk-man, I got to be prowling on. The way you mention him, I better meet him early and talk till late if I want to haul me down a job."

B.J. smiled shrewdly. "That might be the hardest part of it, sure enough. But there ain't no sense you walking up to the Blue Dive. I got to go right by there on my way back to the cotton gin and I can give you a ride, drop you off right at the door."

"It wouldn't be out of your way, you sure?"

"Go right past it," B.J. said. "And it's dinnertime and you got to eat anyhow, so you'll just have to come on in and sit down with us."

"I couldn't put you out," Stovebolt said. "Your wife wasn't figuring on no stranger coming to her table, descending down on her like a turkey buzzard to eat up her food."

"Well, I know Darlene and you don't. She'd purely skin my head, you didn't sit down and eat a bite." He touched Stovebolt's elbow, steering him toward the screen door.

"Daddy," Rafer shrieked, "ain't you going to make him play? I want you to hear it, what he does."

* * *

Halfway back to the highway where the car lane smoothed out a bit, B.J. slowed the truck and looked across the seat admiringly at Stovebolt, who sat with his guitar resting on the floorboard between his knees. "Lord a mercy," he said. "I never seen anything like that."

"What you mean?" Stovebolt asked. His voice was thick and drowsy.

"How much you eat, what I'm talking I never seen a man put it down like that. Is that the way you eat normal?"

"First homecooked rations I've had since I don't know when. Man, I hope Darlene ain't excited against me. I guess I ate about everything in the house."

B.J. grinned and punched him lightly on the shoulder. "Don't you worry none," he said. "That just warmed her heart to you."

Three miles farther up the highway they came to the Blue Dive. B.J. swerved the truck across the road into the parking lot, spraying up dust and noisy gravel. "This is it," he said. "I hope you a lot of luck here."

Stovebolt shook hands with him once more. "Don't know how to properly thank you," he said. "You've been so awful kindhearted to me. It was nothing I ever expected."

"Nothing to it," B.J. said. "We're happy to see you."

When the truck pulled away, Stovebolt stood in the parking lot observing, taking his time. The Blue Dive was something like he'd expected from what had been described to him, but there were differences too. For one thing, it was larger than he'd thought. It was a rectangular concrete block building, sure enough painted a mild blue, but there were yellow lights at every edge and he supposed that at night the place would look greenish. No big plate glass windows in front, but a row of six slotted windows high up, as if the occupants were readying to fight off an Indian attack. And no neon lights but just a painted sign, black on white, over the door, fixed into the blocks with mortar nails. BLUE DIVE.

"Mm hmm," Stovebolt murmured, though as yet he really didn't know what he thought.

Carrying the guitar at the base of the neck he walked to the door and entered. Inside, it was more familiar-seeming. A concrete floor, damp in places, and patched here and there with new pourings of cement; a long bar a little taller than waist high with no rail and with wooden stools lined before; a streaky mirror with scraps of paper taped up in various spots, surrounded with red and white bulbs enclosed in a plywood frame painted probably blue. It was a good-sized place, sixty feet long maybe; lots of room for dancing—and fighting too, if it was that kind of joint. Stovebolt searched the bar-ends and the ceiling corners for a television set without finding one. There was, however, a jukebox against the righthand wall, emitting fluorescent light like a hospital corridor.

He advanced to the bar. Behind the cash register in the center of the bar, a middle-aged man wearing goldrimmed spectacles sat reading a newspaper. He didn't look up, asking, "What can I get you?"

"Excuse me," Stovebolt said, "but I'm looking for the man name of Mr. Locklear Hawkins."

The man raised his head, and with the light behind him, Stovebolt couldn't see his eyes behind his glasses. "Who you say now?" he asked.

"A Mr. Locklear Hawkins, I believe."

"He ain't here." He didn't return to reading but kept his hardly discernible face motionless, waiting.

"Well, is he ever here, or is he at some other part of the world?"

"This here is his place. He'll be coming in after while."

"About when would that be?"

"Hard to tell about him. Might be a little while, might be a mighty long while."

He ought to be here right now, Stovebolt thought, studying the good manners of his help. "Well, I think I'll wait on him, if it's all right with you."

"Ever what you like," the man said. "Wouldn't you want a beer while you're waiting?"

"Maybe so," Stovebolt said, "maybe so." He patted his righthand pants pocket automatically, though he knew he had twenty-seven cents there. "How much will it run these days?"

"Fifty cents."

"All right. I'll take a cold Blue Ribbon."

From his left pocket he produced a small tight roll of bills secured with a grimy cotton string. He untied the string carefully and unsheaved a five dollar bill and tied the roll back just as it had been.

The dripping can was before him and the man stood there,

his face still unreadable; but Stovebolt could sense the amusement in him. He tendered the bill slowly and the man opened the cash register and smacked his change down in front of him.

Now Stovebolt felt himself growing nettled, and he thought he had better make what overture he could. The way things smelled here it would be a long roll uphill. "If you don't mind telling me something," he said, "why do they call this here place the Blue Dive?"

"Because it was painted blue from the start."

"But what I mean to say, why not a little more high class name? Like The Top Hat maybe, or The High Society? I recall a place in Mobile called The Duke that the people seemed to appreciate."

The barman leaned forward, melting a bit. "That was the name of it before the present management," he said. "The people around here used to it. You ain't landed in Detroit city, you know."

"I was just speculating," Stovebolt said.

"Well, I believe Hawk did have some ideas along that line and then went and decided that folks was too familiar to it to change."

"Let me ask you something. The people that come in here, what kind of music do they like?"

"They like it all. On a good hard night they'll play every last song on that jukebox."

"Mm hmm," Stovebolt said.

"But what ain't on it, I don't know whether they're going to care for or not. I see you're a musician, you hauling that guitar, but why ain't you hauling it in a case? That old totesack."

"Used to have a case. Red leather."

"Where's it at?"

"Huh," Stovebolt said. "If I know where that case is at, I know where there's three hundred and fifty dollars of my good money. But that particular night time is long gone away, and I ain't never going to know what direction it took."

"That right?" the barman said. "Well, I can understand that. I been there myself."

The door opened; an oblong of gray light fell across the room. A slight soft-looking man seated himself on a stool. When the barman went to him he ordered a Schlitz.

Stovebolt lifted his beer and sucked down about half of it. "Mm hmm." He couldn't precisely recall the last time he had drunk a beer, but it had been a few years, of course. I want to be careful, he thought. I could start gobbling this stuff and wind up here no better off than a stray dog. He carried the can across to the jukebox and noted the selections. Dionne Warwick. James Brown. The O'Kaysions. Major Lance. It was to a T what he'd expected. He used a dime to punch up *Dancing in the Streets,* by Martha and the Vandellas, and then returned to his stool. He knew the song he had paid for. That's an old time song, he thought, old fast blues. They've just silvered it over with a big shiny arrangement. He sat listening, mentally picking out the changes, until the record ended.

With the music gone the Blue Dive seemed hushed, sunk at the bottom of an ocean of daze, and no one moved except to take a short reflective sip of beer.

Finally the slight man who had lately come in spoke to Stovebolt. "You play that guitar?"

"Yes I do," Stovebolt said, but he was in a spell, and his voice came out thoughtless and dreamy.

"What kind is it, a Gibson?"

"No sir. This one is a Ginger." He unshucked the instrument and dropped the floursack on the bar beside his beer can. He extended the bottom of it, where the name Ginger was burned in a thin spidery hand.

"I never heard of no Ginger."

Stovebolt roused himself, shook off his momentary lethargy. "It was an old time man made me this guitar," he said, "an old-time banjo-maker. He asked me did I want him to write *Gibson* or *Martin* on the front of it when he was finished. Says, a lot of folks want them a storebought name on it if they going to play in front of people. I told him, Hell, you making it, put your own name on it. Ginger Parham, and he put Ginger. Tickled him to do it. He was a redheaded white man, a mountain man."

"You don't tell me," said the other. "What kinds of things you play, what kinds of songs?"

"I play whatever there is," Stovebolt said. "I play the best music in the world."

"That right?"

"It surely is." He laid it across his lap and jimmied with the tuning. No tuning needed, but he wanted to cancel out some of the effect of the jukebox. "What you want to hear?"

"How about *My Girl?*" the man said.

Mm hmmm, Stovebolt thought, now I know who you are.

"Don't recollect that one right off," he said. "Play you a little old song called *Yellow Gal.*"

He started it off as fast as he could make it go, playing as many notes as he could stick in anywhere. He played three choruses before he even thought of singing, and when he sang it was with a metallic low-tenor timbre quite unlike his natural baritone talking voice.

"O yellow gal, come see me tonight
Yellow gal, when the moon is bright
Yellow gal, we gonna do up right
Yellow O yellow O yellow gal

Yellow O yellow O yellow gal
Yellow O yellow O yellow gal
O yellow O yellow O yellow gal
Yellow O yellow O yellow gal."

He whacked the side of his heel against the bar stool leg, driving it along. Now pay me some mind, Stovebolt thought, because I'm going to do me something right here. His hand slipped like water up the neck to the high registers. Mm hmm. And now get yourself ready, because I'm going to drop it off short right . . . *here.* The strings trembled buzzing for a moment and then he laid his finger across them.

Again the Blue Dive was suspended in a ghostly deep silence. The other two men didn't move and seemed not even to breathe until Stovebolt picked up his beer and drank down the last of it. He placed the empty on the bar and said, "I'll have me another if you don't mind. That one kind of parched my throat."

"Jim," said the slight man, "I'm going to buy him that beer, and I don't care if he wants to drink the whole cooler-full if I got the money."

Stovebolt chuckled. "I oughtn't to do that. It don't suit me when I drink too much."

"Well then," the other told the barman, "what is it he wants let him have."

"I'm thanking you. I believe I'll have me just one more Blue Ribbon."

"Where did you ever learn to play like that?"

"Well," Stovebolt said, "for the most part I figured it and worked it out myself. But back when I was starting off, I used to go anywhere I heard of that somebody good was making music. Back then it wasn't nothing to me to travel anyway I could two, three hundred miles to pick up on somebody I admired. You ever hear Big Bill Broonzy?"

"Can't say so."

"He was one. I went all the way to Jacksonville, Florida, one time he was playing. He was a famous man and wound up in Paris, France. It ain't a style like mine, but I surely did admire to hear that man. He was a hard-drinking man too, and always had a bottle by him. Folks that don't like this stuff is crazy, he used to say."

"Well now, how you think of B.B. King?" the slight man asked.

"He's all right," said Stovebolt, "he does fine. But I don't know what I agree with the electric guitar. A man can make it do a lot of different things, but that ain't hard, and the sound of it comes funny the way I listen. Best man on electric I ever hear is John Lee Hooker."

"Don't believe I've heard him either."

"He's a good one. He's rough and tough."

"Um," the man said. "I guess you know a lot of musicians I never heard, it being your business and all. What are you doing in these parts here?"

"I'm trying to pull me down a job. I'm waiting in this bar to see a Mr. Hawkins to see couldn't he use some live music, some hard-driving guitar like I can play for him and the people like to hear."

"Now that would be all right, if you was to play here. I'd be willing to sit a good long time to hear it."

Stovebolt turned to the barman. "You hear what this man says?"

"I hear him."

Stovebolt went on. "And there's a man name of B.J. and his wife Darlene, and they said they'd be willing to come and listen."

"I know B.J. a long time," the barman said.

"They mighty fine folks," Stovebolt said. "Mighty fine."

Three others came in, two young men and a girl, shy-eyed and silent. When they saw Stovebolt, a stranger, sitting at the bar with his guitar in his lap, they showed surprise. They went to a table near the end of the bar and sat, sneaking glances at Stovebolt and whispering to one another. When the barman had brought their beer they bent their heads over the table and murmured.

Stovebolt fingered the strings, jotting up riffs and disjointed phrases. He had no notion of playing a whole tune just yet; he was simply preventing the newcomers from playing the juke-box.

In a while one of the young men rose and approached him. "Hello," he said. "What's your name?"

"I'm Stovebolt Johnson."

"Oh yeah," he said, but he seemed disappointed. "I thought maybe I heard of you, but I guess I ain't."

"Don't let it trouble you," Stovebolt said. "There's a whole raft of people never have heard of me."

"Do you play that guitar?"

"Yes he plays it," said the slight man. "He plays it, Billy, so as you'd never want to hear nobody else."

"Well, Mandy over there was wishing you might play us something on it."

Stovebolt looked across at the girl and she dropped her eyes to the table. "What you say her name was?"

"Mandy. Mandy Owens is her name."

He had a tune which in his mind he called *Stovebolt's Blues,* with innumerable verses he could shift about to fit almost any occasion. "Seems like I know a song called *Mandy,*" he said. "Maybe she'd like to hear the one about her own name."

"For a fact she would," the young man said. "I'll go and tell her."

Stovebolt closed his eyes and sidled into the song, soft and lifting. Mm hmm, he thought, not too slow now, and let it hang over the edges like that. But not too slow . . . He played along until the words came strong into his mind.

"Now Mandy, Mandy, where was you last night?
Mandy, Mandy, Mandy, where was you last night?
The stars was all a-shining and the moon was big and bright."

Now, he thought, I might better be careful what words I'm singing. I could get them down on me, stirring up bad feelings. Stovebolt thought the words were important, and you never knew when somebody might take these old time words personally.

"Oh Mandy now, you the apple of my eye.
Listen, pretty Mandy, you the apple of my eye.
You know I'm the man that loves you till the day I die."

While he was singing the door opened and someone entered, but Stovebolt didn't open his eyes. He kept caressing the blues song, to make it sweet and enticing. Playing for these young people, he thought, it's almost like courting a skittish woman. He sang three more verses and played one chorus and stopped.

He opened his eyes and looked at them. They smiled, still embarrassed, and then applauded softly and timidly. "We thank you a lot," the young man said.

"Glad to play for you," Stovebolt said. "That's my business, to be amusing folks."

"It was real good," the young man said. "We intending to buy you some beer."

"Awful good of you, but I'm a little bit ahead already."

The barman came and touched him on the arm. "Hawk came in while you doing that last piece. I mentioned you want to talk to him and he says to sit down and wait at the table yonder and he'll be out in just a minute." He indicated a table in the dim far corner.

"All right," Stovebolt said. He picked up one of the three full cans of beer that sat in front of him and carried that and his guitar over and sat. He drank almost half the beer before a man pushed through a doorway strung with beaded curtains and came toward him.

Uh huh, Stovebolt thought, this is him, all right.

He was a tall thin man, very light-skinned, with an aquiline nose and a large but well-groomed Afro haircut. He was dressed like no one else in the room, perhaps like no other man in the county. He wore a green velvet shirt and tight-fitting maroon pants secured by a wide black patent leather belt. On each hand were two rings and on his left wrist three thin silver bracelets. The green shirt was open halfway down his chest.

Stovebolt thought, This here is Mr. Brains, if ever I see him. I had better watch where I'm walking.

Mr. Hawkins slid into the chair on the other side of the table. His movements were easy, cool and silky, and he had about him an air of calm control. His voice too was cool but firm at the edges when he said, "I understand you've been looking for me, Mr. Johnson."

"It didn't start that way," Stovebolt said. "I begun looking for Pointy Childress, but I been told he's long gone away from these parts here."

"That's so. Mr. Childress now owns an establishment in Norfolk, Virginia."

"Well, I might be needing to get the location of that, but I hope not. Pointy offered me a job here at the Blue Dive, it was—oh three years back, maybe. In fact, he right-out promised me a job when I would come by here."

"Mm." Mr. Hawkins leaned back in his chair and crossed his hands on the table. "I'm sure you realize, Mr. Johnson, that the present management can't be responsible for the business arrangements of past managements. It's a whole new set-up entirely."

"Sure-now," Stovebolt said quickly. "I wouldn't be coming to you on what Pointy said." I see you before, he thought. Talk like a bank president till it suits your pocketbook to talk like a black man. "I'd be coming to you as my own man every time."

Mr. Hawkins smiled. "What is it you want then, Mr. Johnson, with me?"

"I'm still looking for that job. I take notice here, and I see that there ain't no live music. And I was thinking, Pointy or not, you could step up your business some, especially when word gets around as I'm playing, and I was playing here regular."

"Well, I don't know, Mr. Johnson." His eyes were half-closed, and Stovebolt saw in them a dark sharp light. "It might be more complicated than you think. What kind of music do you offer?"

"I play whatever music there is," Stovebolt said. "I play the best music in the world."

"You mean you play the blues."

"I can play you some *blues.*"

"You mean you play those old-time nigger whining songs about how you're mean and broke and dog-ass miserable."

Stovebolt managed to stop off his rage in his throat, but his free hand under the table clenched and trembled. When he spoke at last his voice was turgid and congealed. "I don't know how you listen the blues, but there's all different kinds of blues songs. There's one kind and then there's another."

Mr. Hawkins touched his fingertips together in front of his face, resting his elbows against his chest. "But that's the kind of music you play, though."

"Wait a minute," Stovebolt said. He pushed his empty aside with the back of his wrist and rose and walked very deliberately to the bar. He picked up another can and drank from it, feeling all the eyes in the room on him. Then he walked back to the table, carrying the beer in his right hand, the guitar dangling limply in the other. He sat down heavily. "Wait a minute," he said, "I play any kind of music. You name it, and if I ever hear it I can play it for you right off."

Mr. Hawkins was aloofly amused. He seemed to be growing thinner and sharper before Stovebolt's eyes. "But why would I need you? I've got a jukebox right over there, and it seems to do well enough. No one complains to me about it."

"Machine music," Stovebolt said. "It's purely hateful to me."

"But it does well enough. And then there's the revenue it brings in. Quarters and dimes add up, you know."

"That might be, but it ain't bringing you in any *new* business. Ain't nobody going to drive fifteen, twenty miles to listen to it. They'll just go to another place that's closer by and plug into another machine just exactly like it."

The thin man nodded slightly. "Could be that you have a point there, Mr. Johnson. But it could be too that there are other complications you haven't thought about. You see, there's a law in this state that if I offer live music here in the Blue Dive I have to buy a cabaret license. That would cost me something a little over three hundred dollars."

"I know about that law. I been playing in different places maybe more years than you've been born. And I know the white law don't bother messing with a black man's little old concrete block roadhouse for such a reason as that. And anyway, you would be making up for that too if I stayed here a good fair while."

"It may be that you're right again, Mr. Johnson. It may be that they wouldn't bother to enforce that particular law, or it may be that I have a way of sliding by it. But they'd hear about you, and then they'd be asking about you." He leaned forward and pressed his hands flat on the table. "So I'll ask you beforehand: *How long is it since you've been out of prison?*"

Then it seemed to Stovebolt that he had gone blind for a moment, not angry blind or blind from sickness, but that a wall had risen all round him, soft and black and deafening, a hopeless wall of darkness he could never scale nor tear through. He felt the strength leaking from his body and his will, so that he wanted to lay his head back and howl like an animal in pain . . . He ought to have known that it must come to this, and perhaps he had known, but had managed to thrust it away while gripped by the wide hallucinatory fever of once more being free for a while. But when this Hawk-man asked him that question the whole sense of his gray destiny washed over him.

But still he fought back. His will power flickered, then flamed up again. Where did this storebought dude get off, anyhow? What belonged to Stovebolt was his own, and that included most certainly every day he had lived fretting behind the concrete walls. This Hawk-man here was nobody he ever had to account to, and the main thing was that he could pick up and go. Hadn't been any promises made here.

"This-now last time they gave me three years in, four years off," Stovebolt said. "What you minding it for, anyhow? I pulled it and have come away clean and I ain't never going back. I'm making clear to you that that is my business and not another soul's."

"All right," the thin man said. "Calm down. But you must have known that if I was going to hire you I would have to find out anyway."

"Well then," he said, "but that's the meat of the question, whether or not you going to hire me."

"I'll have to think about it," he said. "Say you can play other kinds of music besides the slow blues?"

"Sure I can." He began immediately a fast dance tune, sloppily and a bit crazily, not even getting some of the notes right.

Hawkins held up his hand. "Wait," he said. "Don't play at me. Play for the people. They'll be the ones making the judgment."

Stovebolt looked back past the bar and saw that the room was almost half-filled with people. He was surprised, not having noticed that anyone had come in. He had been concentrating on the man across the table. Mr. Brains here, he reflected, he sure will take it out of you. "Sure-now I will," he said, "and you can listen in and make up your mind."

"Don't worry about that. I'll be keeping an eye out."

And what do you mean by that? Stovebolt thought. The Hawk-man can't stop making threats the way some dogs can't help chasing cars. "All right," he said. "I appreciate you taking the time and consideration." He got up and went back to the bar.

The slight man was still sitting next to his stool and he peered at him brightly as he came up. "What did Hawkins say?" he asked. "Is he going to take you on?"

"Couldn't tell you a thing," Stovebolt said. "We still negotiating on it."

"Man, I hope he does. This place could stand to have some good live music."

"That was the way I put it to him."

"Well, here's hoping." He lifted his beer and saluted Stovebolt.

Stovebolt grinned. "Right." There were now four full cans of beer waiting on the bar and he took one and drank it down, the whole can, with one deep breath.

"How about playing us another tune?"

Stovebolt belched silently. The gas bubble went like needles through his palate. "Right," he said. "What you wanting to hear?" But now he didn't want to play; he simply didn't feel like it, tired and irritated. "First off, though, where is the john in this place?"

"Over there."

He laid the guitar carefully across the bar and walked through and found the dark green door and went in. After he had urinated, he washed his hands and rubbed water on his face. Then he leaned with his back against the wall and pondered, his eyes hooded. He was feeling down now, and it seemed to him that no matter where he walked or how carefully he was always stepping into a hole full of snakes. There had been a bad luck over his life like a dark tent roof, and he could travel a thousand miles any direction the wind blew and he would still be underneath. This man Hawkins, where could he have come from, to be so uptown and tightass? What kind of people did he think he had out front every night drinking beer? It was nothing but field workers here, and Stovebolt knew them and they knew Stovebolt. But this sharp man had another kind of idea, sure enough. Hell with him, Stovebolt thought. The blues is the blues. When I'm in for playing the blues, I'm going to play it.

He went back to the bar and resumed his seat.

The slight man was waiting. "You look different now someway," he observed.

"Washed my face," Stovebolt said. "Feel like a new man." He took up his guitar. "There's a real old-time song name of *John Henry.* You ever hear that?"

"Oh yeah." He smiled without enthusiasm. "It's old enough for sure."

"Well, I ain't going to play it, but while I was back there washing up it come into my mind. You know why?"

He shook his head.

Stovebolt nodded at the jukebox. "Because it's a song about a down-home nigger just like me that's got to beat the machine. That's what it's about . . . You get to studying on it sometimes, you see the men that made up some of these old songs, they had them a notion. It's the truth they did."

"Never thought about it like that."

He wagged his head solemnly. "Every time, when you think about it, the old folks way ahead of us."

Now he started playing. He played and sang like a man fighting off droves of devils. No sooner would somebody name a song than he would ply into it and sing with such resonance that his voice could be felt humming in the wood of the bar. Fast dance tunes and slow ballads and blues. Sometimes the people would dance frenziedly, or on the slow songs they would move in slow circles, languidly linked together. When they ran short of tunes to suggest, Stovebolt kept right on going, picking up the first one that entered his mind, and laying it out for them, precise and easy and thunderous. His voice began to get hoarse and raspy at the edges, but that didn't harm anything, and only gave the lyrics piquancy.

They kept putting beers on the bar for him and he kept gulping them down, drinking hard and steady, but feeling no effect except for a calm sweet uplifting of his spirits. While he was draining another one, B.J. came up with Darlene on his arm. She smiled shyly and nodded, and B.J. slapped him on the shoulder. "Stovebolt, man," he said, "what my boy Rafer said about you, he was *right.* I maybe wouldn't have believed anybody could do it like you do. There ain't no way in the world you ain't got this job sewed up in a toe sack."

He grinned and shook B.J.'s hand. "I'm still remembering that fine dinner you gave me," he said to Darlene.

She looked at her feet.

"You got to come by again tomorrow or when you can," B.J. said. "My kids like to driving me crazy, asking about you, when you be back."

"Handsome younguns," Stovebolt said. "But I don't expect I'll be here tomorrow to meet them. I'll be someplace down the road."

"What you talking?" B.J. said. "He got to hire you. There ain't been nothing like this around here, never."

"This Mr. Hawkins don't have to do *nothing.* I done figured it out that he ain't got no use for me. That is clear as daylight. But I thought one time before I got gone I would give the people a taste of what they be missing. That's a private arrangement I got in my mind for Mr. Hawkins."

B.J. shook his head. "I can't understand it all. I'm telling you the people would flock in here like bees to clover."

Stovebolt smiled. "Yes," he said. "I can play you some music. But the Hawk-man has got another purpose about things."

"I don't understand it nohow."

"What I'll do now is, I know a song that's got Darlene's name in it, and if she would like it, I'll sing it for her."

"It would tickle her to death," B.J. said. "Just look at her."

She was still gazing at the floor and smiling.

"That's what I'll do then. Here." He reached behind him to the bar and held out two cans of beer. "See if you can't take care of these for me while I'm singing."

"Well, thank you now," B.J. said.

He gave a different version of *Stovebolt's Blues,* singing pretty things about Darlene. He sang five more songs, slowly and softly now, winding himself down gently. It was 12:30 and the people began to drift away awkwardly and unwillingly, sometimes lingering by the door to hear the end of a chorus or the last notes of a tune.

Finally everyone was gone but three or four young men, and Jim the barman wiped his face on his sleeve and flicked on the harsh white ceiling lights. "Man, I tell you," he said, "if you keep on here, we going to have to take on more help. I never seen people put down so much and come up so happy from it."

The thin sharp Mr. Hawkins pushed through the beaded curtains at the back and came in behind the bar. He stood there waiting for Stovebolt to make his move.

"I guess it's Good Evening, Mr. Hawkins and Goodbye,

Mr. Hawkins," Stovebolt said. "I don't believe I'm going to give you the satisfaction of asking just in order to be turned down."

He nodded carefully. "Mr. Johnson, I think you must have known already what my judgment was going to be."

"Indeed I did. But I thought you might have a few words about it."

The thin man in his velvet shirt took a deep breath. He looked the squat powerful singer up and down, measuring the whole man. "Mr. Johnson, this is my place bought with my money and what I borrowed from the bank. I have certain plans in mind. And in my plans there is no room in this nightclub for any Rastuses or any Sambos." His hands moved behind the bar, and it was obvious that he had some sort of weapon there. "And there's no room for anybody named *Stovebolt.*"

Some other time, he thought, and I would lay this dude flat out on the floor with a busted something. But the instant of anger flickered away. He was still happy, though washed out, and he still felt free and easy. So he grinned. "I think I do understand you, Mr. Hawkins, and maybe I would even agree. You're right that one of us is behind the times. I'm just not so simple-certain which one of us it is." As he got the sack and wrapped the guitar, he kept his eyes fixed on the man. Then he turned his back on him and went out the door into the chilly night.

Stovebolt Johnson was walking again, under the midnight sky, under the stars. The highway shone a dim grainy gray in the starlight, before and behind him stretching away forever. He didn't have to walk; he was planning to flag down and board the first bus that came either way. But he liked the motion of it, the easy rocking forward that set up a rhythm in his head. He hummed aimlessly, his body still warm even in the cold wind.

In a little while new words to *Stovebolt's Blues* came to him, and he tried them out as he walked along, not singing but murmuring almost tonelessly.

Now I been down to the place call Hawk's Blue Dive.
Yes I been down now, place call Hawk's Blue Dive.
I got to tell you, baby, I didn't know if I'd come back alive.

* * *

He thought about the words and then decided that they would do all right. Yes indeed, they would do just fine.

There was one clear yellow star that stood in the sky directly behind the twiggy tip of a wild cherry tree. As the wind moved, the tip kept brushing through the light of it. But, Stovebolt knew, it was never going to brush that light away. He reached into his shirt pocket and took out the bar of chewing tobacco and began to unwrap it.

OVER THE HILL

by *Andre Dubus*

❀

1

Her hand was tiny. He held it gently, protectively, resting in her lap, the brocaded silk of her kimono against the back of his hand, the smooth flesh gentle and tender against his palm. He looked at her face, which seemed no larger than a child's and she smiled.

"You buy me another drink?" she said.

"Sure."

He motioned to the bartender, who filled the girl's shot glass with what was supposedly whiskey, though Gale knew it was not and didn't care, then mixed bourbon and water for Gale, using the fifth of Old Crow that three hours earlier he had brought into the bar.

"I'll be right back," he said to the girl.

She nodded and he released her hand and slid from the stool.

"You stay here," he said.

"Sure I stay."

He walked unsteadily past booths where Japanese girls drank with sailors. In the smelly, closet-sized restroom he closed the door and urinated, reading the names of sailors and ships written on the walls, some of them followed by obscenities scrawled by a different, later hand. The ceiling was bare. He stepped onto the toilet and reaching up, his coat tightening at the armpits and bottom rib, he printed with a ballpoint pen, stopping often to shake ink down to the point again: *Gale Castete, Pvt. USMC, Marine Detachment, USS Vanguard Dec. 1961.* He stood on the toilet with one hand against the door in front of him, reading his name. Then he thought of her face tilted back, the roots of her hair brown near the forehead when it was time for the

Clairol again, the rest of it spreading pale blonde around her head, the eyes shut, the mouth half open, teeth visible, and the one who saw this now was not him—furiously he reached up to write an obscenity behind his name, then stopped; for reading it again, he felt a gentle stir of immortality, faint as a girl's whispering breath into his ear. He stepped down, was suddenly nauseated, and left the restroom, going outside into the alley behind the bar, where he leaned against the wall and loosened his tie and collar and raised his face to the cold air. Two Japanese girls entered the alley from a door to his left and walked past him as if he were not there, arms folded and hands in their kimono sleeves, their lowered heads jabbering strangely, like sea gulls.

He took out his billfold, which bulged with wide folded yen and tried unsuccessfully to count it in the dark. He thought there should be around thirty-six thousand, for the night before—at sea—he had received the letter, and that morning when they tied up in Yokosuka he had drawn one hundred and fifty dollars, which was what he had saved since the cruise began in August because she wanted a Japanese stereo (and china and glassware and silk and wool and cashmere sweaters and a transistor radio) and in two more paydays she would have had at least the stereo. That evening he had left the ship with his money and two immediate goals: to get falling, screaming drunk and to get laid, two things he had not done on the entire cruise because he had had reason not to; or so he thought. But first he called home—Louisiana—to hear from her what his mother had already told him in the letter, and her vague answers cost him thirty dollars. Then he bought the Old Crow and went into the bar and the prettiest hostess came and stood beside him, her face level with his chest though he sat on a barstool, and she placed a hand on his thigh and said *Can I sit down?* and he said *Yes, would you like a drink?* and she said *Yes, sank you* and sat down and signaled the bartender and said *My name Betty-san* and he said *What is your Japanese name?* She told him but he could not repeat it, so she laughed and said *You call me Betty-san;* he said *Okay, I am Gale. Gale-san? Is girl's name. No,* he said, *it's a man's.*

Now he buttoned his collar and slipped his tie knot into place and went inside.

"You gone long time," she said. "I sink you go back ship."

"No. S'koshi sick. Maybe I won't go back ship."

"You better go. They put you in monkey house."

"Maybe so."

He raised his glass to the bartender and nodded at Betty, then looked at the cuff of his sleeve, at the red hashmark which branded him as a man with four years' service and no rank—three years in the Army and eighteen months in the Marines—although eight months earlier he had been a private first class, nearly certain that he would soon be a lance corporal, then walking back to the ship one night in Alameda, two sailors called him a jarhead and he fought them both and the next day he was reduced to private. He was twenty-four years old.

"I sink you have sta'side wife," Betty said.

"How come?"

"You all time quiet. All time sink sink sink."

She mimicked his brooding, then giggled and shyly covered her face with both hands.

"My wife is butterfly girl," he said.

"Dat's true?"

He nodded.

"While you in Japan she butterfly girl?"

"Yes."

"How you know?"

"My mama-san write me a letter."

"Dat's too bad."

"Maybe I take you home tonight, okay?"

"We'll see."

"When?"

"Bar close soon."

"You're very pretty."

"You really sink so?"

"Yes."

She brought her hands to her face, moved the fingertips up to her eyes.

"You like Japanese girl?"

"Yes," he said. "Very much."

2

Now he could not sleep and he wished they had not gone to bed so soon, for at least as they walked rapidly over strange, winding, suddenly quiet streets he had thought of nothing but Betty and his passion, stifled for four and a half months, but now he lay smoking, vaguely conscious of her foot touching his calf, knowing the Corporal of the Guard had already recorded his absence, and he felt helpless before the capricious forces which governed his life.

Her name was Dana. He had married her in June, two months before the cruise, and their transition from courtship to marriage involved merely the assumption of financial responsibility and an adjustment to conflicting habits of eating, sleeping, and using the bathroom, for they had been making love since their third date, when he had discovered that he not only was not her first, but probably was not even her fourth or fifth. In itself, her lack of innocence did not disturb him. His moral standards were a combination of Calvinism (greatly dulled since leaving home four and a half years earlier), the pragmatic workings of the service, and the ability to think rarely in terms of good and evil. Also, he had no illusions about girls and so on that third date he was not shocked. But afterward he was disturbed. Though he was often tormented by visions of her past, he never asked her about it and he had no idea of how many years or boys, then men, it entailed; but he felt that for the last two or three or even four years (she was nineteen) Dana had somehow cheated him, as if his possession of her was retroactive. He also feared comparison. But most disturbing of all was her casual worldliness: giving herself that first time as easily as, years before, high school girls had given a kiss, and her apparent assumption that he did not expect a lengthy seduction any more than he expected to find that she was a virgin. It was an infectious quality, sweeping him up, making him feel older and smarter, as if he had reached the end of a prolonged childhood. But at the same time he sensed his destruction and, for moments, he looked fearfully into her eyes.

They were blue. When she was angry they became suddenly hard, harder than any Gale had ever seen, and looking at them he always yielded, afraid that if he did not she would scream at him the terrible silent things he saw there. His memories of the last few days before the cruise—the drive in his old Plymouth from California to Louisiana, the lack of privacy in his parents' home—were filled with images of those eyes as they reacted to the heat and dust or a flintless cigarette lighter or his inability to afford a movie or an evening of drinking beer.

He took her home because in Alameda she had lived with her sister and brother-in-law (she had no parents: she told him they were killed in a car accident when she was fifteen; but for some reason he did not believe her) and she did not like her sister; she wanted to live alone in their apartment, but he refused, saying it was a waste of money when she could live with her sister or his parents without paying rent. They talked for days, often quarreling, and finally, reluctantly, she decided to go to Louisiana, saying even *that* would be better than her sister's. So he took her home, emerging from his car on a July afternoon, hot and tired but boyishly apprehensive, and taking her hand he led her up the steps and onto the front porch where nearly five years before, his father—a carpenter—had squinted down at him standing in the yard and said: *So you joined the Army. Well, maybe they can make something out of you. I shore couldn't do no good.*

3

Strange fish and octopus and squid were displayed uncovered in front of markets, their odors pervading the street. The morning was cold, damp, and gray: so much like a winter day in Louisiana that Gale walked silently with Betty, thinking of rice fields and swamps and ducks in a gray sky, and of the vanished faces and impersonal bunks which, during his service years, had been his surroundings but not his home.

They walked in the street, dodging through a succession of squat children with coats buttoned to their throats and women in kimonos, stooped with the weight of babies on their backs, and young men in business suits who glanced at Gale and Betty, and young girls who looked like bar hostesses and, like Betty, wore sweaters and skirts; men on bicycles, their patient faces incongruous with their fast-pumping legs, rode heedlessly through all of them, and small taxis sounded vain horns and braked and swerved and shifted gears until they had moved through the passive faces and were gone. Bars with American names were on both sides of the street. Betty entered one of the markets and, after pausing to look at the fish outside, Gale followed her and looked curiously at rows of canned goods with Japanese labels, then stepped into the street again. Above the market a window slid open and a woman in a kimono looked down at the street, then slowly laid her bedding on the market roof and, painfully, Gale felt the serenity of the room behind her. Betty came out of the market, carrying a paper bag.

"Now I make you sukiyaki," she said.

"Good. I need some shaving gear first."

"Okay. We go Japanese store."

"Where is it?"

"Not far. You sink somebody see you?"

"Naw. Everybody's on the ship now. They'll be out this afternoon."

"What they do when you go back? Put you in monkey house?"

"Right."

"When you go back?"

"Next week. Before she goes to sea."

"Maybe you better go now."

"They'd lock me up anyhow. One day over the hill or six, it doesn't matter."

"Here's store."

"You buy 'em. They wouldn't understand me."

"What you want?"

"Shaving cream, razor, and razor blades."

He gave her a thousand yen.

"Dat's too much."

"Keep the rest."

"Sank you. You nice man."

She went into the drugstore. He waited, then took her bags when she came out and, walking back to her house, treating her with deference and marveling at her femininity and apparent purity and honesty, he remembered how it was with Dana at first, how he had gone to the ship each morning feeling useful and involved with the world and he had had visions of himself as a salty, leather-faced, graying sergeant-major.

4

—and she was gone for a week before we could even find her and even when we got out there she told us she wasn't coming with us, she was going to stay with him and it took your daddy about a hour to talk her into coming with us and you know how mad he gets, I don't see how he didn't whip her good right there, that's what I felt like doing, and it's a good thing that boy wasn't there or I know your daddy would killed him. I don't know how long it was going on before, she used to go out at night in your car, she'd tell us she was going to a show and I guess we should have said no or followed her or something but you just don't know at the time, then Sunday she didn't come home and her suitcase was gone so I guess she packed it while I was taking a nap and stuck it in the car. I hate to be writing this but I don't know what else a mothers supposed to do when her boys wife is running around like that. We'll keep her here til you tell us what your going to do, she don't have any money and daddy has the car keys. Tell us what your going to do, I hope its divorse because she's no good for you. I hate to say it but I could tell soon as I seen her, there's something about a girl of her kind and you just married too fast. Its no good around here, she stays in your room most of the time and just goes to the kitchen when she feels like it at all hours and gets something to eat by herself and I don't think we said three words since we got her back—

He returned the letter to his pocket, lighted a cigarette, poured another glass of dark, burning rum that a British sailor had left with Betty months before, and looked at his watch. It was seven o'clock; Betty had been gone an hour, promising to wake him when she came home from the bar. During the afternoon they had eaten sukiyaki, Betty kneeling on the opposite side of the low table, cooking and serving as he ate, shaking her head each time he asked her to eat instead of cook, assuring him that in Japan the woman ate last; he ate, sitting cross-legged on the floor until his legs cramped, then he straightened them and leaned back on one arm, the other hand proudly and adeptly manipulating a pair of chopsticks or lifting a tumbler of hot *sake* to his lips. After eating she turned on the television set and they sat on the floor and watched it for the rest of the afternoon. She reacted like a child: laughing, frowning, watching intently. He understood nothing and merely held her hand and smoked until near evening, when they watched an American Western with Japanese dialogue and he smiled.

Now he rose, brought the rum and his glass to the bedroom, undressed, went back to the living room for an ash tray and cigarettes, then lay in bed and pulled the blankets up to his throat. He lay in the dark, his hands on his belly, knowing that he could not take her back and could not divorce her; then he started drinking rum again, with the final knowledge that he did not want to live.

5

He stood in the Detachment office, his legs spread, his hands behind his back, and stared at the white bulkhead behind the Marine captain. That afternoon, as his defense counsel told the court why he had gone over the hill, he had felt like crying and now, faced with compassion, he felt it again. But he would not. He had waited two weeks at sea for his court-martial and every night, sober and womanless and without mail, he had lain in bed with clenched jaws and finally slept without crying. Now he shut his eyes, then opened them again to the bulkhead and the voice.

"If you had told me about it, I would've got you off the ship. Emergency leave. I'd have flown you back. Why didn't you tell us?"

"I don't know, sir."

"All right, it's done. Now I want you to know what's going to happen. They gave you three months confinement today. We don't keep people in the ship's brig over thirty days, so you'll be sent to Yokosuka when we get back there and you'll serve the rest of your sentence in the Yokosuka brig. So we'll have to transfer you to the Marine Barracks at Yokosuka. When you get out of the brig, you'll report there for duty. Do you understand all that?"

"No, sir."

"What don't you understand?"

"When will I get back to the States?"

"You'll finish your overseas tour with the Barracks at Yokosuka. You'll be there about a year."

"A year, sir?"

"Yes. I'm sorry. But by the time you get out of the brig, the ship will be back in the States."

"Yes, sir."

"One other thing. You've worked in this brig. You know my policies and you know the duties of the turnkeys and prisoner chasers. While you're down there, I expect you to be a number one prisoner. Don't give your fellow Marines a hard time."

"Yes, sir."

"All right. If you need any help with your problem, let me know."

"Yes, sir."

He waited, blinking at the bulkhead.

"That's all," the captain said.

He clicked his heels together, pivoted around, and strode out. A chaser with a nightstick was waiting for him outside the door. Gale stopped.

"Son of a bitch," he whispered. "They're sending me to Yokosuka."

"Go to your wall locker and get your toilet articles and cigarettes and stationery," the chaser said.

Gale marched to his bunk, the chaser behind him, and squatted, opening the small bulkhead locker near the head of his bunk, which was the lower one, so that his hands were concealed by the two bunks above his and he was able to slide one razor blade from the case and hide it in his palm. He packed his shaving kit with one hand and brought the other to his waist and tucked the razor blade under his belt.

He rose and the chaser marched him to the brig on the third deck, where Fisher, the turnkey, took his shaving kit and stationery and cigarettes from him and put them in a locker.

"It's letter-writing time now," Fisher said. "You can sit on the deck and write a letter."

"Sir, Prisoner Castete would like to smoke."

"Only after meals. You missed the smoke break."

"Sir, Prisoner Castete will write a letter."

Fisher gave him his stationery and pen and he sat on the deck beside two sailors who glanced at him, then continued their writing.

He did not write. He sat for half an hour thinking of her scornful, angry, blue eyes looking at him or staring at the living room wall in Louisiana as she spoke loudly into the telephone:

What do you expect me to do when you're off on that damn boat? I bet you're not just sitting around over there in Japan.

No I haven't done a damn thing. Goddamnit, Dana. I love you. Do you love me?

I don't know.

Do you love him?

I don't know.

What are you going to do?

What do you mean, what am I going to do?

Well, you have to do something!

It looks like I'm going to sit right here in this house.

That's not what—oh you Goddamn bitch, you dirty Goddamn bitch, how could you do it to me when I love you and I never even looked at these gooks, you're killing me, Dana, sonofabitch you're killing me—

Son. Son!

Mama?

She was going to hang up on you and you calling all the way from Japan and spending all that money—

Were you standing right there?

Yes, and I couldn't stand it, the way she was talking to you—

Why were you standing there?

Well, why shouldn't I be there when the phone rings in my own house and my boy's—

Never mind. Where's Dana?

In the bedroom, I guess. I don't know.

Let me talk to her.

She won't come.

You didn't ask her.

Gale, you're wasting time and money.

Mama, would you please call her to the damn phone?

All right, wait a minute.

What do you want?

Dana, we got to talk.

How can we talk when your mother's standing right here and you're across the ocean spending a fortune?

If I write you a letter, will you answer it?

Yes.

What?

Yes!

I got to know everything, all about it. Did you think you loved him?

I don't know.

Is he still hanging around?

No.

Dana, I love you. Have you ever run around on me before this?

No.

Why did you do it?

I told you I don't know! Why don't you leave me alone!

I'll write to you.

All right.

Bye. Answer my letter. I love you.

Bye.

The letter-writing period ended and he handed the blank paper and pen to Fisher, who started to say something but did not.

Gale did not start crying until after he was put into a cell and the door was locked behind him and he had unfolded his rubber mattress and was holding one end of it under his chin and with both hands was working it into a mattress cover and he thought of Dana, then of himself, preparing his bed in a cell thousands of miles away, then he started, the tears flowing soundlessly down his cheeks until he was blinded and could not see his hands or even the mattress and it seemed that he would never get the cover on it and he desperately wanted someone to do it for him and lay the mattress on the deck and turn back the blanket and speak his name. He dropped the mattress, threw the cover against the bulkhead, unfolded the blanket, and lay down and covered himself, then gingerly took the razor blade from under his belt, touching it to his left wrist, for a moment just touching, then pressing, then he slashed, knowing in that instant of cutting that he did not want to; that if he had, he would have cut an artery instead of the veins where now the blood was warm and fast, going down his forearm, and when it reached the inside of his elbow he said:

"Fisher."

But there was no answer, so he threw off the blanket and stood up, this time yelling it:

"Fisher!"

Fisher came to the door and looked through the bars and Gale showed him the wrist; he said sonofabitch and was gone, coming back with the keys and opening the door, pulling Gale out into the passageway and grabbing the wrist and tying a handkerchief around it, muttering.

"You crazy bastard. What are you? Crazy?"

Then he ran to the phone and dialed the dispensary, watching Gale, and when he hung up he said:

"Lie on your back. I oughta treat you for shock."

Gale lay on the deck and Fisher turned a wastebasket on its side and rolled it under his legs, then threw a blanket over him.

"Son of a bitch!" he said. "They'll hang me. How'd you get that Goddamn razor?"

6

The doctor was tall, with short gray hair and a thin gray moustache. He was a commander, so at least there was that much, at least they didn't send a lieutenant. The doctor filled his cup at the percolator, then faced Gale and looked at him, then came closer until Gale could smell the coffee.

"You didn't do a very good job, did you, son?"

"No, sir."

"Do you ever do a good job at anything?"

"No, sir."

The doctor's eyes softened and he raised his cup to his lips, watching Gale over its rim, then he lowered the cup and swallowed and wiped his mouth with the back of his hand.

"You go on and sleep now," he said, "without any more silly ideas. I'll see you tomorrow and we'll talk about it."

"Yes, sir."

Gale stepped into the passageway where the chaser was waiting and they marched down the long portside passageway, empty and darkened save for small red lights, Gale staring ahead, conscious of the bandage on his wrist as though it were an emblem of his uncertainty and his inability to change his life. He knew only that he faced a year of waiting for letters that would rarely come, three months of that in the brig where he would lie awake and wonder who shared her bed and, once released from the brig, he would have to return to Betty or find another girl so he would not have to think of Dana every night (although, resolving to do this, he already knew it would be in vain); and that, when he finally returned to the States, his life would be little more than a series of efforts to avoid being deceived and finally, perhaps years later, she would —with one last pitiless glare—leave him forever. All this stretched before him, as immutable as the long passageway where he marched now, the chaser in step behind him, yet he not only accepted it, but chose it. He figured that it was at least better than nothing.

PANTALOON IN BLACK

by *William Faulkner*

❀

1

He stood in the worn, faded clean overalls which Mannie herself had washed only a week ago, and heard the first clod strike the pine box. Soon he had one of the shovels himself, which in his hands (he was better than six feet and weighed better than two hundred pounds) resembled the toy shovel a child plays with at the shore, its half cubic foot of flung dirt no more than the light gout of sand the child's shovel would have flung. Another member of his sawmill gang touched his arm and said, "Lemme have hit, Rider." He didn't even falter. He released one hand in midstroke and flung it backward, striking the other across the chest, jolting him back a step, and restored the hand to the moving shovel, flinging the dirt with that effortless fury so that the mound seemed to be rising of its own volition, not built up from above but thrusting visibly upward out of the earth itself, until at last the grave, save for its rawness, resembled any other marked off without order about the barren plot by shards of pottery and broken bottles and old brick and other objects insignificant to sight but actually of a profound meaning and fatal to touch, which no white man could have read. Then he straightened up and with one hand flung the shovel quivering upright in the mound like a javelin and turned and began to walk away, walking on even when an old woman came out of the meagre clump of his kin and friends and a few old people who had known him and his dead wife both since they were born, and grasped his forearm. She was his aunt. She had raised him. He could not remember his parents at all.

"Whar you gwine?" she said.

"Ah'm goan home," he said.

"You dont wants ter go back dar by yoself," she said. "You needs to eat. You come on home and eat."

"Ah'm goan home," he repeated, walking out from under her hand, his forearm like iron, as if the weight on it were no more than that of a fly, the other members of the mill gang whose head he was giving way quietly to let him pass. But before he reached the fence one of them overtook him; he did not need to be told it was his aunt's messenger.

"Wait, Rider," the other said. "We gots a jug in de bushes—" Then the other said what he had not intended to say, what he had never conceived of himself saying in circumstances like these, even though everybody knew it—the dead who either will not or cannot quit the earth yet although the flesh they once lived in has been returned to it, let the preachers tell and reiterate and affirm how they left it not only without regret but with joy, mounting toward glory: "You dont wants ter go back dar. She be wawkin yit."

He didn't pause, glancing down at the other, his eyes red at the inner corners in his high, slightly back-tilted head. "Lemme lone, Acey," he said. "Doan mess wid me now," and went on, stepping over the three-strand wire fence without even breaking his stride, and crossed the road and entered the woods. It was middle dusk when he emerged from them and crossed the last field, stepping over that fence too in one stride, into the lane. It was empty at this hour of Sunday evening—no family in wagon, no rider, no walkers churchward to speak to him and carefully refrain from looking after him when he had passed—the pale, powder-light, powder-dry dust of August from which the long week's marks of hoof and wheel had been blotted by the strolling and unhurried Sunday shoes, with somewhere beneath them, vanished but not gone, fixed and held in the annealing dust, the narrow, splay-toed prints of his wife's bare feet where on Saturday afternoons she would walk to the commissary to buy their next week's supplies while he took his bath; himself, his own prints, setting the period now as he strode on, moving almost as fast as a smaller man could have trotted, his body breasting the air her body had vacated, his eyes touching the objects—post and tree and field and house and hill—her eyes had lost.

The house was the last one in the lane, not his but rented

from Carothers Edmonds, the local white landowner. But the rent was paid promptly in advance, and even in just six months he had refloored the porch and rebuilt and roofed the kitchen, doing the work himself on Saturday afternoon and Sunday with his wife helping him, and bought the stove. Because he made good money: sawmilling ever since he began to get his growth at fifteen and sixteen and now, at twenty-four, head of the timber gang itself because the gang he headed moved a third again as much timber between sunup and sundown as any other moved, handling himself at times out of the vanity of his own strength logs which ordinarily two men would have handled with cant hooks; never without work even in the old days when he had not actually needed the money, when a lot of what he wanted, needed perhaps, didn't cost money—the women bright and dark and for all purposes nameless he didn't need to buy and it didn't matter to him what he wore and there was always food for him at any hour of day or night in the house of his aunt who didn't even want to take the two dollars he gave her each Saturday—so there had been only the Saturday and Sunday dice and whiskey that had to be paid for until that day six months ago when he saw Mannie, whom he had known all his life, for the first time and said to himself: "Ah'm thu wid all dat," and they married and he rented the cabin from Carothers Edmonds and built a fire on the hearth on their wedding night as the tale told how Uncle Lucas Beauchamp, Edmonds' oldest tenant, had done on his forty-five years ago and which had burned ever since; and he would rise and dress and eat his breakfast by lamplight to walk the four miles to the mill by sunup, and exactly one hour after sundown he would enter the house again, five days a week, until Saturday. Then the first hour would not have passed noon when he would mount the steps and knock, not on post or doorframe but on the underside of the gallery roof itself, and enter and ring the bright cascade of silver dollars onto the scrubbed table in the kitchen where his dinner simmered on the stove and the galvanised tub of hot water and the baking powder can of soft soap and the towel made of scalded flour sacks sewn together and his clean overalls and shirt waited, and Mannie would gather up the money and walk the half-mile to the commissary and buy their next week's supplies and bank the rest of the money in Edmonds' safe and return and they would eat once again without haste or hurry after five days—the sidemeat, the greens, the cornbread, the buttermilk from the well-house, the cake which she baked every Saturday now that she had a stove to bake in.

But when he put his hand on the gate it seemed to him suddenly that there was nothing beyond it. The house had never been his anyway, but now even the new planks and sills and shingles, the hearth and stove and bed, were all a part of the memory of somebody else, so that he stopped in the half-open gate and said aloud, as though he had gone to sleep in one place and then waked suddenly to find himself in another: "Whut's Ah doin hyar?" before he went on. Then he saw the dog. He had forgotten it. He remembered neither seeing nor hearing it since it began to howl just before dawn yesterday—a big dog, a hound with a strain of mastiff from somewhere (he had told Mannie a month after they married: "Ah needs a big dawg. You's de onliest least thing whut ever kep up wid me one day, leff alone fo weeks.") coming out from beneath the gallery and approaching, not running but seeming rather to drift across the dusk until it stood lightly against his leg, its head raised until the tips of his fingers just touched it, facing the house and making no sound; whereupon, as if the animal controlled it, had lain guardian before it during his absence and only this instant relinquished, the shell of planks and shingles facing him solidified, filled, and for the moment he believed that he could not possibly enter it. "But Ah needs to eat," he said. "Us bofe needs to eat," he said, moving on though the dog did not follow until he turned and cursed it. "Come on hyar!" he said. "Whut you skeered of? She lacked you too, same as me," and they mounted the steps and crossed the porch and entered the house—the dusk-filled single room where all those six months were now crammed and crowded into one instant of time until there was no space left for air to breathe, crammed and crowded about the hearth where the fire which was to have lasted to the end of them, before which in the days before he was able to buy the stove he would enter after his four-mile walk from the mill and find her, the shape of her narrow back and haunches squatting, one narrow spread hand shielding her face from the blaze over which the other hand held the skillet, had already fallen to a dry, light soilure of dead ashes when the sun rose yesterday—and himself standing there while the last of light died about the strong and indomitable beating of his heart and the deep steady arch and collapse of his chest which walking fast over the rough going of woods and fields had not increased and standing still in the quiet and fading room had not slowed down.

Then the dog left him. The light pressure went off his flank; he heard the click and hiss of its claws on the wooden floor as it surged away and he thought at first that it was fleeing. But it stopped just outside the front door, where he could see it now, and the upfling of its head as the howl began, and then he saw her too. She was standing in the kitchen door, looking at him. He didn't move. He didn't breathe nor speak until he knew his voice would be all right, his face fixed too not to alarm her. "Mannie," he said. "Hit's awright. Ah aint afraid." Then he took a step toward her, slow, not even raising his hand yet, and stopped. Then he took another step. But this time as soon as he moved she began to fade. He stopped at once, not breathing again, motionless, willing his eyes to see that she had stopped too. But she had not stopped. She was fading, going. "Wait," he said, talking as sweet as he had ever heard his voice speak to a woman: "Den lemme go wid you, honey." But she was going. She was going fast now, he could actually feel between them the insuperable barrier of that very strength which could handle alone a log which would have taken any two other men to handle, of the blood and bones and flesh too strong, invincible for life, having learned at least once with his own eyes how tough, even in sudden and violent death, not a young man's bones and flesh perhaps but the will of that bone and flesh to remain alive, actually was.

Then she was gone. He walked through the door where she had been standing, and went to the stove. He did not light the lamp. He needed no light. He had set the stove up himself and built the shelves for the dishes, from among which he took two plates by feel and from the pot sitting cold on the cold stove he ladled onto the plates the food which his aunt had brought yesterday and of which he had eaten yesterday though now he did not remember when he had eaten it nor what it was, and carried the plates to the scrubbed bare table beneath the single small fading window and drew two chairs up and sat down, waiting again until he knew his voice would be what he wanted it to be. "Come on hyar, now," he said roughly. "Come on hyar and eat yo supper. Ah aint gonter have no—" and ceased, looking down at his plate, breathing the strong, deep pants, his chest arching and collapsing until he stopped it presently and held himself motionless for perhaps a half minute, and raised a spoonful of the cold and glutinous peas to his mouth. The congealed and lifeless mass seemed to bounce on contact with his lips. Not even warmed from mouth-heat, peas and spoon spattered and rang upon the plate; his chair crashed backward and he was standing, feeling the muscles of his jaw beginning to drag his mouth open, tugging upward the top half of his head. But he stopped that too before it became sound, holding himself again while he rapidly scraped the food from his plate onto the other and took it up and left the kitchen, crossed the other room and the gallery and set the plate on the bottom step and went on toward the gate.

The dog was not there, but it overtook him within the first half mile. There was a moon then, their two shadows flitting broken and intermittent among the trees or slanted long and intact across the slope of pasture or old abandoned fields upon the hills, the man moving almost as fast as a horse could have moved over that ground, altering his course each time a lighted window came in sight, the dog trotting at heel while their shadows shortened to the moon's curve until at last they trod them and the last far lamp had vanished and the shadows began to lengthen on the other hand, keeping to heel even when a rabbit burst from almost beneath the man's foot, then lying in the gray of dawn beside the man's prone body, beside the labored heave and collapse of the chest, the loud harsh snoring which sounded not like groans of pain but like someone engaged without arms in prolonged single combat.

When he reached the mill there was nobody there but the fireman—an older man just turning from the woodpile, watching quietly as he crossed the clearing, striding as if he were going to walk not only through the boiler shed but through (or over) the boiler too, the overalls which had been clean yesterday now draggled and soiled and drenched to the knees with dew, the cloth cap flung onto the side of his head, hanging peak downward over his ear as he always wore it, the whites of his eyes rimmed with red and with something urgent and strained about them. "Whar yo bucket?" he said. But before the fireman could answer he had stepped past him and lifted the polished lard pail down from a nail in a post. "Ah just wants a biscuit," he said.

"Eat hit all," the fireman said. "Ah'll eat outen de yuthers' buckets at dinner. Den you gawn home and go to bed. You dont looks good."

"Ah aint come hyar to look," he said, sitting on the ground, his back against the post, the open pail between his knees, cramming the food into his mouth with his hands, wolfing it—peas again, also gelid and cold, a fragment of yesterday's Sunday fried chicken, a few rough chunks of this morning's fried sidemeat, a biscuit the size of a child's cap—indiscriminate, tasteless. The rest of the crew was gathering now, with voices and sounds of movement outside the boiler shed; presently the white foreman rode into the clearing on a horse. He did not look up, setting the empty pail aside, rising, looking at no one, and went to the branch and lay on his stomach and lowered his face to the water, drawing the water into himself with the same deep, strong, troubled inhalations that he had snored with, or as when he had stood in the empty house at dusk yesterday, trying to get air.

Then the trucks were rolling. The air pulsed with the rapid beating of the exhaust and the whine and clang of the saw, the trucks rolling one by one up to the skidway, he mounting the trucks in turn, to stand balanced on the load he freed, knocking the chocks out and casting loose the shackle chains and with his cant hook squaring the sticks of cypress and gum and oak one by one to the incline and holding them until the next two men of his gang were ready to receive and guide them, until the discharge of each truck became one long rumbling roar punctuated by grunting shouts and, as the morning grew and the sweat came, chanted phrases of song tossed back and forth. He did not sing with them. He rarely ever did, and this morning might have been no different from any other—himself man-height again above the heads which carefully refrained from looking at him, stripped to the waist now, the shirt removed and the overalls knotted about his hips by the suspender straps, his upper body bare except for the handkerchief about his neck and the cap clapped and clinging somehow over his right ear, the mounting sun sweat-glinted steel-blue on the midnight-colored bunch and slip of muscles until the whistle blew for noon and he said to the two men at the head of the skidway: "Look out. Git out de way," and rode the log down the incline, balanced erect upon it in short rapid backward-running steps above the headlong thunder.

His aunt's husband was waiting for him—an old man, as tall as he was, but lean, almost frail, carrying a tin pail in one hand and a covered plate in the other; they too sat in the shade beside the branch a short distance from where the others were opening their dinner pails. The bucket contained a fruit jar of buttermilk packed in a clean damp towsack. The covered dish was a peach pie, still warm. "She baked hit fer you dis mawin," the uncle said. "She say fer you to come home." He didn't answer, bent forward a little, his elbows on his knees, holding the pie in both hands, wolfing at it, the syrupy filling smearing and trickling down his chin, blinking rapidly as he chewed, the whites of his eyes covered a little more by the creeping red. "Ah went to yo house last night, but you want dar. She sont me. She wants you to come on home. She kept de lamp burnin all last night fer you."

"Ah'm awright," he said.

"You aint awright. De Lawd guv, and He tuck away. Put yo faith and trust in Him. And she kin help you."

"Whut faith and trust?" he said. "Whut Mannie ever done ter Him? What He wanter come messin wid me and——"

"Hush!" the old man said. "Hush!"

Then the trucks were rolling again. Then he could stop needing to invent to himself reasons for his breathing, until after a while he began to believe he had forgot about breathing since now he could not hear it himself above the steady thunder of the rolling logs; whereupon as soon as he found himself believing he had forgotten it, he knew that he had not, so that instead of tipping the final log onto the skidway he stood up and cast his cant hook away as if it were a burnt match and in the dying reverberation of the last log's rumbling descent he vaulted down between the two slanted tracks of the skid, facing the log which still lay on the truck. He had done it before—taken a log from the truck onto his hands, balanced, and turned with it and tossed it onto the skidway, but never with a stick of this size, so that in a complete cessation of all sound save the pulse of the exhaust and the light free-running whine of the disengaged saw since every eye there, even that of the white foreman, was upon him, he nudged the log to the edge of the truckframe and squatted and set his palms against the underside of it. For a time there was no movement at all. It was as if the unrational and inanimate wood had invested, mesmerised the man with some of its own primal inertia. Then a voice said quietly: "He got hit. Hit's off de truck," and they saw the crack and gap of air, watching the infinitesimal straightening of the braced legs until the knees locked, the movement mounting infinitesimally through the belly's insuck, the arch of the chest, the neck cords, lifting the lip from the white clench of teeth in passing, drawing the whole head backward and only the bloodshot fixity of the eyes impervious to it, moving on up the arms and the straightening elbows until the balanced log was higher than his head. "Only he aint gonter turn wid dat un," the same voice said. "And when he try to put hit back on de truck, hit gonter kill him." But none of them moved. Then—there was no gathering of supreme effort—the log seemed to leap suddenly backward over his head of its own volition, spinning, crashing and thundering down the incline; he turned and stepped over the slanting track in one stride and walked through them as they gave way and went on across the clearing toward the woods even though the foreman called after him: "Rider!" and again: "You, Rider!"

At sundown he and the dog were in the river swamp four miles away—another clearing, itself not much larger than a room, a hut, a hovel partly of planks and partly of canvas, an unshaven white man standing in the door beside which a shotgun leaned, watching him as he approached, his hand extended with four silver dollars on the palm. "Ah wants a jug," he said.

"A jug?" the white man said. "You mean a pint. This is Monday. Aint you all running this week?"

"Ah laid off," he said. "Whar's my jug?" waiting, looking at nothing apparently, blinking his bloodshot eyes rapidly in his high, slightly back-tilted head, then turning, the jug hanging from his crooked middle finger against his leg, at which moment the white man looked suddenly and sharply at his eyes as though seeing them for the first time—the eyes which had been strained and urgent this morning and which now seemed to be without vision too and in which no white showed at all—and said,

"Here. Gimme that jug. You dont need no gallon. I'm going to give you that pint, give it to you. Then you get out of here and stay out. Dont come back until—" Then the white man reached and grasped the jug, whereupon the other swung it behind him, sweeping his other arm up and out so that it struck the white man across the chest.

"Look out, white folks," he said. "Hit's mine. Ah done paid you."

The white man cursed him. "No you aint. Here's your money. Put that jug down, nigger."

"Hit's mine," he said, his voice quiet, gentle even, his face quiet save for the rapid blinking of the red eyes. "Ah done paid for hit," turning on, turning his back on the man and the gun both, and recrossed the clearing to where the dog waited beside the path to come to heel again. They moved rapidly on between the close walls of impenetrable cane-stalks which gave a sort of blondness to the twilight and possessed something of that oppression, that lack of room to breathe in, which the walls of his house had had. But this time, instead of fleeing it, he stopped and raised the jug and drew the cob stopper from the fierce duskreek of uncured alcohol and drank, gulping the liquid solid and cold as ice water, without either taste or heat until he lowered the jug and the air got in. "Hah," he said. "Dat's right. Try me. Try me, big boy. Ah gots something hyar now dat kin whup you."

And, once free of the bottom's unbreathing blackness, there was the moon again, his long shadow and that of the lifted jug slanting away as he drank and then held the jug poised, gulping the silver air into his throat until he could breathe again, speaking to the jug: "Come on now. You always claim you's a better man den me. Come on now. Prove it." He drank again, swallowing the chill liquid tamed of taste or heat either while the swallowing lasted, feeling it flow solid and cold with fire, past then enveloping the strong steady panting of his lungs until they too ran suddenly free as his moving body ran in the silver solid wall of air he breasted. And he was all right, his striding shadow and the trotting one of the dog travelling swift as those of two clouds along the hill; the long cast of his motionless shadow and that of the lifted jug slanting across the slope as he watched the frail figure of his aunt's husband toiling up the hill.

"Dey tole me at de mill you was gone," the old man said. "Ah knowed whar to look. Come home, son. Dat ar cant help you."

"Hit done awready hope me," he said. "Ah'm awready home. Ah'm snakebit now and pizen cant hawm me."

"Den stop and see her. Leff her look at you. Dat's all she axes: just leff her look at you—" But he was already moving. "Wait!" the old man cried. "Wait!"

"You cant keep up," he said, speaking into the silver air, breasting aside the silver solid air which began to flow past him almost as fast as it would have flowed past a moving horse. The faint frail voice was already lost in the night's infinitude, his shadow and that of the dog scudding the free miles, the deep strong panting of his chest running free as air now because he was all right.

Then, drinking, he discovered suddenly that no more of the liquid was entering his mouth. Swallowing, it was no longer passing down his throat, his throat and mouth filled now with a solid and unmoving column which without reflex or revulsion sprang, columnar and intact and still retaining the mold of his gullet, outward glinting in the moonlight, splintering, vanishing into the myriad murmur of the dewed grass. He drank again. Again his throat merely filled solidly until two icy rills ran from his mouth-corners; again the intact column sprang silvering, glinting, shivering, while he panted the chill of air into his throat, the jug poised before his mouth while he spoke to it: "Awright. Ah'm gwy try you again. Soon as you makes up yo mind to stay whar I puts you, Ah'll leff you alone." He drank, filling his gullet for the third time and lowered the jug one instant ahead of the bright intact repetition, panting, indrawing the cool of air until he could breathe. He stoppered the cob carefully back into the jug and stood, panting, blinking, the long cast of his solitary shadow slanting away across the hill and beyond, across the mazy infinitude of all the night-bound earth. "Awright," he said. "Ah just misread de sign wrong. Hit's done done me all de help

Ah needs. Ah'm awright now. Ah doan needs no mo of hit."

He could see the lamp in the window as he crossed the pasture, passing the black-and-silver yawn of the sandy ditch where he had played as a boy with empty snuff-tins and rusted harness-buckles and fragments of trace-chains and now and then an actual wheel, passing the garden patch where he had hoed in the spring days while his aunt stood sentry over him from the kitchen window, crossing the grassless yard in whose dust he had sprawled and crept before he learned to walk. He entered the house, the room, the light itself, and stopped in the door, his head back-tilted a little as if he could not see, the jug hanging from his crooked finger, against his leg. "Unc Alec say you wanter see me," he said.

"Not just to see you," his aunt said. "To come home, whar we kin help you."

"Ah'm awright," he said. "Ah doan needs no help."

"No," she said. She rose from the chair and came and grasped his arm as she had grasped it yesterday at the grave. Again, as on yesterday, the forearm was like iron under her hand. "No! When Alec come back and tole me how you had wawked off de mill and de sun not half down, Ah knowed why and whar. And dat cant help you."

"Hit done awready hope me. Ah'm awright now."

"Dont lie to me," she said. "You aint never lied to me. Dont lie to me now."

Then he said it. It was his own voice, without either grief or amazement, speaking quietly out of the tremendous panting of his chest which in a moment now would begin to strain at the walls of this room too. But he would be gone in a moment.

"Nome," he said. "Hit aint done me no good."

"And hit cant! Cant nothing help you but Him! Ax Him! Tole Him about hit! He wants to hyar you and help you!"

"Efn He God, Ah dont needs to tole Him. Efn He God, He awready know hit. Awright. Hyar Ah is. Leff Him come down hyar and do me some good."

"On yo knees!" she cried. "On yo knees and ax Him!"

But it was not his knees on the floor, it was his feet. And for a space he could hear her feet too on the planks of the hall behind him and her voice crying after him from the door: "Spoot! Spoot!"—crying after him across the moon-dappled yard the name he had gone by in his childhood and adolescence, before the men he worked with and the bright dark nameless women he had taken in course and forgotten until he saw Mannie that day and said, "Ah'm thu wid all dat," began to call him Rider.

It was just after midnight when he reached the mill. The dog was gone now. This time he could not remember when nor where. At first he seemed to remember hurling the empty jug at it. But later the jug was still in his hand and it was not empty, although each time he drank now the two icy runnels streamed from his mouth-corners, sopping his shirt and overalls until he walked constantly in the fierce chill of the liquid tamed now of flavor and heat and odor too even when the swallowing ceased. "Sides that," he said, "Ah wouldn't thow nothin at him. Ah mout kick him efn he needed hit and was close enough. But Ah wouldn't ruint no dog chunkin hit."

The jug was still in his hand when he entered the clearing and paused among the mute soaring of the moon-blond lumber-stacks. He stood in the middle now of the unimpeded shadow which he was treading again as he had trod it last night, swaying a little, blinking about at the stacked lumber, the skidway, the piled logs waiting for tomorrow, the boiler shed all quiet and blanched in the moon. And then it was all right. He was moving again. But he was not moving, he was drinking, the liquid cold and swift and tasteless and requiring no swallowing, so that he could not tell if it were going down inside or outside. But it was all right. And now he was moving, the jug gone now and he didn't know the when or where of that either. He crossed the clearing and entered the boiler shed and went on through it, crossing the junctureless backloop of time's trepan, to the door of the tool-room, the faint glow of the lantern beyond the plank-joints, the surge and fall of living shadow, the mutter of voices, the mute click and scutter of the dice, his hand loud on the barred door, his voice loud too: "Open hit. Hit's me. Ah'm snakebit and bound to die."

Then he was through the door and inside the tool-room. They were the same faces—three members of his timber gang, three or four others of the mill crew, the white night-watchman with the heavy pistol in his hip pocket and the small heap of coins and worn bills on the floor before him, one who was called Rider and was Rider standing above the squatting circle, swaying a little, blinking, the dead muscles of his face shaped into smiling while the white man stared up at him. "Make room, gamblers," he said. "Make room. Ah'm snakebit and de pizen cant hawm me."

"You're drunk," the white man said. "Get out of here. One of you niggers open the door and get him out of here."

"Dass awright, boss-man," he said, his voice equable, his face still fixed in the faint rigid smiling beneath the blinking of the red eyes; "Ah aint drunk. Ah just cant wawk straight fer dis yar money weighin me down."

Now he was kneeling too, the other six dollars of his last week's pay on the floor before him, blinking, still smiling at the face of the white man opposite, then, still smiling, he watched the dice pass from hand to hand around the circle as the white man covered the bets, watching the soiled and palm-worn money in front of the white man gradually and steadily increase, watching the white man cast and win two doubled bets in succession then lose one for twenty-five cents, the dice coming to him at last, the cupped snug clicking of them in his fist. He spun a coin into the center.

"Shoots a dollar," he said, and cast, and watched the white man pick up the dice and flip them back to him. "Ah lets hit lay," he said. "Ah'm snakebit. Ah kin pass wid anything," and cast, and this time one of the negroes flipped the dice back. "Ah lets hit lay," he said, and cast, and moved as the white man moved, catching the white man's wrist before his hand reached the dice, the two of them squatting, facing each other above the dice and the money, his left hand grasping the white man's wrist, his face still fixed in the rigid and deadened smiling, his voice equable, almost deferential: "Ah kin pass even wid miss-outs. But dese hyar yuther boys—" until the white man's hand sprang open and the second pair of dice clattered onto the floor beside the first two and the white man wrenched free and sprang up and back and reached the hand backward toward the pocket where the pistol was.

The razor hung between his shoulder-blades from a loop of cotton string round his neck inside his shirt. The same motion of the hand which brought the razor forward over his shoulder flipped the blade open and freed it from the cord, the blade opening on until the back edge of it lay across the knuckles of his fist, his thumb pressing the handle into his closing fingers, so that in the second before the half-drawn pistol exploded he actually struck at the white man's throat not with the blade but with a sweeping blow of his fist, following through in the same motion so that not even the first jet of blood touched his hand or arm.

2

After it was over—it didn't take long; they found the prisoner on the following day, hanging from the bell-rope in a negro schoolhouse about two miles from the sawmill, and the coroner had pronounced his verdict of death at the hands of a person or persons unknown and surrendered the body to its next of kin all within five minutes—the sheriff's deputy who had been officially in charge of the business was telling his wife about it. They were in the kitchen. His wife was cooking supper. The deputy had been out of bed and in motion ever since the jail delivery shortly before midnight of yesterday and had covered considerable ground since, and he was spent now from lack of sleep and hurried food at hurried and curious hours and, sitting in a chair beside the stove, a little hysterical too.

"Them damn niggers," he said. "I swear to godfrey, it's a wonder we have as little trouble with them as we do. Because why? Because they aint human. They look like a man and they walk on their hind legs like a man, and they can talk and you can understand them and you think they are understanding you, at least now and then. But when it comes to the normal human feelings and sentiments of human beings, they might just as well be a damn herd of wild buffaloes. Now you take this one today——"

"I wish you would," his wife said harshly. She was a stout woman, handsome once, graying now and with a neck definitely too short, who looked not harried at all but composed in fact, only choleric. Also, she had attended a club rook-party that afternoon and had won the first, the fifty-cent, prize until another member had insisted on a recount of the scores and the ultimate throwing out of one entire game. "Take him out of my kitchen, anyway. You sheriffs! Sitting around that courthouse all day long, talking! It's no wonder two or three men can walk in and take prisoners out from under your very noses. They would take your chairs and desks and window sills too if you ever got your feet and backsides off of them that long."

"It's more of them Birdsongs than just two or three," the deputy said. "There's forty-two active votes in that connection. Me and Maydew taken the poll-list and counted them one day. But listen—" The wife turned from the stove, carrying a dish. The deputy snatched his feet rapidly out of the way as she passed him, passed almost over him, and went into the dining room. The deputy raised his voice a little to carry the increased distance: "His wife dies on him. All right. But does he grieve? He's the biggest and busiest man at the funeral. Grabs a shovel before they even got the box into the grave they tell me, and starts throwing dirt onto her faster than a slip scraper could have done it. But that's all right—" His wife came back. He moved his feet again and altered his voice again to the altered range: "—maybe that's how he felt about her. There aint any law against a man rushing his wife into the ground, provided he never had nothing to do with rushing her to the cemetery too. But here the next day he's the first man back at work except the fireman, getting back to the mill before the fireman had his fire going, let alone steam up; five minutes earlier and he could even have helped the fireman wake Birdsong up so Birdsong could go home and go back to bed again, or he could even have cut Birdsong's throat then and saved everybody trouble.

"So he comes to work, the first man on the job, when McAndrews and everybody else expected him to take the day off since even a nigger couldn't want no better excuse for a holiday than he had just buried his wife, when a white man would have took the day off out of pure respect no matter how he felt about his wife, when even a little child would have had sense enough to take a day off when he would still get paid for it too. But not him. The first man there, jumping from one log truck to another before the starting whistle quit blowing even, snatching up ten-foot cypress logs by himself and throwing them around like matches. And then, when everybody had finally decided that that's the way to take him, the way he wants to be took, he walks off the job in the middle of the afternoon without by-your-leave or much obliged or goodbye to McAndrews or nobody else, gets himself a whole gallon of bust-skull white-mule whiskey, comes straight back to the mill and to the same crap game where Birdsong has been running crooked dice on them mill niggers for fifteen years, goes straight to the same game where he has been peacefully losing a probably steady average ninety-nine percent of his pay ever since he got big enough to read the spots on them miss-out dice, and cuts Birdsong's throat clean to the neckbone five minutes later." The wife passed him again and went to the dining room. Again he drew his feet back and raised his voice:

"So me and Maydew go out there. Not that we expected to do any good, as he had probably passed Jackson, Tennessee, about daylight; and besides, the simplest way to find him would be just to stay close behind them Birdsong boys. Of course there wouldn't be nothing hardly worth bringing back to town after they did find him, but it would close the case. So it's just by the merest chance that we go by his house; I dont even remember why we went now, but we did; and there he is. Sitting behind the barred front door with a open razor on one knee and a loaded shotgun on the other? No. He was asleep. A big pot of field peas et clean empty on the stove, and him laying in the back yard asleep in the broad sun with just his head under the edge of the porch in the shade and a dog that looked like a cross between a bear and a Polled Angus steer yelling fire and murder from the back door. And we wake him and he sets up and says, 'Awright, white folks. Ah done it. Jest dont lock me up,' and Maydew says, 'Mr Birdsong's kinfolks aint going to lock you up neither. You'll have plenty of fresh air when they get hold of you,' and he says, 'Ah done it. Jest dont lock me up'—advising, instructing the sheriff not to lock him up; he done it all right and it's too bad but it aint convenient for him to be cut off from the fresh air at the moment. So we loaded him into the car, when here come the old woman—his ma or aunt or something—panting up the road at a dog-trot, wanting to come with us too, and Maydew trying to explain to her what would maybe happen to her too if them Birdsong kin catches us before we can get him locked up, only she is coming anyway, and like Maydew says, her being in the car too might be a good thing if the Birdsongs did happen to run into us, because after all interference with the law cant be condoned even if the Birdsong connection did carry that beat for Maydew last summer.

"So we brought her along too and got him to town and into the jail all right and turned him over to Ketcham and

Ketcham taken him on up stairs and the old woman coming too, right on up to the cell, telling Ketcham, 'Ah tried to raise him right. He was a good boy. He aint never been in no trouble till now. He will suffer for what he done. But dont let the white folks get him,' until Ketcham says, 'You and him ought to thought of that before he started barbering white men without using no lather first.' So he locked them both up in the cell because he felt like Maydew did, that her being in there with him might be a good influence on the Birdsong boys if anything started if he should happen to be running for sheriff or something when Maydew's term was up. So Ketcham come on back down stairs and pretty soon the chain gang come in and went on up to the bull pen and he thought things had settled down for a while when all of a sudden he begun to hear the yelling, not howling: yelling, though there wasn't no words in it, and he grabbed his pistol and run back up stairs to the bull pen where the chain gang was and Ketcham could see into the cell where the old woman was kind of squinched down in one corner and where that nigger had done tore that iron cot clean out of the floor it was bolted to and was standing in the middle of the cell, holding the cot over his head like it was a baby's cradle, yelling, and says to the old woman, 'Ah aint goan hurt you,' and throws the cot against the wall and comes and grabs holt of that steel barred door and rips it out of the wall, bricks hinges and all, and walks out of the cell toting the door over his head like it was a gauze window-screen, hollering, 'It's awright. It's awright. Ah aint trying to git away.'

"Of course Ketcham could have shot him right there, but like he said, if it wasn't going to be the law, then them Birdsong boys ought to have the first lick at him. So Ketcham dont shoot. Instead, he jumps in behind where them chain gang niggers was kind of backed off from that steel door, hollering, 'Grab him! Throw him down!' except the niggers hung back at first too until Ketcham gets in where he can kick the ones he can reach, batting at the others with the flat of the pistol until they rush him. And Ketcham says that for a full minute that nigger would grab them as they come in and fling them clean across the room like they was rag dolls, saying, 'Ah aint tryin to git out. Ah aint tryin to git out,' until at last they pulled him down—a big mass of nigger heads and arms and legs boiling around on the floor and even then Ketcham says every now and then a nigger would come flying out and go sailing through the air across the room, spraddled out like a flying squirrel and with his eyes sticking out like car headlights, until at last they had him down and Ketcham went in and began peeling away niggers until he could see him laying there under the pile of them, laughing, with tears big as glass marbles running across his face and down past his ears and making a kind of popping sound on the floor like somebody dropping bird eggs, laughing and laughing and saying, 'Hit look lack Ah just cant quit thinking. Look lack Ah just cant quit.' And what do you think of that?"

"I think if you eat any supper in this house you'll do it in the next five minutes," his wife said from the dining room. "I'm going to clear this table then and I'm going to the picture show."

THE SKY IS GRAY
by *Ernest Gaines*

❀

1

Go'n be coming in a few minutes. Coming round that bend down there full speed. And I'm go'n get out my handkerchief and wave it down, and we go'n get on it and go.

I keep on looking for it, but Mama don't look that way no more. She's looking down the road where we just come from. It's a long old road, and far 's you can see you don't see nothing but gravel. You got dry weeds on both sides, and you got trees on both sides, and fences on both sides, too. And you got cows in the pastures and they standing close together. And when we was coming out here to catch the bus I seen the smoke coming out of the cows's noses.

I look at my mama and I know what she's thinking. I been with Mama so much, just me and her, I know what she's thinking all the time. Right now it's home—Auntie and them. She's thinking if they got enough wood—if she left enough there to keep them warm till we get back. She's thinking if it go'n rain and if any of them go'n have to go out in the rain. She's thinking 'bout the hog—if he go'n get out, and if Ty and Val be able to get him back in. She always worry like that when she leaves the house. She don't worry too much if she leave me there with the smaller ones, 'cause she know I'm go'n look after them and look after Auntie and everything else. I'm the oldest and she say I'm the man.

I look at my mama and I love my mama. She's wearing that black coat and that black hat and she's looking sad. I love my mama and I want put my arm round her and tell her. But I'm not supposed to do that. She say that's weakness and that's crybaby stuff, and she don't want no crybaby round her. She don't want you to be scared, either. 'Cause Ty's scared of ghosts and she's always whipping him. I'm scared of the dark, too, but I make 'tend I ain't. I make 'tend I ain't 'cause I'm the oldest, and I got to set a good sample for the rest. I can't ever be scared and I can't ever cry. And that's why I never said nothing 'bout my teeth. It's been hurting me and hurting me close to a month now, but I never said it. I didn't say it 'cause I didn't want act like a crybaby, and 'cause I know we didn't have enough money to go have it pulled. But, Lord, it been hurting me. And look like it wouldn't start till at night when you was trying to get yourself little sleep. Then soon 's you shut your eyes—ummm-ummm, Lord, look like it go right down to your heartstring.

"Hurting, hanh?" Ty'd say.

I'd shake my head, but I wouldn't open my mouth for nothing. You open your mouth and let that wind in, and it almost kill you.

I'd just lay there and listen to them snore. Ty there, right 'side me, and Auntie and Val over by the fireplace. Val younger than me and Ty, and he sleeps with Auntie. Mama sleeps round the other side with Louis and Walker.

I'd just lay there and listen to them, and listen to that wind out there, and listen to that fire in the fireplace. Sometimes it'd stop long enough to let me get little rest. Sometimes it just hurt, hurt, hurt. Lord, have mercy.

2

Auntie knowed it was hurting me. I didn't tell nobody but Ty, 'cause we buddies and he ain't go'n tell nobody. But some kind of way Auntie found out. When she asked me, I told her no, nothing was wrong. But she knowed it all the time. She told me to mash up a piece of aspirin and wrap it in some cotton and jugg it down in that hole. I did it, but it didn't do no good. It stopped for a little while, and started right back again. Auntie wanted to tell Mama, but I told her, "Uh-uh." 'Cause I knowed we didn't have any money, and it just was go'n make her mad again. So Auntie told Monsieur Bayonne, and Monsieur Bayonne came over to the house and told me to kneel down 'side him on the fireplace. He put his finger in his mouth and made the Sign of the Cross on my jaw. The tip of Monsieur Bayonne's finger is some hard, 'cause he's always playing on that guitar. If we sit outside at night we can always hear Monsieur Bayonne playing on his guitar. Sometimes we leave him out there playing on the guitar.

Monsieur Bayonne made the Sign of the Cross over and over on my jaw, but that didn't do no good. Even when he prayed and told me to pray some, too, that tooth still hurt me.

"How you feeling?" he say.

"Same," I say.

He kept on praying and making the Sign of the Cross and I kept on praying, too.

"Still hurting?" he say.

"Yes, sir."

Monsieur Bayonne mashed harder and harder on my jaw. He mashed so hard he almost pushed me over on Ty. But then he stopped.

"What kind of prayers you praying, boy?" he say.

"Baptist," I say.

"Well, I'll be—no wonder that tooth still killing him. I'm going one way and he pulling the other. Boy, don't you know any Catholic prayers?"

"I know 'Hail Mary,' " I say.

"Then you better start saying it."

"Yes, sir."

He started mashing on my jaw again, and I could hear him praying at the same time. And, sure enough, after while it stopped hurting me.

Me and Ty went outside where Monsieur Bayonne's two hounds was and we started playing with them. "Let's go hunting," Ty say. "All right," I say; and we went on back in the pasture. Soon the hounds got on a trail, and me and Ty followed them all 'cross the pasture and then back in the woods, too. And then they cornered this little old rabbit and killed him, and me and Ty made them get back, and we picked up the rabbit and started on back home. But my tooth had started hurting me again. It was hurting me plenty now, but I wouldn't tell Monsieur Bayonne. That night I didn't sleep a bit, and first thing in the morning Auntie told me to go back and let Monsieur Bayonne pray over me some more. Monsieur Bayonne was in his kitchen making coffee when I got there. Soon 's he seen me he knowed what was wrong.

"All right, kneel down there 'side that stove," he say. "And this time make sure you pray Catholic. I don't know nothing 'bout that Baptist, and I don't want know nothing 'bout him."

3

Last night Mama say, "Tomorrow we going to town."

"It ain't hurting me no more," I say. "I can eat anything on it."

"Tomorrow we going to town," she say.

And after she finished eating, she got up and went to bed. She always go to bed early now. 'Fore Daddy went in the Army, she used to stay up late. All of us sitting out on the gallery or round the fire. But now, look like soon 's she finish eating she go to bed.

This morning when I woke up, her and Auntie was standing 'fore the fireplace. She say, "Enough to get there and get back. Dollar and a half to have it pulled. Twenty-five for me to go, twenty-five for him. Twenty-five for me to come back, twenty-five for him. Fifty cents left. Guess I get little piece of salt meat with that."

"Sure can use it," Auntie say. "White beans and no salt meat ain't white beans."

"I do the best I can," Mama say.

They was quiet after that, and I made 'tend I was still asleep.

"James, hit the floor," Auntie say.

I still made 'tend I was asleep. I didn't want them to know I was listening.

"All right," Auntie say, shaking me by the shoulder. "Come on. Today's the day."

I pushed the cover down to get out, and Ty grabbed it and pulled it back.

"You, too, Ty," Auntie say.

"I ain't getting no teef pulled," Ty say.

"Don't mean it ain't time to get up," Auntie say. "Hit it, Ty."

Ty got up grumbling.

"James, you hurry up and get in your clothes and eat your food," Auntie say. "What time y'all coming back?" she say to Mama.

"That 'leven o'clock bus," Mama say. "Got to get back in that field this evening."

"Get a move on you, James," Auntie say.

I went in the kitchen and washed my face, then I ate my breakfast. I was having bread and syrup. The bread was warm and hard and tasted good. And I tried to make it last a long time.

Ty came back there grumbling and mad at me.

"Got to get up," he say. "I ain't having no teefes pulled. What I got to be getting up for?"

Ty poured some syrup in his pan and got a piece of bread. He didn't wash his hands, neither his face, and I could see that white stuff in his eyes.

"You the one getting your teef pulled," he say. "What I got to get up for. I bet if I was getting a teef pulled, you wouldn't be getting up. Shucks; syrup again. I'm getting tired of this old syrup. Syrup, syrup, syrup. I'm go'n take with the sugar diabetes. I want me some bacon sometime."

"Go out in the field and work and you can have your bacon," Auntie say. She stood in the middle door looking at Ty. "You better be glad you got syrup. Some people ain't got that—hard 's time is."

"Shucks," Ty say. "How can I be strong."

"I don't know too much 'bout your strength," Auntie say; "but I know where you go'n be hot at, you keep that grumbling up. James, get a move on you; your mama waiting."

I ate my last piece of bread and went in the front room. Mama was standing 'fore the fireplace warming her hands. I put on my coat and my cap, and we left the house.

4

I look down there again, but it still ain't coming. I almost say, "It ain't coming yet," but I keep my mouth shut. 'Cause that's something else she don't like. She don't like for you to say something just for nothing. She can see it ain't coming, I can see it ain't coming, so why say it ain't coming. I don't say it, I turn and look at the river that's back of us. It's so cold the smoke's just raising up from the water. I see a bunch of pool-doos not too far out—just on the other side the lilies. I'm wondering if you can eat pool-doos. I ain't too sure, 'cause I ain't never ate none. But I done ate owls and blackbirds, and I done ate redbirds, too. I didn't want kill the redbirds, but she made me kill them. They had two of them back there. One in my trap, one in Ty's trap. Me and Ty was go'n play with them and let them go, but she made me kill them 'cause we needed the food.

"I can't," I say. "I can't."

"Here," she say. "Take it."

"I can't," I say. "I can't. I can't kill him, Mama, please."

"Here," she say. "Take this fork, James."

"Please, Mama, I can't kill him," I say.

I could tell she was go'n hit me. I jerked back, but I didn't jerk back soon enough.

"Take it," she say.

I took it and reached in for him, but he kept on hopping to the back.

"I can't, Mama," I say. The water just kept on running down my face. "I can't," I say.

"Get him out of there," she say.

I reached in for him and he kept on hopping to the back. Then I reached in farther, and he pecked me on the hand.

"I can't, Mama," I say.

She slapped me again.

I reached in again, but he kept on hopping out my way. Then he hopped to one side and I reached there. The fork got him on the leg and I heard his leg pop. I pulled my hand out 'cause I had hurt him.

"Give it here," she say, and jerked the fork out my hand.

She reached in and got the little bird right in the neck. I heard the fork go in his neck, and I heard it go in the ground. She brought him out and helt him right in front of me.

"That's one," she say. She shook him off and gived me the fork. "Get the other one."

"I can't, Mama," I say. "I'll do anything, but don't make me do that."

She went to the corner of the fence and broke the biggest switch over there she could find. I knelt 'side the trap, crying.

"Get him out of there," she say.

"I can't, Mama."

She started hitting me 'cross the back. I went down on the ground, crying.

"Get him," she say.

"Octavia?" Auntie say.

'Cause she had come out of the house and she was standing by the tree looking at us.

"Get him out of there," Mama say.

"Octavia," Auntie say, "explain to him. Explain to him. Just don't beat him. Explain to him."

But she hit me and hit me and hit me.

I'm still young—I ain't no more than eight; but I know now; I know why I had to do it. (They was so little, though. They was so little. I 'member how I picked the feathers off them and cleaned them and helt them over the fire. Then we all ate them. Ain't had but a little bitty piece each, but we all had a little bitty piece, and everybody just looked at me 'cause they was so proud.) Suppose she had to go away? That's why I had to do it. Suppose she had to go away like Daddy went away? Then who was go'n look after us? They had to be somebody left to carry on. I didn't know it then, but I know it now. Auntie and Monsieur Bayonne talked to me and made me see.

5

Time I see it I get out my handkerchief and start waving. It's still 'way down there, but I keep waving anyhow. Then it come up and stop and me and Mama get on. Mama tell me go sit in the back while she pay. I do like she say, and the people look at me. When I pass the little sign that say "White" and "Colored," I start looking for a seat. I just see one of them back there, but I don't take it, 'cause I want my mama to sit down herself. She comes in the back and sit down, and I lean on the seat. They got seats in the front, but I know I can't sit there, 'cause I have to sit back of the sign. Anyhow, I don't want sit there if my mama go'n sit back here.

They got a lady sitting 'side my mama and she looks at me and smiles little bit. I smile back, but I don't open my mouth, 'cause the wind'll get in and make that tooth ache. The lady take out a pack of gum and reach me a slice, but I shake my head. The lady just can't understand why a little boy'll turn down gum, and she reach me a slice again. This time I point to my jaw. The lady understands and smiles little bit, and I smile little bit, but I don't open my mouth, though.

They got a girl sitting 'cross from me. She got on a red overcoat and her hair's plaited in one big plait. First, I make 'tend I don't see her over there, but then I start looking at her little bit. She make 'tend she don't see me, either, but I catch her looking that way. She got a cold, and every now and then she h'ist that little handkerchief to her nose. She ought to blow it, but she don't. Must think she's too much a lady or something.

Every time she h'ist that little handkerchief, the lady 'side her say something in her ear. She shakes her head and lays her hands in her lap again. Then I catch her kind of looking where I'm at. I smile at her little bit. But think she'll smile back? Uh-uh. She just turn up her little old nose and turn her head. Well, I show her both of us can turn us head. I turn mine too and look out at the river.

The river is gray. The sky is gray. They have pool-doos on the water. The water is wavy, and the pool-doos go up and down. The bus go round a turn, and you got plenty trees hiding the river. Then the bus go round another turn, and I can see the river again.

I look toward the front where all the white people sitting. Then I look at that little old gal again. I don't look right at her, 'cause I don't want all them people to know I love her. I just look at her little bit, like I'm looking out that window over there. But she knows I'm looking that way, and she kind of look at me, too. The lady sitting 'side her catch her this time, and she leans over and says something in her ear.

"I don't love him nothing," that little old gal says out loud.

Everybody back there hear her mouth, and all of them look at us and laugh.

"I don't love you, either," I say. "So you don't have to turn up your nose, Miss."

"You the one looking," she say.

"I wasn't looking at you," I say. "I was looking out that window, there."

"Out that window, my foot," she say. "I seen you. Everytime I turned round you was looking at me."

"You must of been looking yourself if you seen me all them times," I say.

"Shucks," she say, "I got me all kind of boyfriends."

"I got girlfriends, too," I say.

"Well, I just don't want you getting your hopes up," she say.

I don't say no more to that little old gal 'cause I don't want have to bust her in the mouth. I lean on the seat where Mama sitting, and I don't even look that way no more. When we get to Bayonne, she jugg her little old tongue out at me. I make 'tend I'm go'n hit her, and she duck down 'side her mama. And all the people laugh at us again.

6

Me and Mama get off and start walking in town. Bayonne is a little bitty town. Baton Rouge is a hundred times bigger than Bayonne. I went to Baton Rouge once—me, Ty, Mama, and Daddy. But that was 'way back yonder, 'fore Daddy went in the Army. I wonder when we go'n see him again. I wonder when. Look like he ain't ever coming back home. . . . Even the pavement all cracked in Bayonne. Got grass shooting right out the sidewalk. Got weeds in the ditch, too; just like they got at home.

It's some cold in Bayonne. Look like it's colder than it is home. The wind blows in my face, and I feel that stuff running down my nose. I sniff. Mama says use that handkerchief. I blow my nose and put it back.

We pass a school and I see them white children playing in the yard. Big old red school, and them children just running and playing. Then we pass a café, and I see a bunch of people in there eating. I wish I was in there 'cause I'm cold. Mama tells me keep my eyes in front where they belong.

We pass stores that's got dummies, and we pass another café, and then we pass a shoe shop, and that bald-head man in there fixing on a shoe. I look at him and I butt into that white lady, and Mama jerks me in front and tells me stay there.

We come up to the courthouse, and I see the flag waving there. This flag ain't like the one we got at school. This one here ain't got but a handful of stars. One at school got a big pile of stars—one for every state. We pass it and we turn and there it is—the dentist office. Me and Mama go in, and they got people sitting everywhere you look. They even got a little boy in there younger than me.

Me and Mama sit on that bench, and a white lady come in there and ask me what my name is. Mama tells her and the white lady goes on back. Then I hear somebody hollering in there. Soon 's that little boy hear him hollering, he starts hollering, too. His mama pats him and pats him, trying to make him hush up, but he ain't thinking 'bout his mama.

The man that was hollering in there comes out holding his jaw. He is a big old man and he's wearing overalls and a jumper.

"Got it, hanh?" another man asks him.

The man shakes his head—don't want open his mouth.

"Man, I thought they was killing you in there," the other man says. "Hollering like a pig under a gate."

The man don't say nothing. He just heads for the door, and the other man follows him.

"John Lee," the white lady says. "John Lee Williams."

The little boy juggs his head down in his mama's lap and holler more now. His mama tells him go with the nurse, but he ain't thinking 'bout his mama. His mama tells him again, but he don't even hear her. His mama picks him up and takes him in there, and even when the white lady shuts the door I can still hear little old John Lee.

"I often wonder why the Lord let a child like that suffer," a lady says to my mama. The lady's sitting right in front of us on another bench. She's got on a white dress and a black sweater. She must be a nurse or something herself, I reckon.

"Not us to question," a man says.

"Sometimes I don't know if we shouldn't," the lady says.

"I know definitely we shouldn't," the man says. The man looks like a preacher. He's big and fat and he's got on a black suit. He's got a gold chain, too.

"Why?" the lady says.

"Why anything?" the preacher says.

"Yes," the lady says. "Why anything?"

"Not us to question," the preacher says.

The lady looks at the preacher a little while and looks at Mama again.

"And look like it's the poor who suffers the most," she says. "I don't understand it."

"Best not to even try," the preacher says. "He works in mysterious ways—wonders to perform."

Right then little John Lee bust out hollering, and everybody turn they head to listen.

"He's not a good dentist," the lady says. "Dr. Robillard is much better. But more expensive. That's why most of the colored people come here. The white people go to Dr. Robillard. Y'all from Bayonne?"

"Down the river," my mama says. And that's all she go'n say, 'cause she don't talk much. But the lady keeps on looking at her, and so she says, "Near Morgan."

"I see," the lady says.

7

"That's the trouble with the black people in this country today," somebody else says. This one here's sitting on the same side me and Mama's sitting, and he is kind of sitting in front of that preacher. He looks like a teacher or somebody that goes to college. He's got on a suit, and he's got a book that he's been reading. "We don't question is exactly our problem," he says. "We should question and question and question—question everything."

The preacher just looks at him a long time. He done put a toothpick or something in his mouth, and he just keeps on turning it and turning it. You can see he don't like that boy with that book.

"Maybe you can explain what you mean," he says.

"I said what I meant," the boy says. "Question everything. Every stripe, every star, every word spoken. Everything."

"It 'pears to me that this young lady and I was talking 'bout God, young man," the preacher says.

"Question Him, too," the boy says.

"Wait," the preacher says. "Wait now."

"You heard me right," the boy says. "His existence as well as everything else. Everything."

The preacher just looks across the room at the boy. You can see he's getting madder and madder. But mad or no mad, the boy ain't thinking 'bout him. He looks at that preacher just 's hard 's the preacher looks at him.

"Is this what they coming to?" the preacher says. "Is this what we educating them for?"

"You're not educating me," the boy says. "I wash dishes at night so that I can go to school in the day. So even the words you spoke need questioning."

The preacher just looks at him and shakes his head.

"When I come in this room and seen you there with your book, I said to myself, 'There's an intelligent man.' How wrong a person can be."

"Show me one reason to believe in the existence of a God," the boy says.

"My heart tells me," the preacher says.

" 'My heart tells me,' " the boy says. " 'My heart tells me.' Sure, 'My heart tells me.' And as long as you listen to what your heart tells you, you will have only what the white man gives you and nothing more. Me, I don't listen to my heart. The purpose of the heart is to pump blood throughout the body, and nothing else."

"Who's your paw, boy?" the preacher says.

"Why?"

"Who is he?"

"He's dead."

"And your mom?"

"She's in Charity Hospital with pneumonia. Half killed herself, working for nothing."

"And 'cause he's dead and she's sick, you mad at the world?"

"I'm not mad at the world. I'm questioning the world. I'm questioning it with cold logic, sir. What do words like Freedom, Liberty, God, White, Colored mean? I want to know. That's why *you* are sending us to school, to read and to ask questions. And because we ask these questions, you call us mad. No, sir, it is not us who are mad."

"You keep saying 'us'?"

" 'Us.' Yes—us. I'm not alone."

The preacher just shakes his head. Then he looks at everybody in the room—everybody. Some of the people look down at the floor, keep from looking at him. I kind of look 'way myself, but soon 's I know he done turn his head, I look that way again.

"I'm sorry for you," he says to the boy.

"Why?" the boy says. "Why not be sorry for yourself? Why are you so much better off than I am? Why aren't you sorry for these other people in here? Why not be sorry for the lady who had to drag her child into the dentist office?

Why not be sorry for the lady sitting on that bench over there? Be sorry for them. Not for me. Some way or the other I'm going to make it."

"No, I'm sorry for you," the preacher says.

"Of course, of course," the boy says, nodding his head. "You're sorry for me because I rock that pillar you're leaning on."

"You can't ever rock the pillar I'm leaning on, young man. It's stronger than anything man can ever do."

"You believe in God because a man told you to believe in God," the boy says. "A white man told you to believe in God. And why? To keep you ignorant so he can keep his feet on your neck."

"So now we the ignorant?" the preacher says.

"Yes," the boy says. "Yes." And he opens his book again.

The preacher just looks at him sitting there. The boy done forgot all about him. Everybody else make 'tend they done forgot the squabble, too.

Then I see that preacher getting up real slow. Preacher's a great big old man and he got to brace himself to get up. He comes over where the boy is sitting. He just stands there a little while looking down at him, but the boy don't raise his head.

"Get up, boy," preacher says.

The boy looks up at him, then he shuts his book real slow and stands up. Preacher just hauls back and hit him in the face. The boy falls back 'gainst the wall, but he straightens himself up and looks right back at that preacher.

"You forgot the other cheek," he says.

The preacher hauls back and hit him again on the other side. But this time the boy braces himself and don't fall.

"That hasn't changed a thing," he says.

The preacher just looks at the boy. The preacher's breathing real hard like he just run up a big hill. The boy sits down and opens his book again.

"I feel sorry for you," the preacher says. "I never felt so sorry for a man before."

The boy makes 'tend he don't even hear that preacher. He keeps on reading his book. The preacher goes back and gets his hat off the chair.

"Excuse me," he says to us. "I'll come back some other time. Y'all, please excuse me."

And he looks at the boy and goes out the room. The boy h'ist his hand up to his mouth one time to wipe 'way some blood. All the rest of the time he keeps on reading. And nobody else in there say a word.

8

Little John Lee and his mama come out the dentist office, and the nurse calls somebody else in. Then little bit later they come out, and the nurse calls another name. But fast 's she calls somebody in there, somebody else comes in the place where we sitting, and the room stays full.

The people coming in now, all of them wearing big coats. One of them says something 'bout sleeting, another one says he hope not. Another one says he think it ain't nothing but rain. 'Cause, he says, rain can get awful cold this time of year.

All round the room they talking. Some of them talking to people right by them, some of them talking to people clear 'cross the room, some of them talking to anybody'll listen. It's a little bitty room, no bigger than us kitchen, and I can see everybody in there. The little old room's full of smoke, 'cause you got two old men smoking pipes over by that side door. I think I feel my tooth thumping me some, and I hold my breath and wait. I wait and wait, but it don't thump me no more. Thank God for that.

I feel like going to sleep, and I lean back 'gainst the wall. But I'm scared to go to sleep. Scared 'cause the nurse might call my name and I won't hear her. And Mama might go to sleep, too, and she'll be mad if neither one of us heard the nurse.

I look up at Mama. I love my mama. I love my mama. And when cotton come I'm go'n get her a new coat. And I ain't go'n get a black one, either. I think I'm go'n get her a red one.

"They got some books over there," I say. "Want read one of them?"

Mama looks at the books, but she don't answer me.

"You got yourself a little man there," the lady says.

Mama don't say nothing to the lady, but she must've smiled, 'cause I seen the lady smiling back. The lady looks at me a little while, like she's feeling sorry for me.

"You sure got that preacher out here in a hurry," she says to that boy.

The boy looks up at her and looks in his book again. When I grow up I want be just like him. I want clothes like that and I want keep a book with me, too.

"You really don't believe in God?" the lady says.

"No," he says.

"But why?" the lady says.

"Because the wind is pink," he says.

"What?" the lady says.

The boy don't answer her no more. He just reads in his book.

"Talking 'bout the wind is pink," that old lady says. She's sitting on the same bench with the boy and she's trying to look in his face. The boy makes 'tend the old lady ain't even there. He just keeps on reading. "Wind is pink," she says again. "Eh, Lord, what children go'n be saying next?"

The lady 'cross from us bust out laughing.

"That's a good one," she says. "The wind is pink. Yes, sir, that's a good one."

"Don't you believe the wind is pink?" the boy says. He keeps his head down in the book.

"Course I believe it, honey," the lady says. "Course I do." She looks at us and winks her eye. "And what color is grass, honey?"

"Grass? Grass is black."

She bust out laughing again. The boy looks at her.

"Don't you believe grass is black?" he says.

The lady quits her laughing and looks at him. Everybody else looking at him, too. The place quiet, quiet.

"Grass is green, honey," the lady says. "It was green yesterday, it's green today, and it's go'n be green tomorrow."

"How do you know it's green?"

"I know because I know."

"You don't know it's green," the boy says. "You believe it's green because someone told you it was green. If someone had told you it was black you'd believe it was black."

"It's green," the lady says. "I know green when I see green."

"Prove it's green," the boy says.

"Sure, now," the lady says. "Don't tell me it's coming to that."

"It's coming to just that," the boy says. "Words mean nothing. One means no more than the other."

"That's what it all coming to?" that old lady says. That old lady got on a turban and she got on two sweaters. She got a green sweater under a black sweater. I can see the green sweater 'cause some of the buttons on the other sweater's missing.

"Yes, ma'am," the boy says. "Words mean nothing. Action is the only thing. Doing. That's the only thing."

"Other words, you want the Lord to come down here and show Hisself to you?" she says.

"Exactly, ma'am," he says.

"You don't mean that, I'm sure?" she says.

"I do, ma'am," he says.

"Done, Jesus," the old lady says, shaking her head.

"I didn't go 'long with that preacher at first," the other lady says; "but now—I don't know. When a person say the grass is black, he's either a lunatic or something's wrong."

"Prove to me that it's green," the boy says.

"It's green because the people say it's green."

"Those same people say we're citizens of these United States," the boy says.

"I think I'm a citizen," the lady says.

"Citizens have certain rights," the boy says. "Name me one right that you have. One right, granted by the Constitution, that you can exercise in Bayonne."

The lady don't answer him. She just looks at him like she don't know what he's talking 'bout. I know I don't.

"Things changing," she says.

"Things are changing because some black men have begun to think with their brains and not their hearts," the boy says.

"You trying to say these people don't believe in God?"

"I'm sure some of them do. Maybe most of them do. But they don't believe that God is going to touch these white people's hearts and change things tomorrow. Things change through action. By no other way."

Everybody sit quiet and look at the boy. Nobody says a thing. Then the lady 'cross the room from me and Mama just shakes her head.

"Let's hope that not all your generation feel the same way you do," she says.

"Think what you please, it doesn't matter," the boy says.

"But it will be men who listen to their heads and not their hearts who will see that your children have a better chance than you had."

"Let's hope they ain't all like you, though," the old lady says. "Done forgot the heart absolutely."

"Yes, ma'am, I hope they aren't all like me," the boy says. "Unfortunately, I was born too late to believe in your God. Let's hope that the ones who come after will have your faith—if not in your God, then in something else, something definitely that they can lean on. I haven't anything. For me, the wind is pink, the grass is black."

9

The nurse comes in the room where we all sitting and waiting and says the doctor won't take no more patients till one o'clock this evening. My mama jumps up off the bench and goes up to the white lady.

"Nurse, I have to go back in the field this evening," she says.

"The doctor is treating his last patient now," the nurse says. "One o'clock this evening."

"Can I at least speak to the doctor?" my mama asks.

"I'm his nurse," the lady says.

"My little boy's sick," my mama says. "Right now his tooth almost killing him."

The nurse looks at me. She's trying to make up her mind if to let me come in. I look at her real pitiful. The tooth ain't hurting me at all, but Mama say it is, so I make 'tend for her sake.

"This evening," the nurse says, and goes on back in the office.

"Don't feel 'jected, honey," the lady says to Mama. "I been round them a long time—they take you when they want to. If you was white, that's something else; but we the wrong color."

Mama don't say nothing to the lady, and me and her go outside and stand 'gainst the wall. It's cold out there. I can feel that wind going through my coat. Some of the other people come out of the room and go up the street. Me and Mama stand there a little while and we start walking. I don't know where we going. When we come to the other street we just stand there.

"You don't have to make water, do you?" Mama says.

"No, ma'am," I say.

We go on up the street. Walking real slow. I can tell Mama don't know where she's going. When we come to a store we stand there and look at the dummies. I look at a little boy wearing a brown overcoat. He's got on brown shoes, too. I look at my old shoes and look at his'n again. You wait till summer, I say.

Me and Mama walk away. We come up to another store and we stop and look at them dummies, too. Then we go on again. We pass a café where the white people in there eating. Mama tells me keep my eyes in front where they belong, but I can't help from seeing them people eat. My stomach starts to growling 'cause I'm hungry. When I see people eating, I get hungry; when I see a coat, I get cold.

A man whistles at my mama when we go by a filling station. She makes 'tend she don't even see him. I look back and I feel like hitting him in the mouth. If I was bigger, I say; if I was bigger, you'd see.

We keep on going. I'm getting colder and colder, but I don't say nothing. I feel that stuff running down my nose and I sniff.

"That rag," Mama says.

I get it out and wipe my nose. I'm getting cold all over now—my face, my hands, my feet, everything. We pass another little café, but this'n for white people, too, and we can't go in there, either. So we just walk. I'm so cold now I'm 'bout ready to say it. If I knowed where we was going I wouldn't be so cold, but I don't know where we going. We go, we go, we go. We walk clean out of Bayonne. Then we cross the street and we come back. Same thing I seen when I got off the bus this morning. Same old trees, same old walk, same old weeds, same old cracked pave—same old everything.

I sniff again.

"That rag," Mama says.

I wipe my nose real fast and jugg that handkerchief back in my pocket 'fore my hand gets too cold. I raise my head and I can see David's hardware store. When we come up to it, we go in. I don't know why, but I'm glad.

It's warm in there. It's so warm in there you don't ever want to leave. I look for the heater, and I see it over by them barrels. Three white men standing round the heater talking in Creole. One of them comes over to see what my mama want.

"Got any axe handles?" she says.

Me, Mama, and the white man start to the back, but Mama stops me when we come up to the heater. She and the white man go on. I hold my hands over the heater and look at them. They go all the way to the back, and I see the white man pointing to the axe handles 'gainst the wall. Mama takes one of them and shakes it like she's trying to figure how much it weighs. Then she rubs her hand over it from one end to the other end. She turns it over and looks at the other side, then she shakes it again, and shakes her head and puts it back. She gets another one and she does it just like she did the first one, then she shakes her head. Then she gets a brown one and do it that, too. But she don't like this one, either. Then she gets another one, but 'fore she shakes it or anything, she looks at me. Look like she's trying to say something to me, but I don't know what it is. All I know is I done got warm now and I'm feeling right smart better. Mama shakes this axe handle just like she did the others, and shakes her head and says something to the white man. The white man just looks at his pile of axe handles, and when Mama pass him to come to the front, the white man just scratch his head and follows her. She tells me come on and we go on out and start walking again.

We walk and walk, and no time at all I'm cold again. Look like I'm colder now 'cause I can still remember how good it was back there. My stomach growls and I suck it in to keep Mama from hearing it. She's walking right 'side me, and it growls so loud you can hear it a mile. But Mama don't say a word.

10

When we come up to the courthouse, I look at the clock. It's got quarter to twelve. Mean we got another hour and a quarter to be out here in the cold. We go and stand 'side a building. Something hits my cap and I look up at the sky. Sleet's falling.

I look at Mama standing there. I want stand close 'side her, but she don't like that. She say that's crybaby stuff. She say you got to stand for yourself, by yourself.

"Let's go back to that office," she says.

We cross the street. When we get to the dentist office I try to open the door, but I can't. I twist and twist, but I can't. Mama pushes me to the side and she twist the knob, but she can't open the door, either. She turns 'way from the door. I look at her, but I don't move and I don't say nothing. I done seen her like this before and I'm scared of her.

"You hungry?" she says. She says it like she's mad at me, like I'm the cause of everything.

"No, ma'am," I say.

"You want eat and walk back, or you rather don't eat and ride?"

"I ain't hungry," I say.

I ain't just hungry, but I'm cold, too. I'm so hungry and cold I want to cry. And look like I'm getting colder and colder. My feet done got numb. I try to work my toes, but I don't even feel them. Look like I'm go'n die. Look like I'm go'n stand right here and freeze to death. I think 'bout home. I think 'bout Val and Auntie and Ty and Louis and Walker. It's 'bout twelve o'clock and I know they eating dinner now. I can hear Ty making jokes. He done forgot 'bout getting up early this morning and right now he's probably making jokes. Always trying to make somebody laugh. I wish I was right there listening to him. Give anything in the world if I was home round the fire.

"Come on," Mama says.

We start walking again. My feet so numb I can't hardly feel them. We turn the corner and go on back up the street. The clock on the courthouse starts hitting for twelve.

The sleet's coming down plenty now. They hit the pave and bounce like rice. Oh, Lord; oh, Lord, I pray. Don't let me die, don't let me die, don't let me die, Lord.

11

Now I know where we going. We going back of town where the colored people eat. I don't care if I don't eat. I been hungry before. I can stand it. But I can't stand the cold.

I can see we go'n have a long walk. It's 'bout a mile down there. But I don't mind. I know when I get there I'm go'n warm myself. I think I can hold out. My hands numb in my pockets and my feet numb, too, but if I keep moving I can hold out. Just don't stop no more, that's all.

The sky's gray. The sleet keeps on falling. Falling like rain now—plenty, plenty. You can hear it hitting the pave. You can see it bouncing. Sometimes it bounces two times 'fore it settles.

We keep on going. We don't say nothing. We just keep on going, keep on going.

I wonder what Mama's thinking. I hope she ain't mad at me. When summer come I'm go'n pick plenty cotton and get her a coat. I'm go'n get her a red one.

I hope they'd make it summer all the time. I'd be glad if it was summer all the time—but it ain't. We got to have winter, too. Lord, I hate the winter. I guess everybody hate the winter.

I don't sniff this time. I get out my handkerchief and wipe my nose. My hands's so cold I can hardly hold the handkerchief.

I think we getting close, but we ain't there yet. I wonder where everybody is. Can't see a soul but us. Look like we the only two people moving round today. Must be too cold for the rest of the people to move round in.

I can hear my teeth. I hope they don't knock together too hard and make that bad one hurt. Lord, that's all I need, for that bad one to start off.

I hear a church bell somewhere. But today ain't Sunday. They must be ringing for a funeral or something.

I wonder what they doing at home. They must be eating. Monsieur Bayonne might be there with his guitar. One day Ty played with Monsieur Bayonne's guitar and broke one of the strings. Monsieur Bayonne was some mad with Ty. He say Ty wasn't go'n ever 'mount to nothing. Ty can go just like Monsieur Bayonne when he ain't there. Ty can make everybody laugh when he starts to mocking Monsieur Bayonne.

I used to like to be with Mama and Daddy. We used to be happy. But they took him in the Army. Now, nobody happy no more. . . . I be glad when Daddy comes home.

Monsieur Bayonne say it wasn't fair for them to take Daddy and give Mama nothing and give us nothing. Auntie say, "Shhh, Etienne. Don't let them hear you talk like that." Monsieur Bayonne say, "It's God truth. What they giving his children? They have to walk three and a half miles to school hot or cold. That's anything to give for a paw? She's got to work in the field rain or shine just to make ends meet. That's anything to give for a husband?" Auntie say, "Shhh, Etienne, shhh." "Yes, you right," Monsieur Bayonne say. "Best don't say it in front of them now. But one day they go'n find out. One day." "Yes, I suppose so," Auntie say. "Then what, Rose Mary?" Monsieur Bayonne say. "I don't know, Etienne," Auntie say. "All we can do is us job, and leave everything else in His hand . . ."

We getting closer, now. We getting closer. I can even see the railroad tracks.

We cross the tracks, and now I see the café. Just to get in there, I say. Just to get in there. Already I'm starting to feel little better.

12

We go in. Ahh, it's good. I look for the heater; there 'gainst the wall. One of them little brown ones. I just stand there and hold my hands over it. I can't open my hands too wide 'cause they almost froze.

Mama's standing right 'side me. She done unbuttoned her coat. Smoke rises out of the coat, and the coat smells like a wet dog.

I move to the side so Mama can have more room. She opens out her hands and rubs them together. I rub mine together, too, 'cause this keep them from hurting. If you let them warm too fast, they hurt you sure. But if you let them warm just little bit at a time, and you keep rubbing them, they be all right every time.

They got just two more people in the café. A lady back of the counter, and a man on this side the counter. They been watching us ever since we come in.

Mama gets out the handkerchief and count up the money. Both of us know how much money she's got there. Three dollars. No, she ain't got three dollars, 'cause she had to pay us way up here. She ain't got but two dollars and a half left. Dollar and a half to get my tooth pulled, and fifty cents for us to go back on, and fifty cents worth of salt meat.

She stirs the money round with her finger. Most of the money is change 'cause I can hear it rubbing together. She stirs it and stirs it. Then she looks at the door. It's still sleeting. I can hear it hitting 'gainst the wall like rice.

"I ain't hungry, Mama," I say.

"Got to pay them something for they heat," she says.

She takes a quarter out the handkerchief and ties the handkerchief up again. She looks over her shoulder at the people, but she still don't move. I hope she don't spend the money. I don't want her spending it on me. I'm hungry, I'm almost starving I'm so hungry, but I don't want her spending the money on me.

She flips the quarter over like she's thinking. She's must be thinking 'bout us walking back home. Lord, I sure don't want walk home. If I thought it'd do any good to say something, I'd say it. But Mama makes up her own mind 'bout things.

She turns 'way from the heater right fast, like she better hurry up and spend the quarter 'fore she change her mind. I watch her go toward the counter. The man and the lady look at her, too. She tells the lady something and the lady walks away. The man keeps on looking at her. Her back's turned to the man, and she don't even know he's standing there.

The lady puts some cakes and a glass of milk on the counter. Then she pours up a cup of coffee and sets it 'side the other stuff. Mama pays her for the things and comes on back where I'm standing. She tells me sit down at the table 'gainst the wall.

The milk and the cakes's for me; the coffee's for Mama. I eat slow and I look at her. She's looking outside at the sleet. She's looking real sad. I say to myself, I'm go'n make all this up one day. You see, one day, I'm go'n make all this up. I want say it now; I want tell her how I feel right now; but Mama don't like for us to talk like that.

"I can't eat all this," I say.

They ain't got but just three little old cakes there. I'm so hungry right now, the Lord knows I can eat a hundred times three, but I want my mama to have one.

Mama don't even look my way. She knows I'm hungry, she knows I want it. I let it stay there a little while, then I get it and eat it. I eat just on my front teeth, though, 'cause if cake touch that back tooth I know what'll happen. Thank God it ain't hurt me at all today.

After I finish eating I see the man go to the juke box. He

drops a nickel in it, then he just stand there a little while looking at the record. Mama tells me keep my eyes in front where they belong. I turn my head like she say, but then I hear the man coming toward us.

"Dance, pretty?" he says.

Mama gets up to dance with him. But 'fore you know it, she done grabbed the little man in the collar and done heaved him 'side the wall. He hit the wall so hard he stop the juke box from playing.

"Some pimp," the lady back of the counter says. "Some pimp."

The little man jumps up off the floor and starts toward my mama. 'Fore you know it, Mama done sprung open her knife and she's waiting for him.

"Come on," she says. "Come on. I'll gut you from your neighbo to your throat. Come on."

I go up to the little man to hit him, but Mama makes me come and stand 'side her. The little man looks at me and Mama and goes on back to the counter.

"Some pimp," the lady back of the counter says. "Some pimp." She starts laughing and pointing at the little man. "Yes, sir, you a pimp, all right. Yes sir-ree."

13

"Fasten that coat, let's go," Mama says.

"You don't have to leave," the lady says.

Mama don't answer the lady, and we right out in the cold again. I'm warm right now—my hands, my ears, my feet—but I know this ain't go'n last too long. It done sleet so much now you got ice everywhere you look.

We cross the railroad tracks, and soon's we do, I get cold. That wind goes through this little old coat like it ain't even there. I got on a shirt and a sweater under the coat, but that wind don't pay them no mind. I look up and I can see we got a long way to go. I wonder if we go'n make it 'fore I get too cold.

We cross over to walk on the sidewalk. They got just one sidewalk back here, and it's over there.

After we go just a little piece, I smell bread cooking. I look, then I see a baker shop. When we get closer, I can smell it more better. I shut my eyes and make 'tend I'm eating. But I keep them shut too long and I butt up 'gainst a telephone post. Mama grabs me and see if I'm hurt. I ain't bleeding or nothing and she turns me loose.

I can feel I'm getting colder and colder, and I look up to see how far we still got to go. Uptown is 'way up yonder. A half mile more, I reckon. I try to think of something. They say think and you won't get cold. I think of that poem, "Annabel Lee." I ain't been to school in so long—this bad weather—I reckon they done passed "Annabel Lee" by now. But passed it or not, I'm sure Miss Walker go'n make me recite it when I get there. That woman don't never forget nothing. I ain't never seen nobody like that in my life.

I'm still getting cold. "Annabel Lee" or no "Annabel Lee," I'm still getting cold. But I can see we getting closer. We getting there gradually.

Soon 's we turn the corner, I see a little old white lady up in front of us. She's the only lady on the street. She's all in black and she's got a long black rag over her head.

"Stop," she says.

Me and Mama stop and look at her. She must be crazy to be out in all this bad weather. Ain't got but a few other people out there, and all of them's men.

"Y'all done ate?" she says.

"Just finish," Mama says.

"Y'all must be cold then?" she says.

"We headed for the dentist," Mama says. "We'll warm up when we get there."

"What dentist?" the old lady says. "Mr. Bassett?"

"Yes, ma'am," Mama says.

"Come on in," the old lady says. "I'll telephone him and tell him y'all coming."

Me and Mama follow the old lady in the store. It's a little bitty store, and it don't have much in there. The old lady takes off her head rag and folds it up.

"Helena?" somebody calls from the back.

"Yes, Alnest?" the old lady says.

"Did you see them?"

"They're here. Standing beside me."

"Good. Now you can stay inside."

The old lady looks at Mama. Mama's waiting to hear what she brought us in here for. I'm waiting for that, too.

"I saw y'all each time you went by," she says. "I came out to catch you, but you were gone."

"We went back to town," Mama says.

"Did you eat?"

"Yes, ma'am."

The old lady looks at Mama a long time, like she's thinking Mama might be just saying that. Mama looks right back at her. The old lady looks at me to see what I have to say. I don't say nothing. I sure ain't going 'gainst my mama.

"There's food in the kitchen," she says to Mama. "I've been keeping it warm."

Mama turns right around and starts for the door.

"Just a minute," the old lady says. Mama stops. "The boy'll have to work for it. It ain't free."

"We don't take no handout," Mama says.

"I'm not handing out anything," the old lady says. "I need my garbage moved to the front. Ernest has a bad cold and can't go out there."

"James'll move it for you," Mama says.

"Not unless you eat," the old lady says. "I'm old, but I have my pride, too, you know."

Mama can see she ain't go'n beat this old lady down, so she just shakes her head.

"All right," the old lady says. "Come into the kitchen."

She leads the way with that rag in her hand. The kitchen is a little bitty little old thing, too. The table and the stove just 'bout fill it up. They got a little room to the side. Somebody in there laying 'cross the bed—'cause I can see one of his feet. Must be the person she was talking to: Ernest or Alnest—something like that.

"Sit down," the old lady says to Mama. "Not you," she says to me. "You have to move the cans."

"Helena?" the man says in the other room.

"Yes, Alnest?" the old lady says.

"Are you going out there again?"

"I must show the boy where the garbage is, Alnest," the old lady says.

"Keep that shawl over your head," the old man says.

"You don't have to remind me, Alnest. Come, boy," the old lady says.

We go out in the yard. Little old back yard ain't no bigger than the store or the kitchen. But it can sleet here just like it can sleet in any big back yard. And 'fore you know it, I'm trembling.

"There," the old lady says, pointing to the cans. I pick

up one of the cans and set it right back down. The can's so light, I'm go'n see what's inside of it.

"Here," the old lady says. "Leave that can alone."

I look back at her standing there in the door. She's got that black rag wrapped round her shoulders, and she's pointing one of her little old fingers at me.

"Pick it up and carry it to the front," she says. I go by her with the can, and she's looking at me all the time. I'm sure the can's empty. I'm sure she could've carried it herself—maybe both of them at the same time. "Set it on the sidewalk by the door and come back for the other one," she says.

I go and come back, and Mama looks at me when I pass her. I get the other can and take it to the front. It don't feel a bit heavier than that first one. I tell myself I ain't go'n be nobody's fool, and I'm go'n look inside this can to see just what I been hauling. First, I look up the street, then down the street. Nobody coming. Then I look over my shoulder toward the door. That little old lady done slipped up there quiet 's mouse, watching me again. Look like she knowed what I was go'n do.

"Ehh, Lord," she says. "Children, children. Come in here, boy, and go wash your hands."

I follow her in the kitchen. She points toward the bathroom, and I go in there and wash up. Little bitty old bathroom, but it's clean, clean. I don't use any of her towels; I wipe my hands on my pants legs.

When I come back in the kitchen, the old lady done dished up the food. Rice, gravy, meat—and she even got some lettuce and tomato in a saucer. She even got a glass of milk and a piece of cake there, too. It looks so good, I almost start eating 'fore I say my blessing.

"Helena?" the old man says.

"Yes, Alnest?"

"Are they eating?"

"Yes," she says.

"Good," he says. "Now you'll stay inside."

The old lady goes in there where he is and I can hear them talking. I look at Mama. She's eating slow like she's thinking. I wonder what's the matter now. I reckon she's thinking 'bout home.

The old lady comes back in the kitchen.

"I talked to Dr. Bassett's nurse," she says. "Dr. Bassett will take you as soon as you get there."

"Thank you, ma'am," Mama says.

"Perfectly all right," the old lady says. "Which one is it?"

Mama nods toward me. The old lady looks at me real sad. I look sad, too.

"You're not afraid, are you?" she says.

"No, ma'am," I say.

"That's a good boy," the old lady says. "Nothing to be afraid of. Dr. Bassett will not hurt you."

When me and Mama get through eating, we thank the old lady again.

"Helena, are they leaving?" the old man says.

"Yes, Alnest."

"Tell them I say good-bye."

"They can hear you, Alnest."

"Good-bye both mother and son," the old man says. "And may God be with you."

Me and Mama tell the old man good-bye, and we follow the old lady in the front room. Mama opens the door to go out, but she stops and comes back in the store.

"You sell salt meat?" she says.

"Yes."

"Give me two bits worth."

"That isn't very much salt meat," the old lady says.

"That's all I have," Mama says.

The old lady goes back of the counter and cuts a big piece off the chunk. Then she wraps it up and puts it in a paper bag.

"Two bits," she says.

"That looks like awful lot of meat for a quarter," Mama says.

"Two bits," the old lady says. "I've been selling salt meat behind this counter twenty-five years. I think I know what I'm doing."

"You got a scale there," Mama says.

"What?" the old lady says.

"Weigh it," Mama says.

"What?" the old lady says. "Are you telling me how to run my business?"

"Thanks very much for the food," Mama says.

"Just a minute," the old lady says.

"James," Mama says to me. I move toward the door.

"Just one minute, I said," the old lady says.

Me and Mama stop again and look at her. The old lady takes the meat out of the bag and unwraps it and cuts 'bout half of it off. Then she wraps it up again and juggs it back in the bag and gives the bag to Mama. Mama lays the quarter on the counter.

"Your kindness will never be forgotten," she says. "James," she says to me.

We go out, and the old lady comes to the door to look at us. After we go a little piece I look back, and she's still there watching us.

The sleet's coming down heavy, heavy now, and I turn up my coat collar to keep my neck warm. My mama tells me turn it right back down.

"You not a bum," she says. "You a man."

TIME OF BITTER CHILDREN

by *George Garrett*

❀

The truck slowed to a hissing stop on the shoulder of the highway. The driver left the engine running. He pushed back away from the wheel, yawned and stretched, and, seeing that the man next to him in the cab was still sound asleep, hunched up in a small round ball of himself like a sleeping animal, he reached across and touched him lightly on the shoulder to wake him. At his touch the man uncoiled and sat up straight—alert, tense, red-eyed, and suspicious.

"This is far as I go," the driver said. "I'm turning north."

"You just going to dump me out here right in the middle of nowhere?"

"You suit yourself," the driver said. "Stay with me if you want to end up in Knoxville."

"I ain't bound for Knoxville. I'm headed south."

"That's what I thought you said," the driver said, grinning, easy. He was a big man, gentle in the knowledge of his own great strength and power. "You already told me you was going south."

The small man squinted at him, and his sharp rodent's face worked itself into a mask of fine wrinkles, sly and dangerous.

"Why do I have to get out then? It's cold and lonesome up here in the mountains. Ain't nobody else on the road. What are you trying to do to me?"

The very idea made the driver laugh.

"Like I say, you can ride all the way to Knoxville if you want to. Suit yourself."

"You'll be going the wrong direction."

"From here on I will."

"Goddamnit!" the little man said. "Don't that beat all?"

The driver was still more tickled than anything else, but he looked at his watch to see how much time he was wasting. It was past midnight already. He was going to have to put down a heavy foot on the gas as it was.

"Would you just turn a man loose in open country? There's probably wild animals and Lord knows what else up here. You'd just stop your truck and make a fellow get out and shiver in the cold?"

"I didn't tell you to get out yet, but I'm fixing to."

"See there? See what I'm talking about? You don't give a hoot. What happened to all the charity in the world?"

"My charity, such as it is, goes as far as this turnoff. I guess I'm through talking. Time to get off."

The driver shoved a long arm around behind the little man, who had backed himself up against the cab door like a cornered animal. The man twitched and winced away from the arm as if he were dodging a blow, but the driver merely flicked the door handle and pushed it open. Then he had to be quick. The little man, with all his weight against the door, would have pitched out of the high cab if the driver hadn't seized him in a tight grip. For an instant they were locked there in a reluctant embrace.

"I guess somebody will be coming along pretty soon," the driver said.

"Who would stop and give me a ride?"

"What are you complaining about? I give you a ride, didn't I? You're just as bad as an old woman."

The driver shook his head, dismay now added to his natural curiosity. He refused to let himself be moved or troubled by the tears silently falling from the red-rimmed, bloodshot, phlegm-colored eyes, making jagged streaks along his dusty face.

"I see you've made up your mind," he said to the driver at last. "Invincible ignorance, I call it. Well, could you do me one thing?"

"What's that?"

"Lemme have a couple of cigarettes and a pack of matches."

The driver sighed with relief. He hadn't been able to guess what was coming next, and anyway this was going to make it simple and final. He took the half-empty pack from his pocket and fumbled for matches.

"Here," he said. "Keep the pack. I got another one."

The little man took them with his left hand, still keeping the other one out of sight as he had all along, jammed in his pants pockets. No "thank you," nothing. Just took the pack of cigarettes and the matches in his free left hand, slipped sidewise off the seat, and dropped down to the ground. The driver had to reach all the way across and pull the door to. He shifted into low and pulled the big truck off the shoulder and back onto the road, shifted again, made his turn, and drove north.

For a moment he thought about it. Then he laughed out loud to himself.

"It does beat all," he said, "the way some people you run into these days act."

Then, with all that over and done with, he started thinking about the diner up the road, up near Knoxville, where he would treat himself to a great big breakfast. There were a couple of cute little waitresses who worked there, and you could joke with them if you felt like it. Driving a truck on long hauls wasn't such a lonesome job as a man might think.

The small man left behind stood in the middle of the road, stamping his feet in a fierce little dance, partly against the sudden chill of the night after the close warmth of the cab, but equally out of an excess of puzzled frustration. He watched the red taillights of the truck and trailer vanish into the dark, swallowed whole. He spat on the road and cursed the driver and the truck and all of Creation. Clenching his fist, he felt the crackle of the cellophane on the half-empty pack of cigarettes and relaxed, feeling in the privacy of the dark a slow, sly grin forming itself on his lips.

He moved off the road, hopped lightly over a yawning ditch, sat down on the other side, and dangled his legs. Expertly with his left hand he opened the pack of paper matches, folded one match back, struck it and lit a cigarette, staring into the blue heart of the little flame, letting his cupped palm feel the warmth of it until the match was burned almost down to the end. He puffed and blinked and let his eyes become accustomed to the dark again. Gradually the stars grew bright and the bulked shapes of the mountains loomed like huge, crouching beasts around him. He hunched down as small as he could, as if to draw in against the dark and the cold, as if somehow to conserve and protect, like the cupped match flame he had stared at, the invisible heat of his body and soul. He was like a drab little sparrow there. He smoked and chuckled to himself.

"Well," he said, "if worse comes to worse, you could always get yourself a job as a scarecrow."

The picture of himself in a lonely field, arms outstretched, scaring the crows away, tickled him no end.

Then, more sober, shouting into the dark: "You foxed him! You foxed that fool out of half a pack of ready-made cigarettes!"

Lee Southgate was already on the road at that time. He was driving fast because he had some business in eastern Tennessee in the morning, and he wasn't sleeping well in hotels and motels anyway. He had stopped once, east of Ashville, and had an order of bacon and eggs and toast and coffee, even though he hadn't been the least bit hungry. A traveling man just had to stop every so often to get the feel of solid ground under his feet again, the earth he spent so much of his waking time and energy lightly skimming and scorning. Like a dainty-legged water bug swift across the surface of a pond, he thought. Sometimes, for no special need or reason, you had to light somewhere and take a look around.

So he stopped at the roadside diner, knowing the long, winding, lonely drive through the mountains lay in a dark ambush ahead of him. He had eaten, played the jukebox, talked a while with the waitress and shown her the snapshots in his wallet, pictures of his wife, his two young children, his dog, and his new ranch-style house in the Tall Oaks subdivision. It had been a nice time. The waitress was big, plain, and sympathetic, motherly. He always got along easy with big, plain women.

Lee Southgate was a salesman for a sporting-goods firm. He made a good living at it, but his territory in this part of the country had to be large. He was on the road a lot of the time and it was hard on him, wore him down. He was a natural salesman, much the same as some are natural actors; selling came easy to him; but the trips alone, the vague gaps of time between meeting people and performing, for every sale was a performance, troubled him.

Even though he had promised his wife to be careful about picking up hitchhikers, for terrible things happened these days, he usually ended up keeping his eyes peeled for figures by the side of the road. They almost always turned out to be college students or young men going in search of some adventure. He was reminded of himself and his own youth in the drab days of the Depression.

By now it was almost dawn with the sky already gray and lightened. Lee Southgate's headlights leapt to discover and reveal a small shape, like a boy's, standing by the side of the road. Surprised, then relieved, he slowed down and stopped, opened the door.

When the man climbed in, a small man, almost a kind of dwarf, old and dirty, his right hand jammed in his pocket, and without a word, just climbed in, pulled the door to and looked straight ahead waiting to get going, Lee Southgate wished that he had passed by.

He just might have a knife in that pocket, Lee Southgate was thinking. *A crazy, twisted, little old man like that might do most anything.*

He drove on.

"Been waiting long?"

The man twisted to look at him, to look him over, scornful, surprised, and maybe even outraged at being asked a direct question. He did not reply for a while. He waited so long to answer that Lee Southgate wondered if he had really heard him at all.

"Long enough," he said. "I like to have froze down to the bones waiting for you to get here."

"Well, well! Well, then. Let me just turn the heater on and see if we can't take the chill off."

The man grunted at that and looked away again, staring at the dark nothing out of the window. As if to say it would take more than a heater and a few kind, impersonal words to get rid of his chill. Lee Southgate stifled a belch. He was beginning to suffer from indigestion. He almost always did have indigestion after he had eaten without really being hungry and when he was very tired. A man could change all that, lose the slump of sheer fatigue and the growl in his stomach, once he found a motel, took himself a good hot shower, and changed his clothes.

Furtively he sized up his passenger. One thing was for sure, he hadn't been near a bath or a basin of water for quite a while. He had noticed his clothes in the quick, impersonal, complete manner of a salesman when the door opened for him to get in and the overhead light briefly bathed the car in a yellow glow. Now without even looking he could see the separate parts. The shoes, worn, run down flat at the heels, scuffed and paper-thin. The pants dirty, ragged, and stained. Then the strange thing was the jacket, an expensive one, suede, a genuine luxury item. It had looked to be fairly clean too and didn't come close to fitting him. The sleeve almost hid his thumb. Maybe somebody down the road had given it to him. Then again maybe he stole it. If he had a knife in his pocket he might have just taken it off somebody. It would be a big man too.

"Where are you headed, old-timer?"

"South, if it's anybody's business but my own."

"You don't say," Lee Southgate said, for the moment too pleased with the sound of another voice to care what was said.

"And another thing."

"What's that?"

"My name is not old-timer."

"No offense meant," he said, smiling. "My name's Lee Southgate."

"Okay. Pleased to meet you. But just never mind who I am."

"Is it supposed to be a secret?"

"A secret? What do you mean making a crack like that?"

The old man turned again to stare at him with that same leathery crinkled expression of suspicion, curiosity, outrage, and incredulity. A mad look. Small as a boy or a jockey he was all right. Lee Southgate was drawn irresistibly, as to a kind of magnetic appeal, to think about that hidden right hand in its pocket. *Who knows? He might even have some kind of a little zip gun. Or maybe an old-fashioned set of brass knuckles. Most likely a knife though, one with an edge like a straight razor.*

He reached over and punched on the radio. If he wasn't going to be able to share a decent conversation, he could at least listen to something. They could listen together. That would be sharing something. Lee Southgate fiddled with the dial until he picked up, faint and static-clouded, an all-night disc-jockey show. He hummed along with the music and watched the road ahead swimming in the glare of his headlights. He felt better.

After a while he realized that his companion was still staring at him, waiting for something, maybe for the answer to the question he'd asked that Lee Southgate had already forgotten.

Lee Southgate looked at him and flashed an amiable smile.

"It ain't a secret. You'd know it. You'd know it in a minute if I was to tell you."

"Is that a fact?" Lee Southgate began. Then, as if on second thought: "Sure now, I guess I would."

That seemed to satisfy the old man. He nodded solemnly, looked away, and eased back in the seat again. Lee Southgate shrugged and kept his mind on the driving. When the old man decided to speak again, it was so soft, almost a whisper against the noise of the radio, that Lee Southgate wasn't sure whether he had heard him say something or not.

"What's that? Excuse me, did you say something?"

"You could hear fine if it wasn't for that damn noise on the radio."

"Oh, I'm sorry." He twisted a knob on the radio and then the only noise was the slight whisper of the heater and its whirring fan.

"Thibault, I said. Battling Bill Thibault from New Orleans."

"Is that a fact?"

"Battling Bill Thibault, that's who I am."

There was a kind of patronizing smile about the way he said it though his fierce expression did not change.

"You don't say. What's your line of work, Mr. Thibault?"

"My what?"

"Line of work. Occupation."

The old man gasped in simple amazement.

"You don't know? You mean to tell me that you ain't never heard of me? Where the hell have you been?"

"Excuse me," Lee Southgate started to say, "I'm sorry, but—"

"Where were you hiding when I took on Brakeman Shriver in Mobile? Didn't you even hear what I done to Burr Beaver in Houston, Texas? And you know damn well that Beaver, he went on to fight for the Championship of the World. You know they let that Burr Beaver have a shot at the Championship and I had already proved I was twice the man Beaver was."

So that's it! Just a punchy old prizefighter!

"That must have been quite a while ago, Mr. Thibault."

The old man giggled.

"Well, I guess so. I would say so. Likely you weren't even born yet, a young fellow like you."

"I guess that's why I never heard of you."

"That's no excuse. It isn't like I was just nobody. I was famous."

"Sure," Lee Southgate said, irritated. "You may be famous yet for all I know. I don't follow the fight game."

To Lee Southgate's surprise the old man winced away at that. He pressed his face flat against the glass of the rolled-up window.

"What's the use?"

It was a rhetorical question.

"Those were the days," the old man went on. "That was the time. It was the time of tall men. You won't believe it, but even me, a little old bird like me, I was a tall man in those days. It was good to be alive then. Nowadays there's nothing. This here is a bad time, a time of bitter children. There's not one good man among you anymore."

Then Lee Southgate was left with the heater to listen to and the road to watch and the sense that even though he had hurt the old man's feelings—and he was sensitive to other people's feelings and hated, usually, to hurt them—that he had accidentally saved himself from something bad, discomfort, trouble, some kind of real disaster. He could have been more polite with the old bum, feigned an interest anyway, but, obscurely threatened, he had told the truth. Lee Southgate was perplexed, baffled with himself. Why had he been compelled to offend the old man so?

It was early morning now. They had come out of the mountains of North Carolina and were in Tennessee, passing small farms and coming on toward Johnson City. Lee Southgate's appointment was in Chattanooga, but he felt so tired he decided after all that he would stop off in Johnson City at least long enough to get a barbershop shave.

"How far did you say you were going, old-timer?"

"I didn't say. But I'm trying to get as far as Chattanooga."

"I'm stopping off in Johnson City. I'll let you off anywhere you want."

"I want to go to Chattanooga."

Here we go, Lee Southgate thought. *Here we go again.*

"Oh, you'll get a ride easy from here on."

"I'm sick and tired of having to get in and out of cars and trucks and standing by the road and waiting for rides to come along. All I want to do is get where I'm going."

"You ought to take the bus or the train."

The old man certainly brought out the worst in him. Maybe he was just tired out, worn beyond endurance, down to the bone marrow and the raw edges of his nerves. Truly he couldn't wait to get the old man out of the car and out of his sight.

As soon as they were in town, he pulled over and parked. People were already on the way to work, moving with purpose along the sidewalks to shops and offices. The mountains, the lonesome road, and the night seemed far behind. He felt much better.

"All right, Mr. Battling Bill Thibault, this is where you get off. End of the line."

Thibault, or whatever his name was, started to ease himself out of the car without a word.

"Why don't you take the bus from here on?"

No answer, but he stopped moving and waited.

"I'll tell you what," Lee Southgate said. "I'll give you enough money to have breakfast and buy yourself a bus ticket."

"What for? I ain't done nothing for you. What do I have to do for it?"

"Nothing."

"People don't give money for nothing."

Lee Southgate had an inspiration. Why not?

"Okay, I'll tell you what," he said. "I'll give you the money for your knife."

"What knife? I ain't got one. What do I need a knife for?"

"Show me what you're hiding in your right-hand pocket and I'll give you the money."

The old man's rat-face wrinkled with curiosity. Thibault had to think about it.

"You gonna give me some money just to look at my bad hand?"

Delicately he slipped his hand out of his pocket and showed it to the salesman. It was puffed and swollen out of all shape and proportion, red as a cooked lobster and the skin stretched taut, terribly infected. Southgate looked and saw that it seemed to throb with each pulse beat. The old man looked at it too for a moment, but impersonally, as if it were a separate thing, maybe a small sick animal, no part of him.

Lee Southgate, sickened and ashamed, fumbled for a wad

of dollar bills without counting them. The old man snatched them and, without a word, stepped out of the car.

Southgate started the car and drove away in a hurry, not willing to glance back. And so he never saw, would never even imagine, the expression of simple childish pleasure and victory on the old man's face.

REVENGE

by *Ellen Gilchrist*

It was the summer of the Broad Jump Pit.

The Broad Jump Pit, how shall I describe it! It was a bright orange rectangle in the middle of a green pasture. It was three feet deep, filled with river sand and sawdust. A real cinder track led up to it, ending where tall poles for pole-vaulting rose forever in the still Delta air.

I am looking through the old binoculars. I am watching Bunky coming at a run down the cinder path, pausing expertly at the jump-off line, then rising into the air, heels stretched far out in front of him, landing in the sawdust. Before the dust has settled Saint John comes running with the tape, calling out measurements in his high, excitable voice.

Next comes my thirteen-year-old brother, Dudley, coming at a brisk jog down the track, the pole-vaulting pole held lightly in his delicate hands, then vaulting, high into the sky. His skinny tanned legs make a last, desperate surge, and he is clear and over.

Think how it looked from my lonely exile atop the chicken house. I was ten years old, the only girl in a house full of cousins. There were six of us, shipped to the Delta for the summer, dumped on my grandmother right in the middle of a world war.

They built this wonder in answer to a V-Mail letter from my father in Europe. The war was going well, my father wrote, within a year the Allies would triumph over the forces of evil, the world would be at peace, and the Olympic torch would again be brought down from its mountain and carried to Zurich or Amsterdam or London or Mexico City, wherever free men lived and worshiped sports. My father had been a participant in an Olympic event when he was young.

Therefore, the letter continued, Dudley and Bunky and Philip and Saint John and Oliver were to begin training. The United States would need athletes now, not soldiers.

They were to train for broad jumping and pole-vaulting and discus throwing, for fifty-, one-hundred-, and four-hundred-yard dashes, for high and low hurdles. The letter included instructions for building the pit, for making pole-vaulting poles out of cane, and for converting ordinary saw-horses into hurdles. It ended with a page of tips for proper eating and admonished Dudley to take good care of me as I was my father's own dear sweet little girl.

The letter came one afternoon. Early the next morning they began construction. Around noon I wandered out to the pasture to see how they were coming along. I picked up a shovel.

"Put that down, Rhoda," Dudley said. "Don't bother us now. We're working."

"I know it," I said. "I'm going to help."

"No, you're not," Bunky said. "This is the Broad Jump Pit. We're starting our training."

"I'm going to do it too," I said. "I'm going to be in training."

"Get out of here now," Dudley said. "This is only for boys, Rhoda. This isn't a game."

"I'm going to dig if I want to," I said, picking up a shovelful of dirt and throwing it on Philip. On second thought I picked up another shovelful and threw it on Bunky.

"Get out of here, Ratface," Philip yelled at me. "You German spy." He was referring to the initials on my Girl Scout uniform.

"You goddamn niggers," I yelled. "You niggers. I'm digging this if I want to and you can't stop me, you nasty niggers, you Japs, you Jews." I was throwing dirt on everyone now. Dudley grabbed the shovel and wrestled me to the ground. He held my arms down in the coarse grass and peered into my face.

"Rhoda, you're not having anything to do with this Broad Jump Pit. And if you set foot inside this pasture or come around here and touch anything we will break your legs and drown you in the bayou with a crowbar around your neck." He was twisting my leg until it creaked at the joints. "Do you get it, Rhoda? Do you understand me?"

"Let me up," I was screaming, my rage threatening to split open my skull. "Let me up, you goddamn nigger, you Jap, you spy. I'm telling Grannie and you're going to get the worst whipping of your life. And you better quit digging this hole for the horses to fall in. Let me up, let me up. Let me go."

"You've been ruining everything we've thought up all summer," Dudley said, "and you're not setting foot inside this pasture."

In the end they dragged me back to the house, and I ran screaming into the kitchen where Grannie and Calvin, the black man who did the cooking, tried to comfort me, feeding me pound cake and offering to let me help with the mayonnaise.

"You be a sweet girl, Rhoda," my grandmother said, "and this afternoon we'll go over to Eisenglas Plantation to play with Miss Ann Wentzel."

"I don't want to play with Miss Ann Wentzel," I screamed. "I hate Miss Ann Wentzel. She's fat and she calls me a Yankee. She said my socks were ugly."

"Why, Rhoda," my grandmother said. "I'm surprised at you. Miss Ann Wentzel is your own sweet friend. Her momma was your momma's roommate at All Saint's. How can you talk like that?"

"She's a nigger," I screamed. "She's a goddamned nigger German spy."

"Now it's coming. Here comes the temper," Calvin said, rolling his eyes back in their sockets to make me madder. I threw my second fit of the morning, beating my fists into a door frame. My grandmother seized me in soft arms. She led me to a bedroom where I sobbed myself to sleep in a sea of down pillows.

The construction went on for several weeks. As soon as they finished breakfast every morning they started out for the pasture. Wood had to be burned to make cinders, sawdust brought from the sawmill, sand hauled up from the riverbank by wheelbarrow.

When the pit was finished the savage training began. From my several vantage points I watched them. Up and down, up and down they ran, dove, flew, sprinted. Drenched with sweat they wrestled each other to the ground in bitter feuds over distances and times and fractions of inches.

Dudley was their self-appointed leader. He drove them like a demon. They began each morning by running around the edge of the pasture several times, then practicing their hurdles and dashes, then on to discus throwing and calisthenics. Then on to the Broad Jump Pit with its endless challenges.

They even pressed the old mare into service. Saint John was from New Orleans and knew the British ambassador and was thinking of being a polo player. Up and down the pasture he drove the poor old creature, leaning far out of the saddle, swatting a basketball with my grandaddy's cane.

I spied on them from the swing that went out over the bayou, and from the roof of the chicken house, and sometimes from the pasture fence itself, calling out insults or attempts to make them jealous.

"Guess what," I would yell, "I'm going to town to the Chinaman's store." "Guess what, I'm getting to go to the beauty parlor." "Doctor Biggs says you're adopted."

They ignored me. At meals they sat together at one end of the table, making jokes about my temper and my red hair, opening their mouths so I could see their half-chewed food, burping loudly in my direction.

At night they pulled their cots together on the sleeping porch, plotting against me while I slept beneath my grandmother's window, listening to the soft assurance of her snoring.

I began to pray the Japs would win the war, would come marching into Issaquena County and take them prisoners, starving and torturing them, sticking bamboo splinters under their fingernails. I saw myself in the Japanese colonel's office, turning them in, writing their names down, myself being treated like an honored guest, drinking tea from tiny blue cups like the ones the Chinaman had in his store.

They would be outside, tied up with wire. There would be Dudley, begging for mercy. What good to him now his loyal gang, his photographic memory, his trick magnet dogs, his perfect pitch, his camp shorts, his Baby Brownie camera.

I prayed they would get polio, would be consigned forever to iron lungs. I put myself to sleep at night imagining their labored breathing, their five little wheelchairs lined up by the store as I drove by in my father's Packard, my arm around the jacket of his blue uniform, on my way to Hollywood for my screen test.

* * *

Meanwhile, I practiced dancing. My grandmother had a black housekeeper named Baby Doll who was a wonderful dancer. In the mornings I followed her around while she dusted, begging for dancing lessons. She was a big woman, as tall as a man, and gave off a dark rich smell, an unforgettable incense, a combination of Evening in Paris and the sweet perfume of the cabins.

Baby Doll wore bright skirts and on her blouses a pin that said REMEMBER, then a real pearl, then HARBOR. She was engaged to a sailor and was going to California to be rich as soon as the war was over.

I would put a stack of heavy, scratched records on the record player, and Baby Doll and I would dance through the parlors to the music of Glenn Miller or Guy Lombardo or Tommy Dorsey.

Sometimes I stood on a stool in front of the fireplace and made up lyrics while Baby Doll acted them out, moving lightly across the old dark rugs, turning and swooping and shaking and gliding.

Outside the summer sun beat down on the Delta, beating down a million volts a minute, feeding the soybeans and cotton and clover, sucking Steele's Bayou up into the clouds, beating down on the road and the store, on the pecans and elms and magnolias, on the men at work in the fields, on the athletes at work in the pasture.

Inside Baby Doll and I would be dancing. Or Guy Lombardo would be playing "Begin the Beguine" and I would be belting out lyrics.

"Oh, let them begin . . . we don't care,
America all . . . ways does its share,
We'll be there with plenty of ammo,
Allies . . . don't ever despair . . ."

Baby Doll thought I was a genius. If I was having an especially creative morning she would go running out to the kitchen and bring anyone she would find to hear me.

"Oh, let them begin any warrr . . ." I would be singing, tapping one foot against the fireplace tiles, waving my arms around like a conductor.

"Uncle Sam will fight
for the underrr . . . doggg.
Never fear, Allies, never fear."

A new record would drop. Baby Doll would swoop me into her fragrant arms, and we would break into an improvisation on Tommy Dorsey's "Boogie-Woogie."

But the Broad Jump Pit would not go away. It loomed in my dreams. If I walked to the store I had to pass the pasture. If I stood on the porch or looked out my grandmother's window, there it was, shimmering in the sunlight, constantly guarded by one of the Olympians.

Things went from bad to worse between me and Dudley. If we so much as passed each other in the hall a fight began. He would hold up his fists and dance around, trying to look like a fighter. When I came flailing at him he would reach underneath my arms and punch me in the stomach.

I considered poisoning him. There was a box of white powder in the toolshed with a skull and crossbones above the label. Several times I took it down and held it in my hands, shuddering at the power it gave me. Only the thought of the electric chair kept me from using it.

Every day Dudley gathered his troops and headed out for the pasture. Every day my hatred grew and festered. Then, just about the time I could stand it no longer, a diversion occurred.

One afternoon about four o'clock an official-looking sedan clattered across the bridge and came roaring down the road to the house.

It was my cousin, Lauralee Manning, wearing her WAVE uniform and smoking Camels in an ivory holder. Laurelee had been widowed at the beginning of the war when her young husband crashed his Navy training plane into the Pacific.

Lauralee dried her tears, joined the WAVES, and went off to avenge his death. I had not seen this paragon since I was a small child, but I had memorized the photograph Miss Onnie Maud, who was Lauralee's mother, kept on her dresser. It was a photograph of Lauralee leaning against the rail of a destroyer.

Not that Lauralee ever went to sea on a destroyer. She was spending the war in Pensacola, Florida, being secretary to an admiral.

Now, out of a clear blue sky, here was Lauralee, home on leave with a two-carat diamond ring and the news that she was getting married.

"You might have called and given some warning," Miss Onnie Maud said, turning Lauralee into a mass of wrinkles with her embraces. "You could have softened the blow with a letter."

"Who's the groom," my grandmother said. "I only hope he's not a pilot."

"Is he an admiral?" I said, "or a colonel or a major or a commander?"

"My fiancé's not in uniform, Honey," Lauralee said. "He's in real estate. He runs the war-bond effort for the whole state of Florida. Last year he collected half a million dollars."

"In real estate!" Miss Onnie Maud said, gasping. "What religion is he?"

"He's Unitarian," she said. "His name is Donald Marcus. He's best friends with Admiral Semmes, that's how I met him. And he's coming a week from Saturday, and that's all the time we have to get ready for the wedding."

"Unitarian!" Miss Onnie Maud said. "I don't think I've ever met a Unitarian."

"Why isn't he in uniform?" I insisted.

"He has flat feet," Lauralee said gaily. "But you'll love him when you see him."

Later that afternoon Lauralee took me off by myself for a ride in the sedan.

"Your mother is my favorite cousin," she said, touching my face with gentle fingers. "You'll look just like her when you grow up and get your figure."

I moved closer, admiring the brass buttons on her starched uniform and the brisk way she shifted and braked and put in the clutch and accelerated.

We drove down the river road and out to the bootlegger's shack where Lauralee bought a pint of Jack Daniel's and two Cokes. She poured out half of her Coke, filled it with whiskey, and we roared off down the road with the radio playing.

We drove along in the lengthening day. Lauralee was chain-smoking, lighting one Camel after another, tossing the butts out the window, taking sips from her bourbon and Coke. I sat beside her, pretending to smoke a piece of rolled-up paper, making little noises into the mouth of my Coke bottle.

We drove up to a picnic spot on the levee and sat under a tree to look out at the river.

"I miss this old river," she said. "When I'm sad I dream about it licking the tops of the levees."

I didn't know what to say to that. To tell the truth I was afraid to say much of anything to Lauralee. She seemed so splendid. It was enough to be allowed to sit by her on the levee.

"Now, Rhoda," she said, "your mother was matron of honor in my wedding to Buddy, and I want you, her own little daughter, to be maid of honor in my second wedding."

I could hardly believe my ears! While I was trying to think of something to say to this wonderful news I saw that Lauralee was crying, great tears were forming in her blue eyes.

"Under this very tree is where Buddy and I got engaged," she said. Now the tears were really starting to roll, falling all over the front of her uniform. "He gave me my ring right where we're sitting."

"The maid of honor?" I said, patting her on the shoulder, trying to be of some comfort. "You really mean the maid of honor?"

"Now he's gone from the world," she continued, "and I'm marrying a wonderful man, but that doesn't make it any easier. Oh, Rhoda, they never even found his body, never even found his body."

I was patting her on the head now, afraid she would forget her offer in the midst of her sorrow.

"You mean I get to be the real maid of honor?"

"Oh, yes, Rhoda, Honey," she said. "The maid of honor, my only attendant." She blew her nose on a lace-trimmed handkerchief and sat up straighter, taking a drink from the Coke bottle.

"Not only that, but I have decided to let you pick out your own dress. We'll go to Greenville and you can try on every dress at Nell's and Blum's and you can have the one you like the most."

I threw my arms around her, burning with happiness, smelling her whiskey and Camels and the dark Tabu perfume that was her signature. Over her shoulder and through the low branches of the trees the afternoon sun was going down in an orgy of reds and blues and purples and violets, falling from sight, going all the way to China.

Let them keep their nasty Broad Jump Pit I thought. Wait till they hear about this. Wait till they find out I'm maid of honor in a military wedding.

Finding the dress was another matter. Early the next morning Miss Onnie Maud and my grandmother and Lauralee and I set out for Greenville.

As we passed the pasture I hung out the back window making faces at the athletes. This time they only pretended to ignore me. They couldn't ignore this wedding. It was going to be in the parlor instead of the church so they wouldn't even get to be altar boys. They wouldn't get to light a candle.

"I don't know why you care what's going on in that pasture," my grandmother said. "Even if they let you play with them all it would do is make you a lot of ugly muscles."

"Then you'd have big old ugly arms like Weegie Toler," Miss Onnie Maud said. "Lauralee, you remember Weegie Toler, that was a swimmer. Her arms got so big no one would take her to a dance, much less marry her."

"Well, I don't want to get married anyway," I said. "I'm never getting married. I'm going to New York City and be a lawyer."

"Where does she get those ideas?" Miss Onnie Maud said.

"When you get older you'll want to get married," Lauralee said. "Look at how much fun you're having being in my wedding."

"Well, I'm never getting married," I said. "And I'm never having any children. I'm going to New York and be a lawyer and save people from the electric chair."

"It's the movies," Miss Onnie Maud said. "They let her watch anything she likes in Indiana."

We walked into Nell's and Blum's Department Store and took up the largest dressing room. My grandmother and Miss Onnie Maud were seated on brocade chairs and every saleslady in the store came crowding around trying to get in on the wedding.

I refused to even consider the dresses they brought from the "girls' " department.

"I told her she could wear whatever she wanted," Lauralee said, "and I'm keeping my promise."

"Well, she's not wearing green satin or I'm not coming," my grandmother said, indicating the dress I had found on a rack and was clutching against me.

"At least let her try it on," Lauralee said. "Let her see for herself." She zipped me into the green satin. It came down to my ankles and fit around my midsection like a girdle, making my waist seem smaller than my stomach. I admired myself in the mirror. It was almost perfect. I looked exactly like a nightclub singer.

"This one's fine," I said. "This is the one I want."

"It looks marvelous, Rhoda," Lauralee said, "but it's the wrong color for the wedding. Remember I'm wearing blue."

"I believe the child's color-blind," Miss Onnie Maud said. "It runs in her father's family."

"I am not color-blind," I said, reaching behind me and unzipping the dress. "I have twenty-twenty vision."

"Let her try on some more," Lauralee said. "Let her try on everything in the store."

I proceeded to do just that, with the salesladies getting grumpier and grumpier. I tried on a gold gabardine dress with a rhinestone-studded cummerbund. I tried on a pink ballerina-length formal and a lavender voile tea dress and several silk suits. Somehow nothing looked right.

"Maybe we'll have to make her something," my grandmother said.

"But there's no time," Miss Onnie Maud said. "Besides first we'd have to find out what she wants. Rhoda, please tell us what you're looking for."

Their faces all turned to mine, waiting for an answer. But I didn't know the answer.

The dress I wanted was a secret. The dress I wanted was dark and tall and thin as a reed. There was a word for what I wanted, a word I had seen in magazines. But what was that word? I could not remember.

"I want something dark," I said at last. "Something dark and silky."

"Wait right there," the saleslady said. "Wait just a minute." Then, from out of a prewar storage closet she brought a black-watch plaid recital dress with spaghetti straps and a white piqué jacket. It was made of taffeta and rustled when I touched it. There was a label sewn into the collar of the jacket.

Little Miss Sophisticate, it said. *Sophisticate,* that was the word I was seeking.

I put on the dress and stood triumphant in a sea of ladies and dresses and hangers.

"This is the dress," I said. "This is the dress I'm wearing."

"It's perfect," Lauralee said. "Start hemming it up. She'll be the prettiest maid of honor in the whole world."

All the way home I held the box on my lap thinking about how I would look in the dress. Wait till they see me like this, I was thinking. Wait till they see what I really look like.

I fell in love with the groom. The moment I laid eyes on him I forgot he was flat-footed. He arrived bearing gifts of music and perfume and candy, a warm dark-skinned man with eyes the color of walnuts.

He laughed out loud when he saw me, standing on the porch with my hands on my hips.

"This must be Rhoda," he exclaimed, "the famous red-haired maid of honor." He came running up the steps, gave me a slow, exciting hug, and presented me with a whole album of Xavier Cugat records. I had never owned a record of my own, much less an album.

Before the evening was over I put on a red formal I found in a trunk and did a South American dance for him to Xavier Cugat's "Poinciana." He said he had never seen anything like it in his whole life.

The wedding itself was a disappointment. No one came but the immediate family and there was no aisle to march down and the only music was Onnie Maud playing "Liebestraum."

Dudley and Philip and Saint John and Oliver and Bunky were dressed in long pants and white shirts and ties. They had fresh military crew cuts and looked like a nest of new birds, huddled together on the blue velvet sofa, trying to keep their hands to themselves, trying to figure out how to act at a wedding.

The elderly Episcopal priest read out the ceremony in a gravelly smoker's voice, ruining all the good parts by coughing. He was in a bad mood because Lauralee and Mr. Marcus hadn't found time to come to him for marriage instruction.

Still, I got to hold the bride's flowers while he gave her the ring and stood so close to her during the ceremony I could hear her breathing.

* * *

The reception was better. People came from all over the Delta. There were tables with candles set up around the porches and sprays of greenery in every corner. There were gentlemen sweating in linen suits and the record player playing every minute. In the back hall Calvin had set up a real professional bar with tall, permanently frosted glasses and ice and mint and lemons and every kind of whiskey and liqueur in the world.

I stood in the receiving line getting compliments on my dress, then wandered around the rooms eating cake and letting people hug me. After a while I got bored with that and went out to the back hall and began to fix myself a drink at the bar.

I took one of the frosted glasses and began filling it from different bottles, tasting as I went along. I used plenty of crème de menthe and soon had something that tasted heavenly. I filled the glass with crushed ice, added three straws, and went out to sit on the back steps and cool off.

I was feeling wonderful. A full moon was caught like a kite in the pecan trees across the river. I sipped along on my drink. Then, without planning it, I did something I had never dreamed of doing. I left the porch alone at night. Usually I was in terror of the dark. My grandmother had told me that alligators come out of the bayou to eat children who wander alone at night.

I walked out across the yard, the huge moon giving so much light I almost cast a shadow. When I was nearly to the water's edge I turned and looked back toward the house. It shimmered in the moonlight like a jukebox alive in a meadow, seemed to pulsate with music and laughter and people, beautiful and foreign, not a part of me.

I looked out at the water, then down the road to the pasture. The Broad Jump Pit! There it was, perfect and unguarded. Why had I never thought of doing this before?

I began to run toward the road. I ran as fast as my Mary Jane pumps would allow me. I pulled my dress up around my waist and climbed the fence in one motion, dropping lightly down on the other side. I was sweating heavily, alone with the moon and my wonderful courage.

I knew exactly what to do first. I picked up the pole and hoisted it over my head. It felt solid and balanced and alive. I hoisted it up and down a few times as I had seen Dudley do, getting the feel of it.

Then I laid it ceremoniously down on the ground, reached behind me, and unhooked the plaid formal. I left it lying in a heap on the ground. There I stood, in my cotton underpants, ready to take up pole-vaulting.

I lifted the pole and carried it back to the end of the cinder path. I ran slowly down the path, stuck the pole in the wooden cup, and attempted throwing my body into the air, using it as a lever.

Something was wrong. It was more difficult than it appeared from a distance. I tried again. Nothing happened. I sat down with the pole across my legs to think things over.

Then I remembered something I had watched Dudley doing through the binoculars. He measured down from the end of the pole with his fingers spread wide. That was it, I had to hold it closer to the end.

I tried it again. This time the pole lifted me several feet off the ground. My body sailed across the grass in a neat arc and I landed on my toes. I was a natural!

I do not know how long I was out there, running up and down the cinder path, thrusting my body further and further through space, tossing myself into the pit like a mussel shell thrown across the bayou.

At last I decided I was ready for the real test. I had to vault over a cane barrier. I examined the pegs on the wooden poles and chose one that came up to my shoulder.

I put the barrier pole in place, spit over my left shoulder, and marched back to the end of the path. Suck up your guts, I told myself. It's only a pole. It won't get stuck in your stomach and tear out your insides. It won't kill you.

I stood at the end of the path eyeballing the barrier. Then, above the incessant racket of the crickets, I heard my name being called. Rhoda . . . the voices were calling. Rhoda . . . Rhoda . . . Rhoda . . . Rhoda.

I turned toward the house and saw them coming. Mr. Marcus and Dudley and Bunky and Calvin and Lauralee and what looked like half the wedding. They were climbing the fence, calling my name, and coming to get me. Rhoda . . . they called out. Where on earth have you been? What on earth are you doing?

I hoisted the pole up to my shoulders and began to run down the path, running into the light from the moon. I picked up speed, thrust the pole into the cup, and threw myself into the sky, into the still Delta night. I sailed up and was clear and over the barrier.

I let go of the pole and began my fall, which seemed to last a long, long time. It was like falling through clear water. I dropped into the sawdust and lay very still, waiting for them to reach me.

Sometimes I think whatever has happened since has been of no real interest to me.

THE BRILLIANT LEAVES
by *Caroline Gordon*

❀

At three o'clock he came out on the gallery. His mother and his aunt were at the far end, knitting. He had half an hour to kill and he stood, leaning against a post and listening to their talk. They liked to sit there in the afternoons and gossip about all the people who had come to this summer resort in the last thirty years. The Holloways—he was the grandson of a South Carolina bishop and she allowed her children to go barefooted and never attended vesper services; that Mrs. Paty who had had a fit one day in the post office; the mysterious boarder who came every summer to the Robinsons. They knew them all. They were talking now about something that had happened a long time ago. A girl named Sally Mainwaring had climbed down a rope ladder to meet her sweetheart while her father stood at another window, shotgun in hand. When she got to the ground the lover had scuttled off into the bushes, "and so," his aunt concluded dramatically, "she came back into the house through the front door and was an old maid the rest of her life."

"Those Mainwaring girls were all fast," his mother said reflectively.

"Not fast, Jenny, wild."

"High-spirited," his mother conceded. "Come to think of it, Sally Mainwaring was the first woman I ever saw ride astride. I remember. I was about ten years old and she came by the house on a big black horse. I thought about Queen Elizabeth reviewing the troops at Banbury."

"Tilbury, Jenny. You always get things wrong."

"Tilbury or Banbury," his mother said. "It's all one. Kate, do you throw over a stitch here or just keep on purling?"

He had his watch open in his hand and now he snapped it shut and stepped off the gallery onto the ground. His mother looked up quickly. "Aren't you going to play tennis this afternoon, Jimmy?"

"No," he said. "I thought I'd just take a turn in the woods," and he was gone up the path before she could speak again.

The path took him quickly into the woods. The mountain arched up its western brow here and it was all wooded, but the cottage—the cottage to which his family had come every summer since he was born—was on an open slope facing north. When you stood on the gallery and looked out, you had the roofs of all those little white houses spread below you. He halted once imperceptibly and glanced back. They always looked just alike, those houses. He wondered how his mother and his aunt could sit there every afternoon talking about the people who lived in them.

He took his watch out again. "Meet me at half past three," Evelyn had said. It was only ten minutes past now. He didn't want to get there first and just stand waiting. He slowed his pace. This part of the woods he was in now was full of black gums. The ground under his feet was red with the brilliant, fallen leaves. "Spectacular," his aunt called it. He had come here yesterday on a duty walk with her and with his mother. His aunt kept commenting on the colors of the leaves, and every now and then she would make him pick one up for her. "The entrance to the woods is positively spectacular," she told everybody when she got home.

All the time he had been wondering when Evelyn would get there. And then this morning her letter had come. ". . . We're leaving Friday morning. I've got to get up in a minute and start packing. . . ."

He said over to himself the part about the train. "I'm telling you which one it is, but don't come to meet it. Don't even come to the house—first. I'll meet you at our tree. I can be there by half past . . ."

He came to a log and, standing flat-footed, jumped over it. When he landed on the other side he broke into a run, hands held chest high, feet beating the ground in a heavy rhythm, the kind of stride you used in track. He ran four or five hundred yards then stopped, grinning and looking about him as if there might have been somebody there to see.

Another five hundred yards carried him to the tree. Evelyn was already there, walking up and down, her hands in the pockets of her brown sweater. She heard him, turned and came running, so fast that they bumped into each other. She recoiled but he caught her to him and held her awkwardly until he had pressed his mouth on hers. Her lips, parting beneath his, felt firm and cool, not warm and soft as they had been when they kissed good-by in June under this same tree.

His arm was still about her, but she was pulling away to look up into his face. "Dimmy!" she said.

They both laughed because that was what his aunt called him sometimes and it made him mad. Then they drew apart and started walking down the road. Her brown hair was long, now, and done up in a knot, and she had on Girl Scout shoes and bright red socks and she kept scuffling the leaves up as she went. He walked beside her, his hands in his pockets. Now that he didn't have his arms around her he felt awkward. That was because she was silent, like the picture he had at home on his dresser, not laughing and talking or turning her head the way she really did.

She looked up at him, sidewise. "It's different, isn't it?" she said.

His impulse was to stop short but he made himself walk on. He spoke and was surprised to find his voice so deep. "Why is it different, Evelyn?"

Color burned in her smooth cheek. She fixed bright, shy eyes on his. "*Silly!*" she said.

He thought that he must have sounded silly. Still she didn't have any business to say what she had. His face hardened. "Why is it different?" he persisted in the same controlled voice.

She jumped up, high enough to snatch a wine-colored leaf from the bough over her head. "Everything was green, then," she said. "Last time we were here the woods were just turning green."

He remembered the June woods. His face, which some people thought too heavy, lightened. "I know a place where it's still green," he said. "I was there the other day. There's some yellow leaves but it's mostly green. Like summer."

"Come on," she said and caught his extended hand. They raced down the road, scattering the brilliant leaves from under their feet. After a little they came out on the brow of the mountain. There was no red carpet there. What trees could be seen, stunted hackberries mostly, grew in crevices of the rock. They went forward and stood on the great ledge that was called Sunset Point. Below them the valley shimmered in autumn haze. They could see the Murfreesboro road cutting its way through fields of russet sedge, or suddenly white against a patch of winter oats. They watched a black car spin along past the field and disappear into the tunnel of woods that marked the base of the mountain. Suddenly she stretched her arms out and tilted her head back so that she was looking straight into the sky. "The sky's on fire," she cried and laughed out loud like a child.

He touched her arm. "Let's go down there," he said and pointed to the road which wound along the side of the ledge.

They stepped over the drift of dead leaves which choked the entrance and started down. The road slanted steeply along the mountainside. The boughs of the trees met over it in some places. Frail grass grew in the ruts and there were ferns along the edge. What sun got through lay in bright coins on the frail grass and the ferns. The air was cool, not with autumn chill but with the coolness of the deep shade.

The rock they sat down on was tufted with moss. She laid her hand on it, fingers outspread and curving downward. "Look," she said, "every one's like a little pine tree."

"Sometimes they have little flowers on them," he said.

He watched the slim, tanned fingers sink deeper among the little green sprays. "I thought you might not come today," he said. "I heard the train and I thought maybe you didn't come."

"We almost didn't," she said. "Mother got a telegram at the last minute."

"Who from?"

"Aunt Sally Mainwaring. She's always coming to see us."

"Is that the old lady that stays at the Porters'?"

She nodded indifferently. "She's awful crabby."

"I heard mother and my aunt talking about her. They said she climbed out of a window to elope."

She nodded again. "But he was gone when she got down there, so she was an old maid. That's what makes her so crabby."

They both laughed. Off in the woods a bird called, an unbearably sweet note that seemed to belong to summer rather than autumn. She was looking at the road where it disappeared around a great boulder whose base was thick with ferns. "Where does it go?"

"To Cowan. They call it the old Confederate road. My grandfather came along here once."

"What for?"

"I don't know," he answered vaguely. "He said it was a night attack."

She had got up and was moving over to the place where the ferns grew most luxuriantly. She stood and looked down at them. "Just like summer," she said. "It's just like summer in here, isn't it, Jimmy?"

"Yes, it is," he said.

She walked on. He followed her around the corner of the great boulder. "Have you been playing much tennis?" she asked.

"There wasn't anything else to do," he said.

"How's your backhand?"

"Pretty good. There was a new fellow here this summer could beat me two out of three."

"That Jerrold boy from Atlanta?"

"How'd you know about him?"

"Pinky Thomas wrote me."

He was silent. He had not known that she corresponded with Pinky Thomas. "I don't reckon I'll be playing so much tennis from now on," he said at length.

She made no comment. He leaned down and pulled some beggar's lice from his trouser leg. "I don't reckon I'll be up here much next summer. Not more'n two weeks anyhow. You lay off all summer and it shows on you all right. But I don't reckon that makes much difference."

"Why won't you be up here next summer?" she asked in a low voice.

"Dad wants me to go in his office," he said. "I reckon I better start. I suppose—I suppose if you're ever going to make a living you better get started at it."

She did not answer, then suddenly she stepped up on the edge of the rock. He jumped up beside her. "Evelyn," he said, "would you marry me?"

She was looking off through the woods. "They wouldn't let us," she said; "we're too young."

"I know," he said, "but if I go in dad's office. I mean . . . pretty soon I'd get a raise. I mean . . . you would, wouldn't you?"

She turned her head. Their eyes met. Hers were a light, clear brown like the leaves that lie sometimes in the bed of a brook. "I'm perfectly *crazy* about you," she said.

He lifted her in his arms and jumped from the rock. They sank down in the bed of ferns. When he kissed her she kissed him back. She put her arms around his neck and laid her cheek against his, but when he slipped his hand inside the V of her sweater to curve it into the soft hollow under her arm she drew away. "Don't," she said, "please, Jimmy."

"I won't," he said.

She let him kiss her again, then she got to her knees. He sat up straight beside her and caught her hand and held it tight. Her hand fluttered in his then broke away. "It's still in here," she said. "No, it isn't either. I hear running water."

"It's the falls," he said. "Bridal Veil Falls is round the corner of that big ledge."

"I never have seen it," she said.

"It's not very pretty around there," he said.

She was laughing and her eyes had more than ever that look of leaves in a running brook. "I bet it's prettier than it is here," she said.

He stood up, straightened his tie and passed a hand over his hair then stretched a hand out to her. She jumped up beside him lightly. "It's this way," he said and struck off on a path through the ferns. She followed close. Sometimes they could walk side by side. Sometimes when he had to go in front he put his hand back and she held on to it.

He stopped abruptly beside a big sycamore. She was walking fast and ran into him. He embraced her and kissed her, hard. "You're so sweet," he whispered.

She said again, "I'm *crazy* about you," and then she pulled away to look up at him. "Don't you—don't you like doing things together, Jimmy?"

"Some things," he said and they laughed and after that stepped side by side for a while.

They came out of the hollow and were on the brow of the mountain again. In front of them was a series of limestone ledges that came down one after another like steps. Gushing out from one of them, filling the whole air with the sound of its rushing, was the white waterfall they called the Bridal Veil.

She drew her breath in sharply. "I never was here before," she cried.

He led her past one of the great boulders which were all about them. They set their feet on the ledge from which the water sprang.

"Look," he said, "you can see where it comes out." She leaned forward in the curve of his arm. The water came down out of a fissure in the highest ledge. It was pure and colorless at first, but it whitened as it struck the first rock step. She leaned farther forward, still with his arm curving about her. Far below were a few pools of still water, fringed with ferns, but most of the water kept white with its dashing from ledge to ledge. She turned quickly, and he felt the cold drops of moisture as her cheek brushed his. "It is like a bridal veil," she said.

He was eyeing the great shelf that made the first falls. "There's a place in there where you can stand and be dry as a bone," he said.

"Have you been there?"

He nodded. "Bill Thompson and I climbed through once. Long time ago. We must have been about ten years old."

She was still turned away from the water, facing him. Her eyes brightened. "Would you do it again?" she asked.

He hesitated, conscious of his body that seemed now to belong more to the ground than it had eight years ago. "I reckon I could if I had to," he said.

Her fingers closed on his arm. "Let's do it now."

He stared at her. "Are you crazy?" he asked.

She did not answer. Her face was bent down. He could see that her eyes were traveling along the main ledge. "How did you go?" she asked.

He pointed to a round rock that rose in the middle of the shelf. "We climbed up over that and then when you get back in there it's like a little path."

Her fingers were softly opening and closing on his arm. She reached up suddenly and gave his cheek a feather-light touch. "I *like* doing things together," she said.

He was looking at her steadily. The color had risen in his cheeks. Suddenly he bent and began untying her shoelaces. "You'll have to take these off if you're going along there," he said.

She stood on one foot and drew off, one after another, shoes and socks. He took his own shoes off and tied them around his neck, then slung hers around, too. "You're the doctor," he said. "Come on."

They climbed to the top of the round rock. He jumped down, then stood braced while she jumped beside him. They stood there and looked down the great black staircase. She squeezed his arm and then she leaned out a little way over the ledge. "Look how the ferns follow the water all the way down," she said.

"Don't try to see too much," he told her and made her straighten up. They stepped carefully along the ledge over the place that he had said was like a little path. The falls were not three feet away, now. He could feel the cold spray on his cheek, could see the place under the water where you could stand and be dry. "Come on," he said. "One more rock to get around."

The second rock did not jut out as far as the other, but the rock under their feet was wet and a little slippery in places. He thought he would go first and then he decided he could help her better from his side. "Go easy," he said.

She stepped lightly past him. He saw her foot go out and her body swing around the rock and then—he never knew. She might have slipped or she might have got scared, but her foot went down, sickeningly, and she was falling backward from the rock. He clutched at her and touched only the smooth top of her head. Her face was before him, thrown sharply backward, white, with staring eyes—and then he had to lean out to see, lying far below among the ferns—the brown heap.

He got down there—he never could tell them afterward what way he took—but he got down there, slipping, sliding, over the wet rocks. She was lying by one of those little pools on her back, her brown hair tangled in the ferns. He knelt beside her. "Evelyn," he said, "are you hurt? Are you hurt very bad?" Her eyes were open but she did not answer except for a moan. He bent over farther, put his hand on her shoulder. "Could you stand up?" he asked. "Oh, darling, couldn't you just stand up?" The moaning sound went on and now he knew that she did not see him and he started up, his hands swinging at his sides. Then he knelt down again and tried to lift her up. She screamed twice horribly. He laid her back. The screaming had stopped. He could hear the water rushing down onto the rocks. He passed his hand over his trembling lips. "I got to get some help," he said.

He said that but he took another step toward her before he turned away. His hands, still hanging at his sides, danced as though he were controlling invisible marionettes. He stared at the gray mountain ledge. "I reckon this is the way," he said and started upward, stumbling over the wet rocks.

Fifteen minutes later he came up over the top of the ledge onto the western brow. One of his trouser legs was torn off and blood showed through the fluttering rags of his shirt. He stood on the ledge and put his hand up and wiped the sweat from his forehead and shut his eyes for a second. Then he plunged into the underbrush. A few more minutes and he came out onto the woods road. He ran slower now, lurching sometimes from side to side, but he ran on. He ran and the brilliant, the wine-colored leaves crackled and broke under his feet. His mouth, a taut square, drew in, released whining breaths. His staring eyes fixed the ground, but he did not see the leaves that he ran over. He saw only the white houses that no matter how fast he ran kept always just ahead of him. If he did not hurry they would slide off the hill, slide off and leave him running forever through these woods, over these dead leaves.

THE FACES OF BLOOD KINDRED
by *William Goyen*

James came to stay in his cousin's house when his mother was taken to the hospital with arthritis. The boys were both fourteen. James was blond and faintly hare-lipped, and he stuttered. His cousin was brown and shy. They had not much in common beyond their mysterious cousinhood, a bond of nature which they instinctively respected; though James mocked his cousin's habits, complained that he worried too much about things and was afraid of adventure. James owned and loved a flock of bantams, fought the cocks secretly, and his pockets jingled with tin cockspurs. His hands even had pecked places on them from fighting cocks in Mexican towns.

James' father had run away to St. Louis some years ago, and his mother Macel had gone to work as a seamstress in a dress factory in the city of Houston. Macel was blond and gay and good-natured, though the cousin's mother told his father that she had the Ganchion spitfire in her and had run her husband away and now was suffering for it with arthritis. When they went to the hospital to see Aunt Macel, the cousin looked at her hands drawn like pale claws against her breast and her stiffened legs braced down in splints. The cousin, white with commiseration, stood against the wall and gazed at her and saw her being tortured for abusing his uncle and driving him away from home and from his cousin James. James, when taken along by force, would stand at his mother's bedside and stare at her with a look of careless resignation. When she asked him questions he stammered incoherent answers.

James was this mysterious, wandering boy. He loved the woods at the edge of his cousin's neighborhood and would spend whole days there while his aunt called and searched for him by telephone. She would call the grandmother's house, talk to a number of little grandchildren who passed the phone from one to another and finally to the deaf old grandmother who could scarcely understand a word. But James was not there and no one had seen him. Once Fay, one of the young aunts living in the grandmother's house, called at midnight to say they had just discovered James sleeping under the fig trees in the back yard. Jock her husband had almost shot him before he had called out his name. Years later, when the cousin was in high school, he heard talk between his mother and father about Fay's hiding in the very same place while the police looked for her in the house—why, he did not know. At any rate, they had not found her.

He was a wild country boy brought to live in the city of Houston when his parents moved there from a little town down the road south. He said he wanted to be a cowboy, but it was too late for that; still, he wore boots and spurs. He hated the city, the schools, played away almost daily. The cousin admired James, thought him a daring hero. When he listened to his mother and father quarrel over James at night after they had gone to bed, his tenderness for him grew and grew. "He's like all the rest of them," his mother accused his father.

"They are my folks," the cousin's father said with dignity. "Macel is my sister."

"Then let some of the other folks take care of James. Let Fay. I simply cannot handle him."

Poor James, the cousin thought, poor homeless James. He has no friend but me.

One afternoon James suggested they go to see some Cornish fighting cocks on a farm at the edge of the city. The cousin did not tell his mother and they stole away against his conscience. They hitchhiked to the farm out on the highway to Conroe, and there was a rooster-like man sitting barefooted in a little shotgun house. He had rooster feet, thin and with spread-out toes, and feathery hair. His wife was fat and loose and was barefooted, too. She objected to the cousin being there and said, "Chuck, you'll get yourself in trouble." But Chuck asked the cousin to come out to his chicken yard to see his Cornish cocks.

In a pen were the brilliant birds, each in its own coop, some with white scars about their jewel eyes. Stretching out beyond the chicken pen was the flat, rainy marshland of South Texas over which a web of gray mist hung. The sad feeling of after-rain engulfed the cousin and, mixed with the sense of evil because of the fighting cocks and his guilt at having left home secretly, made him feel speechless and afraid. He would not go in the pen but stood outside and watched James and Chuck spar with the cocks and heard Chuck speak of their prowess. Then the cousin heard James ask the price of a big blue cock with stars on its breast. "Fifteen dollars," Chuck said, "and worth a lot more. He fights like a fiend." To the cousin's astonishment he heard James say he would take the blue one, and he saw him take some bills from his pocket and separate fifteen single ones. When they left they heard Chuck and his wife quarreling in the little house.

They went on away to the highway to thumb a ride, and James tucked the blue cock inside his lumberjacket and spoke very quietly to him with his stuttering lips against the cock's blinking and magnificent ruby eye.

"But where will we keep him?" the cousin asked. "We can't at my house."

"I know a place," James said. "This Cornish will make a lot of money."

"But I'm afraid," the cousin said.

"You're always 'f-f-fraid," James said with a tender, mocking smile. And then he whispered something else to the black tip that stuck out from his jacket like a spur of ebony.

A pickup truck stopped for them shortly and took them straight to the Houston Heights where James said they would get out. James said they were going to their grandmother's house.

Their grandmother and grandfather had moved to the city, into a big rotten house, from the railroad town of Palestine, Texas. They had brought a family of seven grown children and the married children's children. In time, the grandfather had vanished and no one seemed to care where. The house was like a big boarding house, people in every room, the grandmother rocking, deaf and humped and shriveled, in the dining room. There was the smell of mustiness all through the house, exactly the way the grandmother smelled. In the back yard were some fig trees dripping with purple figs, and under the trees was a secret place, a damp and musky cove. It was a hideaway known to the children of the house, to the blackbirds after the figs, and to the cats stalking the birds. James told his cousin that this was the place to hide with the Cornish cock. He told the cock that he would have to be quiet for one night and made a chucking sound to him.

The cousins arrived at the grandmother's house with its sagging wooden front porch and its curtainless windows where some of the shades were pulled down. The front door was always open and the screen door sagged half-open. In the dirt front yard, which was damp and where cans and papers were strewn, two of the grandchildren sat quietly together: they were Jack and Little Sister whose mother was divorced and living there with her mother. They seemed special to the cousin because they were Catholics and had that strangeness about them. Their father had insisted that they be brought up in his church, though he had run away and left them in it long ago; and now they seemed to the cousin to have been abandoned in it and could never change back. No one would take them to Mass, and if a priest appeared on the sidewalk, someone in the house would rush out and snatch at the children or gather them away and shout at the priest to mind his own business and go away, as if he were a kidnapper.

"Our mother is sick in bed," Jack said to James and the cousin as they passed him and Little Sister in the yard. Their mother, Beatrice, was a delicate and wild woman who could not find her way with men, and later, when the cousin was in college, she took her life. Not long after, Little Sister was killed in an automobile crash—it was said she was running away to Baton Rouge, Louisiana, to get married to a Catholic gambler. But Jack went on his way somewhere in the world, and the cousin never saw him again. Years later he heard that Jack had gone to a Trappist Monastery away in the North, but no one knew for sure. James grumbled at Jack and Little Sister and whispered, "If-f-f you tell anybody we were here, then a bear will come tonight and e-e-*eat* you up in bed." The two little alien Catholics, alone in a churchless house, looked sadly and silently at James and the cousin. They were constantly together and the cousin thought how they protected each other, asked for nothing in their orphan's world; they were not afraid. "My pore little Cathlicks," the grandmother would sometimes say over them when she saw them sleeping together on the sleeping-porch, as if they were cursed.

James and the cousin went around the house and into the back yard. Now it was almost dark. They crept stealthily, James with the Cornish cock nestled under his lumberjacket. Once it cawed. Then James hushed it by stroking its neck and whispering to it.

Under the fig trees, in the cloying sweetness of the ripe fruit, James uncovered the Cornish cock. He pulled a fig and ate a bite of it, then gave a taste of it to the cock who snapped it fiercely. Before the cousins knew it he had leapt to the ground and, as if he were on springs, bounced up into a fig tree. The Cornish cock began at once to eat the figs. Jim murmured an oath and shook the tree. Figs fat and wet fell upon him and the cousin.

"Stop!" the cousin whispered. "You'll ruin Granny's figs."

"Shut up." James scowled. "You're always 'f-f-fraid."

The cousin picked up a rock from the ground and threw it into the tree. He must have hurled it with great force, greater than he knew he possessed, for in a flash there shuddered at his feet the dark leafy bunch of the Cornish cock. In a moment the feathers were still.

"I didn't mean to, I didn't mean to!" the cousin gasped in horror, and he backed farther and farther away, beyond the deep shadows of the fig trees. Standing away, he saw in the dark luscious grove the figure of James fall to the ground and kneel over his Cornish cock and clasp the tousled mass like a lover's head. He heard him sob softly; and the cousin backed away in anguish.

As he passed the curtainless windows of the dining room where the light was now on, he saw his old grandmother hunched in her chair, one leg folded under her, rocking gently and staring at nothing; and she seemed to him at that moment to be bearing the sorrow of everything—in her house, under the fig trees, in all the world. And then he heard the soft cries of Beatrice from her mysterious room, "Somebody help me, somebody go bring me a drink of water." He went on, past the chaos of the sleeping-porch that had so many beds and cots in it—for Beatrice's two children the little Catholics, for Fay's two, for his grandmother, for his grandfather who would not stay home, for Fay and for Jock the young seaman, her third husband, with tattoos and still wearing his sailor pants. He thought of Jock who cursed before everybody, was restless, would come and go or sprawl on the bed he and Fay slept in on the sleeping-porch with all the rest; and he remembered when he had stayed overnight in this house once how he had heard what he thought was Jock beating Fay in the night, crying out to her and panting, "you f . . ."; how Jock the sailor would lie on the bed in the daytime smoking and reading from a storage of battered *Western Stories* and *Romance Stories* magazines that were strewn under the bed, while Fay worked at the Palais Royale in town selling ladies' ready-to-wear, and the voice of Beatrice suddenly calling overall, "Somebody! Please help me, I am so sick." Once the cousin had gone into her sad room when no one else would and she had pled, startled to see him there, and with a stark gray face scarred by the delicate white cleft of her lip, "Please help your Aunt Bea get a little ease from this headache; reach under the mattress—don't tell anybody—your Aunt Bea has to have some rest from this pain —reach right yonder under the mattress and give her that little bottle. That's it. This is our secret, and you mustn't ever tell a soul." Within five years she was to die, and why should this beautiful Beatrice have to lie in a rest home, alone and none of her family ever coming to see her, until the home sent a message that she was dead? But he thought, hearing of her death, that if he had secretly helped ease her suffering, he had that to know, without ever telling— until he heard them say that she had died from taking too many pills from a hidden bottle.

The cousin walked away from the grandmother's house and went the long way home under the fresh evening sky, his fingers sticky with fig musk, leaving James and the dead cock under the fig trees. If he could one day save all his kindred from pain or help them to some hope! "I will, I will!" he promised. But what were they paying penance for? What was their wrong? Later he knew it bore the ancient name of lust. And as he walked on he saw, like a sparkling stone hurling toward him over the Natural Gas Reservoir, the first star break the heavens—who cast it?—and he wished he might die by it. When he approached the back door of his house, there was the benevolent figure of his mother in the kitchen fixing supper and he wondered how he would be able to tell her and his father where he had been and what had happened to James. "We went to the woods," he cried, "and James ran away." Later that night when James did not come back, his father telephoned the grandmother's house. But no one there had seen him.

The cousin cried himself to sleep that night, lonely and guilty, grieving for much more than he knew, but believing, in that faithful way of children, that in time he might know what it all meant, and that it was a matter of waiting, confused and watchful, until it came clear, as so much of everything promised to, in a long time; and he dreamt of a blue rooster with stars on its breast sitting in a tree of bitter figs, crowing a doom of suffering over the house of his kinfolks.

James stayed away for three days and nights; and on the third night they had a long-distance call from James' father in St. Louis, saying that James had come there dirty and tired and stuttering. They had not seen each other for seven years.

Long later the cousin was in a large Midwestern city where some honor was being shown him. Suddenly in the crowded hall a face emerged from the gathering of strangers and moved toward him. It seemed the image of all his blood kin: was it that shadow-face that tracked and haunted him? It was James' face, and at that glance there glimmered over it some dreamlike umbrageous distortion of those long-ago boy's features, as if the cousin saw that face through a pane of colored glass or through currents of time that had deepened over it as it had sunk into its inheritance.

There was something James had to say, it was on his face; but what it was the cousin never knew, for someone pulled him round, his back to James, to shake his hand and congratulate him—someone of distinction. When he finally turned, heavy as stone, as if he were turning to look back into the face of his own secret sorrow, James was gone; and the cousins never met again.

But the look upon James' face that moment that night in a strange city where the cousin had come to passing recognition and had found a transient homage, bore the haunting question of ancestry; and though he thought he had at last found and cleared for himself something of identity, a particle of answer in the face of the world, had he set anything at peace, answered any speechless question, atoned for the blind failing, the outrage and the pain on the face of his blood kindred? That glance, struck like a blow against ancestral countenance, had left a scar of resemblance, ancient and unchanging through the generations, on the faces of the grandmother, of the aunts, the cousins, his own father, and his father's father; and would mark his own face longer than the stamp of any stranger's honor that would change nothing.

TESTIMONY OF PILOT
by *Barry Hannah*

When I was ten, eleven and twelve, I did a good bit of my play in the backyard of a three-story wooden house my father had bought and rented out, his first venture into real estate. We lived right across the street from it, but over here was the place to do your real play. Here there was a harrowed but overgrown garden, a vine-swallowed fence at the back end, and beyond the fence a cornfield which belonged to someone else. This was not the country. This was the town, Clinton, Mississippi, between Jackson on the east and Vicksburg on the west. On this lot stood a few water oaks, a few plum bushes, and much overgrowth of honeysuckle vine. At the very back end, at the fence, stood three strong nude chinaberry trees.

In Mississippi it is difficult to achieve a vista. But my friends and I had one here at the back corner of the garden. We could see across the cornfield, see the one lone tin-roofed house this side of the railroad tracks, then on across the tracks many other bleaker houses with rustier tin roofs, smoke coming out of the chimneys in the late fall. This was niggertown. We had binoculars and could see the colored children hustling about and perhaps a hopeless sow or two with her brood enclosed in a tiny boarded-up area. Through the binoculars one afternoon in October we watched some men corner and beat a large hog on the brain. They used an ax and the thing kept running around, head leaning toward the ground, for several minutes before it lay down. I thought I saw the men laughing when it finally did. One of them was staggering, plainly drunk to my sight from three hundred yards away. He had the long knife. Because of that scene I considered Negroes savage cowards for a good five more years of my life. Our maid brought some sausage to my mother and when it was put in the pan to fry, I made a point of running out of the house.

I went directly across the street and to the back end of the garden behind the apartment house we owned, without my breakfast. That was Saturday. Eventually, Radcleve saw me. His parents had him mowing the yard that ran alongside my dad's property. He clicked off the power mower and I went over to his fence, which was storm wire. His mother maintained handsome flowery grounds at all costs; she had a leaf-mold bin and St. Augustine grass as solid as a rug.

Radcleve himself was a violent experimental chemist. When Radcleve was eight, he threw a whole package of .22 shells against the sidewalk in front of his house until one of them went off, driving lead fragments into his calf, most of them still deep in there where the surgeons never dared tamper. Radcleve knew about the sulfur, potassium nitrate and charcoal mixture for gunpower when he was ten. He bought things through the mail when he ran out of ingredients in his chemistry sets. When he was an infant, his father, a quiet man who owned the Chevrolet agency in town, bought an entire bankrupt sporting-goods store, and in the middle of their backyard he built a house, plain-painted and neat, one room and a heater, where Radcleve's redundant toys forevermore were kept—all the possible toys he would need for boyhood. There were things in there that Radcleve and I were not mature enough for and did not know the real use of. When we were eleven, we uncrated the new Dunlop golf balls and went on up a shelf for the tennis rackets, went out in the middle of his yard, and served new golf ball after new golf ball with blasts of the rackets over into the cornfield, out of sight. When the strings busted we just went in and got another racket. We were absorbed by how a good smack would set the heavy little pills on an endless flight. Then Radcleve's father came down. He simply dismissed me. He took Radcleve into the house and covered his whole body with a belt. But within the week Radcleve had invented the mortar. It was a steel pipe into which a flashlight battery fit perfectly, like a bullet into a muzzle. He had drilled a hole for the fuse of an M-80 firecracker at the base, for the charge. It was a grand cannon, set up on a stack of bricks at the back of my dad's property, which was the free place to play. When it shot, it would back up violently with thick smoke and you could hear the flashlight battery whistling off. So that morning when I ran out of the house protesting the hog sausage, I told Radcleve to bring over the mortar. His ma and dad were in Jackson for the day, and he came right over with the pipe, the batteries and the M-80 explosives. He had two gross of them.

Before, we'd shot off toward the woods to the right of niggertown. I turned the bricks to the left; I made us a very fine cannon carriage pointing toward niggertown. When Radcleve appeared, he had two pairs of binoculars around his neck, one pair a newly plundered German unit as big as a brace of whiskey bottles. I told him I wanted to shoot for that house where we saw them killing the pig. Radcleve loved the idea. We singled out the house with heavy use of the binoculars.

There were children in the yard. Then they all went in. Two men came out of the back door. I thought I recognized the drunkard from the other afternoon. I helped Radcleve fix the direction of the cannon. We estimated the altitude we needed to get down there. Radcleve put the M-80 in the breech with its fuse standing out of the hole. I dropped the flashlight battery in. I lit the fuse. We backed off. The M-80 blasted off deafeningly, smoke rose, but my concentration was on that particular house over there. I brought the binoculars up. We waited six or seven seconds. I heard a great joyful wallop on tin. "We've hit him on the first try, the first try!" I yelled. Radcleve was ecstatic. "Right on his roof!" We bolstered up the brick carriage. Radcleve remembered the correct height of the cannon exactly. So we fixed it, loaded it, lit it and backed off. The battery landed on the roof, blat, again, louder. I looked to see if there wasn't a great dent or hole in the roof. I could not understand why niggers weren't pouring out distraught from that house. We shot the mortar again and again, and always our battery hit the tin roof. Sometimes there was only a dull thud, but other times there was a wild distress of tin. I was still looking through the binoculars, amazed that the niggers wouldn't even come out of their house to see what was hitting their roof. Radcleve was on to it better than me. I looked over at him and he had the huge German binocs much lower than I did. He was looking straight through the cornfield, which was all bare and open, with nothing left but rotten stalks. "What we've been hitting is the roof of that house just this side of the tracks. White people live in there," he said.

I took up my binoculars again. I looked around the yard of that white wooden house on this side of the tracks, almost next to the railroad. When I found the tin roof, I saw four significant dents in it. I saw one of our batteries lying in the middle of a sort of crater. I took the binoculars down into the yard and saw a blond middle-aged woman looking our way.

"Somebody's coming up toward us. He's from that house and he's got, I think, some sort of fancy gun with him. It might be an automatic weapon."

I ran my binoculars all over the cornfield. Then, in a line with the house, I saw him. He was coming our way but having some trouble with the rows and dead stalks of the cornfield.

"That is just a boy like us. All he's got is a saxophone with him," I told Radcleve. I had recently got in the school band, playing drums, and had seen all the weird horns that made up a band.

I watched this boy with the saxophone through the binoculars until he was ten feet from us. This was Quadberry. His name was Ard, short for Arden. His shoes were foot-square wads of mud from the cornfield. When he saw us across the fence and above him, he stuck out his arm in my direction.

"My dad says stop it!"

"We weren't doing anything," says Radcleve.

"Mother saw the smoke puff up from here. Dad has a hangover."

"A what?"

"It's a headache from indiscretion. You're lucky he does. He's picked up the poker to rap on you, but he can't move further the way his head is."

"What's your name? You're not in the band," I said, focusing on the saxophone.

"It's Ard Quadberry. Why do you keep looking at me through the binoculars?"

It was because he was odd, with his hair and its white

ends, and his Arab nose, and now his name. Add to that the saxophone.

"My dad's a doctor at the college. Mother's a musician. You better quit what you're doing. . . . I was out practicing in the garage. I saw one of those flashlight batteries roll off the roof. Could I see what you shoot 'em with?"

"No," said Radcleve. Then he said: "If you'll play that horn."

Quadberry stood out there ten feet below us in the field, skinny, feet and pants booted with black mud, and at his chest the slung-on, very complex, radiant horn.

Quadberry began sucking and licking the reed. I didn't care much for this act, and there was too much desperate oralness in his face when he began playing. That was why I chose the drums. One had to engage himself like suck's revenge with a horn. But what Quadberry was playing was pleasant and intricate. I was sure it was advanced, and there was no squawking, as from the other eleven-year-olds on sax in the band room. He made the end with a clean upward riff, holding the final note high, pure and unwavering.

"Good!" I called to him.

Quadberry was trying to move out of the sunken row toward us, but his heavy shoes were impeding him.

"Sounded like a duck. Sounded like a girl duck," said Radcleve, who was kneeling down and packing a mudball around one of the M-80s. I saw and I was an accomplice, because I did nothing. Radcleve lit the fuse and heaved the mudball over the fence. An M-80 is a very serious firecracker; it is like the charge they use to shoot up those sprays six hundred feet on July Fourth at country clubs. It went off, this one, even bigger than most M-80s.

When we looked over the fence, we saw Quadberry all muck specks and fragments of stalks. He was covering the mouthpiece of his horn with both hands. Then I saw there was blood pouring out of, it seemed, his right eye. I thought he was bleeding directly out of his eye.

"Quadberry?" I called.

He turned around and never said a word to me until I was eighteen. He walked back holding his eye and staggering through the cornstalks. Radcleve had him in the binoculars. Radcleve was trembling . . . but intrigued.

"His mother just screamed. She's running out in the field to get him."

I thought we'd blinded him, but we hadn't. I thought the Quadberrys would get the police or call my father, but they didn't. The upshot of this is that Quadberry had a permanent white space next to his right eye, a spot that looked like a tiny upset crown.

I went from sixth through half of twelfth grade ignoring him and that wound. I was coming on as a drummer and a lover, but if Quadberry happened to appear within fifty feet of me and my most tender, intimate sweetheart, I would duck out. Quadberry grew up just like the rest of us. His father was still a doctor—professor of history—at the town college; his mother was still blond, and a musician. She was organist at an Episcopalian church in Jackson, the big capital city ten miles east of us.

As for Radcleve, he still had no ear for music, but he was there, my buddy. He was repentant about Quadberry, although not so much as I. He'd thrown the mud grenade over the fence only to see what would happen. He had not really wanted to maim. Quadberry had played his tune on the sax, Radcleve had played his tune on the mud grenade. It was just a shame they happened to cross talents.

Radcleve went into a long period of nearly nothing after he gave up violent explosives. Then he trained himself to copy the comic strips, *Steve Canyon* to *Major Hoople*, until he became quite a versatile cartoonist with some very provocative new faces and bodies that were gesturing intriguingly. He could never fill in the speech balloons with the smart words they needed. Sometimes he would pencil in "Err" or "What?" in the empty speech places. I saw him a great deal. Radcleve was not spooked by Quadberry. He even once asked Quadberry what his opinion was of his future as a cartoonist. Quadberry told Radcleve that if he took all his cartoons and stuffed himself with them, he would make an interesting dead man. After that, Radcleve was shy of him too.

When I was a senior we had an extraordinary band. Word was we had outplayed all the big A.A.A. division bands last April in the state contest. Then came news that a new blazing saxophone player was coming into the band as first chair. This person had spent summers in Vermont in music camps, and he was coming in with us for the concert season. Our director, a lovable aesthete named Richard Prender, announced to us in a proud silent moment that the boy was joining us tomorrow night. The effect was that everybody should push over a seat or two and make room for this boy and his talent. I was annoyed. Here I'd been with the band and had kept hold of the taste among the whole percussion section. I could play rock and jazz drum and didn't even really need to be here. I could be in Vermont too, give me a piano and a bass. I looked at the kid on first sax, who was going to be supplanted tomorrow. For two years he had thought he was the star, then suddenly enters this boy who's three times better.

The new boy was Quadberry. He came in, but he was meek, and when he tuned up he put his head almost on the floor, bending over trying to be inconspicuous. The girls in the band had wanted him to be handsome, but Quadberry refused and kept himself in such hiding among the sax section that he was neither handsome, ugly, cute or anything. What he was was pretty near invisible, except for the bell of his horn, the all-but-closed eyes, the Arabian nose, the brown hair with its halo of white ends, the desperate oralness, the giant reed punched into his face, and hazy Quadberry, loving the wound in a private dignified ecstasy.

I say dignified because of what came out of the end of his horn. He was more than what Prender had told us he would be. Because of Quadberry, we could take the band arrangement of Ravel's *Bolero* with us to the state contest. Quadberry would do the saxophone solo. He would switch to alto sax, he would do the sly Moorish ride. When he played, I heard the sweetness, I heard the horn which finally brought human *talk* into the realm of music. It could sound like the mutterings of a field nigger, and then it could get up into inhumanly careless beauty, it could get among mutinous helium bursts around Saturn. I already loved *Bolero* for the constant drum part. The percussion was always there, driving along with the subtly increasing triplets, insistent, insistent, at last outraged and trying to steal the whole show from the horns and the others. I knew a large boy with dirty blond hair, name of Wyatt, who played viola in the Jackson Symphony and sousaphone in our band

—one of the rare closet transmutations of my time—who was forever claiming to have discovered the central *Bolero* one Sunday afternoon over FM radio as he had seven distinct sexual moments with a certain B., girl flutist with black bangs and skin like mayonnaise, while the drums of Ravel carried them on and on in a ceremony of Spanish sex. It was agreed by all the canny in the band that *Bolero* was exactly the piece to make the band soar—now especially as we had Quadberry, who made his walk into the piece like an actual lean Spanish bandit. This boy could blow his horn. He was, as I had suspected, a genius. His solo was not quite the same as the New York Phil's saxophonist's, but it was better. It came in and was with us. It entered my spine and, I am sure, went up the skirts of the girls. I had almost deafened myself playing drums in the most famous rock and jazz band in the state, but I could hear the voice that went through and out that horn. It sounded like a very troubled forty-year-old man, a man who had had his brow in his hands a long time.

The next time I saw Quadberry up close, in fact the first time I had seen him up close since we were eleven and he was bleeding in the cornfield, was in late February. I had only three classes this last semester, and went up to the band room often, to loaf and complain and keep up my touch on the drums. Prender let me keep my set in one of the instrument rooms, with a tarpaulin thrown over it, and I would drag it out to the practice room and whale away. Sometimes a group of sophomores would come up and I would make them marvel, whaling away as if not only deaf but blind to them, although I wasn't at all. If I saw a sophomore girl with exceptional bod or face, I would do miracles of technique I never knew were in me. I would amaze myself. I would be threatening Buddy Rich and Sam Morello. But this time when I went into the instrument room, there was Quadberry on one side, and, back in a dark corner, a small ninth-grade euphonium player whose face was all red. The little boy was weeping and grinning at the same time.

"Queerberry," the boy said softly.

Quadberry flew upon him like a demon. He grabbed the boy's collar, slapped his face, and yanked his arm behind him in a merciless wrestler's grip, the one that made them bawl on TV. Then the boy broke it and slugged Quadberry in the lips and ran across to my side of the room. He said "Queerberry" softly again and jumped for the door. Quadberry plunged across the room and tackled him on the threshold. Now that the boy was under him, Quadberry pounded the top of his head with his fist made like a mallet. The boy kept calling him "Queerberry" throughout this. He had not learned his lesson. The boy seemed to be going into concussion, so I stepped over and touched Quadberry, telling him to quit. Quadberry obeyed and stood up off the boy, who crawled on out into the band room. But once more the boy looked back with a bruised grin, saying "Queerberry." Quadberry made a move toward him, but I blocked it.

"Why are you beating up on this little guy?" I said. Quadberry was sweating and his eyes were wild with hate; he was a big fellow now, though lean. He was, at six feet tall, bigger than me.

"He kept calling me Queerberry."

"What do you care?" I asked.

"I care," Quadberry said, and left me standing there.

We were to play at Millsaps College Auditorium for the concert. It was April. We got on the buses, a few took their cars, and were a big tense crowd getting over there. To Jackson was only a twenty-minute trip. The director, Prender, followed the bus in his Volkswagen. There was a thick fog. A flashing ambulance, snaking the lanes, piled into him head on. Prender, who I would imagine was thinking of *Bolero* and hearing the young horn voices in his band —perhaps he was dwelling on Quadberry's spectacular gypsy entrance, or perhaps he was meditating on the percussion section, of which I was the king—passed into the airs of band-director heaven. We were told by the student director as we set up on the stage. The student director was a senior from the town college, very much afflicted, almost to the point of drooling, by a love and respect for Dick Prender, and now afflicted by a heartbreaking esteem for his ghost. As were we all.

I loved the tough and tender director awesomely and never knew it until I found myself bawling along with all the rest of the boys of the percussion. I told them to keep setting up, keep tuning, keep screwing the stands together, keep hauling in the kettledrums. To just quit and bawl seemed a betrayal to Prender. I caught some girl clarinetists trying to flee the stage and go have their cry. I told them to get the hell back to their section. They obeyed me. Then I found the student director. I had to have my say.

"Look. I say we just play *Bolero* and junk the rest. That's our horse. We can't play *Brighton Beach* and *Neptune's Daughter*. We'll never make it through them. And they're too happy."

"We aren't going to play anything," he said. "Man, to play is filthy. Did you ever hear Prender play piano? Do you know what a cool man he was in all things?"

"We play. He got us ready, and we play."

"Man, you can't play any more than I can direct. You're bawling your face off. Look out there at the rest of them. Man, it's a herd, it's a weeping herd."

"What's wrong? Why aren't you pulling this crowd together?" This was Quadberry, who had come up urgently. "I got those little brats in my section sitting down, but we've got people abandoning the stage, tearful little finks throwing their horns on the floor."

"I'm not directing," said the mustached college man.

"Then get out of here. You're weak, weak!"

"Man, we've got teen-agers in ruin here, we got sorrowville. Nobody can—"

"Go ahead. Do your number. Weak out on us."

"Man, I—"

Quadberry was already up on the podium, shaking his arms.

"We're right here! The band is right here! Tell your friends to get back in their seats. We're doing *Bolero*. Just put *Bolero* up and start tuning. *I'm* directing. I'll be right here in front of you. You look at *me!* Don't you dare quit on Prender. Don't you dare quit on me. You've got to be heard. *I've* got to be heard. Prender wanted me to be heard. I am the star, and I say we sit down and blow."

And so we did. We all tuned and were burning low for the advent into *Bolero,* though we couldn't believe that Quadberry was going to remain with his saxophone strapped to him and conduct us as well as play his solo. The judges, who apparently hadn't heard about Prender's death, walked down to their balcony desks.

One of them called out "Ready" and Quadberry's hand was instantly up in the air, his fingers hard as if around the stem of something like a torch. This was not Prender's way, but it had to do. We went into the number cleanly and Quadberry one-armed it in the conducting. He kept his face, this look of hostility, at the reeds and the trumpets. I was glad he did not look toward me and the percussion boys like that. But he must have known we would be constant and tasteful because I was the king there. As for the others, the soloists especially, he was scaring them into excellence. Prender had never got quite this from them. Boys became men and girls became women as Quadberry directed us through *Bolero*. I even became a bit better of a man myself, though Quadberry did not look my way. When he turned around toward the people in the auditorium to enter on his solo, I knew it was my baby. I and the drums were the metronome. That was no trouble. It was talent to keep the metronome ticking amidst any given chaos of sound.

But this keeps one's mind occupied and I have no idea what Quadberry sounded like on his sax ride. All I know is that he looked grief-stricken and pale, and small. Sweat had popped out on his forehead. He bent over extremely. He was wearing the red brass-button jacket and black pants, black bow tie at the throat, just like the rest of us. In this outfit he bent over his horn almost out of sight. For a moment, before I caught the glint of his horn through the music stands, I thought he had pitched forward off the stage. He went down so far to do his deep oral thing, his conducting arm had disappeared so quickly, I didn't know but what he was having a seizure.

When *Bolero* was over, the audience stood up and made meat out of their hands applauding. The judges themselves applauded. The band stood up, bawling again, for Prender and because we had done so well. The student director rushed out crying to embrace Quadberry, who eluded him with his dipping shoulders. The crowd was still clapping insanely. I wanted to see Quadberry myself. I waded through the red backs, through the bow ties, over the white bucks. Here was the first-chair clarinetist, who had done his bit like an angel; he sat close to the podium and could hear Quadberry.

"Was Quadberry good?" I asked him.

"Are you kidding? These tears in my eyes, they're for how good he was. He was too good. I'll never touch my clarinet again." The clarinetist slung the pieces of his horn into their case like underwear and a toothbrush.

I found Quadberry fitting the sections of his alto in the velvet holds of his case.

"Hooray," I said. "Hip damn hooray for you."

Arden was smiling too, showing a lot of teeth I had never seen. His smile was sly. He knew he had pulled off a monster unlikelihood.

"Hip hip hooray for me," he said. "Look at her. I had the bell of the horn almost smack in her face."

There was a woman of about thirty sitting in the front row of the auditorium. She wore a sundress with a drastic cleavage up front; looked like something that hung around New Orleans and kneaded your heart to death with her feet. She was still mesmerized by Quadberry. She bore on him with a stare and there was moisture in her cleavage.

"You played well."

"Well? Play well? Yes."

He was trying not to look at her directly. Look at *me*, I beckoned to her with full face: I was the *drums*. She arose and left.

"I was walking downhill in a valley, is all I was doing," said Quadberry. "Another man, a wizard, was playing my horn." He locked his sax case. "I feel nasty for not being able to cry like the rest of them. Look at them. Look at them crying."

True, the children of the band were still weeping, standing around the stage. Several moms and dads had come up among them, and they were misty-eyed too. The mixture of grief and superb music had been unbearable.

A girl in tears appeared next to Quadberry. She was a majorette in football season and played third-chair sax during the concert season. Not even her violent sorrow could take the beauty out of the face of this girl. I had watched her for a number of years—her alertness to her own beauty, the pride of her legs in the majorette outfit—and had taken out her younger sister, a second-rate version of her and a wayward overcompensating nymphomaniac whom several of us made a hobby out of pitying. Well, here was Lilian herself crying in Quadberry's face. She told him that she'd run off the stage when she heard about Prender, dropped her horn and everything, and had thrown herself into a tavern across the street and drunk two beers quickly for some kind of relief. But she had come back through the front doors of the auditorium and sat down, dizzy with beer, and seen Quadberry, the miraculous way he had gone on with *Bolero*. And now she was eaten up by feelings of guilt, weakness, cowardice.

"We didn't miss you," said Quadberry.

"Please forgive me. Tell me to do something to make up for it."

"Don't breathe my way, then. You've got beer all over your breath."

"I want to talk to you."

"Take my horn case and go out, get in my car, and wait for me. It's the ugly Plymouth in front of the school bus."

"I know," she said.

Lilian Field, this lovely teary thing, with the rather pious grace of her carriage, with the voice full of imminent swoon, picked up Quadberry's horn case and her own and walked off the stage.

I told the percussion boys to wrap up the packing. Into my suitcase I put my own gear and also managed to steal drum keys, two pairs of brushes, a twenty-inch Turkish cymbal, a Gretsch snare drum that I desired for my collection, a wood block, kettledrum mallets, a tuning harp and a score sheet of *Bolero* full of marginal notes I'd written down straight from the mouth of Dick Prender, thinking I might want to look at the score sheet sometime in the future when I was having a fit of nostalgia such as I am having right now as I write this. I had never done any serious stealing before, and I was stealing for my art. Prender was dead, the band had done its last thing of the year, I was a senior. Things were finished at the high school. I was just looting a sinking ship. I could hardly lift the suitcase. As I was pushing it across the stage, Quadberry was there again.

"You can ride back with me if you want to."

"But you've got Lilian."

"Please ride back with me . . . us. Please."

"Why?"

"To help me get rid of her. Her breath is full of beer. My father always had that breath. Every time he was friendly, he had that breath. And she looks a great deal like my mother." We were interrupted by the Tupelo band director. He put his baton against Quadberry's arm.

"You were big with *Bolero*, son, but that doesn't mean you own the stage."

Quadberry caught the end of the suitcase and helped me with it out to the steps behind the auditorium. The buses were gone. There sat his ugly ocher Plymouth; it was a failed, gay, experimental shade from the Chrysler people. Lilian was sitting in the front seat wearing her shirt and bow tie, her coat off.

"Are you going to ride back with me?" Quadberry said to me.

"I think I would spoil something. You never saw her when she was a majorette. She's not stupid, either. She likes to show off a little, but she's not stupid. She's in the History Club."

"My father has a doctorate in history. She smells of beer."

I said, "She drank two cans of beer when she heard about Prender."

"There are a lot of other things to do when you hear about death. What I did, for example. She ran away. She fell to pieces."

"She's waiting for us," I said.

"One damned thing I am never going to do is drink."

"I've never seen your mother up close, but Lilian doesn't look like your mother. She doesn't look like anybody's mother."

I rode with them silently to Clinton. Lilian made no bones about being disappointed I was in the car, though she said nothing. I knew it would be like this and I hated it. Other girls in town would not be so unhappy that I was in the car with them. I looked for flaws in Lilian's face and neck and hair, but there weren't any. Couldn't there be a mole, an enlarged pore, too much gum on a tooth, a single awkward hair around the ear? No. Memory, the whole lying opera of it, is killing me now. Lilian was faultless beauty, even sweating, even and especially in the white man's shirt and the bow tie clamping together her collar, when one knew her uncomfortable bosoms, her poor nipples. . . .

"Don't take me back to the band room. Turn off here and let me off at my house," I said to Quadberry. He didn't turn off.

"Don't tell Arden what to do. He can do what he wants to," said Lilian, ignoring me and speaking to me at the same time. I couldn't bear her hatred. I asked Quadberry to please just stop the car and let me out here, wherever he was: this front yard of the mobile home would do. I was so earnest that he stopped the car. He handed back the keys and I dragged my suitcase out of the trunk, then flung the keys back at him and kicked the car to get it going again.

My band came together in the summer. We were the Bop Fiends . . . that was our name. Two of them were from Ole Miss, our bass player was from Memphis State, but when we got together this time, I didn't call the tenor sax, who went to Mississippi Southern, because Quadberry wanted to play with us. During the school year the college boys and I fell into minor groups to pick up twenty dollars on a weekend, playing dances for the Moose Lodge, medical-student fraternities in Jackson, teen-age recreation centers in Greenwood, and such as that. But come summer we were the Bop Fiends again, and the price for us went up to $1,200 a gig. Where they wanted the best rock and bop and they had some bread, we were called. The summer after I was a senior, we played in Alabama, Louisiana and Arkansas. Our fame was getting out there on the interstate route.

This was the summer that I made myself deaf.

Years ago Prender had invited down an old friend from a high school in Michigan. He asked me over to meet the friend, who had been a drummer with Stan Kenton at one time and was now a band director just like Prender. This fellow was almost totally deaf and he warned me very sincerely about deafing myself. He said there would come a point when you had to lean over and concentrate all your hearing on what the band was doing and that was the time to quit for a while, because if you didn't you would be irrevocably deaf like him in a month or two. I listened to him but could not take him seriously. Here was an oldish man who had his problems. My ears had ages of hearing left. Not so. I played the drums so loud the summer after I graduated from high school that I made myself, eventually, stone deaf.

We were at, say, the National Guard Armory in Lake Village, Arkansas, Quadberry out in front of us on the stage they'd built. Down on the floor were hundreds of sweaty teen-agers. Four girls in sundresses, showing what they could, were leaning on the stage with broad ignorant lust on their minds. I'd play so loud for one particular chick, I'd get absolutely out of control. The guitar boys would have to turn the volume up full blast to compensate. Thus I went deaf. Anyhow, the dramatic idea was to release Quadberry on a very soft sweet ballad right in the middle of a long ear-piercing run of rock-and-roll tunes. I'd get out the brushes and we would astonish the crowd with our tenderness. By August, I was so deaf I had to watch Quadberry's fingers changing notes on the saxophone, had to use my eyes to keep time. The other members of the Bop Fiends told me I was hitting out of time. I pretended I was trying to do experimental things with rhythm when the truth was I simply could no longer hear. I was no longer a tasteful drummer, either. I had become deaf through lack of taste.

Which was—taste—exactly the quality that made Quadberry wicked on the saxophone. During the howling, during the churning, Quadberry had taste. The noise did not affect his personality; he was solid as a brick. He could blend. Oh, he could hoot through his horn when the right time came, but he could do supporting roles for an hour. Then, when we brought him out front for his solo on something like "Take Five," he would play with such light blissful technique that he even eclipsed Paul Desmond. The girls around the stage did not cause him to enter into excessive loudness or vibrato.

Quadberry had his own girl friend now, Lilian back at Clinton, who put all the sundressed things around the stage in the shade. In my mind I had congratulated him for getting up next to this beauty, but in June and July, when I was still hearing things a little, he never said a word about her. It was one night in August, when I could hear nothing and was driving him to his house, that he asked me to turn on the inside light and spoke in a retarded deliberate way. He knew I was deaf and counted on my being able to read lips.

"Don't . . . make . . . fun . . . of her . . . or me. . . . We . . . think . . . she . . . is . . . in trouble."

I wagged my head. Never would I make fun of him or her. She detested me because I had taken out her helpless little sister for a few weeks, but I would never think there was anything funny about Lilian, for all her haughtiness. I only thought of this event as monumentally curious.

"No one except you knows," he said.

"Why did you tell me?"

"Because I'm going away and you have to take care of her. I wouldn't trust her with anybody but you."

"She hates the sight of my face. Where are you going?"

"Annapolis."

"You aren't going to any damned Annapolis."

"That was the only school that wanted me."

"You're going to play your saxophone on a boat?"

"I don't know what I'm going to do."

"How . . . how can you just leave her?"

"She wants me to. She's very excited about me at Annapolis. William [this is my name], there is no girl I could imagine who has more inner sweetness than Lilian."

I entered the town college, as did Lilian. She was in the same chemistry class I was. But she was rows away. It was difficult to learn anything, being deaf. The professor wasn't a pantomimer—but finally he went to the blackboard with the formulas and the algebra of problems, to my happiness. I hung in and made a B. At the end of the semester I was swaggering around the grade sheet he'd posted. I happened to see Lilian's grade. She'd only made a C. Beautiful Lilian got only a C while I, with my handicap, had made a B.

It had been a very difficult chemistry class. I had watched Lilian's stomach the whole way through. It was not growing. I wanted to see her look like a watermelon, make herself an amazing mother shape.

When I made the B and Lilian made the C, I got up my courage and finally went by to see her. She answered the door. Her parents weren't home. I'd never wanted this office of watching over her as Quadberry wanted me to, and this is what I told her. She asked me into the house. The rooms smelled of nail polish and pipe smoke. I was hoping her little sister wasn't in the house, and my wish came true. We were alone.

"You can quit watching over me."

"Are you pregnant?"

"No." Then she started crying. "I wanted to be. But I'm not."

"What do you hear from Quadberry?"

She said something, but she had her back to me. She looked to me for an answer, but I had nothing to say. I knew she'd said something, but I hadn't heard it.

"He doesn't play the saxophone anymore," she said.

This made me angry.

"Why not?"

"Too much math and science and navigation. He wants to fly. That's what his dream is now. He wants to get into an F-something jet."

I asked her to say this over and she did. Lilian really was full of inner sweetness, as Quadberry had said. She understood that I was deaf. Perhaps Quadberry had told her.

The rest of the time in her house I simply witnessed her beauty and her mouth moving.

I went through college. To me it is interesting that I kept a B average and did it all deaf, though I know this isn't interesting to people who aren't deaf. I loved music, and never heard it. I loved poetry, and never heard a word that came out of the mouths of the visiting poets who read at the campus. I loved my mother and dad, but never heard a sound they made. One Christmas Eve, Radcleve was back from Ole Miss and threw an M-80 out in the street for old times' sake. I saw it explode, but there was only a pressure in my ears. I was at parties when lusts were raging and I went home with two girls (I am medium handsome) who lived in apartments of the old two-story 1920 vintage, and I took my shirt off and made love to them. But I have no real idea what their reaction was. They were stunned and all smiles when I got up, but I have no idea whether I gave them the last pleasure or not. I hope I did. I've always been partial to women and have always wanted to see them satisfied till their eyes popped out.

Through Lilian I got the word that Quadberry was out of Annapolis and now flying jets off the *Bonhomme Richard,* an aircraft carrier headed for Vietnam. He telegrammed her that he would set down at the Jackson airport at ten o'clock one night. So Lilian and I were out there waiting. It was a familiar place to her. She was a stewardess and her loops were mainly in the South. She wore a beige raincoat, had red sandals on her feet; I was in a black turtleneck and corduroy jacket, feeling significant, so significant I could barely stand it. I'd already made myself the lead writer at Gordon-Marx Advertising in Jackson. I hadn't seen Lilian in a year. Her eyes were strained, no longer the bright blue things they were when she was a pious beauty. We drank coffee together. I loved her. As far as I knew, she'd been faithful to Quadberry.

He came down in an F-something Navy jet right on the dot of ten. She ran out on the airport pavement to meet him. I saw her crawl up the ladder. Quadberry never got out of the plane. I could see him in his blue helmet. Lilian backed down the ladder. Then Quadberry had the cockpit cover him again. He turned the plane around so its flaming red end was at us. He took it down the runway. We saw him leap out into the night at the middle of the runway going west, toward San Diego and the *Bonhomme Richard.* Lilian was crying.

"What did he say?" I asked.

"He said, 'I am a dragon. America the beautiful, like you will never know.' He wanted to give you a message. He was glad you were here."

"What was the message?"

"The same thing. 'I am a dragon. America the beautiful, like you will never know.' "

"Did he say anything else?"

"Not a thing."

"Did he express any love toward you?"

"He wasn't Ard. He was somebody with a sneer in a helmet."

"He's going to war, Lilian."

"I asked him to kiss me and he told me to get off the plane, he was firing up and it was dangerous."

"Arden is going to war. He's just on his way to Vietnam and he wanted us to know that. It wasn't just him he wanted us to see. It was him in the jet he wanted us to see. He *is* that black jet. You can't kiss an airplane."

"And what are we supposed to do?" cried sweet Lilian.

"We've just got to hang around. He didn't have to lift off and disappear straight up like that. That was to tell us how he isn't with us anymore."

Lilian asked me what she was supposed to do now. I told her she was supposed to come with me to my apartment in the old 1920 Clinton place where I was. I was supposed to take care of her. Quadberry had said so. His six-year-old directive was still working.

She slept on the fold-out bed of the sofa for a while. This was the only bed in my place. I stood in the dark in the kitchen and drank a quarter bottle of gin on ice. I would not turn on the light and spoil her sleep. The prospect of Lilian asleep in my apartment made me feel like a chaplain on a visit to the Holy Land; I stood there getting drunk, biting my tongue when dreams of lust burst on me. That black jet Quadberry wanted us to see him in, its flaming rear end, his blasting straight up into the night at mid-runway—what precisely was he wanting to say in this stunt? Was he saying remember him forever or forget him forever? But I had my own life and was neither going to mother-hen it over his memory nor his old sweetheart. What did he mean, *America the beautiful, like you will never know?* I, William Howly, knew a goddamn good bit about America the beautiful, even as a deaf man. Being deaf had brought me up closer to people. There were only about five I knew, but I knew their mouth movements, the perspiration under their noses, their tongues moving over the crowns of their teeth, their fingers on their lips. Quadberry, I said, you don't have to get up next to the stars in your black jet to see America the beautiful.

I was deciding to lie down on the kitchen floor and sleep the night, when Lilian turned on the light and appeared in her panties and bra. Her body was perfect except for a tiny bit of fat on her upper thighs. She'd sunbathed herself so her limbs were brown, and her stomach, and the instinct was to rip off the white underwear and lick, suck, say something terrific into the flesh that you discovered.

She was moving her mouth.

"Say it again slowly."

"I'm lonely. When he took off in his jet, I think it meant he wasn't ever going to see me again. I think it meant he was laughing at both of us. He's an astronaut and he spits on us."

"You want me on the bed with you?" I asked.

"I know you're an intellectual. We could keep on the lights so you'd know what I said."

"You want to say things? This isn't going to be just sex?"

"It could never be just sex."

"I agree. Go to sleep. Let me make up my mind whether to come in there. Turn out the lights."

Again the dark, and I thought I would cheat not only Quadberry but the entire Quadberry family if I did what was natural.

I fell asleep.

Quadberry escorted B-52s on bombing missions into North Vietnam. He was catapulted off the *Bonhomme Richard* in his suit at 100 degrees temperature, often at night, and put the F-8 on all it could get—the tiny cockpit, the immense long two-million-dollar fuselage, wings, tail and jet engine, Quadberry, the genius master of his dragon, going up to twenty thousand feet to be cool. He'd meet with the big B-52 turtle of the air and get in a position, his cockpit glowing with green and orange lights, and turn on his transistor radio. There was only one really good band, never mind the old American rock-and-roll from Cambodia, and that was Red Chinese opera. Quadberry loved it. He loved the nasal horde in the finale, when the peasants won over the old fat dilettante mayor. Then he'd turn the jet around when he saw the squatty abrupt little fires way down there after the B-52s had dropped their diet. It was a seven-hour trip. Sometimes he slept, but his body knew when to wake up. Another thirty minutes and there was his ship waiting for him out in the waves.

All his trips weren't this easy. He'd have to blast out in daytime and get with the B-52s, and a SAM missile would come up among them. Two of his mates were taken down by these missiles. But Quadberry, as on saxophone, had endless learned technique. He'd put his jet perpendicular in the air and make the SAMs look silly. He even shot down two of them. Then, one day in daylight, a MIG came floating up level with him and his squadron. Quadberry couldn't believe it. Others in the squadron were shy, but Quadberry knew where and how the MIG could shoot. He flew below the cannons and then came in behind it. He knew the MIG wanted one of the B-52s and not mainly him. The MIG was so concentrated on the fat B-52 that he forgot about Quadberry. It was really an amateur suicide pilot in the MIG. Quadberry got on top of him and let down a missile, rising out of the way of it. The missile blew off the tail of the MIG. But then Quadberry wanted to see if the man got safely out of the cockpit. He thought it would be pleasant if the fellow got out with his parachute working. Then Quadberry saw that the fellow wanted to collide his wreckage with the B-52, so Quadberry turned himself over and cannoned, evaporated the pilot and cockpit. It was the first man he'd killed.

The next trip out, Quadberry was hit by a ground missile. But his jet kept flying. He flew it a hundred miles and got to the sea. There was the *Bonhomme Richard,* so he ejected. His back was snapped but, by God, he landed right on the deck. His mates caught him in their arms and cut the parachute off him. His back hurt for weeks, but he was all right. He rested and recuperated in Hawaii for a month.

Then he went off the front of the ship. Just like that, his F-6 plopped in the ocean and sank like a rock. Quadberry saw the ship go over him. He knew he shouldn't eject just yet. If he ejected now he'd knock his head on the bottom and get chewed up in the motor blades. So Quadberry waited. His plane was sinking in the green and he could see the hull of the aircraft carrier getting smaller, but he had oxygen through his mask and it didn't seem that urgent a decision. Just let the big ship get over. Down what later proved to be sixty feet, he pushed the ejection button. It fired him away, bless it, and he woke up ten feet under the surface swimming against an almost overwhelming body of underwater parachute. But two of his mates were in a helicopter, one of them on the ladder to lift him out.

Now Quadberry's back was really hurt. He was out of this war and all wars for good.

Lilian, the stewardess, was killed in a crash. Her jet exploded with a hijacker's bomb, an inept bomb which wasn't supposed to go off, fifteen miles out of Havana; the poor pilot, the poor passengers, the poor stewardesses were all splattered like flesh sparklers over the water just out of Cuba. A fisherman found one seat of the airplane. Castro expressed regrets.

Quadberry came back to Clinton two weeks after Lilian and the others bound for Tampa were dead. He hadn't heard about her. So I told him Lilian was dead when I met him at the airport. Quadberry was thin and rather meek in his civvies—a gray suit and an out-of-style tie. The white ends of his hair were not there—the halo had disappeared—because his hair was cut short. The Arab nose seemed a pitiable defect in an ash-whiskered face that was beyond anemic now. He looked shorter, stooped. The truth was he was sick, his back was killing him. His breath was heavy-laden with airplane martinis and in his limp right hand he held a wet cigar. I told him about Lilian. He mumbled something sideways that I could not possibly make out.

"You've got to speak right at me, remember? Remember me, Quadberry?"

"Mom and Dad of course aren't here."

"No. Why aren't they?"

"He wrote me a letter after we bombed Hué. Said he hadn't sent me to Annapolis to bomb the architecture of Hué. He had been there once and had some important experience—French-kissed the queen of Hué or the like. Anyway, he said I'd have to do a hell of a lot of repentance for that. But he and Mom are separate people. Why isn't *she* here?"

"I don't know."

"I'm not asking you the question. The question is to God."

He shook his head. Then he sat down on the floor of the terminal. People had to walk around. I asked him to get up.

"No. How is old Clinton?"

"Horrible. Aluminum subdivisions, cigar boxes with four

thin columns in front, thick as a hive. We got a turquoise water tank; got a shopping center, a monster Jitney Jungle, fifth-rate teenyboppers covering the place like ants." Why was I being so frank just now, as Quadberry sat on the floor downcast, drooped over like a long weak candle? "It's not our town anymore, Ard. It's going to hurt to drive back into it. Hurts me every day. Please get up."

"And Lilian's not even over there now."

"No. She's a cloud over the Gulf of Mexico. You flew out of Pensacola once. You know what beauty those pink and blue clouds are. That's how I think of her."

"Was there a funeral?"

"Oh, yes. Her Methodist preacher and a big crowd over at Wright Ferguson funeral home. Your mother and father were there. Your father shouldn't have come. He could barely walk. Please get up."

"Why? What am I going to do, where am I going?"

"You've got your saxophone."

"Was there a coffin? Did you all go by and see the pink or blue cloud in it?" He was sneering now as he had done when he was eleven and fourteen and seventeen.

"Yes, they had a very ornate coffin."

"Lilian was the Unknown Stewardess. I'm not getting up."

"I said you still have your saxophone."

"No, I don't. I tried to play it on the ship after the last time I hurt my back. No go. I can't bend my neck or spine to play it. The pain kills me."

"Well, *don't* get up, then. Why am I asking you to get up? I'm just a deaf drummer, too vain to buy a hearing aid. Can't stand to write the ad copy I do. Wasn't I a good drummer?"

"Superb."

"But we can't be in this condition forever. The police are going to come and make you get up if we do it much longer."

The police didn't come. It was Quadberry's mother who came. She looked me in the face and grabbed my shoulders before she saw Ard on the floor. When she saw him she yanked him off the floor, hugging him passionately. She was shaking with sobs. Quadberry was gathered to her as if he were a rope she was trying to wrap around herself. Her mouth was all over him. Quadberry's mother was a good-looking woman of fifty. I simply held her purse. He cried out that his back was hurting. At last she let him go.

"So now we walk," I said.

"Dad's in the car trying to quit crying," said his mother.

"This is nice," Quadberry said. "I thought everything and everybody was dead around here." He put his arms around his mother. "Let's all go off and kill some time together." His mother's hair was on his lips. "You?" he asked me.

"Murder the devil out of it," I said.

I pretended to follow their car back to their house in Clinton. But when we were going through Jackson, I took the North 55 exit and disappeared from them, exhibiting a great amount of taste, I thought. I would get in their way in this reunion. I had an unimprovable apartment on Old Canton Road in a huge plaster house, Spanish style, with a terrace and ferns and yucca plants, and a green door where I went in. When I woke up I didn't have to make my coffee or fry my egg. The girl who slept in my bed did that. She was Lilian's little sister, Esther Field. Esther was pretty in a minor way and I was proud how I had tamed her to clean and cook around the place. The Field family would appreciate how I lived with her. I showed her the broom and the skillet, and she loved them. She also learned to speak very slowly when she had to say something.

Esther answered the phone when Quadberry called me seven months later. She gave me his message. He wanted to know my opinion on a decision he had to make. There was this Dr. Gordon, a surgeon at Emory Hospital in Atlanta, who said be could cure Quadberry's back problem. Quadberry's back was killing him. He was in torture even holding up the phone to say this. The surgeon said there was a seventy-five/twenty-five chance. Seventy-five that it would be successful, twenty-five that it would be fatal. Esther waited for my opinion. I told her to tell Quadberry to go over to Emory. He'd got through with luck in Vietnam, and now he should ride it out in this petty back operation.

Esther delivered the message and hung up.

"He said the surgeon's just his age; he's some genius from Johns Hopkins Hospital. He said this Gordon guy has published a lot of articles on spinal operations," said Esther.

"Fine and good. All is happy. Come to bed."

I felt her mouth and her voice on my ears, but I could hear only a sort of loud pulse from the girl. All I could do was move toward moisture and nipples and hair.

Quadberry lost his gamble at Emory Hospital in Atlanta. The brilliant surgeon his age lost him. Quadberry died. He died with his Arabian nose up in the air.

That is why I told this story and will never tell another.

THE FUGITIVES
by Madison Jones

Walt heard the train again. He slowed his steps until the clap of his shoes on the pavement was dimmed to a flesh-like padding. It reached him from far off beyond the field where cotton rows merged at a distance and wove a lush unruffled fabric that fanned out wide under the moon to a dark wall of thicket. From so far away the sound was only a wail, almost painful, like the surge of a childhood memory into the heart. It came to him that way often when on summer nights through his open window he heard the trains heading south out of the city. Then he would half rouse from his pillow and follow in spirit over the rolling farm-checkered land, along the delta that bounded the broad untamed river. Then he would think again of Uncle Tad, an old man hunched in a chair gripping a stick between his knees with hands burly as haunches of meat but strangely tender with mottled old-man's flesh. Walt used to sit at his feet. By the hour he sat there and looked up at him while the old man talked, recounting over and over violent tales of the days when he had been a railroad engineer. Walt used to watch his hands gripping the stick like a lever in his engine, growing white about the knuckles when he told about the time his coaches cut loose; or again, when he ran the barricade, how he throttled up his engine as he came on and hit with a force that knocked him half senseless against the iron-studded panel and yet found strength to lean out of the window and wave goodbye to the mob with a big ruddy hand. Walt used to think what those hands had done. And once he brought him an egg to break, long-ways in one hand like Uncle Tad had said he could. But now he said, "No; no more," because the strength had gone from his grip. Walt wanted his hands to be like Uncle Tad's and he used to pull at his fingers thinking that would help them grow, and hold them out ahead of him in the sun trying to make them red. Now they were big, as long as Uncle Tad's, he guessed. But the brawn and the redness were not there. People didn't have hands like his any more. And sometimes at his drafting table he had mused upon it, looking at his hands and at Walker's next to him that were thin and fragile and capable only of wielding a compass. And then he would think of what they had told him in biology about hands and evolution and he thought about men reverting because they did nothing to develop their hands. Or again, he would look out of the window over the blue tiresome sheet into the sunlight and think of a muscular hand gripping a hot steel lever, whitening at the knuckles, or perhaps twisting a compass about a single finger.

Walt shifted the bag to his other hand and moved on down the empty highway. There had been no car for half an hour. An occasional truck went by droning south to Vicksburg or New Orleans or north Memphis. They wouldn't hail at night. But he didn't care. The air was live and fresh and the pavement stretched away like an unbroken line of soft manila paper. Perhaps he would have to walk all night. It didn't matter. He had a week and some money and a few clothes in the handbag. Maybe he would make New Orleans. It was the going he liked, the feel and privacy of night, the chance he took of catching a ride or being marooned until dawn on the highway. And back home they had no notion of it. By now, his mother was thinking, he was in Nashville at Woody's house asleep. She had kept him at the door what seemed an intolerable time, holding his hand, fondling him with her eyes. When at last he broke away he felt as though he had done her some violence. It made him angry at her. He could feel her eyes as he passed along the hedge, but he did not look back. Perhaps he should have; it did no good to be unkind. They had given him everything; whatever they knew of to do they had done. Except they seemed never to have known, or else to have forgotten, that stifling sense of tedium, of meeting yourself coming back in a tiny circle which was your birthright. And he had inherited a Lilliputian world precisely rendered in minute sketches of bridges and buildings on a sheet of dull blue drawing paper. He could nearly encircle it by extending the arm of his little silver compass. And he had drawn, he knew, a million such circles. They were everywhere in the world, an infinity of circles, only waiting to be drawn. But if you did not draw them—then they were only in the mind; they did not exist. Yet his was drawn already, a little one in which the heart grew calluses from its incessant pounding against the narrow ribs of its cage. The way out was to lower your head and break through and claim your real birthright—the right to draw your own circle, or to draw none at all. And why shouldn't he do that? He was grown now and free and the road stretched out from his feet through a hundred cities where he had never been heard of and nothing was required of him but that he should mind his business. He looked down at his free hand, at the paleness of his outstretched fingers. It was only the wan light, he knew, but somehow the hand looked bigger, broader than before, and harder. He clenched it into a fist and the knuckles, whitening, showed like bulbs of ivory under the moon.

The road curved in a gentle arc and the moon was higher and the shadows not so long as before. Through the cotton to his right an embankment like a tiny levee ran and converged with the road which straightened ahead and paralleled it. On its crest twin rails glimmered away and in the distance came together with a single splash of brightness. Now he was tiring. He sat down, folding his legs up beneath him against the warm pavement. Mosquitoes whined around. One bit his cheek. He slapped it fiercely and got up and went on. There was nothing in sight but fields of cotton. He wondered if he would have to walk all night.

It was late when he saw a town. It lay back from the highway, straggling, still, like a little fortress of impregnable sleep. He stopped at the turn-off where trees cast a ragged shadow. A sign said "Rolling Fork." Up the lane scattered streetlights made vague semicircles on the dark macadam. There was no other sign of life. To try there for a place seemed almost irreverent, as though he would be treading on graves. And besides, it was too late. He stood pondering it, conscious how his legs ached. There was not even a barn nearby. Then his eyes caught something he had not seen before—boxcars, two of them, on the track only a little distance beyond the town.

Somewhere he missed the crossing and had to push through weeds. He felt his pants wet to the hips as he stepped up on the embankment. The boxcar door was sealed. He passed on to the other car. That one too was closed, but he saw that the seal was broken. With his free hand he pushed solidly at the door and it did not budge and he set the bag down and with both hands pulled. The door slid and the rasp of grating steel echoed in the hollow interior. Inside, a rectangle of light extended half across the floor, but beyond, the cargo of darkness seemed piled impenetrably upon itself. He heard no sound from within and about him only the chirping noises of night. He took up the bag and set it inside and tried again to peer through the blackness. His hands rested on the steel sill and he vaulted and stood upright. Here it was still with a silence that muted the pulsing of night beyond. Then he had the feeling of eyes fixed on him out of the dark. Cautiously he turned his head and tried to see into the regions where no light fell. Words formed in his mind. But a timidity restrained him, as though his voice would make a tumult of the silence. He reached for a match. It struck noisily against the cover, but moonlight drowned its glow and he held it far out ahead and inched his way into the darkness. It burned his finger. He dropped it and took another and held it up and struck it. In the first bright flare his eye leaped to a face that watched him from the corner. His pulses sprang; he recoiled and the match fell extinguished from his hand. Half in the light he stood his ground and felt the quick beating of blood in his chest and the scrutiny of eyes from out of the dark. He felt the need for some word or action to break the hold of silence. His own voice startled him.

"I couldn't see you back there. Gave me a start at first." The empty car gave an unfamiliar resonance to his words. He got no answer, but he felt a slack in the tension, as though his speech had thawed a subtle bodiless ice. He waited, listening for some response. Then he said, "Mosquitoes about took me. I thought it'd be better in here." And now he began to wonder. Perhaps it had been his imagination and no one was there at all. He jumped at the sudden voice.

"Air this a town?"

The voice was deep and without inflection, but something in the speech, some uncertain quality, gave him new assurance.

"Just a little village," he said. "This is the road to Vicksburg. We're out on the delta."

He felt a certain awkwardness in his stance and he reached for a cigarette and lit it deliberately and knew that his countenance showed clearly in the blaze of the match. He blew a long puff and watched the smoke vanish into blackness. Then came a sudden rustling and he started again at footsteps which resounded as from a cavern and approached him out of the dark. But he held his ground. He saw a figure, tall, coming into the light. The figure moved past him, an arm's length out, and stopped a little back from the door. Walt turned cautiously and watched him sidelong from his eye. He seemed not to notice Walt's presence. He gazed through the door and out across the delta with the look of a man who watches something far away. He was tall, exceedingly tall. And in the light that reached him he stood with a straightness that seemed unnatural. He appeared to be wrought there, like the far-gazing monuments of soldiers Walt had seen, Confederates mounted on their footings in quiet southern towns. His face looked gaunt, with pockets of shadow settled in hollows beneath the protruding bones. And now Walt was conscious of smoke from his cigarette rising toward the light and the whisper of crickets outside and now, it seemed, a change in that face, a softening. The lips moved barely and the face turned to him. Walt met his gaze and knew that he wasn't afraid any more.

"How far air we from Memphis?" The man's voice had a familiar twang, like the speech of mountaineers Walt had heard over at Lupton's Cove.

"Hundred and fifty miles, I guess. Where are you headed for?"

The man didn't answer for a time. Then,

"A ways on down yet," he murmured.

Walt heard the thin crying of a mosquito and he struck at it with his hand. "I never saw so many of the devils. You can't rest for them out there."

The man didn't reply. He stood there pensively and gazed at the landscape and finally said, "How far's this Vicksburg?"

"I'm not sure. A long way. Seventy miles, I reckon."

"You say that's a town yonder?"

"Yeah. But it's all closed up. It's just a little place."

Again Walt glanced at the face beside him and now he noticed its gauntness, and he wondered if the man was hungry. He had a sandwich in his bag. He hesitated though, waiting for something. Finally he said, "If you're hungry I've got a sandwich you can have. I don't want it."

Walt saw his lips part and an eagerness in his face that touched it with boyishness. He was younger, much younger than he had seemed, Walt's own age perhaps. Walt took the sandwich and put it into the outstretched hand. The man tore it from the paper and ate it savagely. After he had finished he turned his eyes to Walt again and in that instant they caught the moonlight. Walt returned their gaze and he half grinned at the earnest question. There was no mistaking it. He was still a boy. Walt shook his head. "That's all I've got."

The boy smiled a little. "I'm obliged to you." Now his face seemed less grave, as though quickened by something he watched out there. "Do you reckon there's any water here about?"

"I don't know," Walt said. "Unless it's back in that little town."

"Ain't there no creeks?"

"Yeah. But they're not fit to drink, down here in this low country. No telling what you'd catch."

"I've got to have some," he said and stepped to the door and put his hand on the sill and dropped nimbly to the ground. Then he stood motionless outside the car. Walt looked down on his ruffled hair and in the moonlight it seemed to have an auburn tint. It looked like Woody's hair. A truck was passing on the highway a hundred yards beyond and the noisy hum of its engine seemed the only sound in all that still country. The boy was following its progress with a gradual turn of his head. Walt saw that he was waiting.

"Those mosquitoes'll carry you off out there." He thought the boy shifted as though to start and Walt moved forward and came down beside him on the embankment. "Let's go," he said. They started, walking along the embankment. The slope declined from the ends of the crossties and made hard walking and they stepped up onto the track.

"It'd be better down on the road."

For a while the boy didn't speak. Then, "Let's stay up here."

Walt stepped rapidly to keep beside his long striding that covered two ties at a time. He glanced sidelong at him waiting for some apology. But there was none. Gravel crunched beneath their feet. Sometimes a steel track rang from rock they kicked against it. Walt's eyes followed the rails, how they sped away like silver wires into the distance. Now he was sure of it. This boy's was no pleasure jaunt like his own. Why else should he prefer this gravel and ties to the smooth pavement of a highway. And why all that time in a boxcar hungry and thirsty, like a fugitive there in the dark. Maybe that was it. What else would a hill boy be doing there? Walt glanced up suddenly, half expecting to see him anew. But the boy looked far out ahead as though nature steered his feet, and even in the dim light his face seemed full of a strange bright exuberance. Walt watched the ties passing beneath them. Maybe he was right; maybe not. Somehow it didn't matter. Yesterday and what had come before were things shut out by the level horizon that encircled them.

The cotton field to the right never varied and in spite of their rapid walking seemed to have no end. Walt was feeling the weariness he had forgotten. "Let's stop a minute," he said. "I've been walking all night." Walt sat on the track. It was cool and wet with the dew. The boy stood for a time, then seated himself on the opposite track. The mosquitoes were back again. Walt slapped and reached for his cigarettes and held them out and the boy took one and thanked him.

"Smoke's all that'll keep them away," Walt said. He watched the smoke rise thinly from his hand.

"They wasn't hardly this bad back home. 'Less you went down in a hollow." He spoke as though thinking aloud.

"Where do you live?" Walt said.

He hesitated; then, "Point Creek," and then, "It's in Tennessee."

Walt dragged again at his cigarette. "How far is that from Carthage?"

"A right far piece. Fifty mile, I reckon."

After a moment Walt said, "Good fishing up around Carthage. I was up there once."

The boy looked down. "I used to fish all the time in Wolf creek. Used to grab for them—I could catch them, too. Pa said it was 'cause I was so long and gangling I could get back up under them rocks where nobody else couldn't." He paused and a smile was on his lips. "Once I pulled out a snake. Pa said I jumped clean up on the hill." He laughed deep and mellow and Walt laughed too. They were quiet again except for an occasional chuckle from deep inside the boy. Walt blew smoke up into the air. Then the boy looked at him and the moon reflected in his eyes. "Where do you live at?"

"Memphis." The boy seemed to ponder it a moment. "That's a big place," he said. Then he threw down his cigarette. "I got to have some water."

"I could use some myself."

The rest had done Walt good. His legs felt lighter. He caught the swing of his companion's stride, a rhythm like the cadence of marching men. After a long time the boy said, "Don't look like there's no water about."

"Naw it don't. Looks like we'd run on a house or something."

In his mind Walt could picture a spring welling out from rock at the foot of a hill and them on their bellies sucking deep, wetting the ends of their noses. The thought of it made him thirstier. Perhaps the boy too was thinking of a spring where he had drunk back in some mountain hollow. Walt thought how it would look and how pleasant it would be to go with him there and drink from the spring, or grab for fish in the mountain branch. Suddenly the boy began to whistle soft and fine. It was square-dance music, Walt knew; it sounded like "Turkey in the Straw." But he did not know the tune. "What's the name of that?" Walt said.

The boy reflected a moment. Finally, "I've forgot. Pa used to fiddle it all the time."

The tune ran in Walt's head. After a little he was whistling it between his teeth.

"Naw," the boy said. "It goes like this." He whistled a few bars and Walt joined in and then the boy stopped and Walt saw him nodding and heard him say, "Now you got it."

They walked for a long time and once stopped to rest and smoke and the boy sang "Barbara Allen," all of it he could remember, and laughed when he got through. But now their gaiety had passed. The boy was suffering for water, Walt knew, because he kept talking to him about it and twice stopped and pulled blades of the wet grass and put them in his mouth and chewed them. Walt was thirsty too. It had grown upon him in the last hour, as though the boy's thirst had infected him. Then the boy said, "Look," and pointed and Walt saw a roof there at the thicket which bounded the cotton field. They hurried; then they saw that it was a shed without walls and empty.

"Shore we'll find some directly," the boy said. Walt felt his disappointment, its keenness, in the wan hope of his voice.

Still the highway and the open field were on their left, but to the right now a thicket rose and shut out the light but for patches where it broke through the heavy foliage.

"I hear a frog," the boy said. "Must be water." He was right, for now Walt too could hear it. That was the reason for a thicket—because the land was too wet for cotton. "It must be a swamp," Walt said. "We can't drink swamp water."

They went on, peering down into the thicket. Now they heard clearly the frogs, their quiet clamor that swelled and died in a strange grating rhythm, like the pulse of the swamp whose breath reached up and touched their nostrils with its dankness. Here the mosquitoes were worse. Even walking they had to flail at them with their hands. Then, at the thicket's edge where the moon broke through, they saw water, slick and shining under the light. The boy stopped. Quickly Walt said, "You can't drink that. It'll kill you."

"I got to have some water," he said.

"But that stuff's full of fever. It'd be just like drinking poison."

The boy still looked down at it.

"Come on," Walt said. "We're bound to run on a house."

The boy did not answer, only grunted when again Walt warned him against the water. Now they could see that the swamp was not large, that up ahead the thicket broke as abruptly as it had begun onto another field of cotton. Then they saw the stream that fed it, how its bright placid face abruptly vanished into the shadows that darkened the swamp. Ahead it passed under the tracks. Once more Walt set his pace with the boy's, which had quickened at sight of the water.

They stepped onto the bridge and Walt looked down through the ties at the stream. It looked deep. No ripple stirred and the gloss of its surface lay tranquil as ice. Walt tasted the humid air.

"This ain't in the swamp," the boy said.

"It's the same stuff though. Look how still it is."

The boy kept on looking at it.

"Let's go," Walt said. "It'll be day pretty soon. Then we can catch a ride." But his words made him remember.

"Naw," the boy answered. "I got to have some." He started across the bridge and when Walt came up beside him he said, "I got to. I ain't had none since yesterday noon."

Walt followed him down the bank through weeds and onto a clearing beside the stream where someone had watered stock. The boy dropped to his knees and put his hands in the water; mud clouded upward to meet his face. He straightened up again and crawled a little down the bank and leaned out beyond the stance of his spraddled hands. But he paused a moment there above his shadow. Then he began to drink. Walt watched the ripples around his head, how they shimmered the water's face, and he heard the suck of his drinking.

"Don't get too much," Walt said.

The boy did not stop or even seem to hear, as though there was no sound in the world but the noise of water coursing down his throat. Walt went to him and put his hand on his shoulder, the hard muscle that quivered with the strain.

"Don't drink any more."

The boy stopped. Walt looked at his kneeling body, the heaving of his chest, the still head that drooped a little downward toward his shadow with the look of a man in prayer. Now Walt could not hear his breathing any more; only mosquitoes and the witless chorus of frogs. The boy rocked back on his heels and struck at his arm. Walt looked at the water.

"How is it?"

"Better than nothing."

Walt looked at the water, aware that the boy stood up. The coating of light lay like varnish on its pond-quiet face. Looking at the water he heard the boy speak. He answered, "Yeah" and stepped to where the boy had been and knelt and lowered his face. His nose touched warm water; the scent of it rose up rancid and unclean into his nostrils. Beneath his eyes the water was black and lifeless as oil sopping his lips and tongue. He swallowed once, then again. As he came upright he felt the warm languid surge of it downward in his gullet. After a moment it had passed, but he shuddered. He got up and the boy was watching him. Light was in his eyes. They were gray eyes, or seemed to be, gray for looking distances. Walt held out his cigarettes and the boy took one without speaking and Walt lit it for him and then his own.

"Let's get up on the track," Walt said.

The boy sat on the rail beside him. They watched their smoke rising on the windless air. Walt said, "They don't like smoke."

"Naw," the boy answered.

But still Walt could hear mosquitoes about his head and he slapped at his cheek. The boy got up. Walt watched him as he searched about in the weeds and pulled some grass, sage, Walt thought, that looked drier than the rest. He came back with his hands full and arranged it quickly in a criss-cross pile near Walt's feet. He tried to light it, this stem and that, and at length a flame flickered tinily. They nursed it with their breath and bits of grass they dropped on it until a slow flame with gentle hissing consumed its way through the pile.

"That'll fetch them," the boy said.

Walt listened. But now he heard the boy's whistling again, the tune he had whistled before.

"Ain't you going back?" Walt asked.

"Naw. That's the first place they'd look."

"Where you going to?"

The boy threw the stub of his cigarette into the fire. "I don't know. It don't matter. I ain't going back to Nashville."

After a little Walt said, "How long did you have?"

The little blaze was flickering.

"Life."

Walt leaned forward and laid unburnt stems on the

flame. They writhed for an instant in the heat, smoking, then caught.

The boy said, "I'd rather be dead than back there." He watched the fire, its fluctuations like bursts of a dying candle. "But I ain't sorry. I give him fair warning—I told him to stay away from there."

The last of the flames swelled to a moment's brightness and reeled and vanished into embers that pulsed still with an inner fire. The smoke still rose. Walt heard only the frogs. He looked down the silver tracks.

"You might go to New Orleans. They'd have a hard time finding you there."

The boy answered, "Yeah" and yawned and in the middle of it said, "Reckon I will," and reached his hands above his head and stretched. Walt yawned too. "Catching, ain't it?" he said.

The smoke, all but a wisp, was gone. Walt saw him start to move and they stood up together and Walt reached for his handbag and stepped off. But the boy was not at his side. Walt turned back and started at the look of him, the fixed body and half-raised hand and his face rigid. The boy turned his back to him.

"What is it?" Walt said.

"Listen."

That tenseness, the set of his body, stopped Walt's own slow breathing.

"Don't you hear it?" the boy whispered.

"No."

"Listen."

Now he heard it, a distance off up the tracks. Then it sounded again, clearer.

"I hear dogs."

The boy didn't say anything. They heard again the throaty yelps coming intermittently—but not a sound like barking. Walt felt the tension, the strain of gazing through light that was too unsure. He heard the hasty whisper that spoke the thought in his mind.

"They ain't no ordinary dogs."

Then Walt pointed, "Look"; he saw it glint an instant under the moon. The boy wheeled. Walt read panic in his face. He had no words, but he seized the boy's arm and the bright eyes fixed on him a wild mute appeal.

"The water," Walt said; "they can't track in the water."

Comprehending, he cut his eyes from Walt's face and bolted into the weeds toward the clearing. Walt started to call and did not. He saw the boy drawing away from him with long bounds of his shifting body; he felt sudden loneliness. The yelp of the dogs, clearer now, was advancing on him. Walt sprang into his wake. Striking the weeds he saw the boy reach the stream; he saw something else, a glimpse screened quickly by his descent, a car crawling lightless along the highway beyond. The boy was in water hip-deep wading on toward the road.

"The swamp," Walt hissed; "they're on the highway." The boy heard and wheeled and lurched back like a man dizzy with turning and sprawled in the water. Trying to run he made his way back to Walt and grasped his arm and "Quiet," Walt said, "they'll hear," and the boy's wide eyes crossed his face and Walt struggled on by his side. Under the bridge they crossed its shadow and came into light again. The water grew deeper. It rose up onto Walt's chest. The boy was gaining on him. Walt let go his handbag. The swamp was ahead with its sudden line of shadow and they began to swim a long silent breast stroke. The boy passed into the shadow first and the light was shorn from his hair. They heard the dogs, clear-voiced, nearer now. They slid on through black slick water that swirled in hollow sucks above their hands and the voice of a million frogs dinned in their ears like soft rhythmic thunder. They made for the bank. Mud like paste gave way under their hands, but a vine was there and they seized it, the boy first, and dragged themselves on wet bellies over the shallow bank. They came upright and the boy led blindly off.

"Keep close to the creek," Walt said. They plowed on half stumbling through sticky mud and vines that caught at their feet or slid wetly across their legs. A glooming light was all around, like a spell misguiding their steps. Walt struck another vine and fell to his knees and got up and went on. They were in water, splashing, tugging against the mud. Someone called. "Wait," Walt said and the boy stopped. Above the sounds of the swamp Walt heard the dogs and then on the bridge behind them the voices of men. They waited. The voices still sounded, but they could not distinguish the words. Suddenly mosquitoes were about them thick as from a hive, brushing against their faces, swarming so that Walt held his breath for fear they would enter his nostrils. He heard the boy say, "God," and start again. But now Walt could feel a difference, a sense of something gone, some unclear haze like departed sleep that left him aware of wretchedness, of sweat and his aching legs, and then, of wonder. It was only this morning—or yesterday—he stood on his own front walk—as though it were someone else, not him, who was fleeing here through the swamp; someone who had no memory of the names of books on his shelf, of Litton's voice, the look of his mother's face. He sank in mud to his shins. He tugged free and plunged on again. Then, "Look yonder," the boy cried. He was right. A rim of clear light was there, dissected by trunks that intervened, but deep like crystal water reaching into the distance. They hurried; then they both stopped together. The men were ahead of them; they knew every swamp and thicket, the lay of every field, the habits of men in flight. "They ain't to the creek yet," the boy hissed and started angling toward the stream. Walt fought the mucky space that grew between them, calling to him as loud as he dared. Then a voice sounded beyond the swamp dead on line of their course. The boy stopped. Another voice back behind them answered. Walt came up beside him. The boy did not look at him.

"They're all around," Walt said. He watched the line of the boy's profile, the swamp light on his face. And again he felt the mosquitoes. Abruptly the boy began to flail with heavy wasteful strokes of his hands.

Walt said, "We can't stay here. It's almost day."

He quit beating the air and stood gently fanning with his hands.

"I'm going to try it—in the cotton yonder."

"You can't," Walt said. "It's too light. And besides—those dogs. Even if they missed—"

"I'm going to try it." The words were a whisper, strained, exhausted. But they did not pass; they whispered themselves like faint echoes inside the cavern of Walt's skull. He could hear nothing, think nothing, but the sound of that whispering. The boy's movement startled him; his mind filled up again. He was following through water half to his knees, through mire that sucked at his shoes and strained hot cramps into the muscles of his thighs. He shielded his face with his arms and broke through the vines; his wrists burned like sores. He felt he was blind, compelled on his course by a kind of groping instinct. Once he came hard against a stump and fell to his hands. He felt cool water on his lips, the muck like a cushion under him. Then ahead he saw light. His eyes searched the rim of the thicket, under the roof of foliage, along black trunks that stood like portals opening onto the field. He saw the boy's head. It was framed black as the trees in a square of light. Walt got up and started. The head had vanished, but he found the boy on his hands and knees in the last edge of the shadows. The boy turned his face to him as he came up and kneeled down. But the boy did not speak. His eyes looked almost white. It was dusk over the field. The moon was in the west the feeble color of milk, hung in the interregnum between day and night. Off somewhere the throaty bark of a dog, then a voice. Nothing stirred. It seemed long.

"Hear the owl?"

Walt wasn't sure the boy had said it. His head was turned away, as stiffly fixed as though he were scenting something. Then Walt saw a man. He was standing hip-deep in cotton a distance down the edge of the thicket. He had a gun.

"The creek," the boy whispered.

"They'll be looking for that," Walt answered.

They began to crawl painfully along the shadow to where it touched on the cotton. They paused. The man had not moved. Even the frogs had stopped. On a line with his eyes the cotton spread out like a glistening turgid lake.

"It's dawning," the boy said. The words came on a faint expiration of breath, like something imagined. The boy was gazing at him. Walt strained to see his face, but only the feeble whiteness of his eyes showed through the blur. He could tell when the eyes closed, deliberately, and opened again and then turned away into the field.

They were crawling in the cotton down a narrow aisle of lumpy dirt and uprooted vegetation that rustled against their arms and legs. For long spaces he held his breath and watched his hands passing one another like pale fragile duck's feet against the dark earth. Sometimes he touched the muddy sole of a shoe and hesitated. Sometimes back behind them there were voices calling. A bird in the swamp shattered the dawn with its raucous cry. He knew that they must hurry. A space grew between him and the shoes. He moved faster. Then a sudden noise startled him to a halt; a white tuft of hair bobbed off through the cotton. The rattling of stalks beat for an agonized moment against the membranes of his ears. He could not move; he felt his heart swelled up tight like stuffing against his ribs. Suddenly behind them came another crashing. He knew that this was it, but he felt only confusion, and feebleness in his muscles. Then a voice, thunderous, challenging. He felt the boy come to his feet, the earth tremble at each quick thud of the ponderous shoes. The voice calling "Halt" and again "Halt" shocked Walt into motion. But a shot answered the upward lurch of his body; the noise like a concussion blew him staggering forward in the tracks of the racing figure. He strained at the yielding dirt. And some hard object, it seemed, probed against the small of his back. Then he could not stand it any more. He dove onto his belly and behind him the voice cracked and then the shot. He heard the boy's body strike the ground, as though the gun had discharged some enormous awkward load of pulp. He bolted forward. He half heard the warning shout and came to his knees by the long still body. The boy was lying face down. An arm was crooked clumsily under him. He had the look of having been dropped there from a great height. But now his body was shuddering. Walt felt sudden panic. He hovered over the boy, forming words with his tongue that did not come out. Then, as suddenly, he felt it was all a ridiculous act and he wanted to shout, "Stop it, stop it." But he could not stand to see him lying like that. With a calm that surprised him he was gently turning the boy onto his back, gently murmuring to him in the accents of a lover. The boy's lips were faintly writhing; there was blood on them and Walt's hand was covered with blood. But he hardly noticed it. With the tail of his shirt he wiped the lips and he wiped dirt from the nostrils and forehead. And all the time those pale lidless eyes stared at him. He tried to look deep into them, past that look of white amazement, down through the channels of his mind. But the whiteness blinded him. The boy's body began to strain; a noise like gargling issued from his throat.

"Turn his head 'fore he chokes," a voice said.

He obeyed, unshaken even by the sudden intrusion of that voice. The mouth was open. The teeth looked nearly scarlet, like dirty rubies. He laid his hand on the boy's dark jacket over the heart. It was wet, grimy; it cleaved like paste to his fingers. He took his hand away. There was a sound of rattling foliage and other voices were around him answering quietly to one another. Then he knew he was being spoken to, querulously. He was answering, not looking up, not even thinking, as though the words came by rote to his tongue. Now others were kneeling beside him. They did not speak for a long time. Then one of them stood up.

"Bring him on," the man said.

Two men seized the boy's long arms and hoisted him. His head flopped back and rolled wandering on his shoulders as he came upright. Walt sprang to him. He shouldered the man aside and took the limp wet arm and encircled his own neck with it. He heard the man curse and another coldly answer him. Then he began to think with a kind of pain at his own heart, "We cannot carry him this way, with a hole through his chest." But as they plodded off and the boy's feet dragged behind him and his head toppled aimlessly on the yielding column of his neck, Walt understood that he carried a corpse.

The east was flaming bright when they got up onto the track. The arm about his neck was sticky, suffocating; his wrist and fingers ached from the grip he held on that dead hand which slipped persistently from his own on a slime of sweat and blood. He felt that he could not get his breath. Some object like a round stone seemed lodged in his gullet, swelling up, pressing the air from his lungs. He tried to swallow it back, but it surged up hot and acid into his throat and drenched his tongue. He vomited, bent under the weight of the body. The heaves came violently, knotting his muscles, straining his entrails dry. He did not know so much of that black water was in him.

It seemed a long time he was on his knees retching. When it ceased he felt too tired to get up. It was as though he had waked up from a drugged uneasy sleep and looked out at a new-risen sun. But one of the men was speaking to him. He got to his feet. The body was stretched out, staring. There were no shadows on the face now. It looked older than it had before, the features not so clean of cut. And deep indentations, like scars, angled down from the flanges of the nose past the open mouth. But more than these, death had frozen the face in a look of dull and wanton brutality. He turned away. He could not help to carry the body any more.

They left him there with one silent man and took the corpse away. He did not look after them. The sun threw coppery spangles into a dusty sky. It promised heat. He felt shattered, as though he had run hard against a barrier of stone. And as he looked up the track which they had come down so lustily last night, he imagined he saw his own figure walking slowly north. At the end of his walk his own front door was standing open and they were watching him approach and the expression on their faces was something between placid satisfaction and mild surprise.

THE FIFTH GENERATION

by *Hunter Kay*

❀

1

A drowsiness, like when you've slept too long, hangs over my days here. Driving for hours past midnight through the streets of the deserted town, occasional silver streetlights casting a paralyzing spell over buildings and lawns usually filled with moving people and cars and bright sunlight, but now frozen in the delicate sheen, the languor and the sense of drifting so complete and I so comfortable in it, buoyed and cushioned.

What has been bred out of us? "Takes five generations to make a gentleman," my grandmother used to say. Five generations to purge the barbarity of an upstart forebear who came (no one knows where from) to the pine-oak lands of East Texas and watched his dozen grizzly cattle grow and eat their way into the forests until one day he died and his son found himself a land and cattle baron and doubled it all before going off to kill (to hear him tell it) thousands of Yankees and retire to town (having exchanged land and cattle for the less demanding management of a railroad). Here he built his ostentatious nightmare of a house with turrets and odd buttresses and the whole irregularity covered in Victorian ornamentation like an over-decorated cake. Whose halls my grandfather made respectable by the profession of banking and my father, even less inclined for work, ordered engraved cards which read "Charles Harold Sullivan, Investments" (not the crisp "C. H. Sullivan" of his plutocratic father), which meant that he merely handled the investment interest ("There's nothing like a good interest rate") of assorted widowed aunts and cousins still in their minority, the eventual heirs of that poor white of five generations ago whom most of them wouldn't allow in their front door (coarse muddy boots on pale living-room carpets wall-to-wall) and whose blood, diluted by generations of ease and forgetfulness (of cold nights without firewood and long winters on salted meat), has dribbled down to me.

I have withdrawn to the shadowed corner of my room and carefully I have watched; have introspected my introspections; have stood back, and back further still, and am lonely in the face of the convinced action of those who move in the world. To have cheated the widow of her mite, the church of its alms. I was always such a good little boy.

This morning at the white-painted iron table in the yard under the old trees, low branches long since cut off so you feel protected under great green umbrellas. I peeled the cicada shell I found in the chair, its dead legs still gripping the arm.

Slamming of a screen door somewhere. Grey tailored suit, jaunty smile, slender—"Father."

"Good morning, good morning!" Not a jolly man though he pretends. Looks at the watch. "My goodness, up so early? It's not even eleven yet. Busy day ahead, I guess." Still smiling. Hair carefully barbered. Reaches over for the glass; tastes. "Ah, lemonade. My favorite. Made you a whole pitcher, eh?" Looks around as if inspecting the morning. "Well, off to the salt mines. Don't let the ice melt."

The silent reproach. Eloquent. Could rise and shake off the dust of lethargy and head for the aluminum palaces of Dallas or Atlanta—follow the migration—but lacking his faith in the virtues of finance . . . Where?

Since graduation, for four weeks I have sat here in comfortable limbo until the whole house has taken on the shape of my limp body like a soft mattress where you have lain too long.

The sunset fading from the sky, I followed it out west of town, but it escaped me. In the sudden evening I saw the town coming to an end and only the seldom gas stations before giving way to billboards and cattle.

The Cattleman's Club, multicolored brick front to disguise the cheap cinderblock construction of the shapeless building. Maybe my ancestor's type of place. Perhaps he would have pulled in with the shiny GM pickups and tromped through the couples and men just in from work in the oil fields or the factory. Probably picked a fight . . .

Do they bust chairs over each other's heads and go crashing through windows together in fights over barmaids? I wonder, would the music stop and the talk and laughter fade as if on cue if the door opened hesitantly and I entered; the brawling stop and everyone dust themselves off and stop spitting on the floor?

A delicate question. I turned around at a gas station and went back, parking in the asphalt lot. I approached on foot, with a bristle of fear. I shivered from the sudden cool and found my way in the darkness to a table in the corner across from the bar. A man made for corners. Dark and layered with smoke, the room continued around the corner behind the bar where there must have been a pool table; I heard the dull clock of balls.

My part of the room was almost empty of people, but there was promise. The girl behind the bar, talking to a man, finally noticed me and excused herself from him. "What do you want?" she challenged. Not the sort of service I'm accustomed to. I ordered a daiquiri—a sissy drink, I remembered too late, but no one came over to look at the greenhorn. It was slow coming and lukewarm then. You don't seem to know who I am.

Four times she came back to the table with her demand, probably hoping I would order a real drink. The daiquiris, so sweet and soft and gentle. I stared without seeing into the room, a camera fixed on the edge of a highway, while the traffic passed before me, filling the room with voices, laughter. The juke-box blinked into action, wailing thin music.

I focused on them, my pale vision probing them. I sought violence and the defiance of reckless passion. Potentiality awaited me there. My eyes pushed through the smoke. Pink-faced women with out-of-date hairstyles sprayed up on the top of their heads, and high plastic boots. Lean men with nasal accents one generation out of the hills, their shirts stitched with colors, gawdy-Western.

Couples pulled each other listlessly across the dance floor, Johnny Cash in the background. They drank their beer slowly, with discretion. There was a man wearing an orange pair of sea-turtle boots which everyone admired.

The music changed, and the people in their store-bought costumes talked without raising their voices. The sound of singers moved to the suburbs of Nashville to sing in soundproof glass studios of dust farms and cotton fields and the whistling wind in wintertime before getting in their cars to fight the traffic home and I'm so lonesome I could . . .

Bogus. Even the fabled redneck has failed me. Not a speck of dirt on their pressed jeans nor cow manure on their polished boots. Talk and laughter as empty as a country club luncheon. Their Rotary, their Chamber of Commerce. They have tamed the West. Where is my carefree cowboy? Do I infect everything I touch with my own malady?

It is finished for me so my vision retreated out of focus and the sounds blurred. The girl brought me another daiquiri which I drank without tasting. Time wasted the evening and I felt myself sinking gently, disembodied with only a tingling of nerve-endings to tell me I was there. I floated into the emptiness of the void which was myself.

Someone kicked against the chair across the table and my sticky drink spilled over my hands. Several people were stopped in their movement toward the door. "Now here's a man who'll stay up and drink with me!" I was trying to find a handkerchief to wipe off my hands.

He stood there blocking my sight but I didn't look up. They talked and milled around him. I saw a tarnished "CSA" belt-buckle and faded jeans and his rough boot was on the chair in rude trespass and imposition. Then he bent down to me and I focused on the grinning, bright, tanned face and remembered a day when I was a boy and had gone with my father into the country to the rambling dog-trot house of a prosperous farmer in ante-bellum days and waited in the car while he went inside and there was a boy my age who came around the corner of the barn on a tractor with his shirt open and eating a tomato in the summer sun with the juice running down his chin, and I wished I could ride on the tractor and he looked down haughtily for a moment as he passed as if to say, You're no better than anyone else no matter who your daddy is.

The man smiled down broadly at me and said to those behind him, "Get going; I'll see you all later," and he pulled out the old pocket watch he wore under his belt and said, "It's hardly a decent hour of night and people already wanting to leave," and sat down as though I had invited him. "Believe I will," he said.

"Whatcha drinking?" he asked, picking up my empty glass and sniffing it rudely before I had a chance to answer. "Some kind of punch, huh? You been to a wedding? I'm a beer man myself." He lifted his Schlitz.

"I don't like beer," I said, irritated.

"Takes getting used to. Honey, a beer for the gentleman and me," he called to the waitress as she passed. "Fix us up a tab," he ordered with casual opulence when they came.

"I'll get sick if I drink that," I pouted.

"Naw you won't. Drink it down quick, Charlie," he said and raised his can.

"Charles," I corrected and, since I was beyond caring by that time, raised mine too.

We had two more and he flashed before me bobbing and weaving like a boxer, his mobile face changing quickly from mock horror to seriousness to unrestrained laughter as he recounted outrageous, incredible stories of his adventures, as if his sole purpose for the night was to entertain me, which he did while I drank beer as if I had been doing it all my life.

The table gradually filled with his friends who pulled up extra chairs. "Sit down and have a beer!" he called to everyone who passed.

"I know his daddy," a fat woman said, taking her fourth beer. They were men and women mostly with two first names who slapped me on the back in the middle of laughter over something Gary had said that broke them all up, pointing to him as if to say, He's some boy, isn't he? and I nodding, Yeah, I guess he is. Finally very late they all got up and carried me out the door with them after I paid the tab and Gary was with somebody's robin-red-breasted wife who laughed fully when he pinched her and he winking all the time at me through a grin.

I shivered. Over my head was an air conditioner too big for the room. I lay under a mound of quilts, bedspreads, and World War II olive-green army blankets. A frying sound. Concrete floor, a piece of red carpeting, a box room, old metal garden chairs, windows with fading red curtains, deer head, pictures torn from sporting magazines of charging football players and leaping bass, public park sign over the door "No Loitering," in the tiny bathroom over the tub "No Fishing," and a yearbook photo of him accepting a large athletic trophy. Against the walls there were three low metal campbeds, unmade, like in a disorderly barracks. The throb of a rock record played too loud gutted my head.

"You don't waste any time getting up out of bed, do you?" He stood across the room at the stove, shirtless amid a cloud of grease smoke. "The name's Gary, case you don't remember. You really wowed them last night at the club."

"Can you turn that record down? I think I'm sick."

"How many eggs can you eat?" I focused on the dreadful pile of bacon and toast on the cabinet.

"No, please," I begged. "I'm not much of a breakfast eater."

"Too late," he announced happily, putting the last fried eggs on the platter and it on the table. "Come on. A little food and you'll feel fine." A little food—it looked like a dozen were coming for breakfast. By the time I had dressed and made it to the table he'd set a creamy-looking gallon of milk in the middle and had already heaped my plate. I tried to look enthusiastic.

"I'm sorry if I embarrassed you in front of your friends last night," I said.

"Whatdya mean? You were great. When right before the Club closed up you got real sad and started telling us how you graduated a month ago and that you didn't have a job and didn't really know how to do anything anyway and didn't want to do anything at all," he mimicked a plaintive tone, "and looked so pitiful you had them howling, them knowing your daddy and how really hard-up you all are and all. They ate it up. I promised I'd bring you back tonight."

"You what?"

"Yeah, I told them we were great friends and all, like we'd said more than ten words to each other before last night."

He watched me eat, satisfied. "Boy, you really put it away, don't you. What they been doing to you off there where you been to school, you so skinny and all?" I had a mouthful of food and before I could answer he was talking on a new tack, and by the end of the piece of toast, still without a word from me, he had me moved in with him and working on his shift in the oil fields and what did I say to that?

There was a nighttime picture of a rig, outlined by lights, rising against the black sky. I turned to look at it—to imagine, to consider. But he dove, graceful as a deer, headfirst over the ragged couch and caught my leg with one hand, twisted, throwing me down, and was on top of me gouging my face into the carpet. He wrenched my arm behind my back and I struggled against the weight balanced on top of me.

"Are you a nigger?"

"No!"

"You're not? You said last night I lived like one." He bent my arm back until the pain shot through the nerves into my shoulder and chest.

"I'm a nigger! Now let me up, damnit." Satisfied, he released me and his weight lifted. I stood up and brushed off. I considered the rug-burn on my elbow.

"See, I've already taught you how to cuss. Whatdya say?" I was afraid, and a rich surge of fear shot through me, but suddenly I felt my life fill with potentiality—for danger, for excitement, for spontaneity—like a sickly face regaining color.

"No fishing in the tub?" I asked.

"Nope," he said, standing up and dispensing with his plastic plate by a toss into the sink. He leaned over and prodded me exploringly in my soft stomach. "We'll get you in shape yet," he promised, raising his shirt proudly to display his hard ripples. He stuck out his hand. "Podners?"

I stood and shook it. "Partners."

2

"This is all really unnecessary, you know," my father said as I was carrying a load of clothes to the car. I had told him about Gary and he had said, "Yes, my father and his grandfather were friends; they used to fish together. I hold the note on their farm." I walked past him across the off-white carpet that covered the floor, through the effeminate Victorian furniture, fussily carved and upholstered in pastel cloths. The old outlaw robbed by main force and his grandson seized through cunning, sleuth, guile; but not my father. Opportunity and advantage become his without even the thrill of springing shut the trap. As a spider waits, he waits, spinning and capturing without pleasure.

Gary got me a job on the rig with him and took me across the frontier into another country where everything was alien to me. I doubt if I did half the work they paid me for, that first week; Gary had to work for both of us.

He woke me every morning at 4:30 and, with me still asleep, drove to the wooden dock stretched into the fog of the lake. There a crewboat would appear suddenly close after we had heard its motors for some time and pick up the party of men which grew and shrank in inverse ratio to the intensity of the work or the drunk of the day or night before.

I would be nodding, desperately trying to sleep again, as we ferried across the lake, invisible in the fog. Then the motor would cut almost to an idle because we were entering the narrows of the river and I would give up. On each side of the river neck the wreck of an ancient rig rose out of the mist like gates. The girders were rusted and in some cases had fallen to leave holes in the skeletal ribs. Decades of bird droppings streaked the steel which was charred by the occasional burning of the sludge pits beneath them, and spikes and piles of sheet metal, pipe, and discarded engines littered the sandy banks where no vegetation grew because of the run-off and the fires.

The channel of the river had been dredged wide enough for us to pass through beneath the trees that closed over us. We continued down the river with the waterplants scraping under the hull and our wake slapping against the eroded bank. Then we would be out of the river and into a small lagoon across which would come the splitting sound of the morning whistle, echoing from the rig which stood planted in the water, its height towering above us, a giant, bright obelisk, shining with the lights of thousands of bulbs in the dim morning light.

The night crew, dirty and exhausted, would push onto the boat before we were off and then the giant generators and engines would start and the platform shudder with the noise and vibration that would continue until we shut down our shift at dusk.

I began each morning with new-found muscles still torn from the day before, and the work began immediately after we landed. The main platform was square and covered with a steel grillwork over the girders and you could see the water through the flooring ten feet below. Here were the corrugated dining hall, the equipment shed, and the crane which lifted the red metal boxes of tools up to us on the drilling floor above.

Here we dispersed, Gary and I and three others climbing up another series of ladders to the drilling floor. I had a hardhat which didn't fit but pinched my head or fell over my face when I bent over. After a week of carrying long sections of pipe, the gloves I had bought had already worn through.

The huge bulk of the drilling clamp hung from thick cables until we brought it a new section of pipe. With wrenches more than two feet long we connected them, then the clamp began turning, drilling the section down through the floor while we brought more. Its appetite was insatiable, and there seemed to be no final goal for the work.

I was not a good worker. The sun burned off successive layers of skin until I was raw wherever exposed. Whenever it rained the swampy land around us steamed for days so that it was like breathing through damp cotton. The wind—when there was any—blew clouds of mosquitoes up to us. The sections of pipe were so long that I had to drag them and trying to hold a wrench in each hand straight out in front of me became impossible because of the pain in my forearms.

Gary never told me, but I figured they must have taken me on probation, on his word. I couldn't have looked like much to them; most of the men were bigger and the few my size were hardened with compact strength. They pushed past me when I dropped my section, carrying theirs to feed the drill clamp.

One evening when we were driving home I said, "I think I ought to quit." I knew Gary couldn't go on forever doing his work and mine too. The men acknowledged him as the best worker among them, but that didn't make them like me. I felt their resentment when I faltered or went too often to the water jug. We still sat with them at meals but on the edge of the group with me on the end. If it hadn't been for Gary, they would have known ways of getting rid of me. But they knew he stood with me.

"Nope," he said. "You won't." Anger smoldered for a moment but didn't catch. "Those sorry bastards are taking bets on how many days you'll last, and guess who's the only one betting on a month."

"I would pay you back."

"Yeah, I just bet you would." He turned to look at me and I was afraid we would run off the road in the dark. "You never made enough money in your life to buy a fart. But you could get your daddy to give it to you, couldn't you?" He hated me, or at least that part of me that had spoken, and felt such a contempt for it that I knew he would like to beat it out of me. I hated that part of me too.

And I didn't really want to quit, for amid the defeats of the last two weeks I knew I was being refined, and all that was inessential burnt out of me. Excess flesh was consumed, leaving my body aching but lithe and stretched like a catgut string. Every day I took on the primordial struggle for life (too long forgotten from our blood): resting, eating, and sleeping not for pleasure but to survive until the next.

But the process was not yet complete, and I stood frustrated on the edge of something that didn't quite arrive, the moment when my clumsy fingers would hold and my cramped muscles grip; but most of all when my careful heart would respond. So two days before when I had been hanging high out over the water to screw a gauge into the valve that stuck out from a girder and had lost my grip and in my panic dropped the gauge, I had cried not because Gary came up and said, "Man, be careful, they'd fire *me* if I started dropping things overboard," but because of my frustration at having torn through enough of my cocoon walls to see light yet to be still held inside.

We hadn't had a day off since I started work. The driller was beginning to despair over me. I didn't blame him; he had a schedule to meet and I was putting him behind, to say nothing of the equipment I had lost, the paid man-hours I had wasted, or the food I had eaten. But Gary held him off, although I sensed that even he was beginning to lose patience. He took to the work so naturally and couldn't understand why I didn't.

The next day the sun seemed swollen and giant with its own heat and before noon a fuse blew somewhere in the kitchen and the electric stoves wouldn't work so we had to eat tasteless cold-cuts. Then there was the afternoon and the time when I would start lying to myself about hearing the crewboat coming to relieve us.

The operator told me to fetch the spare bit which was up a ramp in one of the equipment boxes. The bit weighed about fifty pounds of dense, concentrated metal and swirls of teeth pinched me as I walked stooped and bowlegged, carrying the mass in my laced fingers.

I was just thinking how things had gone fairly well all day and maybe I'd make it yet, when the tip of one of the clumsy steel-toed boots I was still trying to get used to stubbed against the edge of the ramp, throwing me down on my face while the bit rolled easily off the ramp. I lay there watching it with morbid curiosity as it fell to the floor of the main platform—not hitting and killing anybody, at least—the sound ringing out above the noise of the engines, and bounced off into the brown water with a dull splash.

The driller raised his arms hopelessly and one of the men strolled over to the rail and stared down, as if to see if the bit had really sunk. I climbed down to the platform deck where Gary was arguing with the angry driller.

"I saw where it went in; I could get it," I offered.

"Shut up," Gary said, noticing me for the first time. They had shut off the motors and the men, taking advantage of the break, were coming down to the platform. I went to the rail and looked down. The bit had fallen into the swirling, eddying water where the channel of the river cut through the artificial lake. The water was brown and I couldn't see anything except occasional sticks and pieces of log floating by.

"Looks like he just bought himself a oneway ticket to the house," one of the men remarked about me. "Goddamn, but the old man's hot!" Otherwise they ignored me. Gary was still trying to placate the driller and the men made jokes about how he was going to freeze his ass when he hit the spring-fed water. I had as effectively removed myself from the scene by the accident as if I had gone under with the bit. I was inconsequential now that things had become serious. They knew that, as usual, Gary would have to do my work and that I was finished. They had only been waiting for a sure bet to come in.

It was over, and I felt the final dissolution spreading through me. I pulled off my boots. The last moment of potentiality for me had passed and I had failed it. I unzipped the coveralls and stepped out of them, then my undershorts.

"Ain't that a pitiful-looking sight," one of the men noticed and they laughed. Thus an insect feels the sudden coming of winter and wanders hopeless in the cold. I was over the rail lightly, falling like a dead fly swept from a table, wondering as I fell if they would make bets on whether I'd come back up.

Hitting the water was a shock and I automatically kicked furiously trying to lift myself out of the cold while my pulse shot up trying to heat my body. Shivering frantically I surfaced yards away from where I had jumped. I faced the current and swam back, hearing Gary yelling and threatening the men for not stopping me.

I took a breath and drove my head into the cold, kicking down and against the current that swept me back. I clawed and kicked myself endlessly down until my hands clutched suddenly into the soft mud and I began digging into the cold, rotten-feeling lumps that squeezed apart and disintegrated. Then I was scrambling for the surface out of breath so quick.

A bundle of weeds floated into me and clung to my legs. "Stay on top of the water!" Gary was yelling. I felt heavy and bloated and drained, the cold of the water entering me and sinking me. This time I seemed to go down easily, digging again through the nails and glass and bits of metal—debris from months of work above—embedded in the mud; digging like a dog with both hands and feet.

I hardly noticed the drill bit when I hit it and it didn't move. By then I didn't care. I was dizzy and let it go, conscious only of the weight crushing my rib cage in the cold, my lungs shrunken and hard and hot. The cold was all through me and I knew only the pain in my chest as I floated up. I relinquished, I surrendered all to the numbness of the cold.

I flowed gently with the current, then in the blackness something hit me hard across the face and grabbed me under the arm, dragging me up. There was light and I was on my back with someone surging under me and Gary gasping over at me, "You could at least kick!"

The blanket scratched against my skin and I dug deeper shivering into it when I felt the hands shaking me and pummelling me awake. It couldn't be time to get up yet and I pulled the blanket farther up over my head for protection against awaking. "He looks like he's gonna make it after all." The blanket was jerked away from my face and the light hit me so I knew it was no use and opened my eyes. Gary was bending over me, his hair wet and dripping on my face. The other men were around me too and I remembered.

"Listen, I know where it is. I found it down there," I tried to tell them before I went back into sleep, hearing somewhere his voice over and over: "You crazy sonofabitch. You crazy sonofabitch."

The blanket was warm against the night breeze which touched us in the boat as we began the slow trip down the river. Gary and I were bundled up in the front of the boat and my hands and feet were bandaged where they had been laced with cuts from the debris in the mud.

After pulling me in, he had gone back and attached a rope to the bit so they could pull it in. The driller had been more upset by the prospect of someone drowning on his shift (inquiries into safety procedures, etc.) than by the near-loss of the bit; and Gary reasoned with him that, since I nearly killed myself trying to get his goddamn precious bit, maybe I should get another chance. About that time I began to show signs of life, so he agreed that I could stay on if I would just promise to stay away from the edges of things.

"Let's me and you get drunk tonight, just the two of us."

"Sure."

"Better still, let's throw a party at the Club. We got plenty of money." He planned it happily. "Boy, you shoulda seen yourself when you went over the side, cool as if you were going for a swim at the goddamn country club. You didn't think or nothing, just dropped right over. I couldn't believe it."

There were clouds in the evening sunset shining with violent orange light from the West. On either side of the river, dug out so we could not see them over the banks, there were several sludge pits full of the thick oil waste, and as we passed between them they were lit and their flames shot up from either side as if out of the ground—harsh orange and red flames pouring out black oily smoke. In the intense heat the pits bubbled and exploded like great cauldrons in new blasts at us where we sat, feeling the heat and watching the sky fill with smoke and fiery light, like conquerors passing through pyres of captured cities, proud in our strength. We rounded a curve and the nesting waterbirds by the thousands rose startled at our approach, swirling and calling over our heads with the sharp orange light on their wings in the black sky.

We passed out of the gates of toppling steel with the men joking about the accident. "We never come that close to losing one of our men before," one of them observed.

I felt full of new strength when we passed out into the calm of the lake where the threads of fog were trailing like distant watchfires, and heard the violent bird-cries dying away in the night.

3

It was as if from that moment I crossed over the boundary of two worlds. From then I moved only in that new land and thought only in its terms, desiring only what those around me desired.

They were men of great appetite. When they ate, they ate without manners, noisily with loud talk and the scraping of chairs and plates, with total disregard of proper diet or calorie count, several meats at a sitting, a ceaseless scooping and knifing of extra helpings and great pink balls of peach ice cream.

Beer men with big bellies who bore them before them like orbs before kings; silent old men with bodies slender and hard like youths from decades of work.

Potent men who claimed greater sexual popularity than a lone bull in a herd of hot cows, to whom fidelity and constancy meant about as much as chastity, boasting daily of the night before, celebrating in happy detail each new consummation of sex performed in total isolation from affection, love, or permanence; each act merely another paean to power which they celebrated daily in feats of strength and endurance on the rig, or another competition with each other like arm-wrestling or drinking.

Proud men who alone of their society retained the hot-blooded honor of the Southerner, who would fight at the word "liar" or any slur against the respectability of their women. Men who, if you were their enemy, could drop half a ton of metal on you from the top of the rig or trip you into the grinding machinery; but if they loved you would fight for you against a dozen others though you would not fight for yourself, or give you money if you asked though they knew it meant they would have to borrow for their own; for whom your enemies meant their enemies, and to whose door you could come at three in the morning if an angry wife had locked you out.

And I lived with the favorite of them all. He was easily the youngest, and the older men looked at him in a way that revealed the wish that their sons, growing up having to wear glasses or too puny to play football or with no love for hunting, had been born like him. He was god-like handsome among a people whom hard work and raw sun dried up and withered early, and he could work on during an extra shift when the toughest of them had to be relieved.

At night in bars they competed to buy him drinks, and were always asking him who he was sleeping with, only to be tantalized by his modest reply that it was fine for old men who couldn't even get a rise to talk about it, but for those who were still getting it every night it really didn't seem important enough to discuss. They took him hunting with their dogs and fishing in their boats and listened respectfully to his latest jokes and outrageous tales, knowing that he was cleverer than they and that if they didn't watch out they might be the victims of his jokes, which they didn't mind, although to be made fun of by anyone else would easily lead to blood. They were older men, and the more they felt themselves cooling with age the more they loved him for the sheer biological vitality of his youth which they knew they were losing.

We continued to live in the little box of a room and even went in together and bought the most expensive color TV we could find and paid on it for months. "Like a couple of niggers," he said. On days off sometimes we would stay in bed until afternoon, propped up on mounds of pillows, Gary constantly switching channels and volume from his bed with the remote-control gadget, while I complained that I couldn't keep up with the program plots, he changed them so much.

In cowboy hats pulled down low over our eyes we wore out decks of cards and bought rule books to learn new games. With the stereo or the TV blaring, and drunk from the beer whose cans lay scattered on the floor near the often-missed wastebasket, we gambled away thousands at poker, hearts, spades, crazy-eights, gin-rummy, old maid, honeymoon bridge—playing with big wads of dollar bills that we tossed on the table with boasts and threats like millionaires, one or the other sometimes winning several hundred dollars and having to support the other on an extravagant allowance until our luck (balanced on the one side by my knowledge of averages and on the other by Gary's outlandish and ever-changing bluff) swung in the opposite direction. On these nights we bloated ourselves on the biggest T-bone steaks that could be put on a plate which Gary, instructed by who-knows-what exotic cook, basted heavily with brown sugar and butter until the taste was the concentrated ultimate of richness in meat, spices, and cream.

We had the day off. I knew it even in my sleep so I slept without fear of the moment when he would come bounce and shake me awake to go to work. When I heard him up and moving, I burrowed deeper into the dark warmth of the covers; I wanted to sleep all day.

I heard the pop of a beer can being opened, and then the stereo began to play. Against my will I counted three more beers while he cooked. Then I could hear him at the table where he began lecturing me on his sexual history while he ate, even though my head was deep under the covers and I pretended to be asleep.

His narrative continued past breakfast—stories of Mexican whores at fifteen and other men's wives at eighteen. Then it began to get irritating because he was talking about girls I had known all my life as friends, talking about them intimately, about what he had done with them, and how they had craved it.

"You're obscene!" I said and threw off the covers, sitting up. He was sitting at the table drinking beer.

"What?"

"It's disgusting the way you talk."

"It's healthy. And you're a good one to talk; I bet you really go after yourself there under the covers at night." A look of horror came over him and he loped over to tickle me off the bed. "My sheets! I bet you've ruined them!"

"No I don't; I sublimate," I said, laughing at him searching the bedclothes.

"You what?" he said, backing away.

"I sublimate." He fled to the other side of the room.

"Of all the perverts, I had to go and get a goddamn 'sublimater' to come live with me."

". . . And whatever happens, don't let me get my hands on those keys," he warned as he got into the car, hinting darkly at the dire fate awaiting us should he, in his drunken state, be allowed to drive. By the time I got in he was already draining the last of a beer he had taken from the cooler that was between us on the seat and took up most of the space in the front of the car.

"Couldn't we put this thing in the back?" I asked; it was going to be practically impossible to shift gears with it in the way. He tossed the empty can casually out the window and sat there biting on the aluminum flip-tab. "Say, why don't you drink those a little slower," I said, obliging him with a tone of caution and concern.

Satisfied, he grabbed another from the ice and pulled the tab open with a dull phop and bent quickly over to slurp up the foam. "Nope," he said, wiping his mouth with his arm, "we're not putting it in the back. When the police start chasing us I'm going to take it and run while you lure them away in the car, so I want it handy. And furthermore,"—he took a long chug—"I keep you around to drive me, not to give me lectures on my drinking problem."

His car was so old and had been wrecked or modified so many times and re-painted and re-chromed that its make and year were a total mystery. The mufflers had long been removed so that it could be heard long before seen, and its horn bleated a sound much like an animal in desperate heat. Today was Saturday and he wanted to go to the pool hall in Jacksonville, a small town about thirty miles away where, he announced, there were several "sorry sonofabitches whose ass I'm gonna whip."

So off we went with Gary turning up the radio until the speakers were vibrating fuzzily and then shouting over it.

He directed me into a decaying part of town near the old railroad depot, an area frequented by negroes on Saturday afternoons. The pool hall was a converted restaurant which had probably been converted from a hat shop and still bore the traces of the former name stenciled elegantly on the large windows in front, though now mostly obscured by election posters and rodeo announcements pasted in haphazard arrangement, the newer ones gradually covering the wind-ripped and rain-faded slogans of sheriff candidates long retired.

As I parked the car in front, I knew the scenario already: Gary would swagger in, threaten to beat hell out of anyone in sight, and a friend or two would recognize him and buy him a beer and the pool room would grow warmer with his laughter and tales.

But still I was uneasy about stalking through yet another strange door in another neighboring town, and when we were inside (I following close beside), the empty echo of cue-balls striking in the barren wood room and the erratic flashing and hollow ringing of pinball machines gradually died away as the tough-looking country boys paused to pick up their cigarettes and look us over.

Satisfied that he had their attention, Gary strutted further into the middle of the room contemptuously looking the place over, but I saw none of the usual reassuring grins of those who knew him and understood the ritual, and I wished he would come back closer to the door. Then he stopped and proudly launched into his usual ridiculous boast:

"I'm Number 2 in Texas City!" like this would awe anyone within hearing, though where on earth Texas City was I'm sure no one out of a twenty-mile radius of the place could say, and I never heard anyone brag about being Number 2 in any town. But he kept going, even though a couple of boys had put down their sticks and were moving toward him.

"I'm the meanest, roughest, strongest, toughest sonofabitch in this-here town!" he announced, delivering it in his best mock-Western style, which had them hesitating and looking puzzled at one another. I think he was about ready for "There ain't room here for both of us" or "Be outa town by sundown" when there was a movement to my left and I turned and saw the man behind the counter, short and crew-cut with nasty-looking tattoos on his arm, coming towards me and, involuntarily in a voice that sounded whining and helpless, I heard myself pleading, "Gary . . ." and he turned around to see what was the matter. Which was a mistake, for an old gentleman who had been sitting crouched paralytically against the wall near him suddenly stood up and unfolded into a large man and took two steps towards Gary, on the second stepping in with his fist into the side of Gary's jaw with a sound like a mule kicking a barn and I thought Gary was going through the wall, but before he could the crew-cut man seemed to fly through the air at him, all fists and elbows when he connected with Gary's already falling carcass and I thought Gary was never going to make it to the floor but remain propped up by the fierce jabs windmilling into his body and face like a fast-draw gunman can keep a tin can in the air.

Then suddenly it was over. The old man was feebly slumping in his chair like he had never moved and would never be able to, the crew-cut was back at his counter, and all around the room lungs exhaled long-held smoke and the pinball machines and pool games whirred and clacked into motion again, except that on the floor near the second table Gary lay like a dusty pile of burlap bags so that the next pool shooter had to step over him when lining up his shot.

I thawed out my fear and got to him just as he began to move. I pulled him over on his back and his eyes opened although the left one was already beginning to puff up and there was blood running from his nose and the side of his mouth. "Get me up," he whispered through gritting teeth and I dragged him to his feet and supported him quickly to the door. But there he gripped my shoulder and stopped me and said, "I have a final word to deliver to my constituents," with a parody of a smile on his messed-up face. I couldn't believe it.

"Are you *crazy*!" I hissed, trying to get him through the door before he provoked a repeat performance, but he shoved me off and took a couple of steps back into the room. There was immediate silence and he bent over to spit blood elaborately in several spurts from his mouth. Then he drew up proudly straight.

"I let you off easy this time. But I'm gonna get me some new teeth put in and then we'll come back and see if one of you sonofabitches can knock *them* out!" That shook them up. He turned his back, strutted to the door, and held it open for me as we left. But once outside I had to help him into the car, all the time looking back uneasily at the pool hall door.

He hadn't really lost any teeth at all, but convincing blood ran down the front of his shirt, so I got a towel and began mopping the mess off his face.

He lay silently on his back with his feet out the window, biting his lip and frowning while I drove out of town towards home; and though he made no effort to reproach me I felt, worse than any reprimand, that I had put something between us. I had seen the danger and considered the outcome and had been afraid, so afraid that I had made him get hurt when he turned to help me while in my fear I made no effort to help him. I had not followed him completely into unhesitating action.

He pulled out the gold watch and opened the case. "This was my great-great-granddaddy's," he said. The case was dented and I saw that the time was wrong. "He went off to fight in the War same as yours did. And he took his own horse, too," he added. Then he settled back in silence while I drove on.

Then, as if a new thought had come to him, he sat up and turned to me. "Listen now. Say we were somewhere and things didn't go so fast like they did today"—he was making it sound almost attractive, agreeable—"and some guys jumped us. I mean, you and me. Would you fight them with me? You know, really haul in there and bust-ass with me? Huh?"

I spoke quickly while I could. "Yeah. Yeah, I think I would."

"Really?" he said, satisfied like a kid you've told that next year you'll take him to the circus. He lay back down. "That'd really be something, all right. You and me," he muttered happily, striking his palm with his other fist in anticipation of our battle. "Yeah." He was content and soon fell asleep.

I uncurled slowly from my ball and in the dream-recall of first waking remembered unhappily another recurrence of a dream type that had all but disappeared until a few nights ago. In the dreams I am a mercenary soldier, an international spy, or a modern guerrilla, the beneficiary of brilliant intuitions and sudden mental dodges which unhesitatingly lead me to encircle or escape my enemy, and in these mornings I wake still excited first with the thrill of haphazard danger and then with a longing for the careless activity of that imaginary self.

I looked over to Gary's bed where he lay sprawled with his arms and legs slung out in awkward grace and his head thrown back. As I looked at him the alarm went off and I let it ring until he began to stretch himself in the bed. He propped up on his elbows and, looking down where he rose like a young sapling under the sheet, laughed apologetically. I knew that the eagerness was on him again, to give, spend, and exhaust himself with one of the women who called up often on the phone.

Downtown later that morning I ran into my father outside the bank and had a demoralizing talk with him.

"Well, if it isn't Texas's leading oil man!" he said brightly, shaking my hand. "Spindletop come in yet?" And with him before me all the events of the recent months fell away from me, into perspective, and I considered them in light of what had been before and what might come after. There was the tailored suit from a full closet, the trimmed gray hair, the tanned face with the purposeless purposeful look of a man watching over a fortune made by other men which, like the perpetual-motion machine, ticks with a great deal of inner motion but is in reality going nowhere, neither growing nor declining. The usurer has his place, though I have none.

My new life seemed suddenly temporary.

That evening the stereo filled the room and the night beyond the windows with music, and the steaks in the oven sizzled moist odors into the dark, but I was held in the cold grip of my thoughts. I could not stay here living like this much longer, and the old dread and uncertainty began chilling me again.

Gary was singing with the record when he brought the steaks and when he sat down announced, "Guess who's coming by to pick us up in about an hour?" I turned up my nose at the smell of his cologne and made no response. "Give? Well, hang onto your hat, kid; we'll get you bred yet." He easily cancelled my virginity. "Two of the fattest, ugliest, dirtiest sluts in the business." He continued with a catalogue of their stamina and acrobatic abilities.

I barely tasted the steak. "You go on," I said. "I think I'll stay."

"Whatdya mean?" He was betrayed. I just shook my head. "What's wrong?"

"Nothing's wrong," I said, trying without conviction to sound convincing. "You just go on without me and have a good time." I was holding out on him and lying about it.

"Okay I will, goddamnit." We ate in silence and I climbed into my bed to read. There was a knock at the door and assured female voices mixed with his good-time laughter, hesitation in my direction, the door slam, and silence.

When he came back it was late and the TV had gone off into color patterns. He was happy with himself as he went around turning off the porch light and locking the door. He took off his clothes and got a beer and sat on the edge of his bed facing me. "Been having a good time with yourself?" he teased. "It was rough on me taking on two at one time, but they thought I did okay."

I put my book down. "I've been thinking." I got up and walked over to the sink for a glass of water.

"About what?"

"About what I'm going to do when I leave here."

"Why don't you stay?"

I turned and looked at him, but it was like through the wrong end of the telescope. "You know I can't do that."

"But I can?"

It had all seemed very right to me once, that I should stay there with him. But it was more like a vacation, a well-planned tour where you get to live among the savage natives and know briefly their way of life. But it is all over soon and you go back and take a bath and change to your street clothes and read about it all in *National Geographic* where it becomes about as real for you as the life of a thieving ancestor, made respectable by squeamish ladies in Richmond who write bloodless family histories.

"I think so. We're different. I come from another world; you belong here. I can't stay here and work in the oil fields and drink beer the rest of my life." My voice grew abstracted and cold, like a lecture to an anonymous class. He had become a thing bodiless; it was like talking to myself.

"Our time is very short. We buzz and fly and crawl for a summer and then die. The cold kills us. We're not like you;

we have no blood to warm ourselves. And summer is over."

"Talk sense, damnit."

"I am," I said and looked at him and was sad with the last of my feeling for him.

His anger was quick and surprised me, coming out of nowhere. He stood and grabbed my arm and shoved me against the cabinet. "Don't you talk at me like that." I felt the glass slip from my hand and heard it break and felt the splash of water against my feet, but didn't look down. "What is it you want anyway? You want a woman? I'll get you one." Then his snarl of disgust changed to a demand, almost an entreaty. "Come on. I'll get us one for tomorrow. The same one for both of us." The last was vicious again and accompanied by a shove. But I didn't want anything, at least nothing I could find there.

I walked around the table, but he followed me and his fist loomed out before me and I felt a sharp stinging on my arm like when a hypodermic needle is removed. "Whatdya want?" he pleaded, his voice a rage of anguish. He hit me again as I backed away, on the other arm at the shoulder.

"That hurt?" he growled, and hit me again, the blow bringing sudden hot light into my eyes like waking up in the morning or water thrown in your face. "Sting a little?" He struck again and I staggered back from the blow.

"Make you wanta hit me back?" A dull smashing again. "Come on." A blow. "Right here." He pointed to the shoulder he offered me. Another. "Hard." Again.

But I was slipping away, dissolving; and he shrank smaller and smaller the further I got, like a wasp disappearing into the sky. Only his fists ballooning large as they hit me were close and pulled me back, but my arms were growing numb and the pain dulled and the light faded, each jab in succession growing dimmer. And he must have realized this, seen me slipping further away, for he began hitting me harder and harder and then less from rage than in a desperate attempt to reach me, begging, "Ple-ease! Hit me back! Please! Just once!" until, staring at him with unseeing eyes, I turned and walked over to my bed and lay face down on the pillow as if asleep.

A minute later the bed rocked gently in the silence. I vaguely felt his hands on my back and shoulders, kneading them and rubbing them like he'd learned when playing football, squeezing and flexing them to relieve the pain, which I no longer felt. I thought I heard his voice somewhere, faintly: "I'm sorry I hit you." And then a silence. "Say, you hear me, kid? I didn't hurt you none, did I?" Silence. "We're still podners, ain't we?" But I was too far away by then to hear.

THE SINGER
by *David Madden*

Thank You, Reverend Bullard. Your introduction was exaggerated, of course, but I won't say it made me mad. Ladies and gentlemen, I want to say first what splendid work your church has been doing. And I'm speaking now not as a P.R. man but as a citizen and a Christian. As the reverend was saying, the church must play a role in the important issues of this changing world of ours. Now don't anybody go away and tell it on me that Pete Simpkins talked here tonight like some radical. Politics is one thing, and the hard facts of social life is another. You can't legislate morality. But now you *can* educate people about the facts of their state government and where it's not doing right by the people. So "Christian Program on Politics" is a good, 100 per cent American name for what you're doing in this election year. Now with the ward your church is in, I don't have to guess how most of you folks have voted for the last half-century, but tonight I just want to *show* you some of the mistruths that the present administration is forsting upon the people, and you can vote accordingly. Because this movie I'm going to show you—which I was in on making—is to show you the truth, instead of what you read in the papers, about how they're wiping out poverty in eastern Kentucky.

You know, in spring, when the floods aren't raging, in summer when there isn't a drought, and in the fall, when the mountain slopes aren't ablaze, eastern Kentucky is beautiful. In the winter, though, I don't hesitate to call it a nightmare landscape: nature hides herself under a mossy rock and you see the human landscape come into focus, especially in *this* winter's record cold and hunger. We took these movies all this summer and fall, off and on, up the narrow valleys, creeks, and hollers of the counties of eastern Kentucky: McCreary, Owsley, Bell, Breathitt, Perry, Pike, Laurel, Lee, Leslie, Letcher, Clay, Harlan, Knott, Floyd, and let's see, Magoffin, Martin, Whitley, and Wolfe.

So let me show you what we saw in eastern Kentucky. Now, you understand, we're in the early stages of working on this movie. We got a lot of work and a heap of fund-raising ahead of us yet, before we can get it in shape to release to the general public on TV and at rallies where it can do the damage. So, Fred, if you're ready to roll. . . .

Wayne, you want to get up here with me, so if there's any questions I can't answer, maybe you can? Come on up. You had more to do with this project than I did. As the reverend told you, ladies and gentlemen, Wayne was our advance man. We sent him ahead to prepare the people for the cameras—set things up. I got my poop sheets laying on the pulpit here, Wayne, else I'd let you see how it feels to stand in the preacher's shoes.

You're doing fine, Pete.

Then let's start, Fred. . . . Ha! Can you all see through me okay? Those numbers show up awful clear on my shirt. I better scoot off to the side a little. Now, soon's those numbers stop flashing, you'll see what the whole national uproar is about. People better quit claiming credit before it's due, just because they're trying to win an election.

Now these washed-out shoulders you can blame on the Department of Highways and Politics. Coming down the steep mountainsides, you have to swerve to miss holes that look to been made by hand grenades, and then around the curve you try to miss the big trucks. Hard freezes, sudden thaws, and coal truck traffic too heavy for the roads they travel can tear up a cheap narrow road. But if the administration kept its promises to maintain certain standards of construction . . .

Folks, that's not an Indian mound, that's a slag heap. Something else that greets you around every curve: slate dumps from shut-down mines and sawdust piles from abandoned wood-pecker mills, smoldering, thousands of them, smoldering for ten years or more. The fumes from these dumps'll peel the paint off your house. A haze always hangs over the towns and the taste of coal is in the air you breathe. That smell goes away with you in your clothes.

Good shot of one of those gas stations from the 1930s. Remember those tall, skinny, old-timey orange pumps with the glass domes? This station was lived in for about twenty-five years before it was abandoned. They don't demolish anything around there. Plenty of room to build somewhere else. Look at that place. You know, traveling in eastern Kentucky makes you feel you're back in the '30s.

Ah! Now this is a little ghost town called Blackey.

I think this is Decoy, Pete.

Decoy. And I mean, there's not a soul lives there. But plenty of evidence a lot of them once did. You get there up fifteen miles of dirt road. Millions of dollars were mined out of there. That's the company store, there's the hospital, post office, jail, schoolhouse—turned coal camp gray, and may as well be on the dark side of the moon. See the old mattress draped over the tree limb, and all the floors—see that—covered with a foot of wavy mud that's hardened over the summer. That crust around the walls close to the ceiling marks the level of the flood that bankrupted what was left of the company. Ripped couches in the yard there, stink weeds all around, rusty stovepipes, comic books, romance magazines, one shoe in the kitchen sink, the other somewhere out in the yard under the ropes where they've hacked the swing down. Rooms full of mud daubers building nests, dead flies on the sills and half-eaten spiderwebs. And over the crusts of mud in the houses and in the yards is strowed about a bushel of old letters from boys that joined the services out of desperation or hoping for adventure, and photographs the people left behind when they fled to God knows where. So it's just out there in the middle of the wilderness, doing nothing. Decoy.

Here we are in a typical eastern Kentucky town. Harlan, wudn't it, Wayne?

Hazard.

Hard to tell them apart. Well, next time we show this thing, God willing, it'll have one of the biggest TV announcers in Louisville narrating.

See the way the slopes of the mountains kindly make a bowl around Harlan? Houses cover the hillsides—just sort of flung up there. No streets or even dirt roads leads up to some of them. Swaying staircases and crooked paths go up to those porches that hover above the road there. Go along the highway, and see washing machines and refrigerators parked on the front porches. See high up, just below the clouds, that brown house with the long porch—just clinging to the cliffside? Houses like that all over, deserted, some of them just charred shells, the roofs caved in under tons of snow, the junk spewed out the front door.

Now *this* you see everywhere you go: old folks sitting on the front porch in half-deserted coal camps. On relief, on the dole, *been* on the dole since the war. That old man isn't near as old as he looks. Worked in the mines before they laid him off and idleness went to work on him like erosion. Wife got no teeth, no money to get fitted. Dipped snuff and swigged RCs to kill the pain of a mouth full of cavities till the welfare jerked them all out for her. And there comes the little baby—right through the ripped screen door—grandchild the daughter left behind when she went to Chicago or Cincinnati or *De*troit or Baltimore, which is where they all go. Didn't they say this baby's momma had it, Wayne, just had it, so they could collect on it?

Yeah.

And another girl, under twenty-one, had four babies and drew on *all* of them. Why, the government takes an interest in her that no husband could hope to match. Look at that baby's little tummy, swollen out there like a—Fred, you shoulda held on that one.

And this is a general view of how high the mountains are. *Way* up high . . . (What *was* the point of that, Wayne?)

(I don't know.)

See that stream? Watch . . . See that big splash of garbage? Fred, did you get a good shot of that woman? *There* you go! She just waltzed out in her bare feet and tossed that lard bucket of slop over the back banister without batting an eye.

Even the industries dump—

Well . . . And that stream—Big Sandy, I think. See how low it runs? Well, every spring it climbs those banks and pours down that woman's chimney and washes out every home along that valley. See the strips of red cloth left hanging on the branches of the trees? Like flagging a lot of freight trains. And rags and paper and plastic bleach jugs dangle from the bushes and from the driftwood that juts up out of the riverbed mud. In the summer those banks swarm with green, but don't let it fool you. See how wavy that mud is? And that little bright trickle of poisoned water. Fish *die* in that stuff, so leave your pole at home. And stay away from the wells. Lot of them polluted.

This is a trash dump on a slope high above Harlan where whole families go to root for "valuables." Look like bats clinging to a slanting wall, don't they? But if you go in among them, why, seems like it's just a Sunday family outing.

Most of the graveyards are up on a hill like this one, to escape the floods, I guess. But living on the mountains, maybe the natural way of thinking is up. Look close under that inscription: it's a photograph, sealed in glass, showing the deceased sitting in the front-porch swing with his wife, morning-glories climbing the trellis.

With that red sky behind them, those kadziu vines crawling all over the hillsides, dripping from the trees, look like big lizards rising up out of the mud. Come around a bend on a steep mountain highway and they've crept to the edge. Those kadziu vines are the last green to go.

Here we are up in the mountains again. (Who said to shoot the scenic overlooks, Wayne?)

(Nobody. Fred loved to shoot the view, I suppose.)

(That'd be fine if this was called "Vacation in Eastern Kentucky.") Now, this part, Wayne, I don't remember at all.

This is Cumberland. You were still asleep and Fred and I went out for coffee and passed this big crowd— Wait a minute . . .

Actually, folks, this is the first time I've had a chance to see the stuff. I told Fred just to throw it together for tonight. The real editing comes later.

Just a bunch of miners standing on a street corner. You might take notes on some of this stuff, Fred, stuff to cut out, and, ladies and gentlemen, I hope *you* will suggest what—

Good Lord, Fred!

(Watch your language, Wayne. I saw it.) Fred, I think you got some black-and-white footage accidentally mixed in. Folks, please excuse this little technical snafu, but as I say we wanted to get this *on* the screen for you, get your reactions, and I think Fred here— He's worked pretty hard and late hours, these past three weeks especially, and we only got back to Louisville a few days ago. . . . Ha! Ha. Fred, how much of this? . . . As some of you folks may know, Fred is mute.

Now this, ladies and gentlemen, is the girl some of you have been reading about in the *Courier*. And the other girl, the one leaning against the front of that empty pool hall, is——

Wayne, I don't think—I'm sure these fine people aren't interested in hearing any more about *that* little incident. Listen, Fred, that machine has a speed-up on it, as I recall.

I think he brought the old Keystone, Pete.

Oh. Well, folks, I don't know how long this part lasts, and I apologize for Fred, but we'll just have to wait till it runs out.

In the meantime, what I could do is share with you some facts I've collected from eyewitnesses and that my research staff has dug out for me. Barely see my notes in this dim light. The Cumberland Mountains are a serrated upland region that was once as pretty as the setting of that old *Trail of the Lonesome Pine* movie. It has a half-million inhabitants. But there's been about a 28 per cent decline in population of people between the ages of twenty and twenty-four, and an *increase* of about 85 per cent old people. In some counties about half the population is on relief and it's predicted that some day about 80 per cent of the whole region will be drawing commodities. There's about 25 per cent illiteracy for all practical purposes, and those that *do* get educated leave. And something that surprises me is that there's only about 15 per cent church affiliation. All in all, I'd say the poverty is worse than Calcutta, India, and the fertility rate is about as high, seems like to me. In other words, the people are helpless and the situation is hopeless. The trouble with this administration is that they *think* a whole lot *can* be done, and then they claim credit even before they do it, to make *us* look bad. We don't make no such promises. Because we see that the facts——

I think a lady in the audience has her hand up, Pete.

Ma'am? . . . I'm sorry, that old moving-picture machine makes such a racket, you'll have to speak louder.

Pete, I think what she asked was, "Did any of us get to talk with her?"

With who? Oh. Ma'am, that really isn't what this movie is about. We went in there with the best color film money can buy to shoot poverty, and where Fred got this cheap black-and-white newsreel stock——

I think it was from that New York crew.

Now, Wayne, this is not the place to drag all *that* business in. We came here tonight to show what it's like to live in the welfare state where all a body's got is promises instead of bread to put on the table. *I* know. I *come* from those people. Now there *are* some legitimate cripples, caused by explosions, fires, roof-falls, and methane gas poisoning in the mines, and some have been electrocuted and blinded and afflicted with miner's asthma. But a majority that's on relief are welfare malingerers who look forward to getting "sick enough to draw," and whose main ambition is to qualify for total and permanent disability. For those people, all these aids, gifts, grants, and loans are the magic key to the future, but I see it as what's undermining public morals and morale. That's the story I was hired to get, and as I remember that's the story we *got,* on those thousands of feet of expensive color film. And if——

Well, now we're back at the heart of the matter. Here we are on Saturday in Hazard.

> Pete.

What?

> I think *that's* Harlan.

Wayne, I was *born* in Harlan.

> Well, Pete, there's that twelve-foot pillar of coal in the middle of the intersection, which you told us to shoot because it belonged to your childhood.

Fred's got the whole thing so fouled up, he's probably spliced Hazard and Harlan together.

> Okay. . . .

Now the shot's *gone.* That, as you could see, folks, *was* the bread line. The monthly rations.

I guess Wayne was right, after all. Says WORK, THINK, BUY COAL, painted right across the top of the town's highest building.

Here you see a mother and her four kids standing beside the highway, waiting for her goldbricking husband to row across the river and pick her up and take the rations and the donated clothes over to the old log cabin—calked with mud, see that, and ambushed by briars and weeds. That's their swinging bridge, dangling in the water from the flood last spring that he's too lazy to——

Now this is *really* the kind of thing we went in there to get. That's not a desert, that's a dry riverbed those two women are crossing. What they're lugging on their backs is tow-sacks full of little pieces of shale coal that——Now see that steep ridge? You can just barely make them out on the path now. See that? See that man under the bridge? A little too dark . . . Get down under there, Fred. *There* we go! Squatting on the bottom of that dry riverbed with his five kids, actually rooting in the dirt for pieces of coal no bigger than a button that the floods washed down from the mountains. Whole family grubbing for coal, looking toward winter. Sunday. Bright fall morning. Church bells ringing in Harlan while we were shooting. Kids dirty. Noses and sores running. Don't that one remind you of pictures of children liberated from Auschwitz? Look at the way he stares at you. I offered to *buy* the man a truckload of coal. What he said, I won't repeat. Who's he talking to now, Wayne?

Fred.

Sure got a good close-up of him, Fred. The eye that belongs in that empty socket is under tons of coal dust in some choked-up mine shaft, and when he lifts those buckets and starts to follow the women, he'll limp.

Black-and-white again, Fred! Now where did this stuff *come* from? Who's paying for this waste?

That other crew, Pete, when they went back to New York, they practically gave it to Fred in exchange for a tank of gas.

(Wayne, I wouldn't be surprised if Fred put up as much as he made on the whole expedition.)

(Frankly, I think he did.)

Fred, shut off the dang picture and let the thing wind ahead by itself.

This is the old machine, Pete.

(I don't understand how he could make such a mistake. Anybody can see when they've got color and when——)

Pete, young man in the back has his hand up.

Yes? . . . Listen, son, I don't know one thing about that girl. In fact, I'd be happy to forget what little I *do* know. All three of them, in fact, and the motorsickle and the whole mess. . . . I'm sorry, you'll have to talk louder . . . (Wayne, you should have *pre*viewed this movie!) Now, son, I don't have a thing to say about that girl.

(Well, somebody better say *some*thing, Pete. It's only human for them to be interested.)

(Then *you* tell them. You're as bad as Fred was—*is*.)

To answer your question, young man. No one has yet located the parents of the two girls.

These shots show them walking along the highway between Whitesburg and Millstone. The smoke you see is coming from one of those slag heaps Pete was telling about. It's the first light of morning before the coal trucks begin to roll. Later, on down the road, one of those trucks, going around a hairpin curve, turned over and slung coal almost 200 feet. That's The Singer, as she was called, the one with the guitar slung over her shoulder, and there's the friend, who always walked a few steps behind, like a servant. These black-and-white shots were taken by the crew from New York. I don't think *they* were mentioned in the newspaper stories, though. But they crossed paths with the girls in Wheelright, Lovely, Upper Thousand Sticks, Dalna, Coal Run, Highsplint, and other towns along the way. Yes, Reverend Bullard?

What did he say?

He said no smoking on church premises, Pete.

Oh. Sorry, reverend. Nervous habit, I guess.

Somewhere in here is a shot of the preacher who started it all. Soon after people started talking about The Singer, he described himself as God's transformer. Claimed God's electricity flowed through *him* into *her*. The day they found the girls, he put it a different way—said he was only God's impure vessel.

Ladies and gentlemen, I would like to focus your attention on a really fine shot of a rampaging brush fire that—

Hey, Fred, I didn't know you got those girls in color!

Okay, Fred, okay, okay! Just throw the switch! Lights, somebody! Lights!

Fred, Pete said to cut the projector off!

Folks, I apologize for Fred, but I had no way of knowing. Fred, this is what I call a double cross, a real live double cross, Fred! You promised that if I'd hire you back, you'd stay away from that New York outfit and those two girls.

(Pete, aren't you doing more harm than good by just cutting the thing off?)

(This stuff don't belong in the picture.)

(Just look at their faces. They want to know all about it, they want to *see* every inch of film on that reel.)

(This ain't what I come to show.)

(She couldn't be in *all* of it. We didn't run into her that often, and neither did that New York bunch.)

(It's distracting as hell.)

(The poverty footage is *on* the reel, too, you know.)

(You *want* to tell them, don't you? *He* wants to *show* them and *you* want to tell all about it. Admit it.)

(Look, Pete, it's only natural——)

(Yeah, like looking for a job when you're out of one. Go ahead. Tell them. If Fred wasn't a mute, he'd furnish the sound track in person.)

Folks, this is just our little joke tonight. We thought we'd experiment. You know, give you a double feature, both on the same reel.

Here, Fred got a shot of the revival tent in Blue Diamond where she first showed up about five weeks ago, early in September. That's a blown-up photograph of Reverend Daniel in front of the tent. Sun kind of bleached it out, but the one in the paper was clear.

That's the old company store at Blue Diamond and the photographs you see on the bulletin board there are of miners killed in the war. Maybe one of them was The Singer's brother.

The tent again . . .

The way people tell it, Reverend Daniel was preaching pretty hard, lashing out at sinners, when he suddenly walked straight to the back, pointing at a girl that he said he knew wanted to be saved because she had committed a terrible sin that lay heavy on her heart. And standing where the tent flap was pulled back, dripping rain, was this girl. Thin and blond, with the biggest eyes you ever saw.

Good footage on that wrecked car in the creek, Fred. You know, the young men go to *De*troit to work awhile, get homesick and drive some broken-down Cadillac or Buick back home and leave it where it crashed in the river or broken down in the front yard, and the floods ship it on to the next town. Hundreds of roadside scrap yards like this one where cars look like cannibals have been at them. Good panoramic shot. Fred's pictures are worth a thousand words when he's got his mind on his work.

> And here's Fred shooting the mountains again. Couldn't get enough of those look-offs.
>
> So there she stood, a little wet from walking to the tent in the rain, and Reverend Daniel led her up front, and pretty soon he began to heal the afflicted. They say he was great that night. Had them all down on the ground. He laid hands on them, and there was speaking in tongues, and those who weren't on the ground were singing or doing a sort of dance-like walk they do. And when it was all over, he went among them with his portable microphone and asked them to testify.
>
> Then he came to *her*. And instead of talking, she began to sing. A man that lived nearby was sitting on his porch, and he said he thought it was the angels, coming ahead of Gabriel.
>
> She sang "Power in the Blood" for an hour, and when she stopped, Reverend Bullard—excuse me—Reverend *Daniel* asked her what she suffered from. And when she didn't speak, he said he bet it was rheumatic fever, and when she still didn't speak——

Moving on now, we see a typical country schoolhouse. In the middle of the wilderness, a deserted schoolhouse is not just an eyesore, it's part of the country. When people live on the front porch, relics of the past are always in view, reminding them of times that's gone: the era of the feuds, of the timber industry, of the coming of the railroad, of the moonshine wars, and of the boom and bust days of coal.

Ha! Fooled you, didn't I? Thought it was deserted. Ha. There's the teacher in her overcoat, and the kids all bundled up in what little clothes they have. See that one girl with rags wrapped around her legs in place of boots? That's the reason: gaps between the boards a foot wide. And believe me, it gets cold in those mountains. Now what's the administration going to say to the voters about *that* when they go to the polls in November? They claim they're *improving* conditions.

From the highway, you don't often see the scars in the earth from strip mines and the black holes where the augers have bored. I suppose those New York boys are trying here to give you an impression of the landscape The Singer wandered over. On the highways, you may pass a truck hauling big augers, but to watch the auger rig boring, you have to climb steep dirt roads. That's where The Singer and her friend seem to be going now—not on purpose, I don't think. Just aimlessly wandering, those New York boys following close behind with their black-and-white. Now who's *that* girl? Oh, yeah, the one that starred in *their* movie. What was her name? Deirdre. . . . Back to The Singer again. Going on up the winding road, and those black eyes staring at you out of that far hillside—auger holes seven feet in diameter. The dust those trucks stir up barreling down the mountain is from spoil banks that get powder-dry in the summer and it sifts down, along with coal grit, onto the little corn and alfalfa and clover that still grows in the worn-out land. With its trees cut down by the stripping operation, its insides ripped out by the augers, this mountain is like some mangy carcass, spewing out fumes that poison the air and the streams.

Where these augers and the strip mining have been, snows, rains, floods, freezes and thaws cause sheet erosion, and rocks big as tanks shoot down on people's cabins. This used to be rich bottomland. Now it's weeds, broomsedge, and thickets. Don't look for an old bull-tongue plow on *those* hillsides. And the big trees are gone. Of course, the blight got the chestnuts, but what do you call *this?*

Wayne, let's keep in mind the money that helped make this movie possible.

Well, this, friends, was once called Eden. Some people have reason to call it dark and bloody ground. There's places that look like the petrified forest, places like the painted desert, but it's a wasteland, whatever you call it, and the descendants of the mountaineers are trespassers on company property that their fathers sold for a jug, ignorant as a common Indian of its long-term value. And they can't look to the unions any more. The UMWA has all but abandoned them, some say, while the bulldozers that made that road and which drag that auger apparatus into place for another boring every hour continue what some people call the rape of the Appalachians . . . I'm sorry, I didn't hear the question?

Young lady wants to know what happened next.

Next? Oh. You mean about The Singer? Oh, yes. Well, the story, which we got piece by piece, has it that when the girl didn't speak, Reverend Daniel got a little scared and looked around for someone that knew her.

In the entrance to the tent, where The Singer had stood, was another girl: black-haired, sort of stocky, just a little cross-eyed, if you remember the picture, but pretty enough to attract more men than was good for her. She didn't know The Singer but was staring at her in a strange way, and several boys in leather jackets were trying to get her to come away from the tent and go off with them.

Now this is a shot of the girls drinking from a spring that gushes out of the mountain with enough force to knock a man down. Her friend sees the cameraman and steps behind The Singer to block her from the camera. Those New York boys would barge right in without blinking an eye.

Well, Reverend Daniel did find someone who knew her and who said there was absolutely nothing wrong with her, physically or mentally, that when she saw her the day before The Singer was just fine. That made everybody look at Reverend Daniel a little worried, and he turned pale, but an old, old woman began to do that dance and speak in tongues and when she calmed down she said *she* knew what had come over the girl. Said she had what they call——

Now here we see the Negro section of Harlan. Notice——

Just a second, Pete.

The old lady said that the girl had got a *calling,* to sing for Jesus. And The Singer began to sing again, and the girl that travels with Reverend Daniel *gave* The Singer her guitar, said, "Take it, keep it, use it to sing for Jesus." Then *she* took up the tambourine, the whole tent began to shake with singing, The Singer's voice soaring above it all, and listen, ladies and gentlemen, before that night nobody in that area knew a thing about her singing.

You pass this condemned swimming pool and that graveyard of school buses and go over a concrete-railing bridge that humps in the middle and there you are in the Negro slums. The cement street turns into a dirt road a country block long, and the houses are identical, and the ones that haven't turned brown are still company green. See, the street is just a narrow strip between that hill and the river that floods the houses every year. At each end, wild bushes reach up to the tree line. At the back steps, a steep hill starts up. There's no blackness like midnight dark in the Cumberland Mountains, but the white man can walk this street safely. No one wants to discourage him from buying the white lightnin' and the black women. And here we are inside the dance hall where the Negroes are having a stomping Saturday night good time. Awful dim, but if you strain a little . . .

Want to let me finish, Pete?

Then The Singer walked out of the tent and they followed her up the highway, but she kept walking, higher and higher into the mountains, and the people kept falling back, until only one person walked behind her—that black-haired girl with the slightly crossed eyes.

You through?

Sure, go ahead.

(They just *missed* the greatest shot in the whole movie.)

(They saw it, Pete.)

(The hell. They were listening to *you,* 'stead of looking at the *move*-ee. For an Ohio Yankee you sure act like you know it all. Now when *my* part is on, *you* shut up.)

(Fair enough, Pete.)

More of the black-and-white. . . . Shots of The Singer at a coal tipple near Paintsville. Truck mine. No railroad up this branch, so they just pop-shoot it with dynamite and truck it out.

Anyway, what would happen was that The Singer and the other girl would walk along and whenever and *wherever* the spirit moved her, The Singer would sing. Just sing, though. She couldn't, wouldn't, anyway *didn't* speak a word. Only sing. And while she sang, she never sat down or leaned against anything. Hardly any expression on her face. Sometimes she seemed to be in a trance, sometimes a look on her face like she was trying to hide pain, sometimes a flicker of a smile, but what got you in a funny way was that the song hardly ever called for the little things she did, except the happy songs, "I Love to Tell the Story," or "Just as I Am," you know—those she'd plunge into with a smile at first, until she would be laughing almost hysterically in a way that made you want to hug her, but, of course, nobody, not even the kind of women that'll take hold of a sweating girl full of the Holy Ghost and drench her with tears, really dared to. No, not The Singer. She wasn't touched, that I know of, though people sort of reached for her as she passed. But then sometimes you'd feel that distance between you and her and next thing you knew she'd be so close in among people you could smell her breath, like cinnamon. She had ways of knocking you off balance, but so you only fell deeper into her song. Like she'd be staring into your eyes, and her lids would drop on a note that was going right through you. Or coming out of a pause between verses, she'd suddenly take three steps toward you.

They walked, they never rode They walked thousands of miles through those hills, aimlessly: through Sharondale, Vicco, Kingdom Come, Cumberland Gap, Cody, along Hell-for-Certain Creek, and up through Pine Mountain.

And here we are in a jailhouse in Manchester. Handle a lot of coal around there. And these boys you see looking through the bars are teenagers the sheriff rounded up the night before. Out roving the highways in these old cars, shooting up road signs. They loved having their picture taken—a mob of little Jesse Jameses.

Now, I ask you: can the administration just *give* these youngsters jobs?

Winding road . . . coiled up like a rattlesnake. See where those boys—WATCH FOR FALLEN ROCK. Just shot it all to pieces. Most of them will end up in the penitentiary *making* road signs.

Now in this shot—in Hellier, I think—The Singer has wandered into a church and they've followed her. And off to the side there, among the parked cars and pickup trucks, you can see the other girl, leaning against the door of a car, talking to some men and boys. Can't see them for the car. There. See them? Talking to her? Well, that's the way it was, after awhile.

A boy told one of the young men on the New York crew that he was outside the tent at Blue Diamond that first night, and that the black-haired girl was going from car to car where the men were waiting for their wives to come out of the revival tent and the young boys were waiting for the girls to come out. But *this* girl never made it *in*. They always waited for her outside, and she went with all of them. And then—I don't know who or where I got it—the girl heard the singing and left the cab of a coal truck and went to the entrance of the tent, and then when The Singer went out to the highway, she followed her. Then after about a week——

Oh. Go ahead, Pete.

Folks, here we are, back on the track, with a shot we were afraid wouldn't come out. Good job, Fred. A carload of pickets waiting to join a caravan. Eight young men in that car, all of them armed. You can hear them at night, prowling up and down the highways in long caravans, waking you up, and if you look between the sill and the shade by your bed, you can see lights flashing against Black Mountain under the cold sky, full of stars.

And here we are swinging down the mountainside. . . . Some of the early September shots before this record cold drove people indoors. We just suddenly, in the bright morning sunlight, came upon this train, derailed in the night by dynamite. Don't it look like an exhibit out in that big open space, all those crowded porches huddled around on the bare hillside?

Going along the highway, you can expect to find anything in the yards, even in front of inhabited houses. See that car? Pulled up by a block and tackle tossed over a tree limb—looks like an old-time lynching. This man's taken the junk that the floods leave on his porch—sometimes on his roof—and arranged a *dis*play of it all in his yard.

You look up and see those long porches, hanging over the road, seems like, clinging to the steep slopes, and what it reminds *me* of is little villages in Europe when I was in the army. Whole family sitting out there, on the railing, on car seats jerked out of wrecks on the highway, on cane-bottom chairs salvaged from their cabin home places far in the mountains, talking and swirling RCs and watching the road. For *what*?

Well, for *her,* wouldn't you say, Pete? Word of her singing ran ahead of her, and since nobody knew where she'd turn up next . . . One time she even walked right into a congregation of snake handlers and started singing. But not even that brazen New York crew got any shots of *that*. And sometimes she'd walk right out of the wildest woods, the other girl a little behind, both of them covered with briars and streaked with mud.

Here—somewhere along the Poor Fork of the Cumberland River—Fred seems to be trying to give an impression of the road, the winding highway The Singer walked. Pretty fall leaves stripped from the branches now. Abandoned coal tipples, bins, chutes, ramps, sheds, clinging to the bare hillsides like wild animals flayed and nailed to an old door. Those stagnant yellow ponds where the rain collects breed mosquitoes and flies the way the abandoned towns and the garbage on the hillsides breed rats. You may leave this region, but the pictures of it stick in your mind like cave drawings.

Here you see The Singer and her friend walking along one of those mountain roads again. Too bad those New York boys couldn't afford color. A light morning rain has melted most of the snow that fell the night before. This is along Troublesome Creek and they've already been through Cutshin, Diablock, Meta, Quicksand, Jeff, and Carbon Glow, Lynch, and Mayking. By the way, the reason the girls are dressed that way—style of the '30s—is because they're wearing donated clothes. Remember the appeal that came over television and filled the fire stations with clothes after last spring's flood?

These artificial legs were displayed in a window near our *ho*tel next to the railroad depot in Harlan. Nice, hazy Sunday morning sunlight, but *that,* and this shot of a pawnshop window—little black-muzzled, pearl-handled revolvers on pretty little satin cushions—reminds you of what kind of life these people have in the welfare state. And those windows piled high with boots and shoes beyond repair are something else you see at rest on Sunday in Harlan.

> There they are in front of a movie theater—— What's that showing? Oh, yeah, an old Durango Kid movie. Fred and I saw that in another town—Prestonsburg, I think. Never forget the time she walked into a movie theater and started to sing right in the middle of a showdown in some cowboy shoot-out, and one big lummox started throwing popcorn at her till the singing reached him and he just left his hand stuffed in the bag like it was a bear trap.

> Anyway, as I was telling before, the other girl, after about a week, took to luring the men away from The Singer because they began to follow her and bother her and try to start something with her, so the friend had to distract them from her, and ended up doing the very thing she had tried to stop herself from doing by going with The Singer. They say The Singer never seemed to know what was going on. She'd walk on up the highway or on out of town and the other girl would catch up.

See how they just nail their political posters to the nearest tree? Sun sure bleached that man out, didn't it?

> Here, Fred got a shot of the New York movie crew getting out of their station wagon. Three young men and a girl. Looks like somebody scraped the bottom of a barrel full of Beatniks, doesn't it? The local boys and men kept teasing them about their beards and they tried to laugh along, but finally they would get into fights, and we'd come into a town just after they had gone, with the police trying to get people out of the street, or the highway patrol escorting the crew into the next county. They came down to shoot what they called an art movie. They told Fred the story once and I listened in, but I can't remember a thing about it, except that this girl named Deirdre was going to be in it. She *was* in it. Yeah, this is one of the scenes! Shot her *in front of* a lot of things, and she would kind

of sway and dip around among some local people—just like that—and everybody—— Yeah, see the big grins on their faces? And the director kept begging them to look serious, look serious.

That one's *yours,* Pete.

Shots of old men in front of the courthouse. . . . Young boys, too. . . . No work. Bullet holes around the door from the '30s. Bad time, bad time.

What those guys did, Wayne, was make everybody mad, so that when *we* came rolling into town, they were ready to shoot anybody that even *looked* like he wanted to pull out a camera.

Yeah. Always pointing those loaded cameras at things and running around half-cocked, shoot, shoot, shooting.

Then they ran into The Singer and her friend, and——Yeah, this is the one, this is actually the *first* shot they took of The Singer. First, this is a close-up of *their* girl—Deirdre—you're looking at, long stringy hair, soulful eyes. One time they even put something *in* her eyes to make the tears run. And in just a second they'll swing to catch The Singer. That's it! See the camera jerk? The script writer saw The Singer on the opposite corner and jerked the cameraman around. Here you can see The Singer's friend standing off to the side, on the lookout for trouble-makers—front of a little café in Frenchberg. Cameraman got her in the picture by accident, but later when the director caught on to what she was *doing* with The Singer, he hounded her to death. Made her very angry a couple of times. Deirdre in *his* movie though——

Pete . . .

What's you want?

Your part's on.

Well . . . that's, as you can see . . . the garbage in the streams there . . . kids with rickets . . . brush fire in the mountains . . .

I was about to say about the folk singer from Greenwich Village—Deirdre—she got very angry, too, over the way the movie boys took after The Singer, so she threatened to get a bus back to New York. But after they had listened to people tell about The Singer in the towns they came into, not long after she had gone on, and after they had tracked her down a few times, and after Deirdre had heard her sing, she got so she tried to *follow* The Singer. Deirdre ran away from the movie boys once, and when they caught up with her the black-haired girl was trying to fight off some local boys who thought Deirdre was like *her.* But she wasn't. Not after The Singer got to her, anyway. I don't know *what* Deirdre was like in New York, but in the Cumberland Mountains she heard one song too many. I never saw her after she changed, either. Finally, the New York boys had to lock her in a room at the Phoenix Hotel in Salyersville and one stayed behind to watch over her. Wish we had a shot of that hotel. White, a century old, or more, three stories in front, four in back, little creek running behind it. Three porches along the front. Sit in a broken chair and watch the people go by below. If you're foolish, you sit on the rail. If you leave the windows open in the room at the back, you wake up covered with dew and everything you touch is damp.

Pete.

Shots of another abandoned shack . . .

Go ahead, Pete.

They can see it okay . . . same old thing . . .

Oh. Now *that's* Reverend Daniel, the one that ministered to The Singer in Blue Diamond. He'd moved his tent to Pikeville and that's where we saw him, and got these shots of his meeting. Promised him a stained-glass window for his tent if he'd let us, didn't we, Wayne? Ha! Anyway, next time we saw him was a week ago, just before the accident, and he told me how he had offered to make The Singer rich if she would sing here in Louisville. Told her people all over Kentucky had read about the wandering singer for Jesus, and that he could make her famous all over the world, and they could build the biggest church in the country, and stuff like that. She just looked at him and walked on. He pestered her awhile, but finally gave up after about six miles of walking. Wayne, you saw him after it happened, didn't you?

> Yeah. He blames himself. Thinks he should have looked after her. As though God meant him to be not just a transformer but a guardian angel, too. He'll never put up another tent as long as he lives.

And that girl—Deirdre—that come down from New York, she could be dead for all we know. The boy that was guarding her——

> Said he shouldn't have told her about what happened on the highway.

Slipped out of the Phoenix *Ho*tel somehow and vanished.

> She *may* turn up in New York.

And she might turn up alongside some highway in the mountains, too.

> This is one of Fred's few shots of the girls. He hated to disturb them. Actually, The Singer never paid any attention to us or to the other crew, did she, Pete? Mostly, Fred listened to her sing, standing in the crowds in Royalton, Hardburley, Coalville, Chevrolet, Lothair, his camera in his case, snapped shut. Right, Fred? But here, while they sat on a swinging bridge, eating—well, the friend eating, because nobody ever saw The Singer put a bite of food in her mouth, just drink at the mountain springs—Fred got them with his telephoto lens from up on one of those look-offs beside the road.

Kind of grainy and the color's a little blurred, but it looks like it's from a long way off through a fine blue mist at about twilight. Nice shot, Fred.

There's those numbers on my shirt again. What about that? Fred, you want to catch that thing—film flapping that way gets on my nerves.

> Personally, I'm glad nobody's got the *end* on film.

Know what you mean, Wayne.

> What the papers didn't tell was——

That the boy on the motorsickle? . . .

> Wasn't *looking* for the girls.

And he wasn't a member of some wild California gang crossing the country, either.

> Go ahead and tell them, Pete.

That's okay. You tell it, Wayne.

> The way Fred got the story—— Fred, this is one time when I really wish you could speak for *yourself*. Fred was the one who kept his arms around the boy till he stopped crying.

Tell them where it happened.

> Outside Dwarf on highway 82. The girls were walking along in the middle of the highway at about three o'clock in the morning and a thin sheet of ice was forming, and this motorcycle came down the curve, and if he hadn't slammed on his brakes——

More or less as a reflex——

> It wouldn't have swerved and hit them.

You see, Fred had set out to catch up with them. Me and Wayne'd left him to come on back to Louisville alone, because he said he was going to stop off a day or two to visit his cousin in Dwarf, and when he pulled in for coffee at Hindman and some truck driver told him he *thought* he had seen the girls walking, out in the middle of nowhere, Fred got worried, it being so cold, and——

So he tried to catch up with them.

The girls and the boy were lying in the road.

Kid come all the way from Halifax, Nova Scotia.

Yeah, that's where they got the facts wrong in the paper. Saying he was some local hoodlum, then switching to the claim that he was with a gang from California. The fact is that the boy had quit school and bought a brand new black Honda, and he had set out to see the United States.

Wait a second, Wayne. Fred's trying to hand you a note.

Thanks, Fred. Oh. Ladies and gentlemen, Fred says here that it wasn't *Halifax,* Nova Scotia. He says, "It was *Glasgow,* Nova Scotia. Not that it matters a damn."

THE BEST TEACHER IN GEORGIA

by *John McCluskey, Jr.*

The Musing

As Dora fell off the back porch, next door Miss Mary Lou Hunter was turning the selector to a rerun of "The Rockford Files." In her front room Miss Mary settled down in her favorite sitting chair, a steaming cup of sassafras tea, sweetened with two teaspoons of honey, resting on a carefully folded square of newspaper. To make sure that she did not miss a word of her favorite afternoon show, the set was turned up loud, so Dora's first shout for help, an embarrassed yelp more than anything else, was drowned in the twangy guitar crescendo of the opening theme. Then Miss Mary blew into her tea, took two sips, and set her cup down. Scratching down an arm, she sat back and waited for the first chase scene.

Dora had tried to catch herself on her hands, then her elbows, but had failed. Her knees and chin were the three points that absorbed the impact of her fall. She was as surprised at the lack of pain as she was by the fall itself, surprised even that her glasses stayed on. The world had been spinning when she stepped to the back porch. There were plenty of pecans under the great tree and she wanted to bring them in for a pie. That spinning that she had now been so accustomed to for the past eight months started again as the back door slammed and she had stopped at the edge of the porch and, already falling, was reaching for the railing. She heard a *crack* before the ground rushed up fast. The ground was still spinning as she lay there even now, the faint smell of packed dirt in her nostrils.

She tried to get up, but could not. She could not feel her arms, though she could see them tensing. It was as if they had fallen asleep during some nightmare and she was armless. She remembered screams in such dreams and knew that the one she recalled from just seconds ago was her own.

Her weight was on her neck now and she slid forward and to one side quickly to relieve the pain. But her shawl tightened deeply across a shoulder. She struggled to lessen the strain, but could not. Finally, she managed to turn just enough so that she could free one end of it. She let out a sigh. Again, she could compare this to only a bad dream. Occasionally there would be one—whether someone was chasing her or she was shut up in a closet didn't matter. She would be suffocating and one part of her could tell the other that she was face down in the pillow and all she had to do was roll over. The feeling was so strange, because there would be the great will to breathe again and the easy urge to lie like that as sweet resignation washed over her. And she would turn, in some mighty effort, just enough to breathe fresh air, then search back quickly for the episode in her dream that made her realize that she was suffocating. She could never find it.

Bunny had brought the shawl home from a trip to Philadelphia two years ago. Bunny and her husband had spent the Christmas away, so the gift was not presented until New Year's Eve. That was the day before the coming of the deer. New Year's Day was unseasonably warm and from the thick woods over a mile away a small band of deer found Dora's backyard. Fawns were frolicking about the pecan tree by the time Dora came to the back window. They played close to the porch while two larger does kept to the edge of the yard, watchful. With potato chips or soda crackers in their hands a few of the kids like little Calvin, Thomasina's loud boy, tried to tiptoe up on one of the fawns. When they saw a big buck step out of the woods and start digging at the ground with one of his front legs—well, those children just backed on off and went up to the porch to watch the show like everybody else. The deer stayed out there for ten, twenty minutes and then, one by one, they were gone. Just like ice storms in that part of Georgia, they appeared as swift and silencing miracles and then, with no trace, they left. That was the morning of the day Bunny and her husband returned. She brought the shawl over after dinner. It was in a deep-red box hidden beneath the wrapping paper, and inside the blue and cream shawl rested on crinkly paper. Dora had been connecting the shawl to the deer to ice storms ever since.

She reached down suddenly. A gust of wind had started up

the back of her legs and she felt the hem of her skirt rising, then the skirt ballooning up from behind. She quickly smoothed down her skirt. Don't want that Mr. Leroy to look down here and see me with my bloomers showing to the sky. Just like him, too, to look out of his window and stay up there grinning like a fool and trying to see what all he could see while I'm down here rolling around. I've caught him a dozen times riding that old piece of bicycle he got, riding past the porches and trying to look up some woman's dress. He bends down like he cocking his head to say "hello" but he got something else on his mind. That man's got to be ninety if he's a day and still carrying on all sorts of foolishness. He's the loudest one in church on Sunday mornings and he shouts "amen" loud enough to shake the rooftop when the preacher starts in talking about the lust in some men's hearts. Yes, he'd see all he could see first before he would get over here to help out, nasty thing. She tried to push up, but failed.

"Lord, I've got to get up from here," she heard herself say.

What else might be going on? She thought of how some young fool could break right in the front door while she was out here and steal the television set or those pretty brass lamps that she had bought her mother on her seventieth birthday. Her mother would be in the bedroom humming to herself and not hear or see a thing. Then Dora let her body go limp. As the sound of her heavy breathing faded, she could hear a car or two passing out front. Before too long there would be the four o'clock whistle from the paper mill. She could hear now, as plain as the ticking of a clock coming closer, the wooden heels of someone walking past the house. She wanted to scream but decided against it. And what would that whistling somebody with the loud heels find? Just an old woman without her hair piece who fell off her back porch and could not get up again. About as bad as Humpty-Dumpty with all the king's men. She saw knights in dull grey armor attempt to pull her up, fail in their grunting, then mount their glorious black horses, liveried in silver, and move slowly off in single file. She laughed drily. "Well, I'm not that bad off and I want everyone to know it."

She thought that if she stayed still for just a short while longer the ground would stop spinning and she could roll to one side, then sit up. Last spring she had fallen and she had had several dizzy spells since then, spells which made her sit up for minutes until her head cleared. The first time she was in the backyard where she had finished hanging out some sheets to dry. From here, she could see the spot where she fell, and she remembered how she caught herself on her hands and waited there on all fours, her knees sinking into the soft ground, until the world stopped. She didn't tell her mother about that time. Would her mother have understood? She who, until her own blindness, never knew a sick day or a knock-down illness in her life?

At some time in her late years her mother must have fallen. But now with her cane, the fingers of her free hand walking the rough plaster walls, she knew every dangerous step, every corner, every table in the house. And Dora, twenty years younger and fading already, it seemed, was given to dizzy spells that a smart-aleck doctor with a beard could not cure. Her mother had already outlived a husband and son and it looked like she would outlast the only one she had left.

She gained an elbow about the time Miss Mary whooped when the private investigator, after hitting a lumbering goon on the chin, doubled up in pain, then blew across and kissed his aching knuckles. The giant merely blinked, rocked slightly on his heels, and chased Rockford off with a lead pipe. Miss Mary sipped again from her tea, then glanced to the window where the end of a branch was scraping. She could not hear it, however.

Still on one elbow, Dora concluded that her mother must be in the dim sitting room listening to the late afternoon symphony from a classical music station out of Atlanta. "The only colored woman in Spalding County, Georgia, to listen to the opera," she once boasted. But it was the news, the details of all events national and international, that kept her by the radio. She feared losing touch, feared not knowing the names of those who made the news. ("We as a people have got to get our heads out of the sand and realize there's a whole world out there. How come colored can't care about what's happening in India or Poland?")

Two squirrels skittered around the trunk of a burr oak in Mr. Leroy's yard. From somewhere a crow cawed and she could smell the smoke from someone's burning trash. At a two-year-old's height she could see the backyard. It was large enough for a child to run about, to feel small in. When she was growing up here, it always seemed that the yard was large enough for a dozen cows to graze in. The day she returned from Atlanta to live here she was shocked at the game her memory had played. It was still a large backyard dominated by one huge pecan tree at its center but three full-grown Herefords would have made it appear a pen.

Now she could only look. Just months earlier she had been hoeing in the garden which ran the length of the back fence. Now the green beans and most of the tomatoes had been picked. A few collards were left, but the sweet potatoes, somehow forgotten this year, might be a lost cause. Of course, as predictable as early November frost, there were the plentiful pecans. Each year, as an additional Christmas gift, she would send a large box of them to her daughter and her family in Milwaukee. The daughter would call on Christmas Day to thank her for the gifts, usually not mentioning the pecans. She called, too, after the arrival of flowery cards on Mother's Day and her birthday. Every two years the daughter with her family would visit and every other trip they would arrive in a new car. Dora would have appreciated a long letter on no special occasion and failed to convince herself that they were too busy adding on rooms, buying appliances, getting promotions on time. Had she as a mother failed to do something right when her daughter was six, or thirteen, or twenty? She wondered.

Adjusting her glasses, she tried to focus on the pecan tree now. During the late mornings of last August's brutal heat she would read in the shade of the great tree, its trunk cool along the length of her spine. Last summer she had stuck to poetry—Shakespeare's sonnets, the Brownings, and Countee Cullen. Six years before she retired she had been voted the best teacher in Georgia and she could recite Cullen poems with a voice pitched to the middle register of a flute: *These are no wind-blown rumors, soft say-sos/no garden-whispered hearsays, lightly heard . . .*

When she finished, her eyes often moist, the fifth-graders would look at one another in confusion. One or two might cover their mouths and roll their eyes, not knowing any better, and the silence would then beg for a snicker, a dry cough—anything to bring the room back to normal. How did she ever hope to successfully explain the weight behind the words she recited, the moons and suns those words created and softly landed upon? She hoped to merely provide them a form which their experiences would fill. In the all-white school where she taught during the last five years before her retirement, they would giggle. Somehow she would expect it there, though. She imagined they took the sight and her words home with them to be brought up over dinner. ("Mama, we got this strange colored woman for a teacher and she can stare out the window and say poems by heart. And sometimes she seemed to be about ready to cry over them.") Aside from screams barely audible over guitars, they had no stories, no songs. It was even getting that way for the black children. She confessed to herself many times that she pitied the young with their anthems of screaming guitars and runaway saxophones. Many gave them noise for music, but few gave them a poem.

She was almost up now, but, leaning too far forward, slipped and fell to her other side with a groan. ("Mama, Mama, don't come now and learn I'm like this!") A door slammed; Mr. Leroy's dog barked twice. Her view was once again that of a toddler's. She listened to the beating of her heart. It was not racing. Her breathing was normal. The ground had stopped spinning. She was relieved by at least that much. She managed to turn over on her back, not caring how her dress and sweater would look when she finally did get up. She relaxed and looked up through the limbs of the tree to the sky. She had not lain on her back looking at the sky for nearly fifty years.

Though it was summer that time, she could not remember the heat. Her high school friend Alphonso had introduced her to George, who attended Morehouse and visited town that summer after his junior year. With Alphonso's fiancée, they had all bicycled out to a small lake for a picnic. Then they walked, the couples separating, and she and George found a hill all their own. After they shared their future plans, they relaxed in a silence. She closed her eyes and saw red against the insides of her eyelids. Clover was sweet and she smelled his cologne, a faint lemon it was, before he kissed her lightly. The next day they returned alone and kissed many times, she recalled now. They made love quickly, awkwardly. Afterwards, briefly, she let the sunlight again paint the insides of her eyelids red. By the next summer he urged marriage, but she could not accept then. She would remember that hill, that red, those smells forever, but it had only been a few brief moments and she had imagined love to be a string of such moments, palpable, infinite in length.

Horace, however, was October, a vivid splash of color. She married him the year she found her first teaching job. It was a hard marriage. She grew to crave consistency. She fought for sameness, though it was the sudden peaks and valleys of emotions that raced her blood. He died fifteen years ago and she lived alone in Atlanta until she retired. Her daughter invited her to join her and her young family in Milwaukee. "Too cold," she had lied, not wanting to be a burden and, besides, her mother needed someone close by.

Perhaps it was the rush of those long ago moments, the slant of the afternoon light on this day, that had sent her to the back window before she decided that the fallen pecans were worth her trouble. Yes, perhaps that, before the porch started spinning. Resting on an elbow, she concluded once more that she would seek more moments, more vivid splashes of color. Just three days ago she had reserved a flight to New Orleans. She had planned the trip with Gladys, another retired teacher, but Gladys died suddenly in September. A local travel agency had made travel arrangements, reserved a seat at two plays, and was forwarding a listing of preferred restaurants with the ticket. ("You'll just love New Orleans, Mrs. Wright," said an agent over the phone, cool efficiency sugared by admiration. "We've got you a room in an elegant and quiet hotel on Royal. It's what we call a 'C and C,' clean and classy. All our clients just love the place. It's near everything in the Quarter. You're a mighty lucky lady.")

She and Horace had planned to visit New Orleans for two weeks around their fortieth anniversary. From the stories of clubwomen who had traveled there in groups or with their husbands, she knew all about the food, all about the balcony ironwork magically spun by slaves. This time of the year there would be no crowds and she would not be jostled on the sidewalks. But what if she had a spell there among strangers, collapsing on those ancient sidewalks before ancient cafés? She winced. Please hurry, ticket. With ticket and travel plans in hand, only then would she tell her mother. Another breeze swept up and terror was that sudden chill at the base of her neck.

And Fond Memory

She was sitting upright now. She could hear her mother working her way through the kitchen. She shook her shawl out and placed it around her shoulders. She brought her legs together and smoothed down her skirt and apron. After a glance at Mr. Leroy's window, she found a few pecans nearby and dropped them in her lap one by one, as she might drop stones in a pond.

"Dora? Dora child, where you at? I been calling you for the past ten minutes and can't get a word out of you."

"Out here, Mama. I'm out back."

"What you doing out there so long?" came her mother's voice.

"I'm just out here enjoying the weather."

Her mother pushed through the back door and came onto the porch. She tapped her cane against a chair, then against the wooden pillar that supported the railing. "You going to catch a cold out there. This fall weather can fool you."

She smiled. Over a long checkered dress her mother wore a faded brown sweater. She was a neat woman who dressed up and wore small gold earrings every day.

"I want to get supper started and I need you to slice a little of that ham off. Come on now. You ain't getting no younger and too much of this sitting around on the wet ground can give you arthritis. I know what I'm talking about."

"I'm on my way, Mama."

As her mother started to turn, the sleeve of her sweater caught a nail on the back post. In trying to pull away and misjudging her own strength, she pulled a hole in the sweater sleeve and, losing her balance, fell backward against, then through, the railing.

"Mama! Mama, the rail . . . !"

The old woman fell on her side, no scream, and her body made a dull sound when it landed, like that of a hundred-pound bag of seed.

"Mama, you all right?" She tried to inch forward on her elbows and stomach. "Mama, say something!"

Her mother was bleeding from the elbow and the forehead, a trickle of blood snaking between the eyebrows already. Her eyes wide—though her daughter felt the stare of such eyes long past fear—she looked to the sound of her daughter's voice as a child would. The blood, a thin crooked line, found the bridge of her nose.

"Oh, I'm all right. Just a scratch, child." She patted her own cheek.

"Still . . . no, you're bleeding, Mama!" She was close now, close enough to touch her. Then with the hem of her skirt she wiped the blood from her mother's face, dabbed at the cut lip she had just noticed.

Her mother shook her head as if to push her away, the way an embarrassed child anticipates a rough kiss.

"Help me up, Dora."

"I can't."

"What do you mean 'you can't'?"

"I can't. Mama, I can't get up my own self."

Her mother bowed her head as if in prayer. "Dora, how long you been out here like this?"

"Fifteen, twenty minutes maybe. My arms and legs just went numb for a while . . ."

Her mother's soft shriek came as if she had been hit suddenly. Then her face tightened. Dora thought she was going to cry.

"Well, I'll be. How come you didn't call me, Dora?"

"There wasn't any need. It's happened to me once before and I got right up, quicker than a cat. If it keeps happening, I better learn to pull up some kind of way."

"You better to see a doctor is what you 'better' do. Why, you could just drop down at the shopping center or at church or anywhere. Whatever it is, you better not play with it."

"I have seen a doctor. He just gave me some pills. He said if they didn't do any good to come back around Thanksgiving for some tests." She glanced off. By Thanksgiving she would have been to New Orleans. Maybe the trip would cure her. She had heard of spells that just went away mysteriously after coming on once or twice.

Her mother was silent for a moment, then spoke softly to no one in particular. "You ain't getting no younger. You can't all the time be hoping to pull yourself up." Then to her daughter: "Can you see anybody around? Let's call somebody over."

"Mama, just give me a minute. I'll have both of us up."

"Well, just one minute then. This cold ground cause arthritis sure as we sittin' here." She snorted, patted a thigh. "At least I ain't broke nothing. Women fallin' at my age break a hip the same way you break a toothpick. Remember Lila's girl, Hattie, slipped and fell on her steps that time and broke her hip in two places? That's been what—two, three years, ain't it? You ain't broke nothing, did you?"

"I better not break anything. Can you imagine me on crutches?"

"There's worse things than crutches," her mother said.

Then Dora chuckled. "We must look quite the pair. Two women plopped down in the backyard and can't even get up."

"It won't be funny an hour from now and we still sittin' here."

"Just another min . . . the front door locked? You sure everything's off the stove?" Dora suddenly imagined the house on fire, smoke billowing from the kitchen. Sirens before loud-talking, heavy-booted firemen intruding, crashing through the kitchen to find them in the backyard.

"Nothing's on the stove and I 'spect the front door is still fastened. I locked it right back after the mailman done handed me the mail." (The ticket! The ticket!)

Dora turned to her side, pushing, but her arms were numb, muscleless. She sighed. She wanted to laugh. She wanted to cry.

"This telling me I'm getting old," Dora said.

"You got to use your common sense, Dora. You got to fall off the porch to find out you ain't thirty no more? Or even sixty?"

She looked at her mother's sightless eyes. They were hazel. Younger, Dora felt that when she looked directly at her mother the light eyes gave the impression of pools that you looked into. Her own eyes, dark brown and like most of her features, were those of her father. She fidgeted.

"Well, I don't like this. I don't like this feeling where you can't control what your body's going to do the next minute."

"What you gon' do about it? I don't like it either, but ain't nothing neither one of us can do about it. You gon' stop the clock?"

"I mean I'm scared, Mama. I been scared for a long time, but it took this to make it plain."

She brushed dirt from her mother's shoulders, then dabbed again at her forehead. The trickle of blood had slowed.

"Scared?" her mother asked. "I tell you what scared is. I'm talking after the change of life and after your teeth go bad and your hair thin. I do have to thank the good Lord my hair stayed thick as it was when I was fifty. But then your hearing go on you and you get tired of bothering folks all the time, asking them to repeat what they say. So you just shake your head at them and go ahead and say something to what you think they be saying. And you remember how it was early morning when you hear the birds just starting up, just before daybreak? Well, you get so you can hardly make out the sounds. 'Bout the only thing you can catch is some big ole crow or Mr. Leroy's loud rooster. Then before you get used to not hearing as good as you used to, your smell give out on you. Oh, you can still make out cabbage all right, but what happened to cinnamon and thyme and just plain ole coffee? You see something that could be a rose or a apple, but unless it's right up against your nose, it might as well be plastic. Dora, you hear what I'm telling you?"

"I can hear you."

Her mother cleared her throat. "Then if all that ain't enough to make you scared and mad at the same time, you might get some real bad luck and get the cataracts on your eyes so bad that even after operations . . ."

"Mama, I know about what happened. You don't . . ."

". . . listen good, now—after the operations you still can't see and over months you can't see nothing, not one blessed thing. You can tell light from dark, but you see things like they was ghosts or something and you know you'll be that way—even if you believe every jack-leg preacher between here and Nashville who say he got the cure for you—know you'll be seeing ghosts for the rest of your life. And all the while your bones drying out and getting like . . . like chalk. Every little bump you pay for, every fall. You and me gon' feel this fall clear into next week."

Dora was shaking her head. She tried to see herself in ten years, fifteen, twenty. Wondered what her luck would be. Would she be able to see the morning light sparkling on heavy frost? Would she be able to see her amaryllis in bloom? Would she be able to do for herself alone? But her mother continued, reaching to pat her arm.

"Ain't no time to be scared, child. We just got to get on up from here before we have everybody laughing at us out here. They'll laugh first, then come running over here asking if they can help."

"They're not that bad."

"I tell you I know them, I know how they do."

She wanted to tell her mother that it was not just the embarrassment and confusion of a body failing, growing stranger. It was death, of course, that frightened her, that chilled her again that afternoon with terror. And when she finally brought herself to say it, she was alarmed at how still her mother became. A truck rumbled down the street out front.

"Don't be so scary, will you? You talk like you got one foot in the grave already. Plus, it ain't too late for a woman like you to have men to come calling."

Dora snickered. "Only eligible men 'way out here are not doing so well, in and out of the hospital every day. You talking about them calling and they can barely make it back and forth from the bedroom to the kitchen table to the bathroom . . ."

Her mother threw up her hands. "There you go again talking like you too good."

"I'm not too good. Don't you think I'd like to have a man to talk to, to have dinner with and dance with, all these years?"

"All I'm saying is that a woman like you—educated and who think about things—a woman like you need friends, educated friends. I know there ain't much here for you. Maybe for somebody like myself, when I was your age, there were one or two. You remember I used to see that Mr. Coates? Now he was a nice decent man to come courting and like me he just barely finished high school."

"Mama, college by itself doesn't mean a person's nice or decent or even educated."

Her mother talked on, low. Dora didn't know whether her mother heard her this time. Softening, she pitied her in that instant, pitied them both. After Horace's death, there had been a special friend once and, now, the sun flooding the yard with its dying light, she spoke of him. She had promised herself never to tell.

He had been five years younger and his wife was in poor health. Downtown Atlanta had only recently opened up for blacks and three nights a week they would meet at a small restaurant off Peachtree. They kept to the side streets, hand in hand. Once even they checked into a downtown hotel, avoiding the popular Paschal's Motel, as husband and wife. As excited as teenagers, they had been. But their affair lasted only three months. Except for her award, it was the most exciting time of her last fifteen years.

Her mother's face had registered curiosity when she first started. By the end of Dora's confession, however, her face revealed horror. Her head snapped once, as one shakes from a sudden chill or as if slapped from a trance.

"Shame on you, running around like some hot-blooded Jezebel! Rochelle Louise Fields didn't raise no child to run around with married men. Taking advantage of some sick woman that way and you a respectable schoolteacher and all. I bet you got plenty of secrets."

Dora's shoulders sagged under a heavy load. She saw herself in New Orleans alone on Rue Royal. The knocking of her shoes was the loudest noise in the world as she walked. She stepped into a puddle of light, scattering pigeons. There was a spring in her step as she moved on. The background music was not Dixieland, but Ella Fitzgerald's "A Tisket-A Tasket." Lilac was strong in the air, though it was autumn.

"I was lonely, Mama. He was, too. That was all it was." She dared not tell her that for six of those ten daring weeks it had been much, much more. Then as if some bright monarch butterfly skimming the tops of grass and grain, love had skipped away.

"You don't know how lonely I've been these last fifteen years. There have been times I've wanted to walk over to the woods and just scream like some crazy woman. You hear that clock ticking, cars passing out front with people on their way to . . . to something—work, a family, somebody to touch and talk to. And you know all you can do is sit or dress up to walk downtown or around the mall. Crowds make you feel even more lonely so you come back home and sit. Maybe you find a book every once in awhile to take your mind off things. Even then you want to share it."

"That don't mean you take up with a married man," her mother said. "They're plenty of folks lonely—I can tell you a thing or two 'bout loneliness—but they ain't dabblin' in no other folkses' home business. And you don't have to talk about me on the sly, talking about what I didn't learn. I only got past high school. I know I never got the chance to go to college or nothing. My folks barely had enough to send one off and that was your uncle who just wasted his time and your grandpa's money . . ."

Dora clapped both hands to her ears, for she had heard many times the tale of the ungrateful son who had gone up to Fisk to be a doctor and had ignored his studies. He had been dismissed and worked in Nashville over a year before he found the nerve to tell the family what had happened. Meanwhile Rochelle had worked and bought second-hand books to know the worlds she thought only available to the formally educated. She learned manners from books of etiquette and from the languid gestures of young white women she served during lawn parties. Grew defensive, then rigid about what she learned in solitude. So when her brother returned to confess his failure, she wanted to throw a pot at him. She, not he, should have been the one to go to college. Later her carpenter husband would stand mute before her monologues on good manners.

How quickly we forget! Rochelle's own daughter took her own good fortune in stride. Why, even after she had been voted Teacher of the Year for the entire state and shifted to a formerly all-white school as something of a reward, Dora was not pleased. Dora's hands came down quickly when she heard.

"Mama, how many times I have to tell you that I made my way teaching among my own? I was happy at Phillis Wheatley. I didn't need white folks to tell me I was good. My students and other teachers and principal nominated me. That made me the proudest."

But her mother was convinced that such matter-of-factness before so astounding an achievement—she had been voted best out of the "colored" and the white!—was unnatural. Was vanity.

Dora now thought of the plaque, a gold-plated square on a walnut-stained shield, hanging on the front room wall where no one could miss it. Her mother had insisted that it be hung there. Dora thought of the telegram that she tore open with trembling hands and the long, flowery letter that followed. This, before the award ceremony and the plaque.

"Oh, Mama, remember how you came to Atlanta with Miss Mary and everybody? How I wore my best dress—it was the baby-blue one with the lace at the collar and sleeves, remember?—I put on so much rosewater I bet they could smell me clear to Macon. And, when that skinny man with the big belly announced my name, how I walked up—I don't know 'til this day how my legs carried me up there—and I had to practically tear the plaque away from him."

Her mother nodded and managed a smile. "He acted like you was taking gold." It was one of her mother's last sights. In a brief silence they sat. That night in an auditorium in downtown Atlanta had been one of the last genuinely happy moments they had shared. Now her mother cleared her throat.

"Dora, we ain't got all day. The past is dead and gone."

"Maybe." In two weeks, her ticket clutched against one side, she would board a gleaming silver jet with royal blue trim. Two stewardesses would flash smiles and point her to her seat. Her mother would be here in this house where she would be cared for by Miss Mary until Dora returned. By then she would understand why Dora needed the trip. By then all her questions would be exhausted.

She got to her knees and leaned on her mother. "Mama, just stay still. I need your shoulder here to help me up." Trying to put as little weight on the shoulder as she could, she pressed down and gained one foot, then the other.

"Glory," she sighed. "Mama, I'm up. I'll come from behind you and pull you up."

Slipping her arms inside her mother's, she pulled her up in one mighty effort. Then she brushed the dirt from both of them and led her mother to the porch.

"You smell good today, Mama."

"You saying I don't always smell good?"

"No, I'm just saying you smell special. It's that new Avon you ordered? You got somebody special to come calling?"

"Don't sass," her mother said.

Smiling, Dora did not look back as they opened the door. The pecans were still scattered behind. She would come back for them soon. Right now there was a supper to start.

Miss Mary turned off the set as the last of the theme song died out. She climbed upstairs to her bedroom and walked to the window. She heard the back door slam next door at the Fields's. Their backyard seemed to float up toward her. There was a spot just beyond the porch that was favored by the sun. Pecans had rained there. The yard looked like a meadow left shimmering after a morning mist had just lifted. She recalled that years ago a flock of pink flamingoes had played near that very same spot.

Or was it peacocks or rabbits or . . . deer?

THE SOJOURNER
by *Carson McCullers*

The twilight border between sleep and waking was a Roman one this morning: splashing fountains and arched, narrow streets, the golden lavish city of blossoms and age-soft stone. Sometimes in this semi-consciousness he sojourned again in Paris, or war German rubble, or Swiss skiing and a snow hotel. Sometimes, also, in a fallow Georgia field at hunting dawn. Rome it was this morning in the yearless region of dreams.

John Ferris awoke in a room in a New York hotel. He had the feeling that something unpleasant was awaiting him—what it was, he did not know. The feeling, submerged by matinal necessities, lingered even after he had dressed and gone downstairs. It was a cloudless autumn day and the pale sunlight sliced between the pastel skyscrapers. Ferris went into the next-door drugstore and sat at the end booth next to the window glass that overlooked the sidewalk. He ordered an American breakfast with scrambled eggs and sausage.

Ferris had come from Paris to his father's funeral which had taken place the week before in his home town in Georgia. The shock of death had made him aware of youth already passed. His hair was receding and the veins in his now naked temples were pulsing and prominent and his body was spare except for an incipient belly bulge. Ferris had loved his father and the bond between them had once been extraordinarily close—but the years had somehow unraveled this filial devotion; the death, expected for a long time, had left him with an unforseen dismay. He had stayed as long as possible to be near his mother and brothers at home. His plane for Paris was to leave the next morning.

Ferris pulled out his address book to verify a number.

He turned the pages with growing attentiveness. Names and addresses from New York, the capitals of Europe, a few faint ones from his home state in the South. Faded, printed names, sprawled drunken ones. Betty Wills: a random love, married now. Charlie Williams: wounded in the Hürtgen Forest, unheard of since. Grand old Williams—did he live or die? Don Walker: a B.T.O. in television, getting rich. Henry Green: hit the skids after the war, in a sanitarium now, they say. Cozie Hall: he had heard that she was dead. Heedless, laughing Cozie—it was strange to think that she too, silly girl, could die. As Ferris closed the address book, he suffered a sense of hazard, transience, almost of fear.

It was then that his body jerked suddenly. He was staring out of the window when there, on the sidewalk, passing by, was his ex-wife. Elizabeth passed quite close to him, walking slowly. He could not understand the wild quiver of his heart, nor the following sense of recklessness and grace that lingered after she was gone.

Quickly Ferris paid his check and rushed out to the sidewalk. Elizabeth stood on the corner waiting to cross Fifth Avenue. He hurried toward her meaning to speak, but the lights changed and she crossed the street before he reached her. Ferris followed. On the other side he could easily have overtaken her, but he found himself lagging unaccountably. Her fair brown hair was plainly rolled, and as he watched her Ferris recalled that once his father had remarked that Elizabeth had a 'beautiful carriage.' She turned at the next corner and Ferris followed, although by now his intention to overtake her had disappeared. Ferris questioned the bodily disturbance that the sight of Elizabeth aroused in him, the dampness of his hands, the hard heartstrokes.

It was eight years since Ferris had last seen his ex-wife. He knew that long ago she had married again. And there were children. During recent years he had seldom thought of her. But at first, after the divorce, the loss had almost destroyed him. Then after the anodyne of time, he had loved again, and then again. Jeannine, she was now. Certainly his love for his ex-wife was long since past. So why the unhinged body, the shaken mind? He knew only that his clouded heart was oddly dissonant with the sunny, candid autumn day. Ferris wheeled suddenly and, walking with long strides, almost running, hurried back to the hotel.

Ferris poured himself a drink, although it was not yet eleven o'clock. He sprawled out in an armchair like a man exhausted, nursing his glass of bourbon and water. He had a full day ahead of him as he was leaving by plane the next morning for Paris. He checked over his obligations: take luggage to Air France, lunch with his boss, buy shoes and an overcoat. And something—wasn't there something else? Ferris finished his drink and opened the telephone directory.

His decision to call his ex-wife was impulsive. The number was under Bailey, the husband's name, and he called before he had much time for self-debate. He and Elizabeth had exchanged cards at Christmastime, and Ferris had sent a carving set when he received the announcement of her wedding. There was no reason *not* to call. But as he waited, listening to the ring at the other end, misgiving fretted him.

Elizabeth answered; her familiar voice was a fresh shock to him. Twice he had to repeat his name, but when he was identified, she sounded glad. He explained he was only in town for that day. They had a theater engagement, she said—but she wondered if he would come by for an early dinner. Ferris said he would be delighted.

As he went from one engagement to another, he was still bothered at odd moments by the feeling that something necessary was forgotten. Ferris bathed and changed in the late afternoon, often thinking about Jeannine: he would be with her the following night. 'Jeannine,' he would say, 'I happened to run into my ex-wife when I was in New York. Had dinner with her. And her husband, of course. It was strange seeing her after all these years.'

Elizabeth lived in the East Fifties, and as Ferris taxied uptown he glimpsed at intersections the lingering sunset, but by the time he reached his destination it was already autumn dark. The place was a building with a marquee and a doorman, and the apartment was on the seventh floor.

'Come in, Mr. Ferris.'

Braced for Elizabeth or even the unimagined husband, Ferris was astonished by the freckled red-haired child; he had known of the children, but his mind had failed somehow to acknowledge them. Surprise made him step back awkwardly.

'This is our apartment,' the child said politely. 'Aren't you Mr. Ferris? I'm Billy. Come in.'

In the living room beyond the hall, the husband provided another surprise; he too had not been acknowledged emotionally. Bailey was a lumbering red-haired man with a deliberate manner. He rose and extended a welcoming hand.

'I'm Bill Bailey. Glad to see you. Elizabeth will be in, in a minute. She's finishing dressing.'

The last words struck a gliding series of vibrations, memories of the other years. Fair Elizabeth, rosy and naked before her bath. Half-dressed before the mirror of her dressing table, brushing her fine, chestnut hair. Sweet, casual intimacy, the soft-fleshed loveliness indisputably possessed. Ferris shrank from the unbidden memories and compelled himself to meet Bill Bailey's gaze.

'Billy, will you please bring that tray of drinks from the kitchen table?'

The child obeyed promptly, and when he was gone Ferris remarked conversationally, 'Fine boy you have there.'

'We think so.'

Flat silence until the child returned with a tray of glasses and a cocktail shaker of Martinis. With the priming drinks they pumped up conversation: Russia, they spoke of, and the New York rain-making, and the apartment situation in Manhattan and Paris.

'Mr. Ferris is flying all the way across the ocean tomorrow,' Bailey said to the little boy who was perched on the arm of his chair, quiet and well behaved. 'I bet you would like to be a stowaway in his suitcase.'

Billy pushed back his limp bangs. 'I want to fly in an airplane and be a newspaperman like Mr. Ferris.' He added with sudden assurance, 'That's what I would like to do when I am big.'

Bailey said, 'I thought you wanted to be a doctor.'

'I do!' said Billy. 'I would like to be both. I want to be a atom-bomb scientist too.'

Elizabeth came in carrying in her arms a baby girl.

'Oh, John!' she said. She settled the baby in the father's lap. 'It's grand to see you. I'm awfully glad you could come.'

The little girl sat demurely on Bailey's knees. She wore a pale pink crepe de Chine frock, smocked around the yoke with rose, and a matching silk hair ribbon tying back her pale soft curls. Her skin was summer tanned and her brown eyes flecked with gold and laughing. When she reached up and fingered her father's horn-rimmed glasses, he took them off and let her look through them a moment. 'How's my old Candy?'

Elizabeth was very beautiful, more beautiful perhaps than he had ever realized. Her straight clean hair was shining. Her face was softer, glowing and serene. It was a madonna loveliness, dependent on the family ambiance.

'You've hardly changed at all,' Elizabeth said, 'but it has been a long time.'

'Eight years.' His hand touched his thinning hair self-consciously while further amenities were exchanged.

Ferris felt himself suddenly a spectator—an interloper among these Baileys. Why had he come? He suffered. His own life seemed so solitary, a fragile column supporting nothing amidst the wreckage of the years. He felt he could not bear much longer to stay in the family room.

He glanced at his watch. 'You're going to the theater?'

'It's a shame,' Elizabeth said, 'but we've had this engagement for more than a month. But surely, John, you'll be staying home one of these days before long. You're not going to be an expatriate, are you?'

'Expatriate,' Ferris repeated. 'I don't much like the word.'

'What's a better word?' she asked.

He thought for a moment. 'Sojourner might do.'

Ferris glanced again at his watch, and again Elizabeth apologized. 'If only we had known ahead of time——'

'I just had this day in town. I came home unexpectedly. You see, Papa died last week.'

'Papa Ferris is dead?'

'Yes, at Johns Hopkins. He had been sick there nearly a year. The funeral was down home in Georgia.'

'Oh, I'm so sorry, John. Papa Ferris was always one of my favorite people.'

The little boy moved from behind the chair so that he could look into his mother's face. He asked, 'Who is dead?'

Ferris was oblivious to apprehension; he was thinking of his father's death. He saw again the outstretched body on the quilted silk within the coffin. The corpse flesh was bizarrely rouged and the familiar hands lay massive and joined above a spread of funeral roses. The memory closed and Ferris awakened to Elizabeth's calm voice.

'Mr. Ferris' father, Billy. A really grand person. Somebody you didn't know.'

'But why did you call him *Papa* Ferris?'

Bailey and Elizabeth exchanged a trapped look. It was Bailey who answered the questioning child. 'A long time ago,' he said, 'your mother and Mr. Ferris were once married. Before you were born—a long time ago.'

'Mr. Ferris?'

The little boy stared at Ferris, amazed and unbelieving. And Ferris' eyes, as he returned the gaze, were somehow unbelieving too. Was it indeed true that at one time he had called this stranger, Elizabeth, Little Butterduck during nights of love, that they had lived together, shared perhaps a thousand days and nights and—finally—endured in the misery of sudden solitude the fiber by fiber (jealousy, alcohol and money quarrels) destruction of the fabric of married love.

Bailey said to the children, 'It's somebody's suppertime. Come on now.'

'But Daddy! Mama and Mr. Ferris—I——'

Billy's everlasting eyes—perplexed and with a glimmer of hostility—reminded Ferris of the gaze of another child. It was the young son of Jeannine—a boy of seven with a shadowed little face and nobby knees whom Ferris avoided and usually forgot.

'Quick march!' Bailey gently turned Billy toward the door. 'Say good night now, son.'

'Good night, Mr. Ferris.' He added resentfully, 'I thought I was staying up for the cake.'

'You can come in afterward for the cake,' Elizabeth said. 'Run along now with Daddy for your supper.'

Ferris and Elizabeth were alone. The weight of the situation descended on those first moments of silence. Ferris asked permission to pour himself another drink and Elizabeth set the cocktail shaker on the table at his side. He looked at the grand piano and noticed the music on the rack.

'Do you still play as beautifully as you used to?'

'I still enjoy it.'

'Please play, Elizabeth.'

Elizabeth arose immediately. Her readiness to perform when asked had always been one of her amiabilities; she never hung back, apologized. Now as she approached the piano there was the added readiness of relief.

She began with a Bach prelude and fugue. The prelude was as gaily iridescent as a prism in a morning room. The first voice of the fugue, an announcement pure and solitary, was repeated intermingling with a second voice, and again repeated within an elaborated frame, the multiple music, horizontal and serene, flowed with unhurried majesty. The principal melody was woven with two other voices, embellished with countless ingenuities—now dominant, again submerged, it had the sublimity of a single thing that does not fear surrender to the whole. Toward the end, the density of the material gathered for the last enriched insistence on the dominant first motif and with a chorded final statement the fugue ended. Ferris rested his head on the chair back and closed his eyes. In the following silence a clear, high voice came from the room down the hall.

'Daddy, how *could* Mama and Mr. Ferris——' A door was closed.

The piano began again—what was this music? Unplaced, familiar, the limpid melody had lain a long while dormant in his heart. Now it spoke to him of another time, another place—it was the music Elizabeth used to play. The delicate air summoned a wilderness of memory. Ferris was lost in the riot of past longings, conflicts, ambivalent desires. Strange that the music, catalyst for this tumultuous anarchy, was so serene and clear. The singing melody was broken off by the appearance of the maid.

'Miz Bailey, dinner is out on the table now.'

Even after Ferris was seated at the table between his host and hostess, the unfinished music still overcast his mood. He was a little drunk.

'L'improvisation de la vie humaine,' he said. 'There's nothing that makes you so aware of the improvisation of human existence as a song unfinished. Or an old address book.'

'Address book?' repeated Bailey. Then he stopped, noncommittal and polite.

'You're still the same old boy, Johnny,' Elizabeth said with a trace of the old tenderness.

It was a Southern dinner that evening, and the dishes were his old favorites. They had fried chicken and corn pudding and rich, glazed candied sweet potatoes. During the meal Elizabeth kept alive a conversation when the silences were overlong. And it came about that Ferris was led to speak of Jeannine.

'I first knew Jeannine last autumn—about this time of the year—in Italy. She's a singer and she had an engagement in Rome. I expect we will be married soon.'

The words seemed so true, inevitable, that Ferris did not at first acknowledge to himself the lie. He and Jeannine had never in that year spoken of marriage. And indeed, she was still married—to a White Russian money-changer in Paris from whom she had been separated for five years. But it was too late to correct the lie. Already Elizabeth was saying: 'This really makes me glad to know. Congratulations, Johnny.'

He tried to make amends with truth. 'The Roman autumn is so beautiful. Balmy and blossoming.' He added. 'Jeannine has a little boy of six. A curious trilingual little fellow. We go to the Tuileries sometimes.'

A lie again. He had taken the boy once to the gardens. The sallow foreign child in shorts that bared his spindly legs had sailed his boat in the concrete pond and ridden the pony. The child had wanted to go in to the puppet show. But there was not time, for Ferris had an engagement at the Scribe Hotel. He had promised they would go to the guignol another afternoon. Only once had he taken Valentin to the Tuileries.

There was a stir. The maid brought in a white-frosted cake with pink candles. The children entered in their night clothes. Ferris still did not understand.

'Happy birthday, John,' Elizabeth said. 'Blow out the candles.'

Ferris recognized his birthday date. The candles blew out lingeringly and there was the smell of burning wax. Ferris was thirty-eight years old. The veins in his temples darkened and pulsed visibly.

'It's time you started for the theater.'

Ferris thanked Elizabeth for the birthday dinner and said the appropriate good-byes. The whole family saw him to the door.

A high, thin moon shone above the jagged, dark skyscrapers. The streets were windy, cold. Ferris hurried to Third Avenue and hailed a cab. He gazed at the nocturnal city with the deliberate attentiveness of departure and perhaps farewell. He was alone. He longed for flighttime and the coming journey.

The next day he looked down on the city from the air, burnished in sunlight, toylike, precise. Then America was left behind and there was only the Atlantic and the distant European shore. The ocean was milky pale and placid beneath the clouds. Ferris dozed most of the day. Toward dark he was thinking of Elizabeth and the visit of the previous evening. He thought of Elizabeth among her family with longing, gentle envy and inexplicable regret. He sought the melody, the unfinished air, that had so moved him. The cadence, some unrelated tones, were all that remained; the melody itself evaded him. He had found instead the first voice of the fugue that Elizabeth had played—it came to him, inverted mockingly and in a minor key. Suspended above the ocean the anxieties of transience and solitude no longer troubled him and he thought of his father's death with equanimity. During the dinner hour the plane reached the shore of France.

At midnight Ferris was in a taxi crossing Paris. It was a clouded night and mist wreathed the lights of the Place de la Concorde. The midnight bistros gleamed on the wet pavements. As always after a transocean flight the change of continents was too sudden. New York at morning, this midnight Paris. Ferris glimpsed the disorder of his life: the succession of cities, of transitory loves; and time, the sinister glissando of the years, time always.

'*Vite! Vite!*' he called in terror. '*Dépêchez-vous.*'

Valentin opened the door to him. The little boy wore pajamas and an outgrown red robe. His grey eyes were shadowed and, as Ferris passed into the flat, they flickered momentarily.

'*J'attends Maman.*'

Jeannine was singing in a night club. She would not be home before another hour. Valentin returned to a drawing, squatting with his crayons over the paper on the floor. Ferris looked down at the drawing—it was a banjo player with notes and wavy lines inside a comic-strip balloon.

'We will go again to the Tuileries.'

The child looked up and Ferris drew him closer to his knees. The melody, the unfinished music that Elizabeth had played, came to him suddenly. Unsought, the load of memory jettisoned—this time bringing only recognition and sudden joy.

'Monsieur Jean,' the child said, 'did you see him?'

Confused, Ferris thought only of another child—the freckled, family-loved boy. 'See who, Valentin?'

'Your dead papa in Georgia.' The child added, 'Was he okay?'

Ferris spoke with rapid urgency: 'We will go often to the Tuileries. Ride the pony and we will go into the guignol. We will see the puppet show and never be in a hurry any more.'

'Monsieur Jean,' Valentin said. 'The guignol is now closed.'

Again, the terror, the acknowledgement of wasted years and death. Valentin, responsive and confident, still nestled in his arms. His cheek touched the soft cheek and felt the brush of the delicate eyelashes. With inner desperation he pressed the child close—as though an emotion as protean as his love could dominate the pulse of time.

GOOD COUNTRY PEOPLE

by *Flannery O'Connor*

Besides the neutral expression that she wore when she was alone, Mrs. Freeman had two others, forward and reverse, that she used for all her human dealings. Her forward expression was steady and driving like the advance of a heavy truck. Her eyes never swerved to left or right but turned as the story turned as if they followed a yellow line down the center of it. She seldom used the other expression because it was not often necessary for her to retract a statement, but when she did, her face came to a complete stop, there was an almost imperceptible movement of her black eyes, during which they seemed to be receding, and then the observer would see that Mrs. Freeman, though she might stand there as real as several grain sacks thrown on top of each other, was no longer there in spirit. As for getting anything across to her when this was the case, Mrs. Hopewell had given it up. She might talk her head off. Mrs. Freeman could never be brought to admit herself wrong on any point. She would stand there and if she could be brought to say anything, it was something like, "Well, I wouldn't of said it was and I wouldn't of said it wasn't," or letting her gaze range over the top kitchen shelf where there was an assortment of dusty bottles, she might remark, "I see you ain't ate many of them figs you put up last summer."

They carried on their most important business in the kitchen at breakfast. Every morning Mrs. Hopewell got up at seven o'clock and lit her gas heater and Joy's. Joy was her daughter, a large blonde girl who had an artificial leg. Mrs. Hopewell thought of her as a child though she was thirty-two years old and highly educated. Joy would get up while her mother was eating and lumber into the bathroom and slam the door, and before long, Mrs. Freeman would arrive at the back door. Joy would hear her mother call, "Come on in," and then they would talk for a while in low voices that were indistinguishable in the bathroom. By the time Joy came in, they had usually finished the weather report and were on one or the other of Mrs. Freeman's daughters, Glynese or Carramae. Joy called them Glycerin and Caramel. Glynese, a redhead, was eighteen and had many admirers; Carramae, a blonde, was only fifteen but already married and pregnant. She could not keep anything on her stomach. Every morning Mrs. Freeman told Mrs. Hopewell how many times she had vomited since the last report.

Mrs. Hopewell liked to tell people that Glynese and Carramae were two of the finest girls she knew and that Mrs. Freeman was a *lady* and that she was never ashamed to take her anywhere or introduce her to anybody they might meet. Then she would tell how she had happened to hire the Freemans in the first place and how they were a godsend to her and how she had had them four years. The reason for her keeping them so long was that they were not trash. They were good country people. She had telephoned the man whose name they had given as a reference and he had told her that Mr. Freeman was a good farmer but that his wife was the nosiest woman ever to walk the earth. "She's got to be into everything," the man said. "If she don't get there before the dust settles, you can bet she's dead, that's all. She'll want to know all your business. I can stand him real good," he had said, "but me nor my wife neither could have stood that woman one more minute on this place." That had put Mrs. Hopewell off for a few days.

She had hired them in the end because there were no other applicants but she had made up her mind beforehand exactly how she would handle the woman. Since she was the type who had to be into everything, then, Mrs. Hopewell had decided, she would not only let her be into everything, she would *see to it* that she was into everything—she would give her the responsibility of everything, she would put her in charge. Mrs. Hopewell had no bad qualities of her own but she was able to use other people's in such a constructive way that she never felt the lack. She had hired the Freemans and she had kept them four years.

Nothing is perfect. This was one of Mrs. Hopewell's favorite sayings. Another was: that is life! And still another, the most important, was: well, other people have their opinions too. She would make these statements, usually at the table, in a tone of gentle insistence as if no one held them but her, and the large hulking Joy, whose constant outrage had obliterated every expression from her face, would stare just a little to the side of her, her eyes icy blue, with the look of someone who has achieved blindness by an act of will and means to keep it.

When Mrs. Hopewell said to Mrs. Freeman that life was like that, Mrs. Freeman would say, "I always said so myself." Nothing had been arrived at by anyone that had not first been arrived at by her. She was quicker than Mr. Freeman. When Mrs. Hopewell said to her after they had been on the place a while, "You know, you're the wheel behind the wheel," and winked, Mrs. Freeman had said, "I know it. I've always been quick. It's some that are quicker than others."

"Everybody is different," Mrs. Hopewell said.

"Yes, most people is," Mrs. Freeman said.

"It takes all kinds to make the world."

"I always said it did myself."

The girl was used to this kind of dialogue for breakfast and more of it for dinner; sometimes they had it for supper too. When they had no guest they ate in the kitchen because that was easier. Mrs. Freeman always managed to arrive at some point during the meal and to watch them finish it. She would stand in the doorway if it were summer but in the winter she would stand with one elbow on top of the refrigerator and look down on them, or she would stand by the gas heater, lifting the back of her skirt slightly. Occasionally she would stand against the wall and roll her head from side to side. At no time was she in any hurry to leave. All this was very trying on Mrs. Hopewell but she was a woman of great patience. She realized that nothing is perfect and that in the Freemans she had good country people and that if, in this day and age, you get good country people, you had better hang onto them.

She had had plenty of experience with trash. Before the Freemans she had averaged one tenant family a year. The wives of these farmers were not the kind you would want to be around you for very long. Mrs. Hopewell, who had divorced her husband long ago, needed someone to walk over the fields with her; and when Joy had to be impressed for these services, her remarks were usually so ugly and her face so glum that Mrs. Hopewell would say, "If you can't come pleasantly, I don't want you at all," to which the girl, standing square and rigid-shouldered with her neck thrust slightly forward, would reply, "If you want me, here I am—LIKE I AM."

Mrs. Hopewell excused this attitude because of the leg (which had been shot off in a hunting accident when Joy was ten). It was hard for Mrs. Hopewell to realize that her child was thirty-two now and that for more than twenty years she had had only one leg. She thought of her still as a child because it tore her heart to think instead of the poor stout girl in her thirties who had never danced a step or had any *normal* good times. Her name was really Joy but as soon as she was twenty-one and away from home, she had had it legally changed. Mrs. Hopewell was certain that she had thought and thought until she had hit upon the ugliest name in any language. Then she had gone and had the beautiful name, Joy, changed without telling her mother until after she had done it. Her legal name was Hulga.

When Mrs. Hopewell thought the name, Hulga, she thought of the broad blank hull of a battleship. She would not use it. She continued to call her Joy to which the girl responded but in a purely mechanical way.

Hulga had learned to tolerate Mrs. Freeman who saved her from taking walks with her mother. Even Glynese and Carramae were useful when they occupied attention that might otherwise have been directed at her. At first she had thought she could not stand Mrs. Freeman for she had found that it was not possible to be rude to her. Mrs. Freeman would take on strange resentments and for days together she would be sullen but the source of her displeasure was always obscure; a direct attack, a positive leer, blatant ugliness to her face—these never touched her. And without warning one day, she began calling her Hulga.

She did not call her that in front of Mrs. Hopewell who would have been incensed but when she and the girl happened to be out of the house together, she would say something and add the name Hulga to the end of it, and the big spectacled Joy-Hulga would scowl and redden as if her privacy had been intruded upon. She considered the name her personal affair. She had arrived at it first purely on the basis of its ugly sound and then the full genius of its fitness had struck her. She had a vision of the name working like the ugly sweating Vulcan who stayed in the furnace and to whom, presumably, the goddess had to come when called. She saw it as the name of her highest creative act. One of her major triumphs was that her mother had not been able to turn her dust into Joy, but the greater one was that she had been able to turn it herself into Hulga. However, Mrs. Freeman's relish for using the name only irritated her. It was as if Mrs. Freeman's beady steel-pointed eyes had penetrated far enough behind her face to reach some secret fact. Something about her seemed to fascinate Mrs. Freeman and then one day Hulga realized that it was the artificial leg. Mrs. Freeman had a special fondness for the details of secret infections, hidden deformities, assaults upon children. Of diseases, she preferred the lingering or incurable. Hulga had heard Mrs. Hopewell give her the details of the hunting accident, how the leg had been literally blasted off, how she had never lost consciousness. Mrs. Freeman could listen to it any time as if it had happened an hour ago.

When Hulga stumped into the kitchen in the morning (she could walk without making the awful noise but she made it—Mrs. Hopewell was certain—because it was ugly-sounding), she glanced at them and did not speak. Mrs. Hopewell would be in her red kimono with her hair tied around her head in rags. She would be sitting at the table, finishing her breakfast and Mrs. Freeman would be hanging by her elbow outward from the refrigerator, looking down at the table. Hulga always put her eggs on the stove to boil and then stood over them with her arms folded, and Mrs. Hopewell would look at her—a kind of indirect gaze divided between her and Mrs. Freeman—and would think that if she would only keep herself up a little, she wouldn't be so bad looking. There was nothing wrong with her face that a pleasant expression wouldn't help. Mrs. Hopewell said that people who looked on the bright side of things would be beautiful even if they were not.

Whenever she looked at Joy this way, she could not help but feel that it would have been better if the child had not taken the Ph.D. It had certainly not brought her out any and now that she had it, there was no more excuse for her to go to school again. Mrs. Hopewell thought it was nice for girls to go to school to have a good time but Joy had "gone through." Anyhow, she would not have been strong enough to go again. The doctors had told Mrs. Hopewell that with the best of care, Joy might see forty-five. She had a weak heart. Joy had made it plain that if it had not been for this condition, she would be far from these red hills and good country people. She would be in a university lecturing to people who knew what she was talking about. And Mrs. Hopewell could very well picture her there, looking like a scarecrow and lecturing to more of the same. Here she went about all day in a six-year-old skirt and a yellow sweat shirt with a faded cowboy on a horse embossed on it. She thought this was funny; Mrs. Hopewell thought it was idiotic and showed simply that she was still a child. She was brilliant but she didn't have a grain of sense. It seemed to Mrs. Hopewell that every year she grew less like other people and more like herself—bloated, rude, and squint-eyed. And she said such strange things! To her own mother she had said—without warning, without excuse, standing up in the middle of a meal with her face purple and her mouth half full—"Woman! do you ever look inside? Do you ever look inside and see what you are *not?* God!" she had cried sinking down again and staring at her plate, "Malebranche was right: we are not our own light. We are not our own light!" Mrs. Hopewell had no idea to this day what brought that on. She had only made the remark, hoping Joy would take it in, that a smile never hurt anyone.

The girl had taken the Ph.D. in philosophy and this left Mrs. Hopewell at a complete loss. You could say, "My daughter is a nurse," or "My daughter is a school teacher," or even, "My daughter is a chemical engineer." You could not say, "My daughter is a philosopher." That was something that had ended with the Greeks and Romans. All day Joy sat on her neck in a deep chair, reading. Sometimes she went for walks but she didn't like dogs or cats or birds or flowers or nature or nice young men. She looked at nice young men as if she could smell their stupidity.

One day Mrs. Hopewell had picked up one of the books the girl had just put down and opening it at random, she read, "Science, on the other hand, has to assert its soberness and seriousness afresh and declare that it is concerned solely with what-is. Nothing—how can it be for science anything but a horror and a phantasm? If science is right, then one thing stands firm: science wishes to know nothing of nothing. Such is after all the strictly scientific approach to Nothing. We know it by wishing to know nothing of Nothing." These words had been underlined with a blue pencil and they worked on Mrs. Hopewell like some evil incantation in gibberish. She shut the book quickly and went out of the room as if she were having a chill.

This morning when the girl came in, Mrs. Freeman was on Carramae. "She thrown up four times after supper," she said, "and was up twict in the night after three o'clock. Yesterday she didn't do nothing but ramble in the bureau drawer. All she did. Stand up there and see what she could run up on."

"She's got to eat," Mrs. Hopewell muttered, sipping her coffee, while she watched Joy's back at the stove. She was wondering what the child had said to the Bible salesman. She could not imagine what kind of a conversation she could possibly have had with him.

He was a tall gaunt hatless youth who had called yesterday to sell them a Bible. He had appeared at the door, carrying a large black suitcase that weighted him so heavily on one side that he had to brace himself against the door facing. He seemed on the point of collapse but he said in a cheerful voice, "Good morning, Mrs. Cedars!" and set the suitcase down on the mat. He was not a bad-looking young man though he had on a bright blue suit and yellow socks that were not pulled up far enough. He had prominent face bones and a streak of sticky-looking brown hair falling across his forehead.

"I'm Mrs. Hopewell," she said.

"Oh!" he said, pretending to look puzzled but with his eyes sparkling, "I saw it said 'The Cedars,' on the mailbox so I thought you was Mrs. Cedars!" and he burst out in a pleasant laugh. He picked up the satchel and under cover of a pant, he fell forward into her hall. It was rather as if the suitcase had moved first, jerking him after it. "Mrs. Hopewell!" he said and grabbed her hand. "I hope you are well!" and he laughed again and then all at once his face sobered completely. He paused and gave her a straight earnest look and said, "Lady, I've come to speak of serious things."

"Well, come in," she muttered, none too pleased because

her dinner was almost ready. He came into the parlor and sat down on the edge of a straight chair and put the suitcase between his feet and glanced around the room as if he were sizing her up by it. Her silver gleamed on the two sideboards; she decided he had never been in a room as elegant as this.

"Mrs. Hopewell," he began, using her name in a way that sounded almost intimate, "I know you believe in Chrustian service."

"Well, yes," she murmured.

"I know," he said and paused, looking very wise with his head cocked on one side, "that you're a good woman. Friends have told me."

Mrs. Hopewell never liked to be taken for a fool. "What are you selling?" she asked.

"Bibles," the young man said and his eye raced around the room before he added, "I see you have no family Bible in your parlor, I see that is the one lack you got!"

Mrs. Hopewell could not say, "My daughter is an atheist and won't let me keep the Bible in the parlor." She said, stiffening slightly, "I keep my Bible by my bedside." This was not the truth. It was in the attic somewhere.

"Lady," he said, "the word of God ought to be in the parlor."

"Well, I think that's a matter of taste," she began. "I think . . ."

"Lady," he said, "for a Chrustian, the word of God ought to be in every room in the house besides in his heart. I know you're a Chrustian because I can see it in every line of your face."

She stood up and said, "Well, young man, I don't want to buy a Bible and I smell my dinner burning."

He didn't get up. He began to twist his hands and looking down at them, he said softly, "Well, lady, I'll tell you the truth—not many people want to buy one nowadays and besides, I know I'm real simple. I don't know how to say a thing but to say it. I'm just a country boy." He glanced up into her unfriendly face. "People like you don't like to fool with country people like me!"

"Why!" she cried, "good country people are the salt of the earth! Besides, we all have different ways of doing, it takes all kinds to make the world go 'round. That's life!"

"You said a mouthful," he said.

"Why, I think there aren't enough good country people in the world!" she said, stirred. "I think that's what's wrong with it!"

His face had brightened. "I didn't inraduce myself," he said. "I'm Manley Pointer from out in the country around Willohobie, not even from a place, just from near a place."

"You wait a minute," she said. "I have to see about my dinner." She went out to the kitchen and found Joy standing near the door where she had been listening.

"Get rid of the salt of the earth," she said, "and let's eat."

Mrs. Hopewell gave her a pained look and turned the heat down under the vegetables. "*I* can't be rude to anybody," she murmured and went back into the parlor.

He had opened the suitcase and was sitting with a Bible on each knee.

"You might as well put those up," she told him. "I don't want one."

"I appreciate your honesty," he said. "You don't see any more real honest people unless you go way out in the country."

"I know," she said, "real genuine folks!" Through the crack in the door she heard a groan.

"I guess a lot of boys come telling you they're working their way through college," he said, "but I'm not going to tell you that. Somehow," he said, "I don't want to go to college. I want to devote my life to Chrustian service. See," he said, lowering his voice, "I got this heart condition. I may not live long. When you know it's something wrong with you and you may not live long, well then, lady . . ." He paused, with his mouth open, and stared at her.

He and Joy had the same condition! She knew that her eyes were filling with tears but she collected herself quickly and murmured, "Won't you stay for dinner? We'd love to have you!" and was sorry the instant she heard herself say it.

"Yes, mam," he said in an abashed voice, "I would sher love to do that!"

Joy had given him one look on being introduced to him and then throughout the meal had not glanced at him again. He had addressed several remarks to her, which she had pretended not to hear. Mrs. Hopewell could not understand deliberate rudeness, although she lived with it, and she felt she had always to overflow with hospitality to make up for Joy's lack of courtesy. She urged him to talk about himself and he did. He said he was the seventh child of twelve and that his father had been crushed under a tree when he himself was eight year old. He had been crushed very badly, in fact, almost cut in two and was practically not recognizable. His mother had got along the best she could by hard working and she had always seen that her children went to Sunday School and that they read the Bible every evening. He was now nineteen year old and he had been selling Bibles for four months. In that time he had sold seventy-seven Bibles and had the promise of two more sales. He wanted to become a missionary because he thought that was the way you could do most for people. "He who losest his life shall find it," he said simply and he was so sincere, so genuine and earnest that Mrs. Hopewell would not for the world have smiled. He prevented his peas from sliding onto the table by blocking them with a piece of bread which he later cleaned his plate with. She could see Joy observing sidewise how he handled his knife and fork and she saw too that every few minutes, the boy would dart a keen appraising glance at the girl as if he were trying to attract her attention.

After dinner Joy cleared the dishes off the table and disappeared and Mrs. Hopewell was left to talk with him. He told her again about his childhood and his father's accident and about various things that had happened to him. Every five minutes or so she would stifle a yawn. He sat for two hours until finally she told him she must go because she had an appointment in town. He packed his Bibles and thanked her and prepared to leave, but in the doorway he stopped and wrung her hand and said that not on any of his trips had he met a lady as nice as her and he asked if he could come again. She had said she would always be happy to see him.

Joy had been standing in the road, apparently looking at something in the distance, when he came down the steps toward her, bent to the side with his heavy valise. He stopped where she was standing and confronted her directly. Mrs. Hopewell could not hear what he said but she trembled to think what Joy would say to him. She could see that after a minute Joy said something and that then the boy began to speak again, making an excited gesture with his free hand. After a minute Joy said something else at which the boy began to speak once more. Then to her amazement, Mrs. Hopewell saw the two of them walk off together, toward the gate. Joy had walked all the way to the gate with him and Mrs. Hopewell could not imagine what they had said to each other, and she had not yet dared to ask.

Mrs. Freeman was insisting upon her attention. She had moved from the refrigerator to the heater so that Mrs. Hopewell had to turn and face her in order to seem to be listening. "Glynese gone out with Harvey Hill again last night," she said. "She had this sty."

"Hill," Mrs. Hopewell said absently, "is that the one who works in the garage?"

"Nome, he's the one that goes to chiropracter school," Mrs. Freeman said. "She had this sty. Been had it two days. So she says when he brought her in the other night, he says, 'Lemme get rid of that sty for you,' and she says, 'How?' and he says, 'You just lay yourself down acrost the seat of that car and I'll show you.' So she done it and he popped her neck. Kept on a-popping it several times until she made him quit. This morning," Mrs. Freeman said, "she ain't got no sty. She ain't got no traces of a sty."

"I never heard of that before," Mrs. Hopewell said.

"He ast her to marry him before the Ordinary," Mrs. Freeman went on, "and she told him she wasn't going to be married in no *office*."

"Well, Glynese is a fine girl," Mrs. Hopewell said. "Glynese and Carramae are both fine girls."

"Carramae said when her and Lyman was married Lyman said it sure felt sacred to him. She said he said he wouldn't take five hundred dollars for being married by a preacher."

"How much would he take?" the girl asked from the stove.

"He said he wouldn't take five hundred dollars," Mrs. Freeman repeated.

"Well, we all have work to do," Mrs. Hopewell said.

"Lyman said it just felt more sacred to him," Mrs. Freeman said. "The doctor wants Carramae to eat prunes. Says instead of medicine. Says them cramps is coming from pressure. You know where I think it is?"

"She'll be better in a few weeks," Mrs. Hopewell said.

"In the tube," Mrs. Freeman said. "Else she wouldn't be as sick as she is."

Hulga had cracked her two eggs into a saucer and was bringing them to the table along with a cup of coffee that she had filled too full. She sat down carefully and began to eat, meaning to keep Mrs. Freeman there by questions if for any reason she showed an inclination to leave. She could perceive her mother's eye on her. The first round-about question would be about the Bible salesman and she did not wish to bring it on. "How did he pop her neck?" she asked.

Mrs. Freeman went into a description of how he had popped her neck. She said he owned a '55 Mercury but that Glynese said she would rather marry a man with only a '36 Plymouth who would be married by a preacher. The girl asked what if he had a '32 Plymouth and Mrs. Freeman said what Glynese had said was a '36 Plymouth.

Mrs. Hopewell said there were not many girls with Glynese's common sense. She said what she admired in those girls was their common sense. She said that reminded her that they had had a nice visitor yesterday, a young man selling Bibles. "Lord," she said, "he bored me to death but he was so sincere and genuine I couldn't be rude to him. He was just good country people, you know," she said, "—just the salt of the earth."

"I seen him walk up," Mrs. Freeman said, "and then later—I seen him walk off," and Hulga could feel the slight shift in her voice, the slight insinuation, that he had not walked off alone, had he? Her face remained expressionless but the color rose into her neck and she seemed to swallow it down with the next spoonful of egg. Mrs. Freeman was looking at her as if they had a secret together.

"Well, it takes all kinds of people to make the world go 'round," Mrs. Hopewell said. "It's very good we aren't all alike."

"Some people are more alike than others," Mrs. Freeman said.

Hulga got up and stumped, with about twice the noise that was necessary, into her room and locked the door. She was to meet the Bible salesman at ten o'clock at the gate. She had thought about it half the night. She had started thinking of it as a great joke and then she had begun to see profound implications in it. She had lain in bed imagining dialogues for them that were insane on the surface but that reached below to depths that no Bible salesman would be aware of. Their conversation yesterday had been of this kind.

He had stopped in front of her and had simply stood there. His face was bony and sweaty and bright, with a little pointed nose in the center of it, and his look was different from what it had been at the dinner table. He was gazing at her with open curiosity, with fascination, like a child watching a new fantastic animal at the zoo, and he was breathing as if he had run a great distance to reach her. His gaze seemed somehow familiar but she could not think where she had been regarded with it before. For almost a minute he didn't say anything. Then on what seemed an insuck of breath, he whispered, "You ever ate a chicken that was two days old?"

The girl looked at him stonily. He might have just put this question up for consideration at the meeting of a philosophical association. "Yes," she presently replied as if she had considered it from all angles.

"It must have been mighty small!" he said triumphantly and shook all over with little nervous giggles, getting very red in the face, and subsiding finally into his gaze of complete admiration, while the girl's expression remained exactly the same.

"How old are you?" he asked softly.

She waited some time before she answered. Then in a flat voice she said, "Seventeen."

His smiles came in succession like waves breaking on the surface of a little lake. "I see you got a wooden leg," he said. "I think you're real brave. I think you're real sweet."

The girl stood blank and solid and silent.

"Walk to the gate with me," he said. "You're a brave sweet little thing and I liked you the minute I seen you walk in the door."

Hulga began to move forward.

"What's your name?" he asked, smiling down on the top of her head.

"Hulga," she said.

"Hulga," he murmured, "Hulga. Hulga. I never heard of anybody name Hulga before. You're shy, aren't you, Hulga?" he asked.

She nodded, watching his large red hand on the handle of the giant valise.

"I like girls that wear glasses," he said. "I think a lot. I'm not like these people that a serious thought don't ever enter their heads. It's because I may die."

"I may die too," she said suddenly and looked up at him. His eyes were very small and brown, glittering feverishly.

"Listen," he said, "don't you think some people was meant to meet on account of what all they got in common and all? Like they both think serious thoughts and all?" He shifted the valise to his other hand so that the hand nearest her was free. He caught hold of her elbow and shook it a little. "I don't work on Saturday," he said. "I like to walk in the woods and see what Mother Nature is wearing. O'er the hills and far away. Pic-nics and things. Couldn't we go on a pic-nic tomorrow? Say yes, Hulga," he said and gave her a dying look as if he felt his insides about to drop out of him. He had even seemed to sway slightly toward her.

During the night she had imagined that she seduced him. She imagined that the two of them walked on the place until they came to the storage barn beyond the two back fields and there, she imagined, that things came to such a pass that she very easily seduced him and that then, of course, she had to reckon with his remorse. True genius can get an idea across even to an inferior mind. She imagined that she took his remorse in hand and changed it into a deeper understanding of life. She took all his shame away and turned it into something useful.

She set off for the gate at exactly ten o'clock, escaping without drawing Mrs. Hopewell's attention. She didn't take anything to eat, forgetting that food is usually taken on a picnic. She wore a pair of slacks and a dirty white shirt, and as an afterthought, she had put some Vapex on the collar of it since she did not own any perfume. When she reached the gate no one was there.

She looked up and down the empty highway and had the furious feeling that she had been tricked, that he had only meant to make her walk to the gate after the idea of him. Then suddenly he stood up, very tall, from behind a bush on the opposite embankment. Smiling, he lifted his hat which was new and wide-brimmed. He had not worn it yesterday and she wondered if he had bought it for the occasion. It was toast-colored with a red and white band around it and was slightly too large for him. He stepped from behind the bush still carrying the black valise. He had on the same suit and the same yellow socks sucked down in his shoes from walking. He crossed the highway and said, "I knew you'd come!"

The girl wondered acidly how he had known this. She pointed to the valise and asked, "Why did you bring your Bibles?"

He took her elbow, smiling down on her as if he could not stop. "You can never tell when you'll need the word of God, Hulga," he said. She had a moment in which she doubted that this was actually happening and then they began to climb the embankment. They went down into the pasture toward the woods. The boy walked lightly by her side, bouncing on his toes. The valise did not seem to be heavy today; he even swung it. They crossed half the pasture without saying anything and then, putting his hand easily on the small of her back, he asked softly, "Where does your wooden leg join on?"

She turned an ugly red and glared at him and for an instant the boy looked abashed. "I didn't mean you no harm," he said. "I only meant you're so brave and all. I guess God takes care of you."

"No," she said, looking forward and walking fast, "I don't even believe in God."

At this he stopped and whistled. "No!" he exclaimed as if he were too astonished to say anything else.

She walked on and in a second he was bouncing at her side, fanning with his hat. "That's very unusual for a girl," he remarked, watching her out of the corner of his eye. When they reached the edge of the wood, he put his hand on her back again and drew her against him without a word and kissed her heavily.

The kiss, which had more pressure than feeling behind it, produced that extra surge of adrenalin in the girl that enables one to carry a packed trunk out of a burning house, but in her, the power went at once to the brain. Even before he released her, her mind, clear and detached and ironic anyway, was regarding him from a great distance, with amusement but with pity. She had never been kissed before and she was pleased to discover that it was an unexceptional experience and all a matter of the mind's control. Some people might enjoy drain water if they were told it was vodka. When the boy, looking expectant but uncertain, pushed her gently away, she turned and walked on, saying nothing as if such business, for her, were common enough.

He came along panting at her side, trying to help her when he saw a root that she might trip over. He caught and held back the long swaying blades of thorn vine until she had passed beyond them. She led the way and he came breathing heavily behind her. Then they came out on a sunlit hillside, sloping softly into another one a little smaller. Beyond, they could see the rusted top of the old barn where the extra hay was stored.

The hill was sprinkled with small pink weeds. "Then you ain't saved?" he asked suddenly, stopping.

The girl smiled. It was the first time she had smiled at him at all. "In my economy," she said, "I'm saved and you are damned but I told you I didn't believe in God."

Nothing seemed to destroy the boy's look of admiration. He gazed at her now as if the fantastic animal at the zoo had put its paw through the bars and given him a loving poke. She thought he looked as if he wanted to kiss her again and she walked on before he had the chance.

"Ain't there somewheres we can sit down sometime?" he murmured, his voice softening toward the end of the sentence.

"In that barn," she said.

They made for it rapidly as if it might slide away like a train. It was a large two-story barn, cool and dark inside. The boy pointed up the ladder that led into the loft and said, "It's too bad we can't go up there."

"Why can't we?" she asked.

"Yer leg," he said reverently.

The girl gave him a contemptuous look and putting both hands on the ladder, she climbed it while he stood below, apparently awestruck. She pulled herself expertly through the opening and then looked down at him and said, "Well, come on if you're coming," and he began to climb the ladder, awkwardly bringing the suitcase with him.

"We won't need the Bible," she observed.

"You never can tell," he said, panting. After he had got into the loft, he was a few seconds catching his breath. She had sat down in a pile of straw. A wide sheath of sunlight, filled with dust particles, slanted over her. She lay back against a bale, her face turned away, looking out the front opening of the barn where hay was thrown from a wagon into the loft. The two pink-speckled hillsides lay back against a dark ridge of woods. The sky was cloudless and cold blue. The boy dropped down by her side and put one arm under her and the other over her and began methodically kissing her face, making little noises like a fish. He did not remove his hat but it was pushed far enough back not to interfere. When her glasses got in his way, he took them off of her and slipped them into his pocket.

The girl at first did not return any of the kisses but presently she began to and after she had put several on his cheek, she reached his lips and remained there, kissing him again and again as if she were trying to draw all the breath out of him. His breath was clear and sweet like a child's and the kisses were sticky like a child's. He mumbled about loving her and about knowing when he first seen her that he loved her, but the mumbling was like the sleepy fretting of a child being put to sleep by his mother. Her mind, throughout this, never stopped or lost itself for a second to her feelings. "You ain't said you loved me none," he whispered finally, pulling back from her. "You got to say that."

She looked away from him off into the hollow sky and then down at a black ridge and then down farther into what appeared to be two green swelling lakes. She didn't realize he had taken her glasses but this landscape could not seem exceptional to her for she seldom paid any close attention to her surroundings.

"You got to say it," he repeated. "You got to say you love me."

She was always careful how she committed herself. "In a sense," she began, "if you use the word loosely, you might say that. But it's not a word I use. I don't have illusions. I'm one of those people who see *through* to nothing."

The boy was frowning. "You got to say it. I said it and you got to say it," he said.

The girl looked at him almost tenderly. "You poor baby," she murmured. "It's just as well you don't understand," and she pulled him by the neck, face-down, against her. "We are all damned," she said, "but some of us have taken off our blindfolds and see that there's nothing to see. It's a kind of salvation."

The boy's astonished eyes looked blar kly through the ends

of her hair. "Okay," he almost whined, "but do you love me or don'tcher?"

"Yes," she said and added, "in a sense. But I must tell you something. There mustn't be anything dishonest between us." She lifted his head and looked him in the eye. "I am thirty years old," she said. "I have a number of degrees."

The boy's look was irritated but dogged. "I don't care," he said. "I don't care a thing about what all you done. I just want to know if you love me or don'tcher?" and he caught her to him and wildly planted her face with kisses until she said, "Yes, yes."

"Okay, then," he said, letting her go. "Prove it."

She smiled, looking dreamily out on the shifty landscape. She had seduced him without even making up her mind to try. "How?" she asked, feeling that he should be delayed a little.

He leaned over and put his lips to her ear. "Show me where your wooden leg joins on," he whispered.

The girl uttered a sharp little cry and her face instantly drained of color. The obscenity of the suggestion was not what shocked her. As a child she had sometimes been subject to feelings of shame but education had removed the last traces of that as a good surgeon scrapes for cancer; she would no more have felt it over what he was asking than she would have believed in his Bible. But she was as sensitive about the artificial leg as a peacock about his tail. No one ever touched it but her. She took care of it as someone else would his soul, in private and almost with her own eyes turned away. "No," she said.

"I known it," he muttered, sitting up. "You're just playing me for a sucker."

"Oh no no!" she cried. "It joins on at the knee. Only at the knee. Why do you want to see it?"

The boy gave her a long penetrating look. "Because," he said, "it's what makes you different. You ain't like anybody else."

She sat staring at him. There was nothing about her face or her round freezing-blue eyes to indicate that this had moved her; but she felt as if her heart had stopped and left her mind to pump her blood. She decided that for the first time in her life she was face to face with real innocence. This boy, with an instinct that came from beyond wisdom, had touched the truth about her. When after a minute, she said in a hoarse high voice, "All right," it was like surrendering to him completely. It was like losing her own life and finding it again, miraculously, in his.

Very gently he began to roll the slack leg up. The artificial limb, in a white sock and brown flat shoe, was bound in a heavy material like canvas and ended in an ugly jointure where it was attached to the stump. The boy's face and his voice were entirely reverent as he uncovered it and said, "Now show me how to take it off and on."

She took it off for him and put it back on again and then he took it off himself, handling it as tenderly as if it were a real one. "See!" he said with a delighted child's face. "Now I can do it myself!"

"Put it back on," she said. She was thinking that she would run away with him and that every night he would take the leg off and every morning put it back on again. "Put it back on," she said.

"Not yet," he murmured, setting it on its foot out of her reach. "Leave it off for a while. You got me instead."

She gave a little cry of alarm but he pushed her down and began to kiss her again. Without the leg she felt entirely dependent on him. Her brain seemed to have stopped thinking altogether and to be about some other function that it was not very good at. Different expressions raced back and forth over her face. Every now and then the boy, his eyes like two steel spikes, would glance behind him where the leg stood. Finally she pushed him off and said, "Put it back on me now."

"Wait," he said. He leaned the other way and pulled the valise toward him and opened it. It had a pale blue spotted lining and there were only two Bibles in it. He took one of these out and opened the cover of it. It was hollow and contained a pocket flask of whiskey, a pack of cards, and a small blue box with printing on it. He laid these out in front of her one at a time in an evenly-spaced row, like one presenting offerings at the shrine of a goddess. He put the blue box in her hand. THIS PRODUCT TO BE USED ONLY FOR THE PREVENTION OF DISEASE, she read, and dropped it. The boy was unscrewing the top of the flask. He stopped and pointed, with a smile, to the deck of cards. It was not an ordinary deck but one with an obscene picture on the back of each card. "Take a swig," he said, offering her the bottle first. He held it in front of her, but like one mesmerized, she did not move.

Her voice when she spoke had an almost pleading sound. "Aren't you," she murmured, "aren't you just good country people?"

The boy cocked his head. He looked as if he were just beginning to understand that she might be trying to insult him. "Yeah," he said, curling his lip slightly, "but it ain't held me back none. I'm as good as you any day in the week."

"Give me my leg," she said.

He pushed it farther away with his foot. "Come on now, let's begin to have us a good time," he said coaxingly. "We ain't got to know one another good yet."

"Give me my leg!" she screamed and tried to lunge for it but he pushed her down easily.

"What's the matter with you all of a sudden?" he asked, frowning as he screwed the top on the flask and put it quickly back inside the Bible. "You just a while ago said you didn't believe in nothing. I thought you was some girl!"

Her face was almost purple. "You're a Christian!" she hissed. "You're a fine Christian! You're just like them all—say one thing and do another. You're a perfect Christian, you're . . ."

The boy's mouth was set angrily. "I hope you don't think," he said in a lofty indignant tone, "that I believe in that crap! I may sell Bibles but I know which end is up and I wasn't born yesterday and I know where I'm going!"

"Give me my leg!" she screeched. He jumped up so quickly that she barely saw him sweep the cards and the blue box back into the Bible and throw the Bible into the valise. She saw him grab the leg and then she saw it for an instant slanted forlornly across the inside of the suitcase with a Bible at either side of its opposite ends. He slammed the lid shut and snatched up the valise and swung it down the hole and then stepped through himself.

When all of him had passed but his head, he turned and regarded her with a look that no longer had any admiration in it. "I've gotten a lot of interesting things," he said. "One time I got a woman's glass eye this way. And you needn't to think you'll catch me because Pointer ain't really my name. I use a different name at every house I call at and don't stay nowhere long. And I'll tell you another thing, Hulga," he said, using the name as if he didn't think much of it, "you ain't so smart. I been believing in nothing ever since I was born!" and then the toast-colored hat disappeared down the hole and the girl was left, sitting on the straw in the dusty sunlight. When she turned her churning face toward the opening, she saw his blue figure struggling successfully over the green speckled lake.

Mrs. Hopewell and Mrs. Freeman, who were in the back pasture, digging up onions, saw him emerge a little later from the woods and head across the meadow toward the highway. "Why, that looks like that nice dull young man that tried to sell me a Bible yesterday," Mrs. Hopewell said, squinting. "He must have been selling them to the Negroes back in there. He was so simple," she said, "but I guess the world would be better off if we were all that simple."

Mrs. Freeman's gaze drove forward and just touched him before he disappeared under the hill. Then she returned her attention to the evil-smelling onion shoot she was lifting from the ground. "Some can't be that simple," she said. "I know I never could."

TRILOBITES

by *Breece D'J Pancake*

I open the truck's door, step onto the brick side street. I look at Company Hill again, all sort of worn down and round. A long time ago it was real craggy and stood like an island in the Teays River. It took over a million years to make that smooth little hill, and I've looked all over it for trilobites. I think how it has always been there and always will be, at least for as long as it matters. The air is smoky with summertime. A bunch of starlings swim over me. I was born in this country and I have never very much wanted to leave. I remember Pop's dead eyes looking at me. They were real dry, and that took something out of me. I shut the door, head for the café.

I see a concrete patch in the street. It's shaped like Florida, and I recollect what I wrote in Ginny's yearbook: "We will live on mangoes and love." And she up and left without me—two years she's been down there without me. She sends me postcards with alligator wrestlers and flamingos on the front. She never asks me any questions. I feel like a real fool for what I wrote, and go into the café.

The place is empty, and I rest in the cooled air. Tinker Reilly's little sister pours my coffee. She has good hips. They are kind of like Ginny's and they slope in nice curves to her legs. Hips and legs like that climb steps into airplanes. She goes to the counter end and scoffs down the rest of her sundae. I smile at her, but she's jailbait. Jailbait and black snakes are two things I won't touch with a window pole. One time I used an old black snake for a bullwhip, snapped the sucker's head off, and Pop beat hell out of me with it. I think how Pop could make me pretty mad sometimes. I grin.

I think about last night when Ginny called. Her old man drove her down from the airport in Charleston. She was already bored. Can we get together? Sure. Maybe do some brew? Sure. Same old Colly. Same old Ginny. She talked through her beak. I wanted to tell her Pop had died and Mom was on the warpath to sell the farm, but Ginny was talking through her beak. It gave me the creeps.

Just like the cups give me the creeps. I look at the cups hanging on pegs by the storefront. They're decal-named and covered with grease and dust. There's four of them, and one is Pop's, but that isn't what gives me the creeps. The cleanest one is Jim's. It's clean because he still uses it, but it hangs there with the rest. Through the window, I can see him crossing the street. His joints are cemented with arthritis. I think of how long it'll be before I croak, but Jim is old, and it gives me the creeps to see his cup hanging up there. I go to the door to help him in.

He says, "Tell the truth, now," and his old paw pinches my arm.

I say, "Can't do her." I help him to his stool.

I pull this globby rock from my pocket and slap it on the counter in front of Jim. He turns it with his drawn hand, examines it. "Gastropod," he says. "Probably Permian. You buy again." I can't win with him. He knows them all.

"I still can't find a trilobite," I say.

"There are a few," he says. "Not many. Most of the outcrops around here are too late for them."

The girl brings Jim's coffee in his cup, and we watch her pump back to the kitchen. Good hips.

"You see that?" He jerks his head toward her.

I say, "Moundsville Molasses." I can spot jailbait by a mile.

"Hell, girl's age never stopped your dad and me in Michigan."

"Tell the truth."

"Sure. You got to time it so you nail the first freight out when your pants are up."

I look at the windowsill. It is speckled with the crisp skeletons of flies. "Why'd you and Pop leave Michigan?"

The crinkles around Jim's eyes go slack. He says, "The war," and sips his coffee.

I say, "He never made it back there."

"Me either—always wanted to—there or Germany—just to look around."

"Yeah, he promised to show me where you all buried that silverware and stuff during the war."

He says, "On the Elbe. Probably plowed up by now."

My eye socket reflects in my coffee, steam curls around my face, and I feel a headache coming on. I look up to ask Tinker's sister for an aspirin, but she is giggling in the kitchen.

"That's where he got that wound," Jim says. "Got it on the Elbe. He was out a long time. Cold, Jesus, it was cold. I had him for dead, but he came to. Says, 'I been all over the world'; says, 'China's so pretty, Jim.' "

"Dreaming?"

"I don't know. I quit worrying about that stuff years ago."

Tinker's sister comes up with her coffeepot to make us for a tip. I ask her for an aspirin and see she's got a pimple on her collarbone. I don't remember seeing pictures of China. I watch little sister's hips.

"Trent still wanting your place for that housing project?"

"Sure," I say. "Mom'll probably sell it, too. I can't run the place like Pop did. Cane looks bad as hell." I drain off my cup. I'm tired of talking about the farm. "Going out with Ginny to-night," I say.

"Give her that for me," he says. He takes a poke at my whang. I don't like it when he talks about her like that. He sees I don't like it, and his grin slips. "Found a lot of gas for her old man. One hell of a guy before his wife pulled out."

I wheel on my stool, clap his weak old shoulder. I think of Pop, and try to joke. "You stink so bad the undertaker's following you."

He laughs. "You were the ugliest baby ever born, you know that?"

I grin, and start out the door. I can hear him shout to little sister: "Come on over here, honey, I got a joke for you."

The sky has a film. Its heat burns through the salt on my skin, draws it tight. I start the truck, drive west along the highway built on the dry bed of the Teays. There's wide bottoms, and the hills on either side have yellowy billows the sun can't burn off. I pass an iron sign put up by the WPA: "Surveyed by George Washington, the Teays River Pike." I see fields and cattle where buildings stand, picture them from some long-off time.

I turn off the main road to our house. Clouds make the sunshine blink light and dark in the yard. I look again at the spot of ground where Pop fell. He had lain spread-eagled in the thick grass after a sliver of metal from his old wound passed to his brain. I remember thinking how beaten his face looked with prints in it from the grass.

I reach the high barn and start my tractor, then drive to the knob at the end of our land and stop. I sit there, smoke, look again at the cane. The rows curve tight, but around them is a sort of scar of clay, and the leaves have a purplish blight. I don't wonder about the blight. I know the cane is too far gone to worry about the blight. Far off, somebody chops wood, and the ax-bites echo back to me. The hillsides are baked here and have heat ghosts. Our cattle move to the wind gap, and birds hide in caps of trees where we never cut the timber for pasture. I look at the wrinkly old boundary post. Pop set it when the hobo and soldier days were over. It is a locust-tree post and will be there a long time. A few dead morning glories cling to it.

"I'm just not no good at it," I say. "It just don't do to work your ass off at something you're not no good at."

The chopping stops. I listen to the beat of grasshopper wings, and strain to spot blight on the far side of the bottoms.

I say, "Yessir, Colly, you couldn't grow pole beans in a pile of horseshit."

I squash my cigarette against the floor plate. I don't want a fire. I press the starter, and bump around the fields, then down to the ford of the drying creek, and up the other side. Turkles fall from logs into stagnant pools. I stop my machine. The cane here is just as bad. I rub a sunburn into the back of my neck.

I say, "Shot to hell, Gin. Can't do nothing right."

I lean back, try to forget these fields and flanking hills. A long time before me or these tools, the Teays flowed here. I can almost feel the cold waters and the tickling the trilobites make when they crawl. All the water from the old mountains flowed west. But the land lifted. I have only the bottoms and stone animals I collect. I blink and breathe. My father is a khaki cloud in the canebrakes, and Ginny is no more to me than the bitter smell in the blackberry briers up on the ridge.

I take up my sack and gaff for a turkle. Some quick chubs flash under the bank. In the moss-dapples, I see rings spread where a turkle ducked under. This sucker is mine. The pool smells like rot, and the sun is a hardish brown.

I wade in. He goes for the roots of a log. I shove around, and feel my gaff twitch. This is a smart turkle, but still a sucker. I bet he could pull liver off a hook for the rest of his days, but he is a sucker for the roots that hold him while I work my gaff. I pull him up, and see he is a snapper. He's got his stubby neck curved around, biting at the gaff. I lay him on the sand, and take out Pop's knife. I step on the shell, and press hard. That fat neck gets skinny quick, and sticks way out. A little blood oozes from the gaff wound into the grit, but when I slice, a puddle forms.

A voice says, "Get a dragon, Colly?"

I shiver a little, and look up. It's only the loansman standing on the creekbank in his tan suit. His face is splotched pink, and the sun is turning his glasses black.

"I crave them now and again," I say. I go on slitting gristle, skinning back the shell.

"Aw, your daddy loved turtle meat," the guy says.

I listen to scratching cane leaves in the late sun. I dump the tripes into the pool, bag the rest, and head up the ford. I say, "What can I do for you?"

This guy starts up: "I saw you from the road—just came down to see about my offer."

"I told you yesterday, Mr. Trent. It ain't mine to sell." I tone it down. I don't want hard feelings. "You got to talk to Mom."

Blood drips from the poke to the dust. It makes dark paste. Trent pockets his hands, looks over the cane. A cloud blocks the sun, and my crop glows greenish in the shade.

"This is about the last real farm left around here," Trent says.

"Blight'll get what the dry left," I say. I shift the sack to my free hand. I see I'm giving in. I'm letting this guy go and push me around.

"How's your mother getting along?" he says. I see no eyes behind his smoky glasses.

"Pretty good," I say. "She's wanting to move to Akron." I swing the sack a little toward Ohio, and spray some blood on Trent's pants. "Sorry," I say.

"It'll come out," he says, but I hope not. I grin and watch the turkle's mouth gape on the sand. "Well, why Akron?" he says. "Family there?"

I nod. "Hers," I say. "She'll take you up on the offer." This hot shadow saps me, and my voice is a whisper. I throw the sack to the floor plate, climb up to grind the starter. I feel better in a way I've never known. The hot metal seat burns through my jeans.

"Saw Ginny at the post office," this guy shouts. "She sure is a pretty."

I wave, almost smile, as I gear to lumber up the dirt road. I pass Trent's dusty Lincoln, move away from my bitten cane. It can go now; the stale seed, the drought, the blight—it can go when she signs the papers. I know I will always be to blame, but it can't just be my fault. "What about you?" I say. "Your side hurt all that morning, but you wouldn't see no doctor. Nosir, you had to see that your dumb boy got the crop put proper in the ground." I shut my trap to keep from talking like a fool.

I stop my tractor on the terraced road to the barn and look back across the cane to the creekbed. Yesterday Trent said the bottoms would be filled with dirt. That will put the houses above flood, but it'll raise the flood line. Under all those houses, my turkles will turn to stone. Our Herefords make rusty patches on the hill. I see Pop's grave, and wonder if the new high waters will get over it.

I watch the cattle play. A rain must be coming. A rain is always coming when cattle play. Sometimes they play for snow, but mostly it is rain. After Pop whipped the daylights out of me with that black snake, he hung it on a fence. But it didn't rain. The cattle weren't playing, and it didn't rain, but I kept my mouth shut. The snake was bad enough, I didn't want the belt too.

I look a long time at that hill. My first time with Ginny was in the tree-cap of that hill. I think of how close we could be then, and maybe even now, I don't know. I'd like to go with Ginny, fluff her hair in any other field. But I can see her in the post office. I bet she was sending postcards to some guy in Florida.

I drive on to the barn, stop under the shed. I wipe sweat from my face with my sleeve, and see how the seams have slipped from my shoulders. If I sit rigid, I can fill them again. The turkle is moving in the sack, and it gives me the creeps to hear his shell clinking against the gaff. I take the poke to the spigot to clean the game. Pop always liked turkle in a mulligan. He talked a lot about mulligan and the jungles just an hour before I found him.

I wonder what it will be like when Ginny comes by. I hope she's not talking through her beak. Maybe she'll take me to her house this time. If her momma had been anybody but Pop's cousin, her old man would let me go to her house. Screw him. But I can talk to Ginny. I wonder if she remembers the plans we made for the farm. And we wanted kids. She always nagged about a peacock. I will get her one.

I smile as I dump the sack into the rusty sink, but the barn smell—the hay, the cattle, the gasoline—it reminds me. Me and Pop built this barn. I look at every nail with the same dull pain.

I clean the meat and lay it out on a piece of cloth torn from an old bed sheet. I fold the corners, walk to the house.

The air is hot, but it sort of churns, and the set screens in the kitchen window rattle. From inside, I can hear Mom and Trent talking on the front porch, and I leave the window up. It is the same come-on he gave me yesterday, and I bet Mom is eating it up. She probably thinks about tea parties with her cousins in Akron. She never listens to what anybody says. She just says all right to anything anybody but me or Pop ever said. She even voted for Hoover before they got married. I throw the turkle meat into a skillet, get a beer. Trent softens her up with me; I prick my ears.

"I would wager on Colly's agreement," he says. I can still hear a hill twang in his voice.

"I told him Sam'd put him on at Goodrich," she says. "They'd teach him a trade."

"And there are a good many young people in Akron. You know he'd be happier." I think how his voice sounds like a damn TV.

"Well, he's awful good to keep me company. Don't go out none since Ginny took off to that college."

"There's a college in Akron," he says, but I shut the window.

I lean against the sink, rub my hands across my face. The smell of turkle has soaked between my fingers. It's the same smell as the pools.

Through the door to the living room, I see the rock case Pop built for me. The white labels show up behind the dark gloss of glass. Ginny helped me find over half of those. If I did study in a college, I could come back and take Jim's place at the gas wells. I like to hold little stones that lived so long ago. But geology doesn't mean lick to me. I can't even find a trilobite.

I stir the meat, listen for noise or talk on the porch, but

there is none. I look out. A lightning flash peels shadows from the yard and leaves a dark strip under the cave of the barn. I feel a scum on my skin in the still air. I take my supper to the porch.

I look down the valley to where bison used to graze before the first rails were put down. Now those rails are covered with a highway, and cars rush back and forth in the wind. I watch Trent's car back out, heading east into town. I'm afraid to ask right off if he got what he wanted.

I stick my plate under Mom's nose, but she waves it off. I sit in Pop's old rocker, watch the storm come. Dust devils puff around on the berm, and maple sprigs land in the yard with their white bellies up. Across the road, our windbreak bends, rows of cedars furling every which way at once.

"Coming a big one?" I say.

Mom says nothing and fans herself with the funeral-home fan. The wind layers her hair, but she keeps that cardboard picture of Jesus bobbing like crazy. Her face changes. I know what she thinks. She thinks how she isn't the girl in the picture on the mantel. She isn't standing with Pop's garrison cap cocked on her head.

"I wish you'd of come out while he's here," she says. She stares across the road to the windbreak.

"I heard him yesterday," I say.

"It ain't that at all," she says, and I watch her brow come down a little. "It's like when Jim called us askin' if we wanted some beans an' I had to tell him to leave 'em in the truck at church. I swan how folks talk when men come 'round a widow."

I know Jim talks like a dumb old fart, but it isn't like he'd rape her or anything. I don't want to argue with her. "Well," I say, "who owns this place?"

"We still do. Don't have to sign nothin' till tomorrow."

She quits bobbing Jesus to look at me. She starts up: "You'll like Akron. Law, I bet Marcy's youngest girl'd love to meet you. She's a regular rock hound too. 'Sides, your father always said we'd move there when you got big enough to run the farm."

I know she has to say it. I just keep my mouth shut. The rain comes, ringing the roof tin. I watch the high wind snap branches from the trees. Pale splinters of light shoot down behind the far hills. We are just brushed by this storm.

Ginny's sports car hisses east on the road, honking as it

passes, but I know she will be back.

"Just like her momma," Mom says, "racin' the devil for the beer joints."

"She never knew her momma," I say. I set my plate on the floor. I'm glad Ginny thought to honk.

"What if I's to run off with some foreman from the wells?"

"You wouldn't do that, Mom."

"That's right," she says, and watches the cars roll by. "Shot her in Chicago. Shot hisself too."

I look beyond the hills and time. There is red hair clouding the pillow, blood-spattered by the slug. Another body lies rumpled and warm at the bed foot.

"Folks said he done it cause she wouldn't marry him. Found two weddin' bands in his pocket. Feisty little I-taliun."

I see police and reporters in the tiny room. Mumbles spill into the hallway, but nobody really looks at the dead woman's face.

"Well," Mom says, "at least they was still wearin' their clothes."

The rain slows, and for a long time I sit watching the blue chicory swaying beside the road. I think of all the people I know who left these hills. Only Jim and Pop came back to the land, worked it.

"Lookee at the willow-wisps." Mom points to the hills.

The rain trickles, and as it seeps in to cool the ground, a fog rises. The fog curls little ghosts into the branches and gullies. The sun tries to sift through this mist, but is only a tarnished brown splotch in the pinkish sky. Wherever the fog is, the light is a burnished orange.

"Can't recall the name Pop gave it," I say.

The colors shift, trade tones.

"He had some funny names all right. Called a tomcat a 'pussy scat.' "

I think back. "Cornflakes were 'pone-rakes,' and a chicken was a 'sick-un.' "

We laugh.

"Well," she says, "he'll always be a part of us."

The glommy paint on the chair arm packs under my fingernails. I think how she could foul up a free lunch.

Ginny honks again from the main road. I stand up to go in, but I hold the screen, look for something to say.

"I ain't going to live in Akron," I say.

"An' just where you gonna live, Mister?"

"I don't know."

She starts up with her fan again.

"Me and Ginny's going low-riding," I say.

She won't look at me. "Get in early. Mr. Trent don't keep no late hours for no beer drinkers."

The house is quiet, and I can hear her out there sniffling. But what to hell can I do about it? I hurry to wash the smell of turkle from my hands. I shake all over while the water flows down. I talked back. I've never talked back. I'm scared, but I stop shaking. Ginny can't see me shaking. I just walk out to the road without ever looking back to the porch.

I climb in the car, let Ginny kiss my cheek. She looks different. I've never seen these clothes, and she wears too much jewelry.

"You look great," she says. "Haven't changed a bit."

We drive west along the Pike.

"Where we going?"

She says, "Let's park for old times' sake. How's the depot?"

I say, "Sure." I reach back for a can of Falls City. "You let your hair grow."

"You like?"

"Um, yeah."

We drive. I look at the tinged fog, the colors changing hue.

She says, "Sort of an eerie evening, huh?" It all comes from her beak.

"Pop always called it a fool's fire or something."

We pull in beside the old depot. It's mostly boarded up. We drink, watch the colors slip to gray dusk in the sky.

"You ever look in your yearbook?" I gulp down the rest of my City.

She goes crazy laughing. "You know," she says, "I don't even know where I put that thing."

I feel way too mean to say anything. I look across the railroad to a field sown in timothy. There are wells there, pumps to suck the ancient gases. The gas burns blue, and I wonder if the ancient sun was blue. The tracks run on till they're a dot in the brown haze. They give off clicks from their switches. Some tankers wait on the spur. Their wheels are rusting to the tracks. I wonder what to hell I ever wanted with trilobites.

"Big night in Rock Camp," I say. I watch Ginny drink. Her skin is so white it glows yellowish, and the last light makes sparks in her red hair.

She says, "Daddy would raise hell. *Me* this close to the wells."

"You're a big girl now. C'mon, let's walk."

We get out, and she up and grabs my arm. Her fingers feel like ribbons on the veins of my hand.

"How long you in for?" I say.

"Just a week here, then a week with Daddy in New York. I can't wait to get back. It's great."

"You got a guy?"

She looks at me with this funny smile of hers. "Yeah, I got a guy. He's doing plankton research."

Ever since I talked back, I've been afraid, but now I hurt again. We come to the tankers, and she takes hold on a ladder, steps up.

"This right?" She looks funny, all crouched in like she's just nailed a drag on the fly. I laugh.

"Nail the end nearest the engine. If you slip, you get throwed clear. Way you are a drag on the fly'd suck you under. 'Sides, nobody'd ride a tanker."

She steps down but doesn't take my hand. "He taught you everything. What killed him?"

"Little shell fragment. Been in him since the war. Got in his blood . . ." I snap my fingers. I want to talk, but the picture won't become words. I see myself scattered, every cell miles from the others. I pull them back and kneel in the dark grass. I roll the body face-up, and look in the eyes a long time before I shut them. "You never talk about your momma," I say.

She says, "I don't want to," and goes running to an open window in the depot. She peeks in, turns to me. "Can we go in?"

"Why? Nothing in there but old freight scales."

"Because it's spooky and neat and I want to." She runs back, kisses me on the cheek. "I'm bored with this glum look. Smile!"

I give up and walk to the depot. I drag a rotten bench under the broken window and climb in. I take Ginny's hand to help her. A blade of glass slices her forearm. The cut path is shallow, but I take off my T-shirt to wrap it. The blood blots purple on the cloth.

"Hurt?"

"Not really."

I watch a mud dauber land on the glass blade. Its metal-blue wings flick as it walks the edge. It sucks what the glass has scraped from her skin. I hear them working in the walls.

Ginny is at the other window, and she peers through a knothole in the plywood.

I say, "See that light green spot on the second hill?"

"Yeah."

"That's the copper on your-all's roof."

She turns, stares at me.

"I come here lots," I say. I breathe the musty air. I turn away from her and look out the window to Company Hill, but I can feel her stare. Company Hill looks bigger in the dusk, and I think of all the hills around town I've never set foot on. Ginny comes up behind me, and there's a glass-crunch with her steps. The hurt arm goes around me, the tiny spot of blood cold against my back.

"What is it, Colly? Why can't we have any fun?"

"When I was a young punk, I tried to run away from home. I was walking through this meadow on the other side of the Hill, and this shadow passed over me. I honest to god thought it was a pterodactyl. It was a damned airplane. I was so damn mad, I came home." I peel chips of paint from the window frame, wait for her to talk. She leans against me, and I kiss her real deep. Her waist bunches in my hands. The skin of her neck is almost too white in the faded evening. I know she doesn't understand.

I slide her to the floor. Her scent rises to me, and I shove crates aside to make room. I don't wait. She isn't making love, she's getting laid. All right, I think, all right. Get laid. I pull her pants around her ankles, rut her. I think of Tinker's sister. Ginny isn't here. Tinker's sister is under me. A wash of blue light passes over me. I open my eyes to the floor, smell that tang of rain-wet wood. Black snakes. It was the only time he had to whip me.

"Let me go with you," I say. I want to be sorry, but I can't.

"Colly, please . . ." She shoves me back. Her head is rolling in splinters of paint and glass.

I look a long time at the hollow shadows hiding her eyes. She is somebody I met a long time ago. I can't remember her name for a minute, then it comes back to me. I sit against the wall and my spine aches. I listen to the mud daubers building nests, and trace a finger along her throat.

She says, "I want to go. My arm hurts." Her voice comes from someplace deep in her chest.

We climb out. A yellow light burns on the crossties, and the switches click. Far away, I hear a train. She gives me my shirt, and gets in her car. I stand there looking at the blood spots on the cloth. I feel old as hell. When I look up, her taillights are reddish blurs in the fog.

I walk around to the platform, slump on the bench. The evening cools my eyelids. I think of how that one time was the only airplane that ever passed over me.

I picture my father—a young hobo with the Michigan sunset making him squint, the lake behind him. His face is hard from all the days and places he fought to live in, and of a sudden, I know his mistake was coming back here to set that locust-tree post on the knob.

"Ever notice how only blue lightning bugs come out after a rain? Green ones almost never do."

I hear the train coming. She is highballing all right. No stiffs in that blind baggage.

"Well, you know the Teays must of been a big river. Just stand on Company Hill, and look across the bottoms. You'll see."

My skin is heavy with her noise. Her light cuts a wide slice in the fog. No stiff in his right mind could try this one on the fly. She's hell-bent for election.

"Jim said it flowed west by northwest—all the way up to the old Saint Lawrence Drain. Had garfish—ten, maybe twenty foot long. Said they're still in there."

Good old Jim'll probably croak on a lie like that. I watch her beat by. A worn-out tie belches mud with her weight. She's just too fast to jump. Plain and simple.

I get up. I'll spend tonight at home. I've got eyes to shut in Michigan—maybe even Germany or China, I don't know yet. I walk, but I'm not scared. I feel my fear moving away in rings through time for a million years.

1934

by *Jayne Anne Phillips*

In 1934 I was seven years old. Bellington, Virginia, was a Depression town. My mother was twenty-eight, my father fifty, my grandmother sixty-two. We lived in a big falling house in the center of town; but in those days, forty years ago, even town people had some land, barns in back. We had cows, some chickens. If it weren't for them we'd have starved because my father was crazy.

All morning my grandmother, Jocasta Andora, churned butter on the porch. I believed she had a rat in the tall urn. Determined, scowling, she beat it to death every day. Nonstop, blunt tick of a clock. She kept her white hair twisted in braids and wore a man's wire glasses with bent frames. She got up at five with Lacey, my mother, and started as soon as the cows were milked: pounding, pounding, pounding. She kept on until eight when we left in the cart and she walked over the hill to give blind Aunt Jenny her insulin shot. Until then I had to stand beside her while she molded the pale yellow bricks. I had to run them to the icehouse while she flicked at my heels with a broom.

"Run! Run! Before the mold smears! You'll be your father's daughter yet . . ."

Lacey and I delivered milk and butter and eggs in a cart. Some mornings our neighbor Johannes helped us load up. Tall and blond, Swedish, he said our names in a singsong. He had the high, broad forehead of a child, and a wife who seldom spoke. As we rattled away in the cart he raised an arm and held it, motionless, until we were out of sight. Lacey never turned.

She had a red account book the size of my palm. I held it in my lap, read names and orders over clinks and grumbles of the cart. Lacey's chestnut hair strayed in her eyes. She had one muslin dress she saved to deliver orders; said she refused to look poor in the shops. Storekeepers on Main Street stopped us, asked after J.T. She'd say he was improving thank you. They shook their heads, he was a compatriot who'd deserted them. Besides, everyone in town knew he was only getting worse. Weekly, he'd start downtown in the middle of the street, shirtless, in his nightcap. He wouldn't budge for horses or autos. Just kept striding, shaking back his long hair, probably to the bank to demand his money. Of which there'd been none for five years.

"Take off your pants, J.T.!" Jocasta snarled it from the kitchen, sometimes she yelled it from the window. "If you take off your pants, they'll make her put you away!"

Lacey rushed to the door after him.

"No, Lacey," sighed Jocasta. "Let the child."

So I was sent.

"Pop, the Gypsies are at the house."

"Eh, what? What?"

"The Gypsies, Pop, they're ready to pay."

He'd mumble about settling accounts, let me take his hand, lead him to the wooden sidewalk. We'd go home.

Some days he appeared to be lucid, though he never acknowledged he was poor. Every morning after breakfast he went to his office on the top floor, dressed in his old spats and a bow tie. He had all his account books up there, boxes of them, and he notated every page. He'd been through them all several times; drawing minute red lines and arrows through the words, and quotes from Shakespeare. He imagined I was a boy, his partner in the business. I had one of his cigars I'd chew and pretend to smoke. He'd light it for me, leaning forward, rippling his thick brows, intent on his hand and a cupped flame which wasn't there. His close breath smelled of soap and tobacco. Fine black hair thickened at his wrists. He wore gold cuff links on his shabby shirts.

We could see the whole town from our third-floor windows: Main Street curving down under oaks to where the river curled in a turn, gas-lit globes on the bridge, the junkman on his bicycle. Our tall windows were set thickly in walnut; dark stain dried and flaking to let the wood show naked. Dust floated in the shafted light. J.T.'s lips were the dark pink of sexual flush. He had begun to age with a strength and promise of frailty, flesh across his broad-boned face gone a faint rose in the blue shadow of his beard. He called me Frank instead of Francine.

"Now, Frank. Mr. Southern will arrive here approximately noon. I want you to go down by the river and oversee the cutting. I'll keep him busy here until the wood is stacked."

Southern was a big New England account he'd lost before the mill dissolved. J.T. was once a rich man, owned the biggest lumber operation in the state. He had a whole town of look-alike workers' shacks down by the river in Hampton, ten miles from town. Now they were empty, all the blind cracked glass broken out. My mother eloped with him when he had four grown kids older than she, the finest house in Bellington (historical societies offered to buy us out every year), and lumber operations in six towns. When they came into the station on the train after the wedding trip, his workers lined the tracks and cheered.

"Tail chaser," Jocasta sneered at him. "Out chasing tail every spare minute. No wonder you lost everything. Credit to Gypsies!" she snorted.

"Mother," said Lacey. "What's done is done."

"Yes, and it's done to us. You ought to put him away. He's nothing but a cross."

She and J.T. had fights. Sometimes he'd sneak up and pretend to pick lice off her clothes. I liked that. He would nip at her hair with his fingers until her combs fell out, Jocasta's silver hair falling down all around her. She screamed in fury. Her erotic hair was dangerous; loosened only late at night in her room, thick, blue-silver halfway to her knees. She stayed alone, combing, behind the locked door. Brushing, she watched her circular mirror; sang her high wheedling hum that floated up to my third-floor bed. Across the hall in his room my father listened too. He seemed never to sleep; all night his dim light burned. I saw Jocasta's hair hanging to the rungs of her chair. Yes, I believed I saw it. I wanted to touch her hair. I wanted to wrap myself up in her secretive hair. Ten years later when Jocasta died, I helped Lacey comb out the long and menacing hair. It felt like the mane of a horse.

J.T. used his full charmed strength against Jocasta. She threw every pot in the kitchen at him. Occasionally he threw them back. Lacey and I stood and watched, she yelling "Mother! Not the breakables!" Jocasta picked up something to throw every time he came near her. When she churned, he came up behind her. She'd grab one of the heavy butter molds.

"J.T., you'd look well if I hit you between the eyes with this." She stood facing him, brandishing the mold and holding to her glasses with one hand.

Lacey's father, Jocasta's husband, Herbert, owned a hotel where J.T. used to stay the night on business trips. The first time Lacey saw J.T. she was sixteen, night clerk at the check-in desk. J.T. was thirty-eight, a powerful full-chested man with jet-black hair, a boutonniere and gold-tipped cane. He gave Lacey a diamond wrapped in a handkerchief and said she would marry him. For a year Jocasta kept it from happening, then Herbert died of cirrhosis and Lacey eloped. Jocasta raved on about cursed women and bad choice.

"God knows your father was a wretch. You should have done a sight better in picking one for this child."

Lacey had brown eyes of a depth and shine that always looked welled with tears. "Mother," she said, "you know they were both so charming and fine."

"And what does charm get you? A lunatic or a drunkard. If you'd had a decent father yourself you'd never have tried to marry one, an old man."

"Mother, he wasn't old. He's still not old."

"To a girl of sixteen a man near forty is old, or should be. I tried to tell you that too, a dog that'll carry a bone will bring one. You were a child. He was six years younger than your own father."

"That's just because you robbed the cradle."

"It's best for a woman to marry a younger man. Women outlast men, we're both proof. They don't have our stamina. Marry a young one and you can count on him to bury you."

"Mother, Herbert died long before you will."

"Only because he drank." She sniffed and lifted her chin.

Jocasta kept a locked iron box under her bed. She kept all the baubles J.T. had lavished on Lacey during their courtship. She maintained that those jewels were our security. She even bought back necklaces and watches J.T. had given his mistresses. Wrote letters all over the state offering to buy or trade for them. Then she wrapped them in clean rags and put them in the box. Kept her door locked, carried a long skeleton key on a thin gold chain fastened to her belt.

Jocasta was obsessed with money. All her life she'd barely held on to it, managing the hotel while Herbert drank away the profits. Over and over, she tried to talk Lacey into selling J.T.'s old car, a 1928 Ford locked in the garage. J.T. had it polished until light glanced off like a knife, but he kept driving it top speed down the sidewalks and the town council got out an injunction. Sometimes he walked out at night, looked in the round garage window at the car shining in old smells and dark.

"That car sits out there for six years while we struggle to feed ourselves. That money could roof the barn and buy us another cow. Francine's getting old enough to milk, she can assume her share of the load—"

"Assume her share? She's seven years old and she's seen to J.T. this past year, something you nor I can manage."

"Well, I mean with the economy of the household. If we don't sell that car soon, there won't be a soul left in town with money to buy it."

"There isn't a soul now."

"Yes there is. John Simpson asked me about the car yesterday. I was down at the bank and—"

"Simpson! Just the one J.T. would hate to have it. That man profits on trouble, he's a sniveling crook. I still think there was something shady about the Trust."

The Trust was a fairy tale of which I often heard. When I was born, my father set up a trust to be awarded me when I was ten. Simpson said that when J.T. got so deep in debt that the mill was at stake, he revoked the trust to cover deficits. He lost the mill anyway. Simpson had papers J.T. had supposedly signed, but Lacey thought he'd signed them himself and embezzled the money, covered it somehow with his shifty lawyer mind. She called in other lawyers.

"Gentlemen," Simpson told them. "A shame J.T., a man of stature surely, lost his reason, but the facts speak for themselves. Fifty thousand dollars for a child of ten? Isn't that in itself a little illogical? I tended J.T.'s business as long as possible. We were friends for years, but you can't save a man who's drowning."

Lacey told how he sat there in his big chair looking sorrowful. Simpson weighed three hundred pounds. His limpid blue eyes slanted almost Asian at the corners; he moved his big body with a feline ease. His lips had a swollen look. He pursed them, touched my neck when I delivered milk on Main Street.

He stroked me, lightly, with his manicured hand. Lacey looked stiffly away. Once he leaned into the cart, got close to her over my head and talked to her low and breathy.

"You needn't be so high and mighty," he said. "I could do things for you in this town."

I kicked him hard in the center of his fleshy chest. My boot left a black print that pointed at his throat as he cursed and we drove off. "Damn you! She's the seed of her father! They'll both end in the asylum! To hell with you!"

Bottles bounced and clinked in the cart. I asked if it was true I'd go crazy.

"Of course not. You're like the women in the family, sound as a dollar."

"But Grandmother says I'm like him."

"Don't pay mind to that. She's just jealous because she didn't love her father like you love yours."

"Why not?"

"Because he was an invalid who smelled of camphor and never got out of bed. He used to make her tie her wrist to the arm of her chair and do needlepoint while he took his naps. He lectured her on demons. He was an evil old man."

"Lacey," I said. "I don't know if I love my father. He doesn't even know I'm a girl. Sometimes I hate him."

"I know, Francie, sometimes I do too."

My father's secrets chased us all. At fifty he was still a big man with powerful arms. His grayed hair curled thick and long over his collar before he'd let Lacey cut it. Every few weeks he'd get to drinking. Be docile, childish, speak to Lacey as though she were his mother. She'd tie a bib around his neck, sit him down, shave him and cut his hair.

After he was spruced up he'd grow thoughtful. Walk slowly upstairs in his bare feet, shower, put on aftershave and his green silk vest. He'd put on his straw boater, still almost new because he seldom wore it, and walk to the drugstore after candy.

"Oh, Lord," groaned Jocasta as he came down the steps.

Lacey hushed her, said, "Francie, go after him."

And I'd walk him downtown. "Frank, my boy," he'd say, and put his arm around me. He'd tip his hat to all the women. He was a very handsome man, my father. He'd fairly swagger with happiness, and everyone on the street spoke to him.

They'd nod and shake hands eagerly, the men anxious to talk. At the dry goods store, he'd ask Mrs. Carvey about her children.

"How's Bill doing in the sand lots? That boy has a genuine pitcher's arm, Miranda, he should have training, it's a fact."

Bill had grown and gone before my father married my mother, but Mrs. Carvey went on just like he was nine years old. Her husband was dead; she was lonely. She'd get feeling so good she'd pile me up with remnants to take home. That was how Lacey made my clothes.

Then we'd go down to Farmer's Drug. Cy gave J.T. a box of candy and put it on the imaginary bill. Cy loved J.T. He even slipped Lacey sleeping powders to sedate him in the bad times. J.T. had staked Cy in pharmacy school and again when he started his store. Cy gave me sodas so J.T. would stay and talk to him. Pop always thought it was Sunday when he was in the drugstore and he'd ask for a paper.

"Nope, not in yet this morning, J.T. Come back this afternoon."

"Well, I'll do that, Cy."

They'd shake hands and clap each other's shoulders. Once Cy started tearing up.

"Now, boy, none of that," said J.T. "Times ae getting better, you'll see. And if you have trouble with the store, you know I'm right here with whatever you need."

Out front we'd sit down to discuss the stock market with the men.

"I tell you, boys, the market won't go down. It may waver, but it stands firm."

Of course everyone but he was painfully aware the market had crashed in '29, but they sat discussing the possibility very seriously. They took sides, argued loudly. J.T. and his supporters usually won. They all sat believing in futures.

Finally J.T. got up and stretched, winked, said someone waited for him. He'd whistle all the way home and seem to forget me. He knew the way, he owned the street, I walked behind him. He'd begin to smooth his now-cropped hair and clear his throat.

We could smell our kitchen from down the block. Butter-fried chicken, new potatoes, Jocasta's buttermilk biscuits. Flowers on the swept porch. J.T. made his entrance, swept off his hat grandly, flourished the box. When he spoke to Lacey, white in her muslin dress, J.T. stuttered; something tugged in his brain but he got past it. He took Lacey's hand and folded it to his mouth.

Through dinner she glanced at him, small penetrating glances, as he argued quietly to Jocasta about Galsworthy, whose collected green-bound volumes he read alone in his room at night. Lacey watched them both, twisting her dress beneath the table.

I cleared the plates and she turned on the phonograph, handled heavy waxen records until the old waltzes tinkled out at the right speed. J.T.'s eyes were bright; he whirled her around the room while Jocasta sat downcast. Finally they'd go upstairs as soon as it was decently dark, Lacey's hair falling from the dancing. The record finished and kept scratching, needle bouncing back and forth.

The wind blew the curtains in billowed forms. The glories closed on their vines. We could hear the old brass bed upstairs beginning, rocking very gently. Sometimes Jocasta turned the music on again. Sometimes we just sat, looking at each other, while the rocking went on; small swooning cries, sharp jabs of the bed against the wall.

During a summer storm, lightning struck the barn. Out the back window a rosy flame burned its petaled center, a cauliflower of fire and smoke. We ran outside, the neighbors came, we passed buckets for twenty minutes. J.T. supervised in his pajamas, lined up the men and women, pumped water at the trough. Stark-faced in the jumping light, his voice booming, he yelled directions.

"Get the lions and tigers out!" he kept shouting. "Don't let the big cats burn!"

But the hay caught, the rain slacked. Everything burned except a few chickens and one cow Lacey saved at the risk of her skin.

At the end of it, she stood transfixed by the trough as all the people dispersed. Our neighbor Johannes went to her in the dark and took hold of her. He held her and rubbed her back. "There now, there." She clung to him, grabbed one of his hands behind her and held it. His ashed face nearly shone with some power. He said to come, let him give her some coffee and whiskey. But she said no, she only wanted to stand here for a while. Johannes touched her face, stroked her hair. Picked me up and carried me to his house, and his wife gave me a bath.

Johannes's wife was a wispy woman considerably older than he. She was actually his cousin once removed. They had left Sweden together, she thirty-one and he seventeen, both unmarried virgins. It was a long hard trip, and lonely. When they got to New York he married her. She thought she carried a child but she was wrong. Johannes's wife was barren; she had female problems. Some weeks she stayed in bed.

But that night she bathed me. She smelled of lavender. She lit the bathroom with candles, she sprinkled potpourri and spearmint in the steaming water. She made it bubble with bath salts. Rubbed me with a sponge as big as two hands and I was drunk with flowers. All the time she sang and muttered in her broken English. "Fire no good, poor fire."

She lifted me out of the tub, swaddled me in towels and carried me, though she was frail, into a room where she kept her dolls from Sweden. More lamps, she lit them all, on the floor and the windowsills. Tall globes threw tangled shadows about the walls. Shadows of the dolls' limbs loomed huge across the floor. Dolls, twenty or thirty, in big gossamer hats or bonnets with feathered parakeets, long tulle dresses, buttoned shoes. Their rose faces were perfect in a shadow of curled lashes. They posed sitting, standing, walking, running, holding dishes, bouquets, smaller dolls. One wore roller skates, another walked a stuffed Scottish terrier on a leash. That night was my first hallucination. The dolls began moving around the room, rolling hoops with sticks and talking in their whispery, breathless voices. Johannes's wife was talking too. Her Swedish got faster and faster. She went walking around with the dolls, their glass eyes glazed. They kicked their feet out straight in front. I saw it, the goose-stepping dolls, naked and seven in that room.

"Gerta!" Johannes's voice. He switched on the electric light. Spoke to her with harsh resignation and came to me on the rotating carpet. He pressed my face to his blond beard. The dolls' faces still moved, secretly.

Lacey's face was drawn and tight. She came to get me at Johannes's house the next morning, my best white dress folded on her arm. She stood in the doorway, her hair pulled back severely and her muslin dress freshly ironed.

"Francie," she said. "We're going to the bank."

We turned, walking. Wet grass spattered her stockings. At

the garage she stopped, opened the old locks and let the creaking doors swing wide. The earthen floor rose its buried scent around our heads. When Lacey closed us inside, a powdered light sifted through the dirty window. I saw the board walls grown with chartreuse moss, old sleigh bells hung on leather straps, and something massive glinting in the middle of the room. It seemed to palpitate and breathe, then I saw the movement was only a casting of light on its hard black sides. Chrome and patent black. My eyes grew accustomed to shadows and the car emerged glimmering its saucered headlights. Smells of wax and leather mingled in the dark. Lacey knelt and stripped me. She fastened the dress, nails of her cool fingers scratching my skin. She stood then and walked around the car, touching it with one extended finger.

In the bank we waited, Lacey staring straight ahead. Simpson's secretary, Bedelia, sucked her pencil. Two bright red spots in her cheeks jumped out. She watched Lacey and hated her. Bedelia wore long chains of fake pearls like the women in New York City, but in truth Simpson had found her not twenty miles from town when he foreclosed the mortgage on her father's gritty farm. Bedelia kept a magazine picture of the Eiffel Tower on her desk. She looked at the Eiffel Tower. She looked at Lacey. When Simpson told her to send us in, she nodded at the door and a nerve jumped in her jaw.

Simpson sat in his fat like something cooked.

"My dear Lacey, some brandy, perhaps a sweet liqueur. And Francie needs a sarsaparilla."

"Francine needs nothing. Mr. Simpson, I've come about the car."

"Oh yes, I heard about the fire. Such a misfortune. I'm sure I can be of some help."

Simpson twisted his moustache. Topaz and diamonds choked his little finger. Lacey was impressive; she clutched my hand and left a pale bruise on my wrist. Simpson went on in his honeyed voice.

"J.T. and I were very close, you know. Once I looked after his interests very well. I can do so again."

Lacey was silent. Simpson smiled and watched her. His long black lashes brushed his cheeks, slowly. He blinked once, then again. Opened a drawer in his vast mahogany desk and pulled out a roll of bills. He tossed it in the air, caught it in his fist.

"And there's the matter of that shack property down by the

river. Surely you have no illusions that J.T. will ever work the mill again. I know you ran his business those last years; you have the know-how, I have the means. Perhaps we may arrive at a workable situation . . ."

Simpson was sweating now, his hair gleamed pomaded and perfect. He held out the money and Lacey didn't move. I stepped forward and took it.

We put the money in the iron box; Lacey gave up the deed to the mill. I remember J.T. staying in his room, and the sound of the rocking chair creaking for hours as he sat, rocking, with his arms crossed, staring at the wall. Jocasta was not singing. Lacey had locked her door and the house was weighted with silence, sinking in the dark. I fell asleep.

I saw my father standing over me in his checkered cap, red silk scarf, old suede driving coat. He had a pistol in his hand.

"Frank," he said. "It's time to go."

He lifted me so softly I thought I dreamed him. He pulled my nightgown down to cover my thighs and we crept quietly down two flights of stairs past the sleepers. Everything slept; trees drooped close to the house, no insects sounded. My father's face above me took on an ivory cast. The moon was gone and it was nearly dawn.

At the garage he fired two quick shots at the locks. The sharp report of the gun echoed back and forth. I saw Lacey's light go on but I was in the car and the car was roaring. J.T. eased it down the street and gathered speed. He smiled, his hair blew back. The old bridge rattled under us and moved its lamps; their twelve whirled reflections wobbled in the river. J.T. flexed his beautiful hands and muttered. He touched the leather dash and the steering wheel laced with calfskin. We went faster out the bridge road to the mill.

"Pop?" I said. "Pop, where we going?"

"Straight home, boy. Straight home."

The motor revved. At top speed the car began to shake. We were moving up Tucker Mountain and we shuddered at the crest. A sharp quick crack. I didn't feel myself jump but I saw the wheel spin off, I saw the black Ford fly off the mountain and my father's red scarf streaming.

I looked down two ledges at the overturned car. The wheels whined and smoked. I scrambled down but J.T. was nowhere. I called for him, choking on the smell of the car, then I saw him above me climbing back to the road. He had the steering wheel in one hand. At the top he turned and looked down.

"Frank," he yelled. "Hurry, it's getting late."

The mill was on the other side of Tucker Mountain. We walked. The light came up. Mist rose off the river and the rows of empty shacks seemed to float.

"There they are," said J.T. "They're always here this time of day."

"Who, Pop? Who's here?"

"They are, boy. Look at them, they know who you are."

He raised his arm in the direction of the shacks. His hand hung limp and crooked.

"Where, Pop?"

"The windows, Frank. Look at the windows."

They were slanted in their rotted sills. Broken glass stood out in jagged angles; what was left pearled at odd curves in the light. Something moved, then I knew it was true; I was as crazy as him. The faces shimmered like they were coming up out of water. They rose up from some place existing alongside and suddenly visible. Their blurry features held the same expression, they moved in and out of each other. Wind rushed, whispering sounds I couldn't make out; more and more whispering, louder and louder . . . then they made one sound. "Francine," they said, "Francine."

"Francine. Francine, come here. Over here."

I saw my mother at the edge of the woods. She had J.T.'s old deer rifle and she had it pointed at him. Beyond her Jocasta sat in the delivery cart and didn't look at us. Lacey called me again and I tried to move. She fired the gun in the air; while the sharp boom moved around in the trees I ran to her. I knew the faces watched me. J.T. still looked at them, smiling. My mother held me away from him, tightly, until the faces faded. I must have talked, I must have said I saw them. Her eyes were hard with light. The butt of the gun pressed into her stomach. She put J.T. in the cart and tied him in with a thick rope. He smoothed his torn clothes while she walked me through the shacks. Empty, every one of them. Rats thumped across the porches.

After that we had to have him put away. The morning they came and got him, he turned at the door.

"Lacey," he said calmly, "aren't you coming with me?"

HOLIDAY
by *Katherine Anne Porter*

At that time I was too young for some of the troubles I was having, and I had not yet learned what to do with them. It no longer can matter what kind of troubles they were, or what finally became of them. It seemed to me then there was nothing to do but run away from them, though all my tradition, background, and training had taught me unanswerably that no one except a coward ever runs away from anything. What nonsense! They should have taught me the difference between courage and foolhardiness, instead of leaving me to find it out for myself. I learned finally that if I still had the sense I was born with, I would take off like a deer at the first warning of certain dangers. But this story I am about to tell you happened before this great truth impressed itself upon me—that we do not run from the troubles and dangers that are truly ours, and it is better to learn what they are earlier than later. And if we don't run from the others, we are fools.

I confided to my friend Louise, a former schoolmate about my own age, not my troubles but my little problem: I wanted to go somewhere for a spring holiday, by myself, to the country, and it should be very simple and nice and, of course, not expensive, and she was not to tell anyone where I had gone; but if she liked, I would send her word now and then, if anything interesting was happening. She said she loved getting letters but hated answering them; and she knew the very place for me, and she would not tell anybody anything. Louise had then—she has it still—something near to genius for making improbable persons, places, and situations sound attractive. She told amusing stories that did not turn grim on you until a little while later, when by chance you saw and heard for yourself. So with this story. Everything was just as Louise had said, if you like, and everything was, at the same time, quite different.

"I know the very place," said Louise. "A family of real old-fashioned German peasants, in the deep blackland Texas farm country, a household in real patriarchal style—the kind of thing you'd hate to live with but is very nice to visit. Old father, God Almighty himself, with whiskers and all; old mother, matriarch in men's shoes; endless daughters and sons and sons-in-law, and fat babies falling about the place; and fat puppies—my favorite was a darling little black thing named Kuno—cows, calves, and sheep and lambs and goats and turkeys and guineas roaming up and down the shallow green hills, ducks and geese on the ponds. I was there in the summer when the peaches and watermelons were in—"

"This is the end of March," I said, doubtfully.

"Spring comes early there," said Louise. "I'll write to the Müllers about you, you just get ready to go."

"Just where is this paradise?"

"Not far from the Louisiana line," said Louise. "I'll ask them to give you my attic—oh, that was a sweet place! It's a big room, with the roof sloping to the floor on each side, and the roof leaks a little when it rains, so the shingles are all stained in beautiful streaks, all black and gray and mossy green, and in one corner there used to be a stack of dime novels, The Duchess, Ouida, Mrs. E.D.E.N. Southworth, Ella Wheeler Wilcox's poems—one summer they had a lady boarder who was a great reader, and she went off and left her library. I loved it! And everybody was so healthy and goodhearted, and the weather was perfect. . . . How long do you want to stay?"

I hadn't thought of this, so I said at random, "About a month."

A few days later I found myself tossed off like an express package from a dirty little crawling train onto the sodden platform of a country station, where the stationmaster emerged and locked up the waiting room before the train had got round the bend. As he clumped by me he shifted his wad of tobacco to his cheek and asked, "Where you goin'?"

"To the Müller farm," I said, standing beside my small

trunk and suitcase with the bitter wind cutting my shoulders through my thin coat.

"Anybody meet you?" he asked, not pausing.

"They *said* so."

"All right," he said, and got into his little ragged buckboard with a sway-backed horse and drove away.

I turned my trunk on its side and sat on it facing the wind and the desolate mud-colored shapeless scene and began making up my first letter to Louise. First I was going to tell her that unless she meant to be a novelist, there was no excuse for her having so much imagination. In daily life, I was going to tell her, there are also such useful things as the plain facts that should be stuck to, through thick and thin. Anything else led to confusion like this. I was beginning to enjoy my letter to Louise when a sturdy boy about twelve years old crossed the platform. As he neared me, he took off his rough cap and bunched it in his thick hand, dirt-stained at the knuckles. His round cheeks, his round nose, his round chin were a cool, healthy red. In the globe of his face, as neatly circular as if drawn in bright crayon, his narrow, long, tip-tilted eyes, clear as pale-blue water, seemed out of place, as if two incompatible strains had collided in making him. They were beautiful eyes, and the rest of the face was not to be taken seriously. A blue woolen blouse buttoned up to his chin ended abruptly at his waist as if he would outgrow it in another half hour, and his blue drill breeches flapped about his ankles. His old clodhopper shoes were several sizes too big for him. Altogether, it was plain he was not the first one to wear his clothes. He was a cheerful, detached, self-possessed apparition against the tumbled brown earth and ragged dark sky, and I smiled at him as well as I could with a face that felt like wet clay.

He smiled back slightly without meeting my eye, motioning for me to take up my suitcase. He swung my trunk to his head and tottered across the uneven platform, down the steps slippery with mud, where I expected to see him crushed beneath his burden like an ant under a stone. He heaved the trunk into the back of his wagon with a fine smash, took my suitcase and tossed it after, then climbed up over one front wheel while I scrambled my way up over the other.

The pony, shaggy as a wintering bear, eased himself into

a grudging trot, while the boy, bowed over with his cap pulled down over his ears and eyebrows, held the reins slack and fell into a brown study. I examined the harness, a real mystery. It met and clung in all sorts of unexpected places; it parted company in what appeared to be strategic seats of jointure. It was mended sketchily in risky places with bits of hairy rope. Other seemingly unimportant parts were bound together irrevocably with wire. The bridle was too long for the pony's stocky head, so he had shaken the bit out of his mouth at the start, apparently, and went his own way at his own pace.

Our vehicle was an exhausted specimen of something called a spring wagon, who knows why? There were no springs, and the shallow enclosed platform at the back, suitable for carrying various plunder, was worn away until it barely reached midway of the back wheels, one side of it steadily scraping the iron tire. The wheels themselves spun not dully around and around in the way of common wheels, but elliptically, being loosened at the hubs, so that we proceeded with a drunken, hilarious swagger, like the rolling motion of a small boat on a choppy sea.

The soaked brown fields fell away on either side of the lane, all rough with winter-worn stubble ready to sink and become earth again. The scanty leafless woods ran along an edge of the field nearby. There was nothing beautiful in those woods now except the promise of spring, for I detested bleakness, but it gave me pleasure to think that beyond this there might be something else beautiful in its own being, a river shaped and contained by its banks, or a field stripped down to its true meaning, plowed and ready for the seed. The road turned abruptly and was almost hidden for a moment, and we were going through the woods. Closer sight of the crooked branches assured me that spring was beginning, if sparely, reluctantly; the leaves were budding in tiny cones of watery green besprinkling all the new shoots; a thin sedate rain began again to fall, not so opaque as a fog, but a mist that merely deepened overhead, and lowered, until the clouds became rain in one swathing, delicate gray.

As we emerged from the woods, the boy roused himself and pointed forward, in silence. We were approaching the farm along the skirts of a fine peach orchard, now faintly colored with young buds, but there was nothing to disguise the gaunt and aching ugliness of the farmhouse itself. In this Texas valley, so gently modulated with small crests and shallows, "rolling country" as the farmers say, the house was set on the peak of the barest rise of ground, as if the most infertile spot had been thriftily chosen for building a shelter. It stood there staring and naked, an intruding stranger, strange even beside the barns ranged generously along the back, low-eaved and weathered to the color of stone.

The narrow windows and the steeply sloping roof oppressed me; I wished to turn away and go back. I had come a long way to be so disappointed, I thought, and yet I must go on, for there could be nothing here for me more painful than what I had left. But as we drew near the house, now hardly visible except for the yellow lamplight in the back, perhaps in the kitchen, my feelings changed again toward warmth and tenderness, or perhaps just an apprehension that I could feel so, maybe, again.

The wagon drew up before the porch, and I started climbing down. No sooner had my foot touched ground than an enormous black dog of the detestable German shepherd breed leaped silently at me, and as silently I covered my face with my arms and leaped back. "Kuno, down!" shouted the boy, lunging at him. The front door flew open and a young girl with yellow hair ran down the steps and seized the ugly beast by the scruff. "He does not mean anything," she said seriously in English. "He is only a dog."

Just Louise's darling little puppy Kuno, I thought, a year or so older. Kuno whined, apologized by bowing and scraping one front paw on the ground, and the girl holding his scruff said, shyly and proudly, "I teach him that. He has always such bad manners, but I teach him!"

I had arrived, it seemed, at the moment when the evening chores were about to begin. The entire Müller household streamed out of the door, each man and woman going about the affairs of the moment. The young girl walked with me up the porch steps and said, "This is my brother Hans," and a young man paused to shake hands and passed by. "This is my brother Fritz," she said, and Fritz took my hand and dropped it as he went. "My sister Annetje," said the young girl, and a quiet young woman with a baby draped loosely like a scarf over her shoulder smiled and held out her hand. Hand after hand went by, their palms variously younger or older, broad or small, male or female, but all thick hard decent peasant hands, warm and strong. And in every face I saw again the pale, tilted eyes, on every head that taffy-colored hair, as though they might all be brothers and sisters, though Annetje's husband and still another daughter's husband had gone by after greeting me. In the wide hall with a door at front and back, full of cloudy light and the smell of soap, the old mother, also on her way out, stopped to offer her hand. She was a tall strong-looking woman wearing a three-cornered black wool shawl on her head, her skirts looped up over a brown flannel petticoat. Not from her did the young ones get those water-clear eyes. Hers were black and shrewd and searching, a band of hair showed black streaked with gray, her seamed dry face was brown as seasoned bark, and she walked in her rubber boots with the stride of a man. She shook my hand briefly and said in German English that I was welcome, smiling and showing her blackened teeth.

"This is my girl Hatsy," she told me, "and she will show you to your room." Hatsy took my hand as if I were a child needing a guide. I followed her up a flight of steps steep as a ladder, and there we were, in Louise's attic room, with the sloping roof. Yes, the shingles were stained all the colors she had said. There were the dime novels heaped in the corner. For once, Louise had got it straight, and it was homely and familiar, as if I had seen it before. "My mother says we could give you a better place on the downstairs," said Hatsy, in her soft blurred English, "but *she* said in her letter you would like it so." I told her indeed I did like it so. She went down the steep stairs then, and her brother came up as if he were climbing a tree, with the trunk on his head and the suitcase in his right hand, and I could not see what kept the trunk from crashing back to the bottom, as he used the left hand to climb with. He put his burden down and straightened up, wriggling his shoulders and panting only a little. I thanked him and he pushed his cap back and pulled it forward again, which I took for some sort of polite response, and clattered out hugely. Looking out of my window a few minutes later, I saw him setting off across the fields carrying a lighted lantern and a large steel trap.

I began changing my first letter to Louise. "I'm going to like it here. I don't quite know why, but it's going to be all right. Maybe I can tell you later—"

The sound of the German speech in the household below was part of the pleasantness, for they were not talking to me and did not expect me to answer. All the German I understood then was contained in five small deadly sentimental songs of Heine's, learned by heart; and this was a very different tongue, Low German corrupted by three generations in a foreign country. A dozen miles away, where Texas and Louisiana melted together in a rotting swamp whose sluggish undertow of decay nourished the roots of pine and cedar, a colony of French immigrants had lived out two hundred years of exile, not wholly incorruptible, but mystically faithful to the marrow of their bones, obstinately speaking their old French, by then as strange to the French as it was to the English. I had known many of these families during a certain long summer happily remembered, and here, listening to another language nobody could understand except those of this small farming community, I knew that I was again in a house of perpetual exile. These were solid, practical, hard-bitten, landholding German peasants who stuck their mattocks into the earth deep and held fast wherever they were, because to them life and the land were one indivisible thing; but never in any wise did they confuse nationality with habitation.

I liked the thick warm voices, and it was good not to have to understand what they were saying. I loved that silence which means freedom from the constant pressure of other minds and other opinions and other feelings, that freedom to fold up in quiet and go back to my own center, to find out again, for it is always a rediscovery, what kind of creature it is that rules me finally, makes all the decisions no matter who thinks they make them, even I; who little by little takes everything away except the one thing I cannot live without, and who will one day say, "Now I am all you have left—take me." I paused there a good while listening to this muted unknown language which was silence with music in it; I could be moved and touched but not troubled by it, as by the crying of frogs or the wind in the trees.

The catalpa tree at my window would, I noticed, when it

came into leaf, shut off my view of the barns and the fields beyond. When in bloom the branches would almost reach through the window. But now they were a thin screen through which the calves, splotchy red and white, moved prettily against the weathered darkness of the sheds. The brown fields would soon be green again; the sheep would not look then as they did now, merely lumps of moving earth, but would be washed by the rains and become clean gray. All the beauty of the landscape now was in the harmony of the valley rolling fluently away to the wood's edge. It was an inland country, with the forlorn look of all unloved things; winter in this part of the South is a moribund coma, not the Northern death sleep with the sure promise of resurrection. But in my South, my loved and never-forgotten country, after her long sickness, with only a slight stirring, an opening of the eyes between one breath and the next, between night and day, the earth revives and bursts into the plenty of spring with fruit and flowers together, spring and summer at once under the hot shimmering blue sky.

The freshening wind promised another light sedate rain to come at evening. The voices below-stairs dispersed, rose again, separately calling from the yards and barns. The old woman strode down the path toward the cow sheds, Hatsy running behind her. The woman wore her wooden yoke, with the milking pails covered and closed with iron hasps, slung easily across her shoulders, but her daughter carried two tin milking pails on her arm. When they pushed back the bars of cedar which opened onto the fields, the cows came through lowing and crowding, and the calves scampered each to his own dam with reaching, opened mouths. Then there was the battle of separating the hungry children from their mothers when they had taken their scanty share. The old woman slapped their little haunches with her open palm, Hatsy dragged at their halters, her feet slipping wide in the mud, the cows bellowed and brandished their horns, the calves bawled like rebellious babies. Hatsy's long yellow braids whisked round her shoulders, her laughter was a shrill streak of gaiety above the angry cow voices and the raucous shouting of the old woman.

From the kitchen porch below came the sound of splashing water, the creaking of the pump handle, and the stamping boots of men. I sat in the window watching the darkness come on slowly. All the sounds of the place gathered under the roof while the lamps were being lighted. My own small lamp had a handle on the oil bowl, like a cup's. There was also a lantern with a frosted chimney hanging by a nail on the wall. A voice called to me from the foot of my stairs and I looked down into the face of a dark-skinned, flaxen-haired young woman, far advanced in pregnancy, and carrying a prosperous year-old boy on her hip, one arm clutching him to her, the other raised above her head so that her lantern shone upon their heads. "The supper is now ready," she said, and waited for me to come down before turning away.

In the large square room the whole family was gathering at a long table covered with a red checkered cotton cloth, heaped-up platters of steaming food at either end. A crippled and badly deformed servant girl was setting down pitchers of milk. Her head was so bowed over, her face was almost hidden, and her whole body was maimed in some painful, mysterious way, probably congenital, I supposed, though she seemed wiry and tough. Her knotted hands shook continually, her wagging head kept pace with her restless elbows. She ran unsteadily around the table scattering plates, dodging whoever stood in her way; no one moved aside for her, or spoke to her, or even glanced after her when she vanished into the kitchen.

The men moved forward to their chairs. Father Müller took his patriarch's place at the head of the table, Mother Müller looming behind him like a dark boulder. The young men ranged themselves about one side, the married ones with their wives standing back of their chairs to serve them, for three generations in this country had not made them self-conscious or disturbed their ancient customs. The two sons-in-law and three sons rolled down their shirt sleeves before beginning to eat. Their faces were polished with recent scrubbing and their open collars were damp.

Mother Müller pointed to me, then waved her hand at her household, telling off their names rapidly once more. I was a stranger and a guest, so was seated on the men's side of the table, and Hatsy, whose real name turned out to be Huldah, the maiden of the family, was seated on the children's side of the board, attending to them and keeping them in order. These infants ranged from two years to ten, five in number—not counting the one still straddling his mother's hip behind his father's chair—divided between the two married daughters. The children ravened and gorged and reached their hands into the sugar bowl to sprinkle sugar on everything they ate, solemnly elated over their food and paying no attention to Hatsy, who struggled with them only a little less energetically than she did with the calves, and ate almost nothing. She was about seventeen years old, pale-lipped and too thin, and her sleek fine butter-yellow hair, streaked light and dark, real German peasant hair, gave her an air of fragility. But she shared the big-boned structure, the enormous energy and animal force that was like a bodily presence itself in the room; and seeing Father Müller's pale-gray deep-set choleric eyes and high cheekbones, it was easy to trace the family resemblance around the table: it was plain that poor Mother Müller had never had a child of her own—black-eyed, black-haired South Germany people. True, she had borne them, but that was all; they belonged to their father. Even the tawny Gretchen, expecting another baby, obviously the pet of the family, with the sly smiling manner of a spoiled child, who wore the contented air of a lazy, healthy young animal, seeming always about to yawn, had hair like pulled taffy and those slanted clear eyes. She stood now easing the weight of her little boy on her husband's chair back, reaching with her left arm over his shoulder to refill his plate from time to time.

Annetje's baby drooled comfortably down her back, while she spooned things from platters and bowls for her husband. Whenever their eyes met, they smiled with a gentle, reserved warmth in their eyes, the smile of long and sure friendship.

Father Müller did not in the least believe in his children's marrying and leaving home. Marry, yes, of course; but must that take a son or daughter from him? He always could provide work and a place in the household for his daughters' husbands, and in time he would do the same for his sons' wives. A new room had lately been built on, to the northeast, Annetje explained to me, leaning above her husband's head and talking across the table, for Hatsy to live in when she should be married. Hatsy turned very beautifully pink and ducked her head almost into her plate, then looked up boldly and said, "*Jah, jah*, I am marrit now soon!" Everybody laughed except Mother Müller, who said in German that girls at home never knew when they were well off—no, they must go bringing in husbands. This remark did not seem to hurt anybody's feelings, and Gretchen said it was nice that I was going to be here for the wedding. This reminded Annetje of something, and she spoke in English to the table at large, saying that the Lutheran pastor had advised her to attend church oftener and put her young ones in Sunday School, so that God would give her a blessing with her next child. I counted around again, and sure enough, with Gretchen's unborn, there were eight children at that table under the age of ten; somebody was going to need a blessing in all that crowd, no doubt. Father Müller delivered a short speech to his daughter in German, then turned to me and said, "What I say iss, it iss all craziness to go to church and pay a preacher goot money to talk his nonsense. Say rather that he pay me to come and lissen, then I vill go!" His eyes glared with sudden fierceness above his square speckled gray and yellow beard that sprouted directly out from the high cheekbones. "He thinks, so, that my time maybe costs nothing? That iss goot! Let him pay me!"

Mother Müller snorted and shuffled her feet. "Ach, you talk, you talk! Now you vill make the pastor goot and mad if he hears. Vot ve do, if he vill not chrissen the babies?"

"You give him goot money, he vill chrissen," shouted Father Müller. "You vait und see!"

"Ah sure, dot iss so," agreed Mother Müller. "Only do not let him hear!"

There was a gust of excited talk in German, with much rapping of knife handles on the table. I gave up trying to understand, but watched their faces. It sounded like a pitched battle, but they were agreeing about something. They were united in their tribal skepticisms, as in everything else. I got a powerful impression that they were all, even the sons-in-law, one human being divided into several separate appearances. The crippled servant girl brought in more food and gathered up plates and went away in her limping run, and she seemed to me the only individual in the house. Even I felt divided into many fragments, having left or lost a part of myself in every place I had traveled, in every life mine had touched, above all, in every death of someone near to me that had carried into the grave some part of my living cells. But the servant, she was whole, and belonged nowhere.

I settled easily enough into the marginal life of the household ways and habits. Day began early at the Müllers', and we ate breakfast by yellow lamplight, with the gray damp winds blowing with spring softness through the open windows. The men swallowed their last cups of steaming coffee standing, with their hats on, and went out to harness the horses to the plows at sunrise. Annetje, with her fat baby slung over her shoulder, could sweep a room or make a bed with one hand, all finished before the day was well begun; and she spent the rest of the day outdoors, caring for the chickens and the pigs. Now and then she came in with a shallow box full of newly hatched chickens, abject dabs of wet fluff, and put them on a table in her bedroom where she might tend them carefully on their first day. Mother Müller strode about hugely, giving orders right and left, while Father Müller, smoothing his whiskers and lighting his pipe, drove away to town with Mother Müller calling out after him final directions and instructions about household needs. He never spoke a word to her or looked at her and appeared not to be listening, but he always returned in a few hours with every commission performed exactly. After I had made my own bed and set my attic in order, there was nothing at all for me to do, and I walked out of this enthusiastic bustle into the lane, feeling extremely useless. But the repose, the almost hysterical inertia of their minds in the midst of this muscular life, communicated itself to me little by little, and I absorbed it gratefully in silence and felt all the hidden knotted painful places in my own mind beginning to loosen. It was easier to breathe, and I might weep, if I pleased. In a very few days I no longer felt like weeping.

One morning I saw Hatsy spading up the kitchen garden plot, and my offer to help, to spread the seeds and cover them, was accepted. We worked at this for several hours each morning, until the warmth of the sun and the stooping posture induced in me a comfortable vertigo. I forgot to count the days, they were one like the other except as the colors of the air changed, deepening and warming to keep step with the advancing season, and the earth grew firmer underfoot with the swelling tangle of crowding roots.

The children, so hungry and noisy at the table, were peaceable little folk who played silent engrossed games in the front yard. They were always kneading mud into loaves and pies and carrying their battered dolls and cotton rag animals through the operations of domestic life. They fed them, put them to bed; they got them up and fed them again, set them to their chores making more mud loaves; or they would harness themselves to their carts and gallop away to a great shady chestnut tree on the opposite side of the house. Here the tree became the *Turnverein,* and they themselves were again human beings, solemnly ambling about in a dance and going through the motions of drinking beer. Miraculously changed once more into horses, they harnessed themselves and galloped home. They came at call to be fed and put to sleep with the docility of their own toys or animal playmates. Their mothers handled them with instinctive, constant gentleness; they never seemed to be troubled by them. They were as devoted and care-taking as a cat with her kittens.

Sometimes I took Annetje's next to youngest child, a baby of two years, in her little wagon, and we would go down through the orchard and into the lane for a short distance. I would turn again into a smaller lane, smoother because less traveled, and we would go slowly between the aisles of mulberry trees where the fruit was beginning to hang and curl like green furry worms. The baby would sit in a compact mound of flannel and calico, her pale-blue eyes tilted and shining under her cap, her little lower teeth showing in a rapt smile. Sometimes several of the other children would follow along quietly. When I turned, they all turned without question, and we would proceed back to the house as sedately as we had set out.

The narrow lane, I discovered, led to the river, and it became my favorite walk. Almost every day I went along the edge of the naked wood, passionately occupied with looking for signs of spring. The changes there were so subtle and gradual, I found one day that branches of willows and sprays of blackberry vine alike were covered with fine points of green; the color had changed overnight, or so it seemed, and I knew that tomorrow the whole valley and wood and edge of the river would be quick and feathery with golden green blowing in the winds.

And it was so. On that day I did not leave the river until after dark and came home through the marsh with the owls and nightjars crying over my head, calling in a strange broken chorus in the woods until the farthest answering cry was a ghostly echo. When I went through the orchard the trees were freshly budded out with pale bloom, the branches were immobile in the thin darkness, but the flower clusters shivered in a soundless dance of delicately woven light, whirling as airily as leaves in a breeze, as rhythmically as water in a fountain. Every tree was budded out with this living, pulsing fire as fragile and cool as bubbles. When I opened the gate their light shone on my hands like fox fire. When I looked back, the shimmer of golden light was there, it was no dream.

Hatsy was on her knees in the dining room, washing the floor with heavy dark rags. She always did this work at night, so the men with their heavy boots would not be tracking it up again and it would be immaculate in the morning. She turned her young face to me in a stupor of fatigue. "Ottilie! Ottilie!" she called loudly, and before I could speak, she said, "Ottilie will give you supper. It is waiting, all ready." I tried to tell her that I was not hungry, but she wished to reassure me. "Look, we all must eat. Now, or then, it's no trouble." She sat back on her heels, and raising her head, looked over the window sill at the orchard. She smiled and paused for a moment and said happily, "Now it is come spring. Every spring we have that." She bent again over the great pail of water with her mops.

The crippled servant came in, stumbling perilously on the slippery floor, and set a dish before me, lentils with sausage and red chopped cabbage. It was hot and savory and I was truly grateful, for I found I was hungry, after all. I looked at her—so her name was Ottilie?—and said, "Thank you." "She can't talk," said Hatsy, simply, stating a fact that need not be emphasized. The blurred, dark face was neither young nor old, but crumpled into crisscross wrinkles, irrelevant either to age or suffering; simply wrinkles, patternless blackened seams as if the perishable flesh had been wrung in a hard cruel fist. Yet in that mutilated face I saw high cheekbones, slanted water-blue eyes, the pupils very large and strained with the anxiety of one peering into a darkness full of danger. She jarred heavily against the table as she turned, her bowed back trembling with the perpetual working of her withered arms, and ran away in aimless, driven haste.

Hatsy sat on her heels again for a moment, tossed her braids back over her shoulder, and said, "That is Ottilie. She is not sick now. She is only like that since she was sick when she was baby. But she can work so well as I can. She cooks. But she cannot talk so you can understand." She went up on her knees, bowed over, and began to scrub again, with new energy. She was really a network of thin taut ligaments and long muscles elastic as woven steel. She would always work too hard, and be tired all her life, and never know that this was anything but perfectly natural; everybody worked all the time, because there was always more work waiting when they had finished what they were doing then. I ate my supper and took my plate to the kitchen and set it on the table. Ottilie was sitting in a kitchen chair with her feet in the open oven, her arms folded, and her head waggling a little. She did not see or hear me.

At home, Hatsy wore an old brown corduroy dress and galoshes without stockings. Her skirts were short enough to show her thin legs, slightly crooked below the knees, as if she had walked too early. "Hatsy, she's a good, quick girl," said Mother Müller, to whom praising anybody or anything did not come easily. On Saturdays, Hatsy took a voluminous bath in a big tub in the closet back of the kitchen, where also were stored the extra chamber pots, slop jars, and water jugs. She then unplaited her yellow hair and bound up the crinkled floss with a wreath of pink cotton rosebuds, put on her pale-blue China silk dress, and went to the *Turnverein* to dance and drink a seidel of dark-brown beer with her devoted suitor, who resembled her brothers enough to be her brother. On Sundays, the entire family went to the *Turnverein* after copious washings, getting into starched dresses and shirts, and getting the baskets of food stored in the wagons. The servant, Ottilie, would rush out to see them off, standing with both shaking arms folded over her forehead, shading her troubled eyes to watch them to the turn of the lane. Her muteness seemed nearly absolute; she had no coherent language of signs. Yet three times a day she spread that enormous table with solid food, freshly baked bread, huge platters of vegetables, immoderate roasts of meat, extravagant tarts, strudels, pies—enough for twenty people. If neighbors came in for an afternoon on some holiday, Ottilie would stumble into the big north room, the parlor, with its golden-oak melodeon, a harsh-green Brussels carpet, Nottingham lace curtains, crocheted lace antimacassars on the chair backs, to serve them coffee with cream and sugar and thick slices of yellow cake.

Mother Müller sat but seldom in her parlor, and always with an air of formal unease, her knotted big fingers cramped in a cluster. But Father Müller often sat there in the evenings, where no one ventured to follow him unless commanded; he sometimes played chess with his elder son-in-law, who had learned a good while ago that Father Müller was a good player who abhorred an easy victory, and he dared not do less than put up the best fight he was able, but even so, if Father Müller felt himself winning too often, he would roar, "No, you are not trying! You are not doing your best. Now we stop this nonsense!" and the son-in-law would find himself dismissed in temporary disgrace.

Most evenings, however, Father Müller sat by himself and read *Das Kapital*. He would settle deeply into the red plush base rocker and spread the volume upon a low table before him. It was an early edition in blotty black German type, stained and ragged in its leather cover, the pages falling apart, a very bible. He knew whole chapters almost by heart, and added nothing to, took nothing from, the canonical, once-delivered text. I cannot say at that time of my life I had never heard of *Das Kapital*, but I had certainly never known anyone who had read it, though if anyone mentioned it, it was always with profound disapproval. It was not a book one had to read in order to reject it. And here was this respectable old farmer who accepted its dogma as a religion—that is to say, its legendary inapplicable precepts were just, right, proper, one must believe in them, of course; but life, everyday living, was another and unrelated thing. Father Müller was the wealthiest man in his community; almost every neighboring farmer rented land from him, and some of them worked it on the share system. He explained this to me one evening after he had given up trying to teach me chess. He was not surprised that I could not learn, at least not in one lesson, and he was not surprised either that I knew nothing about *Das Kapital*. He explained his own arrangements to me thus: "These men, they cannot buy their land. The land must be bought, for *Kapital* owns it, and *Kapital* will not give back to the worker the land that is his. Well, somehow, I can always buy land. Why? I do not know. I only know that with my first land here I made good crops to buy more land, and so I rent it cheap, more than anybody else I rent it cheap, I lend money so my neighbors do not fall into the hands of the bank, and so I am not *Kapital*. Someday these workers, they can buy land for me, for less than they can get it anywhere else. Well, that is what I can do, that is all." He turned over a page, and his angry gray eyes looked out at me under his shaggy brows. "I buy my land with my hard work, all my life, and I rent it cheap to my neighbors, and then they say they will not elect my son-in-law, my Annetje's husband, to be sheriff because I am atheist. So then I say, all right, but next year you pay more for your land or more shares of your crops. If I am atheist, I will act like one. So, my Annetje's husband is sheriff, that is all."

He had put a stubby forefinger on a line to mark his place, and now he sank himself into his book, and I left quietly without saying good night.

The *Turnverein* was an octagonal pavilion set in a cleared space in a patch of woods belonging to Father Müller. The German colony came here to sit about in the cool shade, while a small brass band played cloppity country dances. The girls danced with energy and direction, their starched petticoats rustling like dry leaves. The boys were more awkward, but willing; they clutched their partners' waists and left crumpled sweaty spots where they clutched. Here Mother Müller took her ease after a hard week. Her gaunt limbs would relax, her knees spread squarely apart, and she would gossip over her beer with the women of her own generation.

On the other side of the pavilion. Father Müller would sit with the sober grandfathers, their long curved pipes wagging on their chests as they discussed local politics with profound gravity, their hard peasant fatalism tempered only a little by a shrewd worldly distrust of all officeholders not personally known to them, all political plans except their own immediate ones. When Father Müller talked, they listened respectfully, with faith in him as a strong man, head of his own house and his community. They nodded slowly whenever he took his pipe from his mouth and gestured, holding it by the bowl as if it were a stone he was getting ready to throw.

On our way back from the *Turnverein* one evening, Mother Müller said to me, "Well, now, by the grace of Gott it is all settled between Hatsy and her man. It is next Sunday by this time they will be marrit."

All the folk who usually went to the *Turnverein* on Sundays came instead to the Müller house for the wedding. They brought useful presents, mostly bed linen, pillow covers, a white counterpane, with a few ornaments for the bridal chamber; and the bridegroom's gift to the bride was a necklace, a double string of red coral twigs. Just before the short ceremony began, he slipped the necklace over her head with trembling hands. She smiled up at him shakily and helped him disentangle her short veil from the coral, then they joined hands and turned their faces to the pastor, not letting go until time for the exchange of rings—the widest, thickest, reddest gold bands to be found, no doubt—and at that moment they both stopped smiling and turned a little pale. The groom recovered first, and bent over—he was considerably taller than she—and kissed her on the forehead. His eyes were a deep blue, and his hair not really Müller taffy color, but a light chestnut; a good-looking, gentle-tempered boy, I decided, and he looked at Hatsy as if he liked what he saw. They knelt and clasped hands again for the final prayer, then stood together and exchanged the bridal kiss, a very chaste reserved one, still not on the lips. Then everybody came to shake hands and the men all kissed the bride and the women all kissed the groom. Some of the women whispered in Hatsy's ear, and all burst out laughing except Hatsy, who turned red from her forehead to her throat. She whispered in turn to her husband, who nodded in agreement. She then tried to slip away quietly, but the watchful young girls were after her, and shortly we saw her running through the blossoming orchard, holding up her white ruffled skirts, with all the girls in pursuit, shrieking and calling like excited hunters, for the first to overtake and touch her would be the next bride. They returned, breathless, dragging the lucky one with them, and held her, against her ecstatic resistance, while all the young boys kissed her.

The guests stayed on for a huge supper, and Ottilie came in, wearing a fresh blue apron, sweat beaded in the wrinkles of her forehead and around her formless mouth, and passed the food around the table. The men ate first, and then Hatsy came in with the women for the first time, still wearing her square little veil of white cotton net bound on her hair with peach blossoms shattered in the bride's race. After supper, one of the girls played waltzes and polkas on the melodeon, and everyone danced. The bridegroom drew gallons of beer from a keg set up in the hall, and at midnight everybody went away, warmly emotional and happy. I went down to the kitchen for a pitcher of hot water. The servant was still setting things to rights, hobbling between table and cupboard. Her face was a brown smudge of anxiety, her eyes were wide and dazed. Her uncertain hands rattled among the pans, but nothing could make her seem real, or in any way connected with the life around her. Yet when I set my pitcher on the stove, she lifted the heavy kettle and poured the scalding water into it without spilling a drop.

The clear honey green of the early morning sky was a mirror of the bright earth. At the edge of the woods there had sprung a reticent blooming of small white and pale-colored flowers. The peach trees were now each a separate nosegay of shell rose and white. I left the house, meaning to take the short path across to the lane of mulberries. The women were deep in the house, the men were away to the fields, the animals were turned into the pastures, and only Ottilie was visible, sitting on the steps of the back porch peeling potatoes. She gazed in my direction with eyes that fell short of me, and seemed to focus on a point midway between us, and gave no sign. Then she dropped her knife and rose, her mouth opened and closed several times, she strained toward me, motioning with her right hand. I went to her, her hands came out and clutched my sleeve, and for a moment I feared to hear her voice. There was no sound from her, but she drew me along after her, full of some mysterious purpose of her own. She opened the door of a dingy, bitter-smelling room, windowless, which opened off the kitchen, beside the closet where Hatsy took her baths.

A lumpy narrow cot and a chest of drawers supporting a blistered looking-glass almost filled the space. Ottilie's lips moved, struggling for speech, as she pulled and tumbled over a heap of rubbish in the top drawer. She took out a photograph and put it in my hands. It was in the old style, faded to a dirty yellow, mounted on cardboard elaborately clipped and gilded at the edges.

I saw a girl child about five years old, a pretty smiling German baby, looking curiously like a slightly elder sister of Annetje's two-year-old, wearing a frilled frock and a prodigious curl of blonde hair on the crown of her head. The strong legs, round as sausages, were encased in long white ribbed stockings, and the square firm feet were laced into old-fashioned soft-soled black boots. Ottilie peered over the picture, twisted her neck, and looked up into my face. I saw the slanted water-blue eyes and the high cheekbones of the Müllers again, mutilated, almost destroyed, but unmistakable. This child was what she had been, and she was without doubt the elder sister of Annetje and Gretchen and Hatsy; in urgent pantomime she insisted that this was so—she patted the picture and her own face, and strove terribly to speak. She pointed to the name written carefully on the back, Ottilie, and touched her mouth with her bent knuckles. Her head wagged in her perpetual nod; her shaking hand seemed to flap the photograph at me in a roguish humor. The bit of cardboard connected her at once somehow to the world of human beings I knew; for an instant some filament lighter than cobweb spun itself out between that living center in her and in me, a filament from some center that held us all bound to our inescapable common source, so that her life and mine were kin, even a part of each other, and the painfulness and strangeness of her vanished. She knew well that she had been Ottilie, with those steady legs and watching eyes, and she was Ottilie still within herself. For a moment, being alive, she knew she suffered, for she stood and shook with silent crying, smearing away her tears with the open palm of her hand. Even while her cheeks were wet, her face changed. Her eyes cleared and fixed themselves upon that point in space which seemed for her to contain her unaccountable and terrible troubles. She turned her head as if she had heard a voice and disappeared in her staggering run into the kitchen, leaving the drawer open and the photograph face downward on the chest.

At midday meal she came hurrying and splashing coffee on the white floor, restored to her own secret existence of perpetual amazement, and again I had become a stranger to her like all the rest, but she was no stranger to me, and could not be again.

The youngest brother came in, holding up an opossum he had caught in his trap. He swung the furry body from side to side, his eyes fairly narrowed with pride as he showed us the mangled creature. "No, it is cruel, even for the wild animals," said gentle Annetje to me, "but boys love to kill, they love to hurt things. I am always afraid he will trap poor Kuno." I thought privately that Kuno, a wolfish, ungracious beast, might well prove a match for any trap. Annetje was full of silent, tender solicitudes. The kittens, the puppies, the chicks, the lambs and calves were her special care. She was the only one of the women who caressed the weanling calves when she set the pans of milk before them. Her child seemed as much a part of her as if it were not yet born. Still, she seemed to have forgotten that Ottilie was her sister. So had all the others. I remembered how Hatsy had spoken her name but had not said she was her sister. Their silence about her was, I realized, exactly that—simple forgetfulness. She moved among them as invisible to their imaginations as a ghost. Ottilie their sister was something painful that had happened long ago and now was past and done for; they could not live with that memory or its visible reminder—they forgot her in pure self-defense. But I could not forget her. She drifted into my mind like a bit of weed carried in a current and caught there, floating but fixed, refusing to be carried away. I reasoned it out. The Müllers, what else could they have done with Ottilie? By a physical accident in her childhood, she had been stripped of everything but her mere existence. It was not a society or a class that pampered its invalids and the unfit. So long as one lived, one did one's share. This was her place, in this family she had been born and must die; did she suffer? No one asked, no one looked to see. Suffering went with life, suffering and labor. While one lived one worked, that was all, and without complaints, for no one had time to listen, and everybody had his own troubles. So, what else could they have done with Ottilie?

As for me, I could do nothing but promise myself that I would forget her, too; and to remember her for the rest of my life.

Sitting at the long table, I would watch Ottilie clattering about in her tormented haste, bringing in that endless food that represented all her life's labors. My mind would follow her into the kitchen, where I could see her peering into the great simmering kettles, the crowded oven, her ruined hands always lifting and stirring, and paring and chopping, her whole body a mere machine of torture. Straight up to the surface of my mind the thought would come urgently, clearly, as if driving time toward the desired event: Let it be now, let it be *now*. Not even tomorrow, no, today. Let her sit down quietly in her rickety chair by the stove and fold those arms, and let us find her there like that, with her head fallen forward on her knees. I would wait, hoping she might not come again, ever again, through that door I gazed at with wincing eyes, as if I might see something unendurable enter. Then she would come, and it was only Ottilie, after all, in the bosom of her family, and one of its most useful and competent members; and they with a deep right instinct had learned to live with her disaster on its own terms, and hers; they had accepted and then made use of what was for them only one more painful event in a world full of troubles, many of them much worse than this. So, a step at a time, I followed the Müllers as nearly as I could in their acceptance of Ottilie and the use they made of her life, for in some way that I could not quite explain to myself, I found great virtue and courage in their steadiness and refusal to feel sorry for anybody, least of all for themselves.

Gretchen bore her child, a son, conveniently between the hours of supper and bedtime, one evening of friendly domestic-sounding rain. The next day brought neighboring women from miles around, and the child was bandied about among them as if he were a new kind of medicine ball. Sedate and shy at dances, emotional at weddings, they were ribald and jocose at births. Over coffee and beer the talk grew broad, the hearty gutturals were swallowed in the belly of laughter; those honest hard-working wives and mothers saw life for a few hours as a hearty low joke, and it did them good. The baby bawled and suckled like a young calf, and the men of the family came in for a look and added their joyful improprieties.

Cloudy weather drove them home earlier than they had meant to go. The whole sky was lined with smoky black and gray vapor hanging in ragged wisps like soot in a chimney. The edges of the woods turned dull purple as the horizon reddened slowly, then faded, and all across the sky ran a deep shuddering mumble of thunder. All the Müllers hurried about getting into rubber boots and oilcloth overalls, shouting to each other, making their plan of action. The youngest boy came over the ridge of the hill with Kuno helping him to drive the sheep into the fold. Kuno was barking, the sheep were baaing and bleating, the horses freed from the plows were excited; they whinnied and trotted at the lengths of their halters, their ears laid back. The cows were bawling in distress and the calves cried back to them. All the men went out among the animals to round them up and quiet them and get them enclosed safely. Even as Mother Müller, her half-dozen petticoats looped about her thighs and tucked into her hip boots, was striding to join them in the barns, the cloud rack was split end to end by a shattering blow of lightning, and the cloudburst struck the house with the impact of a wave against a ship. The wind broke the windowpanes and the floods poured through. The roof beams strained and the walls bent inward, but the house stood to its foundations. The children were huddled into the inner bedroom with Gretchen. "Come and sit on the bed with me now," she told them calmly, "and be still." She sat up with a shawl around her, suckling the baby. Annetje came then and left her baby with Gretchen, too; and standing at the doorstep with one arm caught over the porch rail, reached down into the furious waters which were rising to the very threshold and dragged in a half-drowned lamb. I followed her. We could not make ourselves heard above the cannonade of thunder, but together we carried the creature into the hall under the stairs, where we rubbed the drowned fleece with rags and pressed his stomach to free him from the water and finally got him sitting up with his feet tucked under him. Annetje was merry with triumph and kept saying in delight, "Alive, alive! Look!"

We left him there when we heard the men shouting and beating at the kitchen door and ran to open it for them.

They came in, Mother Müller among them, wearing her yoke and milk pails. She stood there with the water pouring from her skirts, the three-cornered piece of black oilcloth on her head dripping, her rubber boots wrinkled down with the weight of her petticoats. She and Father Müller stood near each other, looking like two gnarled lightning-struck old trees, his beard and oilcloth garments streaming, both their faces suddenly dark and old and tired, tired once for all; they would never be rested again in their lives. Father Müller suddenly roared at her, "Go get yourself dry clothes. Do you want to make yourself sick?"

"Ho," she said, taking off her milk yoke and setting the pails on the floor. "Go change yourself. I bring you dry socks." One of the boys told me she had carried a day-old calf on her back up a ladder against the inside wall of the barn and had put it safely in the hayloft behind a barricade of bales. Then she had lined up the cows in the stable, and sitting on her milking stool in the rising water, she had milked them all. She seemed to think nothing of it.

"Hatsy," she called, "come help with this milk!" Little pale Hatsy came flying, barefoot because she had been called in the midst of taking off her wet shoes. Her new husband followed her, rather shy of his mother-in-law.

"Let me," he said, wishing to spare his dear bride such heavy work, and started to lift the great pails. "No!" shouted Mother Müller, so the poor young man nearly jumped out of his shirt. "Not you. The milk is not business for a man." He fell back and stood there with dark rivulets of mud seeping from his boots, watching Hatsy pour the milk into pans. Mother Müller started to follow her husband to attend him, but said at the door, "Where is Ottilie?", and no one knew, no one had seen her. "Find her," said Mother Müller. "Tell her we want supper, now."

Hatsy motioned to her husband, and together they tiptoed to the door of Ottilie's room and opened it silently. The light from the kitchen showed them Ottilie, sitting by herself, folded up on the edge of the bed. Hatsy threw the door wide open for more light and called in a high penetrating voice as if to a deaf person or one at a great distance, "Ottilie! Suppertime. We are hungry!", and the young pair left the kitchen to look under the stairway to see how Annetje's lamb was getting on. Then Annetje,

Hatsy, and I began sweeping the dirty water and broken glass from the floors of the hall and dining room.

The storm lightened gradually, but the flooding rain continued. At supper there was talk about the loss of animals and their replacement. All the crops must be replanted, the season's labor was for nothing. They were all tired and wet, but they ate heartily and calmly, to strengthen themselves against all the labor of repairing and restoring which must begin early tomorrow morning.

By morning the drumming on the roof had almost ceased; from my window I looked upon a sepia-colored plain of water moving slowly to the valley. The roofs of the barns sagged like the ridgepoles of a tent, and a number of drowned animals floated or were caught against the fences. At breakfast, Mother Müller sat groaning over her coffee cup. "Ach," she said, "what it is to have such a pain in the head. Here too." She thumped her chest. "All over. Ach, Gott, I'm sick." She got up sighing hoarsely, her cheeks flushed, calling Hatsy and Annetje to help her in the barn.

They all came back very soon, their skirts draggled to the knees, and the two sisters were supporting their mother, who was speechless and could hardly stand. They put her to bed, where she lay without moving, her face scarlet. Everybody was confused; no one knew what to do. They tucked the quilts about her, and she threw them off. They offered her coffee, cold water, beer, but she turned her head away. The sons came in and stood beside her and joined the cry: "*Mütterchen, Mutti, Mutti,* what can we do? Tell us, what do you need?" But she could not tell them. It was impossible to ride the twelve miles to town for a doctor; fences and bridges were down, the roads were washed out. The family crowded into the room, unnerved, in panic, lost unless the sick woman should come to herself and tell them what to do for her. Father Müller came in, and kneeling beside her, he took hold of her hands and spoke to her most lovingly, and when she did not answer him, he broke out crying openly, in a loud voice, the great tears rolling, "Ach, Gott, Gott. A hundert tousand tollars in the bank"—he glared around at his family and spoke broken English to them, as if he were a stranger to himself and had forgotten his own language—"and tell me, tell, what goot does it?"

This frightened them, and all at once, together, they

screamed and called and implored her in a tumult utterly beyond control. The noise of their grief and terror filled the place. In the midst of this, Mother Müller died.

In the midafternoon the rain passed, and the sun was a disk of brass in a cruelly bright sky. The waters flowed thickly down to the river, leaving the hill bald and brown, with the fences lying in a flattened tangle, the young peach trees stripped of bloom and sagging at the roots. In the woods had occurred a violent eruption of ripe foliage of a jungle thickness, glossy and burning, a massing of hot peacock green with cobalt shadows.

The household was in such silence, I had to listen carefully to know that anyone lived there. Everyone, even the younger children, moved on tiptoe and spoke in whispers. All afternoon the thud of hammers and the whine of a saw went on monotonously in the barn loft. At dark, the men brought in a shiny coffin of new yellow pine with rope handles and set it in the hall. It lay there on the floor for an hour or so, where anyone passing had to step over it. Then Annetje and Hatsy, who had been washing and dressing the body, appeared in the doorway and motioned. "You bring it in now."

Mother Müller lay in state in the parlor throughout the night, in her black silk dress with a scrap of white lace at the collar and a small lace cap on her hair. Her husband sat in the plush chair near her, looking at her face, which was very contemplative, gentle, and remote. He wept at intervals, silently, wiping his face with a big handkerchief. His daughters brought him coffee from time to time. He fell asleep there toward morning.

The light burned in the kitchen nearly all night, too, and the sound of Ottilie's heavy boots thumping about unsteadily was accompanied by the locust whirring of the coffee mill and the smell of baking bread. Hatsy came to my room. "There's coffee and cake," she said, "you'd better have some," and turned away crying, crumbling her slice in her hand. We stood about and ate in silence. Ottilie brought in a fresh pot of coffee, her eyes bleared and fixed, her gait as aimless-looking and hurried as ever, and when she spilled some on her own hand, she did not seem to feel it.

For a day longer they waited; then the youngest boy

went to fetch the Lutheran pastor, and a few neighbors came back with them. By noon many more had arrived, spattered with mud, the horses heaving and sweating. At every greeting the family gave way and wept afresh, as naturally and openly as children. Their faces were drenched and soft with their tears; there was a comfortable relaxed look in the muscles of their faces. It was good to let go, to have something to weep for that nobody need excuse or explain. Their tears were at once a luxury and a cure of souls. They wept away the hard core of secret trouble that is in the heart of each separate man, secure in a communal grief; in sharing it, they consoled each other. For a while, they would visit the grave and remember, and then life would arrange itself again in another order, yet it would be the same. Already the thoughts of the living were turning to tomorrow, when they would be at the work of rebuilding and replanting and repairing—even now, today, they would hurry back from the burial to milk the cows and feed the chickens, and they might weep again and again for several days, until their tears should heal them at last.

On that day I realized, for the first time, not death, but the terror of dying. When they took the coffin out to the little country hearse and I saw that the procession was about to form, I went to my room and lay down. Staring at the ceiling, I heard and felt the ominous order and purpose in the movements and sounds below—the creaking harness and hoofbeats and grating wheels, the muted grave voices—and it was as if my blood fainted and receded with fright, while my mind stayed wide-awake to receive the awful impress. Yet when I knew they were leaving the yard, the terror began to leave me. As the sounds receded, I lay there not thinking, not feeling, in a mere drowse of relief and weariness.

Through my half-sleep I heard the howling of a dog. It seemed to be in a dream, and I was troubled to awaken. I dreamed that Kuno was caught in the trap; then I thought he was really caught, it was no dream and I must wake, because there was no one but me to let him out. I came broad awake, the cry rushed upon me like a wind, and it was not the howl of a dog. I ran downstairs and looked into Gretchen's room. She was curled up around her baby, and they were both asleep. I ran to the kitchen.

Ottilie was sitting in her broken chair with her feet in the edge of the open oven, where the heat had died away. Her hands hung at her sides, the fingers crooked into the palm; her head lay back on her shoulders, and she howled with a great wrench of her body, an upward reach of the neck, without tears. At sight of me she got up and came over to me and laid her head on my breast, and her hands dangled forward a moment. Shuddering, she babbled and howled and waved her arms in a frenzy through the open window over the stripped branches of the orchard toward the lane where the procession had straightened out into formal order. I took hold of her arms where the unnaturally corded muscles clenched and strained under her coarse sleeves; I led her out to the steps and left her sitting there, her head wagging.

In the barnyard there remained only the broken-down spring wagon and the shaggy pony that had brought me to the farm on the first day. The harness was still a mystery, but somehow I managed to join pony, harness, and wagon not too insecurely, or so I could only hope; and I pushed and hauled and tugged at Ottilie and lifted her until she was in the seat and I had the reins in hand. We careened down the road at a grudging trot, the pony jolting like a churn, the wheels spinning elliptically in a truly broad comedy swagger. I watched the jovial antics of those wheels with attention, hoping for the best. We slithered into round pits of green mud and jogged perilously into culverts where small bridges had been. Once, in what was left of the main road, I stood up to see if I might overtake the funeral train; yes, there it was, going inchmeal up the road over the little hill, a bumbling train of black beetles crawling helter-skelter over clods.

Ottilie, now silent, was doubled upon herself, slipping loosely on the edge of the seat. I caught hold of her stout belt with my free hand, and my fingers slipped between her clothes and bare flesh, ribbed and gaunt and dry against my knuckles. My sense of her realness, her humanity, this shattered being that was a woman, was so shocking to me that a howl as doglike and despairing as her own rose in me unuttered and died again, to be a perpetual ghost. Ottilie slanted her eyes and peered at me, and I gazed back. The knotted wrinkles of her face were grotesquely changed, she gave a choked little whimper, and suddenly she laughed out, a kind of yelp but unmistakably laughter, and clapped her hands for joy, the grinning mouth and suffering eyes turned to the sky. Her head nodded and wagged with the clownish humor of our trundling lurching progress. The feel of the hot sun on her back, the bright air, the jolly senseless staggering of the wheels, the peacock green of the heavens: something of these had reached her. She was happy and gay, and she gurgled and rocked in her seat, leaning upon me and waving loosely around her as if to show me what wonders she saw.

Drawing the pony to a standstill, I studied her face for a while and pondered my ironical mistake. There was nothing I could do for Ottilie, selfishly as I wished to ease my heart of her; she was beyond my reach as well as any other human reach, and yet, had I not come nearer to her than I had to anyone else in my attempt to deny and bridge the distance between us, or rather, her distance from me? Well, we were both equally the fools of life, equally fellow fugitives from death. We had escaped for one day more at least. We would celebrate our good luck, we would have a little stolen holiday, a breath of spring air and freedom on this lovely, festive afternoon.

Ottilie fidgeted, uneasy at our stopping. I flapped the reins, the pony moved on, we turned across the shallow ditch where the small road divided from the main traveled one. I measured the sun westering gently; there would be time enough to drive to the river down the lane of mulberries and to get back to the house before the mourners returned. There would be plenty of time for Ottilie to have supper ready. They need not even know she had been gone.

THE WARRIOR PRINCESS OZIMBA

by *Reynolds Price*

ꕥ

She was the oldest thing any of us knew anything about, and she had never been near a tennis court, but somewhere around the Fourth of July every year, one of us (it was my father for a long time but for the past two years, just me) rode out to her place and took her a pair of blue tennis shoes. (Blue because that was her favorite color before she went blind and because even now, opening the box and not seeing them, she always asked "Is they blue?") We did it on the Fourth because that was the day she had picked out fifty years ago for her birthday, not knowing what day she had been born and figuring that the Fourth was right noisy anyhow and one more little celebration wouldn't hurt if it pacified my father who was a boy then and who wanted to give her presents. And it was always tennis shoes because they were the only kind she would put on and because with her little bit of shuffling around in the sun, she managed to wear out a pair every year. So now that I was doing it, the time would come, and Vesta, who was her daughter and had taken her mother's place and who didn't have much faith in my memory, would look up at me from stringing beans or waxing the floor and say, "Mr. Ed, Mama's feets going to be flat on the ground by next week," and then I would drive out, and it would be her birthday.

My mother goes out very seldom now, so late in the afternoon of the Fourth, I took the shoes and climbed in the broiling car alone and headed down the Embro road where she lived with Vesta and Vesta's husband, where she had lived ever since she took up with Uncle Ben Harrison in the Year One and started having those children that had more or less vanished. (My grandfather asked her once just when was it she and Ben got married. She smiled and said,

"Mr. Buddy, *you* know we ain't married. We just made arrangements.")

All the way out there the shoulders of the dirt road were full of Negroes dressed up in a lot of light-colored clothes that were getting dustier by the minute, walking nowhere (except maybe to some big baptizing up the creek) slow and happy with a lot of laughing and with children bunched along every now and then, yelling and prancing and important-looking as puppies on the verge of being grown and running away. I waved at several of the struggling knots as I passed just so I could look in the mirror and see the children all stop their scuffling and string out in a line with great wide eyes and all those teeth and watch my car till it was gone, wondering who in the world that waving white man was, flying on by them to the creek.

There was still the creek to cross that I and a little Negro named Walter had dammed up a thousand times for wading purposes. It would follow along on the left, and there would be that solid mile of cool shade and sand and honeysuckle and the two chimneys that had belonged to Lord-knows-what rising from the far end of it and the sawdust pile that had swallowed Harp Hubbard at age eleven so afterwards we couldn't play there except in secret and always had to bathe before going home, and then on the right it would be her place.

About all you could say for her place was it would keep out a gentle rain, balancing on its own low knoll on four rock legs so delicate it seemed she could move once, sitting now tall in her chair on one end of the porch, and send the whole thing—house, dog, flowers, herself, all—turning quietly down past the nodding chickens and the one mulberry tree to the road, if she hadn't been lighter than a fall leaf and nearly as dry. I got out of the car without even waking her dog and started towards her.

She sat there the way she had sat every day for eight years (every day since that evening after supper when she stepped to the living room door and called my father out and asked him, "Mr. Phil, ain't it about time I'm taking me a rest?"), facing whoever might pass and the trees and beyond and gradually not seeing any of them, her hands laid palm up on her knees, her back and her head held straight as any boy and in that black hat nobody ever saw her without but which got changed—by night—every year or so, a little deaf and with no sight at all and her teeth gone and her lips caved in forever, leaving her nothing but those saddles of bone under her eyes and her age which nobody knew (at times you could make her remember when General Lee took up my grandmother who was a baby and kissed her) and her name which my great-grandfather had been called on to give her and which came from a book he was reading at the time—Warrior Princess Ozimba.

I climbed the steps till I stood directly in front of her, level with her shut eyes and blocking the late sun which had made her this year the same as every year the color of bright old pennies that made us all pretend she was an Indian when we were children and spy on her from behind doors and think she knew things she wasn't telling. I wasn't sure she was awake until she said, "Good evening to you," and I said, "Good evening, Aunt Zimby. How are you getting on?"

"Mighty well for an old woman," she said, "with all this good-feeling sunshine."

"Yes, it *is* good weather," I said. "We'll be calling for a little rain soon though."

"Maybe you all will," she said, "but it's the sun and not the rain that helps my misery. And if you just step out of my light, please sir, I can take the last of it." So I sat down on the top step by her feet that were in what was left of last year's shoes, and the sun spread back over her face, and whatever it was my great-grandfather thought the Warrior Princess Ozimba looked like, it must have been something like that.

When she spoke again it seemed to confirm she knew somebody was with her. "I been setting here wondering is my mulberries ripe yet?"

I looked down at her knobby little tree and said "No, not yet."

"My white folks that I works for, they littlest boy named Phil, and he do love the mulberries. One day his Mama was going off somewhere, and she say to him, 'Phil, don't you eat n'er one of them mulberries.' So he say, 'No ma'm' like he swearing in court. Well, I give him his dinner, and he go streaking off down the back of the lot. That afternoon I setting on the kitchen steps, resting my feets, and Phil he come up towards me through the yard, no bigger than a mosquito, and ask me, 'Aunt Zimby, what you studying about?' I say to him I just wondering if them mulberries back yonder is fit to eat yet. And he don't do nothing but stand there and turn up that face of his, round as a dollar watch and just as solemn but with the mulberry juice ringing round his mouth bright as any wreath, and he say, 'I expect they is.' "

I thought she was going to laugh—I did, softly—but suddenly she was still as before, and then a smile broke out on her mouth as if it had taken that long for the story to work from her lips into her mind, and when the smile was dying off, she jerked her hand that was almost a great brown bird's wing paddling the air once across her eyes. It was the first time she had moved, and coming quick as it did, it made me think for a minute she had opened her eyes with her hand and would be turning now to see who I was. But the one move was all, and she was back in her age like sleep so deep and still I couldn't have sworn she was breathing even, if there hadn't been the last of the sun on her face and the color streaming under the skin.

I sat for a while, not thinking of anything except that it was cooling off and that I would count to a hundred and leave if she hadn't moved or spoken. I counted and it seemed she wasn't coming back from wherever she was, not today, so I set the shoe box by the side of her chair and got up to go. Vesta would see them when she came at dark to lead her mother in. I was all the way down the steps, going slow, hoping the dog wouldn't bark, when she spoke, "You don't know my Mr. Phil, does you?"

I walked back so she could hear me and said No, I didn't believe I did. There was no use confusing her now and starting her to remembering my father and maybe crying. Nobody had told her when he died.

She felt for the tin can beside her chair and turned away from me and spat her snuff into it. (She had said before that if she was going sinning on to her grave after dips of snuff, it was her own business, but she wasn't asking nobody else to watch her doing it.) Those few slow moves as gentle and breakable as some long-necked waterfowl brought her to life again, and when she had set her can down, I thought I ought to say something so I got back onto how nice the weather was.

But she held her eyes shut, knowing maybe that if she had opened them and hadn't been blind anyhow, she would have seen I wasn't who she had expected all year long. "Yes sir, this here's the weather you all wants for your dances, ain't it?"

I said, "Yes, it would be ideal for that."

"Well, is you been dancing much lately, Mr. Phil?"

She seemed to think she was talking to me so I said No, there wasn't much of that going on these days.

"You a great one for the dancing, ain't you, Mr. Phil?" All I did was laugh loud enough for her to hear me, but she wiped her mouth with a small yellow rag, and I could see that—not meaning to, not meaning to at all—I had started her.

She began with a short laugh of her own and drummed out a noiseless tune on the arm of the chair and nodded her head and said, "You *is* a case, Mr. Phil."

I asked her what did she mean because I couldn't leave now.

"I was just thinking about that evening you went off to some dance with one of your missy-girls, you in your white trousers looking like snow was on the way. And late that night I was out there on you all's back porch, and it come up a rain, and directly you come strolling up with not a thing on but your underwear and your feets in them white shoes you was putting down like stove lids, and there was your white trousers laid pretty as you please over your arm to keep from getting them muddy. Does you remember that, Mr. Phil?"

I said there were right many things I didn't remember these days.

"The same with me," she said, "except every once in a while . . ." A line of black children passed up the road. They every one of them looked towards us and then towards the older tall yellow girl who led the line and who had been silently deputized to wave and say, "How you this evening, Miss Zimby?"—not looking for an answer surely, not even looking to be heard, just in respect as when you speak to the sea. ". . . What put me to thinking about Mr. Phil is it's time for me some new shoes."

And there I was with the shoes in my hands that I couldn't give her now and wondering what I could do, and while I was wondering she raised her own long foot and stamped the floor three times, and there was considerable noise, as surprising as if that same bird she kept reminding me of had beat the air with its foot and made it thunder. Before I could guess why she had done it, Vesta came to the front door and said, "Lord, Mr. Ed, I didn't know you was out here. Me and Lonnie was in yonder lying down, and I just figured it was Mama going on to herself." Then she said louder to Aunt Zimby, "What you call me for, Mama?"

It took her a little while to remember. "Vesta, when have Mr. Phil been here? It ain't been long is it?"

Vesta looked at me for an answer but I was no help. "No, Mama, it ain't been so long."

"He ain't sick or nothing is he? Because it's getting time for me some new shoes."

"It won't be long, Mama. Mr. Phil ain't never forgot you yet."

And that seemed to settle it for her. The little tune she had been thumping out slowed down and stopped, and next her head began to nod, all as quick as if she had worked the whole day out in the cotton and come home and fixed everybody's supper and seen them to bed and pressed a shirt for Uncle Ben who drove a taxi occasionally and then fallen dead to sleep in the sounding dark with the others breathing all round her.

Vesta and I stayed still by her till we could hear breathing, but when it began, small and slow, I handed Vesta the shoes. She knew and smiled and nodded, and I told her to go on in and let her mother sleep. I stood there those last few minutes, looking through sudden amazed tears at all that age and remembering my dead father.

Evening was coming on but the heat was everywhere still. I took the steps slowly down, and as I expected the old dog came up, and I waited while he decided what to do about me. Over the sounds of his smelling there came a crowd of high rushing nameless notes and her voice among them, low and quiet and firm on the air, "*You* can see them little birds can't you, Mr. Phil? I used to take a joy watching them little fellows playing before they went to sleep."

I knew it would be wrong to answer now, but I looked without a word to where her open eyes rested across the road to the darkening field and the two chimneys, and yes, they were there, going off against the evening like out of pistols, hard dark bullets that arched dark on the sky and curled and showered to the sturdy trees beneath.

ANGEL
by *Eve Shelnutt*

❀

It is a long ride up the mountains. The car is too small, as any car would be, because the mother and the cousin are larger than usual women. It is not *grotesque* cargo. Simply: these two women are oversized enough to be burdensome in a way not easily dismissed, as when a person sniffs an odor he can't place, and suddenly, the nose is all the face remembers of itself.

Then, there's the daughter, in the back with a dress-box.

Inside the box is a dress, almost like another person—compact.

Lois, the mother, and Helen, the cousin, have been fussing over the dress for weeks. The second daughter, the person who is related because they know where to find her, and how her handwriting is, and what color her favorite underwear, is supposed to wear the dress for her recital in the afternoon. If they don't get the chiffon dress to the little college-room in time, she will have to wear a borrowed dress. Then, she would be less related. Already she is distant. Her distance is why they hurry to her. They must get the dress, which they have, on her, whom they haven't.

Of the daughter inside the car—she has thought too much. They don't like her because she thinks. She should hibernate; they need time off. As it is, they keep their eyes on the curves ahead, like beasts taking courage from the feel of muscles inside.

She: she imagines the father they won't speak of is on the car carrier, windfilled. Up there, what does he think of her, quick! before dust fills his mouth? "Never*mind,*" he answers. So she settles for the possible: he wouldn't miss the recital. He, in some way, claims this other daughter more than they. He and she are lost together. Claire, her name is, a bell-sound. Yet, this trio in the car will suit him up when he dies and someone calls (for he has *their* address, not the other way around). Still, they might not know his size; they might have to wire his sister and ask.

And on the chiffon dress, it is the hem which they can't get straight. *His* are the owl-eyes. The whole head moves to a sight. He never over-ate.

Half-way, they stop at an Inn where fish oil is in the air, in the threads of the gingham curtains, in the fibers of the floor, and on the chrome napkin holder. They order fish.

"Amaze me," the daughter says, and she sits opposite to watch.

Really, they have ceased to look at one another when she says something, and this cessation makes her both more distant and more close, or a combination of the two, as in films when the long shot fades to the close-up shot.

Now she sees the down on the cousin's face. Helen is next to the window; sunlight is coming over her left shoulder and onto her left cheek where a thousand tiny hairs cover the acne scars. The same down is on her lip-line and on her arms and, presumably, between her thighs. A soft yellow fur. She looks broader than she is, and nowhere does her dress stick flat on her skin, as if the fur held up the cloth. To go with this yellow, she wears oranges and browns. She puts ketchup on her fish, and her large fingers turn the hush puppies into the red on the plate.

"Pass the salt," they say to each other. They are very much at home here. This is where they stop on each trip to the other daughter, and now the owner of the Inn knows where they are headed.

The mother chews with one hand near her mouth. There are defects on all their bodies. But none of these defects are physical so much as rhythmical—the mother's hand is *arrested* at the mouth when the mouth chews, because once the mother had embarrassing tooth-trouble, and the palm which sought to hush the cracking sound the jaw made (a hollow nothing-crack with the open and shut) failed. And now the mouth condemns the hand by making it stay where it shouldn't when the rest of the body has moved on. And because the father left Lois, her stomach feels too large. She is continuously pressing down on it. When she stands, she feels her ribcage first, as if to locate the last, and missing, rib.

And they are fat, not very fat, but when they sit, their legs sprawl from the weight, and they are always trying to find a place to lie down for rests. Their feet are skinny, more like hands. They like to eat, since, afterwards, the smoking tastes better, and when they smoke, it is the longest part of the meal, with coffee, until the taste of grease is gone, and the taste of smoke is more like it was when they began to smoke. When they smoke in the car, they first take out the thermos of coffee and pour themselves amounts almost measured, and then they light up. Now they pass each other a last shared cigarette. Its filter has two colors of lipstick because this cigarette is the final thing to do in the Inn, after the trip to the bathroom and the stretching behind the chairs to pull the muscles long before bending them short inside the car again.

"Oh my God," Lois says, "look at the time!"

Pauline *knows* this isn't their lives. *She* is small, and when she is younger and first beginning to notice how the body can tell on a person, she imagines her very smallness will save her. She stands on the top of her dressing table, turns backwards, and looks at her face from between the backs of her knees, just to see how a face like hers might look upside down and backwards. She imagines, then, nothing will surprise her, not even a tiny mole such as the father grew after thirty-five years, on his left side and just above the pajama-line, a mole minty-brown and white-flecked.

And there is less of herself to police, not more than five feet and three and one-quarter inches. When Helen and Lois turn to look back at the possum dead on the road, so newly dead his blood marks the tires and the tires mark the road, they hardly see her, in the middle, between the backs of Helen, who never drives, and Lois, who drives. Too, she is quiet, like a string. Nothing moves inside her she doesn't know about. She would leave her address with anyone, her size sewn in any coat, her letters tied in blue ribbons, and everything she has owned laid out on the bed, on the white coverlet, as in wedding rituals and deaths.

What she thinks of the father: is that *when* he dies, it will be like a setting of sterling, burnt mellow with polish, light and dark, the head like a soup spoon laid across the upper part of a butter dish. Then she will come, a promise. And pull all the pieces into a bundle, and wrap it in navy-blue velvet, and put it very carefully back into the mahogany box. The rest of them will laugh, as at a great party where no one knows how to behave when the formal setting is laid.

"What if a tire blows?" the mother asks the cousin.

"I would hitch-hike," the cousin answers.

"You!" the mother laughs. "Light me up one."

When Helen moves, it is slowly, always. She's had three children, who surprise her. She doesn't like to stay home with them. She comes by bus to Lois' house where the child is not really a child and where the piano takes up so much of the living room she fits in with her slow movements. She has yet to break an ashtray. In a way, she is trying to catch up with her children—she pores over the picture album, of Lois and Lois' two girls, and the father—pictured in every kind of light with one hand on the car door and one hand at his necktie. In the album, Lois is last seen holding the girls when the girls are waist-high to Lois, and then, the girls begin to hate the camera; they look at it as if it were a man spying.

Pauline, herself, takes the album out secretly, and on Sundays, when Helen and Lois are in church, she shades the pictures with a lead pencil, very lightly but over and over, at intervals. She leaves his face bright, because she forgets, almost, how it was.

How it was when he brought gifts: he *smiled,* into the money (I was sixteen, myself, he says, before *I* got the goods), and the money showing so that he begins to miss certain other sights around the house that Pauline doesn't miss.

"What I thought of you then . . ." is how she wants to begin now, at this age, maybe over coffee at Howard Johnson's, since he thinks of Howard Johnson's as the place to eat, and she hasn't been able to tell him otherwise, about the color aqua.

He comes in without knocking, barely able to see over the presents, with little, important boxes from jewelry shops sticking from his pockets. "Nevermind your hair," he says to Lois. "*Look.*" He doesn't see the cracks in her lips, or the gray right behind the face-skin, or the fat unless he pinches her fanny.

He thinks the pale-blue satin gown from Atlanta or New

York, with its rhinestone trim from the neck to the floor, and its fringed sash, looks *fine*.

Lois, of course, puts on the satin robe, and sometime later, when he can't be found, as if he had forgotten his manners, she puts the robe on again, to hang herself in, up high, on the chandelier, and Pauline knows it will be something like this to tell him about the robe. It is a *picture:* the neck has creased because the head is to one side, and the neck is swollen, and the hand tucks just inside the rope for breathing space, and it is swollen, and the ankles sticking out from the satin robe are swollen. And the voice is froggish. "*Well,* HELP!"

He doesn't notice, either, how they smell—from what they eat and don't get to eat. He brings the present of a crate of oranges, a crate of grapefruit, tins of liver pate, and boxes of crackers, and cans of oysters, and cans of ham, and a brown mustard, and many kinds of cheese, and sometimes wine, and they eat on the floor, around the presents and his suitcase where something forgotten, some littler present, might be found; and truly, he doesn't notice.

Lois stops the car so fast, it's as if a tire *has* blown, and they are off the pavement into the gravel before Pauline sees the apple stand. But Helen has seen it, maybe miles ahead, or smelled it, and she's got change jingling. She hops out, fast for her, and says, "Peck, red ones," and "Here," and then they eat, three each until the two mouths must taste acid, and the two stomachs must churn. In the car is the smell of apple juice, fine little sprays which catch some light, and fall, and the smell of smoke caught in sunlight, and their Prince Charles perfume, cologne, or powder.

Claire's room, in past-time, smells of the big blue box, on her side of the room, by the bed and under the window, and with no electricity when the bill's not paid, if Pauline wants to see what's new in the box, she sees it in this window-light—pictures from magazines: ladies, lovely ladies with fine hair, and long fingernails, and pink toes, and fine blond hair like Claire's when it is clean, and, sometimes, men standing behind these ladies, darker, with sunglasses in their hands, or wine glasses, or flowers. Or clippings about how to make a curl, or how to pull out the hair over the lip or the eyes. Or drawings of stomachs in which parts of babies are penciled in lighter colors, looking like tadpoles, some with tails and some without. And lists, in Claire's fancy writing:

> "Be kind.
> Be kind regardless.
> Smile at least once a day, to help face muscles.
> Read less; think more.
> Imagine FUTURE.
> Gain five pounds in the legs.
> Learn to play the piano."

In the bottom of the box are two dried apples, studded with cloves and decorated with blue ribbon. And old candy-wrappers, and bobbie pins and lipsticks, a box of Brazil nuts, unopened.

They don't talk, Claire and Pauline. Pauline, in the past, is afraid to talk to her, and Claire doesn't talk to anyone. But Claire leaves the top of the box open. It is the only mystery in the house, and the house is so small there is nowhere to be on days when it rains but in the room with the box, and nowhere to be when Claire is taking wash-ups but in the room, alone with the box.

"She *lies,*" Lois says. "You know she lies—he isn't *fat*, no fatter than me, and you know I wouldn't marry a fat man, not after *him*. Oh God, he was a sexy man. He ruined me, you know that?"

Helen chews on a red nail; she nods.

And it's true: Pauline lies, telling her version when she knows it isn't anything like theirs, feisty-Pauline, who gets Claire the piano by forging Claire's handwriting and making up a new sixteenth-birthday list with "PIANO" first, and second, and third, when Claire can't even imagine a real-live piano. But then, when it's crowded out two stuffed chairs and the bookcaseful of encyclopedias Lois traded for the second-hand piano, and Claire practices what she knew already and the tiny, tiny lessons just made her remember, Lois says, "Look! She has got the longest, the absolute longest fingers. And yellow hair, I swear it's yellow, and she's so skinny! What's that you're playing, dear?"

"I don't know, I don't know."

"God," says Helen, "the hair, I mean she *looks* different."

It will happen, in future-time, that Claire and Pauline will go shopping together, when Claire has gotten married and had two beautiful children, one of each kind to make it explicit, and because Claire likes to, they will go into the ugly stores with bright lights and look at material and patterns and pots and pans, together, only, for a long time, Pauline won't like what Claire picks up to look at; she won't like that it's cheap stuff. Claire won't buy, Pauline right next to her elbow, looking on like a cat.

Lois and Helen will almost cry, saying, "How *could* she! She had what must have been the best figure God put on any one girl, and look! Fat, fat, the arms, even!" They will say, "Look how she moves, like she doesn't know she's fat, not that fat yet, but how *could* she is what I want to know."

And Pauline will first get more and more sleepy-looking in the face, the figure curved in and out, the eyes the only part absolutely awake, and she first believes one side of her face is growing bigger than the other side, because: of how things are.

One time, at a big party, a man will look at her, studying, and later, at night, when the houseguests are supposed to be asleep, this man will knock on her door, and when she goes to see who it is, he will have on a raincoat, and he will say, "Come on, I have something to tell you," and, half-asleep, Pauline will follow him outside, in a drizzle, holding her nightgown close, and shivering, and when they are far from the house, this man will throw her on the ground and put his hands on her breasts, and when she is looking up at him, this time with eyes which seem stopped, he will take off his raincoat and show her he is naked and means to go into her, otherwise why is he so big?

What she will know is he was almost right, because, after she screams and runs, she knows he was just a little off, no words, no introduction to himself, or to her but what he got looking at her feline-like and tense, both. So Pauline's shoulders will start to let loose, and the neck will move more easily, and she will begin to imagine herself keeping a box which is filled with how-to-do clippings.

And she will notice Claire isn't fat like Helen and Lois—it is a bouncy fatness; she sings a lot and still plays, to the children. So they will go shopping, and this time, when Claire says, "You know how little money he gives me, don't you think these would look nice on the stove?" Pauline will say they really would. They will become almost sister-like, and when they put the mother away, they will divide what was in the house evenly, and not once mention that they hate all the odds and ends. In fact, they won't say anything at all that is a lie or a truth. And Pauline will read *Dr. Zhivago* twice, trying to see why it is Claire's favorite book.

And in the future, when the recital is over, Helen and Lois will come back and lie on the sectional sofa with their legs up, and smoke, and their feet will be almost touching, their heads at opposite ends on the sofa so they can look at each other while they talk, and they will say, "My God, I am so tired, these things just wear you out."

But what do *they* know? is what Pauline asks.

Then, they get to the little college town, and go right to the dormitory, and up to the third floor, and into the room, and hug Claire two or three times, squashing her, and look around the room and see the bedspread with the lilac-colored leaves and fuchsia flowers is still on the single bed, and the roommate they never liked who has one hand, a stub so that it seems just curved under so they think of her as sneaky, they will notice she is still the roommate, and that the other girl they don't like with the short haircut and jeans is still popping her head in the room, this time to see how Claire is coming right before her concert.

"Will you look at that figure, will you?" says the girl with the short haircut, from the doorway.

There is the last of the sunlight in the room, on Claire's hair and making her cotton panties and bra look especially white.

"I have simply got to lie down," Lois says, from the bed where she is watching Claire take out the dress. "I am *bushed*."

"Yeah," answers Helen, "let her get dressed."

Pauline now wants something to eat, before the music, but there isn't time. She bites her lip and helps lift the dress over, and pull the long hair out of the neckline. She tries to keep the long skirt moving, flowing, instead of hanging down straight.

"It's pretty, Momma," says Claire. "I like it, I really do, and thank you." And, before the mirror, she fluffs out her hair, and smiles at herself: a picture. She leans over to Pauline and asks, "Isn't the hem crooked? Why couldn't they get it straight?" not meanly, curious.

"I don't know," Pauline whispers back, "the material, the material sags after it's made, I don't know for sure. I'm sorry, but don't say."

"No." She turns, she twirls out in the room, and they all clap and laugh, and Claire keeps turning until she is dizzy, and laughs, and then they have to hurry her over, across the street and into a building, and they leave her rubbing her fingers, a frightened look on her face, the head nodding as they call, Lois and Helen together, "Do good, sugar."

Helen and Lois will get up together, in the middle of a piece by Chopin, and go out for a cigarette.

But now, in present-time, Claire walks in, not slowly—gracefully, with her shoulders back, and her head up but not looking out at the people seated below, the lights shining on the dress which she swishes with her hands so that it is never still. Then she sits and turns to the audience and smiles quickly, but Pauline sees the eyes don't really see; they are remembering, and then the fingers begin to flex. It gets very quiet, and Claire bows her head, and she plays: beautiful, and beautifully.

THE FINDER
by *Elizabeth Spencer*

Dalton was a pleasant town—still is. Lots of shade trees on residential streets, lots of shrubs in all the front yards, ferns in tubs put outside in the summer, birdbaths well attended, and screened side porches with familiar voices going on through the twilight. Crêpe myrtle lined the uptown streets. The old horse troughs on the square were seen by some in authority to be quite fine, so they were never removed but ran with water even after the last mule had died and the last wagon of the dozens that used to creak into town on Saturday from out in the country had fallen apart in somebody's barn or had been chopped up for kindling. So even on the hottest summer day the persistent murmur of water could be heard through still moments, and the lacy shade of crêpe myrtle lay traced on the sidewalks, on the heads of passing ladies, and on the shoulders of shirtsleeved men.

There were several strong families in the town, and Gavin Anderson belonged to one of these. In the nineteen-thirties, there must have been seven or eight branches of the original Anderson parent stem living in and around there, in addition to others who had been taken North or into cities, according to the professions they picked or the men they married, but all of the Andersons had "kept up" and they came back from time to time. No matter where they went, they always said they felt as if they were living right there in Dalton on the Waukahatchie, where all the good picnics were held, down on the sandbar. Since most of the Andersons were from a little distance alike and since nearly all of them were full of the same cordial sayings and the same way of chuckling with forbearance over what they couldn't help, making it funny if possible, it was hard to remember which of them were dead and which had been more recently born. Not that they lacked personality, but only that together they were like one continuous entity, a long table of a family, rather than a history in which the people might be thought of as different shapes and sizes of beads on a string. And the way they talked of one another—with such clarity and wit about the ones who had passed away—you would think the dead were still right there and about to come in any minute.

Gavin Anderson was not different from his family in any discernible way. Looking at him, a stranger would never have guessed what there was about him. It must have started just as a game when he was little, out in the sandpile with all of them. Perhaps somebody had said, "I lost my favorite agate. Now, where is it?" and Gavin's eyes might have been closed just from shutting out the sun as it came too strongly through the cedar limbs, or closed to keep cedar twigs from dropping into them, and maybe the question "Now, where is it?" hadn't been asked of anybody in particular; but lying there with his bright, healthy tan-colored Anderson hair, dry as spun glass, in the remains of a sand castle, and one short practical Anderson hand thrown over his eyes, Gavin suddenly sat up and said, "It's rolled back behind the kindling box in the kitchen. I saw it there." Or if it was a letter that was lost, he would say, "You left it in the ninth-grade history book." Or if it was a book somebody had borrowed, he would say, "It's on Miss Jamie Whittaker's library shelf; she's put it up with her own by mistake." It got to be noticed he was always right. It was further noticed by an old-maid aunt, who had a sharp ear for picking up the flaws and lapses in what was said to her, that when he said he saw something, he had not, in the ordinary sense, seen it at all. Thereupon she questioned him all one afternoon, announced to the family at supper that it was right uncanny, and returned before day the next morning to a town near Jackson where she had taught Latin for twenty-three years. She herself was known to have second sight, and could generally be counted on "to get a feeling" a few days in advance of a death or disaster. Nobody paid much attention to her discovery about Gavin, as it was a busy fall and too much work to do. None of the Andersons were ever spoiled, because there were too many of them. Still, nothing was ever quite forgotten, either.

When Gavin's gift came to general attention, it was over the incident of the seed-pearl star pin that his father, Robert Anderson, had given to his mother and that had been lost so soon they suspected a servant of taking it. They did not want to suspect anybody, of course, and especially not Lulu, who was such a good cook. It was then that Gavin said right where it was—his mother, in her excitement, having hidden it even from herself. Lulu always said that the Lord spared her through that child. She announced this several times, coming once into the living room, and another time out of the kitchen into the dining room while they were eating. She never mentioned any gratitude to Gavin, and when the story was told in later years Gavin would add this observation with the particular little chuckle of the Andersons.

The story stuck. Even in Gavin's young manhood, somebody uptown would stop to ask him about it. "Was that really true about your mama's pin?" they would ask. He shrugged it off: "Should have gone on the stage, I guess. There was somebody up at the Orpheum in Memphis just the other day. Did you see it in the paper? I missed my chance for ever amounting to anything." But by then he was in his rugged, handsome stage and courting the girl he loved. All the Andersons married for love, and they always loved the right kind. One of the girls married a pharmacist who turned to dope and lost his license, but she stuck to him and he finally got over it. Her character was unbeatable; everyone was proud but none surprised.

It was soon after Gavin turned the insurance agency over to his brother and took the local hardware store over from his father—one of the many Anderson interests—and was every day now up on the town square, the father of two fine children, member of the Kiwanis Club, deacon in the church, with a boat on the lake for fishing every day in the summer with his boys, that the stories about him revived. Every once in so often, somebody would come to see him from out in the country or from a neighboring town, and it got to be known that a peculiar kind of worried look, like a bird dog uncertain of the scent, foretold the sort of errand they were on. Sometimes, too, a letter would arrive. He would get a thick packet, and inside, ink- or pencil-written on lined sheets or on cheap-grade blue stationery from the back counters in dusty drugstores, the entire story would come out in every detail. Something was lost: "Where is it? . . . Where is it? I feel like I just got to know—" Gavin's clerk and the bookkeeper would see him glance through page after page, refold the letter hastily, stuff it in his back pocket, and begin at once to do something else, some kind of straightening up he'd never think of otherwise.

One day in autumn, Gavin made a long-distance call to a neighboring town—a call he did not mention. He closed up the store and drove to that town, thirty miles away. He told his wife he had bank business in that part of the country; he didn't say exactly where. She had "a place" in that direction—something she had inherited. He always saw to it for her. She trusted him so much she never was quite sure where it was, and wouldn't have known how to find it if she had tried. Her name was Ethel. He got in the car and drove.

The minister was watching for his car to enter town, and had already reached the silent weekday church grounds before Gavin could cut off the motor. To reach the minister's study they first had to walk through the church itself. They unlocked the door, opened it, and Gavin stepped into the vestibule and encountered smells he had always, from time immemorial, associated with "religion." Hymnbooks, Sunday-school literature, the pulpit Bible, the uncertain cleanliness of aging congregations, the starch of little girls' dresses, the felt in the organ stops, the smell of sunlight filtered by panes of stained glass discoloring the musty maroon carpet. Here there had been flowers sometime recently. He saw some white petals near the stove in passing, and coal dust left scanty by a broom's motion. He passed, following a step or two behind the gray brushed head of the minister—a man he remembered from the time when he had held the pulpit at Dalton but whom he had not seen in twenty-odd years. Dandruff flecked the good brown shoulders of his suit.

"All you all O.K.?" Gavin asked him.

The minister did not turn to answer. "Can't complain. Mrs. Cooper, though, 's got nothing to brag about."

"Serious?"

"Oh, no. Hope not."

The door to the Sunday-school annex stuck. The minister had to push, then rap the base with his toe. Back there it was cold. Gavin remembered his boyhood. Church-cold. Wasn't it always? Voices returned to him—the all-his-life voices. From last Sunday, from thirty years ago: ". . . not enough money to heat the auditorium, much less the Sunday-school annex." . . . "They're only back there a little while; can't they keep their coats on?" And they did, hunched in uncomfortable chairs, snivelling with cold. And voices from those Sunday-school classes: "Yes'm, He meant you had to have faith." . . . "Did He mean faith changes things?" Long pause. Somebody had to answer. If nobody answered, there might not be anymore Sunday school. There had to be more Sunday school. "Oh, yes'm. That is, it might." "Always?" "It might and it might not, I guess." "Does God answer prayer?" "Yes'm, He does." "You mean God does what I tell Him to?" "Guess He don't always. Don't for me." Laughter. "Well, now, to tell you the truth, Billy, He doesn't for me, either." "Sometimes He does, don't He?" "Yes, sometimes He does. So . . . can you summarize?" "Can I what?" "Can you tell me what we've just decided?" Long pause. "Well, uh . . . we decided sometimes He does and sometimes He don't." "There might be a better way to put it. I'd say . . ." The bell rang, a tinkle from the hallway, and the superintendent entered and asked for the collection. The teacher gave it, an envelope already counted and recorded. "We'll be right there. I just want to leave you with this thought for the day. God always answers prayer. Sometimes He says yes, sometimes He says no. And the third answer, we didn't have time to get to. It is this: Wait. Remember that—all week. Now you can go." They would be gone already; there had been a shoving and creaking of chairs from the minute the bell rang.

A country man, a Southern man, a small-town man, not given to book knowledge—he read for entertainment—Gavin Anderson did not recall these things critically. He had a moment's self-doubt—himself and his religion, what did they have to do with one another? If he had once respected, been so impressed by this minister—this Mr. Cooper with the direct sympathies and the earnest plain speech, who could also field in baseball and hit a home run, who had a way of expressing great truths simply and a way of carrying within himself plainly the love of God—

why had he waited twenty-odd years to look him up? Gavin noted that what had stirred a boy of twelve and convinced him of deep truth was almost nothing but a memory to a man of thirty-five. Still, he had come there about something.

They entered the study. The minister snapped on an electric heater. "Bought it myself," he explained. "I come over here to get my sermons up. Couldn't live with a cold all winter. It'll just take a minute to heat up." Theological texts, green-black and red, stood in bookcases covered by protective glass panels.

"Let me take your hat. Have a seat. Now." The minister was back of his desk. Gavin Anderson could not see through the frosted windows. The smell of the electric heat seeped into the room.

"Your family all all right? You've married, I understand? Who was it? Don't tell me—that little old Davis girl."

"You've got some memory."

"She O.K.?"

"Yes, oh, yes—she is. Two boys. All fine. You thought I'd come about somebody being sick." His bemusement vanished. The Anderson charm, always there to save, made a swift return. He smiled warmly.

The minister glowed with relief. "I was just 'fraid it might be—"

"No. Nothing about illness. No, you'd never guess." He laughed his genial uptown chuckle. "It's something worries me. You may not remember; no reason why you should. You might, though. It's right unusual—I don't recall outside the show-business circuit ever hearing of such a thing, and even that might be a fake. Well, to refresh your mind, I always had this certain gift."

"You weren't the one could find things?" The minister broke out laughing.

You'd think I rode all the way over here to have a tea party, Gavin thought. He was very nearly angry. "It ain't funny, Mr. Cooper. I mean, it's true. I really can. I could then and I can still. I'm telling you the truth, Mr. Cooper. There's a world of people in this state that know about me, and when they lose something they write to me. Recently it's got worse. It's never going to stop. I realized that about six months ago. I got three letters in one day—one from way off in Texas somewhere. It's a gift. I can't give it back. Every time I get a letter, I hesitate to open it. Because I don't like to practice it. I think it's a sin."

"Every good gift and every perfect gift is from above," said Mr. Cooper.

"I thought about that, too."

They were silent. What did I ever see in him, thought Gavin Anderson. "It might be the Devil's gift," he suggested.

"Why, I know your family, Gavin. Everybody knows the Andersons. Nothing you folks have got 's ever been near the Devil."

"It's mighty nice of you to say that," said Gavin. "You've helped me a whole lot."

But really the minister had not told him anything. He thought, I went all the way over there to say out loud what I thought myself.

It was later said in Dalton that Gavin Anderson had gone to see a minister and the minister had told him to give up his finding gift, it was a sin. But this had not happened, as Gavin knew. He let it go as truth, but it was not true. So sometimes still he opened the letters. Sometimes he didn't.

Then it was the day of the thunderstorm—a spring day when the sky suddenly got black as pitch around about noon. The tree leaves, which were just coming out, turned an incandescent green in the shift of light; they seemed to be burning with green fire. Just back of the square, a wall of velvet black hung flat as a curtain. The girl who came in to keep books half a day twice a week took off an hour early. "Go on," said Gavin Anderson. "I'll stay here. If you run, you can make it." She was out already, going headlong for her car. There was a short warning jab of lightning. The phone rang. It was the clerk's mother. She had been ailing all winter and now she was scared, up on that hill by herself. "Go on home, Percy," said Gavin Anderson. "Yo' mamma sounds like it's blowing up Judgment Day." "What about you?" Percy Howell inquired. "Oh, I'll either lock up or stick it out. You're 'bout as safe one place as another." He called home, but no one answered. He had just replaced the receiver and stretched to switch a light on as the dark intensified when the phone rang a second time. He reached his hand toward it, but light snapped and thunder exploded simultaneously within the boxed area of the store. Fire leaped from the black mouth of the phone. He felt himself hurled aside, and lost consciousness for a moment or two—or was it longer? A livid turmoil of air stood at the door, loftier than flame. Rain like a white wall was now in swift advance. Not only leaves but the limbs themselves cross-whipped in crazy ways. He had been thinking of his family when the phone had rung and gone dead; now his thought, like an interrupted current, resumed. Where were they? Why, in his own vision, couldn't he find them? It had never occurred to him before; he had never yet tried to find a person, nor had he ever been asked to.

Then he was hastening to close the door, which had blown wide, and the woman shot through half screaming, a scared rabbit of the storm. It wasn't the bookkeeper back. He never thought it was.

The wild smell of the whole spring rushed terrible and vivid through the door, into his face and nostrils, charged with new life, white and cold. Then he slammed it. She stood in mid-floor, drenched, her face screwed up and her hands to her ears while thunder shook at the walls and ceiling, banged against the high transom.

She opened her eyes just long enough to say, "It's a tornado," then shut them tight again.

He'd never seen her before. The protection he felt toward his family, wherever they were, extended suddenly to her. Alone there, he might not have done anything to make himself safer. "Come here," he said.

He led her with him by the hand—she was not tall, and her hand was like a little wood-wet wild paw, trembling—to the back of the store, and, opening a rough wooden door, went down some steps into a storage room, half underground, that his father had built during the Depression for storing potatoes. The walls were earthen and the whole hardly man-high, but as a storm pit he could see it functioning, unless debris fell in to bury them. "Sit down."

He crouched down himself and pulled her down. Drawing herself close to him, she waited in childlike terror, eyes, he could dimly make out, still shut up tight and one hand to her ear, the other hand clutching his hand. "Oh!" and "Oh!" she sobbed, and "Jesus, Jesus!" No woman in his own family said that. She wasn't from around here.

Some minutes later, gently putting her aside, he opened

the door. Store air came into the earthen-smelling dark, and with it the steady beat of rain. "Come on," he said. He shook her. "It's O.K. now."

She opened her eyes—they were large and blue—and pushed her dark hair into place. She smiled, climbed the steps after him, and stood before him in the back area of the store among the crates of stock—a small full-breasted woman in her thirties, smartly dressed in black linen with a wide shiny belt, more than a hint of good living about her. She smoothed her hair a second time. "I've always been like that—storms scare me to death."

"Well, that was a bad one," he said, forgiving her. He gestured toward the store, but she took his hand first and turned it.

"I scratched you." She touched the red marks of her nails—there were three of them, one deeper than the rest.

"I see," he said.

He got out a chair for her and offered her a Coke—all he had. They sat together. The rain still lashed, swaying above the town and countryside. The tree limbs blew freely, and some were broken. The rain sluiced against the store windows and closed doors, but there was something domestic and ample about it now.

"You just passing through?" he asked. "You not from around here."

But she said what he already suspected. She had been looking for a Gavin Anderson, because she had lost something.

It was nothing ordinary. Her grandmother had had it from a man who had died, and some had said he was the real grandfather—here a little laugh—but never mind. The stone was large, and valuable. She had written to Gavin Anderson two weeks ago, but had got no reply. She had the air of a small woman who tried things. If there was a finder to be found, she found him.

"You didn't get my letter."

"I often don't open those letters anymore."

"You mean too many people worry you?"

"Something like that."

"You know, I thought that. I really did imagine it."

"I think—" He stopped. His innermost thoughts, his long struggle. Why give it all away, suddenly, to her? Yet he almost had.

"So I thought if I came and told you that it was special, a special case . . ."

"Everybody's case is special," he said. "Some little girl's pencil box is as important to her as a ruby ring to you."

"How did you know it was a ruby?"

"I didn't know it. Of course I didn't."

He brought matches—store matches—to light her cigarette. The rain beat steadily before the door, on the town square, on the town. As the smoke rose, he closed his eyes. He saw the ring. It had fallen in the crevice of some old, dark broad-boarded floors. A piece of string and the head of a thumbtack lay beside it. The corner of a rug lay over it. He thought, She must have taken it off at night and didn't know she dropped it, going to bed after a party. It lay there in the dark, canted to the side, square-cut, wine red. A little more and he thought he might have seen the silver evening sandals she had probably removed, the stockings fallen beside them. But he opened his eyes. Through the smoke, she was half smiling at him. Now that the danger had come and gone, she looked blue-eyed and young, just out of high school.

He told her where to find the ring.

It was that very evening, after ten, she tried to reach him, but the lines were still down from the storm. She told him this the next morning, excited on the phone, not five minutes after service was resumed. "Right where you said! Can you imagine?"

"Listen," he said. "Please listen. I'm so glad. Yes, I really am, but you've got to listen. I don't want you to tell anybody." For suddenly, vast as an army, scattered out all over the South, maybe all over the country, the numerous connections a woman like that would have stirred to shadowy life in his consciousness. My God, I'll have to explain, he thought, and said, "Listen, are you at home? Will you be at home this evening—afternoon, I mean? Sometime around two or three o'clock?"

"Come to a party tomorrow night! Why don't you? Are you free?"

He was free, but he hesitated. A party was another thing entirely.

"It's nothing fancy," she went on. "Just cocktails and

dinner. We'll have a drink or two, then eat. Some friends from Birmingham are bringing me a horse."

"Well, yes, Ma'am," he found himself saying. "We'll try. It's sort of far for a party, but maybe we can make it." He hung up.

She would go around saying to everybody, "He has this gift, the most remarkable thing, you can't *ima*-gine, honey!" and her eyes, no longer clear blue and just out of high school, would burn overbright from alcohol. He wouldn't see her—not the way she had seemed in the store just with him. And he would be the travelling magician, the oddity led by the wrist. Then he knew the truth about his fears, too—or were they hopes? Even if she did tell that world of people she knew, to them it would just be another of her stories about the backwoods. Most of them wouldn't even believe it. They'd tell the story maybe, but nobody would come look him up. They wouldn't, after an hour, be able to think of his name. And she—after a week or so, would she be able to?

He did not go to the party.

He went to see her instead. He was in that part of the state one afternoon. He got to the town and asked the way from a filling-station attendant. It was out of town, off a side road, over a cattle gap, through a pretty stretch of woods. The fences were all painted white. The house was at the end of a tree-lined path, quite a walk from the car, but the gate to let cars through was closed. He should have telephoned from town. He walked up the path. The trees, though oak, were not imposing, but small instead and rather twisted, as though storm-battered at an early age. And the house, even as it drew closer, was smaller than he had been expecting. It was white with a deep front porch, made private with thickset square pillars and a large bed of azaleas, past their prime. It was hard to get azaleas to bloom in that part of the state. The porch had a swing and white-painted iron furniture with comfortably padded green cushions. There were white-painted iron tables with glass tops, and lamps of wrought iron—all as it should be. No one there. Where was she? Should he stand, like the country man he was, and call? If he called, should he say Mrs. Beris or Naomi? Naomi Beris. It was an odd name. He ascended the front steps and knocked on one of the hollow white pillars. "Anybody home?"

There was a stir from within and a boy came out, tall, in his late teens, with wavy blond hair, wearing beige corduroys and beige suède shoes. The corduroy and suède went with the azaleas in the yard and the shadowy, waxed, thick-carpeted look of the hall. It went with the horses that Gavin Anderson already knew were out back, and would have known about even if she had not mentioned the horse she was getting from Birmingham.

"I'm looking for Mrs. Beris. Is she home?"

"She ought to be back pretty soon." The boy half turned to go inside. "Sit down, if you want to wait." He nodded toward the porch furniture. That was good enough, thought Gavin, feeling himself correctly defined. From a distance, the cattle gap rumbled.

She came in her car through the gate he had thought locked (it was automatic) and, parking in the side yard, got out and started toward the front porch. She was wearing short gloves and a dark cotton dress and carrying, along with her bag, a brown parcel. Near the steps, she paused and, shielding her eyes with one gloved hand, said, "Who is it? Now, don't tell me. It's Mr. Anderson!"

She had a drawling voice that only Southerners who have been away and come to know themselves in another context unconsciously cultivate.

"I was over here on business; just happened to be," he said.

Out back, she had the horses—two of them, a black and a bay. There was a white-fenced area for exercise and mounting, and a building with an open walkway through the middle, two stalls on one side and a tack- and feed-storage room on the other. The horses were small, to scale with everything there, to scale with herself. Perhaps she had a small fortune, Gavin thought. A Negro man who spoke to her pleasantly was cleaning the walkway, humming at his work. Gavin thought maybe the ruby that he had seen only in his vision was the only outsize thing she possessed. He did not ask to see it but, enchanted, listened and watched without seeming to.

"It's mighty pretty here," he said.

"It'd be a shame to part with it, now, wouldn't it?" she asked.

"You going to?"

"What can a lone woman do? My son's here, but after he finishes university he won't want to live here. There's nothing here for him."

"It looks like quite a lot here to me," said Gavin.

"Well, *you* know. . . . It's sweet of you to say so."

"I didn't know you were a lone woman."

"Divorced," she said. "I could face parting with the house, though it's been in the family a long time. But I couldn't sell a house with a ruby in it, now, could I?" He saw the ridiculous side of it. "Well, now," she pressed on, making him laugh more than ever, "how would you feel?"

She gave him a gin drink in a silver cup, fresh mint amidst the ice, and placed a small hand damp from the sweated silver into his as he stood on the steps, taking his leave.

He didn't get back to Dalton till after dark. He told his wife, Ethel, that he'd been up northeast of there to another county to see about some property he might invest in. It was the property, he said, in the ensuing weeks, that took him back up there, time and again. He asked her not to mention it.

"I think you know somebody up there," his wife said one evening. The boys had gone to a school program. It was autumn, the first cold snap. "I don't think you've bought any property up there at all. Anyway, there's plenty of property around here. So I don't believe it."

She was brushing her bobbed hair at the dresser. She had firm shoulders, had played basketball in school that year the girls' team was so attractive they used to get invited everywhere, and all the men turned out for miles around to whistle at their legs. She had short, strong, capable hands, the nails always breaking from housework, and knuckles a little large, a perennial cooking burn somewhere—but still attractive. The gas heater hissed in the room.

Gavin didn't answer her. There was no precedent, as far as he knew, for any Anderson's knowing at this point what to say.

"I just think you're trying to tell me not to go through with it about that property," he said at last. "I've been having some doubts myself. I bet you had a dream."

"I don't have to dream. You think I'm dumb? O.K., I never said anything. That's the way I'm going to act, from now on."

It was the year of the Anderson reunion—the year the Anderson grandmother was ninety-five, the year an Anderson daughter (Gavin's cousin) had twins, the year the Lord spared an Anderson grandson (Gavin's nephew) in a traffic accident in which four were killed and two cars demolished (the boy himself was pitched into a blackberry thicket and woke up not even scratched by briars), the year Gavin's son's calf won the statewide blue ribbon, a year of prosperity in which (everybody hoped) there wouldn't be another German war. The reunion was down on the creek, an Indian summer, and a special moon appeared—a swollen oval at the horizon, so orange, so huge, so mysteriously brushed across with one thin black cloud, that one of the aunts kept saying over and over, "If it wasn't so pretty, it'd be downright scary." The night was warm. The Waukahatchie Creek curled near the bluff opposite the bar, running shallow after a dry fall over ribbed sand. The sandbar lay white beneath the moon, which had risen, grown smaller and radiant. Dozens of children, far and wide, knew just what they wanted to play, and down the path from the house, which wound through the willows, the women came tripping with plates of trimmed sandwiches, platters of fried chicken, bowls of potato salad, warmers full of rolls. Gavin sat with his brothers, harmonizing. They sang about the moon—a dozen moon songs—and clapping came up from the women near the tables. Ethel appeared, a ribbon in her hair, looking like a girl. "Thought you weren't coming," Gavin called to her. She'd had a headache earlier. "Changed my mind," she said, going by. The table spread, they lighted lanterns—somebody, got fancy and prosperous, had bought fashionable glass-shielded hurricane lamps, now sparkling grandly above the food. ("Where'd they come from?" one of the brothers asked. "Harriet," another answered. "Oh," said the first. You had to be one of them to get all there was in this.)

Now the brothers, five in all, were sent up to the house, and the grandmother was carried down in her rocker among them. When they appeared in her room, she was sitting straight and silent, dressed and ready. When she saw them, she broke into tears. "Wonderful boys," she kept saying. "Wonderful, wonderful boys." "Hush, now. Hush, now," they told her. And lightly they bore her down, among the willows.

On the way home, long after midnight, Ethel said, "Why wouldn't you find that bowl for them?" It was a silver bowl she meant. The family had all contributed to give it to the grandmother. Simple, engraved and beautiful, it was to sit on her dresser, a daily offering till she died.

"It wasn't lost," he said. "They were teasing."

"They weren't, either. I saw Marvin. He was just about crazy. So was Pat."

"Well, I didn't b'lieve it. I thought they were kidding. Anyway, you know I don't like to."

"Not even for Gran's birthday!"

"But they found it."

"But they really thought it was lost. It was just in George's car, but he went in for some ice and they didn't know it. But you wouldn't."

"I'm not on the midway. You can't just buy a ticket and have the show commence."

"Seems like if you ever did it in your life you would then. Wasn't your heart just so full with all the Andersons there? It's what you got up and said." This was undercutting of the worst kind—flat country-style.

"Yes, it was. I meant it all. Just like I said."

"You meant it when you said it, that's for sure."

He had got tired. Yet the reunion had finally reached him. His heart, though reluctant at first, had finally filled at that clear spring. The evening had said all the Andersons meant to each other—an eternal table, from the creation onward forever. Now it was plain to him that a tree does not choose to be struck by lightning, and that a plain man—even one who can find a ruby ring and who in consequence is given wine by candlelight and dark nakedness on fine linen—is a plain man still. But who, he thought, knew this better than Ethel? So how could she talk as she had? Well, the answer to that was plain also. He knew how she could, and why.

Next day, he tried all day to write the letter. For two weeks, he stuck strictly around Dalton, and every day he tried to write. At last, he made a phone call.

"I haven't been over," he said. "Listen, I don't think I can anymore. You must have guessed that."

"Guessed? No. No, I didn't guess anything."

The conversation locked them in, close as a last embrace, and down, down they sank with it, till, touching bottom at last, they reversed and rose slowly toward the common light. "Just so long as you know how I feel," he was saying. "That I wanted to. Listen. Would you mind if we both came over? Ethel and me. I just want you to meet her." He hesitated. "I want you both to see." It was a crazy idea, but what he felt like. How did you act? How was an Anderson to know? What did it matter as long as Naomi understood?

"Gavin," said the brave, clear, sophisticated voice over the uncertain connection, "I understand perfectly. Y'all come ahead."

When he let himself out of the drugstore phone booth, a daze fell on him. What had he done? What was he blotting out? Whatever the answers, it was too late to stop. The plan, once agreed to, ticked on like a wound clock.

Ethel rode all the way that Sunday with her pretty face fixed on the road, back straight, her bag and gloves neat in her lap. It was a warm, dusty, early December day.

"How do you do?" said Naomi Beris. She was standing at the top of the steps, in a dress of thin white wool with a gold chain at the neck. "Sit down," she said. Her son came out and offered them Cokes on ice. Everything was Sunday-quiet. The cattle gap rumbled. "Who on earth?" Naomi said. A car appeared, green, larger and newer than average for those days. It paused to allow the gate to open and drew into the side yard beside Naomi's. A man got out. He was heavyset, gray-haired, and florid-faced, dressed in khaki and high-laced riding boots, a worn riding coat over a tan whipcord shirt.

"Mr. Slatton's from Columbus," said Naomi. "He came about the horses. I guess that's right, isn't it, Abe?"

"Are the horses sick?" Ethel asked. Mr. Slatton, certainly not a veterinarian, gave no sign he had heard her.

"No," said Naomi. "I have to sell them eventually, and they show up best before the winter sets in. I didn't mention that, Abe," she said to Slatton. "You see how clever I am."

"Shouldn't mention it now." He did not look at her or at the guests. He drank nothing, not even Coke, and stared out at the avenue of trees.

She was wearing the ruby. Gavin had never seen it before. He had asked her once, and she had said it was in the bank vault; she said the insurance was too expensive to keep up. Now it was just as he had envisioned it. Square-cut, dark as wine, it further shrank her small hand, which rested peacefully on the fine white fabric above her lap. It drank the light, inexhaustibly.

"That's the most beautiful ring," said Ethel, who had never heard of it.

Naomi said, "There's a story about it. My great-grandmother lived in an old house that burned. It was near the Natchez Trace, about a mile over yonder. The road is all fallen in now. Not many people even know that's what it was. This man used to come down it, always going to Jackson and then back to somewhere in Tennessee. He would stop by a spring we had. He was a terrible man—clothes made out of skins, probably smelled like bear grease, nothing to recommend him. My grandmother was a young girl, not but fifteen or sixteen. But he wanted to see her, so he always stopped. He used to wait on his horse in the woods till she went down to the spring to bring some water up for dinner so it would be cool for the table. And how many times he waited and how many times she had to run away from him nobody knew. Who knew if she *didn't* run away from him? Nobody would answer that. He carried a pack and a small blanket roll behind his saddle.

"One day he came through, and he'd had a fight with some men either the day before or the night before. He'd slipped away from them in the early morning. There was blood on him, so my grandmother said. He told her he would come back if he could. Meantime, he unstrapped the rolled blanket from the cantle and gave it to her. He'd come back for it, he said, if he could; if not, it was hers. And he said he trusted her.

"At the house, she unwrapped it—not a blanket but a dirty shawl such as Indians wore against the wind. Was that all he had to sleep in, or did he stay in inns? It was a small roll of things—a pewter cup, a blue glass bottle that smelled like corn whiskey, and then the ruby. She almost missed it; it was tied up in a rag. And he never came back.

She married, or was married to, a Pontotoc boy, soon after. Too soon after, was what they said. So here we are still—and here's the ruby."

All of them were silent.

The man, Abe Slatton, gave no sign that he had listened to her. He had not once looked at her during the story. Finally, still staring out at the line of oak trees, he said, "You got the blood of that *ter*-rible man flowin' in yo' veins."

"Pete wouldn't be home," she said, nodding toward her son, "but the whole Georgia Tech team came down with flu. They had to cancel the Auburn game."

"Everybody's got it there, too," said Pete.

"Do you-all go to the games?" Naomi asked.

"We go to the high-school games," said Ethel. "Our boy is on the team. It keeps us pretty busy, I guess."

Gavin and Ethel Anderson left soon after.

"That man was the rudest thing I ever saw," said Ethel. "He never even said goodbye, glad I met you. Nothing. You didn't talk about the property," she added, sly as a fox.

"I told her on the phone I'd decided against it," he said.

"You believe all that about that ring?" she asked, ten miles farther on.

"I don't know."

"I wonder," said Ethel, "if it's even real."

Back in those days, all the roads in Mississippi, with two exceptions, were either dirt or gravel. The road from Naomi Beris's back to Dalton was sixty winding miles, thick-piled with gravel in the center and along the edges, roiling with dust if another car came by. They stopped in a drab little town—a chain of storefronts facing a railroad track, a few houses scattered up rutted roads along broken sidewalks—and had a sandwich at a café.

"Thank you for taking me, Gavin," said Ethel. She was looking at him tenderly, tears in the wide brown eyes that belonged to him; her slyness and undercutting, he knew, were gone. And she wouldn't talk, wouldn't "tell." Things were righted. He was fit once more to bear a grandmother in a rocking chair, feather-light among five strong men, down to the white sandbar. He could sing once more to the moon. What did he need with a wild witch who had blown up out of a thunderstorm, who writhed like a cat, spitting words out that belonged on the walls of a john? What had she wanted with him? A summer had been enough for both of them.

They came out of the restaurant and got into the car. At a curve in the road, the little town vanished like a thought of itself, something that had never been. Now they faced west, drawn straight into a fiery sun, at first so fierce and blinding through the dust that they had to stop until the worst of the glare had muted. It faded beautifully, from a flaming cauldron to blood to wine to deep red velvet, and sank straight ahead of them, removing its deep tinge almost at once from the sky.

His gift was flawed now. It would be like something from boyhood, put aside in a closet. Was he glad or sorry? He didn't know. Driving the harsh gravel, he felt numb somewhere, and placed one hand to his shoulder. Wet blood still thickly stained the dirty leather of his shirt, and the girl with the bucket of spring water, whose waist and lips he knew, reached up to take the rolled shawl, bound with leather strings. The horse shifted beneath him, and her hands, desperate with love, clung along his thigh, which was that of a horseman in his prime, powerful and bold.

WHAT YOU HEAR FROM 'EM?

by *Peter Taylor*

Sometimes people misunderstood Aunt Munsie's question, but she wouldn't bother to clarify it. She might repeat it two or three times, in order to drown out some fool answer she was getting from some fool white woman, or man, either. "What you hear from 'em?" she would ask. And, then, louder and louder: "What you hear from 'em? *What you hear from 'em?*" She was so deaf that anyone whom she thoroughly drowned out only laughed and said Aunt Munsie had got so deaf she couldn't hear it thunder.

It was, of course, only the most utterly fool answers that ever received Aunt Munsie's drowning-out treatment. She was, for a number of years at least, willing to listen to those who mistook her " 'em" to mean any and all of the Dr. Tolliver children. And for more years than that she was willing to listen to those who thought she wanted just *any* news of her two favorites among the Tolliver children—Thad and Will. But later on she stopped putting the question to all insensitive and frivolous souls who didn't understand that what she was interested in hearing—and *all* she was interested in hearing—was when Mr. Thad Tolliver and Mr. Will Tolliver were going to pack up their families and come back to Thornton for good.

They had always promised her to come back—to come back sure enough, once and for all. On separate occasions, both Thad and Will had actually given her their word. She had not seen them together for ten years, but each of them had made visits to Thornton now and then with his own family. She would see a big car stopping in front of her house on a Sunday afternoon and see either Will or Thad with his wife and children piling out into the dusty street—it was nearly always summer when they came—and then see them filing across the street, jumping the ditch, and unlatching the gate to her yard. She always met them in that pen of a yard, but long before they had jumped the ditch she was clapping her hands and calling out, "Hai-ee! Hai-ee, now! Look-a-here! Whee! Whee! Look-a-here!" She had got so blind that she was never sure whether it was Mr. Thad or Mr. Will until she had her arms around his waist. They had always looked a good deal alike, and their city clothes made them look even more alike nowadays. Aunt Munsie's eyes were so bad, besides being so full of moisture on those occasions, that she really recognized them by their girth. Will had grown a regular wash pot of a stomach and Thad was still thin as a rail. They would sit on her porch for twenty or thirty minutes—whichever one it was and his family—and then they would be gone again.

Aunt Munsie would never try to detain them—not seriously. Those short little old visits didn't mean a thing to her. He—Thad or Will—would lean against the banister rail and tell her how well his children were doing in school or college, and she would make each child in turn come and sit beside her on the swing for a minute and receive a hug around the waist or shoulders. They were timid with her, not seeing her any more than they did, but she could tell from their big Tolliver smiles that they liked her to hug them and make over them. Usually, she would lead them all out to her back yard and show them her pigs and dogs and chickens. (She always had at least one frizzly chicken to show the children.) They would traipse through her house to the back yard and then traipse through again to the front porch. It would be time for them to go when they came back, and Aunt Munsie would look up at *him*—Mr. Thad or Mr. Will (she had begun calling them "Mr." the day they married)—and say, "Now, look-a-here. When you comin' back?"

Both Thad and Will knew what she meant, of course, and whichever it was would tell her he was making definite plans to wind up his business and that he was going to buy a certain piece of property, "a mile north of town" or "on the old River Road," and build a jim-dandy house there. He would say, too, how good Aunt Munsie's own house was looking, and his wife would say how grand the zinnias and cannas looked in the yard. (The yard was all flowers—not a blade of grass, and the ground packed hard in little paths between the flower beds.) The visit was almost over then. There remained only the exchange of presents. One of the children would hand Aunt Munsie a paper bag containing a pint of whiskey or a carton of cigarettes. Aunt Munsie would go to her back porch or to the pit in the yard and get a fern or a wandering Jew, potted in a rusty lard bucket, and make Mrs. Thad or Mrs. Will take it along. Then the visit was over, and they would leave. From the porch Aunt Munsie would wave goodbye with one hand and lay the other hand, trembling slightly, on the banister rail. And sometimes her departing guests, looking back from the yard, would observe that the banisters themselves were trembling under her hand—so insecurely were those knobby banisters attached to the knobby porch pillars. Often as not Thad or Will, observing this, would remind his wife that Aunt Munsie's porch banisters and pillars had come off a porch of the house where he had grown up. (Their father, Dr. Tolliver, had been one of the first to widen his porches and remove the gingerbread from his house.) The children and their mother would wave to Aunt Munsie from the street. Their father would close the gate, resting his hand a moment on its familiar wrought-iron frame, and wave to her before he jumped the ditch. If the children had not gone too far ahead, he might even draw their attention to the iron fence which, with its iron gate, had been around the yard at the Tolliver place till Dr. Tolliver took it down and set out a hedge, just a few weeks before he died.

But such paltry little visits meant nothing to Aunt Munsie. No more did the letters that came with "her things" at Christmas. She was supposed to get her daughter, Lucrecie, who lived next door, to read the letters, but in late years she had taken to putting them away unopened, and some of the presents, too. All she wanted to hear from *them* was when they were coming back for good, and she had learned that the Christmas letters never told her that. On her daily route with her slop wagon through the square, up Jackson Street, and down Jefferson, there were only four or five houses left where she asked her question. These were houses where the amount of pig slop was not worth stopping for, houses where one old maid, or maybe two, lived, or a widow with one old bachelor son who had never amounted to anything and ate no more than a woman. And so—in the summertime, anyway—she took to calling out at the top of her lungs, when she approached the house of one of the elect, "What you hear from 'em?" Sometimes a Miss

Patty or a Miss Lucille or a Mr. Ralph would get up out of a porch chair and come down the brick walk to converse with Aunt Munsie. Or sometimes one of them would just lean out over the shrubbery planted around the porch and call, "Not a thing, Munsie. Not a thing lately."

She would shake her head and call back, "Naw. Naw. Not a thing. Nobody don't hear from 'em. Too busy, they be."

Aunt Munsie's skin was the color of a faded tow sack. She was hardly four feet tall. She was generally believed to be totally bald, and on her head she always wore a white dust cap with an elastic band. She wore an apron, too, while making her rounds with her slop wagon. Even when the weather got bad and she tied a wool scarf about her head and wore an overcoat, she put on an apron over the coat. Her hands and feet were delicately small, which made the old-timers sure she was of Guinea stock that had come to Tennessee out of South Carolina. What most touched the hearts of old ladies on Jackson and Jefferson Streets were her little feet. The sight of her feet "took them back to the old days," they said, because Aunt Munsie still wore flat-heeled, high button shoes. Where ever did Munsie find such shoes any more?

She walked down the street, down the very center of the street, with a spry step, and she was continually turning her head from side to side, as though looking at the old houses and trees for the first time. If her sight was as bad as she sometimes let on it was, she probably recognized the houses only by their roof lines against the Thornton sky. Since this was nearly thirty years ago, most of the big Victorian and ante-bellum houses were still standing, though with their lovely gingerbread work beginning to go. (It went first from houses where there was someone, like Dr. Tolliver, with a special eye for style and for keeping up with the times.) The streets hadn't yet been broadened—or only Nashville Street had—and the maples and elms met above the streets. In the autumn, their leaves covered the high banks and filled the deep ditches on either side. The dark macadam surfacing itself was barely wide enough for two automobiles to pass. Aunt Munsie, pulling her slop wagon, which was a long, low, four-wheeled vehicle about the size and shape of a coffin, paraded down the center of the street without any regard for, if with any awareness of, the traffic problems she sometimes made. Seizing the wagon's heavy, sawed-off-looking tongue, she hauled it after her with a series of impatient jerks, just as though that tongue were the arm of some very stubborn, overgrown white child she had to nurse in her old age. Strangers in town or trifling high-school boys would blow their horns at her, but she was never known to so much as glance over her shoulder at the sound of a horn. Now and then a pedestrian on the sidewalk would call out to the driver of an automobile, "She's so deaf she can't hear it thunder."

It wouldn't have occurred to anyone in Thornton—not in those days—that something ought to be done about Aunt Munsie and her wagon for the sake of the public good. In those days, everyone had equal rights on the streets of Thornton. A vehicle was a vehicle, and a person was a person, each with the right to move as slowly as he pleased and to stop where and as often as he pleased. In the Thornton mind, there was no imaginary line down the middle of the street, and, indeed, no one there at that time had heard of drawing a real line on *any* street. It was merely out of politeness that you made room for others to pass. Nobody would have blown a horn at an old colored woman with her slop wagon—nobody but some Yankee stranger or a trifling high-school boy or maybe old Mr. Ralph Hadley in a special fit of temper. When citizens of Thornton were in a particular hurry and got caught behind Aunt Munsie, they leaned out their car windows and shouted: "Aunt Munsie, can you make a little room?" And Aunt Munsie didn't fail to hear *them*. She would holler, "Hai-ee, now! Whee! Look-a-here!" and jerk her wagon to one side. As they passed her, she would wave her little hand and grin a toothless, pink-gummed grin.

Yet, without any concern for the public good, Aunt Munsie's friends and connections among the white women began to worry more and more about the danger of her being run down by an automobile. They talked among themselves and they talked to her about it. They wanted her to give up collecting slop, now she had got so blind and deaf. "Pshaw," said Aunt Munsie, closing her eyes contemptuously. "Not me." She meant by that that no one would dare run into her or her wagon. Sometimes when she crossed the square on a busy Saturday morning or on a first Monday, she would hold up one hand with the palm turned outward and stop all traffic until she was safely across and in the alley beside the hotel.

Thornton wasn't even then what it had been before the Great World War. In every other house there was a stranger or a mill hand who had moved up from factory town. Some of the biggest old places stood empty, the way Dr. Tolliver's had until it burned. They stood empty not because nobody wanted to rent them or buy them but because the heirs who had gone off somewhere making money could never be got to part with "the home place." The story was that Thad Tolliver nearly went crazy when he heard their old house had burned, and wanted to sue the town, and even said he was going to help get the Republicans into office. Yet Thad had hardly put foot in the house since the day his daddy died. It was said the Tolliver house had caught fire from the Major Pettigru house, which had burned two nights before. And no doubt it had. Sparks could have smoldered in that roof of rotten shingles for a long time before bursting into flame. Some even said the Pettigru house might have caught from the Johnston house, which had burned earlier that same fall. But Thad knew and Will knew and everybody knew the town wasn't to blame, and knew there was no firebug. Why, those old houses stood there empty year after year, and in the fall the leaves fell from the trees and settled around the porches and stoops, and who was there to rake the leaves? Maybe it was a good thing those houses burned, and maybe it would have been as well if some of the houses that still had people in them burned, too. There were houses in Thornton the heirs had never left that looked far worse than the Tolliver or the Pettigru or the Johnston house ever had. The people who lived in them were the ones who gave Aunt Munsie the biggest fool answers to her question, the people whom she soon quit asking her question of or even passing the time of day with, except when she couldn't help it, out of politeness. For, truly, to Aunt Munsie there were things under the sun worse than going off and getting rich in Nashville or in Memphis or even in Washington, D.C. It was a subject she and her daughter Lucrecie sometimes mouthed at each other about across their back fence. Lucrecie was shiftless, and she liked shiftless white people like the ones who didn't have the ambition to leave Thornton. She thought their shiftlessness showed they were *quality*. "Quality?" Aunt Munsie would echo, her voice full of sarcasm. "Whee! Hai-ee! You talk like *you* was *my* mammy, Crecie. Well, if there be quality, there be quality *and* quality. There's quality and there's *has-been* quality, Crecie." There was no end to that argument Aunt Munsie had with Crecie, and it wasn't at all important to Aunt Munsie. The people who still lived in those houses—the ones she called has-been quality—meant little more to her than the mill hands, or the strangers from up North who ran the Piggly Wiggly, the five-and-ten-cent store, and the roller-skating rink.

There was this to be said, though, for the has-been quality: they knew *who* Aunt Munsie was, and in a limited, literal way they understood what she said. But those *others*—why, they thought Aunt Munsie a beggar, and she knew they did. They spoke of her as Old What You Have for Mom, because that's what they thought she was saying when she called out, "What you hear from 'em?" Their ears were not attuned to that soft "r" she put in "from" or the elision that made "from 'em" sound to them like "for Mom." Many's the time Aunt Munsie had seen or sensed the presence of one of those *other* people, watching from next door, when Miss Leonora Lovell, say, came down her front walk and handed her a little parcel of scraps across the ditch. Aunt Munsie knew what they thought of her—how they laughed at her and felt sorry for her and despised her all at once. But, like the has-been quality, they didn't matter, never had, never would. Not ever.

Oh, they mattered in a way to Lucrecie. Lucrecie thought about them and talked about them a lot. She called them "white trash" and even "radical Republicans." It made Aunt Munsie grin to hear Crecie go on, because she knew Crecie got all her notions from her own has-been-quality people. And so it didn't matter, except that Aunt Munsie knew that Crecie truly had all sorts of good sense and had only been carried away and spoiled by such folks as she had worked for, such folks as had really raised Crecie from the time she was big enough to run errands for them, fifty years back. In her heart, Aunt Munsie knew that even Lucrecie didn't matter to her the way a daughter might. It was because while Aunt Munsie had been raising a family of white children, a different sort of white people from hers had been raising her own child, Crecie. Sometimes, if Aunt Munsie was in her chicken yard or out in her little patch of cotton when Mr. Thad or Mr. Will arrived, Crecie would come out to the fence and say, "Mama, some of your chillun's out front."

Miss Leonora Lovell and Miss Patty Bean, and especially Miss Lucille Satterfield, were all the time after Aunt Munsie to give up collecting slop. "You're going to get run over by one of those crazy drivers, Munsie," they said. Miss Lucille was the widow of old Judge Satterfield. "If the Judge were alive, Munsie," she said, "I'd make him find a way to stop you. But the men down at the courthouse don't listen to the women in this town any more. Not since we got the vote. And I think they'd be most too scared of you to do what I want them to do." Aunt Munsie wouldn't listen to any of that. She knew that if Miss Lucille had come out there to her gate, she must have *something* she was going to say about Mr. Thad or Mr. Will. Miss Lucille had two brothers and a son of her own who were lawyers in Memphis, and who lived in style down there and kept Miss Lucille in style here in Thornton. Memphis was where Thad Tolliver had his Ford and Lincoln agency, and so Miss Lucille always had news about Thad, and indirectly about Will, too.

"Is they doin' any good? What you hear from 'em?" Aunt Munsie asked Miss Lucille one afternoon in early spring. She had come along just when Miss Lucille was out picking some of the jonquils that grew in profusion on the steep bank between the sidewalk and the ditch in front of her house.

"Mr. Thad and his folks will be up one day in April, Munsie," Miss Lucille said in her pleasantly hoarse voice. "I understand Mr. Will and his crowd may come for Easter Sunday."

"One day, and gone again!" said Aunt Munsie.

"We always try to get them to stay at least one night, but they're busy folks, Munsie."

"When they comin' back sure enough, Miss Lucille?"

"Goodness knows, Munsie. Goodness knows. Goodness knows when any of them are coming back to stay." Miss Lucille took three quick little steps down the bank and hopped lightly across the ditch. "They're prospering so, Munsie," she said, throwing her chin up and smiling proudly. This fragile lady, this daughter, wife, sister, mother of lawyers (and, of course, the darling of all their hearts), stood there in the street with her pretty little feet and shapely ankles close together, and holding a handful of jonquils before her as if it were her bridal bouquet.

"They're *all* prospering so, Munsie. Mine *and* yours. You ought to go down to Memphis to see them now and then, the way I do. Or go up to Nashville to see Mr. Will. I understand he's got an even finer establishment than Thad. They've done well, Munsie—yours *and* mine—and we can be proud of them. You owe it to yourself to go and see how well they're fixed. They're rich men by our standards in Thornton, and they're going farther—*all* of them."

Aunt Munsie dropped the tongue of her wagon noisily on the pavement. "What I want to go see 'em for?" she said angrily and with a lowering brow. Then she stooped and, picking up the wagon tongue again, she wheeled her vehicle toward the middle of the street, to get by Miss Lucille, and started off toward the square. As she turned out into the street, the brakes of a car, as so often, screeched behind her. Presently everyone in the neighborhood could hear Mr. Ralph Hadley tooting the insignificant little horn on his mama's coupé and shouting at Aunt Munsie in his own tooty voice, above the sound of the horn. Aunt Munsie pulled over, making just enough room to let poor old Mr. Ralph get by but without once looking back at him. Then, before Mr. Ralph could get his car started again, Miss Lucille was running along beside Aunt Munsie, saying, "Munsie, you be careful! You're going to meet your death on the streets of Thornton, Tennessee!"

"Let 'em," said Aunt Munsie.

Miss Lucille didn't know whether Munsie meant "Let 'em run over me; I don't care" or meant "Let 'em just dare!" Miss Lucille soon turned back, without Aunt Munsie's ever looking at her. And when Mr. Ralph Hadley did get his motor started, and sailed past in his mama's coupé, Aunt Munsie didn't give him a look, either. Nor did Mr. Ralph bother to turn his face to look at Aunt Munsie. He was on his way to the drugstore, to pick up his mama's prescriptions, and he was too entirely put out, peeved, and upset to endure even the briefest exchange with that ugly, uppity old Munsie of the Tollivers.

Aunt Munsie continued to tug her slop wagon on toward the square. There was a more animated expression on her face than usual, and every so often her lips would move rapidly and emphatically over a phrase or sentence. Why should she go to Memphis and Nashville and see how rich they were? No matter how rich they were, what difference did it make; they didn't own any land, did they? Or at least none in Cameron County. She had heard the old Doctor tell them—tell his boys and tell his girls, and tell the old lady, too, in her day—that nobody was rich who didn't own land, and nobody stayed rich who didn't see after his land firsthand. But of course Aunt Munsie had herself mocked the old Doctor to his face for going on about land so much. She knew it was only something he had heard his own daddy go on about. She would say right to his face that she hadn't ever seen *him* behind a plow. And was there ever anybody more scared of a mule than Dr. Tolliver was? Mules or horses, either? Aunt Munsie had heard him say that the happiest day of his life was the day he first learned that the horseless carriage was a reality.

No, it was not really to own land that Thad and Will ought to come back to Thornton. It was more that if they were going to be rich, they ought to come home, where their granddaddy had owned land and where their money counted for something. How could they ever be rich anywhere else? They could have a lot of money in the bank and a fine house, that was all—like that mill manager from Chi. The mill manager could have a yard full of big cars and a stucco house as big as you like, but who would ever take him for rich? Aunt Munsie would sometimes say all these things to Crecie, or something as nearly like them as she could find words for. Crecie might nod her head in agreement or she might be in a mood to say being rich wasn't any good for anybody and didn't matter, and that you could live on just being quality better than on being rich in Thornton. "Quality's better than land or better than money in the bank here," Crecie would say.

Aunt Munsie would sneer at her and say, "It never were."

Lucrecie could talk all she wanted about the old times! Aunt Munsie knew too much about what they were like, for both the richest white folks and the blackest field hands. Nothing about the old times was as good as these days, and there were going to be better times yet when Mr. Thad and Mr. Will Tolliver came back. Everybody lived easier now than they used to, and were better off. She could never be got to reminisce about her childhood in slavery, or her life with her husband, or even about those halcyon days after the old Mizziz had died and Aunt Munsie's word had become law in the Tolliver household. Without being able to book read or even to make numbers, she had finished raising the whole pack of towheaded Tollivers just as the Mizziz would have wanted it done. The Doctor told her she *had* to—he didn't ever once think about getting another wife, or taking in some cousin, not after his "Molly darling"—and Aunt Munsie *did*. But, as Crecie said, when a time was past in her mama's life, it seemed to be gone and done with in her head, too.

Lucrecie would say frankly she thought her mama was "hard about people and things in the world." She talked about her mama not only to the Blalocks, for whom she had worked all her life, but to anybody else who gave her an opening. It wasn't just about her mama, though, that she would talk to anybody. She liked to talk, and she talked about Aunt Munsie not in any ugly, resentful way but as she would about when the sheep-rains would begin or where the fire was last night. (Crecie was twice the size of her mama, and black the way her old daddy had been, and loud and good-natured the way he was—or at least the way Aunt Munsie wasn't. You wouldn't have known they were mother and daughter, and not many of the young people in town did realize it. Only by accident did they live next door to each other; Mr. Thad and Mr. Will had bought Munsie her house, and Crecie had heired hers from her second husband.) *That* was how she talked about her mama—as she would have about any lonely, eccentric, harmless neighbor. "I may be dead wrong, but I think Mama's kind of hardhearted," she would say. "Mama's a good old soul, I reckon, but when something's past, it's gone and done with for Mama. She don't think about day before yestiddy—yestiddy, either. I don't know, maybe that's the way to be. Maybe that's why the old soul's gonna outlive us all." Then, obviously thinking about what a picture of health she herself was at sixty, Crecie would toss her head about and laugh so loud you might hear her all the way out to the fair grounds.

Crecie, however, knew her mama was not honest-to-God mean and hadn't ever been mean to the Tolliver children, the way the Blalocks liked to make out she had. All the Tolliver children but Mr. Thad and Mr. Will had quarreled with her for good by the time they were grown, but they had quarreled with the old Doctor, too (and as if they were the only ones who shook off their old folks this day and time). When Crecie talked about her mama, she didn't spare her anything, but she was fair to her, too. And it was in no hateful or disloyal spirit that she took part in the conspiracy that finally got Aunt Munsie and her slop wagon off the streets of Thornton. Crecie would have done the same for any neighbor. She had small part enough, actually, in that conspiracy. Her part was merely to break the news to Aunt Munsie that there was now a law against keeping pigs within the city limits. It was a small part but one that no one else quite dared to take.

"They ain't no such law!" Aunt Munsie roared back at Crecie. She was slopping her pigs when Crecie came to the fence and told her about the law. It had seemed the most appropriate time to Lucrecie. "They ain't never been such a law, Crecie," Aunt Munsie said. "Every house on Jackson and Jefferson used to keep pigs."

"It's a brand-new law, Mama."

Aunt Munsie finished bailing out the last of the slop from her wagon. It was just before twilight. The last, weak rays of the sun colored the clouds behind the mock orange tree in Crecie's yard. When Aunt Munsie turned around from the sty, she pretended that that little bit of light in the clouds hurt her eyes, and turned away her head. And when Lucrecie said that everybody had until the first of the year to get rid of their pigs, Aunt Munsie was in a spell of deafness. She headed out toward the crib to get some corn for the chickens. She was trying to think whether anybody else inside the town still kept pigs. Herb Mallory did—two doors beyond Crecie. Then Aunt Munsie remembered Herb didn't pay town taxes. The town line ran between him and Shad Willis.

That was sometime in June, and before July came, Aunt Munsie knew all there was worth knowing about the conspiracy. Mr. Thad and Mr. Will had each been in town for a day during the spring. They and their families had been to her house and sat on the porch; the children had gone back to look at her half-grown collie dog and the two hounds, at the old sow and her farrow of new pigs, and at the frizzliest frizzly chicken Aunt Munsie had ever had. And on those visits to Thornton, Mr. Thad and Mr. Will had also made their usual round among their distant kin and close friends. Everywhere they went, they had heard of the near-accidents Aunt Munsie was causing with her slop wagon and the real danger there was of her being run over.

Miss Lucille Satterfield and Miss Patty Bean had both been to the mayor's office and also to see Judge Lawrence to try to get Aunt Munsie "ruled" off the streets, but the men in the courthouse and in the mayor's office didn't listen to the women in Thornton any more. And so either Mr. Thad or Mr. Will—how would which one of them it was matter to Munsie?—had been prevailed upon to stop by Mayor Lunt's office, and in a few seconds' time had set the wheels of conspiracy in motion. Soon a general inquiry had been made in the town as to how many citizens still kept pigs. Only two property owners besides Aunt Munsie had been found to have pigs on their premises, and they, being men, had been docile and reasonable enough to sell what they had on hand to Mr. Will or Mr. Thad Tolliver. Immediately afterward—within a matter of weeks, that is—a town ordinance had been passed forbidding the possession of swine within the corporate limits of Thornton. Aunt Munsie had got the story bit by bit from Miss Leonora and Miss Patty and Miss Lucille and others, including the constable himself, whom she did not hesitate to stop right in the middle of the square on a Saturday noon. Whether it was Mr. Thad or Mr. Will who had been prevailed upon by the ladies she never ferreted out, but that was only because she did not wish to do so.

The constable's word was the last word for her. The constable said yes, it was the law, and he admitted yes, he had sold his own pigs—for the constable was one of those two reasonable souls—to Mr. Thad or Mr. Will. He didn't say which of them it was, or if he did, Aunt Munsie didn't bother to remember it. And after her interview with the constable, Aunt Munsie never again exchanged words with any human being about the ordinance against pigs. That afternoon, she took a fishing pole from under her house and drove the old sow and the nine shoats down to Herb Mallory's, on the outside of town. They were his, she said, if he wanted them, and he could pay her at killing time.

It was literally true that Aunt Munsie never again exchanged words with anyone about the ordinance against pigs or about the conspiracy she had discovered against herself. But her daughter Lucrecie had a tale to tell about what Aunt Munsie did that afternoon after she had seen the constable and before she drove the pigs over to Herb Mallory's. It was mostly a tale of what Aunt Munsie said to her pigs and to her dogs and her chickens.

Crecie was in her own back yard washing her hair when her mama came down the rickety porch steps and into the yard next door. Crecie had her head in the pot of suds, and so she couldn't look up, but she knew by the way Mama flew down the steps that there was trouble. "She come down them steps like she was wasp-nest bit, or like some young'on who's got hisself wasp-nest bit—and her all of eighty, I reckon!" Then, as Crecie told it, her mama scurried around in the yard for a minute or so like she thought Judgment was about to catch up with her, and pretty soon she commenced slamming at something. Crecie wrapped a towel about her soapy head, squatted low, and edged over toward the plank fence. She peered between the planks and saw what her mama was up to. Since there never had been a gate to the fence around the pigsty, Mama had taken the wood ax and was knocking a hole in it. But directly, just after Crecie had taken her place by the plank fence, her mama had left off her slamming at the sty and turned about so quickly and so exactly toward Crecie that Crecie thought the poor, blind old soul had managed to spy her squatting there. Right away, though, Crecie realized it was not *her* that Mama was staring at. She saw that all Aunt Munsie's chickens and those three dogs of hers had come up behind her, and were all clucking and whining to know why she didn't stop that infernal racket and put out some feed for them.

Crecie's mama set one hand on her hip and rested the ax on the ground. "Just look at yuh!" she said, and then she let the chickens and the dogs—and the pigs, too—have it. She told them what a miserable bunch of creatures they were, and asked them what right they had to always be looking for handouts from her. She sounded like the bossman who's caught all his pickers laying off before sundown, and she sounded, too, like the preacher giving his sinners Hail Columbia at camp meeting. Finally, shouting at the top of her voice and swinging the ax wide and broad above their heads, she sent the dogs howling under the house and the chickens scattering in every direction. "Now, g'wine! G'wine widja!" she shouted after them. Only the collie pup, of the three dogs, didn't scamper to the farthest corner underneath the house. He stopped under the porch steps, and not two seconds later he was poking his long head out again and showing the whites of his doleful brown eyes. Crecie's mama took a step toward him and then she halted.

"You want to know what's the commotion about? I reckoned you would," she said with profound contempt, as though the collie were a more reasonable soul than the other animals, and as though there were nothing she held in such thorough disrespect as reason. "I tell you what the commotion's about," she said. "They *ain't* comin' back. They ain't never comin' back. They ain't never had no notion of comin' back." She turned her head to one side, and the only explanation Crecie could find for her mama's next words was that that collie pup did look so much like Miss Lucille Satterfield.

"Why don't I go down to Memphis or up to Nashville and see 'em sometime, like *you* does?" Aunt Munsie asked the collie. "I tell you why. Becaze I ain't nothin' to 'em in Memphis, and they ain't nothin' to me in Nashville. *You* can go!" she said, advancing and shaking the big ax at the dog. "A collie dog's a collie dog anywhar. But Aunt Munsie, she's just their Aunt Munsie here in Thornton. I got mind enough to see *that*." The collie slowly pulled his head back under the steps, and Aunt Munsie watched for a minute to see if he would show himself again. When he didn't, she went and jerked the fishing pole out from under the house and headed toward the pigsty. Crecie remained squatting beside the fence until her mama and the pigs were out in the street and on their way to Herb Mallory's.

That was the end of Aunt Munsie's keeping pigs and the end of her daily rounds with her slop wagon, but it was not the end of Aunt Munsie. She lived on for nearly twenty years after that, till long after Lucrecie had been put away, in fine style, by the Blalocks. Ever afterward, though, Aunt Munsie seemed different to people. They said she softened, and everybody said it was a change for the better. She would take paper money from under her carpet, or out of the chinks in her walls, and buy things for up at the church, or buy her own whiskey when she got sick, instead of making somebody bring her a nip. On the square she would laugh and holler with the white folks the way they liked her to and the way Crecie and all the other old-timers did, and she even took to tying a bandanna about her head—took to talking old-nigger foolishness, too, about the Bell Witch, and claiming she remembered the day General N. B. Forrest rode into town and saved all the cotton from the Yankees at the depot. When Mr. Will and Mr. Thad came to see her with their families, she got so she would reminisce with them about their daddy and tease them about all the silly little things they had done when they were growing up: "Mr. Thad—him still in kilts, too—he says, 'Aunt Munsie, reach down in yo' stockin' and git me a copper cent. I want some store candy.' " She told them about how Miss Yola Ewing, the sewing woman, heard her threatening to bust Will's back wide open when he broke the lamp chimney, and how Miss Yola went to the Doctor and told him he ought to run Aunt Munsie off. Then Aunt Munsie and the Doctor had had a big laugh about it out in the kitchen, and Miss Yola must have eavesdropped on them, because she left without finishing the girls' Easter dresses.

Indeed, these visits from Mr. Thad and Mr. Will continued as long as Aunt Munsie lived, but she never asked them any more about when they were sure enough coming back. And the children, though she hugged them more than ever—and, toward the last, there were the children's children to be hugged—never again set foot in her back yard. Aunt Munsie lived on for nearly twenty years, and when they finally buried her, they put on her tombstone that she was aged one hundred years, though nobody knew how old she was. There was no record of when she was born. All anyone knew was that in her last years she had said she was a girl helping about the big house when freedom came. That would have made her probably about twelve years old in 1865, according to her statements and depictions. But all agreed that in her extreme old age Aunt Munsie, like other old darkies, was not very reliable about dates and such things. Her spirit softened, even her voice lost some of the rasping quality that it had always had, and in general she became not very reliable about facts.

THE GEOLOGIST'S MAID

by *Anne Tyler*

Stand outside his house any morning and you will see her opening the curtains—an energetic, middle-aged black woman hauling on the tasselled cord like a bell ringer. She wears a gray uniform. Her face is so dark that it appears to have no features. Behind her, Dr. Johnson is a mountain of light propped against the pillows, facing the picture window—a large white face and a spray of white hair, pale pajamas, white stringy hands resting on the blankets. This is the living room, though Dr. Johnson's high-crowned mahogany bedstead has ruled it for the last six weeks. Through this window it is possible to see everything: all the columns of roses on his wallpaper and the clutter of get-well cards, geology textbooks, and ungraded papers; the furniture clumped hastily together to make way for the bed. It is possible, without even spying, to observe how Maroon bends to offer a pill, or perhaps a choice of breakfasts, and how Dr. Johnson raises his pale, blind-looking eyes to her face. Maroon straightens up. Dr. Johnson's hair flashes silver, sending glints of light across the room. Here, if nowhere else, care is being taken.

Bennett Johnson waits in an armchair after breakfast this morning while his sheets are changed. Cold white domes billow over his mattress, settle and collapse. Maroon slogs around the bed in shoes from the late fifties with needle-sharp toes, spindly heels worn down to the wood, and slits for her bunions. Her body is boardlike, wide and flat and sparse, and her gray hair is boardlike, too, from all the straightener she has used. Her ankles, however, are small and curved, delicate as wineglasses, a continual surprise to Bennett. He ponders them, disconcerted. Maroon pats and tucks and smooths.

She is talking about her sister, the one with asthma. Violet. All her sisters were named for colors, all her brothers for Presidents. Bennett feels he knows every one of them, though most are dead. Cancer has swept that family like an epidemic, eating them alive. First her mother, then two sisters, then a brother, then another brother. Never, not in even a single case, did the doctors tell them ahead of time. They patched them up, handed out pills much too small and round for the pain involved, and sent them shuffling out of the clinic still bent over and clutching at liver, breast, or stomach.

Now Maroon wonders if Violet's asthma could be cancer also. Bennett knows very well that Violet's asthma dates from her childhood, forty-odd years ago, but he says nothing. He rests on the curve of Maroon's rich voice, her habit of croaking upward suddenly at the end of each sentence. Last night, she says, she was in the emergency room for five and one-quarter hours just soothing and calming Violet, waiting on some doctor to take the time to notice them. In the end, she had to go on home. She needed her rest; there was Dr. Johnson to see to in the morning and you *know*, she said to Violet, how Dr. Johnson is so particular about people being on time. She had to leave Violet all alone there on a bench just hunting up the oxygen for one last breath. And if Violet dies, who will Maroon have left? Her father fell off a construction job eighteen years ago, her last remaining brother lives in New York City with a light-colored wife, her many nieces (all named Cherie, it seems to Bennett) have no time for grownups. Sunday nights now, when she and Violet send out for Chinese, they ask for the smallest order the restaurant will deliver and still it is too much for them. Used to be their family would crowd the dining room and flow on into the parlor and there was never enough Chinese to go round, but not anymore.

When Violet dies, Maroon will be left all alone in her dark rowhouse in downtown Baltimore. She will be, she says, at the mercy of the neighbor boys whose parents never raised them right, no-account niggers strung out on dope and glue and Pam, idling under her street light disturbing her rest, scuffing her stoop, bouncing a basketball beneath her window, and nobody daring to complain for fear of worse. She would like to see them locked up forever, she says, tortured, starved, put to death in electric chairs. (She slaps the pillows hard, with a flat yellow palm.) She would not mind, herself, twisting the knife in their innards. She is a hardworking, church-going woman who has feared the Lord all her life, reads her Bible daily, minds her own business, and she cannot stand to see how some worthless, shiftless bastards will get to take everything like they have it coming to them.

Bennett eases himself between the cool sheets, guarding his heart. He has become all pulse; he is aware, every second, of the beating of his blood in his ears; he weighs it and judges it. But Maroon talks on, and leaves still talking, and does not think to ask him if he can make it through the day.

This morning is so long, and so blank, that Bennett wonders if he has already died and gone to Purgatory. He has nowhere to look but out his picture window: a postcard scene of other people's landscaped ranch houses, occasional glimpses of women in slippers and curlers and raincoats departing and returning in station wagons. Later they will appear wearing very short tennis dresses, looking as perky as the little girls he went to grammar school with; later still, just around lunchtime, in pants suits that turn them square-hipped and bossy. He is measuring out his days with women's clothing. Sometimes he thinks the irritation of it will make him grind his teeth down to a fine, gritty powder. He lifts himself to slam his pillow around, hunting coolness, and then remembers his heart and thinks: calm, level; and sinks back and takes a slow deep breath.

He hears Maroon's radio from the kitchen. She is listening to a revivalist preacher with a voice like a cough. If you send in two dollars, the preacher will mention your name on the air and the name of your affliction; for five, he will mail you a miraculous printed prayer that has solved the problems of countless thousands. But Maroon never settles for second best and she is going to send him not two dollars, not five, but *ten*, as soon as she gets it saved up. She wants the prayer in its parchment version—embedded in Lucite—which will double as a paperweight. What problem does she need solved, Bennett wonders. Her sister's asthma, her brother's light-colored wife? Will she tell God to strike all the neighbor boys dead? Bennett has asked her, but she will not answer. She has her secrets. Today she sits in the kitchen, no doubt thumbing through her Bible—a de-luxe version with a ribbon marker, the *last* thing she saved up for, eight ninety-eight reduced from ten ninety-five at Cut-Rate Drugs and Beauty. (It is written in modern language, she says; perhaps now she will understand the stories better.)

On Sundays, Maroon teaches Sunday school, a class of sullen teen-agers; on Mondays, she comes in and complains about them to Bennett. (She asks them who was Jacob and they answer, What do *they* care who was Jacob?) When she tells him this, Bennett feels that he is drowning in despair. He issues loud angry instructions that are bad for his heart: she mustn't teach that class anymore, mustn't keep buying newer and bigger Bibles, must cease believing in that redneck preacher on the radio. But there she sits in the kitchen with the radio turned full blast. The preacher ends and the hymn begins—"In the Garden," sung by the ladies' choir. Their shrill, mournful voices make him suddenly sad. He would expect Maroon to sing along (she does have a voice, of sorts; she often hums something unrecognizable when she is washing the dishes), but today she is quiet, respectfully quiet, silent and no doubt motionless, perhaps even bowing her head—a fact that makes him sadder still.

Bennett is capable now of going to the bathroom by himself, and at eleven o'clock he does so—the major event of his morning. He rises by degrees and creeps across the corridor, patting each piece of furniture he comes upon. It is amazing how far away and white his feet appear. He has been horizontal for so long—first in the hospital, tented, and now here at home. The doctors keep referring to his heart attack as "massive"—a word that surprises him. He is reminded of "massif." (He is a geology professor.) He thinks of mountainous rock, unveined, uneroded: the very opposite of this heart of his, which must surely be in tatters. Weren't its jagged edges the cause of the pain he first felt? (He was carrying his lunch tray across the cafeteria when fragments suddenly crumpled in his chest and nudged each other. Then broken crockery lay on the floor around his head.) He has been sickly all his life—a pale, rheumatic child desperately dependent upon his mother; it is no news to him that his heart is fragile. Now even his skin seems cracked, his hands transparent, as if everything in him has leached out. He feels weak and pure and helpless. He wonders why Maroon cannot leave her fool radio program long enough to come assist him here. As a self-indulgence, he neglects to raise the toilet seat, although Maroon has spoken to him about that more than once.

Lunch today is chicken noodle soup, unsalted, and fresh fruit and a glass of skim milk. Bennett eats from an enamelled tray, Maroon from a card table set up in the corner. (She will not take a meal alone.) Constantly he cranes his neck to see what she has on her plate, for Maroon is a greedy woman. Also, her taste is surprisingly good. She demands the best—no junk food, nothing canned, everything top quality and natural and *real*. Real butter and cream, real percolated coffee, double-rich French vanilla ice cream for dessert, while his doctor keeps him on margarine. Cremora, weak tea, and D-Zerta. He wishes she would eat in the kitchen. He notices that after finishing each dish she pounds her chest with her fist, bringing up a burp. Her nails are opaque and yellow and too long. If there were any decent help in this city, he would not have her around for another day.

When he asks for his tea, she shoves her chair back and goes to fetch it, still chewing. Now that the radio is off he can hear every slam of cupboard doors and rattle of silver, and he strains his ears to find out if it is a tea-bag she is using or Twinings. No use to ask outright for Twinings; she will pretend not to hear. He must simply wait, enduring her tyranny, tasting Twinings on the center of his tongue (Earl Grey, the taste of comfort). Is she taking so long on *purpose*? He feels that he has never been so thirsty in his life: he is *racked* by thirst; even the soles of his feet are parched. And when she returns, sloshing hot water into the saucer from the cracked blue cup, the little tea-bag banner fluttering in the breeze she makes, he is ready to smash her face in; but he only takes his tea and nods.

In the period after lunch that is supposed to be Bennett's nap, Maroon chooses to straighten his room. She stacks sheaves of paper already stacked, moves books an inch to the right or left, picks up a get-well card to stroke its flocked flower basket, which she has already worn nearly bald. As he watches, Bennett wonders what she wants of *him*, personally—what besides her pay, her meals, and the leftovers she sneaks out of the kitchen every night in a string-handled shopping bag. Maybe she has some question that only he can answer, or some dark admission she is bracing herself to make to him. Perhaps she is considering settling slowly, weightily upon his bed, looming closer and closer until her face connects with his like a shadow. His toes curl. But Maroon merely sets the card down, gives the table a swipe with the dustcloth, and moves on. She retrieves a torn envelope from the floor and lays it upon a bookcase. Are maids trained specifically to throw nothing away, to humor their employers' fondness for old matchbooks, scraps of paper, and ticket stubs? Are maids trained at *all*? Presumably not. Like wives and mothers, they are supposed to just know. He watches her turn a flattened cushion in a cane-bottomed rocker. He listens to her ramble: Violet again, then Cherie's graduation, then the boy who shot her windowpane out. In *her* day, when *she* was that boy's age . . . and on about how hard she worked, a little skinny rag of a girl (he can see her, smaller but just as old), scrubbing white folks' white marble stoops at fifteen cents a throw. Then when she was twelve . . .

He remembers when she was twelve. He remembers every blessed minute as clearly as if he has lived it himself, he has heard it so often. How she worked for Mrs. Jeffrey Simpson-Jones out in Roland Park for seventeen years straight—an admirable record. (Yes, but he is tired of it anyway, and has never understood why some people insist on having hyphenated names.) How she was called in one sunny day with no warning at all: they reckoned she had noticed that for a long time now Mrs. Simpson-Jones had been sleeping in the guest room. Fact was they were getting a divorce, putting the house up for sale, taking away the children that Maroon had raised like her own; they hoped it was no inconvenience.

Bennett's head nods. His eyes droop. He is not so much sleepy as *exhausted*, worn down to the bone, and, for a wonder, Maroon sees it and stops her chattering. She rustles one last thing on the table and then goes to close the curtains. He hears her careful, obvious tiptoeing, and the rasping sound of her stockings, which are so thick and serviceable that they constitute a reproach. He catches her scent of gray scrubwater as she passes. She withdraws herself like a question she has regretted asking, leaving him wide-awake again and staring at the ceiling.

He knows Mrs. Simpson-Jones. (Or might as well.) He knows Violet, whom he has never seen and never wanted to. Also the Cheries: one, two, and three, and four if there is a four. He knows Maroon's husband, now dead—a white lady's chauffeur who did not like fatback in his beans or peas in his potato salad. Who was so house-proud that he would not even have children but must spend his salary on white carpeting and then clear plastic runners for the carpet, white couches and then clear plastic slipcovers for the couches, and a glittering icy chandelier for the dining room, which Maroon spends every Saturday polishing, prism by prism, with newspapers dipped in vinegar. She will polish it until she dies, old and childless and quarrelsome, or until the neighbor boys shoot it down with their .22s. And when the chandelier is polished there is the curly-maple curio cabinet full of dime-store figurines, which she has described to Bennett a thousand times. He is confused by her economic inconsistencies: she will haggle over a fifty-cent crab in Lexington Market and go home without it, shaking her head, but just recently she purchased an overpriced table lamp in the shape of a Greek temple, with a Japanese doll in a real silk kimono standing inside it holding a parasol while twisted strands of catgut shimmer all around her, giving the effect of rain. (At least, Maroon *says* it is catgut. Bennett has never seen it.) He finds her thirst for possessions disturbing; he dislikes the way she sometimes fingers the fabric of his bathrobe while hanging it, or strokes the mottled, jewel-like centers of the agates on his bookshelf. Though he is an intelligent man, and reminds himself daily of all she has been deprived of.

This woman, who until his illness was a mere shadow dusting his study, or a supper left in the oven when he came home at night, has somehow woven all her memories into his so that now it seems he has led *two* lives, not merely one. His own memories—his sickly childhood, sisterless, brotherless, his mother's death, his settled, tranquil bachelor's existence—seem, if anything, less clear to him than Maroon's. Maroon's voice threads in and out of his head, complaining and protesting and discussing. He would like to sleep. Maroon will not let him. He is forced to recall that her husband died of overwork, driving his white lady to a North Carolina hunt club too soon after a minor stroke; that he left no insurance; that his four uppity sisters publish a memorial for him in *Afro* once a year but make no mention of his wife, as they are light-skinned and she is dark. *But*, Bennett wants to say, fighting her with the weapons she has handed him herself. He would like to remind her of the fancy parties she attends, given by friends in church who have risen in the world; those Saturday-night affairs she bores him to death with on Monday morning—every crumb of food described in detail, the potatoes tinted pink to match the carpeting and the pink champagne, and the Chinese carry-out, floral centerpieces costing one hundred and twenty-four dollars, leather-covered bars at each end of the room and an extra one in the basement. He would like to remind her of Cherie's graduation, at which Maroon and Violet cried for joy (the first diploma in the family) and Cherie wore nylon net and had more girl friends than anyone else, some of them white, all of them turning her class ring for her, which was the custom: to turn your class ring a hundred times and make a wish. He does silent battle with her and wins, and sinks back on the pillow to sleep. Then Maroon comes to open his curtains and asks if he has had a good nap. No doubt she is puzzled by the weary way he turns his face from her.

Bennett gathers his strength and makes another trip to the bathroom, after which he tries to grade a few papers. It seems very strange to him that he should ever have been interested in the basalt magma of the Mid-Ocean Ridge. Nevertheless he works steadily, managing to correct four papers before discouragement creeps up on him. Also he answers three telephone calls—neighbor women, returning from their luncheons, dutifully checking to see if he needs anything. He tells them he is fine. He has no needs whatsoever.

At four o'clock two colleagues drop by with his mail and bank papers, their classes over for the day. One is a widower and one divorced. They have plenty of time to spare for him. They make themselves short drinks from the liquor cabinet near his bed—Scotch, neat, no ice because it would trouble Maroon. They settle in armchairs and discuss the new department chairman, then a recent field trip, then a book that one of them is writing. Bennett would like to bring up Maroon (sometimes he lets off a little steam that way, grimaces toward the kitchen like a schoolboy), but it is too late. She has entered the room, carrying two trays. One is for Bennett: toast and frozen orange juice, bland as hospital fare. The other is for her, something hot and meaty. Bennett has never figured out why he needs a snack at this hour, or why she must eat hers while his friends are here, or what excuse she could have for helping herself to what is obviously supper when she is supposed to be *home* by suppertime. He has considered asking her outright, but something stops him—perhaps his friends' stiff, embarrassed expressions as they stare down into their drinks. The only sound now is the clinking of Maroon's silverware upon her plate. Her steady munching and swallowing. A fist thumping her chest. He wishes it were *his* fist. The clinking resumes, louder than he would have thought possible. He cannot tolerate the way she dabs at the corners of her mouth with a napkin like a dustcloth. Most of all he despises her *hunger*, this endless reaching, grasping, chewing, gulping. But all he does is crumble his toast, silently, upon his plate. After a while, his friends make their excuses and leave.

Now the sky is darkening and Maroon closes the curtains again. Bennett's life has become a continual opening and shutting of curtains. She stacks the whiskey glasses and alters, very slightly, the position of the chairs his friends were sitting in. Meanwhile she is talking about last weekend: a neighbor lady said she would pay Maroon good for staying with her little girl. Then what did she pay but a quart of beer gone flat and half a broiled chicken, and here Maroon had already eat and would rather, anyway, have had a dollar or two to make up the cost of the reverend's prayer. She would willingly starve, she says, if she could just get her hands on that prayer, for the radio said it answered all questions and solved all problems and would double as a paperweight. Bennett is still angry with her, too angry to talk, but the professor in him stirs and sits up and he nearly makes her an offer: she could ask *him* her question. He holds his tongue, though. He lies flat, injured and bitter. Maroon lets loose a yellow pool of lamplight and leaves with the trays.

Each distant clatter in the kitchen cuts another notch in Bennett's soul. He wishes to write someone a letter of protest about her name, that ugly, awkward name so unfortunately suited to her face. Her smallest action is a crime: her toast burned black around the edges; her thoughtless hauling upon the fragile curtain-pull; the uncared-for, dismal look of this room with the furniture shoved every which way and the afghan slapped crooked across the foot of the bed. There is nothing satisfactory about her. He cannot name one thing.

Still, he is forced to remember that she lives huddled up in musty dark rooms, fearing for her life. That her Sunday-school superintendent accuses her weekly of stupidity and her one last sister sucks air aloud like someone strangling; that the gas man stole five dollars from her bureau—or so she says—and an electrician promised to rewire her home for safety but left with her deposit and not even his wife knows where he is. That her burial insurance has lapsed, though she swears she has paid her quarter every Saturday of her life. That some time ago, while taking her salary home, she was beaten and robbed by two young men whom she could not identify, and still has a yellow swollen patch below one eye if you look closely. That she does not sleep well, has not for years, but now since the beating has nights when she never even closes her eyes, and at the clinic they made her stop taking paregoric and sent her to a psychiatrist, who asked if she was depressed.

Depressed? (Her voice echoes now in Bennett's memory.) No, she wouldn't say she was depressed. She tries to keep busy, she goes out a lot, she goes to a lot of parties, lot of church affairs. She wouldn't say she was depressed. The psychiatrist prescribed Valium, which does not make her feel as fine as paregoric. Also group therapy. Five dollars an hour—more than she can afford—and anyway she doesn't understand these things. She went only once. There were a lot of people discussing their own affairs, which she didn't see the point of on her five dollars—white girl brooding on suicide, white man saying he don't relate to women, oh she just didn't have *time* for this, so she opened a magazine and read till they took notice of her and then she spoke up. She couldn't sleep, she said. She would lie awake all night, remembering that first blow of the fist just below her eye and then her husband dying alone in North

Carolina, before she could find the money to get to him, and it didn't seem fair when she had never done a soul any harm and only tried to live right—wouldn't even drink beer on Sundays, though her guests might have wished she would offer them some. But the other patients just looked at her (white folks, mostly) like they didn't understand. She has never gone back.

Bennett tosses on his bed, and lays his forearm across his eyes to shut the lamplight out. It seems to him that years have passed since morning.

At five-thirty, the doctor comes—an old friend, hearty and artificial now that Bennett is his patient. He neither listens to Bennett's heart nor takes his pulse but sits on the edge of the bed analyzing a football game that Bennett has not seen and never wanted to see. Nevertheless, it is annoying to have Maroon come stand in the doorway. Is nothing private? The doctor, perhaps jolted into action by her presence, drops the football game and starts probing into details of Bennett's life. He asks about constipation, chest pains, mental attitude, diet. He wants to know if Bennett is still suffering those empty dizzy spells in the night. Also, if he is avoiding eggs, if he needs more sleeping tablets, if he notices any adverse symptoms after drinking tea. Bennett replies carefully, weighing every word before he speaks.

Halfway through the visit, both men are startled by the sudden, eye-batting explosion of the door as Maroon slams off to the kitchen.

Her last act of the day is to bring him his supper. She lays it on his knees and props his pillow. Already she is set to go, wearing a faded dress, a string of pink pearls, and a crocheted hat. Her linty black coat will be waiting in the hall along with her string-handled shopping bag. She is always in such a hurry. But today she pauses, stepping back and swinging her arms from the shoulders in that awkward way she has, almost clapping, which means she is embarrassed. He remembers: it is payday. He sets down his fork and opens the drawer beside him, where he finds the bank envelope his colleagues brought him earlier. He hands it to her, and she accepts it while gazing off at a wall. Not until he has picked up his fork again does she look inside the envelope. She takes a dollar from the sheaf of bills and holds it up. For the prayer, of course: a dollar a week for the prayer in the Lucite paperweight. He has no idea how close she is to her goal. He watches how she purses her lips to study the bill, as if it has somehow turned into a prayer on its own. Her face is furrowed, her invisible eyebrows crinkled. She asks the dollar, "Now, how come things goes so wrong for me and so right for the wicked?"

Then she turns, as she always does, leaving him to his meagre supper. As always she lays a hand on his pillow when she passes, wishing him good night—rough skin catching on the linen, smell of gray water, dress so worn it hardly rustles when she moves, unanswered questions echoing on and on long after she has departed.

STRONG HORSE TEA
by *Alice Walker*

Rannie Toomer's little baby boy Snooks was dying from double pneumonia and whooping cough. She sat away from him gazing into a low fire, her long crusty bottom lip hanging. She was not married. Was not pretty. Was not anybody much. And he was all she had.

"Lawd, why don't that doctor come on here?" she moaned, tears sliding from her sticky eyes. She hadn't washed since Snooks took sick five days before, and a long row of whitish snail tracks laced her ashen face.

"What you ought to try is one of the old home remedies," Sarah urged. She was an old neighboring lady who wore magic leaves around her neck sewed up in possum skin next to a dried lizard's foot. She knew how magic came about and could do magic herself, people said.

"We going to have us a doctor," Rannie Toomer said fiercely, walking over to shoo a fat winter fly from her child's forehead. "I don't believe in none of your swamp magic. The 'old home remedies' I took when I was a child come just short of killing me."

Snooks, under a pile of faded quilts, made a small oblong mound in the bed. His head was like a ball of black putty wedged between the thin covers and the dingy yellow pillow. His eyes were partly open as if he were peeping out of his hard wasted skull at the chilly room, and the forceful pulse of his breathing caused a faint rustling in the sheets near his mouth like the wind pushing damp papers in a shallow ditch.

"What time you reckon he'll git here?" asked Sarah, not expecting an answer. She sat with her knees wide apart under three long skirts and a voluminous Mother Hubbard heavy with stains. From time to time she reached down to sweep her damp skirts away from the live coals. It was almost spring, but the winter cold still clung to her bones, and she had to almost sit in the fireplace to get warm. Her deep, sharp eyes had aged a moist hesitant blue that gave her a quick dull stare like a hawk. She gazed coolly at Rannie Toomer and rapped the hearthstones with her stick.

"White mailman, white doctor," she chanted skeptically.

"They gotta come see 'bout this baby," Rannie Toomer said wistfully. "Who'd go and ignore a little sick baby like my Snooks?"

"Some folks we don't know well as we *thinks* we do might," the old lady replied. "What you want to give that boy of yours is one or two of the old home remedies, arrowsroot or sassyfrass and cloves, or sugar tit soaked in cat's blood."

"We don't need none of your witch's remedies!" said Rannie Toomer. "We going to git some of them shots that makes people well. Cures 'em of all they ails, cleans 'em out and makes 'em strong, all at the same time." She grasped her baby by his shrouded toes and began to gently twist, trying to knead life into him the same way she kneaded limberness into flour dough. She spoke upward from his feet as if he were an altar.

"Doctor'll be here soon, baby. I done sent the mailman." She left him reluctantly to go and stand by the window. She pressed her face against the glass, her flat nose more flattened as she peered out at the rain.

She had gone up to the mailbox in the rain that morning, hoping she hadn't missed the mailman's car. She had sat down on an old milk can near the box and turned her drooping face in the direction the mailman's car would come. She had no umbrella, and her feet shivered inside thin, clear plastic shoes that let in water and mud.

"Howde, Rannie Mae," the red-faced mailman said pleasantly, as he always did, when she stood by his car waiting to ask him something. Usually she wanted to ask what certain circulars meant that showed pretty pictures of things she needed. Did the circulars mean that somebody was coming around later and give her hats and suitcases and shoes and sweaters and rubbing alcohol and a heater for the house and a fur bonnet for her baby? Or, why did he always give her the pictures if she couldn't have what was in them? Or, what did the words say? . . . Especially the big word written in red: "S-A-L-E!"?

He would explain shortly to her that the only way she could get the goods pictured on the circulars was to buy them in town and that town stores did their advertising by sending out pictures of their goods. She would listen with her mouth hanging open until he finished. Then she would exclaim in a dull amazed way that *she* never had any money and he could ask anybody. *She* couldn't ever buy any of the things in the pictures—so why did the stores keep sending them to her?

He tried to explain to her that *everybody* got the circulars whether they had any money to buy with or not. That this was one of the laws of advertising, and he couldn't do anything about it. He was sure she never understood what he tried to teach her about advertising, for one day she asked him for any extra circulars he had, and when he asked her what she wanted them for—since she couldn't afford to buy any of the items advertised—she said she needed them to paper the inside of her house to keep out the wind.

Today he thought she looked more ignorant than usual as she stuck her dripping head inside his car. He recoiled from her breath and gave little attention to what she was saying about her sick baby as he mopped up the water she dripped on the plastic door handle of the car.

"Well, never *can* keep 'em dry; I mean, *warm* enough, in rainy weather like this here," he mumbled absently, stuffing a wad of circulars advertising hair dryers and cold creams into her hands. He wished she would stand back from his car so he could get going. But she clung to the side gabbing away about "Snooks" and "pneumonia" and "shots" and about how she wanted a "*real* doctor!"

To everything she said he nodded. "That right?" he injected sympathetically when she stopped for breath, and then he began to sneeze, for she was letting in wetness and damp, and he felt he was coming down with a cold. Black people as black as Rannie Toomer always made him uneasy, especially when they didn't smell good and when you could tell they didn't right away. Rannie Mae, leaning in over him out of the rain, smelled like a wet goat. Her dark dirty eyes clinging to his with such hungry desperation made him nervous.

"Well, ah, *mighty* sorry to hear 'bout the little fella," he said, groping for the window crank. "We'll see what we can do!" He gave her what he hoped was a big friendly smile. God! *He didn't want to hurt her feelings;* she did look so pitiful hanging there in the rain. Suddenly he had an idea.

"Whyn't you try some of old Aunt Sarah's home remedies?" he suggested brightly. He half believed along with everybody else in the county that the old blue-eyed black woman possessed magic. Magic that if it didn't work on whites probably would on blacks. But Rannie Toomer almost turned the car over shaking her head and body with an emphatic NO! She reached in a wet hand to grasp his shoulder.

"We wants us a doctor, a real doctor!" she screamed. She had begun to cry and drop her tears on him. "You git us a doctor from town!" she bellowed, shaking the solid shoulder that bulged under his new tweed coat.

"Like I say," he drawled patiently, although beginning to be furious with her, "we'll do what we can!" And he hurriedly rolled up the window and sped down the road, cringing from the thought that she had put her nasty black hands on him.

"Old home remedies! Old home remedies!" Rannie Toomer had cursed the words while she licked at the hot tears that ran down her face, the only warmth about her. She turned backwards to the trail that led to her house, trampling the wet circulars under her feet. Under the fence she went and was in a pasture surrounded by dozens of fat whitefolks' cows and an old gray horse and a mule. Cows and horses never seemed to have much trouble, she thought, as she hurried home.

Old Sarah dug steadily at the fire; the bones in her legs ached as if they were outside the flesh that enclosed them.

"White mailman, white doctor. White doctor, white mailman," she murmured from time to time, putting the poker down carefully and rubbing her shins.

"You young ones *will* turn to them," she said, "when it is *us* what got the power."

"The doctor's coming, Aunt Sarah. I know he is," Rannie Toomer said angrily.

It was less than an hour after she had talked to the mailman that she looked up expecting the doctor and saw old Sarah tramping through the grass on her walking stick. She couldn't pretend she wasn't home with the smoke from her fire climbing out the chimney, so she let her in, making her leave her bag of tricks on the porch.

Old woman old as that ought to forgit trying to cure other people with her nigger magic. Ought to use some of it on herself! she thought. She would not let Sarah lay a finger on Snooks and warned her if she tried anything she would knock her over the head with her own cane.

"He coming, all right," Rannie Toomer said again firmly, looking with prayerful eyes out through the rain.

"Let me tell you, child," the old woman said almost gently, sipping the coffee Rannie Toomer had given her. "*He ain't.*"

She had not been allowed near the boy on the bed, and that had made her angry at first, but now she looked with pity at the young woman who was so afraid her child would die. She felt rejected but at the same time sadly *glad* that the young always grow up hoping. It *did* take a long time to finally realize that you could only depend on those who would come.

"But I done told you," Rannie Toomer was saying in exasperation, "I asked the mailman to bring a doctor for my Snooks!"

Cold wind was shooting all around her from the cracks in the window framing; faded circulars blew inward from the walls.

"He done fetched the doctor," the old woman said, softly stroking her coffee cup. "What you reckon brung me over here in this here flood? It wasn't no desire to see no rainbows, I can tell you."

Rannie Toomer paled.

"*I's* the doctor, child. That there mailman didn't git no further with that message of yours then the road in front of my house. Lucky he got good lungs—deef as I is I had myself a time trying to make out *what* he was yelling."

Rannie began to cry, moaning.

Suddenly the breathing from the bed seemed to drown out the noise of the downpour outside. The baby's pulse seemed to make the whole house shake.

"Here!" she cried, snatching the baby up and handing him to Sarah. "Make him well! Oh, my lawd, make him well!"

"Let's not upset the little fella unnecessarylike," Sarah

said, placing the baby back on the bed. Gently she began to examine him, all the while moaning and humming a thin pagan tune that pushed against the sound of the wind and rain with its own melancholy power. She stripped him of his clothes, poked at his fiberless baby ribs, blew against his chest. Along his tiny flat back she ran her soft old fingers. The child hung on in deep rasping sleep, and his small glazed eyes neither opened fully nor fully closed.

Rannie Toomer swayed over the bed watching the old woman touching the baby. She mourned the time she had wasted waiting for a doctor. Her feeling of guilt was a stone.

"I'll do anything you say do, Aunt Sarah," she cried, mopping at her nose with her dress. "Anything you say, just, please God, make him git better."

Old Sarah dressed the baby again and sat down in front of the fire. She stayed deep in thought for several minutes. Rannie Toomer gazed first into her silent face and then at the baby whose breathing seemed to have eased since Sarah picked him up.

"Do something, quick!" she urged Sarah, beginning to believe in her powers completely. "Do something that'll make him rise up and call his mama!"

"The child's dying," said the old woman bluntly, staking out beforehand some limitation to her skill. "But," she went on, "there might be something still we might try . . ."

"What?" asked Rannie Toomer from her knees. She knelt before the old woman's chair, wringing her hands and crying. She fastened herself to Sarah's chair. How could she have thought anyone else could help her Snooks, she wondered brokenly, when you couldn't even depend on them to come! She had been crazy to trust anyone but the withered old magician before her.

"What can I *do?*" she urged fiercely, blinded by her new faith, driven by the labored breathing from the bed.

"It going to take a strong stomach," said Sarah slowly. "It going to take a mighty strong stomach, and most of you young peoples these days don't have 'em!"

"Snooks got a strong stomach," Rannie Toomer said, peering anxiously into the serious old face.

"It ain't him that's got to have the strong stomach," Sarah said, glancing at the sobbing girl at her feet. "*You* the one got to have the strong stomach . . . he won't know *what* it is he's drinking."

Rannie Toomer began to tremble way down deep in her stomach. It sure was weak, she thought. Trembling like that. But what could she mean her Snooks to drink? Not cat's blood! and not any of the other messes she'd heard Sarah specialized in that would make anybody's stomach turn. What did she mean?

"What is it?" she whispered, bringing her head close to Sarah's knee. Sarah leaned down and put her toothless mouth to her ear.

"The only thing that can save this child now is some good strong horse tea!" she said, keeping her eyes turned toward the bed. "The *only* thing. And if you wants him out of that bed you better make tracks to git some!"

Rannie Toomer took up her wet coat and stepped across the porch to the pasture. The rain fell against her face with the force of small hailstones. She started walking in the direction of the trees where she could see the bulky lightish shapes of cows. Her thin plastic shoes were sucked at by the mud, but she pushed herself forward in a relentless search for the lone gray mare.

All the animals shifted ground and rolled big dark eyes at Rannie Toomer. She made as little noise as she could and leaned herself against a tree to wait.

Thunder rose from the side of the sky like tires of a big truck rumbling over rough dirt road. Then it stood a split second in the middle of the sky before it exploded like a giant firecracker, then rolled away again like an empty keg. Lightning streaked across the sky, setting the air white and charged.

Rannie Toomer stood dripping under her tree hoping not to be struck. She kept her eyes carefully on the behind of the gray mare, who, after nearly an hour had passed, began nonchalantly to spread her muddy knees.

At that moment Rannie Toomer realized that she had brought nothing to catch the precious tea in. Lightning struck something not far off and caused a cracking and groaning in the woods that frightened the animals away from their shelter. Rannie Toomer slipped down in the mud trying to take off one of her plastic shoes, and the gray mare, trickling some, broke for a clump of cedars yards away.

Rannie Toomer was close enough to the mare to catch the tea if she could keep up with her while she ran. So, alternately holding her breath and gasping for air, she started after her. Mud from her fall clung to her elbows and streaked her frizzy hair. Slipping and sliding in the mud she raced after the big mare, holding out, as if for alms, her plastic shoe.

In the house Sarah sat, her shawls and sweaters tight around her, rubbing her knees and muttering under her breath. She heard the thunder, saw the lightning that lit up the dingy room, and turned her waiting face to the bed. Hobbling over on stiff legs, she could hear no sound; the frail breathing had stopped with the thunder, not to come again.

Across the mud-washed pasture Rannie Toomer stumbled, holding out her plastic shoe for the gray mare to fill. In spurts and splashes mixed with rainwater she gathered her tea. In parting, the old mare snorted and threw up one big leg, knocking her back into the mud. She rose trembling and crying, holding the shoe, spilling none over the top but realizing a leak, a tiny crack, at her shoe's front. Quickly she stuck her mouth there over the crack, and, ankle deep in the slippery mud of the pasture, and freezing in her shabby wet coat, she ran home to give the good and warm strong horse tea to her baby Snooks.

BLACKBERRY WINTER
by *Robert Penn Warren*

✿

(*To Joseph Warren and Dagmar Beach*)

It was getting into June and past eight o'clock in the morning, but there was a fire—even if it wasn't a big fire, just a fire of chunks—on the hearth of the big stone fireplace in the living room. I was standing on the hearth, almost into the chimney, hunched over the fire, working my bare toes slowly on the warm stone. I relished the heat which made the skin of my bare legs warp and creep and tingle, even as I called to my mother, who was somewhere back in the dining room or kitchen, and said, "But it's June, I don't have to put them on!"

"You put them on if you are going out," she called.

I tried to assess the degree of authority and conviction in the tone, but at that distance it was hard to decide. I tried to analyze the tone, and then I thought what a fool I had been to start out the back door and let her see that I was barefoot. If I had gone out the front door or the side door she would never have known, not till dinner time anyway, and by then the day would have been half gone and I would have been all over the farm to see what the storm had done and down to the creek to see the flood. But it had never crossed my mind that they would try to stop you from going barefoot in June, no matter if there had been a gully-washer and a cold spell.

Nobody had ever tried to stop me in June as long as I could remember, and when you are nine years old, what you remember seems forever; for you remember everything and everything is important and stands big and full and fills up Time and is so solid that you can walk around and around it like a tree and look at it. You are aware that time passes, that there is a movement in time, but that is not what Time is. Time is not a movement, a flowing, a wind then, but is, rather, a kind of climate in which things are, and when a thing happens it begins to live and keeps on living and stands solid in Time like the tree that you can walk around. And if there is a movement, the movement is not Time itself, any more than a breeze is climate, and all the breeze does is to shake a little the leaves on the tree which is alive and solid. When you are nine, you know that there are things that you don't know, but you know that when you know something you know it. You know how a thing has been and you know that you can go barefoot in June. You do not understand that voice from back in the kitchen which says that you cannot go barefoot outdoors and run to see what has happened and rub your feet over the wet shivery grass and make the perfect mark of your foot in the smooth, creamy, red mud and then muse upon it as though you had suddenly come upon that single mark on the glistening auroral beach of the world. You have never seen a beach, but you have read the book and how the footprint was there.

The voice had said what it had said, and I looked savagely at the black stockings and the strong, scuffed brown shoes which I had brought from my closet as far as the hearth rug. I called once more, "But it's June," and waited.

"It's June," the voice replied from far away, "but it's blackberry winter."

I had lifted my head to reply to that, to make one more test of what was in that tone, when I happened to see the man.

The fireplace in the living room was at the end; for the stone chimney was built, as in so many of the farmhouses in Tennessee, at the end of a gable, and there was a window on each side of the chimney. Out of the window on the north side of the fireplace I could see the man. When I saw the man I did not call out what I had intended, but, engrossed by the strangeness of the sight, watched him, still far off, come along the path by the edge of the woods.

What was strange was that there should be a man there at all. That path went along the yard fence, between the fence and the woods which came right down to the yard, and then on back past the chicken runs and on by the woods until it was lost to sight where the woods bulged out and cut off the back field. There the path disappeared into the woods. It led on back, I knew, through the woods and to the swamp, skirted the swamp where the big trees gave way to sycamores and water oaks and willows and tangled cane, and then led on to the river. Nobody ever went back there except people who wanted to gig frogs in the swamp or to fish in the river or to hunt in the woods, and those people, if they didn't have a standing permission from my father, always stopped to ask permission to cross the farm. But the man whom I now saw wasn't, I could tell even at that distance, a sportsman. And what would a sportsman have been doing down there after a storm? Besides, he was coming from the river, and nobody had gone down there that morning. I knew that for a fact, because if anybody had passed, certainly if a stranger had passed, the dogs would have made a racket and would have been out on him. But this man was coming up from the river and had come up through the woods. I suddenly had a vision of him moving up the grassy path in the woods, in the green twilight under the big trees, not making any sound on the path, while now and then, like drops off the eaves, a big drop of water would fall from a leaf or bough and strike a stiff oak leaf lower down with a small, hollow sound like a drop of water hitting tin. That sound, in the silence of the woods, would be very significant.

When you are a boy and stand in the stillness of woods, which can be so still that your heart almost stops beating and makes you want to stand there in the green twilight until you feel your very feet sinking into and clutching the earth like roots and your body breathing slow through its pores like the leaves—when you stand there and wait for the next drop to drop with its small, flat sound to a lower leaf, that sound seems to measure out something, to put an end to something, to begin something, and you cannot wait for it to happen and are afraid it will not happen, and then when it has happened, you are waiting again, almost afraid.

But the man whom I saw coming through the woods in my mind's eye did not pause and wait, growing into the ground and breathing with the enormous, soundless breathing of the leaves. Instead, I saw him moving in the green twilight inside my head as he was moving at that very moment along the path by the edge of the woods, coming toward the house. He was moving steadily, but not fast, with his shoulders hunched a little and his head thrust forward, like a man who has come a long way and has a long way to go. I shut my eyes for a couple of seconds, thinking that when I opened them he would not be there at all. There was no place for him to have come from, and there was no reason for him to come where he was coming, toward our house. But I opened my eyes, and there he was, and he was coming steadily along the side of the woods. He was not yet even with the back chicken yard.

"Mama," I called.

"You put them on," the voice said.

"There's a man coming," I called, "out back."

She did not reply to that, and I guessed that she had gone to the kitchen window to look. She would be looking at the man and wondering who he was and what he wanted, the way you always do in the country, and if I went back there now she would not notice right off whether or not I was barefoot. So I went back to the kitchen.

She was standing by the window. "I don't recognize him," she said, not looking around at me.

"Where could he be coming from?" I asked.

"I don't know," she said.

"What would he be doing down at the river? At night? In the storm?"

She studied the figure out the window, then said, "Oh, I reckon maybe he cut across from the Dunbar place."

That was, I realized, a perfectly rational explanation. He had not been down at the river in the storm, at night. He had come over this morning. You could cut across from the Dunbar place if you didn't mind breaking through a lot of elder and sassafras and blackberry bushes which had about taken over the old cross path, which nobody ever used any more. That satisfied me for a moment, but only for a moment. "Mama," I asked, "what would he be doing over at the Dunbar place last night?"

Then she looked at me, and I knew I had made a mistake, for she was looking at my bare feet. "You haven't got your shoes on," she said.

But I was saved by the dogs. That instant there was a bark which I recognized as Sam, the collie, and then a heavier, churning kind of bark which was Bully, and I saw a streak of white as Bully tore round the corner of the back porch and headed out for the man. Bully was a big, bone-white bull dog, the kind of dog that they used to call a farm bull dog but that you don't see any more, heavy chested and heavy headed, but with pretty long legs. He could take a fence as light as a hound. He had just cleared the white paling fence toward the woods when my mother ran out to the back porch and began calling, "Here you, Bully! Here you!"

Bully stopped in the path, waiting for the man, but he gave a few more of those deep, gargling, savage barks that reminded you of something down a stone-lined well. The red clay mud, I saw, was splashed up over his white chest and looked exciting, like blood.

The man, however, had not stopped walking even when Bully took the fence and started at him. He had kept right on coming. All he had done was to switch a little paper parcel which he carried from the right hand to the left, and then reach into his pants pocket to get something. Then I saw the glitter and knew that he had a knife in his hand, probably the kind of mean knife just made for devilment and nothing else, with a blade as long as the blade of a frog-sticker, which will snap out ready when you press a button in the handle. That knife must have had a button in the handle, or else how could he have had the blade out glittering so quick and with just one hand?

Pulling his knife against the dogs was a funny thing to do, for Bully was a big, powerful brute and fast, and Sam was all right. If those dogs had meant business, they might have knocked him down and ripped him before he got a stroke in. He ought to have picked up a heavy stick, something to take a swipe at them with and something which they could see and respect when they came at him. But he apparently did not know much about dogs. He just held the knife blade close against the right leg, low down, and kept on moving down the path.

Then my mother had called, and Bully had stopped. So the man let the blade of the knife snap back into the handle, and dropped it into his pocket, and kept on coming. Many women would have been afraid with the strange man who they knew had that knife in his pocket. That is, if they were alone in the house with nobody but a nine-year-old boy. And my mother was alone, for my father had gone off, and Dellie, the cook, was down at her cabin because she wasn't feeling well. But my mother wasn't afraid. She wasn't a big woman, but she was clear and brisk about everything she did and looked everybody and everything right in the eye from her own blue eyes in her tanned face. She had been the first woman in the county to ride a horse astride (that was back when she was a girl and long before I was born), and I have seen her snatch up a pump gun and go out and knock a chicken hawk out of the air like a busted skeet when he came over her chicken yard. She was a steady and self-reliant woman, and when I think of her now after all the years she has been dead, I think of her brown hands, not big, but somewhat square for a woman's hands, with square-cut nails. They looked, as a matter of fact, more like a young boy's hands than a grown woman's. But back then it never crossed my mind that she would ever be dead.

She stood on the back porch and watched the man enter the back gate, where the dogs (Bully had leaped back into the yard) were dancing and muttering and giving sidelong glances back to my mother to see if she meant what she had said. The man walked right by the dogs, almost brushing them, and didn't pay them any attention. I could see now that he wore old khaki pants, and a dark wool coat with stripes in it, and a gray felt hat. He had on a gray shirt with blue stripes in it, and no tie. But I could see a tie, blue and reddish, sticking in his side coat-pocket. Everything was wrong about what he wore. He ought to have been wearing blue jeans or overalls, and a straw hat or an old black felt hat, and the coat, granting that he might have been wearing a wool coat and not a jumper, ought not to have had those stripes. Those clothes, despite the fact that they were old enough and dirty enough for any tramp, didn't belong there in our back yard, coming down the path, in Middle Tennessee, miles away from any big town, and even a mile off the pike.

When he got almost to the steps, without having said anything, my mother, very matter-of-factly, said, "Good morning."

"Good morning," he said, and stopped and looked her over. He did not take off his hat, and under the brim you could see the perfectly unmemorable face, which wasn't old and wasn't young, or thick or thin. It was grayish and covered with about three days of stubble. The eyes were a kind of nondescript, muddy hazel, or something like that, rather bloodshot. His teeth, when he opened his mouth, showed yellow and uneven. A couple of them had been knocked out. You knew that they had been knocked out, because there was a scar, not very old, there on the lower lip just beneath the gap.

"Are you hunting work?" my mother asked him.

"Yes," he said—not "yes, mam"—and still did not take off his hat.

"I don't know about my husband, for he isn't here," she said, and didn't mind a bit telling the tramp, or whoever he was, with the mean knife in his pocket, that no man was around, "but I can give you a few things to do. The storm has drowned a lot of my chicks. Three coops of them. You can gather them up and bury them. Bury them deep so the dogs won't get at them. In the woods. And fix the coops the wind blew over. And down yonder beyond that pen by the edge of the woods are some drowned poults. They got out and I couldn't get them in. Even after it started to rain hard. Poults haven't got any sense."

"What are them things—poults?" he demanded, and spat on the brick walk. He rubbed his foot over the spot, and I saw that he wore a black, pointed-toe low shoe, all cracked and broken. It was a crazy kind of shoe to be wearing in the country.

"Oh, they're young turkeys," my mother was saying. "And they haven't got any sense. I oughtn't to try to raise them around here with so many chickens, anyway. They don't thrive near chickens, even in separate pens. And I won't give up my chickens." Then she stopped herself and resumed briskly on the note of business. "When you finish that, you can fix my flower beds. A lot of trash and mud and gravel has washed down. Maybe you can save some of my flowers if you are careful."

"Flowers," the man said, in a low, impersonal voice which seemed to have a wealth of meaning, but a meaning which I could not fathom. As I think back on it, it probably was not pure contempt. Rather, it was a kind of impersonal and distant marveling that he should be on the verge of grubbing in a flower bed. He said the word, and then looked off across the yard.

"Yes, flowers," my mother replied with some asperity, as though she would have nothing said or implied against flowers. "And they were very fine this year." Then she stopped and looked at the man. "Are you hungry?" she demanded.

"Yeah," he said.

"I'll fix you something," she said, "before you get started." She turned to me. "Show him where he can wash up," she commanded, and went into the house.

I took the man to the end of the porch where a pump was and where a couple of wash pans sat on a low shelf for people to use before they went into the house. I stood there while he laid down his little parcel wrapped in newspaper and took off his hat and looked around for a nail to hang it on. He poured the water and plunged his hands into it. They were big hands, and strong looking, but they did not have the creases and the earth-color of the hands of men who work outdoors. But they were dirty, with black dirt ground into the skin and under the nails. After he had washed his hands, he poured another basin of water and washed his face. He dried his face, and with the towel still dangling in his grasp, stepped over to the mirror on the house wall. He rubbed one hand over the stubble on his face. Then he carefully inspected his face, turning first one side and then the other, and stepped back and settled his striped coat down on his shoulders. He had the movements of a man who has just dressed up to go to church or a party—the way he settled his coat and smoothed it and scanned himself in the mirror.

Then he caught my glance on him. He glared at me for an instant out of the bloodshot eyes, then demanded in a low, harsh voice, "What you looking at?"

"Nothing," I managed to say, and stepped back a step from him.

He flung the towel down, crumpled, on the shelf, and went toward the kitchen door and entered without knocking.

My mother said something to him which I could not catch. I started to go in again, then thought about my bare feet, and decided to go back of the chicken yard, where the man would have to come to pick up the dead chicks. I hung around behind the chicken house until he came out.

He moved across the chicken yard with a fastidious, not quite finicking motion, looking down at the curdled mud flecked with bits of chicken-droppings. The mud curled up over the soles of his black shoes. I stood back from him some six feet and watched him pick up the first of the drowned chicks. He held it up by one foot and inspected it.

There is nothing deader looking than a drowned chick. The feet curl in that feeble, empty way which back when I was a boy, even if I was a country boy who did not mind hog-killing or frog-gigging, made me feel hollow in the stomach. Instead of looking plump and fluffy, the body is stringy and limp with the fluff plastered to it, and the neck is long and loose like a little string of rag. And the eyes have that bluish membrane over them which makes you think of a very old man who is sick about to die.

The man stood there and inspected the chick. Then he looked all around as though he didn't know what to do with it.

"There's a great big old basket in the shed," I said, and pointed to the shed attached to the chicken house.

He inspected me as though he had just discovered my presence, and moved toward the shed.

"There's a spade there, too," I added.

He got the basket and began to pick up the other chicks, picking each one up slowly by a foot and then flinging it into the basket with a nasty, snapping motion. Now and then he would look at me out of the blood-shot eyes. Every time he seemed on the verge of saying something, but he did not. Perhaps he was building up to say something to me, but I did not wait that long. His way of looking at me made me so uncomfortable that I left the chicken yard.

Besides, I had just remembered that the creek was in flood, over the bridge, and that people were down there watching it. So I cut across the farm toward the creek. When I got to the big tobacco field I saw that it had not suffered much. The land lay right and not many tobacco plants had washed out of the ground. But I knew that a lot of tobacco round the country had been washed right out. My father had said so at breakfast.

My father was down at the bridge. When I came out of the gap in the osage hedge into the road, I saw him sitting on his mare over the heads of the other men who were standing around, admiring the flood. The creek was big here, even in low water; for only a couple of miles away it ran into the river, and when a real flood came, the red water got over the pike where it dipped down to the bridge, which was an iron bridge, and high over the floor and even the side railings of the bridge. Only the upper iron work would show, with the water boiling and frothing red and white around it. That creek rose so fast and so heavy because a few miles back it came down out of the hills, where the gorges filled up with water in no time when a rain came. The creek ran in a deep bed with limestone bluffs along both sides until it got within three quarters of a mile of the bridge, and when it came out from between those bluffs in flood it was boiling and hissing and steaming like water from a fire hose.

Whenever there was a flood, people from half the county would come down to see the sight. After a gully-washer there would not be any work to do anyway. If it didn't ruin your crop, you couldn't plow and you felt like taking a holiday to celebrate. If it did ruin your crop, there wasn't anything to do except to try to take your mind off the mortgage, if you were rich enough to have a mortgage, and if you couldn't afford a mortgage you needed something to take your mind off how hungry you would be by Christmas. So people would come down to the bridge and look at the flood. It made something different from the run of days.

There would not be much talking after the first few minutes of trying to guess how high the water was this time. The men and kids just stood around, or sat on their horses or mules, as the case might be, or stood up in the wagon beds. They looked at the strangeness of the flood for an hour or two, and then somebody would say that he had better be getting on home to dinner and would start walking down the gray, puddled limestone pike, or would touch heel to his mount and start off. Everybody always knew what it would be like when he got down to the bridge, but people always came. It was like church or a funeral. They always came, that is, if it was summer and the flood unexpected. Nobody ever came down in winter to see high water.

When I came out of the gap in the bodock hedge, I saw the crowd, perhaps fifteen or twenty men and a lot of kids, and saw my father sitting his mare, Nellie Gray. He was a tall, limber man and carried himself well. I was always proud to see him sit a horse, he was so quiet and straight, and when I stepped through the gap of the hedge that morning, the first thing that happened was, I remember, the warm feeling I always had when I saw him up on a horse, just sitting. I did not go toward him, but skirted the crowd on the far side, to get a look at the creek. For one thing, I was not sure what he would say about the fact that I was barefoot. But the first thing I knew, I heard his voice calling, "Seth!"

I went toward him, moving apologetically past the men, who bent their large, red or thin, sallow faces above me. I knew some of the men, and knew their names, but because those I knew were there in a crowd, mixed with the strange faces, they seemed foreign to me, and not friendly. I did not look up at my father until I was almost within touching distance of his heel. Then I looked up and tried to read his face, to see if he was angry about my being barefoot. Before I could decide anything from that impassive, high-boned face, he had leaned over and reached a hand to me. "Grab on," he commanded.

I grabbed on and gave a little jump, and he said, "Up-see-daisy!" and whisked me, light as a feather, up to the pommel of his McClellan saddle.

"You can see better up here," he said, slid back on the cantle a little to make me more comfortable, and then, looking over my head at the swollen, tumbling water, seemed to forget all about me. But his right hand was laid on my side, just above my thigh, to steady me.

I was sitting there as quiet as I could, feeling the faint stir of my father's chest against my shoulders as it rose and fell with his breath, when I saw the cow. At first, looking up the creek, I thought it was just another big piece of driftwood steaming down the creek in the ruck of water, but all at once a pretty good-size boy who had climbed part way up a telephone pole by the pike so that he could see better yelled out, "Golly-damn, look at that-air cow!"

Everybody looked. It was a cow all right, but it might just as well have been driftwood; for it was dead as a chunk, rolling and roiling down the creek, appearing and disappearing, feet up or head up, it didn't matter which.

The cow started up the talk again. Somebody wondered whether it would hit one of the clear places under the top girder of the bridge and get through or whether it would get tangled in the drift and trash that had piled against the upright girders and braces. Somebody remembered how about ten years before so much driftwood had piled up on the bridge that it was knocked off its foundations. Then the cow hit. It hit the edge of the drift against one of the girders, and hung there. For a few seconds it seemed as though it might tear loose, but then we saw that it was really caught. It bobbed and heaved on its side there in a slow, grinding, uneasy fashion. It had a yoke around its neck, the kind made out of a forked limb to keep a jumper behind fence.

"She shore jumped one fence," one of the men said.

And another: "Well, she done jumped her last one, fer a fack."

Then they began to wonder about whose cow it might be. They decided it must belong to Milt Alley. They said that he had a cow that was a jumper, and kept her in a fenced-in piece of ground up the creek. I had never seen Milt Alley, but I knew who he was. He was a squatter and lived up the hills a way, on a shirt-tail patch of set-on-edge land, in a cabin. He was pore white trash. He had lots of children. I had seen the children at school, when they came. They were thin-faced, with straight, sticky-looking, dough-colored hair, and they smelled something like old sour buttermilk, not because they drank so much buttermilk but because that is the sort of smell which children out of those cabins tend to have. The big Alley boy drew dirty pictures and showed them to the little boys at school.

That was Milt Alley's cow. It looked like the kind of cow he would have, a scrawny, old, sway-backed cow, with a yoke around her neck. I wondered if Milt Alley had another cow.

"Poppa," I said, "do you think Milt Alley has got another cow?"

"You say 'Mr. Alley,' " my father said quietly.

"Do you think he has?"

"No telling," my father said.

Then a big gangly boy, about fifteen, who was sitting on a scraggly little old mule with a piece of croker sack thrown across the saw-tooth spine, and who had been staring at the cow, suddenly said to nobody in particular, "Reckin anybody ever et drownt cow?"

He was the kind of boy who might just as well as not have been the son of Milt Alley, with his faded and patched overalls ragged at the bottom of the pants and the mud-stiff brogans hanging off his skinny, bare ankles at the level of the mule's belly. He had said what he did, and then looked embarrassed and sullen when all the eyes swung at him. He hadn't meant to say it, I am pretty sure now. He would have been too proud to say it, just as Milt Alley would have been too proud. He had just been thinking out loud, and the words had popped out.

There was an old man standing there on the pike, an old man with a white beard. "Son," he said to the embarrassed and sullen boy on the mule, "you live long enough and you'll find a man will eat anything when the time comes."

"Time gonna come fer some folks this year," another man said.

"Son," the old man said, "in my time I et things a man don't like to think on. I was a sojer and I rode with Gin'l Forrest, and them things we et when the time come. I tell you. I et meat what got up and run when you taken out yore knife to cut a slice to put on the fire. You had to knock it down with a carbeen butt, it was so active. That-air meat would jump like a bullfrog, it was so full of skippers."

But nobody was listening to the old man. The boy on the mule turned his sullen sharp face from him, dug a heel into the side of the mule and went off up the pike with a motion which made you think that any second you would hear mule bones clashing inside that lank and scrofulous hide.

"Cy Dundee's boy," a man said, and nodded toward the figure going up the pike on the mule.

"Reckin Cy Dundee's young-uns seen times they'd settle fer drownt cow," another man said.

The old man with the beard peered at them both from his weak, slow eyes, first at one and then at the other. "Live long enough," he said, "and a man will settle fer what he kin git."

Then there was silence again, with the people looking at the red, foam-flecked water.

My father lifted the bridle rein in his left hand, and the mare turned and walked around the group and up the pike. We rode on up to our big gate, where my father dismounted to open it and let me myself ride Nellie Gray through. When he got to the lane that led off from the drive about two hundred yards from our house, my father said, "Grab on." I grabbed on, and he let me down to the ground. "I'm going to ride down and look at my corn," he said. "You go on." He took the lane, and I stood there on the drive and watched him ride off. He was wearing cowhide boots and an old hunting coat, and I thought that that made him look very military, like a picture. That and the way he rode.

I did not go to the house. Instead, I went by the vegetable garden and crossed behind the stables, and headed down for Dellie's cabin. I wanted to go down and play with Jebb, who was Dellie's little boy about two years older than I was. Besides, I was cold. I shivered as I walked, and I had gooseflesh. The mud which crawled up between my toes with every step I took was like ice. Dellie would have a fire, but she wouldn't make me put on shoes and stockings.

Dellie's cabin was of logs, with one side, because it was on a slope, set on limestone chunks, with a little porch attached to it, and had a little whitewashed fence around it and a gate with plow-points on a wire to clink when somebody came in, and had two big white oaks in the yard and some flowers and a nice privy in the back with some honeysuckle growing over it. Dellie and Old Jebb, who was Jebb's father and who lived with Dellie and had lived with her for twenty-five years even if they never had got married, were careful to keep everything nice around their cabin. They had the name all over the community for being clean and clever Negroes. Dellie and Jebb were what they used to call "white-folks' niggers." There was a big difference between their cabin and the other two cabins farther down where the other tenants lived. My father kept the other cabins weatherproof, but he couldn't undertake to go down and pick up after the litter they strewed. They didn't take the trouble to have a vegetable patch like Dellie and Jebb or to make preserves from wild plum, and jelly from crab apple the way Dellie did. They were shiftless, and my father was always threatening to get shed of them. But he never did. When they finally left, they just up and left on their own, for no reason, to go and be shiftless somewhere else. Then some more came. But meanwhile they lived down there, Matt Rawson and his family, and Sid Turner and his, and I played with their children all over the farm when they weren't working. But when I wasn't around they were mean sometimes to Little Jebb. That was because the other tenants down there were jealous of Dellie and Jebb.

I was so cold that I ran the last fifty yards to Dellie's

gate. As soon as I had entered the yard, I saw that the storm had been hard on Dellie's flowers. The yard was, as I have said, on a slight slope, and the water running across had gutted the flower beds and washed out all the good black woods-earth which Dellie had brought in. What little grass there was in the yard was plastered sparsely down on the ground, the way the drainage water had left it. It reminded me of the way the fluff was plastered down on the skin of the drowned chicks that the strange man had been picking up, up in my mother's chicken yard.

I took a few steps up the path to the cabin, and then I saw that the drainage water had washed a lot of trash and filth out from under Dellie's house. Up toward the porch, the ground was not clean any more. Old pieces of rag, two or three rusted cans, pieces of rotten rope, some hunks of old dog dung, broken glass, old paper, and all sorts of things like that had washed out from under Dellie's house to foul her clean yard. It looked just as bad as the yards of the other cabins, or worse. It was worse, as a matter of fact, because it was a surprise. I had never thought of all that filth being under Dellie's house. It was not anything against Dellie that the stuff had been under the cabin. Trash will get under any house. But I did not think of that when I saw the foulness which had washed out on the ground which Dellie sometimes used to sweep with a twig broom to make nice and clean.

I picked my way past the filth, being careful not to get my bare feet on it, and mounted to Dellie's door. When I knocked, I heard her voice telling me to come in.

It was dark inside the cabin, after the daylight, but I could make out Dellie piled up in bed under a quilt, and Little Jebb crouched by the hearth, where a low fire simmered. "Howdy," I said to Dellie, "how you feeling?"

Her big eyes, the whites surprising and glaring in the black face, fixed on me as I stood there, but she did not reply. It did not look like Dellie, or act like Dellie, who would grumble and bustle around our kitchen, talking to herself, scolding me or Little Jebb, clanking pans, making all sorts of unnecessary noises and mutterings like an old-fashioned black steam thrasher engine when it has got up an extra head of steam and keeps popping the governor and rumbling and shaking on its wheels. But now Dellie just lay up there on the bed, under the patch-work quilt, and turned the black face, which I scarcely recognized, and the glaring white eyes to me.

"How you feeling?" I repeated.

"I'se sick," the voice said croakingly out of the strange black face which was not attached to Dellie's big, squat body, but stuck out from under a pile of tangled bedclothes. Then the voice added, "Mighty sick."

"I'm sorry," I managed to say.

The eyes remained fixed on me for a moment, then they left me and the head rolled back on the pillow. "Sorry," the voice said, in a flat way which wasn't question or statement of anything. It was just the empty word put into the air with no meaning or expression, to float off like a feather or a puff of smoke, while the big eyes, with the whites like the peeled white of hard-boiled eggs, stared at the ceiling.

"Dellie," I said after a minute, "there's a tramp up at the house. He's got a knife."

She was not listening. She closed her eyes.

I tiptoed over to the hearth where Jebb was and crouched beside him. We began to talk in low voices. I was asking him to get out his train and play train. Old Jebb had put spool wheels on three cigar boxes and put wire links between the boxes to make a train for Jebb. The box that was the locomotive had the top closed and a length of broom stick for a smoke stack. Jebb didn't want to get the train out, but I told him I would go home if he didn't. So he got out the train, and the colored rocks, and fossils of crinoid stems, and other junk he used for the load, and we began to push it around, talking the way we thought trainmen talked, making a chuck-chucking sound under the breath for the noise of the locomotive and now and then uttering low, cautious toots for the whistle. We got so interested in playing train that the toots got louder. Then, before he thought, Jebb gave a good, loud *toot-toot,* blowing for a crossing.

"Come here," the voice said from the bed.

Jebb got up slow from his hands and knees, giving me a sudden, naked, inimical look.

"Come here!" the voice said.

Jebb went to the bed. Dellie propped herself weakly up on one arm, muttering, "Come closer."

Jebb stood closer.

"Last thing I do, I'm gonna do it," Dellie said. "Done tole you to be quiet."

Then she slapped him. It was an awful slap, more awful for the kind of weakness which it came from and brought to focus. I had seen her slap Jebb before, but the slapping had always been the kind of easy slap you would expect from a good-natured, grumbling Negro woman like Dellie. But this was different. It was awful. It was so awful that Jebb didn't make a sound. The tears just popped out and ran down his face, and his breath came sharp, like gasps.

Dellie fell back. "Cain't even be sick," she said to the ceiling. "Git sick and they won't even let you lay. They tromp all over you. Cain't even be sick." Then she closed her eyes.

I went out of the room. I almost ran getting to the door, and I did run across the porch and down the steps and across the yard, not caring whether or not I stepped on the filth which had washed out from under the cabin. I ran almost all the way home. Then I thought about my mother catching me with the bare feet. So I went down to the stables.

I heard a noise in the crib, and opened the door. There was Big Jebb, sitting on an old nail keg, shelling corn into a bushel basket. I went in, pulling the door shut behind me, and crouched on the floor near him. I crouched there for a couple of minutes before either of us spoke, and watched him shelling the corn.

He had very big hands, knotted and grayish at the joints, with calloused palms which seemed to be streaked with rust with the rust coming up between the fingers to show from the back. His hands were so strong and tough that he could take a big ear of corn and rip the grains right off the cob with the palm of his hand, all in one motion, like a machine. "Work long as me," he would say, "and the good Lawd'll give you a hand lak cass-ion won't nuthin' hurt." And his hands did look like cast iron, old cast iron streaked with rust.

He was an old man, up in his seventies, thirty years or more older than Dellie, but he was strong as a bull. He was a squat sort of man, heavy in the shoulders, with remarkably long arms, the kind of build they say the river natives have on the Congo from paddling so much in their boats. He had a round bullet-head, set on powerful shoulders. His skin was very black, and the thin hair on his head was now grizzled like tufts of old cotton batting. He had small eyes and a flat nose, not big, and the kindest and wisest old face in the world, the blunt, sad, wise face of an old animal peering tolerantly out on the goings-on of the merely human creatures before him. He was a good man, and I loved him next to my mother and father. I crouched there on the floor of the crib and watched him shell corn with the rusty cast-iron hands, while he looked down at me out of the little eyes set in the blunt face.

"Dellie says she's might sick," I said.

"Yeah," he said.

"What's she sick from?"

"Woman-mizry," he said.

"What's woman-mizry?"

"Hit comes on 'em," he said. "Hit just comes on 'em when the time comes."

"What is it?"

"Hit is the change," he said. "Hit is the change of life and time."

"What changes?"

"You too young to know."

"Tell me."

"Time come and you find out everything."

I knew that there was no use in asking him any more. When I asked him things and he said that, I always knew that he would not tell me. So I continued to crouch there and watch him. Now that I had sat there a little while, I was cold again.

"What you shiver fer?" he asked me.

"I'm cold. I'm cold because it's blackberry winter," I said.

"Maybe 'tis and maybe 'tain't," he said.

"My mother says it is."

"Ain't sayen Miss Sallie doan know and ain't sayen she do. But folks doan know everything."

"Why isn't it blackberry winter?"

"Too late fer blackberry winter. Blackberries done bloomed."

"She said it was."

"Blackberry winter just a leetle cold spell. Hit come and then hit go away, and hit is growed summer of a sudden lak a gunshot. Ain't no tellen hit will go way this time."

"It's June," I said.

"June," he replied with great contempt. "That what folks say. What June mean? Maybe hit is come cold to stay."

"Why?"

"Cause this-here old yearth is tahrd. Hit is tahrd and ain't gonna perduce. Lawd let hit come rain one time forty days and forty nights, 'cause He wus tahrd of sinful folks. Maybe this-here old yearth say to the Lawd, Lawd, I done plum tahrd, Lawd, lemme rest. And Lawd say, Yearth, you done yore best, you give 'em cawn and you give 'em taters, and all they think on is they gut, and, Yearth, you kin take a rest."

"What will happen?"

"Folks will eat up everything. The yearth won't perduce no more. Folks cut down all the trees and burn 'em cause they cold, and the yearth won't grow no more. I been tellen 'em. I been tellen folks. Sayen, maybe this year, hit is the time. But they doan listen to me, how the yearth is tahrd. Maybe this year they find out."

"Will everything die?"

"Everything and everybody, hit will be so."

"This year?"

"Ain't no tellen. Maybe this year."

"My mother said it is blackberry winter," I said confidently, and got up.

"Ain't sayen nuthin' agin Miss Sallie," he said.

I went to the door of the crib. I was really cold now. Running, I had got up a sweat and now I was worse.

I hung on the door, looking at Jebb, who was shelling corn again.

"There's a tramp came to the house," I said. I had almost forgotten the tramp.

"Yeah."

"He came by the back way. What was he doing down there in the storm?"

"They comes and they goes," he said, "and ain't no tellen."

"He had a mean knife."

"The good ones and the bad ones, they comes and they goes. Storm or sun, light or dark. They is folks and they comes and they goes lak folks."

I hung on the door, shivering.

He studied me a moment, then said, "You git on to the

house. You ketch yore death. Then what yore mammy say?"

I hesitated.

"You git," he said.

When I came to the back yard, I saw that my father was standing by the back porch and the tramp was walking toward him. They began talking before I reached them, but I got there just as my father was saying, "I'm sorry, but I haven't got any work. I got all the hands on the place I need now. I won't need any extra until wheat thrashing."

The stranger made no reply, just looked at my father.

My father took out his leather coin purse, and got out a half-dollar. He held it toward the man. "This is for half a day," he said.

The man looked at the coin, and then at my father, making no motion to take the money. But that was the right amount. A dollar a day was what you paid them back in 1910. And the man hadn't even worked half a day.

Then the man reached out and took the coin. He dropped it into the right side pocket of his coat. Then he said, very slowly and without feeling, "I didn't want to work on your—farm."

He used the word which they would have frailed me to death for using.

I looked at my father's face and it was streaked white under the sunburn. Then he said, "Get off this place. Get off this place or I won't be responsible."

The man dropped his right hand into his pants pocket. It was the pocket where he kept the knife. I was just about to yell to my father about the knife when the hand came back out with nothing in it. The man gave a kind of twisted grin, showing where the teeth had been knocked out above the new scar. I thought that instant how maybe he had tried before to pull a knife on somebody else and had got his teeth knocked out.

So now he just gave that twisted, sickish grin out of the unmemorable, grayish face, and then spat on the brick path. The glob landed just about six inches from the toe of my father's right boot. My father looked down at it, and so did I. I thought that if the glob had hit my father's boot something would have happened. I looked down and saw the bright glob, and on one side of it my father's strong cowhide boots, with the brass eyelets and the leather thongs, heavy boots splashed with good red mud and set solid on the bricks, and on the other side the pointed-toe, broken, black shoes, on which the mud looked so sad and out of place. Then I saw one of the black shoes move a little, just a twitch first, then a real step backward.

The man moved in a quarter circle to the end of the porch, with my father's steady gaze upon him all the while. At the end of the porch, the man reached up to the shelf where the wash pans were to get his little newspaper-wrapped parcel. Then he disappeared around the corner of the house and my father mounted the porch and went into the kitchen without a word.

I followed around the house to see what the man would do. I wasn't afraid of him now, no matter if he did have the knife. When I got around in front, I saw him going out the yard gate and starting up the drive toward the pike. So I ran to catch up with him. He was sixty yards or so up the drive before I caught up.

I did not walk right up even with him at first, but trailed him, the way a kid will, about seven or eight feet behind, now and then running two or three steps in order to hold my place against his longer stride. When I first came up behind him, he turned to give me a look, just a meaningless look, and then fixed his eyes up the drive and kept on walking.

When we had got around the bend in the drive which cut the house from sight, and were going along by the edge of the woods, I decided to come up even with him. I ran a few steps, and was by his side, or almost, but some feet off to the right. I walked along in this position for a while, and he never noticed me. I walked along until we got within sight of the big gate that let on the pike.

Then I said, "Where did you come from?"

He looked at me then with a look which seemed almost surprised that I was there. Then he said, "It ain't none of yore business."

We went on another fifty feet.

Then I said, "Where are you going?"

He stopped, studied me dispassionately for a moment, then suddenly took a step toward me and leaned his face down at me. The lips jerked back, but not in any grin, to show where the teeth were knocked out and to make the scar on the lower lip come white with the tension.

He said, "Stop following me. You don't stop following me and I cut yore throat, you little son-of-a-bitch."

Then he went on to the gate, and up the pike.

That was thirty-five years ago. Since that time my father and mother have died. I was still a boy, but a big boy, when my father got cut on the blade of a mowing machine and died of lockjaw. My mother sold the place and went to town to live with her sister. But she never took hold after my father's death, and she died within three years, right in middle life. My aunt always said, "Sallie just died of a broken heart, she was so devoted." Dellie is dead, too, but she died, I heard, quite a long time after we sold the farm.

As for Little Jebb, he grew up to a mean and ficey Negro. He killed another Negro in a fight and got sent to the penitentiary, where he is yet, the last I heard tell. He probably grew up to be mean and ficey from just being picked on so much by the children of the other tenants, who were jealous of Jebb and Dellie for being thrifty and clever and being white-folks' niggers.

Old Jebb lived forever. I saw him ten years ago and he was about a hundred then, and not looking much different. He was living in town then, on relief—that was back in the Depression—when I went to see him. He said to me, "Too strong to die. When I was a young feller just comen on and seen how things wuz, I prayed the Lawd. I said, Oh, Lawd, gimme strength and meke me strong fer to do and to indure. The Lawd harkened to my prayer. He give me strength. I was in-duren proud fer being strong and me much man. The Lawd give me my prayer and my strength. But now He done gone off and fergot me and left me alone with my strength. A man doan know what to pray fer, and him mortal."

Jebb is probably living yet, as far as I know.

That is what has happened since the morning when the tramp leaned his face down at me and showed his teeth and said: "Stop following me. You don't stop following me and I cut yore throat, you little son-of-a-bitch." That was what he said, for me not to follow him. But I did follow him, all the years.

THE WIDE NET
by *Eudora Welty*

ꕥ

(This story is for John Fraiser Robinson)

1

William Wallace Jamieson's wife Hazel was going to have a baby. But this was October, and it was six months away, and she acted exactly as though it would be tomorrow. When he came in the room she would not speak to him, but would look as straight at nothing as she could, with her eyes glowing. If he only touched her she stuck out her tongue or ran around the table. So one night he went out with two of the boys down the road and stayed out all night. But that was the worst thing yet, because when he came home in the early morning Hazel had vanished. He went through the house not believing his eyes, balancing with both hands out, his yellow cowlick rising on end, and then he turned the kitchen inside out looking for her, but it did no good. Then when he got back to the front room he saw she had left him a little letter in an envelope. That was doing something behind someone's back. He took out the letter, pushed it open, held it out at a distance from his eyes. . . . After one look he was scared to read the exact words, and he crushed the whole thing in his hand instantly, but what it had said was that she would not put up with him after that and was going to the river to drown herself.

"Drown herself. . . . But she's in mortal fear of the water!"

He ran out front, his face red like the red of the picked cotton field he ran over, and down in the road he gave a loud shout for Virgil Thomas, who was just going in his own house, to come out again. He could just see the edge of Virgil, he had almost got in, he had one foot inside the door.

They met half-way between the farms, under the shade-tree.

"Haven't you had enough of the night?" asked Virgil. There they were, their pants all covered with dust and dew, and they had had to carry the third man home flat between them.

"I've lost Hazel, she's vanished, she went to drown herself."

"Why, that ain't like Hazel," said Virgil.

William Wallace reached out and shook him. "You heard me. Don't you know we have to drag the river?"

"Right this minute?"

"You ain't got nothing to do till spring."

"Let me go set foot inside the house and speak to my mother and tell her a story, and I'll come back."

"This will take the wide net," said William Wallace. His eyebrows gathered, and he was talking to himself.

"How come Hazel to go and do that way?" asked Virgil as they started out.

William Wallace said, "I reckon she got lonesome."

"That don't argue—drown herself for getting lonesome. My mother gets lonesome."

"Well," said William Wallace, "it argues for Hazel."

"How long is it now since you and her was married?"

"Why, it's been a year."

"It don't seem that long to me. A year!"

"It was this time last year. It seems longer," said William Wallace, breaking a stick off a tree in surprise. They walked along, kicking at the flowers on the road's edge. "I remember the day I seen her first, and that seems a long time ago. She was coming along the road holding a little frying-size chicken from her grandma, under her arm, and she had it real quiet. I spoke to her with nice manners. We knowed each other's names, being bound to, just didn't know each other to speak to. I says, 'Where are you taking the fryer?' and she says, 'Mind your manners,' and I kept on till after while she says, 'If you want to walk me home, take littler steps.' So I didn't lose time. It was just four miles across the field and full of blackberries, and from the top of the hill there was Dover below, looking sizeable-like and clean, spread out between the two churches like that. When we got down, I says to her, 'What kind of water's in this well?' and she says, 'The best water in the world.' So I drew a bucket and took out a dipper and she drank and I drank. I didn't think it was that remarkable, but I didn't tell her."

"What happened that night?" asked Virgil.

"We ate the chicken," said William Wallace, "and it was tender. Of course that wasn't all they had. The night I was trying their table out, it sure had good things to eat from one end to the other. Her mama and papa sat at the head and foot and we was face to face with each other across it, with I remember a pat of butter between. They had real sweet butter, with a tree drawed down it, elegant-like. Her mama eats like a man. I had brought her a whole hat-ful of berries and she didn't even pass them to her husband. Hazel, she would leap up and take a pitcher of new milk and fill up the glasses. I had heard how they couldn't have a singing at the church without a fight over her."

"Oh, she's a pretty girl, all right," said Virgil. "It's a pity for the ones like her to grow old, and get like their mothers."

"Another thing will be that her mother will get wind of this and come after me," said William Wallace.

"Her mother will eat you alive," said Virgil.

"She's just been watching her chance," said William Wallace. "Why did I think I could stay out all night."

"Just something come over you."

"First it was just a carnival at Carthage, and I had to let them guess my weight . . . and after that . . ."

"It was nice to be sitting on your neck in a ditch singing," prompted Virgil, "in the moonlight. And playing on the harmonica like you can play."

"Even if Hazel did sit home knowing I was drunk, that wouldn't kill her," said William Wallace. "What she knows ain't ever killed her yet. . . . She's smart, too, for a girl," he said.

"She's a lot smarter than her cousins in Beula," said Virgil. "And especially Edna Earle, that never did get to be what you'd call a heavy thinker. Edna Earle could sit and ponder all day on how the little tail of the 'C' got through the 'L' in a Coca-Cola sign."

"Hazel *is* smart," said William Wallace. They walked on. "You ought to see her pantry shelf, it looks like a hundred jars when you open the door. I don't see how she could turn around and jump in the river."

"It's a woman's trick."

"I always behaved before. Till the one night—last night."

"Yes, but the one night," said Virgil. "And she was waiting to take advantage."

"She jumped in the river because she was scared to death of the water and that was to make it worse," he said. "She remembered how I used to have to pick her up and carry her over the oak-log bridge, how she'd shut her eyes and make a dead-weight and hold me round the neck, just for a little creek. I don't see how she brought herself to jump."

"Jumped backwards," said Virgil. "Didn't look."

When they turned off, it was still early in the pink and green fields. The fumes of morning, sweet and bitter, sprang up where they walked. The insects ticked softly, their strength in reserve; butterflies chopped the air, going to the east, and the birds flew carelessly and sang by fits and starts, not the way they did in the evening in sustained and drowsy songs.

"It's a pretty *day* for sure," said William Wallace. "It's a pretty *day* for it."

"I don't see a sign of her ever going along here," said Virgil.

"Well," said William Wallace. "She wouldn't have dropped anything. I never saw a girl to leave less signs of where she's been."

"Not even a plum seed," said Virgil, kicking the grass.

In the grove it was so quiet that once William Wallace gave a jump, as if he could almost hear a sound of himself wondering where she had gone. A descent of energy came down on him in the thick of the woods and he ran at a rabbit and caught it in his hands.

"Rabbit . . . Rabbit . . ." He acted as if he wanted to take it off to himself and hold it up and talk to it. He laid a palm against its pushing heart. "Now . . . There now . . ."

"Let her go, William Wallace, let her go." Virgil, chewing on an elderberry whistle he had just made, stood at his shoulder: "What do you want with a live rabbit?"

William Wallace squatted down and set the rabbit on the ground but held it under his hand. It was a little, old, brown rabbit. It did not try to move. "See there?"

"Let her go."

"She can go if she wants to, but she don't want to."

Gently he lifted his hand. The round eye was shining at him sideways in the green gloom.

"Anybody can freeze a rabbit, that wants to," said Virgil. Suddenly he gave a far-reaching blast on the whistle, and the rabbit went in a streak. "Was you out catching cottontails, or was you out catching your wife?" he said, taking the turn to the open fields. "I come along to keep you on the track."

"Who'll we get, now?" They stood on top of a hill and William Wallace looked critically over the countryside. "Any of the Malones?"

"I was always scared of the Malones," said Virgil. "Too many *of* them."

"This is my day with the net, and they would have to watch out," said William Wallace. "I reckon some Malones, and the Doyles, will be enough. The six Doyles and their dogs, and you and me, and two little nigger boys is enough, with just a few Malones."

"That ought to be enough," said Virgil, "no matter what."

"I'll bring the Malones, and you bring the Doyles," said William Wallace, and they separated at the spring.

When William Wallace came back, with a string of Malones just showing behind him on the hilltop, he found Virgil with the two little Rippen boys waiting behind him, solemn little towheads. As soon as he walked up, Grady, the one in front, lifted his hand to signal silence and caution to his brother Brucie who began panting merrily and untrustworthily behind him.

Brucie bent readily under William Wallace's hand-pat, and gave him a dreamy look out of the tops of his round eyes, which were pure green-and-white like clover tops. William Wallace gave him a nickel. Grady hung his head; his white hair lay in a little tail in the nape of his neck.

"Let's let them come," said Virgil.

"Well, they can come then, but if we keep letting everybody come it is going to be too many," said William Wallace.

"They'll appreciate it, those little-old boys," said Virgil. Brucie held up at arms length a long red thread with a bent pin tied on the end; and a look of helpless and intense interest gathered Grady's face like a drawstring—his eyes, one bright with a sty, shone pleadingly under his white bangs, and he snapped his jaw and tried to speak. . . . "Their papa was drowned in the Pearl River," said Virgil.

There was a shout from the gully.

"Here come all the Malones," cried William Wallace. "I asked four of them would they come, but the rest of the family invited themselves."

"Did you ever see a time when they didn't," said Virgil. "And yonder from the other direction comes the Doyles, still with biscuit crumbs on their cheeks, I bet, now it's nothing to do but eat as their mother said."

"If two little niggers would come along now, or one big nigger," said William Wallace. And the words were hardly out of his mouth when two little Negro boys came along, going somewhere, one behind the other, stepping high and gay in their overalls, as though they waded in honeydew to the waist.

"Come here, boys. What's your names?"

"Sam and Robbie Bell."

"Come along with us, we're going to drag the river."

"You hear that, Robbie Bell?" said Sam.

They smiled.

The Doyles came noiselessly, their dogs made all the fuss. The Malones, eight giants with great long black eyelashes, were already stamping the ground and pawing each other, ready to go. Everybody went up together to see Doc.

Old Doc owned the wide net. He had a house on top of the hill and he sat and looked out from a rocker on the front porch.

"Climb the hill and come in!" he began to intone across the valley. "Harvest's over . . . slipped up on everybody . . . cotton's picked, gone to the gin . . . hay cut . . . molasses made around here. . . . Big explosion's over, supervisors elected, some pleased, some not. . . . We're hearing talk of war!"

When they got closer, he was saying, "Many's been saved at revival, twenty-two last Sunday including a Doyle, ought to counted two. Hope they'll be a blessing to Dover community besides a shining star in Heaven. Now what?" he asked, for they had arrived and stood gathered in front of the steps.

"If nobody is using your wide net, could we use it?" asked William Wallace.

"You just used it a month ago," said Doc. "It ain't your turn."

Virgil jogged William Wallace's arm and cleared his throat. "This time is kind of special," he said. "We got reason to think William Wallace's wife Hazel is in the river, drowned."

"What reason have you got to think she's in the river drowned?" asked Doc. He took out his old pipe. "I'm asking the husband."

"Because she's not in the house," said William Wallace.

"Vanished?" and he knocked out the pipe.

"Plum vanished."

"Of course a thousand things could have happened to her," said Doc, and he lighted the pipe.

"Hand him up the letter, William Wallace," said Virgil. "We can't wait around till Doomsday for the net while Doc sits back thinkin'."

"I tore it up, right at the first," said William Wallace. "But I know it by heart. It said she was going to jump straight in the Pearl River and that I'd be sorry."

"Where do you come in, Virgil?" asked Doc.

"I was in the same place William Wallace sat on his neck in, all night, and done as much as he done, and come home the same time."

"You-all were out cuttin' up, so Lady Hazel has to jump in the river, is that it? Cause and effect? Anybody want to argue with me? Where do these others come in, Doyles, Malones, and what not?"

"Doc is the smartest man around," said William Wallace, turning to the solidly waiting Doyles, "but it sure takes time."

"These are the ones that's collected to drag the river for her," said Virgil.

"Of course I am not going on record to say so soon that *I* think she's drowned," Doc said, blowing out blue smoke.

"Do you think . . ." William Wallace mounted a step, and his hands both went into fists. "Do you think she was *carried off?*"

"Now that's the way to argue, see it from all sides," said Doc promptly. "But who by?"

Some Malone whistled, but not so you could tell which one.

"There's no booger around the Dover section that goes around carrying off young girls that's married," stated Doc.

"She was always scared of the Gypsies." William Wallace turned scarlet. "She'd sure turn her ring around on her finger if she passed one, and look in the other direction so they couldn't see she was pretty and carry her off. They come in the end of summer."

"Yes, there are the Gypsies, kidnappers since the world began. But was it to be you that would pay the grand ransom?" asked Doc. He pointed his finger. They all laughed then at how clever old Doc was and clapped William Wallace on the back. But that turned into a scuffle and they fell to the ground.

"Stop it, or you can't have the net," said Doc. "You're scaring my wife's chickens."

"It's time we was gone," said William Wallace.

The big barking dogs jumped to lean their front paws on the men's chests.

"My advice remains, Let well enough alone," said Doc. "Whatever this mysterious event will turn out to be, it has kept one woman from talking a while. However, Lady Hazel is the prettiest girl in Mississippi, you've never seen a prettier one and you never will. A golden-haired girl." He got to his feet with the nimbleness that was always his surprise, and said, "I'll come along with you."

The path they always followed was the Old Natchez Trace. It took them through the deep woods and led them out down below on the Pearl River, where they could begin dragging it upstream to a point near Dover. They walked in silence around William Wallace, not letting him carry anything, but the net dragged heavily and the buckets were full of clatter in a place so dim and still.

Once they went through a forest of cucumber trees and came up on a high ridge. Grady and Brucie who were running ahead all the way stopped in their tracks; a whistle had blown and far down and far away a long freight train was passing. It seemed like a little festival procession, moving with the slowness of ignorance or a dream, from distance to distance, the tiny pink and gray cars like secret boxes. Grady was counting the cars to himself, as if he could certainly see each one clearly, and Brucie watched his lips, hushed and cautious, the way he would watch a bird drinking. Tears suddenly came to Grady's eyes, but it could only be because a tiny man walked along the top of the train, walking and moving on top of the moving train.

They went down again and soon the smell of the river spread over the woods, cool and secret. Every step they took among the great walls of vines and among the passion-flowers started up a little life, a little flight.

"We're walking along in the changing-time," said Doc. "Any day now the change will come. It's going to turn from hot to cold, and we can kill the hog that's ripe and have fresh meat to eat. Come one of these nights and we can wander down here and tree a nice possum. Old Jack Frost will be pinching things up. Old Mr. Winter will be standing in the door. Hickory tree there will be yellow. Sweet-gum red, hickory yellow, dogwood red, sycamore yellow." He went along rapping the tree trunks with his knuckle. "Magnolia and live-oak never die. Remember that. Persimmons will all get fit to eat, and the nuts will be dropping like rain all through the woods here. And run, little quail, run, for we'll be after you too."

They went on and suddenly the woods opened upon light, and they had reached the river. Everyone stopped, but Doc talked on ahead as though nothing had happened. "Only today," he said, "today, in October sun, it's all gold—sky and tree and water. Everything just before it changes looks to be made of gold."

William Wallace looked down, as though he thought of Hazel with the shining eyes, sitting at home and looking straight before her, like a piece of pure gold, too precious to touch.

Below them the river was glimmering, narrow, soft, and skin-colored, and slowed nearly to stillness. The shining willow trees hung round them. The net that was being drawn out, so old and so long-used, it too looked golden, strung and tied with golden threads.

Standing still on the bank, all of a sudden William Wallace, on whose word they were waiting, spoke up in a voice of surprise. "What is the name of this river?"

They looked at him as if he were crazy not to know the name of the river he had fished in all his life. But a deep frown was on his forehead, as if he were compelled to wonder what people had come to call this river, or to think there was a mystery in the name of a river they all knew so well, the same as if it were some great far torrent of waves that dashed through the mountains somewhere, and almost as if it were a river in some dream, for they could not give him the name of that.

"Everybody knows Pearl River is named the Pearl River," said Doc.

A bird note suddenly bold was like a stone thrown into the water to sound it.

"It's deep here," said Virgil, and jogged William Wallace. "Remember?"

William Wallace stood looking down at the river as if it were still a mystery to him. There under his feet which hung over the bank it was transparent and yellow like an old bottle lying in the sun, filling with light.

Doc clattered all his paraphernalia.

Then all of a sudden all the Malones scattered jumping and tumbling down the bank. They gave their loud shout. Little Brucie started after them, and looked back.

"Do you think she jumped?" Virgil asked William Wallace.

2

Since the net was so wide, when it was all stretched it reached from bank to bank of the Pearl River, and the weights would hold it all the way to the bottom. Jug-like sounds filled the air, splashes lifted in the sun, and the party began to move upstream. The Malones with great groans swam and pulled near the shore, the Doyles swam and pushed from behind with Virgil to tell them how to do it best; Grady and Brucie with his thread and pin trotted along the sandbars hauling buckets and lines. Sam and Robbie Bell, naked and bright, guided the old oarless rowboat that always drifted at the shore, and in it, sitting up tall with his hat on, was Doc—he went along without ever touching water and without ever taking his eyes off the net.

William Wallace himself did everything but most of the time he was out of sight, swimming about under water or diving, and he had nothing to say any more.

The dogs chased up and down, in and out of the water, and in and out of the woods.

"Don't let her get too heavy, boys," Doc intoned regularly, every few minutes, "and she won't let nothing through."

"She won't let nothing through, she won't let nothing through," chanted Sam and Robbie Bell, one at his front and one at his back.

The sandbars were pink or violet drifts ahead. Where the light fell on the river, in a wandering from shore to shore, it was leaf-shaped spangles that trembled softly, while the dark of the river was calm. The willow trees leaned overhead under muscadine vines, and their trailing leaves hung like waterfalls in the morning air. The thing that seemed like silence must have been the endless cry of all the crickets and locusts in the world, rising and falling.

Every time William Wallace took hold of a big eel that slipped the net, the Malones all yelled, "Rassle with him, son!"

"Don't let her get too heavy, boys," said Doc.

"This is hard on catfish," William Wallace said once.

There were big and little fishes, dark and bright, that they caught, good ones and bad ones, the same old fish.

"This is more shoes than I ever saw got together in any store," said Virgil when they emptied the net to the bottom. "Get going!" he shouted in the next breath.

The little Rippens who had stayed ahead in the woods stayed ahead on the river. Brucie, leading them all, made small jumps and hops as he went, sometimes on one foot, sometimes on the other.

The winding river looked old sometimes, when it ran wrinkled and deep under high banks where the roots of trees hung down, and sometimes it seemed to be only a young creek, shining with the colors of wildflowers. Sometimes sandbars in the shapes of fishes lay nose to nose across, without the track of even a bird.

"Here comes some alligators," said Virgil. "Let's let them by."

They drew out on the shady side of the water, and three

big alligators and four middle-sized ones went by, taking their own time.

"Look at their great big old teeth!" called a shrill voice. It was Grady making his only outcry, and the alligators were not showing their teeth at all.

"The better to eat folks with," said Doc from his boat, looking at him severely.

"Doc, you are bound to declare all you know," said Virgil. "Get going!"

When they started off again the first thing they caught in the net was the baby alligator.

"That's just what we wanted!" cried the Malones.

They set the little alligator down on a sandbar and he squatted perfectly still; they could hardly tell when it was he started to move. They watched with set faces his incredible mechanics, while the dogs after one bark stood off in inquisitive humility, until he winked.

"He's ours!" shouted all the Malones. "We're taking him home with us!"

"He ain't nothing but a little-old baby," said William Wallace.

The Malones only scoffed, as if he might be only a baby but he looked like the oldest and worst lizard.

"What are you going to do with him?" asked Virgil.

"Keep him."

"I'd be more careful what I took out of this net," said Doc.

"Tie him up and throw him in the bucket," the Malones were saying to each other, while Doc was saying, "Don't come running to me and ask me what to do when he gets big."

They kept catching more and more fish, as if there was no end in sight.

"Look, a string of lady's beads," said Virgil. "Here, Sam and Robbie Bell."

Sam wore them around his head, with a knot over his forehead and loops around his ears, and Robbie Bell walked behind and stared at them.

In a shadowy place something white flew up. It was a heron, and it went away over the dark treetops. William Wallace followed it with his eyes and Brucie clapped his hands, but Virgil gave a sigh, as if he knew that when you go looking for what is lost, everything is a sign.

An eel slid out of the net.

"Rassle with him, son!" yelled the Malones. They swam like fiends.

"The Malones are in it for the fish," said Virgil.

It was about noon that there was a little rustle on the bank.

"Who is that yonder?" asked Virgil, and he pointed to a little undersized man with short legs and a little straw hat with a band around it, who was following along on the other side of the river.

"Never saw him and don't know his brother," said Doc.

Nobody had ever seen him before.

"Who invited you?" cried Virgil hotly. "Hi . . . !" and he made signs for the little undersized man to look at him, but he would not.

"Looks like a crazy man, from here," said the Malones.

"Just don't pay any attention to him and maybe he'll go away," advised Doc.

But Virgil had already swum across and was up on the other bank. He and the stranger could be seen exchanging a word apiece and then Virgil put out his hand the way he would pat a child and patted the stranger to the ground. The little man got up again just as quickly, lifted his shoulders, turned around, and walked away with his hat tilted over his eyes.

When Virgil came back he said, "Little-old man claimed he was harmless as a baby. I told him to just try horning in on this river and anything in it."

"What did he look like up close?" asked Doc.

"I wasn't studying how he looked," said Virgil. "But I don't like anybody to come looking at me that I am not familiar with." And he shouted, "Get going!"

"Things are moving in too great a rush," said Doc.

Brucie darted ahead and ran looking into all the bushes, lifting up their branches and looking underneath.

"Not one of the Doyles has spoke a word," said Virgil.

"That's because they're not talkers," said Doc.

All day William Wallace kept diving to the bottom. Once he dived down and down into the dark water, where it was so still that nothing stirred, not even a fish, and so dark that it was no longer the muddy world of the upper river but the dark clear world of deepness, and he must have believed this was the deepest place in the whole Pearl

River, and if she was not here she would not be anywhere. He was gone such a long time that the others stared hard at the surface of the water, through which the bubbles came from below. So far down and all alone, had he found Hazel? Had he suspected down there, like some secret, the real, the true trouble that Hazel had fallen into, about which words in a letter could not speak . . . how (who knew?) she had been filled to the brim with that elation that they all remembered, like their own secret, the elation that comes of great hopes and changes, sometimes simply of the harvest time, that comes with a little course of its own like a tune to run in the head, and there was nothing she could do about it—they knew—and so it had turned into this? It could be nothing but the old trouble that William Wallace was finding out, reaching and turning in the gloom of such depths.

"Look down yonder," said Grady softly to Brucie.

He pointed to the surface, where their reflections lay colorless and still side by side. He touched his brother gently as though to impress him.

"That's you and me," he said.

Brucie swayed precariously over the edge, and Grady caught him by the seat of his overalls. Brucie looked, but showed no recognition. Instead, he backed away, and seemed all at once unconcerned and spiritless, and pressed the nickel William Wallace had given him into his palm, rubbing it into his skin. Grady's inflamed eyes rested on the brown water. Without warning he saw something . . . perhaps the image in the river seemed to be his father, the drowned man—with arms open, eyes open, mouth open. . . . Grady stared and blinked, again something wrinkled up his face.

And when William Wallace came up it was in an agony from submersion, which seemed an agony of the blood and of the very heart, so woeful he looked. He was staring and glaring around in astonishment, as if a long time had gone by, away from the pale world where the brown light of the sun and the river and the little party watching him trembled before his eyes.

"What did you bring up?" somebody called—was it Virgil?

One of his hands was holding fast to a little green ribbon of plant, root and all. He was surprised, and let it go.

It was afternoon. The trees spread softly, the clouds hung wet and tinted. A buzzard turned a few slow wheels in the sky, and drifted upwards. The dogs promenaded the banks.

"It's time we ate fish," said Virgil.

On a wide sandbar on which seashells lay they dragged up the haul and built a fire.

Then for a long time among clouds of odors and smoke, all half-naked except Doc, they cooked and ate catfish. They ate until the Malones groaned and all the Doyles stretched out on their faces, though for long after, Sam and Robbie Bell sat up to their own little table on a cypress stump and ate on and on. Then they all were silent and still, and one by one fell asleep.

"There ain't a thing better than fish," muttered William Wallace. He lay stretched on his back in the glimmer and shade of trampled sand. His sunburned forehead and cheeks seemed to glow with fire. His eyelids fell. The shadow of a willow branch dipped and moved over him. "There is nothing in the world as good as . . . fish. The fish of Pearl River." Then slowly he smiled. He was asleep.

But it seemed almost at once that he was leaping up, and one by one up sat the others in their ring and looked at him, for it was impossible to stop and sleep by the river.

"You're feeling as good as you felt last night," said Virgil, setting his head on one side.

"The excursion is the same when you go looking for your sorrow as when you go looking for your joy," said Doc.

But William Wallace answered none of them anything, for he was leaping all over the place and all, over them and the feast and the bones of the feast, trampling the sand, up and down, and doing a dance so crazy that he would die next. He took a big catfish and hooked it to his belt buckle and went up and down so that they all hollered, and the tears of laughter streaming down his cheeks made him put his hand up, and the two days' growth of beard began to jump out, bright red.

But all of a sudden there was an even louder cry, something almost like a cheer, from everybody at once, and all pointed fingers moved from William Wallace to the river. In the center of three light-gold rings across the water was lifted first an old hoary head ("It has whiskers!" a voice cried) and then in an undulation loop after loop and hump after hump of a long dark body, until there were a dozen rings of ripples, one behind the other, stretching all across the river, like a necklace.

"The King of the Snakes!" cried all the Malones at once, in high tenor voices and leaning together.

"The King of the Snakes," intoned old Doc in his profound base

"He looked you in the eye."

William Wallace stared back at the King of the Snakes with all his might.

It was Brucie that darted forward, dangling his little thread with the pin tied to it, going toward the water.

"That's the King of the Snakes!" cried Grady, who always looked after him.

Then the snake went down.

The little boy stopped with one leg in the air, spun around on the other, and sank to the ground.

"Git up," Grady whispered. "It was just the King of the Snakes. He went off whistling. Git up. It wasn't a thing but the King of the Snakes."

Brucie's green eyes opened, his tongue darted out, and he sprang up; his feet were heavy, his head light, and he rose like a bubble coming to the surface.

Then thunder like a stone loosened and rolled down the bank.

They all stood unwilling on the sandbar, holding to the net. In the eastern sky were the familiar castles and the round towers to which they were used, gray, pink, and blue, growing darker and filling with thunder. Lightning flickered in the sun along their thick walls. But in the west the sun shone with such a violence that in an illumination like a long-prolonged glare of lightning the heavens looked black and white; all color left the world, the goldenness of everything was like a memory, and only heat, a kind of glamor and oppression, lay on their heads. The thick heavy trees on the other side of the river were brushed with mile-long streaks of silver, and a wind touched each man on the forehead. At the same time there was a long roll of thunder that began behind them, came up and down mountains and valleys of air, passed over their heads, and left them listening still. With a small, near noise a mockingbird followed it, the little white bars of its body flashing over the willow trees.

"We are here for a storm now," Virgil said. "We will have to stay till it's over."

They retreated a little, and hard drops fell in the leathery leaves at their shoulders and about their heads.

"Magnolia's the loudest tree there is in a storm," said Doc.

Then the light changed the water, until all about them the woods in the rising wind seemed to grow taller and blow inward together and suddenly turn dark. The rain struck heavily. A huge tail seemed to lash through the air and the river broke in a wound of silver. In silence the party crouched and stooped beside the trunk of the great tree, which in the push of the storm rose full of a fragrance and unyielding weight. Where they all stared, past their tree, was another tree, and beyond that another and another, all the way down the bank of the river, all towering and darkened in the storm.

"The outside world is full of endurance," said Doc. "Full of endurance."

Robbie Bell and Sam squatted down low and embraced each other from the start.

"Runs in our family to get struck by lightnin'," said Robbie Bell. "Lightnin' drawed a pitchfork right on our grandpappy's cheek, stayed till he died. Pappy got struck by some bolts of lightnin' and was dead three days, dead as that-there axe."

There was a succession of glares and crashes.

"This'n's goin' to be either me or you," said Sam. "Here come a little bug. If he go to the left, be me, and to the right, be you."

But at the next flare a big tree on the hill seemed to turn into fire before their eyes, every branch, twig, and leaf, and a purple cloud hung over it.

"Did you hear that crack?" asked Robbie Bell. "That were its bones."

"Why do you little niggers talk so much!" said Doc. "Nobody's profiting by this information."

"We always talks this much," said Sam, "but now everybody so quiet, they hears us."

The great tree, split and on fire, fell roaring to earth.

Just at its moment of falling, a tree like it on the opposite bank split wide open and fell in two parts.

"Hope they ain't goin' to be no balls of fire come rollin' over the water and fry all the fishes with they scales on," said Robbie Bell.

The water in the river had turned purple and was filled with sudden currents and whirlpools. The little willow trees bent almost to its surface, bowing one after another down the bank and almost breaking under the storm. A great curtain of wet leaves was borne along before a blast of wind, and every human being was covered.

"Now us got scales," wailed Sam. "Us is the fishes."

"Hush up, little-old colored children," said Virgil. "This isn't the way to act when somebody takes you out to drag a river."

"Poor lady's-ghost, I bet it is scareder than us," said Sam.

"All I hoping is, us don't find her!" screamed Robbie Bell.

William Wallace bent down and knocked their heads together. After that they clung silently in each other's arms, the two black heads resting, with wind-filled cheeks and tight-closed eyes, one upon the other until the storm was over.

"Right over yonder is Dover," said Virgil. "We've come all the way. William Wallace, you have walked on a sharp rock and cut your foot open."

3

In Dover it had rained, and the town looked somehow like new. The wavy heat of late afternoon came down from the watertank and fell over everything like shiny mosquito-netting. At the wide place where the road was paved and patched with tar, it seemed newly embedded with Coca-Cola tops. The old circus posters on the store were nearly gone, only bits, the snowflakes of white horses, clinging to its side. Morning-glory vines started almost visibly to grow over the roofs and cling round the ties of the railroad track, where bluejays lighted on the rails, and umbrella china-berry trees hung heavily over the whole town, dripping intermittently upon the tin roofs.

Each with his counted fish on a string the members of

the river-dragging party walked through the town. They went toward the town well, and there was Hazel's mother's house, but no sign of her yet coming out. They all drank a dipper of the water, and still there was not a soul on the street. Even the bench in front of the store was empty, except for a little corn-shuck doll.

But something told them somebody had come, for after one moment people began to look out of the store and out of the post office. All the bird dogs woke up to see the Doyle dogs and such a large number of men and boys materialize suddenly with such a big catch of fish, and they ran out barking. The Doyle dogs joyously barked back. The bluejays flashed up and screeched above the town, whipping through their tunnels in the chinaberry trees. In the café a nickel clattered inside a music box and a love song began to play. The whole town of Dover began to throb in its wood and tin, like an old tired heart, when the men walked through once more, coming around again and going down the street carrying the fish, so drenched, exhausted, and muddy that no one could help but admire them.

William Wallace walked through the town as though he did not see anybody or hear anything. Yet he carried his great string of fish held high where it could be seen by all. Virgil came next, imitating William Wallace exactly, then the modest Doyles crowded by the Malones, who were holding up their alligator, tossing it in the air, even, like a father tossing his child. Following behind and pointing authoritatively at the ones in front strolled Doc, with Sam and Robbie Bell still chanting in his wake. In and out of the whole little line Grady and Brucie jerked about. Grady, with his head ducked, and stiff as a rod, walked with a springy limp; it made him look forever angry and unapproachable. Under his breath he was whispering, "Sty, sty, git out of my eye, and git on somebody passin' by." He traveled on with narrowed shoulders, and kept his eye unerringly upon his little brother, wary and at the same time proud, as though he held a flying Junebug on a string. Brucie, making a twanging noise with his lips, had shot forth again, and he was darting rapidly everywhere at once, delighted and tantalized, running in circles around William Wallace, pointing to his fish. A frown of pleasure like the print of a bird's foot was stamped between his faint brows, and he trotted in some unknown realm of delight.

"Did you ever see so many fish?" said the people in Dover.

"How much are your fish, mister?"

"Would you sell your fish?"

"Is that all the fish in Pearl River?"

"How much you sell them all for? Everybody's?"

"Three dollars," said William Wallace suddenly, and loud.

The Malones were upon him and shouting, but it was too late.

And just as William Wallace was taking the money in his hand, Hazel's mother walked solidly out of her front door and saw it.

"You can't head her mother off," said Virgil. "Here she comes in full bloom."

But William Wallace turned his back on her, that was all, and on everybody, for that matter, and that was the breaking-up of the party.

Just as the sun went down, Doc climbed his back steps, sat in his chair on the back porch where he sat in the evenings, and lighted his pipe. William Wallace hung out the net and came back and Virgil was waiting for him, so they could say good evening to Doc.

"All in all," said Doc, when they came up, "I've never been on a better river-dragging, or seen better behavior. If it took catching catfish to move the Rock of Gibraltar, I believe this outfit could move it."

"Well, we didn't catch Hazel," said Virgil.

"What did you say?" asked Doc.

"He don't really pay attention," said Virgil. "I said, 'We didn't catch Hazel.' "

"Who says Hazel was to be caught?" asked Doc. "She wasn't in there. Girls don't like the water—remember that. Girls don't just haul off and go jumping in the river to get back at their husbands. They got other ways."

"Didn't you ever think she was in there?" asked William Wallace. "The whole time?"

"Nary once," said Doc.

"He's just smart," said Virgil, putting his hand on William Wallace's arm. "It's only because we didn't find her that he wasn't looking for her."

"I'm beholden to you for the net, anyway," said William Wallace.

"You're welcome to borry it again," said Doc.

On the way home Virgil kept saying, "Calm down, calm down, William Wallace."

"If he wasn't such an old skinny man I'd have wrung his neck for him," said William Wallace. "He had no business coming."

"He's too big for his britches," said Virgil. "Don't nobody know everything. And just because it's his net. Why does it have to be his net?"

"If it wasn't for being polite to old men, I'd have skinned him alive," said William Wallace.

"I guess he don't really know nothing about wives at all, his wife's so deaf," said Virgil.

"He don't know Hazel," said William Wallace. "I'm the only man alive knows Hazel: would she jump in the river or not, and I say she would. She jumped in because I was sitting on the back of my neck in a ditch singing, and that's just what she ought to done. Doc ain't got no right to say one word about it."

"Calm down, calm down, William Wallace," said Virgil.

"If it had been you that talked like that, I'd have broke every bone in your body," said William Wallace. "Just let you talk like that. You're my age and size."

"But I ain't going to talk like that," said Virgil. "What have I done the whole time but keep this river-dragging going straight and running even, without no hitches? You couldn't have drug the river a foot without me."

"What are you talking about! Without who!" cried William Wallace. "This wasn't your river-dragging! It wasn't your wife!" He jumped on Virgil and they began to fight.

"Let me up." Virgil was breathing heavily.

"Say it was my wife. Say it was my river-dragging."

"Yours!" Virgil was on the ground with William Wallace's hand putting dirt in his mouth.

"Say it was my net."

"Your net!"

"Get up then."

They walked along getting their breath, and smelling the honeysuckle in the evening. On a hill William Wallace looked down, and at the same time there went drifting by the sweet sounds of music outdoors. They were having the Sacred Harp Sing on the grounds of an old white church glimmering there at the crossroads, far below. He stared away as if he saw it minutely, as if he could see a lady in white take a flowered cover off the organ, which was set on a little slant in the shade, dust the keys, and start to pump and play. . . . He smiled faintly, as he would at his mother, and at Hazel, and at the singing women in his life, now all one young girl standing up to sing under the trees the oldest and longest ballads there were.

Virgil told him good night and went into his own house and the door shut on him.

When he got to his own house, William Wallace saw to his surprise that it had not rained at all. But there, curved over the roof, was something he had never seen before as long as he could remember, a rainbow at night. In the light of the moon, which had risen again, it looked small and of gauzy material, like a lady's summer dress, a faint veil through which the stars showed.

He went up on the porch and in at the door, and all exhausted he had walked through the front room and through the kitchen when he heard his name called. After a moment, he smiled, as if no matter what he might have hoped for in his wildest heart, it was better than that to hear his name called out in the house. The voice came out of the bedroom.

"What do you want?" he yelled, standing stock-still.

Then she opened the bedroom door with the old complaining creak, and there she stood. She was not changed a bit.

"How do you feel?" he said.

"I feel pretty good. Not too good," Hazel said, looking mysterious.

"I cut my foot," said William Wallace, taking his shoe off so she could see the blood.

"How in the world did you do that?" she cried, with a step back.

"Dragging the river. But it don't hurt any longer."

"You ought to have been more careful," she said. "Supper's ready and I wondered if you would ever come home, or if it would be last night all over again. Go and make yourself fit to be seen," she said, and ran away from him.

After supper they sat on the front steps a while.

"Where were you this morning when I came in?" asked William Wallace when they were ready to go in the house.

"I was hiding," she said. "I was still writing on the letter. And then you tore it up."

"Did you watch me when I was reading it?"

"Yes, and you could have put out your hand and touched me, I was so close."

But he bit his lip, and gave her a little tap and slap, and then turned her up and spanked her.

"Do you think you will do it again?" he asked.

"I'll tell my mother on you for this!"

"Will you do it again?"

"No!" she cried.

"Then pick yourself up off my knee."

It was just as if he had chased her and captured her again. She lay smiling in the crook of his arm. It was the same as any other chase in the end.

"I will do it again if I get ready," she said. "Next time will be different, too."

Then she was ready to go in, and rose up and looked out from the top step, out across their yard where the China tree was and beyond, into the dark fields where the lightning-bugs flickered away. He climbed to his feet too and stood beside her, with the frown on his face, trying to look where she looked. And after a few minutes she took him by the hand and led him into the house, smiling as if she were smiling down on him.

THE YELLOW BIRD
by *Tennessee Williams*

Alma was the daughter of a Protestant minister named Increase Tutwiler, the last of a string of Increase Tutwilers who had occupied pulpits since the Reformation came to England. The first American progenitor had settled in Salem, and around him and his wife, Goody Tutwiler, née Woodson, had revolved one of the most sensational of the Salem witch-trials. Goody Tutwiler was cried out against by the Circle Girls, a group of hysterical young ladies of Salem who were thrown into fits whenever a witch came near them. They claimed that Goody Tutwiler afflicted them with pins and needles and made them sign their names in the devil's book quite against their wishes. Also one of them declared that Goody Tutwiler had appeared to them with a yellow bird which she called by the name of Bobo and which served as interlocutor between herself and the devil to whom she was sworn. The Reverend Tutwiler was so impressed by these accusations, as well as by the fits of the Circle Girls when his wife entered their presence in court, that he himself finally cried out against her and testified that the yellow bird named Bobo had flown into his church one Sabbath and, visible only to himself, had perched on his pulpit and whispered indecent things to him about several younger women in the congregation. Goody Tutwiler was accordingly condemned and hanged, but this was by no means the last of the yellow bird named Bobo. It had manifested itself in one form or another, and its continual nagging had left the Puritan spirit fiercely aglow, from Salem to Hobbs, Arkansas, where the Increase Tutwiler of this story was preaching.

Increase Tutwiler was a long-winded preacher. His wife sat in the front pew of the church with a palm-leaf fan which she would agitate violently when her husband had preached too long for anybody's endurance. But it was not always easy to catch his attention, and Alma, the daughter, would finally have to break into the offertory hymn in order to turn him off. Alma played the organ, the primitive kind of organ that had to be supplied with air by an old Negro operating a pump in a stifling cubicle behind the wall. On one occasion the old Negro had fallen asleep, and no amount of discreet rapping availed to wake him up. The minister's wife had plucked nervously at the strings of her palm-leaf fan till it began to fall to pieces, but without the organ to stop him, Increase Tutwiler ranted on and on, exceeding the two-hour mark. It was by no means a cool summer day, and the interior of the church was yellow oak, a material that made you feel as if you were sitting in the middle of a fried egg.

At last Alma despaired of reviving the Negro and got to her feet. "Papa," she said. But the old man didn't look at her. "Papa," she repeated, but he went right on. The whole congregation was whispering and murmuring. One stout old lady seemed to have collapsed, because two people were fanning her from either side and holding a small bottle to her nostrils. Alma and her mother exchanged desperate glances. The mother half got out of her seat. Alma gave her a signal to remain seated. She picked up the hymnbook and brought it down with such terrific force on the bench that dust and fiber spurted in all directions. The minister stopped short. He turned a dazed look in Alma's direction. "Papa," she said, "it's fifteen minutes after twelve and Henry's asleep and these folks have got to get to dinner, so for the love of God, quit preaching."

Now Alma had the reputation of being a very quiet and shy girl, so this speech was nothing short of sensational. The news of it spread throughout the Delta, for Mr. Tutwiler's sermons had achieved a sort of unhappy fame for many miles about. Perhaps Alma was somewhat pleased and impressed by this little celebration that she was accordingly given on people's tongues the next few months, for she was never quite the same shy girl afterwards. She had not had very much fun out of being a minister's daughter. The boys had steered clear of the rectory, because when they got around there they were exposed to Mr. Tutwiler's inquisitions. A boy and Alma would have no chance to talk in the Tutwiler porch or parlor while the old man was around. He was obsessed with the idea that Alma might get to smoking, which he thought was the initial and, once taken, irretrievable step toward perdition. "If Alma gets to smoking," he told his wife, "I'm going to denounce her from the pulpit and put her out of the house." Every time he said this Alma's mother would scream and go into a faint, as she knew that every girl who is driven out of her father's house goes right into a good-time house. She was unable to conceive of anything in between.

Now Alma was pushing thirty and still unmarried, but about six months after the episode in the church, things really started popping around the minister's house. Alma had gotten to smoking in the attic, and her mother knew about it. Mrs. Tutwiler's hair had been turning slowly gray for a number of years, but after Alma took to smoking in the attic, it turned snow-white almost overnight. Mrs. Tutwiler concealed the terrible knowledge that Alma was smoking in the attic from her husband, and she didn't even dare raise her voice to Alma about it because the old man might hear. All she could do was stuff the attic door around with newspapers. Alma *would* smoke; she claimed it had gotten a hold on her and she couldn't stop it now. At first she only smoked twice a day, but she began to smoke more as the habit grew on her. Several times the old man had said he smelled smoke in the house, but so far he hadn't dreamed that his daughter would dare take up smoking. But his wife knew he would soon find out about it, and Alma knew he would too. The question was whether Alma cared. Once she came downstairs with a cigarette in her mouth, smoking it, and her mother barely snatched it out of her mouth before the old man saw her. Mrs. Tutwiler went into a faint, but Alma paid no attention to her, just went on out of the house, lit another cigarette, and walked down the street to the drugstore.

It was unavoidable that sooner or later people who had seen Alma smoking outside the house, which she now began to do pretty regularly, would carry the news back to the preacher. There were plenty of old women who were ready and able to do it. They had seen her smoking in the White Star drugstore while she was having her afternoon Coke, puffing on the cigarette between sips of the Coke and carrying on a conversation with the soda-jerk, just like anyone from that set of notorious high school girls that the whole town had been talking about for several generations. So one day the minister came into his wife's bedroom and said to her, "I have been told that Alma has taken to smoking."

His manner was deceptively calm. The wife sensed that this was not an occasion for her to go into a faint, so she didn't. She had to keep her wits about her this time—that is, if she had any left after all she had been through with Alma's smoking.

"Well," she said, "I don't know what to do about it. It's true."

"You know what I've always said," her husband replied. "If Alma gets to smoking, out she goes."

"Do you want her to go into a good-time house?" inquired Mrs. Tutwiler.

"If that's where she's going, she can go," said the preacher, "but not until I've given her something that she'll always remember."

He was waiting for Alma when she came in from her afternoon smoke and Coke at the White Star drugstore. Soon as she walked into the door he gave her a good, hard slap, with the palm of his hand on her mouth, so that her front teeth bit into her lip and it started bleeding. Alma didn't blink an eye, she just drew back her right arm and returned the slap with good measure. She had bought a bottle of something at the drugstore, and while her father stood there, stupefied, watching her, she went upstairs with the mysterious bottle in brown wrapping paper. And when she came back down they saw that she had peroxided her hair and put on lipstick. Alma's mother screamed and went into one of her faints, because it was evident to her that Alma was going right over to one of the good-time houses on Front Street. But all the iron had gone out of the minister's character then. He clung to Alma's arm. He begged and pleaded with her not to go there. Alma lit up a cigarette right there in front of him and said, "Listen here, I'm going to do as I please around here from now on, and I don't want any more interference from you!"

Before this conversation was finished the mother came out of her faint. It was the worst faint she had ever gone into, particularly since nobody had bothered to pick her up off the floor. "Alma," she said weakly, "Alma!" Then she said her husband's name several times, but neither of them paid any attention to her, so she got up without any assistance and began to take a part in the conversation. "Alma," she said, "you can't go out of this house until that hair of yours grows in dark again."

"That's what you think," said Alma.

She put the cigarette back in her mouth and went out the screen door, puffing and drawing on it and breathing smoke out of her nostrils all the way down the front walk and down to the White Star drugstore, where she had another Coke and resumed her conversation with the boy at the soda-counter. His name was Stuff—that was what people called him—and it was he who had suggested to Alma that she would look good as a blonde. He was ten years younger than Alma but he had more girls than pimples.

It was astonishing the way Alma came up fast on the outside in Stuff's affections. With the new blond hair you could hardly call her a dark horse, but she was certainly running away with the field. In two weeks' time after the peroxide she was going steady with Stuff; for Alma was smart enough to know there were plenty of good times to be had outside the good-time houses on Front Street, and Stuff knew that, too. Stuff was not to be in sole possession of her heart. There were other contenders, and Alma could choose among them. She started going out nights as rapidly as she had taken up smoking. She stole the keys to her father's Ford sedan and drove to such near-by towns as Lakewater, Sunset, and Lyons. She picked up men on the highway and went out "juking" with them, making the rounds of the highway drinking places; never got home till three or four in the morning. It was impossible to see how one human constitution could stand up under the strain of so much running around to night places, but Alma had all the vigor that comes from generations of firm believers. It could have gone into anything and made a sensation. Well, that's how it was. There was no stopping her once she got started.

The home situation was indescribably bad. It was generally stated that Alma's mother had suffered a collapse and that her father was spending all his time praying, and there was some degree of truth in both reports. Very little sympathy for Alma came from the older residents of the community. Certain little perfunctory steps were taken to curb the girl's behavior. The father got the car-key out of her pocket one night when she came in drunk and fell asleep on the sofa, but Alma had already had some duplicates of it made. He locked the garage one night. Alma climbed through the window and drove the car straight through the closed door.

"She's lost her mind," said the mother. "It's that hair-bleaching that's done it. It went right through her scalp and now it's affecting her brain."

They sat up all that night waiting for her, but she didn't come home. She had run her course in that town, and the next thing they heard from Alma was a card from New Orleans. She had got all the way down there. "Don't sit up," she wrote. "I'm gone for good. I'm never coming back."

Six years later Alma was a character in the old French Quarter of New Orleans. She hung out mostly on "Monkey-Wrench Corner" and picked up men around there. It was certainly not necessary to go into a good-time house to have a good time in the Quarter, and it hadn't taken her long to find that out. It might have seemed to some people that Alma was living a wasteful and profligate existence, but if the penalty for it was death, well, she was a long time dying. In fact she seemed to prosper on her new life. It apparently did not have a dissipating effect on her. She took pretty good care of herself so that it wouldn't, eating well and drinking just enough to be happy. Her face had a bright and innocent look in the mornings, and even when she was alone in her room it sometimes seemed as if she weren't alone—as if someone were with her, a disembodied someone, perhaps a remote ancestor of liberal tendencies who had been displeased by the channel his blood had taken till Alma kicked over the traces and jumped right back to the plumed-hat cavaliers.

Of course, her parents never came near her again, but once they dispatched as emissary a young married woman they trusted.

The woman called on Alma in her miserable little furnished room—or crib, as it actually was—on the shabbiest block of Bourbon Street in the Quarter.

"How do you live?" asked the woman.

"What?" said Alma, innocently.

"I mean how do you get along?"

"Oh," said Alma, "people give me things."

"You mean you accept gifts from them?"

"Yes, on a give-and-take basis," Alma told her.

The woman looked around her. The bed was unmade and looked as if it had been that way for weeks. The two-burner stove was loaded with unwashed pots in some of which grew a pale fungus. Tickets from pawnshops were stuck round the edge of the mirror along with many, many photographs of young men, some splitting their faces with enormous grins while others stared softly at space.

"These photographs," said the woman, "are these—are these your friends?"

"Yes," said Alma, with a happy smile. "Friends and acquaintances, strangers that pass in the night!"

"Well, I'm not going to mention this to your father!"

"Oh, go on and tell the old stick-in-the-mud," said Alma. She lit a cigarette and blew the smoke at her caller.

The woman looked around once more and noticed that the doors of the big armoire hung open on white summer dresses that were covered with grass stains.

"You go on picnics?" she asked.

"Yes, but not church ones," said Alma.

The woman tried to think of something more to ask but she was not gifted with an agile mind, and Alma's attitude was not encouraging.

"Well," she said finally, "I had better be going."

"Hurry back," said Alma, without getting up or looking in the woman's direction.

Shortly thereafter Alma discovered that she was becoming a mother.

She bore a child, a male one, and not knowing who was the father, she named it John after the lover that she had liked best, a man now dead. The son was perfect, very blond and glowing, a lusty infant.

Now from this point on the story takes a strange turn that may be highly disagreeable to some readers, if any still hoped it was going to avoid the fantastic.

This child of Alma's would have been hanged in Salem. If the Circle Girls had not cried out against Alma (which they certainly would have done), they would have gone into fifty screaming fits over Alma's boy.

He was thoroughly bewitched. At half-past six every morning he crawled out of the house and late in the evening he returned with fists full of gold and jewels that smelled of the sea.

Alma grew very rich indeed. She and the child went North. The child grew up in a perfectly normal way to youth and to young manhood, and then he no longer crawled out and brought back riches. In fact that old habit seemed to have slipped his mind somehow, and no mention was ever made of it. Though he and his mother did not pay much attention to each other, there was a great and silent respect between them while each went about his business.

When Alma's time came to die, she lay on the bed and wished her son would come home, for lately the son had gone on a long sea-voyage for unexplained reasons. And while she was waiting, while she lay there dying, the bed began to rock like a ship on the ocean, and all at once not John the Second, but John the First appeared, like Neptune out of the ocean. He bore a cornucopia that was dripping with seaweed and his bare chest and legs had acquired a greenish patina such as a bronze statue comes to be covered with. Over the bed he emptied his horn of plenty which had been stuffed with treasure from wrecked Spanish galleons: rubies, emeralds, diamonds, rings, and necklaces of rare gold, and great loops of pearls with the slime of the sea clinging to them.

"Some people," he said, "don't even die empty-handed."

And off he went, and Alma went off with him.

The fortune was left to The Home For Reckless Spenders. And in due time the son, the sailor, came home, and a monument was put up. It was a curious thing, this monument. It showed three figures of indeterminate gender astride a leaping dolphin. One bore a crucifix, one a cornucopia, and one a Grecian lyre. On the side of the plunging fish, the arrogant dolphin, was a name inscribed, the odd name of Bobo, which was the name of the small yellow bird that the devil and Goody Tutwiler had used as a go-between in their machinations.

CONTRIBUTORS

James Agee (1909–1955)
James Agee was born in Knoxville, Tennessee, in 1909. After graduating from Harvard in 1932, he began a writing career of impressive diversity. His literary documentary, *Let Us Now Praise Famous Men,* published in 1941 with the brilliant photographs of Walker Evans, remains a model of its genre, and is still the most complete portrait of Southern poverty available. In 1951, he published *The Morning Watch,* a novella that Anthony Burgess calls "one of the best books about childhood ever written." An enthusiastic cinema addict, Agee worked in Hollywood as a scriptwriter; his most celebrated script is probably *The African Queen.* He also published a large body of film criticism now available in a two-volume work, *Agee on Film,* and praised by W. H. Auden as among the few writings on film with permanent value. Agee died in New York in 1955 at age forty-five. His only novel, *A Death in the Family,* was published posthumously and awarded a Pulitzer Prize in 1958.

John Barth (1930–   )
John Barth was born in Cambridge, Maryland, in 1930, the grandson of 19th-century German immigrants. He studied briefly at the Juilliard School of Music in New York and subsequently enrolled at Johns Hopkins University where, under the influence of the *Thousand and One Nights,* he began writing short stories. His first novel, *The Floating Opera,* was published in 1956, followed by *The End of the Road* in 1958, *The Sot-Weed Factor* in 1960, *Giles Goat-Boy: or, The Revised New Syllabus* in 1966, and *Letters* in 1979. His collection of interrelated short stories, or "fictions," *Lost in the Funhouse,* appeared in 1968. Barth's second collection of stories, *Chimera,* in which he continued his work on the relations among language, myth, and reality, won the National Book Award in 1972. In 1982, *The Literature of Exhaustion* and *The Literature of Replenishment* and *Sabbatical: A Romance* were published. *The Friday Book: Essays and Other Nonfiction* was published in 1984. Mr. Barth is currently the Alumni Centennial Professor of English and Creative Writing at Johns Hopkins University.

Doris Betts (1932-)
Doris Betts was born in Statesville, North Carolina, in 1932. She attended the University of North Carolina at Chapel Hill and subsequently worked as journalist and editor on various North Carolina newspapers. She has published three collections of short stories: *The Gentle Insurrection* in 1954, *The Astronomer and Other Stories* in 1965, *Beasts of the Southern Wild and Other Stories* in 1973, and is working on another collection. Her novels include *Tall Houses in Winter* (1957), *The Scarlet Thread* (1964), *The River to Pickle Beach* (1972), and *Heading West* (1981). Doris Betts is Alumni Distinguished Professor of English at the University of North Carolina at Chapel Hill.

Truman Capote (1924-1984)
Truman Capote was born in New Orleans, Louisiana, in 1924. Though he lived much of his adult life outside the South, his early short stories owe much to his childhood in Louisiana and Alabama. His collections of stories include *A Tree of Night and Other Stories* (1949) and *Breakfast at Tiffany's: A Short Novel and Three Stories* (1958). He wrote two novels, *Other Voices, Other Rooms* (1948) and *The Grass Harp* (1951); three plays, *The Grass Harp* (1952), *House of Flowers* (1954), and *The Thanksgiving Visitor* (1968); and the well-known literary documentary, *In Cold Blood: A True Account of a Multiple Murder and Its Consequences* (1966). His final work, *Music for Chameleons,* was published in 1980. Mr. Capote died in Los Angeles, California, in 1984 at the age of 59.

Fred Chappell (1936-)
Fred Chappell was born in Canton, North Carolina, in 1936. He graduated from Duke University in 1961 and since 1964 has taught writing and literature at the University of North Carolina at Greensboro. Best known as a poet, he has published several novels and two collections of short stories, *Moments of Light* (1980) and *I Am One of You Forever* (1985). His volumes of poetry include *The World Between the Eyes* (1971), *River: A Poem* (1975), *Bloodfire* (1978), and, most recently, *Castle Tzingal* (1985).

Andre Dubus (1936-)
Andre Dubus was born in Lake Charles, Louisiana, in 1936. He served five years in peacetime Marine Corps before entering the Writers' Workshop at the University of Iowa. His stories have appeared in *The New Yorker, The North American Review, Carleton Miscellany, The Sewanee Review,* and twice in *The Best American Short Stories.* In 1967, he published a novel, *The Lieutenant.* Since then he has published four collections of stories: *Separate Flights* (1975), *Adultery and Other Choices* (1978), *Finding a Girl in America* (1980), and *The Times Are Never So Bad* (1983). In 1984, he published a collection of four novellas, *We*

Don't Live Here Anymore, in addition to a limited edition of *Land Where My Fathers Died* and a novella entitled *Voices from the Moon.* In 1985, Mr. Dubus served as writer-in-residence at the University of Alabama at Tuscaloosa.

William Faulkner (1897–1962)

William Faulkner is generally regarded as one of America's foremost modern novelists. In his own lifetime he moved from relative obscurity to international prominence, and in 1949 was awarded the Nobel Prize for Literature. He was born in New Albany, Mississippi, in 1897, and lived most of his life in nearby Oxford, Mississippi. There he attended high school and the University of Mississippi, although he was never graduated from either. During World War I, he enlisted with the British Royal Air Force but saw no action. While living in New Orleans in the 1920s, he met Sherwood Anderson who encouraged him to write and helped him find a publisher. Faulkner's first two novels, *Soldiers' Pay* (1926) and *Mosquitoes* (1927), show an early mastery of narrative style, but it was with his third novel, *Sartoris* (1929), that he began to create his mythical Southern world, Yoknapatawpha County, and to stamp his work with a voice and subject all his own. Among his many works, the following stand out as vital classics of American prose fiction: *The Sound and the Fury* (1929), *As I Lay Dying* (1930), *Light in August* (1932), *Absalom, Absalom!* (1936), *The Hamlet* (1940), and *Go Down, Moses* (1942). All his life Faulkner was a teller of tales, and many of his longer works are organized around short stories. His own collection of stories, which he selected and arranged himself, was published in 1950 as *Collected Stories.* A. Walton Litz, editor of *Major American Short Stories,* calls the *Collected Stories* "one of the richest volumes in the history of the American short story." Toward the end of his life, Faulkner was writer-in-residence at the University of Virginia. He died July 6, 1962. Garland Publishing Company has announced that it will publish the works of Faulkner in a facsimile edition of 44 volumes.

Ernest Gaines (1933–   )

Ernest J. Gaines was born in Oscar, Louisiana, in 1933. He attended San Francisco State College and Stanford University, and from 1953 to 1955 served in the U.S. Army. Though much of his adult life has been spent outside the South, Gaines writes mainly about black Americans living in the rural Louisiana where he was raised. He is the author of five novels: *Catherine Carmier* (1964), *Of Love and Dust* (1967), *The Autobiography of Miss Jane Pittman* (1971), *In My Father's House* (1978), and *A Gathering of Old Men* (1983). His collection of short stories, *Bloodline,* was published in 1968. Mr. Gaines teaches at the University of Southern Louisiana in Lafayette, where he holds a professorship in creative writing.

George Garrett (1929-)
George Garrett was born in Orlando, Florida, in 1929. After graduating from Princeton University in 1952 he has led an active career as both writer and teacher, and has taught at the University of Virginia, Hollins College, the University of South Carolina, and Princeton University. He has written in many genres, and his collected works include short stories, volumes of poetry, novels, and screenplays. He is probably best known for two highly praised historical novels, *Death of the Fox* (1971) and *The Succession* (1983). The *Collected Poems of George Garrett* were published in 1984. His collected stories have recently been published under the title *An Evening Performance* (1985).

Ellen Gilchrist (1935-)
Ellen Gilchrist was born in Vicksburg, Mississippi, in 1935. She received a B.A. in philosophy from Millsaps College and did graduate work at the University of Arkansas. She has published a book of poems, *The Land Surveyor's Daughter* (1979), a novel, *The Annunciation* (1983), and two collections of stories, *In the Land of Dreamy Dreams* (1981) and *Victory Over Japan* (1984).

Caroline Gordon (1895–1981)
Caroline Gordon was born in Trenton, Kentucky, in 1895. From 1924 to 1959, she was married to Allen Tate, poet and Southern man of letters. Between 1920 and 1924, she was a journalist in Chattanooga, Tennessee. She spent much of her career in academic life as a professor and writer-in-residence at various universities throughout the United States. She is the author of two collections of short stories, *The Forest of the South* (1945) and *Old Red and Other Stories* (1963). Her novels include *Penhally* (1931), *The Garden of Adonis* (1937), *Green Centuries* (1941), *The Women on the Porch* (1944), *The Strange Children* (1951), and *The Malefactors* (1956). She also wrote an impressive body of literary criticism, and published, with Allen Tate, a well-known anthology of the short story, *The House of Fiction* (1950). Robert Penn Warren in his introduction to *The Collected Stories of Caroline Gordon* (1981) said that Caroline Gordon "belongs in that group of Southern women who have been enriching our literature uniquely in this century—all so different in spirit, attitude, and method, but all with the rare gift of the teller of the tale." Miss Gordon died in Chiapas, Mexico, in 1981.

William Goyen (1915–1983)
William Goyen was born in Trinity, Texas, in 1915 and was educated at Rice University. He worked as an editor and a professor, and spent five years in the U.S. Navy. Author of three novels, he is best known for his short stories. Many of them are now available in *The Collected Stories,* published in 1972. His novels are *The House of Breath* (1950), *In a Farther Country* (1955), *The Fair Sister* (1963), *Come, the Restorer* (1974), and *Arcadio* (1982). *Had*

I a Hundred Mouths: New and Selected Stories, 1974-83 appeared in 1985 with an introduction by Joyce Carol Oates.

Barry Hannah (1942-)
Barry Hannah was born in Mississippi in 1942. He graduated from Mississippi College and received an M.A. and an M.F.A. from the University of Arkansas. He was awarded the William Faulkner Prize for his first novel, *Geronimo Rex,* published in 1972. A second novel, *Nightwatchmen* (1973), was followed by *Airships* (1978), a highly praised collection of short stories, and *Ray* (1980), a third novel. His achievement in fiction was honored by the American Academy of Arts and Letters. In 1983, Mr. Hannah published two works: *The Tennis Handsome: A Novel* and *Power and Light,* a novella for the screen from an idea by Robert Altman. His most recent collection of eight stories is *Captain Maximus* (1985).

Madison Jones (1925-)
Madison Jones was born in Nashville, Tennessee, in 1925. He attended Vanderbilt University and the University of Florida. He is presently writer-in-residence at Auburn University in Alabama. His short stories have appeared in *The Best American Short Stories, Perspective,* and *The Sewanee Review.* His many novels include *The Innocent* (1957), *Forest of the Night* (1960), *A Buried Land* (1963), *An Exile* (1970), *A Cry of Absence* (1971), *Passage Through Gehenna* (1978), and *Season of the Strangler* (1982). He has held Guggenheim, Rockefeller, and *Sewanee Review* fellowships. Of *An Exile,* Allen Tate said, "Madison Jones is our Southern Thomas Hardy."

Hunter Kay (1948-)
Hunter Kay was born in 1948 in Palestine, Texas, and received his B.A. and M.A. from Vanderbilt University. Except for some fiction published in college magazines, "The Fifth Generation" is his first story. Mr. Kay lives in a house he built with his own hands in a forest near Nashville, Tennessee. "I have promised everyone from God on down that if I ever finish the house I will start writing again." Presently, Mr. Kay is employed by South Central Bell.

David Madden (1933-)
David Madden was born in Knoxville, Tennessee, in 1933. A former assistant editor of *The Kenyon Review,* he has published seven novels, including *Cassandra Singing* (1969), *Bijou* (1974), *The Suicide's Wife* (1978), *Pleasure-Dome* (1979), and *On the Big Wind* (1980); a collection of short stories, *The Shadow Knows* (1970); and *A Primer of the Novel* (1980). In 1982 a collection of stories, *The New Orleans of Possibilities,* was published. Mr.

Madden is on the faculty of Louisiana State University in Baton Rouge.

John McCluskey, Jr. (1944-)
A native of Middletown, Ohio, McCluskey traces his interest in Southern literature back to his parents and grandparents, all of whom were from Georgia. After graduating from Stanford University, he taught at Miles College, Valparaiso University, and Case Western Reserve before assuming his present position of teaching Afro-American literature and creative writing at Indiana University at Bloomington. He is the author of two books, *Look What They've Done to My Song* (1974) and *Mr. America's Last Season Blues* (1983), in addition to having been a Yaddo Fellow during 1984. At present, he is working on two novels.

Carson McCullers (1917–1967)
Carson McCullers was born in Columbus, Georgia, in 1917. At the age of nineteen, she published her first short story, "Wunderkind," in *Story*. Married, divorced, and remarried to Reeves McCullers, she lived for several years in France where she and her husband owned a house just outside Paris. In 1940, she published her best-known novel, *The Heart Is a Lonely Hunter.* Her other novels include *Reflections in a Golden Eye* (1941), *The Member of the Wedding* (1946), and *Clock Without Hands* (1961). In 1950, her play, a rewritten version of *The Member of the Wedding,* won the New York Critics Award. Another successful play, *The Square Root of Wonderful,* appeared in 1958. Her major short stories are collected in *The Ballad of the Sad Café* (1951). Carson McCullers died in New York in 1967. In 1971, *The Mortgaged Heart,* a collection of her poems, short stories, and essays, was published.

Flannery O'Connor (1925–1964)
Flannery O'Connor was born in Savannah, Georgia, in 1925. She attended the Writers' Workshop at the University of Iowa, and published her first story, "Geranium," at the age of twenty-one. Now considered one of America's finest writers of short fiction, she published only one collection during her lifetime: *A Good Man Is Hard to Find and Other Stories* (1955). She is the author of two novels: *Wise Blood* (1952) and *The Violent Bear It Away* (1960). From 1950, when she was stricken with a lingering, incurable ailment, until her death in 1964, she lived near Milledgeville, Georgia, writing and tending a beloved flock of peacocks. In 1965, her collection of stories, *Everything That Rises Must Converge,* was published. And in 1971 *The Complete Stories* appeared, including twelve previously uncollected stories. *The Complete Stories* won the National Book Award in 1972. Her views on writing, on the Catholic faith, and on other subjects can

be found in her collection of essays, *Mystery & Manners,* edited by Sally and Robert Fitzgerald, and published in 1969. In addition, Sally Fitzgerald selected and edited Miss O'Connor's letters in a volume entitled *The Habit of Being* (1979). An important group of letters, to a friend who is called "A.," brings Miss O'Connor into closest range.

Breece D'J Pancake (1952–1979)
Breece Pancake was born in Milton, West Virginia, in 1952. After attending Marshall University in Huntington, West Virginia, he taught English at two Virginia military schools before entering the creative writing program at the University of Virginia in Charlottesville, where he died in 1979. During his lifetime, his short stories were published primarily in *The Atlantic.*

Jayne Anne Phillips (1952–)
Jayne Anne Phillips was born in West Virginia in 1952. She has taught at the University of Iowa as a Teaching-Writing Fellow and at Humboldt State University in Arcata, California. Two early collections of her work, *Sweethearts* and *Counting,* were published in limited editions. Her two most recent works are a collection of short stories and prose poems, *Black Tickets* (1979), and a highly praised novel, *Machine Dreams* (1984). She lives in Boston, Massachusetts.

Katherine Anne Porter (1890–1980)
Katherine Anne Porter was born in Indian Creek, Texas, in 1890. She taught at many universities in the United States and Europe. Winner of the Pulitzer Prize and the National Book Award, she is chiefly known for her short stories. Robert Penn Warren has written that "many of her stories are unsurpassed in modern fiction." Her three major collections of stories are *Flowering Judas and Other Stories* (1930), *Pale Horse, Pale Rider: Three Short Novels* (1938), and *The Leaning Tower and Other Stories* (1944). In 1964, *Collected Stories of Katherine Anne Porter* appeared, gathering together in one volume her three collections with the addition of other previously uncollected stories. Her novel, *Ship of Fools,* was published in 1962. Among her numerous works are *The Days Before: Collected Essays and Occasional Writings* (1952), *A Defense of Circe* (1955), a book of translations, *French Song Book* (1933), and a memoir of the Sacco-Vanzetti case, *The Never-Ending Wrong* (1977).

Reynolds Price (1933–)
Reynolds Price was born in Macon, North Carolina, in 1933. He studied at Duke University and was a Rhodes Scholar at Merton College, Oxford. He has published two collections of short stories: *The Names and Faces of Heroes* (1963) and *Permanent Errors* (1970). His novels include *A Long and Happy Life* (1962),

A Generous Man (1966), *Love and Work* (1968), and *The Surface of Earth* (1975). In 1978 he published a selection of translations from the Bible, *A Palpable God.* In 1981, a novel, *The Source of Light,* was published, followed by *Vital Provisions* (1982), a collection of poetry; *Mustian* (1983), two novels and a story complete and unabridged; and *Private Contentment* (1984), a play. Since 1958, Mr. Price has been on the faculty at Duke University.

Eve Shelnutt (1942–)
Eve Shelnutt, a native of Spartanburg, South Carolina, was born in 1942. She studied at the University of Cincinnati and the University of North Carolina at Greensboro where she received a Masters of Fine Arts as a Randall Jarrell Fellow. She has published her stories in such magazines as *The Virginia Quarterly Review, Shenandoah, The Carolina Quarterly,* and *Mademoiselle;* her first collection, *The Love Child,* was published in 1978. Two subsequent works have been published: *The Formal Voice* (1982), a collection of stories, and a volume of poetry published in the Carnegie-Mellon series entitled *Air and Salt* (1983). Miss Shelnutt's narrative voice—excessively private, deeply feminine, constantly backlooping, highly elliptical—is one of the most distinctive of today's literary scene. She is presently on the faculty of the University of Pittsburgh.

Elizabeth Spencer (1921–)
Elizabeth Spencer was born in Carrollton, Mississippi, in 1921. She was educated at Belhaven College and Vanderbilt University. She has published several novels: *Fire in the Morning* (1948), *This Crooked Way* (1952), *The Voice at the Back Door* (1956), *The Light in the Piazza* (1960), *Knights and Dragons* (1965), *No Place for An Angel* (1967), and *The Snare* (1972). A collection of her short stories, *Ship Island and Other Stories,* appeared in 1968. In her introduction to Miss Spencer's *The Stories of Elizabeth Spencer* (1981), Eudora Welty wrote that Elizabeth Spencer "can faultlessly set the social scene; she takes delight in making her characters reveal themselves through the most precise and telling particulars." Miss Spencer's latest novel, *The Salt Line,* appeared in 1984. She and her husband live in Chapel Hill, North Carolina.

Peter Taylor (1917–)
Peter Taylor was born in Trenton, Tennessee, in 1917. He has lectured widely in many universities in the United States and Europe. Best known for his short stories, represented in over twenty anthologies, he has published a novel, *A Woman of Means* (1950), and several plays. Seven of his one-act plays are collected in *Presences: Seven Dramatic Pieces* (1973). His major collections of stories include *A Long Fourth and Other Stories* (1948), *Happy Families Are All Alike* (1959), *Miss Leonora When Last Seen and Fifteen Other Stories* (1964), and *In the Miro District and Other Stories* (1977). Many of his stories are now collected in one vol-

ume, *The Collected Stories of Peter Taylor* (1969). His latest collection of stories, *The Old Forest and Other Stories* (1985), won the PEN/Faulkner award. Mr. Taylor teaches at the University of Virginia.

Anne Tyler (1941-)
Anne Tyler was born in Minneapolis, Minnesota, in 1941, and spent her early childhood in North Carolina. She received her education at Duke University and Columbia University. Today, she lives in Baltimore, Maryland, and has been dubbed by Reynolds Price "the nearest thing we have to an urban Southern novelist." A natural storyteller, Miss Tyler has written a number of outstanding works, including *Celestial Navigation* (1974), *Searching for Caleb* (1975), *Earthly Possessions* (1977), *Morgan's Passing* (1979), *Dinner at the Homesick Restaurant* (1982), and *The Accidental Tourist* (1985). In all, Miss Tyler's ten books of fiction make her one of America's most promising writers.

Alice Walker (1944-)
Alice Walker was born in Eatonton, Georgia, in 1944. She has taught at Jackson State College and Tougaloo College in Mississippi, at Wellesley College, and the University of Massachusetts. She is the author of collections of poems entitled *Once* (1968) and *Revolutionary Petunias and Other Poems* (1973); a biography, *Langston Hughes* (1973); and the novels *The Third Life of Grange Copeland* (1970) and *Meridian* (1976). A collection of her short stories, *In Love & Trouble: Stories of Black Women,* appeared in 1973. In 1981, another collection of stories, *You Can't Keep a Good Woman Down,* was published, followed in 1982 by the Pulitzer Prize-winning novel *The Color Purple.* In 1983, Miss Walker published a collection of prose entitled *In Search of Our Mother's Garden,* and in 1984 a collection of poetry entitled *Horses Make a Landscape More Beautiful.*

Robert Penn Warren (1905-)
Robert Penn Warren was born in Guthrie, Kentucky, in 1905. He was educated at Vanderbilt University, the University of California, and at Oxford University as a Rhodes Scholar. One of America's most distinguished men of letters, he has excelled in most literary genres, including the novel, the poem, the short story, and the essay. At Vanderbilt University he was a member of the Fugitives, a group of Southern poets. His books of poems include *Thirty-six Poems* (1936); *Eleven Poems on the Same Theme* (1942); *Selected Poems: 1923–1943* (1944); *Promises: Poems 1954–1956* (1957), winner of the National Book Award in 1958; *Selected Poems New and Old, 1923–1966* (1966), *Incarnations: Poems 1966–1968* (1968); and *Or Else: Poems, 1968–1974* (1975). In 1976, he published a new collection, *Selected Poems 1923–1975.* A well-known university teacher, he was founder,

with Cleanth Brooks, of *The Southern Review.* Also with Cleanth Brooks, he has edited two important college textbooks, *Understanding Poetry* (1938) and *Understanding Fiction* (1943). Warren is the author of many novels, including *Night Rider* (1939); *All the King's Men* (1946), winner of the 1947 Pulitzer Prize; *World Enough and Time* (1950); *Band of Angels* (1955); and, lately, *A Place to Come To* (1977). His short stories can be found in the collection *The Circus in the Attic and Other Stories* (1948). Mr. Warren has concentrated on poetry in more recent years, as witnessed by the following: *Now and Then: Poems 1976–1978* (1978); *Being Here: Poetry 1977–1978* (1980); *Rumor Verified: Poems 1979–1980* (1981); *Chief Joseph of the Nez Perce, Who Called Themselves the Nimipu—"The Real People"* (1983), and *New and Selected Poems: 1923–1985* (1985). On February 26, 1986, he was designated the first official Poet Laureate of the United States. He lives with his wife, the writer Eleanor Clark, in Fairfield, Connecticut.

Eudora Welty (1909-   )
Eudora Welty was born in Jackson, Mississippi, in 1909. She was educated at Mississippi State College for Women and the University of Wisconsin. Her reputation as a writer of short stories now firmly established, she received high praise from fellow writers from the beginning of her career. Katherine Anne Porter has written that she has "an eye and an ear sharp, shrewd, and true as a tuning fork." Welty's major collections of stories include *The Wide Net and Other Stories* (1943), *The Golden Apples* (1949), and *The Bride of the Innisfallen and Other Stories* (1955). She is the author of five novels: *The Robber Bridegroom* (1942); *Delta Wedding* (1946); *The Ponder Heart* (1954); *Losing Battles* (1970); and *The Optimist's Daughter* (1972), winner of the 1973 Pulitzer Prize. She has also written several important essays on the craft of writing, most of which are collected in *The Eye of the Story* (1979). Her *Collected Stories* was published in 1980. In 1984, Harvard University Press published Miss Welty's *One Writer's Beginnings,* the only book published by Harvard to make the Best Sellers List. In a recent tribute to Miss Welty, Cleanth Brooks said that she "has a quality that surpasses generosity and that I must call great-heartedness." Miss Welty continues to live in Jackson, Mississippi.

Tennessee Williams (1911–1983)
Tennessee Williams was born in Columbus, Mississippi, in 1911. One of America's most celebrated dramatists, author of *The Glass Menagerie* (1944), *A Streetcar Named Desire* (1947), *Cat on a Hot Tin Roof* (1955), and *Sweet Bird of Youth* (1959), among others, he also wrote many short stories. Among his collections of stories are *One Arm and Other Stories* (1948), *Three Players of a Summer Game and Other Stories* (1960), and *Eight Mortal Ladies Pos-*

sessed: A Book of Stories (1974). He published his *Memoirs* in 1975, followed in 1981 by a play entitled *Clothes for a Summer Hotel: A Ghost Play.* His letters to Donald Windham (1940–65) were published in 1977. Tennessee Williams died at the age of 71 in New York City and left the bulk of his estate to the University of the South at Sewanee to be used to promote theater and the arts.